Praise for Thirty] You

Notes for mortal readers

Please consider those less fortunate when reading this book. You can help by observing the following guidelines:

- Read in page order and resist any temptation to skip ahead
- Do not read while travelling in automobiles, trains or aircraft
- Try to read in the same location and at the same time each day
- If you know of a change of time or venue in advance, please state the details in a clear loud voice at the end of the current session.

Thank you for your support.

The Campaign for Zonal Enrichment

For those who question the answers to their questions

Today is the first day of the rest of your life. But then so is tomorrow, so why not have today off?

— Oscar Wilde, August 1977

Problems with The Word

Men have written scripture for millennia: instruction, consolation, consequences. Though much was hewn with the highest intention, through the finest of language and at great personal cost, the bulk has been inaccurate, misguided and damaging: intolerance, war, genocide and, of course, BBC Television's *Songs of Praise*.

Most works are now lost or forgotten and much of what has survived has been reduced to curiosity or has drifted into obscurity. But a few notable works became cornerstones of civilisations. Some still are. And the works at the summit have entered the consciousness, for good or ill, of almost everyone alive today, even recruitment consultants and PE teachers. We all know this from our first inklings of mistrust at school – the prayers, the songs, the stories we were told were true. None of us was spared. But what is less known is there was once legend of another far less literary but far more holy work – one you have, it is hoped, never heard of. For it was not written by mortal hand. It is a book not meant for mortal eyes and only half meant for dead ones, and though it contains much that is out of date, unhelpful and uncaring, it scores over the recognised works in two important respects. First, it is not bankrolled by any religion, ideology or mortal agenda; second, it is true. Well, mostly.

Part One

Purgatory

Chapter One

'It was another overcast morning.'
Too dull.

'It was another stormy morning.'
Too dramatic. Think gritty. Think stark.

'It was another drizzly morning.'
Does Costa Rica get drizzly? Is drizzly even a word?

A common nugget of Christian's amassed *how to write fiction* advice was never to open a novel talking about the weather. However, another was that you may break any rule, so long as you are a genius. Christian knew he wasn't a genius, at least not yet, but it was definitely the direction in which to be drifting. So his chosen persona would be the rapier-quilled rule-breaker and his novel would begin with the weather. But so far, he had to admit, it hadn't put much puff in his sails.

He stared again at the waiting screen, the blinking cursor. At least Christmas was behind him. No one does anything at Christmas. January 2015. Yes, a new year, a new page.

He scratched his beard. It was at that itchy needy distracty stage. Go and shave it off? No, write now, shave later, shave tomorrow. Write now, write now right now.

He placed his hands on the keyboard. He lightly drummed the key tops. He thought about taking another shot at the submarine level. He'd been so close to cracking it. If only the airlock door didn't close quite so soon. No, *no*. He was here to write and write is what he would do. First sort the weather, then tackle the submarine level. So, with vice-like determination, he returned his attention to Costa Rican meteorology and reviewed the situation. He'd already tried bright rays breaking through the jungle canopy; driving rain; steamy, hot and humid; experimented briefly with snow, before coming back, yet again, to dabbling with drizzle.

Perhaps give the rays another shot? Perhaps rays breaking through the drizzle?

Alt + Tab.

As Christian navigated Lara into the conning tower, he tried to work out where he was going wrong. The months were slipping by and all he'd managed so far was 2,850 words.

Perhaps he was rushing into it? He recalled his most treasured piece of advice from the writing books: 'Never begin when you feel you want to; always try to hold off a little longer.'

But it wasn't all bad. He had his main setting nailed. Costa Rica: the jungle, the heat, the humidity, the clearings in the jungle, the thicker jungle, the thinner jungle and of course the really really thick jungle. No, what he was struggling with was the story, largely because he didn't have one. But this wasn't a problem, far from it – much of the advice had stressed the importance of letting your characters tell their tale. Christian was fine with this, but wished they would get on with it so he could write it all down.

Of course, this was compounded by the problem of not having any characters either, not good ones anyway. When Christian closed his eyes and asked his imagination to go to work, he always ended up with the same image – his old invisible friend from childhood, the character he used to call Erdygrot. He was a stocky, scruffy, beardy man in his fifties, who hung about, hands in the pockets of his cream corduroy suit, with occasional indifferent glances to his scuffed shoes. He'd always been there. Christian couldn't remember it any other way. It had led to a catalogue of problems for the people in orbit around Christian during his early years. First there was the parental angst when Christian didn't appear to be growing out of Erdy, resulting in numerous trips to priests and, eventually, child psychologists, each one failing to recognise the potentially career-making phenomenon sitting before them. And there were bigger problems when Christian started school, with Erdygrot sometimes cropping up in the margins of Christian's work. Unfortunately, the musty, beardy, leather-elbow-patchy nature of Erdygrot fostered an often striking resemblance to Christian's more musty, beardy, leather-elbow-patchy teachers. This, combined with the vividness of Christian's drawings, led to more than one rumbling of misconduct, culminating in the sacking of Geography teacher Mr Burgess in 1996 – the final straw, in the eyes of the headteacher, being Christian's depiction of a wide-eyed Burgess yahooing like a cowboy astride the Ross of Mull.

As the years passed, Erdygrot receded from Christian's waking thoughts, though remained ever-present in his dreams, albeit only as an extra and even then preferring to skulk in the wings and look to skive off at the first opportunity.

So characters were a bit of a problem for Christian. His solution, he told himself, was an interim one, scaffolding to be removed before the final spell check. But Christian would never get to that last polish because soon he would be dead and that makes it much harder to write. Thus, his work was destined to remain in pre-*find-and-replace* state and this would make much of Christian's legacy perplexing to anyone happening upon it after his passing. Or before for that matter.

Chapter Two

Beatrice poured Christian's tea down the sink and washed up the mugs. She dried her hands and again read the stolen page of A4. It wasn't as shocking, third time around, but was no less troubling. The setting and genre were as expected – those being among the few details Christian had been 'ready to share' – but the cast of characters was dumbfounding: Christian's decrepit father, their neighbour Mrs Kapoor, and Christian himself – 'a lean man with the quiet charisma of a professional snooker player' ... *as if* – all apparently mixed up in the underworld of the Central American cocaine trade. On top of this, the text was speckled with strange spelling mistakes – words you should never get wrong – some corrected with biro, others missed.

A sound from upstairs. She held her breath.

Silence.

Beatrice was classically proportioned, with soft, full features she'd once made much more of. Her hair, too, these days, was restrained – uncoloured, undreadlocked, unremarkable. It was a good thing, emancipating even. She was in her thirties now, she had better things to do with her time. It played better at work, too, and it sat better with Christian, or at least she assumed it did.

They'd been together for almost seven years, engaged for the last four. In the beginning it had been good and in many ways it still was – neither of them wanted pets, for example. And he'd always been dependable –

she'd liked that very much, she reminded herself. Yes, it had all been okay, completely and definitely okay, okay at the very least and without question a worthwhile investment of a quarter of her life. Until last year; until the novel. The hardest part was he'd never offered a rationale. And he owed her one. It wasn't like he'd been writing all his life; he wasn't even well read. Thank God his time was almost up.

The sound of someone bounding down the stairs.

Beatrice put the page safely back with the cleaning products.

Her man bowled in. Noon and still in boxers and T-shirt. Shambolic tousled hair enjoying another free swim. Eyes wide and oblivious.

'I've got it,' said Christian.

'Got what?'

'My second setting. It's been staring me in the face.'

'Wonderful.'

She grabbed a tea towel and began to dry the mugs.

'Well don't you want to know what it is?'

'I don't know. Do I?'

'Yes. It's very exciting.'

Silence. She wasn't going to humour him, not this time.

'Is something wrong?' he asked.

'Why would anything be wrong?'

Christian puffed his cheeks.

She put down the tea towel and gripped the edge of the worktop.

'Oh no ... the tea,' he said. 'Sorry. I forgot.'

'Doesn't matter.'

'Oh, it was a gold label as well,' he said, eyeing the box.

He seemed sincere, which only made it worse. 'It's not about the bloody tea,' she said.

More silence.

She took the band from her wrist and began to tie her matted hair.

'Look,' he said, 'whatever I've done, I'm sorry.'

She didn't reply.

'Hey,' he said, stepping in, 'hey, what's the matter?' He put his hands to her waist.

'You really want to know?' There was an awkward pause before she continued. 'I'm worried, Christian. You've been working on this for eight months now but you never show me a damned thing.'

'Will of Ockham, Beasy, of course I show you. I've just come down now to tell you about the new setting.'

'No words though, no actual writing, not so much as a sentence.' She brushed his hands away and turned to hang up the tea towel.

'Look, I've told you,' he said, 'I'll let you read it when the time is right, but it won't make sense at the moment. You just have to trust me for now.'

No reply.

He stepped in again and tried to put his arms around her but she put up her palms.

'Don't,' she said.

'Don't what?'

'Just. Don't.'

'Okay. Okay I get it, you're finding this hard. So am I.'

She shook her head. 'Don't even think about pushing that line. This was your choice. No one was forcing you.'

'Sorry,' he said, jutting out a hand, 'that came out wrong. It's much harder for you, of course it is.'

No reply.

'All right. What can I do to make it up to you?'

Still no reply.

'Well, how about we finally buy the new TV?' he said. 'I've done all the research.'

She shook her head.

'What then?'

Chapter Three

Tony ushered Christian into his office. The breezeblock vicarage had more in common with the nearby shopping centre than the Victorian church it was bonded to, raising unspoken questions on where its loyalties lay, and to Christian it felt more like a visit to the doctors than an audience with one of God's representatives on Earth. But it was warm inside and the traffic noise didn't invade as much as he'd expected.

Tony looked unruffled as ever. Ten years older than Christian and yet still no grey. Laughter lines bookended knowing eyes but his forehead was wrinkle-free, despite a well-known fondness for sunbeds – Bea suspected Botox, but privately Christian reckoned it was merely the natural consequence of having most of every week off.

'Yes, well to be honest, Bea asked me to come,' said Christian, 'but I suppose it's not a bad idea to swot up ahead of the, well, you know.'

'Um, quite. So you've named a day then? Congratulations. Shall I get the diary?'

Christian shook his head. 'It's more of a date for a date. Sort of.'

'Ah, I see. Um, tea, coffee?'

'Champagne, I'd imagine.'

'No, I mean now, would you like a cup?'

'Oh right. Thanks. Better pass. Four lattes today already.'

'I'm a bit of a caffeine fan myself. Does help summon up the energy on Sunday. Do you mind if I ...'

'Oh no, go ahead.'

Tony ambled over to the kettle.

'Now we do recommend planning at least eight months ahead if you're after a specific day.'

'We'll bear that in mind.'

'Of course we can sometimes work a miracle and squeeze you in at short notice, if the mood takes you. Not that marriage is something you should enter into when you're *in the mood*. Quite the opposite, er ... calmly ... soberly ... wisely' – Tony gave a sort of royal wave with his teaspoon – 'you know the drill.'

'Yes, of course. No, I think eight months sounds like the best option. If we have to wait, we have to wait. Could round it up to an even year, actually. Keep it simple.'

'Custard cream?' said Tony, tearing open a large packet.

'Oh, yes, that woooOOW.' Christian jumped to his feet, sending Tony's cat back to the carpet.

'Welby, there you are,' said Tony.

The fluffy creature let out a purr as it pranced around Christian's feet.

'Sorry,' said Christian.

'No harm done,' said Tony, striding over and bending to take the cat in his arms. 'Naughty Welby.'

'Just I'm not much of a pets person,' said Christian.

'Not your fault. He shouldn't even be in here, should you, Welby?' Tony put the cat out in the hall. 'Right,' said Tony, on his return, 'I expect you've got all sorts of questions?'

'Well. Yes. I do, actually,' said Christian and he opened his notepad. 'Right, the whole virgin birth thing. Is it true it was down to a mistranslation?'

'Um, I don't think so,' said Tony. He retook his seat.

'Yes. Apparently it's the mistranslation of the Hebrew word "almah", to "virgin", when in fact it means "young woman".'

'Really?' said Tony, looking puzzled. 'Well I suppose that is a lot more credible than a virgin giving birth.'

'And that doesn't undermine the faith?'

'Well, I don't think so. It's just a detail, really, isn't it?'

'Oh. Right. Okay, well what about thou shalt not kill – shouldn't it be thou shalt not kill unless it's in the name of God?'

'Ah well you're right there. History is rather peppered with whacking in the name of the Lord, a good portion of it by the Church, it has to be said. But we don't tend to go in for that these days. Not that it was right, even then.' Tony leaned back in his chair and linked his hands behind his head. 'I could never have taken part – I don't have it in me to burn anyone. I once caught Mrs Langley with the waffle iron, gave her such a welt, I could barely forgive myself. To burn a whole person, well, I wouldn't have it in me.'

'And evolution?'

'What of it?'

'What's your stance?'

'It's a sound theory. It explains a lot.'

'Oh.'

'I must say, I was rather expecting questions concerning your impending nuptials,' said Tony. He swivelled in his chair and gazed out of the window. 'Your vows and commitments, our requirements of you and so forth ...'

'Oh. Oh yes, yes of course,' said Christian. 'Fire away.'

Tony swivelled back. 'No, I was thinking you had questions for me?'

'Oh. Right. Well, no, not really.'

'Nothing at all?'

'Well, okay, maybe,' said Christian. He tapped his pen on his teeth. 'All right, let's go for the big one – what if I don't believe in God?'

'Ooh, yes, that is rather a biggie,' said Tony. He sat forward to take a sip of coffee before leaning back in his chair. 'Normally I have a sort of *don't ask, don't tell* policy, you know, like homosexuals on building sites.'

'But I've already told you. I don't believe in God, I'm an atheist, it's all a load of nonsense.'

'Yes, all right, no need to shout about it. Look, perhaps we could, well, pretend you haven't told me?'

'Isn't that a bit disingenuous?'

'I suppose it is, a bit. All right, well, could you accept a metaphorical interpretation?'

'I don't think so. Metaphorical nonsense doesn't seem that different from actual nonsense.'

'Look, you're not making this easy,' said Tony. 'I'd remind you the Church is under no obligation here, despite your fiancée's good standing. We don't marry people willy-nilly.' The reverend grabbed two custard creams at once. 'Can't you do anything to meet us halfway? It's not like we're demanding. You should count yourself lucky Beatrice isn't a Baptist

– then you'd have to be all hallelujah, loud, out and proud. And if she was Jewish or Muslim, you'd be in real trouble – forget it.'

'Okay, okay. It's just principles, you know.'

'Indeed …' said Tony, leaning back.

There was a long pause, filled only with tense munching.

'Well,' said Tony, 'if you really don't believe, then what's the harm in mumbling a few words of claptrap? If a child talks to you about Santa Claus, you just go along with it, don't you. What's the harm? It's not like you get on your high horse and tell them Santa doesn't exist.'

'Well no.'

'Exactly.'

'No, I tell them Santa *probably* doesn't exist. Just like God, or fairies. It's not right to go further because you can't prove anything *doesn't exist*.'

'Well there's your answer,' said Tony, spitting crumbs at Christian. 'Take that spark, breathe on it, let it take hold and instead of struggling on thinking this is all baloney, flip it over and focus on that wafer-thin shred of cast iron certainty that it just might not be. That's what the bishop does, says it's never let him down.'

Chapter Four

'It was a bright morning in Heaven.'

Do they have weather in Heaven? If they do, surely it's stating the obvious to say it's bright.

'It was morning in Heaven.'

Do they have mornings in Heaven? That would suggest they have afternoons, evenings and nights. Would that further suggest the Kingdom is illuminated by a sun? The same sun that shines on the earth? Unless it's artificial, perhaps. What then? Good old incandescent or fluorescent energy savers? Maybe Biblical flaming torches?

Christian's Saturday was going well. Weather aside, his decision to set half his novel in the afterlife and switch the style to comedy-drama was proving productive, his word count for the day having already rocketed to a heady 353. Yes, this was the right track.

There would still be challenges, of course. For one, he wasn't sure how the jokes would fit with Costa Rica – from what he could tell it wasn't a funny place – and he didn't know where to begin with marrying up Heaven with all the various types of jungle.

He knew the new setting gave him opportunities, though, exciting ones to go beyond the standard thriller. Normally when the bad guy dies, that's the end of the story. But with the afterlife now in the mix, Dad could kill himself to continue the chase. Quite why he would wish to do so was still an open question, though one option was to have the bad guy dying too soon and by accident. So instead of Dad shooting him at the dénouement, he gets run over on the way to the shops the day before. Dad would feel cheated; fate and misfortune would have stolen his thunder. And this bad guy has really got under Dad's skin. Dad's staked his whole career on catching him. So Dad kills himself to resume the chase.

Hmm …

Or maybe Dad has late-stage lung cancer? That would make his suicide more convincing. But then if he's terminally ill, would he be able to keep working as a no-nonsense undercover detective on the mean streets of San José? It would, at least, mean revising the chase scene where he's climbing all those wire fences. Now he'd have to nip down a side street on a mobility scooter.

He had to admit, it needed work.

He got up and wandered through to the bathroom. He'd put off the shave long enough. But then again, yes, another day wouldn't hurt.

Perhaps a bath would help his ideas flow. He checked his watch. Have to be just a quick dip – an hour and a half at most if he was going to get to the shopping centre on time. Beatrice would make a start; he'd join her later – that was the best deal he could strike. He'd always loved weekends when he was working, despite the shopping, but now they just buggered up his productivity.

'What about these?' asked Beatrice, pointing out some beige corduroy throws.

'Nice,' said Christian.

'That's what you said about the ones in Debenhams.'

'Well aren't these the same?'

'Christian, those were green.'

'Right. Cool. Shall we get these ones then?'

'You're just saying that so we can stop looking.'

'Of course I'm not. I just … really love these ones.'

Christian hated shopping. The only thing worse was doing it in Bracknell, where they lived. The town's moribund shopping centre looked like it had been excreted, its squat stature matched only by its low horizons. Friends who had moved away and moved on used to joke that the experience was so grim surely there was money to be made bringing in eco-tour groups from Knightsbridge, keen to see how the third world did its shopping. Christian had smiled politely, of course. What else was there to do when the prosecution had a watertight case?

Aside from the reflected ridicule, he was fine with the town. This was his home and though his unconscious mind harboured concerns about the possible role of Stockholm syndrome, this is where he belonged.

'These could work,' said Beatrice, picking up a blue and white striped oversized cushion, 'but then, no ... not quite right.'

'Look, Beasy, do you really need a conservatory? The back garden's pretty small as it is. Plus those things always leak.'

'Christian, we've been through this' – she thrust the cushion into his stomach – 'we *agreed*. I've done my bit, now you need to step up.'

Christian had no reply.

'Cheer up,' she said. 'I've been thinking there may be some other things we could get excited about, for when you're back earning.'

'Such as?'

'Well, for one, I was thinking about the trip, finally doing it.'

'The trip?'

'You know, Anna Puma.'

'*Annapurna.*'

'You've been talking about it for years. The conservatory won't take all the cash, so–'

'Well, yes, it's just that–'

'Christian. I really would like to do it. Come on, let's see if there's any deals on.'

'What, today?'

'Why not?'

'Well we'd need to research it.'

'Okay, shall we pick up some brochures then?'

'No need, it's all online.'

'Right,' she said, and waited for a compromise that didn't come. She gave a micro-shake of the head. 'Okay, BHS next, then Marks.'

'Sounds good, really good, but hey, why don't you continue and maybe I could head back and start the research? You're much better at this than I am, and besides, I've got this great idea for the wheels of afterlife justice.'

'Afterlife justice? What on earth are you talking about?'

'The book.'

'What's that got to do with afterlife justice?'

'My second setting. The afterlife. Did I not tell you?'

'No.'

'Oh.'

Chapter Five

It was a bright morning in Heaven. Just like all mornings in Heaven.

Atop twenty-two storeys, the huge Cumulonimbus Lounge was the crowning glory of the Deital Palace tower which dominated the skyline of True Jerusalem. To the north, the inner walls, grand Cardinal Gatehouse and outer walls, with the lost wastelands beyond. To the east, south and west, the eternal city stretching out far beyond each horizon. With 360-degree views and open to the unbroken azure of Heaven's heavens, it would have been welcome sanctuary from matters of state and the oppression of citrine strip-lighting, were it not for the ever-present *kerfong* rising from the hordes of fans outside the inner gates.

Harold shifted his weight. Eight days on from his emergence into the final plane of existence and he'd got the hang of walking under gravity again but was still struggling with standing on the spot, especially when that was all he was doing because then he'd start thinking about it.

God flicked his last fig roll onto the sky-blue super-lux shag pile, cracked his knuckles and sank low into his cloud sofa.

Harold turned to the expressionless aides for a hint. He didn't get one. He put his hand to his mouth and drew index finger and thumb together to where his toothbrush moustache had been. Shaving it off was the only thing he'd changed since his arrival, but then it had been an easy decision – a second lifetime of being mistaken for a taller-than-expected Charlie

Chaplin, on a good day, or a youthful Adolf Hitler, on others, was enough for anyone.

'So, m-may we know your mind, on this matter?' he asked.

'Eh?' barked God.

'Gabriel would like your opinion, on the birthday plans.'

'Look, I'm not fussed,' said God. His troubled gaze drifted from the distant unmarked sky to one of the ridiculous stalk-mounted, stuffed-cotton clouds dangling above him like drab piñatas. 'He's a grown man for Oomlah's sake. Do you still bother to make a big song and dance on your birthday?'

'W-well, I confess no, in recent decades, but each to their own, I suppose.'

'Each to their own?' said God. 'It's not even a big one. It's not like it's his thousandth or two thousandth, is it?'

'Er, no, well–'

'You know what really shits me?' asked God. He stood and took a swipe at one of the clouds, connecting and sending it shooting off its stalk and over the parapet.

'Er–'

'No one ever stops to think about how I feel. I've never had a birthday party, not even once, not once, not ever, not never.'

'Ah, you prefer the quiet dignity of a modest gathering?' said Harold.

'I've never had a birthday party because I've never had a birthday.'

'Um ...'

'Keep up, son. Can't have a birthday if you've never been born, can you?'

'Oh. Oh yes, I see. Well, have you ever considered having an official one, like the Queen? The Queen of England ...'

God turned his eyes to Harold, where they lingered with disapproval on his patched-up cracked white clothing, before returning to the perfect sky. 'Look,' said God, 'let him have his day, but no fuss, understand? Just do what we did last year.'

'Right, yes, last year ... it's just that, I, well, I wasn't–'

'Ask Gabe.'

'Ah, of course, certainly.'

God lowered an arm, picked up his battered tin from the carpet and began to roll a cigarette. 'Where is Gabe anyway?'

'I believe he's down at Arrivals. I'm told they're expecting that Hitchens fellow.'

'Nice,' said God. He lit up his cigarette and went back to staring out at the sky.

Harold went back to staring at God.

Harold was experiencing the normal difficulties of starting a new job where one is thrust into immediate contact with a senior member of the organisation. The fear of making a mistake, of incurring unchecked wrath. *These people don't get this far by being kind,* he told himself, but then countered with *Calm down, he's just a person, no different from me.* Except he wasn't just a person – they never are. In this case, of course, it was a literal truth. This really wasn't a person. This was the supreme spirit being, God, creator of the earth and all life on it. Which is why Harold kept staring. He'd just imagined, well, someone else. For as long as Harold could remember, he'd been told that the idea of God being an old man with flowing white hair and a long white beard, sitting on a cloud, was acknowledged by all, even evangelical religious types, as an outmoded and juvenile way to picture the Lord of all creation. And yet here he was. Okay, so the hair was a skunkish grey and appeared to not so much flow as sprout; the beard was short and bushy, and the overall look was far more hastily groomed tramp than majestic deity, but even so, a whitish-haired man with a whitish beard, sitting, no, slouching, on a sofa shaped like a cloud.

He had assumed God would be taller, though; for some reason, he'd expected unnaturally tall – perhaps eight or nine feet. Yet the figure before Harold wasn't even average height; he was stocky, five six at best, leaving Harold bending at the knees with embarrassment. And then there were the eyes. Eyes that had witnessed the entirety of history – not just human history, but *history* full stop, there for every event from before the beginning of time. They should have been infinitely jaded, infinitely dark, burdened beyond comprehension with the unending horror of eternity, and yet they appeared fresh as a pair of Polos.

But it wasn't just the man at the top. Nothing about Heaven had been as he'd expected since the day he emerged dazed and confused from judgement. How could humanity have been so adrift of the mark? All the things he hadn't believed in at Sunday school had been wrong. And it wasn't just the Christians who'd run aground. As far as he knew, no religion foretold of the celebrity culture or the hedonism, and they certainly hadn't mentioned the strict fellatial customs.

There were more questions, too, hundreds of them, overflowing his disposition to such an extent that when they resurfaced, each still carried shock and sting. Where were his parents and grandparents? How could he have qualified when they had not? And what had happened to Freda and his old friends from the Queue? For now, though, he was happy to let these gremlins loiter in the cupboards of his mind, because another more immediate malevolence confronted him – for the first time in a long time he was a free man; he had no one's back and no one had to have his, but now walls were walls once again; he was fixed in reality's eye once again.

'I said you can go,' said God.

'My apologies,' said Harold. He half turned, stopped and turned back. 'Beg pardon, a final item,' he said. 'Gabriel said you may find this amusing.' He stepped forward and handed God a few pages of parchment manuscript.

'What's this?' asked God.

'It's being written by a man – a mortal, sir.'

'Son, I know you're new, but drop the sir.'

'Sorry – Terry.'

'Last thing I need is *sir*. That's one small step from *Lord*, then it's *I like what you like, Lord! I love you, Lord! Good idea, Lord!* I'm not a celebrity and you are not here to be a yes-man, okay?'

'Yes, s– I mean, no, s– I mean, no. Terry.'

'If there's one thing I cannot abide, it's being worshipped.'

'Yes, Terry, sorry, Terry.'

'And stop saying sorry. Now, off you trot, son.'

Harold nodded and turned to leave.

'Oi. Soft lad,' said God.

Harold turned round to face the Almighty.

'Show some bloody respect and back out, you know, *like for the Queen of England*. If it's ondollar for her, it's ondollar for me.'

'Certainly, sir, sorry, Sir Terry. Sorry.' Harold shuffled back towards the stairs, felling one of the twin Henry Moore mammatocumulus sculptures as he made his exit.

Chapter Six

Christian and Beatrice were sitting in a slightly overpriced independent coffee shop. It was the well-established yet never actually discussed price for getting Christian to come shopping.

'Whereas in Mark and John there's no mention at all,' said Christian. He took a sip from his cup.

'Where are you getting this from?' asked Beatrice, before draining hers.

'My Bible study group. They're so helpful.'

'You're not serious …'

'Don't panic, it's just an online one. And I'm not on there as me.'

'Well who are you on there as?'

'Maurice Whitecock, apprentice vicar.'

'Honestly?'

'Yes.'

Beatrice shook her head. 'Taking advantage like that, it's not right.'

'Well, fair's fair, they do it all the time.'

'What, the other members? They're all vicar impersonators?'

'No, I mean they use the weapons of the enemy.'

'What are you talking about?'

'Well, I'm using their discussion group – their weapon – for my own ends. But they've been doing this for years, the organised religions. Think about it, down through the ages, religion holds back science at every turn, yet who's first to get a printing press? First to buy up a TV channel, first to set up a website? So this is a tiny bit of payback. And believe me, it's a rare opportunity – they have so few weapons of any use.'

'*The enemy*. So I suppose I'm the enemy too then?'

'Not you, Beasy. Not at all. No, you're a victim of the enemy, an innocent swept up in the melee.'

She folded her arms.

'But even with their help, it's still quite a challenge.'

'Really …'

'Oh yes. You see, I'm having to do what every religion has had to do at some point – make up the rules of the game. And it's tougher than it sounds. It's like when you're trying to set up a Scalextric track with one piece missing – you get everything connected apart from that final gap, so you give it a shove and force it to close, but in doing so you break a connection somewhere else, so you fix that, which creates another break and so on, and sooner or later you're back where you started. It's given me a whole new appreciation for religion, how hard they have to work to hold it all together.'

'And yet they do,' said Beatrice.

'No, I don't think they do at all. They just don't get called out on it.'

'All right, give me an example.'

'Easy. Origin of man, Adam and Eve.'

'Go on.'

'Well, let's start by saying God is all-knowing and all powerful.'

'Right.'

'He's lonely, he wants some company, decides to create people.'

'I'm not sure that's really why, but okay.'

'So he makes Adam, then he makes Eve, from Adam's rib, that's right, isn't it?'

'Yes.'

'And they have children.'

'Yes.'

'Well if Eve came from Adam's rib, then she must be genetically identical – his sister. In fact, worse than that, she'd be the female version of his identical twin. It's incest.'

'But maybe God made Adam's rib special, gave it different DNA.'

'Well, all right, even if you ignore Eve coming from Adam, their children must have got it on with each other, or their parents, to create the population. So it's still incest.'

'Yes, but I think there was an amnesty or something, at the start.'

'Oh come on.'

'Well like you say, there was no other way, what choice did they have?'

'But this is my point. If God was all-knowing and powerful, why didn't he save Adam and Eve and their children all the trauma of having to have sex with each other for a few generations by just creating an initial community of a few thousand people, with a diverse gene pool?'

'Well no one knew science back then.'

'Well presumably God did, or at least should have, if he was all-knowing. Which breaks our assumption at the start. So you see, even on this little Mini Cooper figure-of-eight, that first join of the track has already come apart.'

'Hmm ...'

'Unexplored consequences, you see,' said Christian. 'They didn't think it through. And they're full of this, all the religions. It's staggering they've survived so long.'

'I think we'd better change the subject.'

'Why?'

'Because you forget who you're talking to, darling.'

'No I don't.'

'Christian, I'm a Christian.'

'Well yes, okay, but not *Christian* Christian. Your dad's the warden, you're joining in for family harmony, but you don't believe.'

'Of course I do.'

'Yes, all right you *believe*, but only in a sort of generalised benevolent force, not the literal word of the Bible.'

'Yes I do.'

'What, Adam and Eve?'

'Yes.'

'The burning bush?'

'Yes.'

'Virgin birth?'

'Yes. Yes, yes, *yes*.'

'Since when?'

'Since always.'

'But you rebelled,' said Christian. 'You told me, you said you rejected every–'

'When I was a teenager, Christian, before you even knew me.'

'Really?'

'Yes!'

'Right. And now you ...'

'*Yes*. I do.'

'Wow ... *wow*. Well, not to worry. There are books, brilliant books that can help. You can start with my Dawkins, and the Hitchens, then maybe we can order a bit of backup, er, a Pinker, a Harris, and maybe a short course of Dennetts. Now don't you worry, we'll get you sorted, we'll get through this.'

'Just listen to yourself. I haven't got chlamydia, Christian, I don't want sorting out, I don't need sorting out, it's you who needs sorting out. God, you're so arrogant.'

'I'm not arrogant, I'm just right. There is a difference.'

'No, Christian, on this you are arrogant, and you're belittling too.'

'Oh now that's not fair.'

'Oh no? Well tell me straight then, can you honestly say you don't think I'm a fool for believing?'

'What a dreadful thing to say. Of course I don't think you're a fool.'

Her eyes dropped to her empty cup. 'Oh ...'

'No, you're just deluded. And even the smartest person in the world can be deluded.'

Beatrice opened her mouth to speak but in the end she just shook her head and let out a sort of stuttering chuckle.

'What's so funny?'

'What about insane?' said Beatrice. 'Have you thought about that? Maybe I'm insane.'

'Well I think that's overdoing it a bit. No, I'm sure it's just good old delusion.'

'Christian, how can you be so mean? I'm supposed to be your girl-friend, soon I'll be your wife.'

'But I'm not being mean. I'm not.'

Beatrice sat back.

'Look, I'm on your side for pity's sake,' said Christian. 'You're not a fool, you're not mad. All I'm saying is you're deluded. And it's not like that's even your fault. Some humans are hard-wired for it.'

Beatrice shook her head again.

'What?' said Christian.

She pushed her chair back, got up and went to pay.

Christian puffed out his cheeks. He stood, shrugged at an indifferent old man sitting opposite an old woman a few seats away, and went to wait outside. He felt an urge to get moving but was unsure why, given it would only be to resume the quest for cushions.

Beatrice strode up to him. 'I'm so stupid. This is why you agreed to see Tony, isn't it. Research.'

'Ah ...'

'And that's why you said you'll start coming to church.'

'No, it's ...'

She didn't wait for an answer.

Christian had to jog to catch her up. He got level and was about to attempt a partly sincere apology when he felt an arm interlock with his, jerking him back and turning him round. To his surprise, he found himself clenching a fist. But the arm turned out not to be hostile, at least not in the conventional sense.

'Heh heh heh heeeey,' said the owner of the arm – a chubby-cheeked fat man. 'Christian bloody Bootstrap!'

Christian's memory failed him.

'Christian *bloody* Bootstrap!'

Who was this guy? Chubby-cheeked fat man talking too fast in a high-pitched Lancashire accent, like he'd been overwound. Inane grin. 'Kevin ... *Tooting?*' said Christian, unclenching, clenching, then unclenching his fist.

It had been more than a decade since Christian had seen him and he was unrecognisable, at least in body shape. A trekking pole in school days, Kevin was now an easy XL and perhaps pushing the larger sizes.

Christian and Beatrice now prickled into the uneasy socially mandated ceasefire that would remain in force for the duration of the conversation.

Part one of the *I've not seen you in ages* ritual played out. The tedious exchanges of updates and gossip, the feigned interest, the platitudes. Christian hated every bit, but he played his part, a slave to the dance like anyone else. Anyone else except Kevin, that is. He followed the music, but the moves were all his own, shameless as he revelled in the hints of mediocrity instead of serving up the usual awkward reassurances. The grin widened when he learned that Christian and Beatrice were not only shopping in Bracknell, but lived in the town. Kevin was only here for the pies they sold at the indoor market, so he claimed, being of the opinion they were the best around – not exactly the best this side of Skelmersdale but certainly the best within a thirty-minute drive of his – actually his wife's – massive house in Virginia Water. Others might have been offended, but with Christian it didn't even register because he'd already engaged autopilot at the first opportunity. But this was a bad move, because before he knew it, he'd cruised through part two of the *I've not seen you in ages* ritual – exchange of phone numbers, email addresses and the dénouement: 'We should get together, how about Friday'? And before he knew it, his former friend and his former friend's wife were coming to dinner.

Chapter Seven

God was in lounge 103 – the wedge-shaped Rouge Lounge. There was business to discuss and he wanted to be waffendandy.

With more than 1,700 lounges in the ever-expanding footprint of the Deital Palace compound, God inevitably visited some of his hangouts more than others. But the Rouge Lounge was a stalwart – fashions fade, style is eternal and, according to God, this place had skip-loads of it. At the thin end, the end where God was stretched out on a crimson crushed-velvet daybed, the decor was a cross between a gentleman's club and a brothel, with a strong bias to the latter. At the other was a 117-lane bowling alley, its arms radiating out to give what the designers hoped would be a bold yet pleasing Japanese fan effect.

God clicked his fingers, belched, and ordered more 'nosh' before going back to his cigarette and his clippings – transcribed extracts from *The Secret* by Rhonda Byrne.

Soon there was a knock at the door. An aide answered and Gabriel strolled in.

'Terrence.'

'Gabe.'

The archangel stood and waited before God nodded to the daybed opposite.

Up close, Gabriel looked human. His features were perhaps a little birdlike – the beady eyes, the beaky nose, the comb-crested silver quiff –

and his muscle movements somewhat twitchy, as if he'd had six espressos too many, but still, at a glance, human. Zooming out, the resemblance became more tenuous – the larger chest on lighter frame, the slightly paddle-shaped shoes for slightly paddle-shaped feet, and of course the huge awkward armwings.

'Good read?' asked Gabriel.

'It's a revelation,' said God.

'Really?'

'Yep, says I can get anything I want if I just focus really hard.'

'Is that right ...'

'Good eh? I just picture it, ask for it, the universe listens and then gives it to me.'

'How's it working out so far?'

'Well I've only just started.'

'Right ...'

God put the pages down and glared. 'You're so closed-minded, Gabe. You should have more faith.'

'Surely things can't be that simple,' said Gabriel. 'Besides, I can't imagine the universe cares about what we want.'

'Well not with an attitude like that it won't.'

Two aides arrived, one carrying a silver platter of pallid pastries, the other a fat gourd of gravy. They set them down next to God and hurried off.

God took a pie, dunked it in the gravy and took several large bites.

'So, what did you want to discuss?' asked Gabriel.

'This,' said God. He forced the rest of the pie into his mouth before reaching over for the now gravy-spattered manuscript Harold had passed him a few days earlier – *Costa Rica and Beyond*, by Christian Bootstrap.

'Ah yes, I thought you'd be quizzled.'

'Quizzled? I'm not quizzled. I'm pissed off,' said God, spitting chunks of pastry as he smacked the document.

It was open at page five.

Infallibility

It was a predictably bright morning in Heaven. God was sitting on a cloud, mulling over developments in the afterlife arts scene with Uncle Geoffrey. They had just finished reading Sir Walter 'Shag-Spear' Raleigh's latest play, 'William and Steven', a comedy based on the early days of personal computing. They had formed a consensus that it was probably not his best work (you try being fresh and original after five hundred years of wryting), but decided it should proceed to produxion all the same. Not because they had low standards but because there was just such an appetite in the afterlife – anything that helped stave off the dreadful creeping boredom would do.

'Now,' said Uncle Geoffrey, 'there is one thing I have to bring to your attention.'
'Oh yes?' said God. He didn't need to be omniscyient to see what was coming.

> Note: have it that he's really omniscient or just
> thinks he is?

'Hendrix,' said Uncle Geoffrey.
'Yeah.'
'He says you didn't show up for the private show.'
'Well of course not, it's next week, first Tuesday of the month, we agreed.'
'Well, indeed. The thing is, yesterday was the first

Tuesday of the month.'

'Never?'

'Oh yes, look, check the calendar.'

'Well bugger me with a cherub's trumpet.'

'Also, he says even when you do show, you're always late – very late.'

'Bollox. You know me, Uncle Geoffrey, that's just not true.'

'Well ...'

An earthly observer might see Uncle Geoffrey's role here as somewhat awkward, taking the supreme being to task for his unreliability and tardiness, but in truth he was well used to it. The traditional earthly view of an infallible, reliable and punctual God could not be further from the truth. And in this wildly inaccurate assumption lay a lot of humanity's problems.

'What a cheeky get,' said God, and he belted the document again.

Christian was right, though. Without even realising it, he'd stumbled upon humankind's greatest theological mistake: the problem with the world, this particular world, was that some of the first people to attempt to make sense of it all had started with an incredible moment of sublime insight, but followed it with an equally incredible moment of pitiful blindness.

They had in their hands the ultimate answer, the simple answer to why everything was how it was. And yet they did not see it. It was the original and definitive wood and trees scenario and the most lamentable missed opportunity in all human history.

Their moment of insight was to reason that man was made in God's image. Their moment of blindness was to fail to see that in this was the answer to their question 'Why is man unreliable, fallible and often late for important appointments?' The answer, of course, being 'Because God is unreliable, fallible and often late for important appointments.' Once this is established, there is little further to explain and a comprehensive universal scripture written from this base assertion can be accommodated within one small pamphlet.

But if the false assumption is made, that God is reliable, infallible and never late for important appointments, while holding true the first assumption, that man is made in God's image, the resulting paradox leads to voluminous, contradictory and opaque scripture that even the authors don't really understand. Which leads to terrible suffering when people decide to defend to the death their sacred nonsense over that of others.

So there it was on the page. The answer. A simple truth that would allow humanity to relax, come to terms with itself, and take the rest of the day off.

God wasn't having a bar of it, of course. Not because he didn't want that for his people – or, more accurately, didn't mind them pursuing it so long as it didn't get in the way of his afternoons – but because he didn't believe the answer, even though it was obviously true, a position that underscored the point rather well.

'So who's this Uncle Geoffrey fella then?' asked God, dabbing at least some of the gravy off his beard. 'Sounds like a right pain in the arse.'

'It's just fiction, Tel.'

'Bollocks it is,' said God. He stubbed his cigarette into a limp Cornish pasty. 'We had that bloody discussion last week.'

'Oh, that reminds me,' said Gabriel, 'we've had word on the casting. It seems Gielgud's steadfast on playing Gates and they're looking at John Candy for Steve Ballmer.'

'Very nice. But can we stick to the stocks,' said God. 'Now, how did he get the details, this fella, you know, like Shaky's nickname and getting the play title bang on?'

'There is no how, Tel, he just got lucky – a coincidence.'

'My arse. What about the discussion, we had that bloody discussion.'

'I know it seems that way,' said Gabriel – he stretched out his legs before sitting up straight – 'but you think of all the millions of would-be writers down there, tapping away at all sorts of swill, sometimes it hits on the truth, be odd if it didn't. Think of this fellow as one of the million randomly typing monkeys who after a thousand years finally hammers out a few perfect lines of Hamlet.'

'Maybe we should get him up here as a fluffer for Shaky,' said God, 'might be able to improve the nerd play a bit.'

God began to roll another cigarette.

'Seriously, don't worry,' said Gabriel. He stood and walked to the head of lane fifty-five. The waiting aide held out a bowling ball, which Gabriel took, with difficulty, in his small black clawhands. 'In fact, and you'll like this' – he bowled the ball with the grace of a heron with heavy shopping – 'it appears this Bootstrap fellow is writing this as a comedy.'

The ball limped down the lane and toppled three pins, before a previously unseen team of pit-setters scurried into action.

'Never?' said God.

'Honestly, he is.'

God surprised himself with a snorting belling laugh, exactly the way he had while watching the First Vatican Council. It was enough to make him spill his tobacco.

Several aides sprang into action, one fetching a dustpan and brush from the shoe counter.

'Oh that is classic,' said God, 'that is goldstream.'

Gabriel retook his seat. 'Imagine that,' he said, 'he's captured a snippet of what it's really like up here yet he thinks it's a joke.'

'It's a strange old world I made, eh?' said God. He waved away the attentions of the aides and began fishing about the daybed for his rolling papers. 'That does make me feel a bit better. Worried me there for a minute. But hey, it's not like he got it all bang on, is it? His conclusions were way off.'

'Well hang on, you have to admit you are sometimes tardy when it comes to meetings,' said Gabriel.

'When? Go on, name one. Name one occasion.'

'The Black Death planning meeting. You didn't show up until thirteen sixty-two.'

'You can't let that rest, can you? Honestly, you take a break once in a blue moon and suddenly you're bloody Herod.' In his rummaging, God found a fluff-covered unsmoked cigarette, down in the cushion crack. 'Nice.'

'Look, it's not a criticism, Tel, it's a compliment – it says you're above all that perfection nonsense, perfection is wiffly, flat, it's whiter than white. You transcend all that, you're grounded, you have character.'

'Oh yeah, character,' said God. He lit the cigarette and took a long drag. 'Look, you're absolutely sure this fella ain't dangerous?'

'We're fine, Tel, trust me.'

'Okay. Still, keep an eye on him, yeah?'

'Understood.'

'Hey, one more thing,' said God. He took a swig from the gravy gourd. 'Your new fella, did you run through the rules with him?'

'Of course, Tel, why do you ask?'

'Well he's a bit bloody subservient, isn't he?'

'Is that so? I hadn't noticed.'

'And he's still wearing his blacenta, Gabe, *his blacenta* ... Looks like a fuckin' statue.'

'Tel–'

'Look, I know you think he's bright, and I'm all for giving the lad a chance, but get him straightened out if he wants to keep his place, yeah?'

'No problem. Right, are we done?'

'Yep, I reckon,' said God. He drained the gourd and let out a belch that sounded like the mating call of a demented donkey.

Gabriel rose to his feet and commenced an expert reverse towards the door.

'Hey,' said God.

'Yes, Tel?'

'Think of a number.'

'Okay,' said Gabriel, after a short pause.

'Twelve?' asked God.

'Right as ever,' said Gabriel.

'Hey hey,' said God, 'still got it.'

'Still got it,' said Gabriel, and he completed his exit.

'Still got it,' said God.

Chapter Eight

The number of people alive today who have not heard of Heaven, or something like it, is as near to zero as makes no odds. Every culture, every people since the dawn of civilisation, has put it in their lore in one form or another. And all who've heard of the upper place have heard of the lower place, it forming a natural stick to counterpoint the carrot. However, what few have heard, and even fewer believe, is there is a third, far more populous place beyond the gates of judgement.

For reasons most likely justified on the grounds of maintaining moral tension, Limbo has been written out of earthly belief. Though, when it met its final doctrinal excommunication in 2007, there wasn't much to write out anyway, because it had hardly been written in in the first place. The Catholics had been the only ones to give it a whirl, and even then they didn't really commit. Originally, they didn't think it existed – though strictly this was denial by default, in the same way they didn't think quantum mechanics, DNA or Australia existed – then, in Late Antiquity, they decided it did exist – probably. It was hard to be sure because it never got a mention in the Bible and no one had ever seen a need for it until one hessian-hooded bright spark asked the simple question: '*Sed Papa quid de infantibus qui mori ante sunt baptizatus est.*' It was quite a poser – it wouldn't seem fair to send a babe in arms to the torment of the lower place just because they'd died before they could be baptised, but then original sin is original sin, it's not an unpaid library fine, so you can't very well open the stairgate and give them a free crawl up to the glory of the penthouse, either. And so the middle ground, not-getting-to-the-root-of-the-problem-in-the-slightest solution *Limbo of the Infants* was born – a patronising vanilla middle realm with an extraordinarily youthful demographic who suffer none of the pain and torment of Hell but equally are denied the splendour of Heaven.

Many centuries later, in 2007, another bright spark asked a long overdue follow-up question: 'Look, Benny, doesn't the Limbo of the Infants thing make us seem a bit cruel, having a pop at dead babies and all that?' One of the senior cardinals pointed out they had to keep the wrath and damnation, otherwise it wouldn't be Catholicism, and then they might as well just hang it all and become an extremely well-appointed food bank. But the bright spark replied that they'd still be sending the gays and the suicides to burn in Hell and wasn't that enough to keep up the tough no-nonsense image? Everyone nodded and so they decided to decide that Limbo probably didn't exist after all. Or rather they *hoped* it didn't – presumably taking care with the qualifier in case God did turn out to be the sort of deity they'd been backing all along after all.

But Limbo does exist and always has. As real as beetroot, pubic lice and U2. Limbo – the other great underworld realm. Much like its down-stairs neighbour, it is a colossal, dank cavern of tar sands, mist and haze. It is a place of infinite scale in two dimensions – so long and so wide no one has ever found its edges – and malevolent limitation in the other – as little as ten feet high, in places, and never more than twelve hundred. The only way in is from the realm's arrival gate, the only way out – at least, the only practical way – long since sealed by the lucky few above.

So, physically, perhaps, there are some parallels with the Catholic vision, but that is where the similarities end. For the real Limbo has nothing to do with original sin. Its purpose is pure necessity – because, when you think about it, few people are truly evil, few are truly righteous, but everyone has to end up somewhere.

Dexter Adusei, Vice Chairman of the Board, was standing outside the main office of the third founding deity, his boss: Gordon Swan, King of Limbo, Lord Protector of New Limbinian, the Great Grey City.

The new reception decor didn't help – the Vettrianos and 'calming' mustard wash bang up next to the heavy old dogwood doors. And all to the now more established scent of lavender, which would, of course, be even more pungent on the other side.

He glanced at the digits in the flickering flames of the petunias, another misjudged decorative gesture. What was wrong with the standard knotweed? You know where you are with knotweed.

Ten twenty-eight and twenty seconds.

He checked himself in the mirror. He knew Eathelin – Gordon's diary secretary since 700 AD – was watching, as were the other managers waiting for their own appointments. They probably thought it was vanity. He didn't care.

Dexter had a short but steely form that wore a suit so well, so well it was almost part of him. And in a realm where former mortals were rendered an eternal fifty-ish, it gave him an edge, lucky genes making him appear an eternal thrusting forty-five and a good deal fitter than most.

He met his own exacting gaze. Close-cropped silvered curls on top – always functional, always short – prominent brow and cheekbones cradled bronzite eyes that would have glinted, were he not in Limbo.

Another glance at the clock. Ten twenty-nine and forty-one seconds. A final moment of lamentation as his mind turned back, way back, to those early meetings – the confidence, the testosterone, the shoulder pads, the what might have been. But those days were long gone.

He stepped over to the door, gave it three of his most reassuring knocks, and waited.

A booming 'Come' reverberated through the door, rattling its poorly fitting panels.

He turned the stiff handles, entered and began the familiar stroll to the middle of the room. On the way, he took in the new decor here too, the old new decor having lasted barely a week.

Mustard washed walls – same as in reception, he assumed, but here garnished with large feature blocks of olive green, cream and burnt orange.

A huge oil on canvas of *The Singing Butler*.

Full complement of almost-colour-coordinated furniture.

Anything of greater concern?

Stationery cupboard door still on the far right wall.

Spiral staircase to private roof terrace still where it was last time.

Still no windows … but then, windows, what would be the point?

So, thankfully, nothing structural this time. Small mercies, thought Dexter, small mercies.

The floor-to-ceiling hawthorn hedgerow, which took up the entire left wall of the room, was still in place, too, as was the immense bowled back wall of vertical citrine light-strips, which, along with the more conventional though still numerous ceiling strips, made Gordon's office the brightest room in the city, with illumination levels almost approaching adequate.

The great man himself was sitting in an attempted Jacobsen Egg Chair – already showing signs of repairs – in the middle of his new breakout area. As usual, Gordon wore a plain cream caftan. It was actually pure titanium-white, but here cream was as good as white got – throughout this realm, hues were washed out, colours failed to flourish, and life had the look of a Nordic TV detective series. White, true white, was the stuff of legend. But apart from a few years towards the end of the twentieth century, cream caftans was all Gordon had ever worn, all he'd worn since the beginning. Recently, though, there had been signs of creeping change. Today, for example, he looked a little flushed in the cheeks. Dexter couldn't tell if it was stress or just too much blusher.

'Dexter,' said Gordon, not looking up from his papers.

'Gordon,' said Dexter.

Dexter sat on the divan opposite Gordon. It felt like it had been stuffed with barbed wire and spanners.

'Nice,' said Dexter, patting the dirty-yellow upholstery, 'complements the decor.'

His boss eyeballed him.

Gordon had an erratic side-parting chestnut mane, once again overdue a cut, thought Dexter, the curls so long at the back they bunched on his collar; the eyebrows were chestnut too, but bled out to ginger at the tips, and bristled over a permanent glare that exhausted anyone who didn't know him well.

'Well it does,' said Dexter, gesturing to the room.

'Let's cut the crap and get on with it, shall we?' said Gordon. His voice was cultured and commanding. There was warmth, too, but you had to listen for it.

'Okay. Well, no change,' said Dexter, 'still no sign of our prophet.'

'Fucking still?' bellowed Gordon. He threw down his papers and lurched up onto his flat sandaled feet, the Egg Chair rocking back almost tipping off its base. Gordon was built like a butcher and as graceful as a concussed walrus. Others would have flinched.

'Gordon, what can I say? We have to be patient.'

'Patience my arse,' shouted Gordon. 'We should have heard something by now, we should have heard something years ago.'

'Well, yes. We should.'

'What's that supposed to mean?' said Gordon, suddenly still.

Dexter took a moment before speaking. 'Look, why now?'

'Why now? What do you mean why now?'

'Well you haven't asked for an update in months. Lots of months.'

'It's high time then,' said Gordon. He plodded a few heavy paces. 'I've realised … I've realised my energy for this great endeavour … it's waned, Dex, it really has. I fear all is lost.'

'We have to keep up hope, Gordon.'

'Hope? *Hope?* Do you realise it's been thirty fucking years, man.'

'Of course I know. We all know.'

'Three decades of phoney war.'

'Well, what can I say? We're still watching. Twenty-four-seven. But as ever, if we don't get a sign, it's needles in haystacks.'

'Yes, yes,' snapped Gordon. He turned to the hedgerow, its flickering flames showing an earthly television in full frame, its image showing a home shopping channel showcasing a range of revolutionary beetroot skin care products. 'It's just the pace of things on Earth. Salt in the wound, Dex, salt in the wound. Ten years ago, a child could have worked it out on his home computer, now he could do it on his pocket telephone. Fate is mocking us.'

'It's a tough situation,' said Dexter. 'I only wish there was more we could do.'

'Well, come on, what ideas have you got, what more can we do?'

'Oh, Gordon, please, we've been through this. We're already watching every service in every church, mosque and synagogue in the land, we've even got Speakers' Corner covered. When the prophet clears his throat, we'll be listening. Trust me.'

'And what about …' Gordon's chin dipped. He sat. 'What about the second front?' he asked, his voice softer now. 'I really thought we'd have been able to, to home in on … at least … by now.' He looked down at his planted feet. 'You don't know what it's like. I've abandoned him.'

'We're victims of our own success, in that regard,' said Dexter. 'There's just so many candidates in Britain these days, and not much to tell them apart. They hand out those MBAs like golf sale flyers.'

Gordon shook his head. 'Come on, there must be something else?'

'Well what about you, Gordo, are you still not feeling anything?'

'That's what I don't get,' said Gordon, before standing up again. 'I was told we'd be one and the same, that's how it was sold to me, and yet I still feel just like me, just as I always have.'

'As I understand it,' said Dexter, 'you are fundamentally one and the same, but in day-to-day terms, you are separate. Two consciences, one soul.'

Gordon looked to the ceiling. 'Two hearts living in just one mind,' he said.

'No, two minds living in just one heart.'

'Well, I'm not picking anything up.'

'Yes. Seems the hypnosis drew another blank, too,' said Dexter, flicking through his papers, 'and you're certain "Must buy tam packs" doesn't mean anything?'

'No, no. Already been through that with Grímsson.'

Grímsson: The butterscotch-haired human-half of the double act that cooked all this up. Spitback, aka The Pigeon, had started it but Grímsson had quietly kept it spinning, leaving Dexter holding the baby for three decades. And still Grímsson played his straight-bat defence. After all these years, still the wind beneath The Pigeon's armwings. The gall, the sheer gall of the pair of them.

'And otherwise you feel fine?' asked Dexter.

Gordon sat down again. 'Yes. Why wouldn't I?'

Dexter looked away and then realised he was looking away. He sat forward and brought his hands together. He should mention it: the morbidly obese elephant in the room that Gordon couldn't see or didn't want to see. Of course he should mention it. It would be the ethical thing to do. But he knew he wouldn't. He wouldn't because he never had. And now it was too late, too late by fifteen years. Now he was as culpable as Grímsson and The Pigeon, as culpable as all of them. 'No reason,' he said. 'No reason.'

Chapter Nine

A Brief History of Time

It's easy to forget that telling the time was once a tricky business in Heaven. They'd always been able to remote-view into the mortal realm, of course, right from day one, but that only helps if there's a mortal clock to view. And despite Adam and Steve and Eve being given a pretty good rolling start with God gifting them language, mathematics, the written word, religion, the wheel, knowledge of hunting, farming, fishing, cooking, astronomy, construction, law, trade, footwear, basic tailoring and lots of other handy hints and tips, humanity still took a millennium or two to get going when it came to telling the time. So to begin with, Heaven had to rely on its own methods.

The first was to use a camera obscura, which takes advantage of the sun's movement in the sky. In Heaven, the sun is always overhead but varies in proximity through the course of twenty-four hours, at midday being at a similar distance to its distance from Earth, but at night receding to what new arrivals often mistake for the moon, but locals call the 'manimoon'. To tell the time, all one has to do is step inside the obscura device, close the door, and read off where the sun's disc hits the graduations marked on the floor, the graduations indicating the number of hours from midday. However, several problems exist. The first is it won't tell you if it's before or after the meridian – once a regular gripe of Heaven's late risers, not least of which the commander-in-chief. Second, it won't work well between eight p.m. and four a.m., when the sun becomes the mani-moon and is too dim and too small for a reading. Third, given the geometry involved, to get any kind of accurate reading, your camera obscura needs to be the size of a large shopping centre.

The second method is far simpler and yet is only theoretical: with enough distance from the centre of town and the fixed X and Y axes of the sun's movement (or, more accurately, Heaven's movement relative to the sun – a fact Heaven's astronomers had long since sussed but somehow not quite got around to raising with God), sun-rulers – a variation on the sundial – would be viable. But as that distance needs to be into the tens of thousands of miles, no one has ever journeyed that far to see if anyone is out there, whether they are interested in telling the time, and if they are that this is indeed how they do it. And this is why sun-rulers remain theoretical. Some naysayers – mostly new arrivals – find it staggering anyone would be interested in such a mundane question, with such low chances of finding an answer, and such low potential for heaven-shattering revelations even if they did work out what it was. However, as the centuries have passed, more than one of those cynics has ended up heading out into the wastelands all the same, for no better reason than it offering something to do.

But since the second century BC, most residents have just tuned their window boxes to an earthly source – the Tower of Winds being the early standard, and, in later years, Elizabeth Tower, in London – a trivial and unskilled practice that still leads many of Heaven's old retainers to lament the younger generation's all too willing reliance on newfangled modern technology.

Harold was sitting patiently at allotment thirty-four G, block D. It was his first visit to Blotchley Hall, the oldest if no longer the grandest viewing hall in True Jerusalem.

In the early days, this place was no bigger than a barn and was the Kingdom's only state viewing facility, with space for just sixty observers. But it had been extended numerous times as Heaven's population – and, more importantly, Earth's mortal population – had mushroomed over the last millennium. By the beginning of the thirteenth century, the mighty stone tiered rows could house more than 2,000, and yet, these days, it only ranked among the smaller halls. Heaven had taken its sweet time to build bigger though, to the extent that most people had window boxes in their homes by the time the state began commissioning facilities on a grander scale, and, unknown to them, was still behind the curve now, with even the immense new Turing Building dwarfed by the viewing structures going up in Limbo. But Blotchley was still the original, and God, Gabriel and the cabinet wouldn't conduct their observations anywhere else – at least not their official ones, anyway.

Like all the allotments in Blotchley, thirty-four G, block D consisted of a desk, two chairs, a work surface, a supply of stationery and a small potted juniper bush. Each block was serviced by a complement of support staff, located at the ends of the rows, their stations furnished with larger fig tree window boxes. And at the foot of the lowest tier, on the far wall, to which all allotments faced, was a huge yew hedge, bigger even than the ones in True Jerusalem's largest cinemas.

'Right, how are we doing?' asked Gabriel, as he finally took his seat.

'I believe it's defective,' said Harold.

'Let me see,' said Gabriel, turning the pot towards him.

Gabriel put his right clawhand on the touchstone and with his left he clicked the ignitor.

Clack, clack, clack, clack, clack.

He tried again.

Clack, clack, clack, clack, clack.

'They never work, these things,' said Gabriel, peering at the ignitor. 'Fine for the first few months, then nothing.' He leaned back, clicked his clawfingers and looked across to the support area. An aide caught his eye, and Gabriel enacted a gesture that looked like he was peeling a potato.

Silence.

'They'll just be a moment,' said Gabriel.

'Right,' said Harold.

Gabriel drummed his clawfingers on the table. 'So how's it going then?' he asked. 'The particulars? We haven't had a chance to talk.'

'Oh, fine … it's fine.'

'Doesn't seem fine,' said Gabriel, looking at Harold's single-breasted high-button blacenta, now more cracked and patched than ever, both sleeves and most of one trouser leg now missing. 'I've told you several times now. It can't be waffendandy.'

'I know. I know I'm supposed to let it go. New beginnings and such.'

'It's not just that, Harold. You have to understand, you're not doing yourself any favours – Terry hates anything he can't have.'

'Well, perhaps I could lend him the sleeves? I've kept them, you know.'

'That's not what I mean. Think for a moment – he's eternal, he never had a rebirth, he didn't arrive here from the Spirit Zone encrusted in a brilliant-white blacenta. And besides, it's starting to smell. That Frankincense balm isn't fooling anyone.'

'Oh ...'

'Anyway, he's not known for his patience, so dispose of it and pick out some proper clothes, yes?'

'I will, I will ...'

'And if you're struggling for a look, well, why not go for something like this?' Gabriel showcased his grey knitted waistcoat. It was just as dull as the human equivalent, only cut in the traditional angelic style: split from pit to hip down each side and fastened with buttons to better facilitate the dressing and undressing of the armwinged wearer. 'Obviously you could get sleeves, if you wanted,' said Gabriel. 'Or not – I hear angelwear is quite hip with humans at the moment. Don't go to just any tailor, mind. Most of them don't have their provisioner set up right.'

Provisioners were a standard feature of all three afterlife realms and all were hard-wired to the Judea Essentials range. As well as a selection of simple clothing, tools, plants and basic materials, they were able to produce a few luxury items such as combs, brooches and tasselled felt hats. For the first arrivals, the sight of a smooth shiny cupboard that could summon into being a serviceable pair of sandals had been the stuff of dreams. Not so much these days, though.

'I'll give you my man's details,' continued Gabriel. 'He'll sort you out. He's got his configured beautifully, always a good fit. Well, always an acceptable fit, and really not that painful at all.'

Harold was staring and not at the quality of the weave.

Gabriel flicked his shoulder muscles, giving Harold a start.

'No matter how many humans I've met over the centuries, no one ever seems to get used to us easily.'

'I must apologise,' said Harold, turning away, triggering a fresh rupture in his jacket, 'I didn't mean to–'

'It's alright,' said Gabriel, 'it amuses me, more than anything. After all, what do humans expect to find in Heaven? It's not like we don't get a look-in in the literature.'

'Perhaps it's the disquiet,' said Harold, 'of seeing angels in the flesh.'

'Possibly ...'

'And I suppose your good self, in particular, being the most celebrated.'

'Granted. But there's more, isn't there? Something else. Don't worry, I've heard it a thousand times.'

Harold was silent.

'It's the wings, isn't it?' said Gabriel. 'Wings instead of arms. Wings instead of *wings and arms*. Am I right?'

Harold nodded.

Gabriel smiled. 'Which is a rather silly expectation to have, when you think about it. Men have arms. Birds have wings. Nothing has arms *and* wings.'

'What about dragons?' said Harold, immediately regretting it.

'You see. Silly.'

'Well, how about ants? They have wings and legs.'

'So does a chicken.'

'Yes, but the front legs of ants, they are akin to arms, are they not?'

'Oh right, so angels are like ants then?'

'No, no I meant–'

'The Arch-Ant Gabriel.'

'No–'

'The Ants of Death. The Ant Islington. Ant Delight. *Touched by an Ant.*'

'Again, I must apologise,' said Harold.

'Oh, don't worry. As I say, I've heard it all before. Well, obviously not your ant theory, but anyway, you'll get used to us soon enough.'

He tried the ignitor again.

Clack, clack, clack, clack, clack.

'So are there no female angels?' asked Harold.

'Of course not. Who ever heard of a female angel?'

'Oh. That's a shame.'

'No, not really.'

Harold looked confused.

'We have a saying up here,' said Gabriel. 'Angels are from Heaven ...'

'And?'

'... and so are all the other angels' – he bobbed his chin – 'so much simpler, I think you'll find.'

'But what about, well, reproduction?'

'Different mechanism. In fact, it's more a case of production than reproduction.'

'Oh. I see. So you, well, just pop into existence, do you?'

'*Pop into existence?* This isn't a magic show, Harold.'

'Oh.'

'No, we're formed in the provisioners, in the grottos, like everything else. Set one up, give it an hour or so, and there you go, one juvenile angel.'

'Incredible ...'

Gabriel returned his attention to the window box, fiddling with the settings at the side of the pot.

'Sorry. All my questions must seem rather foolish,' said Harold.

'Yes. Very. Look, it's all there in the book, why do you think he wrote it.'

Clack, clack, clack, clack, clack.

He stopped and turned to Harold, who was now looking rather forlorn. 'Look, what about food? Have you eaten anything yet?'

Harold shook his head.

'What, nothing? Still? Well, have you at least had a drink?'

'No. I'm not thirsty, not even a little.'

'That's not the point, Harold. It'll help you adjust, help you get used to having a body again.'

'I know. They stepped through it at orientation. Oh dear, was I rude to refuse Terry's cheesy footballs?'

'Absolutely not. Wisest move you've made so far.'

'But you just said I should eat?'

'Yes, but food. Not that stuff.'

'It isn't food?'

'Well, technically, yes, I suppose, but you wouldn't want to ingest it. No, tuck into the ambrosia, water's obviously fine, and the nectar's just about palatable too, if you get a good year, but keep well away from anything Terry's munching on.'

'Because it's sacred?'

'Because it's disgusting.'

'Really?'

'Oh yes. It's off, turned, spoiled, all of it. Even when it's fresh it's rotten. Come on, you must have smelled it, what about those vanilla slices he'd got hold of?'

'I thought it was perhaps my senses, you know, still adjusting.'

'No.'

'But why's it spoiled? How? It's just, this is Heaven ...'

'We don't really know,' said Gabriel, 'even after all this time. Perhaps something went wrong with the setup of the grottos, at the start. We've never properly looked into it.'

'Why ever not?'

'Well there's no real need, is there? It's an immortal realm, so no one needs food, for energy, for sustaining life. And besides, Terry likes it as it is.'

'But you said it's disgusting.'

'Oh it is, curdled cream, rancid butter, putrefied meats, and that's before he's got started on his recipes, but then he really will eat anything.'

The aide finally arrived, armed with a piece of flint and a small roughly formed steel bar.

'Ah, here we go,' said Gabriel.

'Now, sir?' asked the aide.

'If you wouldn't mind.'

The aide leaned over between Gabriel and Harold and ran the flint over the bar, like a waiter grating parmesan.

As sparks flew into the foliage, Gabriel returned his clawhand to the touchstone. The bush let out a satisfying *whumph* and it erupted into rich flame, startling Harold.

'Careful there,' said Gabriel, 'these can take your eyebrows.' The archangel gave a curt nod of thanks and the aide retreated. 'Right then, you can drive,' said Gabriel, removing his clawhand.

'But I … I don't know how.'

'Oh it's quite simple. Put your hand here and let your mind's eye do the rest.'

Harold edged his hand onto the touchstone.

'Start with somewhere familiar, a distinctive location, something classic,' said Gabriel. He drummed his chin before turning and pointing to the image of the Gothic opal glass clock face in the flames of the olive tree on the right-hand wall. 'There's your target,' he said, 'central London, Big Ben, show it to me from across the river.'

Harold's arm began to judder.

'May feel a bit queasy at first,' said Gabriel.

The flames flickered and spat before stabilising. A beat and then a rapid sequence of images burst from the centre of the flames: terraced houses, a back yard, a kitchen, a high shelf stacked with tins, bottles, paint-speckled speakers from an old stereo and a food blender.

'My, my old house,' said Harold, his voice thin, 'someone else's now.'

'Not quite Big Ben.'

'I don't– No wait, yes, I remember, we had it on a biscuit tin.'

'Remember, it's where not what,' said Gabriel. 'Well, actually where and what, I suppose.'

More images. A village green, a duck pond. Pan to the left. A modest clock tower.

'Well, it's not Big Ben,' said Gabriel, 'but I suppose it's a start.'

Pan back to the right, back to the pond. Zoom in, a duck, then the clock tower from the duck's point of view, then back to the duck, a jerky zoom into a close-up of its face, then closer still, to its beady eye, full flame.

Harold let go.

'Here, look, I'll start you off,' said Gabriel, taking over.

The fire calmed. A moment later, a pristine image of Elizabeth Tower was filling the flames.

'There you go,' said Gabriel, removing his clawhand.

Harold returned his hand to the touchstone, only to immediately withdraw it. 'Where's the Queue?' he asked. 'Big Ben, the Houses of Parliament. It should be snaking through them both.'

'We can only view the mortal realm,' said Gabriel, 'there's no access to the Spirit Zone.'

Harold looked perturbed.

'Oh dear,' said Gabriel, 'a long time since you saw it all like this, I suppose.'

Harold stared, eyes wide.

'It's a major inconvenience, actually,' said Gabriel. 'Leaves us blind when it comes to zonal affairs.'

'So how do you stay appraised?'

'Well how do you think? We go and take a look.'

Harold looked puzzled.

'We send angels into the field,' said Gabriel.

'Really? But, how? I don't–'

'We have a portal,' said Gabriel. He smiled and gave a quick double lift of his browfeathers. 'One of the privileges of being top realm. It's only one way, but can drop you anywhere in the Zone, pretty much.'

'And it's just for angels?'

'No, any resident of Heaven can use it. With the proper pappywork, of course.'

'But, but I never saw an angel in the Zone. Not even once.'

'And we go to great lengths to keep it that way. Now, come on, I've got you to Big Ben, see if you can have a look around.'

Harold slowly returned his hand to the touchstone. The point of view remained stable for a moment, before cranking back.

'Good,' said Gabriel. 'Now try to imagine gradual transitions, like floating down a river.'

The movements briefly became smoother and steadier but then started to twitch violently.

'Steady, steady ...'

The point of view accelerated towards the Houses of Parliament, skimming the boat wakes as it shot across the Thames, with Harold flinching as it rose to clear the far bank only to impact the old walls head on, then a blink of black before emerging into the Lower House, over the heads of the members on the opposition benches, skimming the eyeballs of the Shadow Secretary of State for Health, as she posed a question on NHS reform, snippets just audible through the window box's scratchy speakers, before arcing up, buzzing wildly around the public gallery, stalling, and then plummeting straight down into the woolsack, the image turning almost black, with only an interference pattern texturising the darkness.

'Here, let me assist,' said Gabriel, placing his clawhand over Harold's trembling fingers.

Harold tried to withdraw his hand, but Gabriel was having none of it.

'Now just relax,' said Gabriel.

A moment later, the image of the clock tower reappeared, closer this time. A brief pause before the point of view started to move, lifting from ground level and circling the tower, keeping it in centre flame all the time.

'Easy, you see.'

Then the point of view stopped circling, but sped up its rotation, revealing a panorama of the Thames and the London skyline.

'Now, watch. You'll like this,' said Gabriel. The view tipped forward, until they were looking face down onto the gardens outside the Houses of Parliament. And then the ground fell away, as the point of view rose, rocketing high above London, above England, above Europe, until the whole planet was visible in the centre of the flames.

'Rather snazzy, don't you think?'

'Extraordinary,' said Harold, for a moment forgetting his queasiness over Gabriel's clawhand.

'Was far more impressive before Google Earth of course,' said Gabriel.

'Anyway, that's the ABC. Now we need to get down to work. So let's see if we can't get a fix on our Mr Bootstrap, shall we?'

Gabriel clicked his clawfingers again to summon assistance.

'Now don't misunderstand me, reports and transcripts are vital, you need to read every single one, but there's still no substitute for getting your own eyes in the game. This is where you fill in the gaps, Harold, this is how you get inside his mind.'

An aide waved a hand of acknowledgement and began making his way over.

'Gabriel, there is, er, one more particular,' said Harold, 'regarding settling in.'

'Oh yes?' said Gabriel, leaning back in his chair.

'It's, well, a discomfiting matter.'

'Come, come, there's nothing you can tell me I haven't heard before.'

'Well, it's just' – Harold's chin dropped forward – 'I'm struggling to become accustomed to the, to the … homosexual procedures. Of course, I know I must recalibrate and accept that ways are different here, you know, grin and bear it – well, obviously not literally grin, while I'm … but it's really not agreeing with me.'

'Homosexual procedures?' said Gabriel, his browfeathers lifting, 'but, I … I had you down for a straight-bat man.'

'Well, um …'

'Bit late in the day to be coming out, isn't it? Though having said that–'

'No, I still am a, a straight-bat man.'

'Oh.'

'It's just I was anxious not to break the sacred wonts and customs.'

'I'm sorry, the wonts and customs?'

'Yes, you know …'

'Harold, have you been talking to some of the junior angels? The ones from the Lower Council?'

'Possibly …'

'A word of advice. Don't believe everything every angel tells you.'

Chapter Ten

Most people struggle with the question of what to do.

What to do?

What to do?

What … to … *do*?

But in every community, in every society, a lucky few will find they have a fair idea, perhaps even a fixed idea, from an early age. And yet there exists a greater level of conviction. In the life of every world, a handful are born who know exactly who they are and what they have to do right from the start. They don't need to be told; they don't need to be taught; they don't need to be encouraged. They just know.

'Come on, we're going to be late,' said Nikki, holding the front door open.

'We're fine, and anyway, it's only dinner.'

'So what if it's only dinner? Why does that make it okay to be late?' Her voice was rich and warm yet full of authority.

Kevin emerged. Jeans, loafers, extra-loud Hawaiian shirt.

She made no comment. To comment would be to take the bait.

He looked her up and down. Three-piece tweed trouser suit, white blouse with navy tie worn low, hair in deep-chestnut shoulder-length layers left in simple loose waves. Stylish, sassy, but no different from a day at the office.

'You not gonna put some heels on?' he said.

'Nope.'

'You gonna tell me why?'

'Nope.'

'Oh great, it's gonna be like that, is it?'

She exhaled. 'I've been wearing them too much,' she said. 'It's not good for your feet, in the long term.' She half smiled, but not for him.

'Well, whatever,' he said, fishing for his house keys.

Nikki unlocked her car – an almost new 7 Series BMW – and got in while Kevin locked the front door.

'Bracknell, yes?' said Nikki, starting the engine.

'Yep,' said Kevin. He tapped the address into the satnav as they began the short journey.

As the countryside gave way to urban scenery, Nikki's mind returned to the rollercoaster that had been the previous week. Kevin's mention of his long-lost friend and the associated impending dinner date had triggered sinking guilt. Somewhere she had made a mistake. She thought she'd accounted for all of them; she *had* accounted for all of them. How could she have missed this one? But the guilt had soon morphed into hope, hope that this lost friend could be the one. She had even allowed herself a brief Charlie Bucket moment to imagine *if*, and indulge the fantasy, before initiating her standard spousal debrief. A debrief which revealed no golden ticket and only served to trigger the resurfacing of undead anger and resentment. The double-check she was now about to execute was mere formality, standard procedure, but Nikki always followed procedure. That it would rile Kevin was merely a bonus.

'I already told you,' said Kevin. 'Christ, you never bloody listen, do you? Head always stuck at work.'

'I'm listening now, aren't I?'

'Look, we just lost touch. He always was antisocial. Total nerd.'

'So why wasn't he in any of your school photos?'

'What? What the ...'

'He isn't in any of them, not a single one.'

'You don't even know what he looks like.'

'But I know what everyone else looks like.'

In the early days of their relationship, Kevin had found the detailed interest in his friends baffling, 'even for a woman', but eventually accepted it as being her way – she was diligent and driven in her business life, and it was the same in her, or rather his, personal life. But as time passed, it had started to trouble him. She'd always said she was doing it because she was interested in him, in his life, and yet she never asked anything about him, only the lives of his friends and acquaintances.

'And you've never met Beatrice?' she asked.

'Only when I bumped into them the other day. Bonny lass, Christ knows what she's doing with Cry.'

'And Christian, he's our age?'

'Well, I went to school with him, so yeah, unless he's been in cryogenic freeze or something.'

'No need to be smart.'

'You know, love, I'd forgotten how nosey you could be.'

'I like a bit of background, you know that. Don't want to put my foot in it.'

'They're a thirty-ish professional couple living in Bracknell, wouldn't think there's much scope for controversy.'

'Well what about religion?'

'Cry? No chance.'

'So sure?'

'Biggest atheist I ever met. Always protesting about prayers in assembly, always forging these letters of support from his parents, other people's parents, even his MP, once.'

'Oh.'

'There was no let-up with him. He'd even make up non-religious swear words, shouting stuff about Russell Grant's teapot instead of saying "Jesus Christ" like anyone else.'

Her heart sank again. Of course she'd already established Christian wasn't devout, but hearing it put like this was the final nail.

'So what else do you want to know?' asked Kevin.

'Nothing,' she said.

'I don't get you any more,' he said. 'For a while it's all questions and you want to know everything, and then it's brick wall time.'

'I thought you didn't want to talk?'

'Imagine if fuckin' Letterman went on like that. Gets the guest cookin', then bloody shuts up shop.'

'Look, can we drop it.'

'Fine by me. Meet them soon enough anyway.' He turned up the radio.

Nikki couldn't stop her thoughts turning back to the search. The exhausting, relentless, fruitless obsession. It hadn't just dominated her life – it was her life. She'd always known it was her reason for being but only came to fully understand why in her late teens, when her intellect matured to deliver the infrastructure for real understanding. It blossomed into an almighty ambition, a vision of what would be, but it had now been denied fuel for a decade and had faded to a flicker.

'You wanna slow down, love? I always find I enjoy me food more when I arrive for dinner still breathing.'

She didn't reply.

Their journey was almost over.

Christian and Beatrice lived in Vestments. Which is not to say they had a liking for fancy religious attire, but to say this was their address. It wasn't Vestments Drive, Vestments Crescent or Vestments Lane, it was just *22 Vestments*, halfway down the cul-de-sac between Vespers and Vestry on the efficiently packed Ringpriest Estate at the southern end of the town. Legally speaking, Beatrice was the homeowner, though Christian did contribute to the mortgage payments and at least some of the bills, sometimes.

Nikki and Kevin got out of the car and approached the grey shoebox house. Small houses can be elegant; small houses can be beautiful. 22 Vestments looked like it was at the end of a long and unsuccessful boxing career followed by an uneasy relationship with plastic surgery: the boss-eyed top windows, the fat-lip porch, the wheelie bin enclosure cut into its left cheek.

Nikki turned to Kevin. He was already smirking.

'What?' he asked.

'Don't even think about it,' she said.

She walked down the path and rang the bell.

Chapter Eleven

'Comin' up ten years,' said Kevin, leaning back and testing the dining chair, 'ain't that right, love?'

Nikki was off in her own world. What she'd seen of Christian so far hadn't given cause for hope to be resuscitated. Now all she wanted was for the evening to end. She topped up her wine glass.

'You?' asked Kevin, turning back to Christian.

'Um, engaged,' said Christian.

'Is that right. When's the big day then?'

'Well, we're, er, working on it,' said Christian, glancing back towards the kitchen. He lowered his voice. 'Sort of on hold at the moment. Bit of a touchy subject.'

Beatrice returned.

'Hey, Cry was saying how you're not married, love,' said Kevin, winking at Christian, 'that's a travesty if you ask me.'

'Yes. It is,' said Beatrice. 'But … we're working on it.' She offered Christian a minimum-wage smile and retook her seat.

'You wanna get yer arse in gear and follow through, Cry,' said Kevin. 'Gorgeous girl like this, I'd have got a finger on her ring by now … if I were you.'

Beatrice smiled again, broader this time.

Kevin took a sip of wine and sat back, not even trying to hide a huge grin.

'Look, can we talk about something else?' said Christian.

'Yeah, perhaps we shouldn't put the fella on the spot,' said Kevin, with a chuckle, 'let's talk about something else.'

'Yes, let's,' said Christian.

'Well,' said Kevin, 'I haven't told you about my real passion yet, have I?'

Nikki turned to Kevin, though wherever this was going, she wasn't interested.

'Yeah, well my day job is just that,' he continued. 'What I really live for is my writing.'

'Writing?' said Christian. 'You?'

'Oh yeah, I've just finished my first screenplay. It's a British take on *Assault on Precinct Thirteen*.'

'Right.'

'It's called *Incident at Dorking Leisure Centre*. I'm thinking of giving it to Quentin Tarantino.'

'Well, well, I don't know what to say,' said Christian. 'I'm stunned. I mean–'

'What on earth are you talking about?' said Nikki to Kevin.

Kevin released a huge raspy guffaw. 'For chrissake, I'm pulling your leg, Cry.'

'Oh ...'

'You muppet, *Incident at Dorking Leisure Centre*? Come on.'

'Ah ...'

Kevin chuckled again, seemingly unconcerned that no one else was joining in.

'What's this about?' asked Nikki.

'Come on, Cry,' said Kevin, 'I couldn't write a screenplay any more than you could write a novel.'

A look of smug self-satisfaction blossomed onto Kevin's face, before he burst into belly laughs once again.

Christian folded his arms.

'Oh, aren't you a mean tease, Kevin,' said Beatrice, through a barely stifled smirk.

'I'm sorry, but what are we talking about?' asked Nikki.

'Christian's writing a novel,' said Beatrice.

Nikki sat forward.

This wasn't in the debriefing. She tried not to get excited. She told herself a desire to write probably didn't mean anything. A novel –

everyone wants to write a novel. But still, it brought the odds down, way down.

'Must admit, Cry, I did set you up there,' said Kevin, 'did some digging before coming over, Jack via Stevie via Ponch, via Daz.'

'Right. Good old Jack,' said Christian.

'You didn't tell me that,' said Nikki to Kevin.

'Need-to-know basis, Nick Nack, need-to-know,' said Kevin, tapping the side of his nose.

'So, *mate*,' said Christian, 'do you always prepare a dossier before a dinner?'

'Of course,' said Kevin, 'crazy not to. You know, *know your enemy* and all that Art of Warcraft crap.'

'Well, I'm glad I can be such a source of amusement to you.'

'I had you going though, didn't I, Cry? Come on, admit it. You really thought I'd written a screenplay, you berk.'

'Will you stop being such a prat, Kevin,' said Nikki.

'Oh come on, I'm only being honest. Cry's always been like this, full of lame ideas – the automatic snooker cue, that robot barber thing, the foot paintings. If he was going to write a novel, he'd have done it by now.'

Nikki watched Christian take a long slow sip of wine, perhaps holding the grotesque of Kevin's distorted smirk in the base of his glass.

'Well,' said Christian, putting his glass down, 'for your information, there is a history of writing in my family. My great-uncle. He wrote a novel. Took him six years and he did it all in secret.'

'Jesus, I bet he got some awkward questions about all those hours alone in the study,' said Kevin, laughing hard again. 'Hey, you got any dirty secrets you want to share, Cry?'

'Shut up,' said Nikki, 'honestly, you don't deserve to have Christian as a friend.'

'No, no, you're quite right,' said Kevin, holding his hands up, 'let's be positive and supportive. What's this book all about then, mate? Come on. Sell it to us.'

'No,' said Christian, folding his arms again. 'I don't want to talk about it.'

'Forget this buffoon,' said Nikki, 'I'm interested, I really am.'

Christian folded his arms tighter, but she held eye contact.

'Um ...'

'Please, Christian,' she said, 'tell us. Where's it set?'

Christian continued to resist, but Nikki continued to hold eye contact. There was only ever going to be one winner.

'Well. Okay,' said Christian, 'so there's two main settings, the first, where it starts, is Costa Rica.'

'Costa Rica?' said Kevin. 'What do you know about Costa bloody Rica?'

'Kevin,' said Nikki, raising a finger to her spouse.

'Lots, actually,' said Christian. 'I've done research.'

'What, flick through the *Lonely Planet*, did you?' said Kevin.

'No, the *Guardian* travel section,' said Beatrice.

'What? That's the research?' said Kevin. 'Oh please tell me you're serious.'

'It was an excellent article,' said Christian, through Kevin's laughter.

'Yes, they're quite an eco-friendly nation, you know,' said Beatrice, with a twinkle.

'Oh well, fair play, Cry, fair play,' said Kevin, and he clapped his hands.

'Hey look, that was just the start,' said Christian, 'I've done lots more since then.'

'That's right,' said Beatrice, 'we watched *Medicine Man*, and what was the other one, *Jumanji*.'

'*Jumanji* ...' said Kevin, failing to get his words out through the laughter. 'Oh dear, oh dear, Cry, whatever happened to write what you know?'

'Oh yes, because that'd work great, wouldn't it,' said Christian, 'really exotic, a novel set in Bracknell and Wokingham, with occasional forays into Yately and Pinkneys fucking Green.'

'Calm down, darling,' said Beatrice.

'Well he started it,' said Christian, and he took another large glug of wine.

'So what's the other setting then?' asked Nikki. 'And please, ignore the clown. I'm interested. I want to know.'

Christian exhaled but Nikki held eye contact once again.

'Okay, well, it's ... it's the afterlife.'

10,000 volts rushed through Nikki's central nervous system, her whole body tensing in near seizure. Time slowed to half speed. She rocked back and then slumped forward, her hand knocking over her glass of wine.

Christian and Beatrice jumped up to steady her.

'Whoa there, you okay, love?' asked Kevin, and he grabbed some serviettes to mop up the wine.

'I'll get some water,' said Beatrice.

'Are you okay?' asked Christian.

'Yes, yes, I'm fine,' said Nikki.

Her mind was racing, trying to make sense of what she'd just heard. Her intellect told her it still probably didn't mean *that*. Apart from anything else, Christian was an atheist. But then this was only on Kevin's say so – she'd not had time to double up with her own research. Maybe Kevin was wrong. Or maybe Kevin was right but Christian was born-again, that could still work, couldn't it? There were still reasons for her intellect to remain sceptical, but in her gut she knew, with complete certainty, it was Christian. The search was over. *It was over.* Another spike of electricity assaulted her nervous system. She clenched her fists.

Keep calm, keep calm, keep calm.

She'd been in adrenaline- and cortisol-fuelled situations before, too many times to recall in her business, but not like this. This was jackpot lottery win, Olympic gold medal, cancer all-clear, and a proposal of marriage from Idris Elba all at once. She was trembling and sweating, and her pulse was galloping away into the distance along with her grip on reality.

'You look really flushed,' said Beatrice, returning with a glass of water, 'are you sure you're okay?'

'Yes, yes, I'm fine, I'm ... wonderful. I just, I just had a bit of a moment. Oh, oh I'm so sorry,' she said, seeing the mess.

'No harm done,' said Christian, helping Kevin mop up the last of the spill.

'Do you want to lie down?' asked Beatrice.

'No, I'm okay. It's nothing. Just a busy week at work catching up with me.'

'What have I been saying, love?' said Kevin. 'She's her own worst enemy this one.'

'Are you sure you're okay?' asked Christian.

She took a sip of water. 'I'm fine, really.'

'Reckon we'll head home,' said Kevin.

'Yes, probably best,' said Christian. 'Shame to cut it short but it's been great. You must come again.'

'No,' said Nikki.

'Come on, love, and I think I'll drive,' said Kevin, and he replaced the cap on the wine bottle.

'I. Said. No.'

They all stood still.

Nikki scanned each pair of eyes.

'I feel fine,' she said, placing her hands on the table. 'I'm not drunk. I'm not ill. I want to stay and I want to hear more about Christian's work.' She took a gulp of water and allowed herself a smile that, though broad, did scant justice to the exaltation overloading her synapses. 'Now, please, Christian, continue.'

'Well, are you sure? It's just–'

'*Christian.*' She held the pause. 'Continue – please.'

The others silently retook their seats. Everyone turned to Christian.

'Okay. Well, as I say, the other location is the afterlife. But the story starts in Costa Rica, with this English guy, a budding writer who's out there doing voluntary work, John is his name, or rather John will be his name, John Milton.'

'*Paradise Lost,*' said Nikki. An exquisite aftershock surged through her, but this time she rode it.

'Indeed,' said Christian.

'Eh?' said Kevin.

'*Paradise Lost,*' said Nikki. 'John Milton was the author.'

'What's that then, book of the series?' said Kevin.

'What series?' asked Christian.

'*Lost,*' said Kevin.

'What's *Lost?*' asked Nikki.

'You know, that American mystery, on the island,' said Beatrice. 'The TV series.'

Nikki shrugged.

'No, Kevin,' said Christian, 'it's a bit older. It's–'

'An epic poem on the temptation of Adam and Eve, and the fall of man,' said Nikki, staring deep into Christian's eyes.

'Yes ...' said Christian, and he looked down at his placemat.

'So you're copying that then?' asked Kevin.

'No, not at all. I'm just including the name as a reference, it's like a tip of the hat.'

'So it's good is it then, this *Paradise Lost?*' asked Kevin.

'It's a masterpiece,' said Christian, 'a classic, apparently.'

'Apparently?'

'Well, yes, I've not read it myself, just yet, but it's on my Kindle.'

'So you've referenced something you've not read? Ah, so people will *think* you've read it? Sneaky.' Kevin lifted his glass in toast.

'No, you don't understand,' said Christian, 'if you don't acknowledge the works that have come before, you'll be seen as arrogant, or naive, or both, and anything you put forward will be dismissed out of hand.'

'I understand perfectly, mate – you're a fake. Nothing wrong with that, loads of people do it, astrologers, ghost hunters, that spoons bloke–'

'No, it's not like that, it's–'

'Just ignore him,' said Nikki. 'Now, what other characters have you got?'

'Look, perhaps we should talk about something else,' said Christian.

'No, please, tell us,' said Nikki.

'Well. All right, there's his uncle, Virgil.'

'Another reference,' said Nikki.

'So what, you copying *Thunderbirds* too?' said Kevin. 'Now I know you watched that.'

'No, birdbrain,' said Nikki, not breaking eye contact with Christian, 'Virgil, the ancient Roman poet, and Dante's guide.'

'Dante?' said Kevin, looking blank.

'*The Divine Comedy*,' said Nikki, turning to Kevin.

Kevin and Beatrice swapped shrugs.

'Yes, in my story, Dad's a bit of a bad apple,' said Christian, 'well, a complex apple anyway – he gets mixed up in the drugs trade, and ends up getting killed, but he redeems himself through becoming John's guide in Hell.'

'Your dad's in this?' asked Kevin.

'What?'

'You said in your story, your dad's a bad apple?'

Beatrice looked like she was about to speak, but said nothing.

'Yes, sorry,' said Christian, 'I sort of use people I know as placeholders for characters, before, of course, changing them, at some point. So at the moment Virgil's character is based on my dad.'

'Why haven't you mentioned this before,' said Beatrice.

'Well it doesn't matter,' said Christian, 'it's temporary, it's–'

'So this character's your old dad,' said Kevin, 'and you're telling me he's got mixed up in the Costa Rican drugs trade? Oh that's a classic, Cry. So what, did he get caught at customs with two hundred mint imperials up his arse?'

'Shut up, Kevin,' said Nikki, 'so who else, Christian?'

'Well, there's his girlfriend, Beatrice.'

'I'm in it? You didn't tell me that,' said Beatrice. 'Look, we need to discuss this. I don't want people to know about us, know our business.'

'Oh no, it's not you, Beasy, or rather it is you, at the moment, but it won't be in the end, then it'll be a mostly different you.'

'Dante again?' said Nikki.

Christian nodded.

'Beatrice is another character from *The Divine Comedy*, Bea,' said Nikki.

'Oh,' said Beatrice. She folded her arms.

'Christian,' said Nikki, 'why do you use people you know as characters, why not make up new ones?'

'Well, I struggle a bit there, to be honest.'

'Really?'

'Yes, well, um, this is going to sound pretty silly, but whenever I try to come up with characters, you know, like from a blank page, my imagination always seems to produce the same image.'

'And what is that image?' asked Nikki, crossing her fingers under the table.

'It's, well, it's an old image from my dreams. A scruffy, stocky, beardy bloke in his mid-fifties, hands in pockets, always looking a bit clueless.'

'Burgess,' said Kevin, 'fuckin' Burgess. Years later and we're all still paying the price. How did he get away with it for so long? I mean, you don't need to be taking showers after a geography field trip, do you?'

'No, Kevin, it's not Burgess,' said Christian.

'Oh. Right. I just thought …'

'No.'

'So … did he ever … with you?'

'No.'

'Oh.'

Nikki was beaming. She was trying to hide it, but she couldn't. The imagery – this was final proof; intellect and instinct were now aligned. She had to stay calm though; this would still need careful handling. She was supposed to have found Christian by the time he was twenty-one, so guiding him at this later stage would be much more difficult. Plus there were still pieces that didn't fit. 'So, Christian,' she said, 'from what Kevin told me, I'd assumed you'd still be an atheist, so what happened?'

'Nothing,' said Christian, looking puzzled, 'I still am.'

A queasy lightness filled her stomach and leached into the lining. 'But you can't be.'

Everyone looked at her.

'It's just …' She took a sip of water. How could he, of all people, be an atheist? It was a contradiction in terms. What on earth did that mean for the plan, for the mission?

'Yes. Still a heathen, I'm afraid,' said Christian, smiling at Beatrice.

'But you're keeping an open mind, aren't you,' said Beatrice, returning the smile in much reduced measure.

'Yes, well, the door's ajar.'

'So,' said Nikki, 'may I ask, why an atheist, with their door ajar, is writing about the afterlife?'

'To take the mickey,' said Beatrice. She smiled, but there was venom in her voice. 'To make fun of people who believe.'

'Your book's a *comedy*?' said Nikki.

'Well,' said Christian, 'that's the way it's going.'

A comedy. It was an outrage, a trashing of common decency. How could he? How could anyone?

Christian looked over at Beatrice. 'I just don't think I could have Heaven and Hell and keep it serious.'

'And Limbo,' said Nikki, 'do you make fun of that too?'

'Limbo?' said Christian.

'The third great afterlife realm.'

Everyone looked blank.

'Three?' said Christian.

'Well of course three,' said Nikki, 'there's always three. Gas, solid, liquid. Past, present, future. Red, green and blue ... the trinity ... the three wise men–'

'The three stooges,' blurted Kevin, '*Three Amigos*, three wheels on a Robin ...'

'Well, I'll think about it,' said Christian, 'but look, what's wrong with making fun? It's just a subject like any other.'

'Because it's people's deepest-held beliefs,' said Beatrice. She held eye contact, her cheeks and lips twitching.

'Well if they truly believe,' said Christian, 'they're not going to fear a bit of a lampooning, are they now?'

'You see, Nikki, he's got an answer for everything.'

Nikki looked over at Christian, but said nothing.

'And of course he's only mocking Christianity,' said Beatrice, 'keeping well clear of Islam, you'll note.'

'Well I'm sure Islam's just as much a load of nonsense, but the truth is I don't know anything about it,' said Christian.

'You know enough to know they wouldn't find your mockery very funny,' said Beatrice.

'Well exactly,' said Christian, 'I don't want a fatwa on me, spend the next ten years under house arrest.'

'To be honest, darling, I think that might suit you rather well.'

Christian took another gulp of wine and folded his arms.

Silence around the table.

'I'm going to put the kettle on,' said Beatrice. She stood and headed for the kitchen.

The silence held until long after she'd left the room.

Christian leaned forward and turned to Nikki. 'Honestly, I'm not being facetious,' he said. 'Well, okay, maybe I am being facetious, but it's more than that. Ever since I struck on this afterlife idea, it's just sort of rung true, I think I'm onto something. Does that make sense?'

'Yes, I suppose,' she said. 'So have you ever been a believer?'

'Never. Well, alright, if you'd asked me when I was seven years old, I'm sure I would have said yes. You couldn't say otherwise in my family, and I was confirmed at about nine, I think, but deep down, even then I think I sort of always knew it wasn't real.'

Nikki didn't understand and wasn't sure how to proceed. But then producing the information was the key; perhaps it didn't matter whether Christian believed it or not. She felt a little better.

For the remainder of the evening, Nikki prevented any other subject getting a look-in.

Christian was worn out and half asleep as he lay in bed with Beatrice.

'Christian,' she said. 'Hey, Christian.'

'What?'

'There's nothing we need to talk about, is there?'

He turned to see her wide awake and staring up at the ceiling. 'What do you mean?' he said.

'Your great-uncle. The novel he wrote. His six years alone in the study.'

'He wasn't in there all the time.'

'It's just … you are writing, aren't you? I mean, we don't have a … problem, do we?'

Christian sat up. 'Look, Bea, my dear, I *am* writing. I'm not bashing the bishop all day if that's what you're suggesting. Thanks for the vote of confidence.' He lay down and turned his back on her.

'I'm sorry. I just … I'm worried.'

He considered saying nothing further but in the end turned back towards her. He put his arms around her and held her tight. 'There's no need to worry, darling. I've got it all under control. Trust me.'

She said nothing further, but hugged him back.

Kevin went straight to bed when he and Nikki got home. Not Nikki though: she was buzzing, wide awake on the biggest and longest high of her life. She said she'd be up in ten minutes, but spent the next four hours in her home office, thinking, planning, speculating, replanning, and rethinking. At five a.m. she phoned Bryan Fishguard, her long-time General Manager and closest aide at her company, iChemiclast, and told him the great search was over. She gave him a list of instructions and changes: she would not be coming into the office for a while; he was to instruct the board to find someone to act as CEO in her stead; he was to hand his General Manager role to his deputy; he was to resurrect and head up the mothballed Person of Interest research department and its first task was to organise an urgent and comprehensive profile on Christian Joshua Bootstrap of 22 Vestments, Bracknell, Berkshire. Finally she told him to reinstate mandatory participation in the company's after-hours all-in wrestling and military history club for all thirteen levels of managers and executives, no exceptions.

Chapter Twelve

A Deeper History of Time

Camera obscuras are useless without sunlight, so in Limbo, water clocks and, later, mechanical clocks came about instead. But their use and prevalence has been in decline for centuries. In the joyless capital, the rise of the current and absolute governing culture had been the final nail, driving out the last of the horologists, along with the few other remaining craftsmen, engineers, artists and dandies. But the real damage had been done centuries earlier with the emergence of modern mortal clocks, because of course, like their brethren in Heaven, Limbo's residents could tune their window boxes to any earthly location, and therefore earthly timepieces. Though in terms of personal timekeeping, even this practice is dying out for those in the Great Grey City because these days no one in New Limbinian is ever far from the time. On every street corner and on the wall of every room of every building you will find a state-supplied knotweed window box, each tuned to a close-up of an unassuming digital display located in an anonymous grey building in a military base in the far northwest of England, Limbo's administration preferring the more prosaic and immaterially more accurate atomic time to that supplied by the clock face of Elizabeth Tower, though that still remains the timepiece of choice for the other places.

But whoever you are, wherever you are, and whenever you are, time keeps ticking by, however you choose to track it.

Dexter was standing, arms folded, eyes low, in the centre of his boss's private rooftop terrace. Four things were bothering him. One, why had Gordon summoned him to a special five forty-five a.m. meeting, before the six a.m. Sunday stand-up they'd both be attending anyway. Two, Gordon never did business up here. Three, this stupid hubristic high terrace was by far Dexter's least comfortable place in the entire city. Four, and most troubling of all, Gordon was late.

Dexter tapped his foot. He hadn't thought Gordon might be tardy, so he hadn't thought to bring some work. No work meant idle time; idle time meant introspection. It was not one of Dexter's loves or fortes, and before he knew it, a fifth darker and more familiar concern eclipsed the others – the future, the endless future.

Dexter had died in 1927 and arrived here from the wilderness of the Spirit Zone in 1974. Even though he'd now been ethereal for the majority of his existence, the memories of his mortal life were still strong, and, as far as he was concerned, that person was still who he was today. He hoped it would stay that way. Not ageing, at least in appearance, would help, his instincts told him. But then he knew this argument was as bogus as trying to stay young in mortal life. No one aged here. A money-lender who'd died in 812 looked as fifty-ish as one who'd died in 1812. Except they didn't. You could see it in the eyes of the older ones – the glazing, the lack of blinking, the distance. More disturbingly, it was often more obvious in their behaviour – the disconnection with mortal affairs, the lack of urgency, and, what worried Dexter more than anything else, the inability to innovate. He rightly suspected this had been a factor in his own rise – his sun appearing all the brighter against what were once the best, the best there had ever been. All good for Dexter in 1974, all good for Dexter now, but how would he be in a hundred years, how would he be in a thousand? Gordon had his back, but then he'd once had Luca Pacioli's, and now all he was good for was fitting skirting boards and he didn't do that very well. Dexter tried not to think about it. And his best method of doing that was the best one of all, just as it had been in mortal life – work. Beautiful, absorbing, ever-expanding work.

He glanced at the digits in the knotweed once again. Five forty-seven and twenty-six seconds. More than two minutes. This was bad.

Creaks of uneven planks under strain and the tinny rattle of poorly fitted iron rods indicated heavy feet on the spiral staircase.

Gordon laboured into view. He clocked Dexter and stopped, appearing almost surprised to see him, before taking the final stair and plodding past and over to lean, with perhaps an unwise degree of confidence, on the section of wooden rails at the edge of the terrace.

Dexter waited but Gordon just stood there with his back to him, gazing out onto the leaden expanse of the city. With reluctance, Dexter made his way over, taking care to shield his eyes from what hung with malice aforethought, just above. He wasn't alone in hating this place. Everyone who came up here felt the same, everyone except Gordon, because everyone except Gordon had at some point known what it was to live under an open sky. The entire realm of Limbo was choked by a low and meandering roof of black basalt, a warped mass of broken column ends, each marbled with vitrified silicon veins that carried small fractions of light from the land above – Limbo living off Heaven's castoffs, once again – such that wherever you were in this oppressive land, you had the sensation of living inside a glow-worm-infested cathedral organ.

All was made worse by the great roof having no visible means of support. Dexter had seen this impossible reality send some on a literal trip to the edge in search of relief, in search of answers. Buried *alive*. A horrific enough prospect for a mortal in some desperate earthly cavern or collapsed building, but for them there was the silver lining that should the worst happen, at least it wouldn't continue to happen for long. Buried *immortal*, now that would be true terror.

Up here on the terrace, those millions of megatonnes were within touching distance. It was the highest point in the realm and sat at the pinnacle of a vast lopsided metropolitan cone. New Limbinian was not like this by design but as a natural consequence of no one apart from Gordon wanting to build higher than their neighbours, but even in Dexter's disquiet, he had to admit, it was still an imposing view. Here they could see almost 300 degrees across the shallow declines to the west, north and east – hundreds of thousands of tightly packed wonky grey roofs radiating out and dropping away through the gloom, the meandering surface broken only by the bulges of the J. Edgar Hoover building, the Bush Rhetoric Centre and the new Trump School of Diplomacy, on and on, in an unbroken grey blanket out to the twisted closed horizon of roof and floor.

Dexter looked across at his boss, who had still said nothing.

'Gordo,' said Dexter, a chill running up his spine as his voice came back at him off the roof.

No reply.

'Gordo. Look, what's this all–'

'Last night,' said Gordon, 'I was at my desk ...'

'So what's new.'

'... I was at my desk and I ... I fainted.'

'Fainted? Are you sure?'

'Sure?' said Gordon, turning to face Dexter, 'of course I'm fucking sure. Came to with half a bottle of nail varnish pooling on my *Men's Health*. Right damned mess.'

'I see.'

'So?'

'So what?'

'So what do you think?'

'That's it?' said Dexter. 'That's what this is about?'

'Yes. Now tell me what you think.'

Dexter relaxed. 'Well, perhaps you've been working too hard.'

'No harder than normal.'

'That's still quite hard.'

'And still quite normal.'

'Fair point. Well, has this ever happened before?'

'Never.'

Dexter puffed out his cheeks. 'Well what does Grímsson say?'

'I've not seen him.'

'Well you should. Gordon, he has a duty of care, him and Spitback, this is all–'

'I've not seen him and I'm not going to.'

'But–'

'You see, there was something else.'

'Oh.'

'Delicate matter.'

'Okay ...' said Dexter.

'I ... I had to change my undergarments.'

'Because you ... didn't like them?'

'Because I had to.'

'And by that you mean ...'

Gordon pursed his lips.

Dexter clenched his teeth. His first thought was incontinence. Not because it was the most likely explanation, but because he didn't want to consider the other one. Gordon had been around a long time, a very long time, but incontinence wasn't possible here, not for deities, not for anyone. So that just left. Oh no, please no ...

'It was a pleasant sensation, admittedly,' said Gordon, 'but I cannot afford to be distracted.'

'Distracted from?'

'Work, man, what else? My work comes first, second and third. Fourth, fifth, sixth and seventh, as it should be. Frivolity is ... is for the other places.'

'Well. Indeed.'

'So what do you think?' asked Gordon, hands clasped.

'I don't know. But it's probably normal, isn't it,' said Dexter, 'healthy even. I expect everyone experiences it now and again.'

'Have you experienced it now and again?'

'No. At least, not ...'

'Not what?'

'Not ... on my own.'

'Oh. Thanks very much.'

'I'm just being honest, Gordo.'

'Right, well, fuck you, Dexter, fuck you.'

Silence.

'Look,' said Dexter, 'how do you feel now?'

'I ... well I feel fine,' said Gordon. 'In fact, aside from the nuts and bolts of the matter, I feel spamtastic. Been a strange week, though. Up and down, very very up and down, but now I'm relaxed, I'm calm.'

'Calm is good,' said Dexter.

'But it's more than that. I feel energised, too.' He stretched his arms above his head and placed his palms flat on the cold rock of the great roof, like he was bracing to take the strain, Atlas style. 'I feel the surge. I know it now, I know we'll get there.'

'Gordon, really, let's not–'

Gordon lowered his arms and leaned in. 'Dexter, I feel it in my waters.'

Dexter held back a grimace.

'You will find them,' said Gordon, 'I know it now. You will find them.'

Chapter Thirteen

Unusually for Christian, and especially because it was Sunday, he'd got up before Beatrice. For the first time in weeks, he'd felt good about the book, though it did unnerve him as to why, given the abuse he and it had endured from Kevin the previous evening. Furthermore, it had been a restless night, Christian's dreams having been occupied by an unusually animated Erdygrot, whining on about the cold reality of the slush pile and the futility of writing anything other than sadomasochistic vampire-werewolf teen romance.

This Sunday was slated to be his first probationary attendance at church (another of Bea's armistice terms). And he would have gone willingly, keen to build bridges as well as study the behaviour of believers in the field, but when Beatrice had got up, she'd informed him she would be going alone. Christian had to stay away 'until he was ready'. It was only when he relived snippets of the conversations from the previous evening that he realised why.

The upside was a free morning to get the new ideas onto the virtual page. Enthused, he made an earlier-than-usual start to his writing day, restricting himself to only one episode of a *Frasier* double bill before sitting down at the keyboard.

.   .   .

For once, words flow with ease. Ideas rise before him, expand, deepen and evolve, deduce their place in the jigsaw and slot themselves in. The pieces begin to join forces; themes and concepts emerge; connections form, arcing between the islands. Child ideas sprout everywhere, so many he switches to pen and paper to scribble each one down, writing furiously for fear of losing the others already evaporating in the stack of his short-term memory. He rarely finds himself in this place, but when he does, he knows he has it in him to be a writer. The world outside, people, time, the room around him, and even his own self have faded away, his universe has collapsed to words and ideas, the pen and the paper. All he has to do is give in to it, try not to overthink, try not to think at all. Just let it flow, yes, trust in the flow. Now words form ever more rapidly, quickly filling the pages, one idea flows into another, and another, and another, over and over. It goes on and on. And then a new element appears in the idea-word-pen-paper universe. It is now an idea-word-pen-paper-doorbell universe. And as easily as he had slipped into the zone, he is wrenched out of it.

As always, he feels dazed, for a second his brain seeing everything around him other than ideas, words, pens, paper and doorbells as exotic and unnatural. A further second and he is back in reality.

The doorbell rang again. For once his frustration at being interrupted was genuine, and as he stomped down the stairs he hoped it would be Jehovah's witnesses, first because he'd be able to quickly get back to his desk and hopefully the zone, and second because he was in the mood to give them a high-velocity, depleted-uranium-tipped piece of his mind. So it was with some surprise, and a little disappointment, that he opened the door to find Nikki standing before him. She was carrying takeaway coffees on a cardboard tray and sporting a smile that would have graced any toothpaste commercial.

She was dressed like a Milan catwalk Lara Croft: cargo pants, spotless trainers, high-cropped black cotton jacket over a white T-shirt. Casual and yet she still looked a million dollars.

He looked about 55p.

'Hi, Christian,'

'Nikki … *hi.*'

'I was passing and I thought I'd drop in and say good morning. Thought you might like a coffee.'

Instant embarrassment at not being dressed and in particular about being in his dressing gown. It was an older-style garment, made of sky-blue terry towelling, and was more at home in the 1976 *Morecombe and*

Wise Christmas Special than the twenty-first century. It was also rather too short and so tended to foster an air of impending indecency. Perfect for embarrassing extra-wide-eyed Jehovah's witnesses into a hasty retreat, but rather a breezily vulnerable choice for receiving a former friend's beautiful wife first thing in the morning.

'Aren't you cold?' asked Christian, the January chill already getting up his gown.

'I don't feel the cold,' said Nikki. 'Now I wasn't sure what you liked, so thought I'd play it safe with semi-skimmed milk lattes, no sugar.'

'Oh, that's perfect,' said Christian, 'most kind.'

He took his coffee.

'So, can I come in?'

'Sorry, yes of course.'

Nikki didn't seem concerned about Christian's mini gown and bounced in. She was lithe and up on her toes. Her hair was tied back into a ponytail and it bobbed along with her quick movements like it didn't have a care in the world. In this moment, she seemed more alive than anyone or anything Christian had ever seen, certainly anything in Bracknell at nine fifteen in the morning.

Nikki headed into the living room and parked herself on one of the twin sofas. Christian followed and sat opposite.

'Bea's at church, I'm afraid, but she won't be too long.'

'That's okay. I came to see you.'

'Really?' said Christian. He closed the gap between his knees.

'Yes, I had a thought on the book, well, two thoughts really.'

'Oh, right.'

'That is if it's okay? I don't want to interfere.'

'No, please go on.'

'Well I loved your ideas, I really did, I just think you may be on the wrong wavelength.'

'Wrong wavelength?'

'Yes. From what you said last night, you've got two problems. Which, of course, are really two opportunities in disguise.'

Christian had heard this sort of drivel hundreds of times over the years at work. It was normally his trigger to begin nodding his head and start thinking about what was on TV tonight. This time he paid attention. But then with Nikki, it was hard not to.

'Your first problem is you're having trouble marrying up Costa Rica with the afterlife.'

'Yep, it's a tricky one.'

'So I was thinking, why don't you drop Costa Rica altogether? Have it all in the afterlife.'

'Well, that's a possibility,' said Christian, already regretting the decision to pay attention. But then he found himself acknowledging it might make sense. The advantage of the afterlife as a setting was that he didn't have to do any location research, because, of course, the location didn't exist … and so if he set the entire book in the afterlife, that would mean he wouldn't have to do any research at all. He glanced over to the *Jumanji* DVD. It would mean writing off that investment, but then it also meant he now had a perfectly good Christmas present for Bea's sister.

'And your other opportunity,' said Nikki, 'is that you struggle with creating characters.'

'I do.'

'So get rid of them.'

Okay, so her first idea was sound, but this was plain daft. How can you have a novel without characters?

'Interesting,' he said.

'Get rid of the characters and turn your book into a rough guide to the afterlife. It would be funny, it would be original.'

This was the second-worst idea he'd ever heard. It was silly, it was stupid, it was … it was … actually, it wasn't too bad … in fact, yes, it was brilliant.

'Interesting,' he said.

They continued to talk further about the book. Christian soon found himself sharing details and ideas he'd not shared with Beatrice, or anyone else, so far. With Nikki, it was easy. She seemed genuinely interested, not just in that he was writing a book, but in what he wanted to write about – she knew not just of the *Commedia*, *Aeneid* and *Paradise Lost*, but of *The Screwtape Letters*, *Good Omens*, *God is Not Great* and *The End of Faith*. What's more, she'd even read them. And she was an atheist, a fact she had not disclosed the previous night but shared now. She confessed to the same loathing and mistrust of organised religion he felt and they spent the next half hour joyfully swapping atheist anecdotes and arguments.

'Christian,' said Nikki, 'can I ask you a personal question?'

'Um, okay.'

'You were at school with Kevin, but I never saw you in his class photos.'

'I'm sorry, what?'

'The annual class photos. I was looking through them. You're not in a single one.'

'No, you must be mistaken. It was a long time ago, I'm quite a bit taller now.'

Nikki held eye contact and shook her head.

Christian said nothing.

'Come on,' she said, 'it's true, isn't it? You're not in any of them.'

'Well. All right. But so what?'

'Will you tell me why?'

He paused. 'No one's ever asked me about this.'

'Come on, you can tell me.'

He waited, but her eyes got him, once again. 'Well, okay,' he said, 'I suppose it hardly matters now. It's not like I can get into trouble with the head. Okay, well, as I'm sure you already know, Kevin and I went to a Catholic school. And you also know I've been an atheist for as long as I can remember. So it was a kind of protest.'

'Against what?'

'The regime. It was so oppressive.'

'Really? Are we talking abuse?'

'Oh no, nothing like that, well, apart from Burgess, of course, or so the rumours went.'

'Of course, but no abuse otherwise?'

'No.'

'So in what way was it oppressive? Did they shoehorn religion into every subject? I don't remember Kevin mentioning anything overt.'

'Well, there was a cross in every classroom, even in the science labs, even in the changing rooms. But I suppose it stopped short of calculating the volume of Noah's ark in maths or intelligent design creeping into biology. So no, it wasn't rammed down our throats, exactly, but you could never fully escape it. No, the problem was the whole mindset of the staff.'

'Ah, right, so staff were picked for their religious conviction rather than their teaching ability?'

'Well no, the subjects were taught well enough, I'd say. Well, obviously apart from sex education, which was bordering on the ridiculous. No, we had some very good teachers. Or at least some very competent teachers.'

'But were they preachy?'

'No, not really.'

'But they were all Catholic?'

'Actually, now you mention it, I'm not sure they were.'

'Right, right. Not *that* oppressive, then?'

'Oh no, no, it was a nightmare. Take my Richard Dawkins Appreciation Society, they tried to make me close it down.'

'You're joking?' she said, through laughter. 'You set up a Richard Dawkins Appreciation Society in a Catholic school?'

'Yes. Why not?'

'Well, all right, fair enough, but you say they *tried* to stop you? So you won that fight?'

'Yes, I suppose.'

'So, again, not quite Stalin's purges then?'

'Well, it could have been. You see, they only called off the dogs because they said I hadn't incited any subversion.'

'How so?'

'Because I was the only member.'

Nikki laughed again. 'You're not serious?'

'Yes. They said technically this meant the society only existed inside my head and so it was a matter for me and my conscience.'

'Hang on, hang on, are you saying you kept going?'

'Of course. I met every Tuesday.'

More laughter. 'Oh, Christian, why on earth did you bother?'

'For the principle,' he said, irritation in his voice, 'this stuff really mattered, it got under my skin. It still does.'

Nikki stopped laughing. 'Yes. Yes, I see that now.'

'It made me feel pretty isolated though.'

'Well what about your classmates? Did no one else think like you?'

'They did and they didn't. Plenty of them were atheists, just none of them wanted to stand up and say so. Kevin, for example, he's not a believer, is he?'

'I don't know what he believes.'

'Well he wasn't a believer back then, I can tell you. I used to see him winking at me as he took the Communion. I think he liked it that I knew he didn't believe while he shamelessly pretended he did, he knew it riled me.'

'Yep. That's my husband.'

'Anyway, he wasn't the only one. Lots of them didn't believe, but none of them, not one, thought it was worth making a stand over. To me, that was worse than the believers. At least the believers had integrity. So that's maybe why I ended up being a bit of a loner.'

'I do know what you mean,' said Nikki. 'I was a loner at school. A loner full stop. But it never bothered me. No one ever achieves anything great by fitting in.'

'Wish I'd felt like that,' said Christian, 'because it did bother me, at the time. I tried to go with the flow, like the rest of them, but I couldn't. Again it was the principle of the thing. We were taught the trinity like we were taught maths or history, like it was fact, and showing any doubt or dissent was treated as a disciplinary issue instead of an intellectual one. How patronising is that?'

'Was there no one you could turn to? No teachers?'

'None, at least none who'd risk taking on that kind of battle.'

'What about your parents?'

'Them? Oh forget it. They were worse than the school, far worse, still are. They'd have had me in one of those ACC schools if they could, but there were none in Britain at the time.'

'ACC?'

'Accelerated Christian Conditioning, hardcore fundamentalist stuff.'

'Oh dear.'

'And I'm not joking, we were even going to move to America at one point, until my dad heard they look up your library records.'

'You poor thing.'

Christian shrugged. 'Ah well, maybe I got off lightly in the end. Didn't feel like it at the time though.'

'So, what's all this got to do with the school photo?' asked Nikki.

'Oh yeah. Well, for me the photo was one of the symbols of our acceptance, tacit agreement that all this was okay. Everyone in their uniform, nice neat rows, all lined up under the statue of the Madonna at the main entrance. So this was my silent protest.'

'So, what, you bunked off each time?'

'Oh no, wasn't my style. I just faked illness.'

'What, seven years in a row?'

'Yes.'

'Wow. Quite a commitment.'

'Well it wasn't hard. We had a different form tutor each year, and despite having a reputation as being theologically difficult, I was never a problem child in the conventional sense, so it wasn't like anyone was going to notice. A kid being off school for the same day of each academic year – who would ever look for that kind of pattern?'

'And is that why you don't appear in the school's records either?'

A moment of silence before Christian spoke. 'How, how could you possibly–'

'Sorry, it's my curious nature. Gets the better of me sometimes. Did I do wrong?'

'Well I don't know. What exactly did you do?'

'It just followed on from you not being in the photos. It was intriguing, I had to know more. Before I knew it, I was on the phone to the school to ask them a few questions, and they said they had no record of you ever attending.'

'Well, that's a bit of an invasion,' said Christian, wondering if she'd uncovered any of his larger skeletons.

'But this isn't news to you, is it? That you're not in their system?'

'No.'

She smiled. 'You wiped the records?'

'Yes.'

'How?'

'I hacked in a few months after I left. It was easy. It wasn't like they had much in the way of security. They were early adopters of computerised records, so hypocritical when you think about it, but they didn't really know what they were doing.'

'So why did you do it? Same reason as not being in the photos?'

'Yes, but this also gave me absolution. It was my way of affirming to myself that even after seven years, they hadn't got to me, hadn't made me religious, let alone Catholic. I just had to do something like this, like an exorcism, you know, lay the ghost, make the ground pure again. You know how many kids from Catholic schools don't believe but still end up as guilty adults?'

'How many?'

'Well, I don't know, but … a lot.'

'So why didn't you wipe everything? Take the whole system down, make a statement?'

'That wasn't the point. Then they would have found out.'

'And fixed it, restored the data, put you back?'

'Exactly. But also it was that I'd put one over on them, proved they didn't know everything. And they never did find out. They still don't, I suppose. There've been lots of times since where I've thought back to that, and it always puts a smile on my face. Kind of reaffirms my faith in not having faith, if you get my meaning.'

It felt good to share this history. It wasn't exactly Watergate or Robert Maxwell stealing from the pension fund, but even so, he'd never told a soul about this, not even Beatrice. Then it occurred to him that she'd never asked – okay, so she could never be expected to ask about whether he'd ever thought about deleting his school data files, but surely she could have asked why he had no school class photos. 'Nikki,' he said, 'I'd like to take on your ideas. I think you're right. An afterlife guide book could really work.'

'Really? Don't joke about this, Christian.'

'I'm not, I'm serious, this is what's been missing.'

'Oh that's amazing,' she said, her eyes wide, 'I'm so glad you liked them. I wasn't sure at first.'

He was surprised she'd picked up on his earlier reticence. 'Yes, sorry about that,' he said. 'I always get a bit defensive when people make suggestions. Normally it's because–'

'Because they're terrible, right?'

He smiled. 'Yes. But yours are, well, brilliant. But, um, I'm not sure what I can offer you in return. I can't just take your ideas.'

'Of course you can. It's your book, Christian, I don't want anything in return, really.'

'Oh. Well, thank you, then.'

'All I want is to see it in print, to see the disgust on the faces of the righteous. I think it could make a real difference, you know.'

'Really?'

She nodded.

'Don't get me wrong,' he said, 'I'm sold on this, but it will still just be a book.'

'Never say that, Christian. This will be no ordinary book.'

It was a throw-away line, hyperbole, and yet he could tell she meant it. There was sudden tension in his neck and shoulders.

But the discomfort passed as they chatted on, making jokes about the absurdity of belief, discussing their favourite atheist books and films, and generally starting to get on rather well.

Beatrice opened the front door to the sound of laughter from the living room and then the voice of Terry Jones as Mandy Cohen.

Now look, he's not the Messiah, he's a very naughty boy.

'Hi, I'm back.'

I'm his mother, that's who.

'Hello?'

'We're in here,' shouted Christian, before muting the TV.

'We?' said Beatrice to herself as she made her way into the living room.

'Hi there,' said Nikki.

'Oh. Hi.'

'Hey, Beasy-Bea,' said Christian, 'we were just watching a bit of *Life of Brian*. How was church?'

'Fine.'

'Nikki's brought us some coffees. There's one for you in the kitchen. It'll be cold so pop it in the mic.'

'Perhaps later.'

'Nikki's been helping me with the book. We've got some fantastic ideas, some exciting new directions.'

'Oh. How delightful for you.'

Silence.

'Well, anyway,' said Nikki, 'I'd better make tracks. Thanks again for last night, you must come to us next. We'll do it soon, I promise.'

'Sounds great,' said Christian.

Beatrice said nothing.

'Right,' said Nikki, 'well, I'll show myself out.'

She skipped past Beatrice, flashed a seemingly sincere smile, and left.

Beatrice waited for the sound of the front door closing.

'What was she doing here?'

'She came round to say good morning. And she had a couple of ideas for the book – good ones.'

'What's that?' said Beatrice, pointing to some printouts.

'Oh just a few pages, nothing really.'

'You showed her?'

'Yes.'

'You showed her your writing. You haven't shown me your writing.'

Beatrice took the takeaway cups into the kitchen, poured her coffee down the sink and threw the cups in the bin.

'Well it was only a couple of pages,' said Christian, following after her. 'You can read them now if you like.'

'I'm not in the mood. And perhaps it's time you put some clothes on. I'm going out.'

'Out? But you've only just got in.'

'Well now I'm going out again.'

Beatrice left, slamming the front door behind her.

Chapter Fourteen

Dexter and Gordon were leaning, though not too hard, on the stone wall of the executive balcony of Henry Ford House, the most important building in the sprawling network of office complexes that was New Limbinian Central Administration. It sat two-thirds of the way up the steeply terraced south side of the cone of the city, the greater clearance from the realm's rock canopy making it a more comfortable meeting place, for Dexter at least.

It was almost midday, not that you would know it. Like Murmansk in winter, Limbo never really had a daytime. There was a rise and fall in the intensity of the points of light that speckled the basalt, tracking the rise and fall of the sun bathing the realm above, but even so it was really just graduations of gloom.

Here, on the south side, the roofs dropped away from Gordon and Dexter like a grey-tiled ski slope. At their foot lay the citadel wall and south barbican, then open ground to a tall wire fence, more open ground and then the thick outer wall that marked the city limits. Then the beginnings of the endless black gravel scrublands and uncharted spaces beyond. All appeared flat and featureless as the closed horizon faded into haze, all apart from a long, thin incline that led up to an expansive flat promontory in the middle distance. On it lay the yellowed pancaked ruins of the old capital, still and silent apart from a small area of intense animation at its centre. For this was still the location of the realm's arrival gate – the only way into this desolate cavern. In size and form it matched its counterparts in the upper place and the lower place, and the Gate of Judgement on Earth, though here the structure itself was never in view, for Limbo's cup runneth over. From Dexter's and Gordon's position on the balcony, it resembled a writhing off-white lava fountain, the lighting rendering the blacentas of Limbo's latest arrivals a troubling mummy-like dirty cream. It was a great vomiting of humanity, spewing souls in such numbers, and with such vigour, that fragments of blacenta rained down like snowflakes and so littered the site they gave the ruins an unbroken smokers' yellow covering, like shit on the cliff of a gannet colony.

'Look at it,' said Gordon, 'our numbers, our metrics, our souls per hour in physical form. Scares a lot of the section heads, you know, in private. Bhakta's the worst, "But what if they attacked?" The man's welnric, I tell you. The masses, the rejects, they don't want what we have. I don't know what those malingerers want. The best, the leaders, they come to us, like you came to us, my friend. Those chaff, out there, they have no leaders. And what nation, what people, have ever done anything without leaders?'

Dexter didn't reply. He was lost in the recall of his own arrival. The fences, the mass of security managers, the orders to 'piss off to the outlands like everyone else'; his protests, his insistence and refusal to go; his eventual admittance and long crawl to the bleak new city, the HR managers looking up from their clipboards, coldly telling him he could get to the interview and assessment centre if he wanted it badly enough. And they'd been right, of course. He was proud of that struggle and the struggles that followed. He owed his success to no one but himself.

'Can you imagine this sight when we win?' said Gordon.

'It'll blow like a geyser,' said Dexter, 'may even hit the roof.'

A rare low belly chuckle from Gordon. 'I dare say it will. Human champagne. Only with scum instead of bubbles.'

'Um. Indeed.'

Gordon turned to look at Dexter.

'Well,' said Gordon.

'Well what?'

'Have we found him?'

'Found who?'

'The prophet, of course, who do you think, fucking Glenn Miller.'

'I'm sorry, but you're seriously asking me that?' said Dexter.

'Yes.'

'Well then no, of course we haven't. You'd have heard about it if we had.'

'We must look harder then,' said Gordon. 'We must redouble our efforts.'

'We have redoubled.'

'We must requadruple then.'

'Gordon–'

'No, not another word. I want everyone on this. We've done the prophet to death, so let's shift our weight and open up on the second front – scan the financial press, Dex, the clues will be there.'

'We already are scanning, Gordon.'

'So scan harder. Find the other end of our trio, find the boy. I tell you, this is our moment.'

'All right, leave it with me,' said Dexter.

'Good. Right, now, while you're here, there is something else I want your opinion on. Delicate matter.'

'Another one? What is it this time?'

'Don't panic, it's nothing sweadly, just not something I could discuss with Grímsson, not his area, and besides, you can never be open with quacks, can you? Then they're inside your head, and then they've got you.'

'Understood,' said Dexter. 'Look, whatever it is, you can trust me.'

'That's the spirit. Right, now, have a look at this.'

Gordon turned and planted his right foot on one of the stone meeting benches behind them. He gave a double flick of his eyebrows then pulled up the hem of his caftan to reveal a pair of lilac linen half stockings.

'Ooh,' said Dexter, with a wince and a step back.

'They're called popsocks,' said Gordon.

He posed his calves for Dexter and pulled his caftan higher still to reveal that each stocking was held in place with a small leather suspender belt, just below the knee. It appeared Gordon had shaved his legs.

'Well, what do you think?'

'I think,' said Dexter, his lips pulling back from his teeth, 'I think it's fine if it makes you comfortable. I mean, they are technically undergarments, aren't they?'

'That's not what I wanted an opinion on.'

'Right, so … what did you want an opinion on?'

'Whether I can get away with them in the lilac.'

'You're asking the wrong man, Gordon.'

'I'm asking *you*, Dexter. Now, can I get away with it? They do also come in powder blue and flamingo pink.'

Dexter closed his eyes and rubbed his brow. 'I don't know what to say, Gordon. I'm strictly, strictly a suit-and-tie man.'

'Don't be so stiff. Haven't you ever heard of the metrosexual?'

'Not in Limbo.'

'Well maybe it's time we made some changes. In fact, yes, I could get you a pair, Grímsson and Spitback too, the section heads, the board …'

'No. Thank you.'

'Honestly, once you try these, you won't go back. They're so smooth – here, just feel.' Gordon stretched out an arm to take Dexter's hand.

Dexter sprang back, almost over the balcony wall. 'I'll take your word for it,' he said.

'What's got into you?'

'Look. I'm concerned, Gordon, about you … The pressure, it's getting to you.'

'Balls, man. I'm as fit as a fiddle.'

'It's just that–'

'I'm fine. I appreciate the concern, but I'm fine. Best thing you can do for me, Dex, aside from giving me a straight answer on my popsocks, is to stop fretting and up the ante on the project. You need to find our prophet, or you need to find my son. No more excuses.'

Chapter Fifteen

It was seven thirty on Monday morning. Throughout Christian's life, this had been his least favourite time of the week. In childhood it signalled nothing but five days of school stretching out before him, with only fleeting respites of summer, Christmas and Easter holidays to break the cycle. Then came the island paradise of university, three years in which Monday morning became a reformed character, relaxed, chilled out, and more than happy to ease you into the week with lie-ins and gentle offerings of low-pressure lifestyle television – that pleasantly toxic Narnia of recipes, chat and parochial phone-ins. Then the reversion to type, the descent into the harsh realities of work – the painful realisation that Bob Ross Monday had been a con, a mask to make the revelation of Chairman Mao Monday all the more horrific. Not only a return to those five days stretching out to the weekend, but longer days, sometimes much longer, and a mere four weeks of holiday a year. Does anyone really not know why they don't like Mondays?

For Christian, that brief period of time before starting the school or work day had always been the worst part of Monday, or any week day. He hated that though this time was his own, it was always too short to do anything with and only served to sharpen the reckoning of what he would spend the rest of the day doing.

But these days it was different. Christian's sabbatical had triggered the miracle. Bob Ross Monday had been resurrected, turning seven thirty

Monday morning from ditch water into fine wine. Now Christian sat on the sofa and watched the rest of the country hurry its way into its week. He enjoyed his coffee. He watched the report on the breakfast TV news about the earthquake in China. He watched the whole report, he took it in, he thought about it. He observed how Beatrice could only catch a headline or two, a random comment from an expert on some unknown topic between showering, dressing, breakfast, makeup, hair, shoe selection and whatever unplanned activities had thrown her off her stride and piled more pressure on getting out of the house by eight fifteen. Then when she left, he continued to sit and take it all in. He delighted in the gradual slowdown of intensity in the broadcast. Once they passed eight thirty they knew all the important people – the ones with jobs – were no longer watching. The next half hour was just filler; you could almost see them shifting into cruise control. The 'lifestyle' guest of the day was delivered to the sofa and the hosts slipped into a more matey vibe. And then his favourite part of all, nine a.m. The official transition. He delighted in picturing all those poor wretches at their desks, the yawny meetings, the sudden return of problems, deadlines and unwelcome pressure, the nagging of the bosses, the bosses having to nag, the whole stupid system. And all the while he could just sit on the sofa and watch the first ten minutes of *Sesame Street*. Today is brought to you by the letters E, A, S and Y. No one was telling him to do anything and he loved it.

After watching Kermit the Frog's live report on the disaster scene following Humpty Dumpty's fall, deciding that, from a journalistic point of view, it was in many ways superior to the Chinese earthquake report from earlier, and speculating that the irony of the sketch would surely be wasted on preschool viewers, he went to make another coffee. As he put the kettle on, the doorbell rang. Toast in hand, he sauntered to the door. For the second time in two days, he was surprised to see Nikki standing before him. Once again she looked a million dollars, and once again he didn't.

Again she'd brought the coffee and again she was soon in his living room.

'Look, it's great to see you again,' said Christian, 'but aren't you going to be late for work?'

'Nope,' she said, and grinned.

'Oh, why so?'

'I've decided to take some time off.'

'Really? Sounded like that place couldn't function without you.'

'Well, it'll have to. I can't remember when I last took a holiday. I deserve a break.'

'So how much time are you taking off?'

'Not sure. As much as I need. That's the nice thing about being the boss.'

'Yes, I expect so.' Christian took a sip of coffee. 'Hey, would you like to see the first page of the new direction? I put it together yesterday.'

'Seriously, you'd let me see it?'

'Of course.' Christian went upstairs to print the page, taking a moment to change into jeans and T-shirt.

Nikki was on her feet when Christian returned with the copy.

'There you go,' he said. 'It's the introduction. Just rough, of course, but I think it works.'

Nikki scanned the page. She smiled, wide and full, then did a couple of small but enthusiastic jumps, and hugged Christian, taking him by surprise. Momentary guilt as he took lungfuls of her perfume. Warm, sophisticated and doubtless not available at the out of town discount chemist warehouse he'd visited with Bea recently.

'Oh it's wonderful, Christian.'

'You really think so?'

'Yes, it is, it really is,' she said. Her eyes returned to the page. 'I'm not sure about the title, but the rest is absolutely spot on.'

'You don't like it? I thought it was fun – you know, a parody of all those dreadful things to do before you're forty books?'

'Yes, I see what you mean, I was just thinking you could maybe change it to something like, oh I don't know, *Terry's Field Guide To the Afterlife.*'

'Who's Terry?'

'Well ... you know what ... forget about it, go with whatever you feel. Always the best approach.'

'Er, right.'

'Look, can I have this?'

'Um. Yes, I suppose so,' said Christian.

'Cool.'

'You, er, you won't show it to anyone, will you?'

'You can trust me, Christian. For my eyes only.'

Nikki had raced home at a speed just above asking for trouble. She was now in the basement rumpus room. Like everything in Nikki's house, it was on a grand scale. Almost 200 square metres of floor space housed a home cinema, pool table, collection of vintage pinball machines, selection of modern games consoles, and, in the centre of the room, a full-size snooker table, under which Nikki was now sitting. Six floor tiles were stacked next to her, as was the blanking panel, and the safe was wide open. For the last minute she'd been holding the large document wallet in her white-cotton-gloved hands, savouring the moment.

She undid the zip and took out the contents – a collection of vellum documents, all yellowed, fragile and ancient, each preserved in their own clear plastic protector. There were a dozen or so pages in all, mostly whole, though some were just fragments. Apart from the title page, all were numbered and this indicated they had come from a work of at least 615 pages. There was nothing else to indicate how many more pages were in the original, though: there was no contents page and the few cross references were of the form *book, chapter, section, verse*. Apart from 615, the pages in Nikki's possession were mostly from the start: in addition to the title page, she had all of pages one to four, and three from the next twenty, with her remaining pages coming from further into the work. She'd taken detailed digital scans of them long ago and must have read each one a hundred times, but this was a moment for the precious originals, not pixels on a screen or learned recollections.

She carefully took page one and placed it on the floor next to its crisp, freshly printed counterpart and began a line-by-line comparison. Her heart was racing. Apart from a few spelling differences, which was to be expected, the texts were identical. She'd already known this of course, when she'd first seen the new page, back at Christian's, but she'd kept her excitement shackled until she could be sure.

Now she finally allowed herself the full acceptance of what she had before her. 'Yes,' she screamed, 'yes, yes, yes.'

She tried to jump to her feet but forgot she was crouching under a slate-bed snooker table. In some part of her brain she knew it hurt, it had to, physics and biology demanded it, but her joy was such that it got shouted down, drowned out by the coup in her neurons. She hopped forward, out from under the table, and ran around the room, skipping like a little girl, leaping between strides, kicking out at the beanbags as she passed by. When she returned to the snooker table, she took the cue ball in her hand and sent it smashing into the perfectly set pack of reds. Civilisation was about to be turned upside down. At last it would happen.

Chapter Sixteen

Gabriel and Harold were in lounge forty-seven, the majestic Library Lounge.

Library *Lounge*. It was a strange name, thought Harold. Wall-to-wall shelves stacked with books; ranks of tables with small moonstone study lamps; a calming musty silence. In other words, a library. The only even slightly loungy feature was the pair of green leather sofas, one of which Gabriel was now sitting on.

'He said he'd be here,' said Gabriel. 'Honestly, he's a law unto himself ...'

Harold stayed standing. It was better for him – for his continuing re-adjustment back to gravity – as well as for the state of his increasingly fragile plaster-cast-like suit. But also he was too excited to sit. He was mesmerised.

'And you say this is just the first chamber?' he said, softly.

'Yes,' said Gabriel, spotting crumbs on the leather opposite, 'first of six hundred.'

'Six ... *hundred*?'

'Yes. Or is it seven hundred. I forget.'

'And all as generously stocked?'

'Yes. Packed to the rafters.'

'But that must be ...' He scanned up the shelves, past the seven-level wooden gantry, craning his neck up to the impossibly high oak-beamed ceiling, and then along the rows to the far wall, more than a hundred yards away. '... hundreds of thousands ... millions.'

'Tens of millions,' said Gabriel, inspecting his clawhands, 'more books than the Library of Congress and growing all the time.'

'A true wonder of Heaven,' said Harold, his eyes wide. He'd been an avid reader in life and, as usually then follows, a frustrated one in death. But now, freshly installed in his brand new immortal body, he could once more linger on the page, he could once more hold the book he was reading. This had quickly become the single ray of hope in this disturbing third phase of existence, even if the only book he had so far acquired was the copy of *Terry's Field Guide To the Afterlife* they'd handed out at orientation.

Now his eyes had been opened. Now he was overwhelmed. But something didn't quite fit. 'I, um ...'

'Yes, Harold?' said Gabriel.

'Nothing.'

'Come on, you were going to say something.'

'Well,' said Harold, lowering his voice to a whisper, 'it's just ... I would never have deduced he was of a literary persuasion.'

'Oh, he's not.'

'Right. Well, *why* then?'

Gabriel smiled. 'He comes here when he wants to feel more learned.'

'And?'

'And mark my words, Harold. *Feel* more learned. Not become more learned. That would not be possible here, well, not unless you brought something to read.'

'But it's a library.'

'Is it?'

'Admittedly, since my arrival there have been few things of which I am certain. But this, plainly, is a library.'

'Take a book then.'

'Which book?'

'Any book. How about a Dickens over there.'

Harold walked to the shelf and looked along the titles. *Hard Times* caught his eye. He placed a finger on the top of the spine but the book would not move. He tried again but it was stuck fast. He tried *Our Mutual Friend*. Also stuck. He moved to the shelf up and tried to release *David Copperfield*, with no success. With urgency, he stumbled across the wide reading area to the opposite wall, where he found the collected works of Anthony Trollope. Not one volume would yield.

'They're not real,' said Harold.

'Oh, they're real all right,' said Gabriel, 'hand-scribed from the mortal originals, every one of them. Pinsprickling work when you think about it.'

'But they're stuck together?'

'Yes,' said Gabriel, with a sigh, 'glued. All of the pages in every book and every book to every shelf.'

'But, why?' asked Harold.

'Why do you think?'

'I … I can't imagine.' Harold put his hands to his cheeks. It was an abomination. Literary vandalism of the highest order.

'You already know enough to work it out,' said Gabriel.

'Well,' said Harold, 'is it … a grand declaration? A grave warning against reading anything other than the Bible?'

'Nope. Actually, I'm not sure we have a copy of that here – gets on his nerves, you know.'

The door creaked open and God, barefoot and wearing a brown suede suit, ambled in carrying a tall papyrus bag that was transparent in places.

'All right, lads.'

'Terrence,' said Gabriel.

Harold turned to God and looked him up and down.

'Doughnut?' asked God, tilting the greasy bag.

Harold returned his troubled stare to the books, seeming not to acknowledge the Almighty or the sweetly rancid whiff. He was fortunate God had had a good morning.

'What's up with him?' asked God, reaching into the bag.

'I think he may be in shock, Tel.' The archangel got to his feet. 'Anyway, there's been a–'

'Awestruck, eh?' said God. He moved behind Harold and placed a hand on his shoulder, triggering yet another suit rupture. 'I've got 'em all here, you know, Chaucer, Shakespeare, Dickens, Cartland …'

Harold shook his head with a judder, almost like he was having a seizure.

'You sure he's okay?' said God, turning briefly to Gabriel. 'Still can't part with the rebirthday suit, I see.' The Almighty leaned in close and took two deep sniffs at Harold's collar. 'He reeks like a ripe cheese.'

'He's perplexed by the gluing of the books, Tel. And we're dealing with the clothing. Now look, can we–'

'Perplexed?'

'Yes. He can't work out why.'

'Thought you said he was smart, Gabe?'

'Tel ...'

'Well it's no big mystery, son, you see, truth is I'm not a big reader. Don't get the time, and there's a lot of books here ...'

This didn't seem to ease Harold's troubles.

'... besides, I know everything anyway.'

Gabriel started chuckling.

God didn't.

Gabriel stopped chuckling.

'Think about it,' said God, 'even with all of eternity to play with, I'd never get through this lot. So imagine how I'd feel coming in here if they hadn't all been glued together ... all those unread books, all crying out, "Read me! Read me!" ... I'm busy, I'm stressed, we all are these days. Last thing I want is a load of needy books hassling me as well.'

'So ...' said Harold. He slowly turned his head as he seemed to come out of his trance. 'The glue means they *can't* be read?'

'Blingo!' said God. 'And if they can't be read, I can't get stressed about not reading them. Pretty clever, eh?'

'But ... but the t-time, the dedication,' said Harold. 'I'm told every work has been hand-scribed?'

'Well it's not like I could order them online, lad,' said God.

'But ... but if you're never going to read them, why not just have a facade?'

'Fakes? What good would that be? How am I going to bask in the glory of literature then?'

'I ... I ...'

'That's the whole beauty of it, son. Here I can bask in it, without the guilt of not reading it. Genius eh? Have me cake and eat it, so to speak.'

He offered the doughnuts again.

Harold sank to the floor, mortally fracturing the seat of his trousers.

'Go on, have a doughnut, lad,' said God, leaning over Harold and thrusting the bag in his face, 'perk you up no end.'

'Look, Tel,' said Gabriel, 'we need to talk.'

'We are talking.'

'It's about Bootstrap ... There's, well, there's been a development.'

'Who?'

'Christian Bootstrap,' said Gabriel, frustration rippling through his plumage, 'the mortal who was writing the book, with the scenes of you, of here.'

'Oh yes, the coincidence monkey.'

'That's the fellow.'

'And?'

'And he's started writing something else.'

'Well I hope it's a bit more complimentary this time.'

'Yes. I, I think you'd better take a look for yourself. You, er, may want to sit down.'

They left Harold on the floor and retired to the sofas. Gabriel handed God the new manuscript.

Thirty Things To Do After You Die
by Christian Bootstrap
Introduxion

Who is this book for?

This book'll be most useful to anyone who's just died.

Who is this book not for?

Can't please everyone. These people best stop reading right now:

  * Deities – you know the answers
  * Philosophers – you think you know the answers
  * Clerics – you think you've been told the answers
  * Physicists – you won't believe the answers.

For everyone else, this book'll fill you in on all those saycred details and customs, and hopefully stop you embarrassing yourself. If you read all these wise words, take note and keep yer head down, you should be okay. First off, the most important rule is don't crack afterlife gags. We've heard 'em. All of 'em. Second, you'll want to get cracking on some creaytive output. Art, music, books, mags. We love all that. Do some of that and you're heading the right way. We're not big on ballet though, or Morris dancing. Line dancing – don't even think about it.

'What the hell,' said God, 'apart from the title, it's bloody word for word. So I suppose you're gonna tell me this is a coincidence, Gabe?'

'Not this time.'

'So where's he getting it? I thought all the earthly copies were destroyed centuries ago?'

'They were. But it's possible someone, perhaps long ago, made an illicit additional copy, and, well, perhaps it's fallen into the hands of this mortal.'

'Bloody hell. So what's his game?'

'Well, we're assuming he's typing it up as a prelude to publication.'

'Publication?' said God, leaping to his feet and sending the doughnuts flying. 'Let the cat out of the bag? Bloody hell. This is bad, Gabe, this is a real hot bobby, we'll have nothing but believers down there ... so no fresh blood coming here, no artists, no writers, no celebrities ... no celebrities, Gabe, no celebrities.'

'Tel, please, calm yourself. I agree it's bad on first glance, but on closer inspection, I don't think we're in too much danger.'

'Oh no?' said God, hands on his hips.

'First of all, he probably won't be able to get it published.'

'But what if he did? Any beefwit can get into print these days, he could do it himself.'

'Well okay, let's suppose he does. So a few people read it, and a handful of them take it seriously and become devout. We lose them to the other places. Big deal, they probably wouldn't have been coming up to us anyway, so end of story.'

'I don't know, Gabe, I don't know ...' said God. He bent down for a doughnut, streaked it on his left lapel and took a bite, chomping with urgency.

'Tel, relax, the wider populous wouldn't give it a second glance. Maybe if it had come to light in the Middle Ages, it could have presented a risk, maybe ... but now? No chance. People are too sophisticated, too savvy, too cynical.'

God ruffled his hair and sat down. 'Well, I trust we're taking a closer interest in him all the same?'

'Absolutely, we've upped the surveillance, we've got him covered at all times, day and night.'

'All right ... all right, well ... keep me posted.'

Chapter Seventeen

It was Wednesday morning. Nikki and Christian were in the living room, in what had already become a daily event.

'It's great,' she said, finishing the second of two pages, the quality so far keeping a lid on productivity concerns.

Christian didn't answer.

She looked across at him.

'You're not convinced?' she asked.

'Not totally.'

'But it's great, what's the problem?'

'I feel uneasy about it.'

'In what way?'

'Well, the words, they feel … odd.'

'They're fine, they flow, they're consistent.' She looked down at the page. 'It's an authentic voice.'

'Exactly my point. The voice, that's what sounds odd.'

She slowly looked up. 'So tell me, how does it sound?'

'It sounds, well … Scouse.'

'Really? I don't see that. Obviously you've got the whole informal conversational thing going on, which works beautifully, but no, I wouldn't say Scouse exactly. But even so, does it matter? If that's how it comes out, that's how it comes out, right?'

'It's just not what I expected.'

'Well, I think it's a sign you're on the right track. All the great writers say their biggest problems are controlling their characters, right?'

'Yes, I suppose ... but then there's the problem of the language itself.'

'I don't follow.'

'Well, take those notes from the other day, the common phrases and sayings.'

Nikki smirked. *'Seize the day after tomorrow.'*

'Exactly,' said Christian.

'What of it? I think they're perfect.'

'Yes, but they wouldn't be in English, would they?'

'Well ... well I don't know.'

'Come on, of course they wouldn't,' said Christian. 'The afterlife would have been there from the start, so they'd speak some ancient language, wouldn't they? Ancient Greek or ... or, you know, one of the other ones.'

'So?'

'So it's not convincing, being in English, it's not credible, it breaks up the suspension of disbelief.'

'I really don't think that's a problem. In science fiction the people on other planets always talk in English, don't they? They even have American accents, but the audience just goes along with it. I'm sure it'll be the same here.'

'Yes, I suppose. But it means wasting a good observation though.'

'And that is?'

'That your average believer doesn't stop to think that they may have to learn ancient Hebrew or whatever to make their way in the afterlife.'

'So what are you thinking then?'

'Well, I suppose I could invent a language of the afterlife, perhaps, you know, like Tolkien did for Middle Earth.'

'Or you could just learn ancient Hebrew and use that?'

'Yes ... yes, I suppose that would be an option too ...'

'Look, how does it feel, leaving it in English? What does your gut say?'

'My gut says it's fine, it says it's right, even. It's my logic that says it's wrong.'

'Well my advice is the same as ever. Don't overthink it. Trust your unconscious and go with what you feel. All the best writers say that's the path to authenticity, so I'm told.'

'I suppose you're right.'

'Well anyway, if these are your only problems, then you can't be doing too much wrong.'

He didn't reply.

'Look, you've made a great start,' she said, 'now you need to seize the moment and make it happen.'

'Actually, there is something else,' said Christian.

She put down the pages. 'Go on.'

'It's just ... when I started out on this, I wanted to write a novel, a serious work, you know, the human condition laid bare, the type of thing they shortlist for the Booker.'

'And?'

'Well, first I converted it to a comedy – they hate comedy – but now I've got rid of the characters and the narrative, too. Trust me, they won't swallow that, no matter how sweeping and expansive it is. It wouldn't even make the longlist.'

'Christian–'

'Don't get me wrong, the ideas, the changes, they're on the money, I know they are. It's just what I have now, well, it's not literature, is it?'

'No. It's something better.'

'*Better than literature?*'

'Yes.'

'How?'

She took a moment before answering. 'People say literature can change the world, but it can't. At best, it's cathartic. How could it ever be more? It's all just words someone made up.'

'So's this,' said Christian, pointing to the pages.

She stood. 'Christian, when the history of this world is written, when life is given its true context, your book will be on page one.'

'That's not funny.'

'I'm not being funny. I'm being serious.'

He looked up at her. She held a poker face, but Christian began to smile. 'You're a bad bad woman,' he said, with a chuckle.

'I am serious,' she said. 'I know you don't believe me, but I am.' Now she smiled too. 'And anyway, those academics, it's only their opinion. Who cares what they think?'

'Well–'

'Bunch of arty-farty liberals in their ivory towers. None of them live in the real world. You ask any one of them to look after a forklift truck business for an afternoon, it'd be chaos.'

'But–'

'Who cares what they think, and who cares if it's not literature? Fuck literature.'

'Fuck literature?'

'Yeah. Come on, I say we load our twelve-gauge, creep up on literature and give it both barrels square in the back.' She picked up her imaginary shotgun and lifted the sights to Bea's bookshelf.

Wuthering Heights. 'Kaboom,' she said as she moved back with the recoil.

Extremely Loud & Incredibly Close. 'Kaboom.'

'Click, click,' she said as she reloaded.

Life of Pi. 'Kaboom.'

The Alchemist. 'Kaboom.'

'Click, click.'

The complete works of Jane Austen. 'Kaboom. Kaboom.'

She extended the massacre to take in *The Notebook, The Art of Loving* and Christian's *2003 Guinness World Records* annual.

'You know ... you know you're right,' said Christian.

'Of course I am.'

'Fuck literature,' he said. He stood. He punched the air. 'Fuck literature!'

The levers were set. The cogs were turning. Soon new would become normal; normal would become routine. All she had to do was wait.

Part Two

The Wilderness

Chapter One

It was Friday morning. And it was early. Harold was sitting naked at the end of his bed, staring through the citrine yellow gloom at, among other things, his sandals.

'Footwear.'

Having been, by anyone's definition, or at least by any mortal's definition, long-term unemployed, before his current role, there were some in the True Jerusalem administration who thought the new boy might take a while to readjust to the world of work. It was often the way, and why they rarely took on freshers. But Harold had proved them wrong, applying himself with such diligence he was rapidly becoming the resident intelligence expert on Christian Bootstrap.

But outside work it was a different story.

He'd had friendships in his mortal life, of course. They'd been of substance, too, the type that can get you through anything. But that was a long time ago and their origins even longer. Now, here in the holy city, he was free to make friends once more. All was opportunity; all was open. The multi-layered delights of True Jerusalem society were just outside his door. And it was terrifying, like the middle-aged divorcee contemplating his first date in twenty-five years. Could he still do it? Did he still know how? It was too much, at least for the time being. And so Harold inevitably drifted into what a lot of lonely new arrivals drift into. He went queuing. It didn't matter what for. Start at the back, get to the front, step out and start again. It wasn't the same, of course, and now it was definitely without point or purpose. But it didn't matter because it was comforting. To feel close contact again; to worry about one's place. But most of all it was the womblike warmth of having your course set by someone else; the submissive solace that is *to follow*. He knew it was corrosive for his state of mind; he knew he had to move on, but the pull to queue was strong, especially when his mind was unoccupied. Thank heavens he was allowed to work weekends.

He looked again at the sandals, at his grey flannels on the chair, the underwear, the white shirt made yellow by this sickly light, and the angel-wear waistcoat hanging behind.

'Getting dressed.'

The motions he'd remembered easily enough, and even after all that time it would be hard to get shoes and socks in the wrong order, but now it all felt so archaic and inefficient, like a return to filling fountain pens and beating carpets. But it felt alien too, like the memories were someone else's, echoes of a past life, long gone.

He couldn't put it off any longer. But then it wasn't like he had much choice. Gabriel had finally made him get rid of his comfort blanket blacenta, and yes, it was Heaven, yes it was the twenty-first century, but striding off to work stark bollock naked just wasn't on.

Nikki glanced again at the dashboard clock as she exited the last roundabout before the long straight drag back to Virginia Water. Ten twenty. Mid-morning and already her day was done, as was her week.

She hated Fridays. She always had, only now for different reasons and now with greater intensity. Now they marked the end of Christian's writing week. Time for him to post another pitiful total, time for her to start another seventy hours of knotted brooding.

They were already into March. Six weeks and all he'd produced was 8,000 words, two beards and a bunch of excuses.

She tried not to think about it. She turned on the radio and flicked through the stations. But inevitably the question that occupied all her waking thoughts, and quite a lot of her sleeping ones, raised its head, yet again – how long?

This week he'd produced 1,252 words, plus 150 today made … just over 1,400 for the week. So, an average of … 200 a day. Dire. As dire as last week. It was bordering on masochistic to continue but she was so used to the extrapolation that she couldn't help herself. She already knew the answer. At 200 words a day, it would take Christian four years and eight months to finish. Even that was assuming there were no more than 800 pages. What if there were 1,000? What if there were 10,000?

She slammed the rim of the steering wheel and let out a long scream.

It was all so easy for him. He really thought he was a writer. The pained artist who couldn't be rushed, who sat way-out beyond reasonable definitions of an honest day's work and apparently happy to savour the long winter as much as the next man with central heating, a well-stocked fridge and no reason to leave the house.

Perhaps she'd encouraged him too much? Been too interested? Or maybe he needed some stick? But then what stick did she have? It wasn't like he was one of her employees.

And direct assistance was out of the question – the game was running, it had to be Christian alone, the pure unadulterated stream, the literal word. Her guidance at the launch, directing him to drop the narrative, to drop Costa Rica and write an afterlife guide, this was her first and final act of direction, and as far as she dared go, the last steadying push after the training wheels come off. Now all she could do was shout from the side-lines. But then shouting from the sidelines was what she was good at. If he'd been an employee, she'd have had his work rate whipped into shape in no time. But he wasn't. He was a mere friend. And even then really just a friend of her husband. She'd tried to create leverage in other ways, of course, to make him obligated, to get him in her pocket. She'd offered to lend him money – *It can't be easy, with just Bea's salary*; she'd tried gifts of a new PC and printer but she couldn't raise his interest in any of it. In a month, all she'd managed to get him on was two reams of A4 and thirty-three lattes. There were other ways and means, of course. She'd seen the way he looked at her, which was the way most men looked at her, but she didn't want to take that path, at least not yet. Not because she wasn't prepared to, but because it was unpredictable. It could get messy; it could make matters worse.

She pounded the steering wheel again in a series of rapid blows, this time catching the horn on the centre pad, proclaiming her frustration to Tesco Express and Oddbins.

She hated that she felt like this. It was weak. In the big scheme of things, a delay, even a long one, just didn't matter. The destination, what lay beyond the final chapter, that was what mattered, that was all that mattered. She should be satisfied with the certainty that he would get there; in fact, she should be permanently euphoric about it. *When* was just a sideshow, a parochial and vulgar distraction. Yet still it was eating her up, the prize teasing her, floating right there just beyond her grasp.

She pulled off the road, stopped the car, and made a resolution. From this point forward, she would walk the straight and narrow path, she would remember her John Bunyan. She would keep her impatience under house arrest and celebrate the little victories. And she would allow herself to hope, too, for there was cause – Christian's butterfly attention offered the prospect of flitting onto the later chapters, perhaps even beyond, to the nectar itself, well before he ran his final spell check. For though he'd only produced 9,423 words, they were scattered across twenty-three chapters, some already from deeper into the work …

Harold had got dressed and was now over at Blotchley Hall. Happy to be back working, happy not to have to think about everything else.

Though still new to the job, he'd soon established a routine:

1. Set up early in one of the quieter allotments
2. Tune into Christian for the final half hour of his sleep
3. Check scribes were on hand, observing and ready
4. Watch Christian's wake-up routine of breakfast and television
5. On weekdays, watch his meeting with the female fan they now knew to be Nikki Tooting
6. Settle in for the long stakeout for anything unusual or interesting
7. Perhaps witness some actual writing
8. Read more of his *Terry's Field Guide To the Afterlife* during the long and frequent periods of inactivity.

But today there had been an unexpected development. Unexpected enough for him to have sent for Gabriel, unexpected enough for Gabriel to have sent for God.

'They managed to capture it,' said Harold, returning from the scribes' desk, 'they're going to run off a legible before Terry gets here.'

'Good,' said Gabriel, looking into the image in the flames. Christian was still at his laptop, only now the screen previously filled with *Microsoft Word* was filled with *Tomb Raider*.

'Where's he getting it from?' said Gabriel. He zoomed the image out, back from Christian's right shoulder, to bring the whole room into view.

'That has perplexed me from the beginning,' said Harold.

Gabriel rotated the image to scan along the cluttered shelves. 'But this is the first time it's not matched?'

'Indeed,' said Harold, 'he's been word for word until now.'

Gabriel released the touchstone.

They sat in silence, watching Christian swim Lara through a long water-filled tunnel, watching her drown, and watching Christian try again. The pattern looked to be set, but after his third failure, Christian switched back to his document.

'There, now ... you see, chapter sixteen B,' said Harold, zooming the image in, 'it doesn't match. There is no sixteen B in "Walk the Earth".' The reference copy – Gabriel's personal signed first edition, on loan to Harold – was already open. Harold flipped the pages. 'Sixteen ... seventeen, there, you see, no sixteen B.'

'I know,' said Gabriel, slowly sitting back in his seat.

'I don't understand,' said Harold.

'It means that this' – Gabriel stretched out an armwing and tapped the tome – 'is not his source.'

'Freeze,' shouted God as he burst in and took the stance of an American TV cop, his hands outstretched together to form a cocked pistol.

In a sort of shock wave rippling down the rows, everyone stopped what they were doing. The only sounds were from the banks of window boxes, tinny chatter from the subjects in the flames. The only movements were from a few users quickly flicking over to Disneyland.

'Hey, I'm only joking, folks,' said God, 'carry on, carry on.'

Everyone slowly went back to their duties.

'We're in luck,' whispered Gabriel, 'he's in a good mood.'

'All right then, lads,' said God as he strode over, 'now, what's this all about?'

'Sorry to call you away, Tel, but there's been another development,' said Gabriel.

'Couldn't it wait, Gabe? It's Friday. I've got Albert lined up for a rematch. Took him to the cleaners this morning.'

'I'm sorry, but you're going to want to see this.'

'Let me guess, the monkey again?'

'I'm afraid so,' said Gabriel. 'It's ... well, it's not good.'

'Go on then, hit me with it.'

Gabriel turned back to the image in the flames. 'Well, if you take a look, we–'

'Hey, they're great, these, aren't they, Harry?' said God, leaning in too close. 'You can see anywhere on Earth with these, son, mortal realm only, of course.'

'He has had the briefing,' said Gabriel.

'Good though, innit,' said God. 'Hey, hey, we should come down here more often, catch a bit of mortal sport, like the old days, eh? Get it up on the big one. Remember the Colosseum, eh, Gabe? They don't do thrills like that any more, real edge of your seat stuff.'

'You do have a viewer almost as big in your quarters, Tel,' said Gabriel, some frustration creeping into his voice.

'True, but I can never get mine to work.'

'Well, um, perhaps I … we,' said Harold, 'could arrange for some assistance.'

'No, no, you're okay, lad. Not really one for the gizmos, me.'

'If I could just get you to look at this, Tel,' said Gabriel, pointing to the flames.

'Wait, wait,' said God, standing back up straight, 'if we're gonna do this, let's do it properly.' He strode off to collar the floor supervisor.

'He does know how to work it, you know,' whispered Gabriel to Harold.

'Oh yes?' said Harold, wondering what penalty whispering about the Almighty might carry, and whether keeping your voice down made you any less likely to get caught.

'Yes. Only uses it when he's on his own though, in the evenings. My advice is to always knock.'

'Now,' said God, to the floor manager, who'd come scampering over, 'I want it up on the big one.'

'Tel, really, they all have their work to do,' said Gabriel, calling across.

'Oh bugger that, put it on the big one. Put it on all of them.'

Gabriel sighed.

The floor manager made a series of rapid gestures to various members of his team.

God returned to Harold and Gabriel. 'So, what's all the drama over then, lads?' he said.

There was a thick powerful *whumph* as the mighty yew hedge fired up.

'Well, I think you'd better tell us what you think of this,' said Gabriel.

All the window boxes switched to the view of Christian, only now he was perusing the results of a 'Lara Croft nude' image search. And then it was on the yew hedge, too – computer, cartoon, airbrushed and reconstructed images of a whole ecosystem of naked Laras plastered sixty-feet high in the foliage.

Cheers and applause rang out.

'What do I think?' asked God. 'I think you boys need to get out more. Though if you pressed me, I'd go with middle row, second from the right.'

'Oh for goodness' sake,' said Gabriel. 'All right, so he's doing ...' Unwisely, Harold had zoomed out to show more of Christian in frame. 'Well, he's doing *what he's doing*, now, but a few minutes ago he was writing more of the book.'

'So what's new?' said God.

'What's new is,' said Gabriel, 'what's ... what's ... I'm sorry, bear with me.' He turned to the floor manager. 'If you wouldn't mind, I think we're done.'

The yew hedge powered down, followed by jeers and boos. Most, though not absolutely everyone, returned their window boxes to their previous subjects.

Gabriel lowered his voice. 'What's new is he's been writing out chapter sixteen B.'

Harold nodded in solemn agreement.

'Really,' said God, 'sixteen B.'

'Sixteen B,' said Harold.

Silence.

'You don't remember what sixteen B is, do you?' said Gabriel.

'Not entirely,' said God.

Gabriel clicked his digits at the scribes. One of them collected up some papyrus pages and brought them over.

'Here, look,' said Gabriel, flicking through. He passed a page to God.

'*Sixteen B*,' said God, '*Fast-Track Process* ... Yeah, so?'

'Well, don't you see,' said Gabriel, 'it's the second edition.'

'Hey, hey, bloody hell, you're right.' God sat down. 'But there's no copies in the mortal realm,' he said, 'not one. How's he got hold of it?'

'We don't know,' said Gabriel.

'Look, copying out the old version, I could live with that, but this, this is a whole different brew.'

'I know, Tel, that's why we got you over here. But don't worry, we're on the case. We're putting together a plan of action.'

'Good. Fill me in.'

'Well, look, shall we retire to somewhere more private?'

God snapped his fingers and pointed at Gabriel. 'Biscilica,' he said.

'No, really, Tel, not there, what about the Library Lounge, we can talk sensibly there, and it's closer.'

'We can talk in the Biscilica,' said God.

'But–'

'The Biscilica,' said God.

Chapter Two

Forty minutes later, Gabriel, God and Harold were in lounge 1,079, otherwise known as Terry's Biscilica. Gabriel was trying to pick the moment to resume the discussion – the serious discussion on how they might go about stopping the mortal who was now somehow copying out chapters of the second edition. But it wasn't easy. Terry's Biscilica was not a place that sat well with seriousness.

But at least they'd now left the sponge-finger loungers and marshmallow footstools, and taken to the tea. Calm, sober, dignified tea, Gabriel told himself, while trying to ignore the wholly un-tea-like meaty aroma.

They continued to paddle out towards the centre, their small splashes amplified under the roof of the chamber. Or at least God and Gabriel paddled out. Harold was still floundering near the twin chocolate log piers, battling for all he was worth to keep his teacup coracle afloat as it wobbled beneath him.

'Stiffen your stance, son,' said God, shouting back.

'And alternate the sides,' added Gabriel, with a shake of the head.

Harold only half heard, and then the echoes arrived, adding to his disorientation.

'What the hell's he gonna be like if it gets choppy?' said God.

'I don't know. Anyway, right, surely this is far enough now, Tel?'

God looked around. 'Yeah, okay.'

They pulled in their oarspoons.

'Right, Tel, we think–'

'Wait,' said God, pointing to the ceiling, 'let's give ourselves a moment, shall we?'

Gabriel sighed.

God gave a single click of his fingers, the sound echoing around the chamber. A moment later, a small band of musicians appeared on the far shore and began playing *Food, Glorious Food*, the sound shimmering with a glassy ring from the lounge's acoustics.

God shifted his weight forward to lie back in his teacup, gesturing for Gabriel to do the same. Under protest, the archangel obliged, tucking his armwings down by his sides to ensure he kept them dry.

And as they lay there, gently bobbing, Gabriel felt the edge being taken off his urgency. He began to calm; he began to relax. He stopped looking through the vista and began to take it in – the stunning collection of ceiling frescoes. It was a masterpiece and definitive proof that beauty can sometimes not only transcend subject but taste as well.

The Biscilica was the largest of God's covered tea lakes, and the vault dome ceiling its crowning glory. It spanned a full fifty metres, eight and a half more than the dome of Saint Peter's. It wasn't as tall as its earthly inspiration, not nearly so, but for good reason – God wanted to be able to really *see* the frescoes. More to the point, he wanted it to be impossible for anyone he brought here *not* to see them and in doing so to be made humble. And they were, because vulgar though it was, it was Michelange-lo's finest work. It had been his most challenging – not just because of the scale, though certainly it was his most grand, but because of his motiva-tion. Not only to be forced to render such lowly themes in his own High Renaissance style, but to reprise – or as God openly demanded, eclipse – his more noble earthly wonders while he did it. It was an outrage. But then, an outrage requested by the Almighty. How could he refuse? How could anyone refuse? And once his decision was made and his disgust corked, he set about his task with gusto. Yes, it would be an abomination, but the most delicate, poignant and sublime abomination Heaven had ever seen (and that was saying something).

Of course, the central theme of crunchy sweet teatime treats had to be centre stage, and the old master had obliged with majestic oversize depic-tions of custard creams, rich tea, caramel wafers, shortbread fingers and digestives, to name but a few. But he'd extended and nuanced the brief, bringing in timeless teatime imagery: tablecloths, teapots and tea trays; sticky buns, scones and sandwiches. And then he'd embellished further with the ingredients of manufacture – mortal manufacture – for the tribute was not to the bland offerings of Heaven, but to the ineffable delights of Earth: sugar, chocolate, butter; single cream, double cream, clotted cream; molasses and mascarpone; caramel and coffee beans, every scene richly adorned with the natural world's finest offerings. And even then he was only warming up. Classical characterisation and drama provided a context for bringing everything to life, with saints and sinners populating the reloaded scenes: the tragedy of Saint Anthony, pursued by gluttonous urchins for the last profiterole; a pensive David, oven glove on shoulder, waiting on his latest batch of macaroons; the wide-eyed grin of Saint Bartholomew as he made off with the skin of the custard. And high in the ceiling, dead centre, directly above where God and Gabriel now bobbed, the majestic plaster-pastry-bordered scene of God himself stretching out to pass Adam a ginger nut. It was a scene that had left many speechless.

'Why have you got a red nose?' asked Gabriel, having never really studied the picture properly before.

'It's a cherry,' said God.

'Are you sure?'

'Course I'm sure, Micky told me himself. Said he did me as a cherry Bakewell.'

'Why?'

'The King of Cakes.'

'I believe I am mastering it,' said Harold, before drifting on past and behind them, unable to stop.

Gabriel shook his head.

'Hey, Harry, whatcha reckon to the ceiling eh?' said God, leaning back. 'My mate Micky did that, whole bloody lot by hand. Took him best part of the twentieth century, that did.'

Harold kept his eyes on the horizon.

'Well bloody look then,' said God.

With visible reluctance, Harold took his hands off his oarspoon, took tight hold of the rim of his teacup, and slowly raised his eyes to the ceiling.

'Hey, hey, what about the lighting, eh? Topaz filtered, that is,' said God.

'Yes, yes, it's–' Harold's teacup lurched, taking on a little tea at the starboard side.

'What the hell are you doing, son?' said God.

'Perhaps we should get down to business, Tel,' said Gabriel.

'Oh all right, if we must,' said God, and he turned back to face the archangel.

'Right, what I was–'

There was a large splash behind them as Harold entered the tea, his teacup coracle disappearing beneath him.

'As I was saying,' continued Gabriel, 'what I was thinking was, what if we–' His train of thought was interrupted by a wobble at his stern. Turning, he found a frantic Harold, low in the tea, with trembling hands gripping the rim of the coracle.

'What in heaven are you doing?' asked Gabriel.

'I went over,' spluttered Harold.

'So it seems,' said Gabriel.

'It tastes foul.'

'You not a fan of Darjeeling?' asked God.

'This is Darjeeling?' said Harold, screwing up his face.

Gabriel shook his head.

'Darjeeling style,' said God, 'meat extract paste, milk and cinnamon.'

'Urgh, urgh, may I come aboard?' asked Harold.

'Absolutely not,' said Gabriel. 'They're one-man vessels, you really should have been more careful with yours.'

'Please, I beg of you.'

'Look, you can hang on to the side, if you keep quiet.'

'Thank you.'

'And if you panic and pull me in, I won't be pleased.'

'Actually, I might be up for a dip,' said God, rubbing his hands, 'probably due a bath.'

'Tel. Please. Can we get back to business.'

'Business?'

'The monkey, Tel, the errant writer, how we're going to stop him.'

'Oh yes yes …'

'Right,' said Gabriel, 'well, what I was thinking was how about we spawn a foresayer, a grade one, we really go Old Testament school, you know, a bit heavy, a bit Moses?'

'You're serious? That's what you've been waiting to tell me?'

'Yes. Get in there, rough him up, tell him what for, shut him up.'

'It's always sayers with you, isn't it,' said God, 'any problem, send a sayer. Well I'm sorry, but the ban stays.'

'Sayer?' said Harold.

'Prophet,' said Gabriel, over his shoulder. He turned back to God. 'Look, are you sure, Tel? It's been centuries. I'm told we understand the settings a lot better these days, or at least a little better.'

'The ban stays,' said God. 'Besides, do you really think we've got twenty years to play with here? We need action now.'

'All right, well, what about you, Tel – fancy another visit?'

'The boy? No chance, never again. Gives me the bloody heebie-jeebies just thinking about it. All that one and the same but not the same rubbish. No bloody thank you. Just not normal being in two places at once.'

'But I thought,' said Harold, 'are you not everywhere at once?'

God lifted his head to peer down at Harold. 'Well that's just perverse.'

Gabriel shook his head at Harold.

They turned back to face front.

'I don't like it any more than you, Tel,' said Gabriel, 'but I think perhaps–'

'No. No more visits for the boy.'

'But–'

'But nothing, Gabe. Come on, how many times has he been down there now? Seven, eight? And they only bloody recognised him once. Never updates his shtick, that's his trouble, never moves with the times. A few flowery words and some seafood extender hasn't cut it for centuries.'

'But this would be a simpler mission, and the lead time, we win on the lead time, it's a fraction of that of a foresayer.'

'Granted, but it's not like our monkey's the type to listen to a precocious toddler, is it now? So you're still looking at fifteen, sixteen years, maybe more, and as I keep saying, we need to act sooner, we need to act now.'

'Well perhaps we could try to influence someone already in the field,' said Gabriel, 'someone the monkey would respect. What about that Dawkins fellow? Bootstrap watches his videos, we've seen him doing it, so how about we get him to, you know, *deliver a message*.' Gabriel hit the palm of his clawhand to make the point.

'That's not gonna work either,' said God, with a sigh. 'First, how are we gonna influence someone like Dawkers? If I pop up among his geraniums, tell him he has to put the frighteners on a computer programmer in Bracknell, he'll just think he's going nuts or eaten a bad pickled egg or something. Second, he's not exactly what you'd call hired muscle, is he?'

'No ... no I suppose not,' said Gabriel.

They all paused in thought.

'Well I'm sorry, but I'm out of ideas,' said Gabriel. 'Harold?'

Harold just shook his head nervously as he clung to the back of the coracle.

God scratched his beard and pursed his lips. 'Well, we could …'

'Could what?' said Gabriel.

'You wanna just er …' said God, nodding back towards Harold.

'Oh, you mean?'

God nodded.

'One moment,' said Gabriel. He turned round to Harold. 'If you'd just like to swim back to the shore, we'll join you soon, yes?'

'But I can't swim,' said Harold.

'Well just let go, and once you've finished sinking, you can trot out along the bottom.'

'No, please no.'

'Yes, come on, now let go.'

'Please, no!'

Gabriel tried to lever Harold's hands off the rim, but his grip was strong. 'Now really, this is most irregular,' said Gabriel.

He picked up his oarspoon and placed it on Harold's forehead, braced his foot on the teacup rim, and began shoving.

'Have mercy,' said Harold, his arms being stretched as his head was forced back.

A further small stabbing shove and Harold's grip was broken.

'Hey, don't splash us,' said Gabriel, as Harold began thrashing in the beef tea.

God leaned his head back and opened his mouth to catch a few drops.

Harold was sinking, but making a valiant effort to learn to swim on the fly, but when Gabriel applied a couple of heavy whacks with the oarspoon, he soon disappeared from view.

Gabriel watched the tea. The ripples died, and the surface returned to calm.

'Right,' said Gabriel. 'Finally.'

'The lad's got heart, Gabe, I'll give him that.'

'Anyway, so, Tel, what's your big idea?'

'Well,' said God, before breaking eye contact. 'What I was thinking was … how about we just … do it the old way?'

'What? A direct appeal? Well there's some fir trees in his garden, I think, but surely it's the same as it would be for Dawkins, he's not the type to go for it.'

'No, Gabe ... *the old way.*'

'I don't follow ... unless ... oh ... really? Are you sure? I thought you said we wouldn't do that any more?'

'Did I?' said God.

'Oh now really,' said Gabriel, 'you know you did. It was your mid-millennium resolution in fifteen hundred.'

'Well I've stuck to it pretty well, haven't I?'

'Exactly. So why go back on it now?'

'Oh come on, it's not like one's gonna hurt, be a treat for my good behaviour.'

'I don't know, slippery slope, Tel, and what's your boy going to say? He won't be happy.'

'Well he doesn't need to know, does he. We'll do it on the quiet.'

'Easier said than done.'

'Well we've got no bloody alternative. So just make it happen, okay?'

'Of course, as you wish.'

'Good. Don't let me keep you then.'

God shifted his weight forward once again and lay back, elbows and knees over the teacup's rim, hands and feet dipping into the beef tea.

Gabriel began reverse-paddling back to the shore.

'Hey, wait up,' said God, his gaze staying fixed on the ceiling, 'the monkey, what's his final destination?'

Gabriel lifted his oarspoon. 'I'll have to commission an assessment. But from what we've seen, I'd say he'd be coming here.'

'Great. Let's collect him as well then. Belt and braces. Besides, I'd like to ask him a few questions.'

'Sounds sensible,' said Gabriel. 'I'll have the pappywork drawn up and we'll get a shepherd allocated.'

'Sweet,' said God.

Gabriel resumed his paddle, but then stopped.

'What's up?' said God.

'The judgement designation. It may not be entirely stable.'

'Meaning?'

'So far he's only written from the introduction, "Death" and "Walk The Earth".' Nothing from the second section, apart from the odd note on the lowest place, but if he were to, well ...'

God continued to stare up at the ceiling but tapped the sides of his coracle. 'Best get on with it then,' he said.

'I will,' said Gabriel.

'And I'll leave you to fill Harry in on the details.'

'Yes, Tel.'

'And impress on him the need for … discretion.'

'Of course, Tel.'

Chapter Three

Nikki looked out at the small garden. The wonky bird table, the white plastic furniture, the green-tinged stump of a plastic parasol.

It was Monday morning. The blessed end to another empty weekend. Renewal. Fresh hope. And perhaps, this time, hope would deliver. According to the BBC, spring was just a week away. This meant nothing for Christian's productivity, of course it didn't, but still, the ground had begun to thaw; there was birdsong; there were buds on the trees.

Christian returned with the tan A4 folder – his daily Oscar envelope – and on Mondays, of course, the prospect of a triple delivery. He reached in, withdrew a solitary page, and passed it across.

She took it and sat. One page. One page and most of it was blank. A paragraph at the top, that was it. The prose was perfect, but then it always was. That wasn't the problem.

'Is this it?' she said.

'Yes.'

'What the fuck were you doing all weekend?'

'Excuse me?'

She paused. 'I'm sorry. That came out wrong. It's just, is everything okay? You sounded so confident on Friday. You were going to have a productive weekend.'

'And I did.'

She glanced at the page in her hands.

'Now,' he said, 'you just see the one page–'

'The one paragraph.'

'Yes, the one paragraph, but there's all the thinking time, the research, the backstory.'

'Backstory? How can there be backstory when there's no narrative?'

'Well, there's still the history of Heaven, creation, Adam, Eve and Steve, you know … it all has to fit, it has to make sense.'

'It's not necessary.'

He smiled. 'Now a lot of non-writers think that. *Why write all that background when it'll never appear in print?* But it is necessary, in fact it's essential.'

'Not in this case.'

He smiled again. 'Okay, well that's certainly one point of view. But I'll be keeping my own counsel in this instance. Though I do appreciate the input, as ever, the … the … Nik, Nik, your jumper.'

She looked down. Her right hand had a full fist of left sleeve, stretched out and twisted in tension, the connecting material tight to her elbow. She released her grip, the material recoiling a little before hanging like an old sock. 'Just a … nervous thing,' she said.

'Is everything okay?'

'Yes. Of course.'

'Okay, look,' he said, 'I could show you something else, if you like? Now I was going to wait until it's finished but, well, what the hell. You see, this isn't all I've been working on this weekend.'

'No?'

He shook his head and grinned. 'Not a bit of it,' he said, and reached back into the folder.

Nikki tried not to get her hopes up. But then the folder did look thicker than before. It did. Perhaps spring had indeed finally sprung.

'Now,' he said, 'take a little look at this.'

He handed her a piece of photo paper, folded down the middle like a birthday card. On the front, in large gold type against a brown woodgrain panel, it said 'Thirty Things To Do After You Die by Christian Bootstrap' and below it a pen-and-ink style drawing of a man and an angel ten-pin bowling amid a cloudy backdrop.

She turned it round. The reverse was edge to edge black, apart from more gold text, listing imagined highlights from rave newspaper reviews:

'Ingenious'
'Audacious and quite brilliant'
'The most ridiculous vision of the afterlife apart from all the others'

There was a flap on the reverse edge, folded inside.

She opened it up to discover a soft-focus, auburn-tinted portrait of Christian looking wistfully into the middle distance.

'I don't believe it,' she said.

'I know. But it's amazing what you can do with graphics packages these days. Now believe it or not, that is not a professional photograph. Just my regular camera and *a lot* of playing around with filters.'

She pinched the bridge of her nose. 'Christian, is this a joke?'

'No. Books need sleeves, sleeves need illustrations, back sleeves need photos. Don't you see? I'm offering the full package, not just a manuscript. Obviously I'll have to drop the comments until after the actual reviews come out, they'd be for the big second print run, but think about it – it's presenting it as a finished product, you know, let a publisher see the vision of it on the shelves. I think it'll really set mine apart.'

'I don't doubt it.'

'Wait, there's more.' His hand went back to the folder and this time withdrew several pages of text. He passed them over. 'This'll go under the photo, eventually, but I probably need to get it under five hundred words. Maybe less actually, the fonts only go so small.'

'What's this?'

'My mini biography. For the jacket sleeve.'

She took a brief glance before letting the pages fall to the carpet.

'Well, like I say, it's not quite the finished article,' he said, stepping across and picking them up, 'but you get the idea.'

'Sorry, I'm just a bit shell-shocked,' she said.

'Well yes, I even surprised myself this time.'

She closed her eyes and pinched her bridge again. 'But, Christian, the writing, the actual writing – one paragraph from a whole weekend's work?' She waited for a reaction, but didn't get one. 'Doesn't that frustrate you, doesn't that torment you? Doesn't it burn your insides with battery acid?'

'Oh yes, a little, for sure. But it's like a Japanese business. You know, it's all in the planning, the preparation.'

'Really …'

'Oh yes. Once it's all straight and crystal clear in your head, then it's just a matter of turning the handle.'

'And how is your handle then? Bit rusty?'

'Not a bit of it. Oiled and ready.'

She didn't reply.

'Well, anyway, the keyboard calls,' said Christian, and he got to his feet.

'Oh sorry. *Sorry*,' she said, 'I didn't know I was standing in the way of the fires of industry.' She got up and headed for the door.

'Yes, well, time waits for no man. I've got to rework the chapter on social norms in the Spirit Zone.'

She stopped and turned back to him. 'It's fine as it is,' she said.

'Really? I just thought–'

'No. It's perfect. You need to move on.' She paused. But then she said it. 'In fact, have you thought about an appendix?'

'An appendix? No, not really ...'

Her stomach clenched in instant regret.

'... why? Do you think we need one?'

What had she done? But it was too late, it was out there now. 'Yes, I think it could be good. Magnificent, even.'

'Oh. Right. What would go in it?'

'Well. I'm not sure – what do you think would go in it?'

Christian looked puzzled. 'I don't know,' he said, 'but come on, it's your idea, why do we need one?'

She drew a breath. She held it. 'Oh no matter,' she said, 'it was just a passing thought.' She made her excuses and left.

On the way out of Bracknell, she twice almost crashed the car. Why had she said it? It was bordering on suggestion, on influence. What was she thinking? She could have ruined everything. It wasn't worth the risk, it wasn't even close to being worth the risk. He would do it, he would get there, even at his glacial pace. So what if it took years, so what if it took decades? What was any finite amount of time in the context of eternity?

Chapter Four

Dexter had not enjoyed his start to the week. Gordon had been prickly and obstructive all day and this was coming off the back of an agitated malaise that had gripped him for weeks. Dexter had thought it couldn't get any worse. He was wrong. In the early hours, he was raised by a pounding at his front door, a pounding that, along with everything else, meant he'd now have to risk asking Central Administration to fit a new lock and door frame.

Having calmed the small and panicked entourage outside, and then addressed his spousal panic inside, Dexter counted to ten, tightened the cord on his dressing gown and went to take his seat in the living room.

'What's her problem then?' asked the slouching Gordon, his nightie riding high up his hips.

'Just a bit of shock,' said Dexter, shielding his eyes, 'she'll be fine.'

'Didn't have her down as the nervous type. Anyway, how was I to know you'd be asleep?'

'It's two in the morning, Gordon.'

'Exactly. Assumed you'd still be working on the … whatsit figures.'

'Finished about an hour ago.'

'Really? Right … well, we'll have to find you more to do then, can't have you slacking.'

'Look, the numbers scan fine, Gordo. And the qualitatives. I'm sure they can wait until–'

'That's not why I'm here,' said Gordon.

'Oh,' said Dexter.

Silence.

'And?' said Dexter.

'And ... and, there is no reason,' said Gordon. 'Nothing you can do about it, nothing I can do about it.'

'Do about what?'

Gordon got up and walked over to the mirror where he flexed his biceps, paused to straighten his hairnet, then began clenching and unclenching his buttocks as if using them to send Morse code.

'I'm a caged bull, Dex. It's boiling me up.'

'What is?' asked Dexter.

'What do you think?' said Gordon, turning to face Dexter. 'The project, the mission.'

'Oh not again, Gordon, please ...'

His boss turned back to the mirror. 'I want to stretch, I want to run. I can feel my reserves rising. But this hangs heavy over everything. We've got Heaven's balls in our hands, Dex. All we need to do is squeeze.'

'Gordon ...'

'But we can't, can we? Not until the prophet shoots his load.'

'There's nothing more we can do, certainly nothing tonight,' said Dexter.

Gordon held his pose, but then his head dipped forward and his muscles relaxed. He returned to his seat, slumping back down, the chair emitting a salvo of pops and snaps as it failed to accommodate his weight. 'I don't sleep these days. I just churn it all over.'

'That's not good.'

'You're telling me. You won't have noticed, but I've been under a bit of a cloud.'

'You don't say.'

'Well it's no picnic, I can tell you. I thought we were getting somewhere, I really did. It felt like the old days, like I could take on Heaven, Hell and all comers, but now ...'

'But now what?'

'Now I feel as limp as a charity.'

'Look, shall I send for Grímsson?'

'No quacks.'

'Just something to help you sleep?'

'*No quacks.*'

More silence.

Gordon's knees drifted apart as he stared into space.

'Gordon,' said Dexter, as he shielded his eyes, once again, 'how long have you been wearing a nightie to bed?'

'Not long, six or seven years I suppose.'

'Right.'

'It's a comfort thing, you understand. Never was one for gown and hat.'

'Well, indeed. And the, er, the silk stockings, you wear them to bed too?'

'Not to bed, of course not to bed. No, I just threw them on for a bit of warmth for the walk over. Chilly in the streets tonight.'

'Chilly enough for stockings, but not chilly enough for ... panties?'

'Panties are for women, Dexter ... though I don't doubt they'd be' – his gaze drifted – 'supremely waffendandy ... No, I don't like to be restricted, not by the board, not by my staff, and certainly not by panties.'

'Well, it's your choice, of course ...'

Gordon's chin dropped. 'All I think about is the boy,' he said, 'out there, somewhere, taking the fight to them, fighting alone.'

Dexter closed his eyes and rubbed his brow. 'Well that always was the deal, Gordon. Us, here, we could only ever be observers.'

'Not so. We could help, work what influence we can.'

'Be barely noticeable.'

'Well at least it would be something. Anything's better than sitting sucking our thumbs in the fucking dark.' He glanced around the room and tapped his fingernails on the arm of the chair. 'Your lighting in here is abysmal.' He sunk back to gaze up at the twin citrine strips. 'You've even got shades up there, man.'

'Janey, she–'

'Like a fucking prison in here.' The Lord of Limbo stood and started trying to remove the tasselled stretched silk.

'Gordon ...'

'You know I've never seen sunlight. Do you know what that's like, to have only existed under this fug?' He gripped the shade and started wrenching at it.

'Gordon, please, can't you just– If you must, there's a clip at the back, it's–'

Gordon stabbed his fingers in at one end, got his hand in and ripped the silk from the frame, tearing it off in one long strip.

'For fuck's sake,' said Dexter.

'There,' said Gordon, as he stood staring into the jaundiced glow. 'What's it like, Dex?'

'What's what like?'

'Sunlight. A full spectrum. Tell me what it's like.'

'It's ...' said Dexter, 'it's overrated, it stops you getting on, stops you putting in the hours.'

'All the same, I'd so like to experience it. To feel my feet on lush grass, to hold a planning meeting under open skies, to see marker pens striking a whiteboard, a true white board, Dex, brilliant and perfect.'

'And you will, when we win. You just need to hang in there.'

'Thought I'd maybe have got a preview by now, you know with ... the connection. He's somewhere out there, you know. Perhaps he stares up at the sun, sometimes, and thinks of me. I just want to share in it, be a part of his life, his experience.'

'Gordon, come on, it's all we ever talk about. It's ...'

'It's what?'

'Well, it's consuming you.'

Gordon made eye contact, appearing to consider the point, but made no comment. He again slumped down into the chair, dealing another body blow to its sub-frame. 'It's the not knowing I can't stand,' he said. 'What if he never found the prophet? Never even found the markerman? What if the prophet resisted his calling? What if the prophet never found the markerman? It's like you said, we needed a hundred things to go right. But only one to go—'

'Gordon, you need to get a grip.'

His boss's head drooped forward.

'You need to get a ... you have to ...'

But the tears were already flowing. That wasn't fair. Dexter wasn't trained for this and it certainly wasn't in his job description.

Seeing this immortal, silk-stockinged, pantie-less alpha hulk sobbing into the sleeve of his nightie was uncomfortable enough, but the spectacle became wretched when Dexter recalled Gordon in his pomp, when Limbo was in its heyday, when the greatest machination of them all was conceived.

It was the middle of the nineteen eighties. Thatcher was crushing the unions; Thatcherism igniting the city. Across the Atlantic, Reaganomics was tearing an even greater divide. Debt, deregulation, speculation. Anything was possible. Limbo watched it all unfold and Limbo lapped it up.

It was Dexter's tenth year in the realm, his tenth year since arriving from the sidelines of the Zone: the regulation of the Queue; the interminable and impotent wait for judgement. But once through, he hadn't hung around. Limbo had no out-of-the-box complement of general staff and no means of making them – angels were yet another privilege exclusive to the upper realm – so everyone there, with the exception of Gordon and a handful of the feathered fallen, had at one point been a mortal human, so Central Administration had no choice but to draw from that pool. Not that they were short of candidates. But even so, Dexter's rise had been exceptional, successively outstripping his peers as he climbed the twenty-three middle layers of management in just eight years to become the first person under the age of three hundred to gain a seat on the board and much-coveted access to the inner circle.

But then Dexter had seen the light sooner than anyone. The first in Limbo to appreciate the power of leverage, to understand the rewards of waiting for the right time, and then going big, with a clear head and the odds on your side. And he had been the first to take on the Wall Street fashion cues: the shoes, the shirts, the suits, the braces – or at least Limbo's best approximations. Everyone ridiculed him at first, but not after the man at the top followed, Gordon stepping into what would become a signature, grey wolf-skin, double-breasted power suit that barked of eighties excess, the first time in 6,000 years he'd been tempted away from his long rack of caftans, and then topping Dexter by going full-Gekko with his hair: short on the collar, but left long at the front, waxed and swept high and back into something resembling a giant prize-winning conker.

Back then, Gordon's office was all blues, blacks and greys, the low-temperature decor regularly complemented by Gordon's tendency to cycle the hedgerow through late-night London, New York or Tokyo neon skylines. Everything said focused free-market success – plenty of shiny surfaces, plenty of designer grandeur, but nothing soft, nothing yielding and definitely nothing in mustard.

'So what's that then?' asked Dexter, pointing to the potted bonsai on Gordon's desk, as his boss put aside his transcribed copies of *Business Week*, *Forbes* and *The Financial Times*.

'Thought you'd spot that,' said Gordon, 'latest thing. Go ahead, take a look.'

Dexter reached over and picked it up. Its foliage was dense, a conifer of some sort, and was otherwise unremarkable apart from two small buttons recessed into either side of its pot.

'Pocket window box, don't you know,' said Gordon.

'Pocket?'

'Yes.'

Dexter passed it between his hands. 'Need a big pocket.'

'I've got a big pocket.'

'Well. Yes.'

'Impressive, isn't it?' said Gordon. 'See how they branded it for me.'

Dexter turned it round. 'Swan TV eighty-four,' he said, reading the silver digital-style font title on the base.

'Watch anywhere on Earth when you're on the go,' said Gordon.

'Where's the touchstone?' said Dexter.

'On the base,' said Gordon. 'Here,' he said, getting up and stretching out a hand.

Dexter stood and passed the gadget across.

Gordon placed it on his palm and clicked the right-hand button.

Nothing happened. He tried it again, and after administering a smack to the pot, there was a thin *whumph* and a soft flame appeared among the foliage, within which appeared a snowy green monochrome image.

'There we go,' he said, turning it so they could both see.

'That's great,' said Dexter, 'really … great. So what exactly are we looking at?'

'What do you mean what are we looking at, what's it look like?'

'A room, maybe, I think, is that a table?'

'It's Levine's office.'

'Levine again?'

'Indeed,' said Gordon, beaming. 'I don't mind telling you, I can't get enough of it.'

'Inside viewing of insider trading.'

'Exactly,' said Gordon as he looked deeper into the flames. 'If you've got the balls to take it, you can have it, you can have it all.'

'And that fuzzy blob?' said Dexter, leaning in.

'That's Levine.'

'Oh right. And the other blob?'

'Chet Halanen Jr.'

'Really?'

'Yes. Either that or a filing cabinet. Anyway, you get the idea.' He clicked a button and the flames died. 'And that's not all that's new,' he said, as he began to wrestle the plant into his trouser pocket.

'Oh yes?' said Dexter, desperately suppressing a smirk.

'Check this out,' said Gordon. He eyed and nodded to his business throne.

'Ah, yes,' said Dexter, noting the poorly stitched ivory leather and the ham-fisted carving on the pommels.

'Arrived today,' said Gordon. He turned the bonsai over and began trying to force it branches first into his trouser pocket.

'So, um, what was wrong with your old one?' asked Dexter.

'Well, apart from being six months old, it didn't swivel.'

'A swivel throne?'

'A swivel business throne.'

'Ah, nice,' said Dexter, 'all looking–'

'Anyway,' said Gordon. He hurled the bonsai at the wall, its pot smashing on impact. He clicked his fingers and sat back down on his throne. 'To business.'

'Of course,' said Dexter, and he sat.

'Spitback,' said Gordon.

'His plan?'

'Indeed. He wants to use the new agents.'

'I know he does,' said Dexter. 'I met with him this morning. Sounds risky.'

'Exactly,' said Gordon, jabbing out a finger, 'that's exactly what I said.'

'I meant risky in a bad way.'

'Balls, man. It's bold, it's exciting. Just the sort of thing you said we should be doing.'

'Yes, but only when it makes sense to do so. El-Mofty took sixty years to prepare those agents, we now have seven capable of ascension, seven. Do you really want to blow them all on this hare-brained scheme?'

'Risk and reward, Dexter, risk and reward. Anyway, Spitzy's confident.'

'He always is.'

'Dexter ...'

'He's ...' Dexter paused to consider the level of frankness. '... It's just he's blue sky. *Very* blue sky.'

'Don't be flasbine. He speaks highly of you.'

'I'm sorry, what?'

'Oh come on, you know it's your passion for calculators that got him thinking on this one.'

'Computers, Gordon, doing calculations.'

'Well, not my area, Dexter. I'm good with ledgers. A lot you can do with ledgers. But that doesn't mean I don't see the potential of these machines, these dark devices, to prise open Pandora's box, bring down the whole damned system. That's why I love this plan. It's of our time. Information as a weapon, launched through their own mechanisms, using their own assets against them ... not to mention exploiting his arrogance and his vanity. It's fucking beautiful.'

'I'm with you, Gordon, one hundred per cent, but we must have control. It's a sound idea but it's not ready.'

'It *is* ready. And now is the time. You said so yourself. In another twenty years, those computers could be as much as fifteen per cent faster than they are today. And that would be enough, wouldn't it?'

'Well yes, I'm sure it would.'

'So we must put the wheels in motion now. Allow for the gestation time.'

'Respectfully, Gordon, I say again, it's being rushed.'

Gordon pulled a lever on his throne and reclined to the sound of crunching cog teeth. 'I understand completely,' he said.

'You do?'

'Of course. You're jealous.'

'Of who?'

'Of Spitback.'

Dexter could not suppress a scowl.

'It's not a criticism,' said Gordon, 'nothing wrong with a bit of the green eye. But it's not a rational objection.'

'You want a rational objection?' said Dexter. 'Fine' – he stood – 'for starters, risks multiply. For it not to go wrong, we'd have to make a hundred things go right.'

'And they will,' said Gordon, 'because this time it'll be properly executed.' He put his hands behind his head before his mouth widened to a genial smile.

'No one can guarantee that,' said Dexter. 'For one, we don't have the personnel. Our agents, they're not made of the right stuff.'

'What do you mean, not the right stuff? El-Mofty handpicked the lot of them. Seven of Limbo's finest.'

'I don't doubt it, but from what pool? Face it, even our best are still bureaucrats, administrators, pen-pushers.'

'Pen-pushers run the mortal world, Dexter.'

'Yes, but they don't go on stealth missions behind enemy lines. This needs steel and courage, not to mention the manipulation of a fair bit of ancient technology. They're not military men, Gordon, they're managers. Neil Armstrong was a former test pilot, not a former assistant to the Head of Regional Advertising.'

'Rubbish. They'll get it right or pay with their lives.'

Dexter retook his seat. 'They already will pay with their lives,' he said, 'even if you can get them in, it's a one-way trip. Spitback's had them swear an oath to throw themselves over the walls the moment they're done.'

'Well what do they expect?' said Gordon. 'About time they put something back, living here rent free in my realm. What do I ever get in return? Statistics and excuses.'

'Precisely my point,' said Dexter. 'They're not doers, none of them are. Now if you sent them to manage others into pulling the right levers and pressing the right buttons up there, okay, fair enough, but actually doing it themselves? I don't know, Gordo, I just don't know.'

The consequences of New Limbinian being populated almost entirely by managers are numerous and far-reaching. Administrative types can blend in like cuttlefish on Earth, moving among us, unseen in our corporations, partnerships and public services. They can, on occasion, appear useful, necessary even, and in extreme cases, vital. But when the only people to manage are other managers, things begin to unravel. The problem is best illustrated by the quintessentially bourgeois world of home improvements and, since the middle of the twentieth century, their near total absence in the Great Grey City. The desire is still there, but the immense risks are not worth it. Because for almost everyone in New Limbinian, as for most people in mortal life, the only option for anything beyond paint and wallpaper is to get someone else to do the work for you. But in modern New Limbinian, the only people available to undertake the work are Central Administration. The experience is just as awful as getting the builders in, but for entirely different reasons, and tends to go something like this: you decide the house would look lovely with a conservatory. You ask Central Administration for a quote. They send round an impeccably turned out official, who nods, smiles, says it will be a straightforward project and gives you a timescale for undertaking the work. On the day committed, a large team of management consultants arrives at exactly nine a.m. and begins to dismantle one side of your house. You ask if they know what they are doing, and they respond with answers that are confident, polished and convincing. They conclude their work, taking exactly the number of days estimated. One week later, your house falls down.

'They will deliver this time,' said Gordon. 'The pressure will focus them.'

'That's not my only concern.'

'Meaning?'

'Meaning what about your involvement, this "visit"?'

'It worked for Terry.'

'No it didn't, they crucified him.'

'Well, yes, apart from that bit.'

'But it's never been tried before,' said Dexter, 'not with a lower-realm deity.'

'Well we've got little choice, according to Spitzy. It's not like the prophet will have Heaven to guide him. On his own, he'll be a ship without a captain.'

'But how can you even be sure of finding him? You won't be able to look him up in the Yellow Pages.'

'Spitzy's got it covered. Says we'll spawn a markerman, too, day-glow bright, loud as Christmas. He will be the link, he will be the staple for our pages.'

'And yet another thing we have to get right.' Dexter shook his head. 'It's already getting more complicated, Gordon.'

'Relax, Dexter. It all feels right. And besides, there's something else I feel, deep in my bones.' He pulled another lever and crunched the throne back to upright. 'You see, there comes a time when a man must become a father.'

'Well, yes,' said Dexter, 'though not normally while he becomes a son at the same time.'

'Well exactly. An unrivalled bond. Next best thing to breastfeeding, according to Spitzy.'

'According to Spitzy ...'

'There's that green eye again,' said Gordon.

'I just don't think he knows what he's doing.'

'Okay, sometimes The Pigeon can overstretch that mighty wingspan. But he's all about ideas, delivery's not his forte ...'

'Well I've been saying that for years.'

'... but that's not a problem any more.'

'Oh no?'

'No. It's Spitzy's baby, but I'm getting someone else to deliver it.'

'Who?'

'You.'

'*Me?*'

'Exactly. I knew you'd love it. Inject some modern professionalism. Risk assessments, audits, compliance policies, all that crap. Yes, yes, you're it, Dexter, the final piece we always needed.'

Dexter stood and turned away. 'Look, Gordon, I'm flattered, of course. But I can't work the miracle you think I can. We'd need to start again from the ground up, take a lot more time to really work it through, put some proper quality standards in place, then yes, maybe then we'd be in business, but as it stands, we're playing with fire.'

He waited for a reply, but was greeted only with a long and strained metal-on-metal screech that ran down to the base of his spine.

'Gordon. Gordon?'

He turned to see his boss leaning back in his throne, having swivelled to face the flames of his hedgerow, now showing the last rays of sun spreading long over lower Manhattan.

'An earthly incarnation,' said Gordon, 'I'm going to be a father, Dex, I'm going to be a father.'

'And a son as well,' said Dexter, with a sigh, 'and a son as well.'

Nothing further was said.

And so it happened. Final preparations were made and the mission was launched. There would be no news straight away, of course: after witnessing the glory of the pure white light of seven ascensions, Gordon and his team were blind to their agents' arrival in Heaven – instantly younger versions of themselves materialising on the roof of the Hoggard's Artisan Sausages Lounge, blind to their successful infiltration of the control rooms, and mostly successful execution of the plan, blind to the bonus that the only ripple seen in Heaven was a report of seven strangely suited men seen shaking hands before throwing themselves over the north perimeter wall. But nine months later, when what was dismissed by Michael Fish as freak aurora borealis were seen across the skies of England on three successive nights, Central Administration threw a party the like of which Limbo had never seen. Kicking off late the following Easter Monday afternoon, some maintained it lasted for more than an hour and twenty minutes, and Cheung had got so carried away he'd allowed grades seventeen and below to go home early, so long as they had completed all their duties for the day and had obtained written line management approval in advance. Heady days ...

Now those times seemed a world away as Dexter looked across at his boss. The same man sitting across from him. Thirty years had passed, Dexter had lived almost all of those days with some sort of contact with Gordon, yet now it was like seeing the transformation for the first time. How had it come to this? The Great Lord of Limbo, Gordon 'Gordo' Swan, slumped in a dribble-stained nightie, hitched up high around his waist, tears running down his cheeks as he stared at the wall.

Dexter was baffled on some things, worryingly assured on others, but certain of only one: that things were getting worse.

Chapter Five

Thursday. Harold was at one of the allotments in Blotchley Hall, as usual, watching Christian watching television, as usual. But Harold's mind was elsewhere, still ruminating on the trauma of going under the brown waves in the Biscilica and the consequent second trip in as many weeks to the almost as terrifying clothing provisioners. Still, that had at least allowed him to get in some proper queuing.

He glanced into the juniper's flames before going back to the book – watching Christian left plenty of time for study – but he was soon interrupted. Gabriel had news.

'He's going to be relocated,' said the archangel, his voice low and measured.

'Really? You mean the London office?' said Harold. 'I've not heard him mention it.' Harold began flicking through his copious notes.

'No, Harold,' said Gabriel. He placed a clawhand on the pages. 'To the Zone. He's going to be relocated to the Zone.'

'I, I don't understand.'

'Do I need to spell it out?'

'Oh no, you don't mean?'

Gabriel nodded.

'They're going to ... kill him?' said Harold.

'Please, keep your voice down,' said Gabriel. 'Terry wants this hush-hush. Cabinet only.'

'Terry knows about it?'

'Of course. Who do you think gave the order.'

'B-but he's God, this is … Heaven.'

Gabriel looked around before speaking. 'All leaders have to make diffi-cult decisions, from time to time,' he said. 'Tel's mortified about it, of course, but his hands are tied. Bootstrap seems intent on continuing the work, and well, that knowledge, it's just too dangerous.'

'But surely there must be another way, another path?'

'There isn't. We have no choice. We can't let this terrorist put every-thing in jeopardy.'

'He doesn't look like a terrorist,' said Harold, turning back to the flames as Christian reached for another macaroon.

'Looks can be deceiving, Harold. This chap's probably deep under cover …'

They looked into the flames again as Christian turned over to *Antiques Road Show*.

'… deep, deep cover.'

'But *relocating him*,' said Harold, 'is that even possible? Isn't killing a sin?'

'Oh yes,' said Gabriel, 'it's a fairly big one.'

'So …'

'Ah, right, I see what you mean. Okay, couple of things here – first, you only face automated judgement at the Gate, on your way in, and actually even then Terry himself would have blanket immunity, but once you're here, well, there's a bit more leeway when it comes to sins. Second, and this is the key point, it's only a sin anyway if you actually do it yourself. Ordering a relocation, or ordering any other sin for that matter, well, there's nothing actually on the statute about that.'

'What?'

'Yes, funny, isn't it? But believe me, that's the way it is.'

'But surely someone will still have to pull the trigger, at the end of the chain of command … So do they pay the price?'

'Well it turns out the same loophole can help you out there too.'

'How?'

'By ensuring there's a few steps between your action and the resultant relocation. You wouldn't just wait for him to leave the house then hit him with a bolt of lightning – well, actually that's a bad example, it's hard to be accurate with weather. No, the point is that even if you could, you wouldn't want to because there would be a pretty direct cause and effect at play – you throw the lightning bolt, he gets relocated, you get implicated.'

'Well how do they do it then?'

'They look for indirect routes,' said Gabriel, 'chain reactions. Let's say you make it rain for forty days and forty nights. All you're guilty of is making it rain. How were you to know some communities would get flooded, how were you to know they didn't have a volunteer lifeboat service and never learned to swim? It's not your fault they weren't prepared.'

'I see ...'

'It's harder than it looks, though, especially for the surgical strike. Your natural disaster's still fine for indiscriminate relocations, but if you're only after one man, well, not so easy.'

Harold sat shaking his head. 'So if you kill someone–'

'Relocate.'

'If you relocate someone, you only go to Hell–'

'Please, Harold, the *lower place* or the *other places*.'

'Beg pardon. You only go to the lower place if you do it by your own hand?'

'Pretty much.'

'But this is, this is an outrage, it's grotesque ... the implications ... did Mr Hitler avoid the lower place?'

'Oh no, no, no.'

'But I don't understand, you said ordering relocations isn't a crime?'

'That's right.'

'But ...'

'But theft is.'

'Theft?'

'Poland, Czechoslovakia, France, the low countries ...'

'So Adolf Hitler is only there on a technicality?'

'Well hardly a technicality. Stealing is very much frowned upon, especially when it's something quite large, like a country, but anyway, that's not the point.'

'What is then?'

'That he is there.'

'But it's like Al Capone being locked up for tax evasion.'

'Well, you have to work within the rules.'

'Forgive me, but doesn't Terry make the rules?'

'Well, yes ... in theory.'

'So why not change them then? Why not update them?'

'Oh we do, from time to time, but it's a tricky business.'

'Why?'

'Well, for one there's a long lead time. Changes take months to kick in and just as long to reverse. So mistakes can be, well, costly.'

'Mistakes?'

'Yes. You see, we don't really understand how the judgement system works. Thousands of coded parameters, all interdependent. So changing it is something of a dark art and even then you need a bit of luck.'

'But you have tried?'

'We have,' said Gabriel. He stretched and flexed his armwings before sitting back. 'The last big change was back in, goodness knows when, to get rid of the believers, it was the cornerstone of the Boot Out the Devout programme.'

'*Boot Out the* … but why?'

'Well, it's obvious really, when you think about it. You imagine being Terry, surrounded by that lot for a few millennia.'

'But, even so.'

'Well, as I recall, I did have my reservations.'

'Quite right,' said Harold. 'It's their kingdom, their inheritance, it's–'

'Oh not on that score, terribly dull lot, your believers, never did care for them. No, my point was that though they may be rhumbolic, chiddle-some and rather rum company, they do have one glowing, redeeming feature.'

'And that is?'

'Loyalty.'

'Yes. Yes I suppose–'

'There is nothing, Harold, nothing in this world that will break the faith of the true-blue literal-word believer. Education, common sense, their own experience, even their own dreadful back-of-the-mind suspicion it's all flapspindle, none of that will create so much as a tremor in that granite-like belief. And there's always plenty of them too, which when combined with the loyalty is reassuring, or rather was reassuring, when we were still admitting them.'

'Reassuring? I don't quite–'

'Whereas your sceptics and your atheists, your questioners, your John Thomases, okay, so they may well be infinitely more charismatic, interesting and creative and entertaining to have round for dinner, but they are not loyal.'

'But surely they're loyal to reason, to logic?'

'Exactly. Show them some new evidence, allow them to verify it and think it all through in a sensible and structured way and they'll turn tail in a heartbeat.'

'I, I don't know what to say.'

'Anyway, we muddled through the changes in the end, but there were side effects.'

'Such as?'

'Well, have you met any Danish people since you arrived?'

'No ...'

'There you go.'

'You're saying no Danish people get into Heaven?'

'Not one, not since the changes, anyway.'

'But that's dreadful.'

'Well, I'm not so sure. How many great Danes can you think of?'

'No, I mean it's dreadful for them.'

'Oh yes ... yes, I suppose. But then it's not a perfect world, is it? There's always going to be collateral damage, as they say these days.'

'Like Mr Bootstrap.'

'Oh no, now don't you start getting sympathetic for our Mr Bootstrap, he's a terrorist through and through, you mark my words.'

Harold's head dropped.

'Oh come, come,' said Gabriel, 'things aren't so bad. You seem to be adjusting ... a bit ... so you're all right, aren't you? You're okay?'

'It's ... it's just nothing here is as I expected.'

'Well, that's life for you.'

'Is there really nothing we can do for Mr Bootstrap?'

'Look, I think you're forgetting something here, Harold.' Gabriel looked around again before lowering his voice, 'Yes, he's going to die, but you and I know dying doesn't mean death, does it now? You didn't *die* when you died, did you? Look at you now, you're dead, but you're not *dead*.'

'But–'

'We're affording him deliverance, Harold, nothing less. We will unburden him from the anguish of mortality, allow him to blossom into an eternal spirit, and then after judgement, take up ownership of a brand new immortal body, just like yours.' Gabriel gently punched Harold on the arm. 'And he's coming here too, to the top table. One of the lucky few, like yourself. And once Tel's had a quiet word with him, got this all ironed out, well I'm sure we'll all be able to have a good laugh about it, Bootstrap too.'

'Somehow I can't see that.'

Gabriel folded his armwings and sat forward. 'Well, either way, the wheels are in motion, so do try to get used to it.'

Harold sank into his seat.

Gabriel got up to leave. 'Tomorrow afternoon,' he said, 'so clear the diary, yes?'

'What, we're going to … watch?'

'Terry's insisting. Look, the way I see it, this way we can at least make sure it's done right. With dignity and compassion.'

Harold said nothing.

'Anyway, Elvis Lounge at four. Don't be late.'

Chapter Six

God's cabinet and the major section heads had assembled for Heaven's first state execution since the Late Middle Ages. So, to the outsider, the tired sapphire-lit blue-suede-everything glitz of the Elvis Lounge might have seemed like an odd choice. Even if you looked past the decor, which was no mean feat, it had poor capacity, the seats were cramped, and its bramble thicket viewer was only half the size of the yew hedge in Blotchley. But with the central section being a combination theatre cinema – flanked by burger bar 'n barbiturate diner to the left and an extensive gallery and museum tribute area to the right – it had a degree of practicality. More importantly, it was, in one specific sense, discreet; it had been built in late '77 to honour the man himself, but after numerous false reports of his impending arrival, was now rarely used, for though this was to be an official state execution, it would be a secret state execution. No records would be kept, no one without clearance would be admitted, and everyone involved, from the most junior usher right up to Gabriel, had been required to swear a special oath of secrecy to Terry himself at the start of the day.

Despite the extensive preparations, the main event would be brief, so to make the most of the occasion, two supporting features had been lined up. First up was some light comedy, the organisers taking advantage of fortunate timing to dip into the proceedings of the Church of England's General Synod. This was followed by a largely unsuccessful trawl for some cheap titillation from various Hollywood celebrity bedrooms. No one cared. It wasn't why they were here.

Harold was the last to show his face, not wanting to make the experience any longer than necessary. By the time he arrived, a thick fatty whiff was the only thing left in the diner, so he headed for the pearl bead and diamante door curtain that led to the banked seating of the theatre cinema. As he stepped through, he felt eyes on him. His heart sank when he spotted Gabriel flapping at him and indicating he'd saved him a seat – right in the centre of the action, row seven and immediately in front of God. As Harold apologised his way towards Gabriel, he realised his boss might not have had to work too hard for the save, as God had his feet up on the top of the seatback and made no attempt to move them when Harold sat down, leaving the new boy no choice but to carefully slot his head in between the Almighty's grease-stained blue suede loafers.

Greetings were exchanged and Harold did his best to settle in. God seemed to be coping with the dark weight of responsibility remarkably well, sending vibrations through the seatback with every chortle.

A large cheer rang out as the wall sliders were closed and the bramble thicket fired up again, this time for the main feature. The flames flickered and crackled before stabilising to reveal an image of Christian. He was in the kitchen making toast while listening to *The Film Programme* on Radio 4. The operators zoomed the point of view in onto Christian's wrist watch to show the time, much to the amusement of the audience. Five minutes to the hour. A wave of Oohs rippled up the rows.

'Popcorn, Harry?' said God, thrusting a greasy bucket of what looked like golf balls of gristle over Harold's shoulder.

'No, thank you,' said Harold.

Back in the brambles, the point of view had been zoomed out to a wide shot that allowed Christian and the kitchen wall clock to be in frame.

'How ... how are they going to do it?' whispered Harold, unable to look at the screen.

'We don't know,' said Gabriel.

'Just how I like it,' said God. 'I love surprises.'

'The Pansies seemed terribly excited though,' added Gabriel.

Harold produced a black band and pinned it around his arm. There were sniggers from the rows behind.

'Chin up,' said Gabriel, placing a clawhand on Harold's shoulder.

With four minutes to go, God produced several boxes of cigars and people began passing them around.

Gabriel checked the aides were ready with the Jeragne – a sort of viscous fizzy mead that chemically peeled the lips yet Terry and tradition insisted everyone ingest at times of celebration.

Three minutes. Two. One.

God rubbed his hands and let out a whoop of excitement. 'Oh it's been a while.'

Harold gripped his seat cushion and dug his nails into the velour.

A hush fell.

Some started calling out the second hand, softly at first, but then louder as others joined. Soon everyone was counting down to the end of Christian's life like it was New Year's Eve.

'Five.'

'Four.'

'Three.'

'Two.'

'One.'

3,208 miles to the west of Bracknell, Foz was waiting for the bus as usual, which was running late, as usual.

He thought again about last night's purchase. He was still apprehensive but feeling better about it now. Maybe it could work? Maybe he really could do it? This wasn't how he'd felt when he woke, an hour earlier, and first recalled his bold investment from the night before. It was enough for him to sink back into the sagging mattress and question his sanity. But it's so easy to commit to a new lifestyle at two in the morning. 'Abs to die for in twelve weeks.' 'Just ten minutes a day.' Who hasn't got ten minutes a day? He definitely had ten minutes a day. In that moment, as always, he'd pictured his new successful self. And in that moment, as always, he knew he could do it, he knew he would do it. But each time, each time until last night, that is, he would hesitate and postpone the call until the morning. And every time, when morning came, he'd feel that sweet relief. Who'd he been kidding? Of course he didn't need a Buck Minglestein exercise station. He wasn't so big, nothing a bit more bowling couldn't sort out, and anyway he had personality – the ultimate get-out-of-exercise-free card. Getting fit is the last throw of the dice for the brainless, he would tell himself. Why did anyone think Minglestein was so obsessed with it in the first place?

But last night had been different. Foz had dialled the number. He'd handed over his details and committed his $149.95. And now, here at the bus stop, the more he thought about it, the more he knew it could work. Yes, it would be tough, yes, it would take a while, but he knew he would do it. He wasn't getting any younger, and life is short. And this wasn't the usual late-night beer and self-pity fuelled pipe dream. This was a real, cold-light-of-day epiphany and this would be the first day of the rest of his life.

He took a last drag on his last cigarette and dropped the butt to the pavement. He took each of the remaining cigarettes from the packet and snapped them in two. He gave a shout, 'Yeah.' It felt good. He looked around. There were a few people going about their day, but he found, with a sweet buzz, that he didn't care. He let out a bigger shout, 'Yeah,' and followed it with a, 'Woo, yeah, woo.' He felt adrenaline squirt through his insulated arteries. That felt good too. He high-fived the bald head of Bruce Willis on his magazine cover. 'Yeah.'

An unusual sound broke his train of thought. It was coming from above, a sort of low corrugated whistle getting closer and louder. His brain trawled his thirty-eight years of experience for candidates for the source of this intrusion, but drew a blank. His brain decided the only course of action was direct investigation, so he looked up. He spotted an object in the sky above him – a bright fiery mass which he reckoned to be about the size of a large bread van. This also failed to register with any of his experiences of life on Earth so far. His experiences of life on Earth so far did, however, allow his brain to establish the approximate position of the fiery mass, its speed and trajectory. Unfortunately, his brain concluded that the fiery mass was about a hundred and fifty feet above his head, travelling at almost a hundred miles an hour, and heading straight for him. His brain added a footnote: a recommendation for evasive action, with a further footnote saying there was only four-fifths of a second in which to take it. This span of time was quite insufficient for any human to retreat to a safe distance, let alone someone in Foz's physical condition. So, four-fifths of a second later, the fiery mass blended him into the pavement, creating, in an instant, a sizzling gumbo of skin, bone, metal, fat, plastics, blood, pavement and brain.

In the Elvis Lounge, the afternoon had been sombre. God had been borderline livid by the time he'd given up, singeing the curtains as he left the room, and most of the cabinet had made their exit soon after. Gabriel and Harold had been told to remain until they had answers, with Gabriel becoming increasingly stressed about the whole situation and feeling the heat as the de facto representative of the Pansies in the absence of their commanding officer. Harold, on the other hand, had perked up. For the moment, at least, Christian Bootstrap was still alive.

Now, late into the evening, a messenger had returned along with Dr Douglas Pringle (BSc, PhD, R.I.P.) of the HFP – the section otherwise known as the Pansies, otherwise known as the Angels of Death.

Pringle wasn't actually an angel and neither were any of his staff. In fact, angels hadn't worked in the section since ancient times, making their most famous name something of an anachronism – all the more so because none of the sections that were still staffed by angels had their genus in the title. But the old name didn't get used much these days anyway; as in all the best totalitarian regimes, the people dishing out the really nasty jobs tended to feel better about it if the people they were dishing them to had a short snappy initialism, allowing the disher to remain verbally and therefore mentally detached from the nature of what would follow, a degree of distance you just can't get when sending the latest batch of pappywork to the Angels of Death. God himself was never troubled by the need to kill people, or the gory details, but the former mortals in his upper administration, who did the actual work of submitting and stamping the S12D execution orders, often found it troubling and so the HFP name was born. Not only did they decide to employ an initialism but the words behind it were chosen to be as soft and inoffensive as possible: 'Happy', 'Fluffy' and 'Pansies' being selected after coming first, second and third in a survey where residents of Heaven were asked, among other questions, what words they felt would be least likely to be associated with state-sanctioned murder.

Originally, the Angels of Death were just that, angels, and they did the job reasonably well for the first 2,000 years. But there were problems – rarely of conscience or moral conflict but often of execution, or rather execution of execution. Because though the angels were willing to do God's bidding, they suffered from a tendency to use their initiative. They would focus on the spirit of the order, rather than the letter, perhaps taking out the true source of a problem, rather than what God thought it was, or changing the timing of a cataclysmic landslide to spare more innocents, or fewer sinners. In other words, they thought for themselves. All of which tended to get God worked into a lather. In the fourth century BC, he swept them aside and restocked the entire force from the ready and growing supply of fanatically devout former mortals (for in the early days it really was the God-fearers, and only the God-fearers, who gained entry to the Kingdom). It was one of his better decisions and blossomed into a golden age for all involved. Grim, heinous and unjust wrath was rained down with not the slightest question or hesitation, reference to internal conscience, or adjustment of the specifics in any way. All was good, and this second generation of the section lasted unchanged for the next two millennia.

But when the devout began to overrun the Kingdom and God decreed their banishment, it spelled the end for the HFP as it then was. All the devout had to go. No exceptions.

And so a third generation was needed. But when angels cannot be trusted to stick to the letter, and with no more believers to blindly obey, where would Heaven go for its dirtiest jobs?

The solution was ingenious. As is often the case when religion leaves a vacuum, philosophy stepped in. For the ranks of the Pansies would be repopulated with the most radical, deceased, causal determinists known to metaphysics. And it worked. Their number believed, with absolute certainty, that the universe ran like clockwork – that everything from atoms to galaxies, was governed by the laws of physics and nothing else. The inclusion was exhaustive and therefore included themselves, their own minds, their own thoughts. To them, free will was an illusion – whether people be mortals, spirits, angels or deities, every detail of their lives was set in stone moments after the big bang and all of reality and time is mechanically playing out along an extraordinarily complex but entirely unalterable path. Whatever influence people think they have on their life, for example whether to have jam or marmalade on their toast on a particular Thursday morning, is merely an illusion. They may think they decided to have jam for a change, but in fact since the dawn of time they were predestined to decide to have jam for a change, because their 'choice' was merely a function of their state of mind and the stimulus acting upon it – those mere products of all the events that had happened so far in the universe – and if their state of mind could be replicated and all stimulus replicated, and if that scenario were to be run a million times, every single time they would decide to have jam for a change. There is no free will; there are no choices, only illusions of choices. And that has consequences (entirely predictable and unalterable ones): Hitler can no more be blamed for his bestiality than Gandhi can be hailed for his humanity. And this was why radical causal determinists made perfect Pansies. They still had to be ruthless, homicidal, radical, causal determinists, but believing the universe was clockwork meant they felt no discomfort about the work of the section, however grim the orders (and over the years, there had been some very grim ones indeed). As they saw it, the events were a natural and unalterable consequence of all the events that preceded them – they couldn't question the orders even if they wanted to because if they had wanted to they would have already done so. It also meant despite being trained ruthless killers, they didn't mind being called Pansies, because it was always what they were going to be called so there was no point getting upset about it. And for the same reason, there was no point in getting upset about having been in a state of stand-down for the last five hundred years. On stand-down until these last couple of days, that is.

'I don't see the problem,' said Pringle. He stood tall in his black tweeds, hands clasped behind his back, and spoke with a slight bark that might have sat better on a sergeant major.

Gabriel and Harold looked at each other.

'That's the problem,' said Gabriel, pointing to the image of Christian and Beatrice enjoying a nice evening not talking to each other.

Pringle looked at the bramble thicket.

'I'm not a technician, Archangel.'

'Not the thicket, what's in the thicket.'

'And your point is ...?'

'Look,' said Gabriel, 'you were supposed to relocate Christian Bootstrap, were you not?'

'No, you told us to kill him.'

'That's what we mean by *relocation*, Doctor.'

'Oh. Right. Yes. We did then.'

Gabriel and Harold looked at each other again.

'Look, my dear man,' said Gabriel to Pringle, 'what aren't you telling us? Did you arrange for a slow, lingering relocation? Poison in the butter, perhaps? Some sort of horrible virus?'

Harold looked queasy.

'Nope, we pulverised him,' said Pringle.

'I don't understand,' said Gabriel.

'Well, it's quite simple,' said Pringle, relaxing his stance, 'we knocked a broadcast satellite off course, just a little nudge and, hey, you'll like this, it was mostly used for evangelical TV stations.' Pringle chuckled. 'Anyway, Isaac Newton did the rest. Well, not literally of course, can never get him interested. Still, beautiful bit of physics, even if I do say so myself. And they say us philosophers can't do real science? Course we can.'

Gabriel clenched his clawhands. 'I'm no expert,' he said, 'but he' – Gabriel pointed to the image of Christian again – 'doesn't look terribly pulverised, not even a little bit.'

'Who's this then?'

'Who do you think? Bootstrap.'

'No it isn't.'

'Yes it is.'

'No, it isn't.'

'Yes, it is.'

'Excuse me,' said Harold, 'Dr Pringle, are you saying that's not who you relocated?'

'Exactly.'

'Oh,' said Gabriel.

'But you did relocate someone today?' said Harold.

'Yes,' said the doctor. 'Thoroughly.'

'My God,' said Harold, and he sat down.

On the outskirts of Hyannis, Massachusetts, Foz was still sitting on his couch, inside a large police tape cordon, next to an impact crater that used to contain the little part of planet Earth he'd stand on while waiting for the bus. The now near silence was broken only by the occasional creek of faux leather as he rocked gently back and forth. He was alone with his thoughts, all of which were hazy and disjointed, and the last of the acrid smell, to which he'd now grown oddly accustomed. At least he was calmer now. Though no less confused.

He kept trying to go over his day, trying to work out what had happened. He remembered leaving the apartment in the late morning, he remembered waiting for the bus, and he thought he remembered looking up at something bright. He also seemed to recall an old man and a tunnel of light, at some point, possibly. The hours after were a blur. He remembered a commotion, cops, the fire department, paramedics, TV crews, but the more time passed, the less real that part of his day now seemed.

Incongruous thoughts flitted through his mind. For one, he knew it was a cold spring afternoon and he'd been sitting out for most of it in just his sweatpants and bowling shirt, yet he didn't feel cold. And that was odd too – his bowling shirt: he was fairly sure, being a work day, he'd been wearing his uniform when he left the apartment. He was sure he hadn't brought the couch with him either. He'd definitely have remembered something like that.

Short on answers, he tried to return to the here and now. What should he do with the rest of his day? There didn't seem much point in going to work. The shift was half over and anyway he was fairly sure they didn't allow furniture on the bus. Perhaps he should head home and take it easy.

But lurking in the wings was something darker, a terrible sense of finality and dread that something quite bad had happened, that though he was still here, he actually sort of might not be – that he'd been somehow booted out of reality and yet still had a ringside seat, not to mention a spare one each side of him. He could see himself, he could touch himself – his arms, his legs, his body, his cushions and his armrests. But the cops, the fire crews the paramedics, the TV people, the onlookers, no one had seemed interested in helping, even when he was screaming at the top of his voice. They had jobs to do, he told himself, and the onlookers, well, they wouldn't want to get involved, they never do. But somewhere not too deep inside, he suspected the awful truth was that they didn't know he was there, that he was invisible to them.

But he was visible to some. In fact, someone was watching him from the cover of the undergrowth across the road and, unusually, had been doing so since before Foz's death. The watcher would make contact, in time, but not today, perhaps not even this week. For now he had to observe his subject, get to know him, understand him. Only then would he move.

Chapter Seven

The next day, Gabriel and Harold were briefing God on the results of their investigation. Gabriel had come armwinged with a large platter of carob and kidney eclairs on a bed of larded prunes in an effort to sweeten the message.

They met the Almighty in the Costa Rica Lounge, where God would often come when things weren't going too well. He found the jungle greens soothing but mostly he liked the way it served as a sauna if you told the staff to turn the climate way up past Tropical Wet Season. Today it was off the scale and it had been hard for Gabriel and Harold to find their boss in all the steam.

'So it was all down to a simple admin error,' said Gabriel, already doubly uncomfortable at having to appear in a semi-public place in just a towel as well as suffer the effects of extreme humidity on his plumage.

'Oh yeah,' said God.

'Well, it seems the Pansies mission office didn't quite check all the details on the S12D during target allocation.'

'I said they'd been too bloody quick.'

'Well, have a heart, Tel, they're just so very keen after the long layoff.'

'My arse,' said God, hurling his eclair, 'keen's good. I like keen, but this is cockhanded, Gabe. Where's the checks and balances? It's not the Wild West, you know.'

'I have spoken to Pringle. He was most apologetic.'

'Made me look like a right turkey,' said God, going for a replacement eclair. 'So are they back on the case then, the real case?'

Harold motioned to speak, but Gabriel got in first.

'Absolutely. They're coming up with a new plan, plus we're maxing out on the shepherds this time, two dozen already signed up.'

'Well I hope it's not gonna involve another satellite. Not exactly hush-hush, was it?'

'No, granted, but look, there's all this splendid technology they've been itching to play with, they've had five centuries on standby, you know how it is.'

'Oh, I know how it is. "Leave it to me," you said. That's how it is, Gabe.'

'We've only lost a few days,' said Gabriel. 'No harm done.'

'No harm done? What about to me? To my reputation? Getting the whole fuckin' cabinet in there to watch ...'

Gabriel had no reply.

'... this whole system's based on their confidence in my competence.'

'Oh, I wouldn't worry, Tel. They'd be loyal however incompetent you seem.'

God stood. He frisbeed the plate of eclairs into the undergrowth and eyeballed Gabriel, forcing him to turn away. 'You forget your place, Archangel.'

Fiery crimson flecks appeared in the Almighty's beard, like burning wire wool; his eyes widened as his pupils shrank to pinpricks.

'Not that you are, in any way incompetent, in any way at all,' said Gabriel, cowering.

God held his scowl for a few beats before retaking his seat. 'Well, I'm not going through that palaver again,' he said.

'You won't have to,' said Gabriel, 'we're proceeding behind closed doors from now on.'

'Good.'

'Look, don't worry, Tel, we'll get him. The Pansies are on top of it.'

'Well I bloody hope so, Gabe,' said God, shaking his head. 'I bloody hope so.'

'Right. Well, we'll leave you in peace,' said Gabriel, and he got up to leave.

Harold stayed seated. 'Terry,' he said.

'Yes, son?'

'The wrong Bootstrap, the American ...'

'Yeah.'

Gabriel gave a warning glare, but Harold either didn't see it or chose to ignore it.

'... what's our plan for him?'

'I don't follow?' said God.

'Harold ...' said Gabriel.

'Let the lad speak,' said God.

'What are we doing about his situation?' said Harold. 'He was an innocent party.'

'This is true,' said God. He paused to search for the right words. 'It was a ...'

'Sad loss?' said Gabriel.

'Yes, a sad loss,' said God, before his eyes turned to the undergrowth, perhaps already regretting his hasty dispatch of the eclairs.

'But what are we going to do about it?' asked Harold.

'Well, what d'ya have in mind?' asked God. 'Memorial service? Apology in the paper?'

'No, no ...'

'*Harold.*'

'Well what then, son?'

'Well shouldn't we put him back?'

'Back where?'

'Back into his mortal body.'

'He hasn't got one any more,' said God. 'It got mashed and burned, remember? It's in the stratosphere now.'

'But, but you're God, Terry, can't you just, make it happen?'

'I don't know where you get your ideas from, son,' said God, shaking his head.

'But he was innocent. We must try, we–'

'*Harold,*' said Gabriel, once again, this time placing a clawhand on his junior's shoulder, but God raised his hand.

'Son ... Harry ... it's tragic. We've all been ... deeply affected by the loss of American Bootstrap, the other day, whenever it was. I for one am quite cut up about it. I nearly didn't finish all me doughnuts this morning, but there's nothing we can do, we have to move on.'

'So you can't ...' said Harold.

God shook his head. 'I'm not a miracle worker, son.'

'Right. I think we'll be heading off, Tel,' said Gabriel, lifting Harold to his feet. They began backing out towards the exit.

'And the other Bootstrap,' said Harold, 'are you certain he's still a danger?'

'Harold,' barked Gabriel, 'that's–'

God held up his hand once again. 'Nothing's changed, son.'

'But–'

'Enough, Harold,' said Gabriel, his plumage bristling, 'that's enough.' Gabriel put his armwing around his charge and led him away.

Chapter Eight

It had only been four days but already the watcher had seen enough, his target trundling around the same triangle – nights in his apartment, mornings at a church, and afternoons where he was now, sitting at the still cordoned off impact crater where four days ago he had ceased to exist in three of the dimensions he'd been living in.

This chubby, bowling-shirted, chesterfield-loving man wasn't what the watcher had expected for this job. He'd thought maybe a major celebrity, a great writer, artist or porn star, perhaps. What the hell did they want with this guy? What the hell did they– He stopped. Forget the what, whats were dangerous. Just do the job. Yes, this one job, and it would all be over. But one step at a time, lots of work to do first. The chesterfield would be a bonus though, a rare creature comfort on the days and nights to come.

It was time. He replaced his helmet and buckled its rear anchor point, then the two at the front. He checked it was well seated on his shoulders before tightening the front straps a further notch.

He set off parallel with the road, keeping the cover of the undergrowth between him and the target, drifting on down fifty yards or so before crossing and making his way back up the other side, closing in until he was just four paces behind his target. Stealth was not the watcher's forte, but over the years he'd found it hardly mattered. It wasn't like you could tread on a twig, and it's amazing how much time the newly dead devote to staring straight ahead. The key was to get in behind and hold off until close. Too much distance and they bolt – too much time to think. Yes, get in close; be heard before you're seen; use their manners against them.

Okay, close enough. 'Could I make an observation, my friend?' The watcher spoke with a Canadian accent and his delivery was authoritative yet honeyed.

Foz jerked round, half craning his neck, half turning his couch. His whole body tensed as he saw the watcher standing over him, but he made no further move. It was not an uncommon reaction.

'So?' said the watcher.

'S-so?' said Foz.

'So could I make an observation?'

'I-I guess,' said Foz.

'Well, to me it looks like you could use a hand, my friend, am I right?'

'Who are you?' asked Foz.

'I'm here to help.'

'W-why've you got a bucket on your head?'

Chapter Nine

Things seemed to be going right for Christian. The new direction still felt good and although the prose wasn't pouring onto the pages, the drip had at least become a trickle. This all changed, however, when on Wednesday morning he received a phone call that burst his bubble the moment he realised who was on the other end of the line. Not only did he not type another word all day, but he didn't even enjoy the second episode of the *Cagney & Lacey* two-parter he'd got so into the day before.

'We have to live in the real world, darling,' said Beatrice, that evening. She told herself not to push too hard. There was now only one way this was going to go. 'You've taken a year, almost. So how far have you got?'

'It's hard to say,' he said. 'I'm not sure where the end will be, I keep finding new topics, you see.'

'Take a guess.'

'Well, I suppose an average novel is about a hundred thousand words, but–'

'And you've written …'

'Ten, no, eleven thousand. But those are finished, done, in the can.'

'So you've done about ten per cent then.'

'Yes …'

'So you only need another nine years to finish.'

'Yes ... no, wait, that can't be right. Look, I only started this one halfway through the year.'

'Another four or five then.'

'Actually, two-thirds through the year.'

'Okay, so that's what, still three more years then.'

'Well maybe it'll only be a short book, fifty thousand–'

'Okay, so another one and a half. One and a half more years.'

'Yes, all right. But if I upped the rate, I'm on the verge of a surge, I can feel it, I–'

'Darling, I'm behind you, always, but we can't do this. We're supposed to be a partnership. You've got to get back to pulling your weight.'

He slumped back into the sofa and exhaled.

'I suppose you're right,' he said.

'But it doesn't mean giving up,' said Beatrice. She knew it would mean giving up. 'You can still do the book in the evenings or at the weekend,' she said. 'I'm sure you'll have the energy.' She knew he wouldn't have the energy. She felt some guilt at her disingenuousness, but she told herself although the book's demise was now certain, only Christian could choose when to let it slip beneath the waves.

'Yes, I suppose so,' said Christian. He picked up a pen and started clicking its button. 'And there's always the holidays, I suppose.'

'Yes, of course. And look, I think it'll do you the world of good getting back to work. You'll regain your self-respect, you'll be able to hold your head up high again.'

'Excuse me, but I have self-respect.'

'Yes, I know, but we all derive our identity from our work, don't we, from having a role, from knowing we're making a difference.'

'How does Quality Assurance in a supermarket IT department make a difference?'

'Well, what was the last thing you worked on?'

'I reviewed an upgrade to the automatic replenishment system for non-perishable small goods.'

'The what?'

'The thing that makes sure the stores don't run out of biscuits.'

'Okay, so if you hadn't done your job, there could have been problems with it, yes?'

'So?'

'Well,' she said, 'it could mean a store runs out of digestives, couldn't it?'

'Yes.'

'So that would impact your customers.'

'Oh yes, be a real crisis. They'd have to buy custard creams instead.'

'But it would still be a problem, one you helped prevent.'

'Not quite solving global warming or curing cancer, is it?'

'All right, so you and I may be small cogs in the wheels of civilisation but we are still vital cogs.'

'Hardly vital.'

'Okay, well, important cogs then.'

'That's still overstating it.'

'Useful?'

'Still a bit much I think,' said Christian. 'Sometimes my efforts made no difference at all – most of the things I work on never even get deployed.'

'Well what would you say then?'

'Dunno. Occasionally useful, perhaps.'

'Okay then, we are occasionally useful small cogs in the wheels of civilisation. But we're still playing our part.'

He ruffled his hair and puffed out his cheeks. 'You're right,' he said. 'Of course you're right.'

She nodded.

'Look, thanks,' he said, 'thanks for, you know, putting up with all this.'

'That's okay, darling. I do support you, and you'll finish the book one day, I want you to, and I know you will.'

She knew he wouldn't.

They hugged.

The next morning, Nikki arrived with the coffees as usual. They discussed the chapter on Heaven's prohibited religions but she could tell Christian's heart wasn't in it, which was strange because he'd done six pages.

'What's up?' she asked.

'What do you mean?'

'Well, you've just put in easily your best spurt so far, yet you seem a bit down.'

'I'm sorry, Nik. It's just, well, I had some bad news yesterday.'

'Oh dear. Can you talk about it?'

'Well, not bad news as such, more of a wake-up call. It was someone from HR at the office, wanting to arrange my return-to-work interview. My time's almost up. I knew it would be, of course, eventually, but I'd kind of put it out of my mind, what with it all going so well.'

'But you're not going back?'

'Well of course I am. We have to face facts.'

'We?'

'Yes, we – me and Bea.'

'Ah, so she's forcing you back.'

'No one's forcing me back. It's my decision. I'm taking responsibility. It's called being an adult.'

'And giving up your dream in the process.'

'Not at all. I can keep going in the evenings, weekends, holidays. It'll just mean a bit of a dip in the work rate, that's all.'

There was a sudden weakness in Nikki's core and she felt herself list onto the arm of the sofa. A dip? What would that mean? Forty words a day? Twenty? Surely not ten? *Less than ten?* She did a quick mental calculation. It suggested Christian might be able to complete three or four more chapters before retirement. Then what? Would he still have his powers? Would he have the motivation to continue?

'No,' said Nikki, 'this won't do. You've come so far.'

'I know, but Bea's right, I have to live in the real world.'

'This is the real world. You're following your dream. All that other stuff, Aston Martins, a châteaux in Provence, yachting off the Côte d'Azur, that's not real, none of it is.'

'But mortgages, food, heating, lighting, nursery fees, they, Nikki, are very real.'

'Nursery fees?'

'Yes. We think it's time to try for a baby. Did I not mention it?'

'No.'

'Oh. Well, we're not getting any younger, so, we're going to give it a shot. And, you know, I think it might do me good to put someone else first for a change. It'll mean less time for the writing, when the baby arrives, what with me going down to number two, but still ...'

Nikki couldn't believe what she was hearing. It meant the end. If Christian and Beatrice had a child, it would drop the word rate to single sentences a year. Even allowing for a pickup once the kid was grown, it was a deal-breaker. Medical science wouldn't be able to keep Christian alive long enough to get halfway, let alone finish.

And then a piece of her own advice smacked her hard on the back of the skull. This wasn't a problem, this was an opportunity. A big one.

'All right,' said Nikki, 'I'm going to fund the book.'

'What?'

'You heard me. I will fund the book. I'll pay you a salary until it's finished. I'll pay you whatever your old job pays, plus say twenty per cent for loss of benefits and career security, and a further twenty on top. What do you say?'

'I say you've lost your mind.'

'I'm serious.'

He paused. 'It's a touching gesture, Nik, but really, how could you afford it, you're not even working yourself at the moment, and besides, how would I ever pay you back?'

'Christian, believe me, I can afford it. Even if it takes four years and eight months, I can afford it. And you can pay me back out of the royalties.'

'But what if ...' He looked down. '... what if I don't finish?'

'You will.'

'Well what if it doesn't sell? We have to face the cold hard reality that there's a slim chance it might not.'

'Christian, I have total faith in you and the book. You've drawn me in. I'm part of this now. We're gonna give literature both barrels, remember? You're cocked and loaded, you're ready to pull the trigger ... you're on the brink, Christian, but now literature's about to sneak out the back door.'

'Not quite sure I'm on the brink.'

'Well maybe the brink of the brink? Look, I know you will finish. I know it will sell. If I'm wrong, then I lose the money. Big deal. Life is for living. One day you'll be dead and it'll get a lot harder to follow your dreams then, believe me. So what do you say?'

'I don't know, Nik, I'm not sure.'

'What's not to be sure about? I take all the risk. For you it's a no-brainer.'

'You're not messing around here, are you? Because if you are, it's not funny.'

'Christian, I've never been more serious about anything in my entire life.' She looked him straight in the eye and held her gaze.

'Will of Ockham , you are serious.'

'Well then?'

'Well then, what can I say? … Okay!'

Nikki shrieked with delight. They jumped up and hugged.

'Sweet Sagan's Cosmos,' said Christian, 'it's gonna happen, I'm gonna finish the book. It's really going to happen.'

'Yes, Christian, and it will sell. It will sell millions.'

They hugged again.

'Okay,' said Nikki, 'let's use this energy, let's ride the wave and really crack on.'

The mutual congratulations went on for a few more minutes before Nikki left to let Christian continue the work.

Christian was so excited he could hardly produce a word all day. And he couldn't wait for Bea to get home so he could tell her the good news.

'She wants to pay you?'

'That's right. She's going to cover my salary until it's finished. I have a benefactor. How cool is that? No one has benefactors these days. I should change my name to Pip!'

'The nerve of that woman … How dare she?'

'What do you mean?'

'Interfering like this. She should mind her own business.'

'But I thought you'd be pleased.'

'Pleased? Why would I be pleased?'

'Because I can finish the book.'

'I don't believe I'm hearing this. I thought we'd agreed you were going back to work?'

'But that was before. Besides, you said you still supported me, you said you wanted me to finish. This is a way to do it.'

'But at what cost, Christian?'

'No cost. In fact, I'm getting a pay rise.' He swept his hand out towards the patio doors. 'You may proceed with the conservatory!'

'This is wrong, Christian. We don't know her, why's she doing this?'

'We do know her. I know her. Look, she's a businesswoman, she knows a sure thing when she sees it, she knows she'll make it all back and more when the book hits the bestseller lists, then there's the movie rights and merchandising. But more than that, she's doing this because it matters, it matters more than software that's quick to spot a run on chocolate fingers, and because she believes in the book, she believes in me.'

'So you're saying I don't?'

Christian gave a shrug and held up his hands. 'You tell me,' he said.

Friday morning began much as the previous evening had finished – in silence. As with all couples, Christian and Beatrice had eventually broken their sincere promise never to go to bed with unresolved differences. At seven years, it had taken them longer than most, but they had finally made it. For Christian, it had led to a night of dreams spent at Erdygrot's marriage counselling services, the therapies mostly involving Christian looking on while Erdy lectured a gagged and chained Beatrice on which gender was supposed to be in charge.

It wasn't absolute silence now, of course. Apart from the usual morning backdrop of the radio and the shower upstairs, the breakfast TV news, kettle and inappropriately chipper pop of the toaster downstairs, there were twelve words of actual speech.

'Morning.'

'Morning.'

'Coffee.'

'Thanks.'

'Toast.'

'Thanks.'

'See you later.'

'See you later.'

Christian watched the rest of the breakfast news as usual but couldn't enjoy it. Even Bert and Ernie couldn't lift his mood at nine. He just found it frustrating. If Ernie wanted to borrow the tricycle that badly, why couldn't Burt just let him have it? It was all so unnecessary.

Nikki arrived at nine fifteen, as usual, but today bounced in with even more vigour than normal. Now she had control, sweet, sweet control.

'Just look at you,' she said. 'Cheer up.'

'Don't, Nik, I'm not in the mood.'

'What's up?'

'Bea.'

'Ah ...'

She handed him his coffee and they made their way through to the living room.

'How did you know?' he said. 'I thought she'd be pleased.'

'I knew because I'm a woman. You thought she'd be pleased because you're a man.'

'Explain it to me then.'

'Well, it's a condition shared by half the population and there's no cure. We could chop off your dangly bits but it wouldn't get to the root of the problem.'

'I said I wasn't in the mood, Nik.'

'Okay, look, it's just a female insecurity thing. She wants dependable, corporate, sense-and-stability Christian. Dynamic, literary, luminary Christian is a bit of a shock for her, that's all. Before, she could tell herself it might not happen, but now, with me behind you, she can see it will. You've got to give her time to adjust.'

'You really think so?'

'Of course. Just give her some space and don't worry.'

'Well, we'll see, I suppose.'

'So. The book. How did you go yesterday?'

'Not great unfortunately. I hardly wrote a word during the day because I was so excited to tell Bea, and then with her reacting so badly, it kind of sapped my motivation.'

'Right ...' said Nikki. 'Well, this couldn't have come at a better time.'

'What?'

'Some changes – we need to make some changes, all for the good of the book, you understand.'

'Okay ... What do you have in mind?'

'Well, first, this is not about the content – the content is wonderful – I don't want to interfere with your creativity at all. But I think we could make some adjustments to your working environment.'

'Such as?'

'Well, I was thinking, why don't you come over to my place during the day to write? There's lots of space, my home office is much more comfortable than your box room, and I've got the gym and the pool so you can get away from the keyboard and refresh your mind now and then.'

'Oh I'm not sure, Nik.'

'You'll be more productive. And some breathing space is always handy when there's tension in the air here.'

'Look, I kinda like my setup here. I'll be fine once Bea calms down.'

'Well, it's your choice, Christian, but I want you to try it once, just to see.'

'I'm not sure.'

'One try. That's all I ask. One day and I won't mention it again. I'll even come and collect you.' She gave him that look, that practised and perfected look. Four, three, two, one.

'Well, okay, I suppose we can give it a try – just once.'

'Great. I'll pick you up Monday then, shall we say eight thirty?'

She would have preferred six thirty or even earlier, but reasoned eight thirty was the earliest pickup time that would still ensure Beatrice had already left for work. Choose your battles.

'Can't we keep to the usual nine fifteen?'

Nikki frowned incredibly pleasantly. 'Eight thirty,' she said.

'Split the difference – eight fifty-ish?'

'Eight thirty.'

'But–'

'Eight thirty.'

Chapter Ten

Foz stared across at the picnic area, his casters low in the grass. Stopping in a park had sounded like a good idea – stopping anywhere had sounded like a good idea – but now it seemed only to bait him with what he'd lost: all this stuff, all this everyday reality he was now excluded from. Despite having preferred pillows, technology and concrete his entire adult life, Foz now felt a desperate yearning to embrace nature: the grass, the trees, the ducks, even. His mood wasn't helped by the wholesome scene he'd watched form and now break up in the picnic area over the last hours. He'd looked on as several well-wrapped families had arrived, picked the best tables, tied silver and pink balloons and a large happy birthday banner in place, and set out a spread of food and hot drinks. It was a warm scene of easy friendship to a backstory of early-spring sunshine, blue jays and pine resin. He tried to console himself with the thought that some of the party would be cold and bored stiff, dragged out by their wives or a vague sense of duty to celebrate some other damn kid's birthday, but it made no difference. Even if they didn't know it, they were alive: living in paradise, lucky bastards.

It had been three days since Foz had met his guide, the man with the bucket on his head who'd introduced himself as Mitch Langford, and in that time Foz had found himself persuaded of the need to undertake this great journey, the first leg of which they had now completed. It made sense, sort of – in the same way that the SmileMax-Professional home dental-hygiene studio had made sense the last time he'd gone shopping for a toothbrush. But then, he reminded himself, the problem of tartar build-up *is* ignored by most people.

He'd accepted he was no longer alive – *no longer alive* seemed a hell of a lot better than *dead* – a day or so after the accident. Once he realised he was no longer able to touch anything apart from himself and his couch, and once he noticed the freakish blue-green glow he and it seemed to emit after dark, he couldn't deny what had happened any longer. His acceptance triggered unexpected concerns: that last slice of deep-pan Hawaiian going to waste in the refrigerator; his inability to turn on the apartment lights or the TV. And then there was the question of his exercise station. It hadn't even arrived but already he was fairly sure he wouldn't be able to use it.

He'd resisted Mitch's line, at first, and tried to reason out a way to keep his old life viable. He didn't give a damn about the job, and it wasn't like he'd be needing the cash any more anyway; his buddies, okay, sure, he'd miss them, but he'd survive, and his family, well, they barely acknowledged him when he was alive. So what did that leave? Not much, but it did leave TV – if he could just find a way to turn it on. He'd burned entire weekends with just TV, so why not go full-time? Hunker down at the apartment, nice and safe, easy as. That could work, even if he couldn't change channels. It could work. Of course Mitch had pointed out it wouldn't be his apartment for much longer, but then as Foz said, he'd shared before and maybe he'd like whoever moved in. Maybe it would be a chick, maybe she'd be hot. Maybe a couple of chicks, smokin' hot lezzers, at it all night long. It could happen. It could.

And yet here he was, exhausted, sitting on his couch in a park by a lake. He knew he wanted to get to Heaven, but he didn't remember anything about there being a mammoth trek to get there. If he had, he'd have bought the exercise station months ago. They must have covered ten miles, maybe more. Foz wasn't used to covering two hundred yards without the aid of motorised transport. And this would be the easy bit, according to Mitch. But then, from the sounds of what lay ahead, it probably was.

He looked again at his sleeping guide sitting next to him, sitting on him, slumped on his left seat cushion and armrest. This Mitch Langford made for a strange sight mid-afternoon in a family picnic spot, but then he would have made for a strange sight anywhere. He wore what even Foz could tell was an expensive tailored, though outdated, charcoal business suit, the jacket sitting over black cashmere. The low-cut black leather boots, reminiscent of original *Star Trek*, also looked like they wouldn't have come cheap. And looking at the guy's hands and fingernails, it didn't seem he'd come from a life outdoors. Not your average adventure tour guide, so it seemed. But all this was overshadowed by the man's headgear – in fact, *overshadowed* wasn't a big enough word but Foz couldn't think of a bigger one – it was clearly not made for this purpose, perhaps having started out as a wooden bucket, or small barrel, and presumably repainted to its present yellow ochre finish. There were no openings, save for two roughly cut eyeholes – both covered on the inside with what appeared to be a thin layer of silk. A large leather collar, which covered the man's entire upper chest and shoulders, was stitched into the bucket's lower rim, and the whole device was secured in place with thick buckled straps down to a sort of rock climber's leather bondage harness around the man's waist, groin and thighs. It was all so primitive, like a civil war superhero's first attempt at an outfit, or at least the top part of it. And matched with the fancy suit, it was plain ridiculous. Who fights crime in their Sunday best?

Foz had bombarded Mitch with questions for the last four days. Why was he stuck to his couch? Why did they glow at night? Why had he lost weight? Where were his more recent tattoos? Where was Jesus? Did they have Coke in Heaven? What about beer, Sam Adams, in particular? Mitch had calmly sidestepped every one, maintaining either he didn't know or the less Foz knew, the better. The only time he'd even hinted at a loss of composure was when Foz raised the subject of the headgear. But then again, thought Foz, no one's going to wear something like that for no reason. Maybe on that score, Mitch was right – maybe he was best off not knowing.

Foz's attention returned again to the small backpack at Mitch's feet and in particular to the book poking out from under the backpack's top flap. It was a hardback, bound in embossed black leather. Lettering on the spine was just visible, in gold hand-scripted Gothic typeface: *Terry's Field Guide To the Afterlife*. Sure, Mitch had warned Foz it was not in his interests to understand what was going on, but he needed answers and from the title, this looked pretty damn likely to provide them.

He checked his companion was still sleeping and then slowly leaned forward, slowly stretching, trying to limit the creaks of his faux leather, until the backpack was within reach. He carefully released its buckles and removed the book. As he did, he glanced into the open pack. Inside he saw a heavy chain and what looked like primitive handcuffs. What the fuck were these for? Was it what this guy was into? Foz looked again at Mitch and mentally scanned back over their conversations, trying to work out if he still believed this guy was here to help. It was impossible to read this guy – how can you see the tells if you can't see the face? Foz couldn't even see the eyes.

He looked down at the book now in his hands. It bulged in the middle and, turning it round, he could see this was at least in part due to an extremely aggressive bookmark – a thick leather strap, looped around the book vertically but passing in between the pages, clamping the back half of the work to the back cover. The book also had a large metal clasp at the front. It was under tension from the bulge, but Foz was able to release it easily enough. He sat back and opened the book, now finding that the bulge was also due to a thick wad of additional pages and documents stuffed into a pouch in the inside cover. He ignored these and flicked forward to a random page. The style of lettering looked hand-scripted and ancient, and the paper was yellowed and rough. On the left were four paragraphs under a heading of 'Social Greetings' and on the right was a fancy black-and-white illustration of what appeared to be a man shaking hands, only the hand he was shaking had no one attached to it. *What the …?* He flipped to other pages at random, finding sections titled 'Risks and Annoyances', 'Prohibited Goods', 'Careless Talk' and, further on, 'Navigation and Travel', where he found numerous maps and star charts.

'I'd put that down if I were you,' said Mitch.

Foz slammed the book shut and began frantically trying to close the clasp. 'I wasn't, I–' He continued the fiddled panic until his companion calmly got up and swiped the book from his hands.

'Did you look in the second section?' said Mitch. He opened the book and held it up level with his eyeholes.

'Second section?' said Foz.

'The strap, did you remove the strap?'

'I was just curious, I only saw like one page.'

'Don't make me ask you again, did you remove the strap securing the second section?'

'No.'

Silence.

'Okay then,' said Mitch.

'Why?' said Foz.

'You don't need to know.' Mitch closed the book and the clasp. 'You're not ready,' he said, waving the book at Foz, 'this is dangerous.'

'I'm sorry, I just wanna know what's going on, man.'

'I've told you what's going on.'

'I need more, my questions, my–'

'Foz, I told you, knowledge could be harmful. So keep your mind clear and follow my lead. Understood?'

'Okay … okay I get it.'

'And why weren't you sleeping?'

'I couldn't. Major head-fuck, man. This journey.' He shook his head. 'I dunno.'

'We can't keep discussing this, Foz. You have to make the journey, you have no choice.'

Foz saw no point in arguing. Instead, he tried to remember what little he'd seen of the book and work out what, if anything, it meant.

'Right,' said Mitch, 'I wasn't gonna do this so soon, but I guess now's as good a time as any.' He bent down and reached into his pack.

Foz thought back to the contents: the chains, the handcuffs, and God knows what else. Fuck. Could he take this guy? Looked like he was in pretty good shape and he'd had no problem completing the route march that morning, so far as he could tell. But then that fancy suit, it's not like he'd know any street-fighting moves … but then neither did Foz. He would have a weight advantage though, especially when you added in the couch, and if he could get round the back, a pretty big field of vision advantage – even Rocky would struggle to fight from inside a bucket. That was the plan then – get round the back, use his weight, fight dirty, fight like Buck Minglestein.

He shifted his weight forward onto his feet and front casters, he bent his knees … steady … steady … gotta pick the moment …

'Now then,' said Mitch, withdrawing a quill and an inkwell from the pack. 'Won't take long, then it's done. And I hate writing at sea, always makes me nauseous.'

'Writing?' said Foz, easing back off his toes.

'Admin,' said Mitch, disdain clear in his voice.

'There's admin in the afterlife?'

'Depressing, ay?'

'You gonna tell me there's taxes too?'

'No, just admin. See, not all bad.' Mitch sat down in the grass, opposite Foz. 'Okay, I'm going to ask you some questions. Now, you gotta be straight with me on these, no bullshit, okay?'

'What questions? What's this got to do with me?'

'It's just your paperwork.'

'My paperwork?'

'Yep. Don't worry, all perfectly regular.'

'What the ...'

Mitch opened the book and withdrew the wad of folded crinkled pages from the pouch inside the front cover. He opened them up and took out the sheet at the back. He took the inkwell, gave it a shake, and opened the lid, before taking his quill, checking the nib and dipping it in, the whole operation being quite laboured because of the restrictions of his headgear.

'Paperwork ... damn paperwork,' said Mitch. 'You know, they could pre-fill most of this, but instead we get lumbered with it.'

'Who's they?'

'Doesn't matter.'

'Who's we?'

'Doesn't matter ... Right then, name?'

'You know my name.'

'I need your full name.'

'Christian Bootstrap.'

'Just that? No middle names?'

'Abel.'

'Good,' said Mitch and made a note. 'Date of birth?'

'November six, seventy-seven.'

'Okay, buddy,' said Mitch, filling that in and pausing before skipping the question on organ donation. 'Now, religious beliefs?'

'Christian.'

'Says here you're an atheist.'

'What do you mean "says here"?' Foz craned his neck. 'What "says here"?'

'Calm down, it's just a bit of pre-fill,' said Mitch, shielding the page from view.

'This is fucked up. How do they know shit about me? Tell me. Who the fuck are they anyway?'

'Sit back. Relax. I told you it doesn't matter.'

'But–'

'Look, there's always a *they*, isn't there. It's common sense. You think this all runs itself? Where there's paperwork, there's records, and where there's records, there's a *they*. Doesn't mean *they* are out to get ya. I mean, what did you do about the *they* in life?'

'I guess I tried not to worry about it.'

'Well there you go,' said Mitch, returning to the form. 'Now, it does say here you're an atheist.'

'I'm a Christian.'

'Buddy, like I said, you gotta be straight with me.'

'I *am* a Christian,' said Foz, slapping his cushions.

Mitch lowered his quill. 'Denomination?'

'Episcopal.'

'When was the last time you went to church?'

'Today, this morning.'

'I mean when you were alive.'

'Ah heck, look, it's not like I went every week.'

Mitch paused. 'Well, I always think this question's really about belief, not what tradition you're from. So maybe you were just going with the flow, yeah?' He picked up his quill and returned to the page.

'No, I believed, I believe, I fuckin' believe! Yea, though I walk through the valley of the shadow of death, I will fear no evil, for thou–'

'Okay, okay,' said Mitch. He crossed out 'Atheist' and make a side note, 'Christian, Episcopal' – and then he stopped, quill hovering above the page. This was his first. How could he not have noticed? Not one believer in twenty years, not a single one. But then, maybe they're the ones who don't need the assistance, maybe they just– He stopped the thought. He'd cut it off at the knees but it had already been allowed to go further than it should.

'Right, so you believe in God,' he said, 'what about new-age shit, astrology, auras, psychic baking, crystal healing.'

'No.'

'Past life experiences?'

'No.'

'Ghosts, sasquatch, the Loch Ness monster, fairies.'

'No. Oh wait, I believe in ghosts.'

'Ghosts,' muttered Mitch, as he made a note.

'Well, isn't that a given?' asked Foz.

'Oh you'd be surprised, buddy,' said Mitch. 'Okay, now have you ever practised magic?'

'What, like witchcraft?'

'No, like card tricks. Rabbits out of hats, sawing people in half, which cup is the pea under.'

'No. Well, my grandpop taught me how to make a coin appear from someone's ear.'

'Okay,' said Mitch, and he made another side note.

'Is that good?'

'I don't know.'

'Well is it bad?'

'Who knows, buddy, who knows.' Mitch scanned back over the page.

'That it?' asked Foz.

'Nearly,' said Mitch. 'I know, I know, pain in the ass, eh, pain in the ass, but what can you do? Can't fight city hall, ay.'

More questions followed, but none offered Foz any sense of comfort or understanding. Some were obscure, others more obvious. Some were very obvious but no less troubling.

'Now,' said Mitch, 'killing, manslaughter, murder?'

'What?'

'Ever committed acts of murder or manslaughter? Ever killed anyone?'

'Who do you think I am?'

'Relax will ya,' said Mitch, 'I know you haven't, of course you haven't, but you know, it's a stock question, I have to ask, you know how it is.'

'Look, I've not killed anyone.'

'Cool, cool … Now, competitive darts?'

'What?'

'Competitive darts. Have you ever played?'

'You're kidding?'

'No.'

'No?'

'No.'

'Oh. Well maybe then, I dunno, what do you mean by competitive?'

'Like in an organised league or a comp or something.'

'Well, no then.'

Mitch looked up at Foz. 'You sure? Says you were first reserve for the … "Happy Hurlers" in the Bracknell & Binfield Men's Darts League, division two, 2008.'

'What? No. Look, I've never heard of the Happy fuckin' Hurlers, I've never heard of Bracknell & Bin-whatever. They up state?'

'No idea,' said Mitch, 'no big deal, I'll cross that out. In any case, it only says you were first reserve, doesn't say you actually played.'

'But why darts? Is playing darts good?'

'I dunno.'

'Well is it bad?'

'No idea.'

'But it's there right alongside theft, killing, murder ...'

'Yes ...'

'Well they're bad.'

'Are they?'

'You don't think so?'

'Well, I don't go in for them myself, but that's just my personal opinion. Who am I to judge?'

'But somebody judges?'

'Well, maybe, but who can say for sure? It's a crazy old world. Best not to think about it. Now, we're nearly there ... let's see, ah yeah, ever worked in sales?'

'What? No, like I say, I'm a chef, always have been.'

'Good, good,' said Mitch, with another flick of the quill, 'and finally ... have you ever preached as a minister of religion?'

'What? No ...'

'Ever attempted to convert people or persons to a religion, reinforce religious beliefs or practices?'

'I don't believe so. No. Is that a problem?'

'No idea, buddy ...'

'I knew you were gonna say that.'

'... and I think we're ... yep, we're done.'

'Look, I've been a good Christian,' said Foz.

'Have you?'

'Yes.'

'That's nice.'

'Aren't you going to write that down?'

'Wasn't planning to.'

'Well can you, please?'

'Er, yeah, I guess,' said Mitch. 'Been ... a ... good ... Christian ...' he muttered, as he made a note.

'Look, can we–'

'Oh I nearly forgot, can I see your soul card?'

'What? This is fuckin' insane, what are you talking about?'

'Like I say, Foz, you have to trust me. Now, please, I need to see your soul card.'

'What's a fuckin' soul card?'

'Your ID. Also doubles as a sort of ethereal birth certificate, for what it's worth. You'll have been given one at the doorway of light, we can at least be sure of that.'

'I don't remember a doorway. I think maybe I remember a kind of tunnel, maybe, I–'

'Yeah, yeah, tunnel, doorway, it's all the same. That's when you got your card.'

'I don't have one.'

'Check your pockets, buddy.'

'There are no pockets in these pants.'

'Try down your cushions,' said Mitch.

Foz stretched left and ran his hand down the back and side of his seat, but found nothing. He turned right to check the other side, this time finding a small white rectangular card and a folded leaflet. 'These are not mine,' he said, pulling them free.

'There you go, that's it,' said Mitch, stretching forward and grabbing the card.

'And this?' asked Foz, holding up the leaflet.

'Ah we don't need that. Read it later if you like.' Mitch studied the card, made a note on the form and then put the form to one side. He got to his feet, took the leaflet from Foz's hands and tucked it and the soul card back behind the couch cushion.

'Look, the questions, that card, what's this all for?'

'You're being fast-tracked, my friend,' said Mitch, 'which means you're very lucky. These are your papers, sort of like a pre-flight check.'

'Fast-tracked, fast-tracked for what?'

'For the Gate, of course.' Mitch placed the lid on the ink and began packing up.

'The gate?' said Foz.

'That's where we're going,' said Mitch. 'Did I not mention it?'

'No.'

'Oh. Well, I'll mention it now then, if you like?'

'Okay.'

'Right,' said Mitch. 'Our destination is the Gate.'

'And?'

'And now I've mentioned it.'

'But why are we going to a gate?'

'The Gate.'

'Okay, why are we going to the gate?'

'So you can go through it of course.'

'Why would I want to do that?'

'To get to the other side. You know, like the chicken.'

'Well, what does it lead to?'

'No idea.'

'I don't understand.'

'Sweet. That's the perfect frame of mind.'

'For what?'

'For what's on the other side.'

'And what is on the other side?'

Mitch shrugged. 'Look, don't sweat it, don't look for certainty, don't look for answers, that's my advice.'

'Why?'

'I don't know,' said Mitch, 'and bear in mind that this advice may not be reliable. Right then, shall we?'

'Shall we what?'

'Make a move.' Mitch slung the pack over his shoulder.

'But it'll be dark soon,' said Foz.

'Exactly,' said Mitch. 'Perfect conditions for navigation.'

'But they've been forecasting storms all week.'

'Look up, buddy, the sky's clear.'

'I dunno, man, I'm not ready. How about we stay here, or head back to my place tonight, think it over?'

'Foz, we agreed.'

'I know, I know, but England, who do I know in England? ... And the fuckin' ocean, man ...'

'Foz ...'

'Look, what about the couch, can't you at least get me outta the couch? I gotta get up, I gotta move.'

Foz thrashed at the seats, trying and failing to push himself free, before throwing himself at his right armrest, gripping it tight and trying to pull himself up.

'Doesn't get any easier, ay?' said Mitch.

'Come on, please, help me, man. Look, maybe if you pull too?'

'It won't work, buddy. Seen it all before. The only way for you to leave the couch is to complete this journey. Possibly.'

'With the fuckin' couch?'

'There's no other way.'

'Oh God, oh God …'

'Foz, this is no time to come apart at the seams.'

'I'm not doing it,' said Foz, 'you hear me? I'm not going in the fuckin' ocean.'

'We have no choice. We have to cross the ocean to get to England, to get to the Gate.'

Foz sat quivering, tension pulsing through his face. 'You think I'm some kinda dumbo?' he said. 'You don't think I don't know what's going on? I've seen the fuckin' handcuffs, man, the fuckin' chains. That why you wanted me to go to sleep?'

Mitch said nothing.

Foz raised his fists.

'All right then,' said Mitch, 'you want to do it this way – fine.' Mitch's stance stiffened. 'Mr Bootstrap, I am here to escort you to the sacred Gate of Judgement. There will be no discussion. There will be no debate, and you will do exactly as you are told. Do you understand?'

'Fuck you, man, fuck you.' Foz's little feet flicked at the grass as he trundled back, spun round, and headed for the road as quickly as he could, which was not quickly.

Mitch breezed past and blocked his path. 'It's your choice how we do this, my friend. But believe me, you do not want to take the hard path.'

'Oh yeah, well it's too late, what you gonna do, butt me with your bucket?'

'You have no concept of the forces you are dealing with.'

'Is that supposed to scare me? Fuuuuck youuuuuu,' said Foz, and he gave Mitch the finger.

A pause and a sigh. 'I was hoping we could be civil about this,' said Mitch. He undid the buckles at his helmet's front anchor points and then, reaching behind, the single one at the back.

'Hey, hey, what are you doing?' said Foz, his speech now faster. 'Wait, just wait.'

Placing hands either side, Mitch lifted the helmet, his body tensing as the headgear came free.

Foz froze in terror. He wanted to scream, but he made no sound. He wanted to flee, he wanted to really get the casters spinning, but his only action was to make a committed but futile attempt to soil himself.

'Now,' said Mitch, 'I trust we'll have no further insubordination?'

Chapter Eleven

Christian woke on Saturday morning to find Beatrice already gone. A note on the kitchen table informed him she had decided to spend the day with Lottie, and she would be back on Sunday morning.

He'd always welcomed the prospect of extra time to himself, and today was no different – not only would he be able to continue with 'Heaven' eighteen and the shortlisting process for his *Desert Island Discs* selection, but there was a *Red Dwarf* marathon starting at midday. However, on this occasion, there was disquiet because he'd still not cleared the air with Beatrice – Friday evening had been a little better than Friday morning, with a few more words exchanged before bed, but there was still six inches of ice on the pond. Now it would be another twenty-four hours. But then perhaps Nikki was right, perhaps Beatrice did just need some space.

Charlotte had suggested they go shopping. Beatrice had accepted readily enough, despite it often being a rollercoaster doing it with this particular friend.

Charlotte had short, lush and architecturally interesting platinum blonde hair. It was stiff and unnatural and yet no one really noticed, because everything about the person it was attached to was stiff and unnatural: the lemon-pursed lips, the neck in ever-skewed tension, the Botox on Botox. Which is not to say she wasn't attractive; indeed, Charlotte was supermodelly photogenic. But in animated form, she always appeared brittle, like she might snap or blow away if you left her out in a strong breeze.

They click-clacked into another shop. It was another place Beatrice would normally walk past, but for Charlotte it was regular territory, slumming it, even. This was the good part about shopping with Charlotte; somehow she legitimised Beatrice's presence, gave her the confidence to cruise into anywhere as if she owned the place.

'You've let him grow a beard?' said Charlotte.

'Well yes, several,' said Beatrice.

'He's got more than one?'

'Well not all at once, obviously. He shaves them off when they get itchy. I'm glad about that, wouldn't want him to get used to it.'

'There you go again, darling, accommodating him. Why did you let him start growing one in the first place?'

'It's his choice, he's a grown man.'

Lottie laughed. 'Get real, my love. Taller, balder boys, that's all they are.'

'Oh come on, surely Daniel's a grown man?'

'Don't you believe it. Head of Procurement by day, submissive little bitch by night.'

'Lottie!'

'It's true.'

'Really?'

'Absolutely. But then I wouldn't have it any other way.'

Beatrice was lost for words.

'Maybe you should try it on Christian,' said Charlotte, 'bring him to heel.'

'Somehow I can't see that,' said Beatrice, screwing up her nose.

'Suit yourself,' said Charlotte. 'But anyway, this confirms what I've been saying. And I take no pleasure in saying this.' She licked her lips. 'He's been selfish from the start.'

'Oh no, I don't think so.'

'Of course he has. It's just like your non-wedding, or when you've talked about him getting you pregnant.'

'Actually we've talked about kids again. I think he's coming round to the idea.'

'Just a smoke screen, like the engagement, just another way to fob you off for a bit longer. Once he gets you into your thirties, you won't leave him whatever he does.'

'That's not true, Lottie.'

'Which bit?'

'All of it.'

'It is true, darling. I know it's painful to hear, but I wouldn't be much of a friend if I didn't tell you about the massive iceberg you're about to hit, would I now?'

'I suppose not.'

Beatrice held up a classic little black dress.

'No,' said Charlotte. 'And I've got nothing against Christian. He's got lots of faults, too many to list, but it's not like he's a rapist or a paedophile, is it now? He's just not the one for you, that's all.'

'But I still think he is the one for me,' said Beatrice. 'Look, maybe I'm the one being unreasonable. Christian's never treated me badly, he's never even raised his voice, not once, and he's never stopped me doing anything. He's always supportive, and always comforting when I'm down. I do love him and I think, despite his ways, he does love me.'

'Who are you trying to convince, babe? And look, those things are all well and good, but they'll count for nothing when you're destitute, having to drive a car that's five years old and going on package deals to Goa. If he really loved you, he'd have kept doing his job, knuckled down and worked his arse off for promotion, whether he liked it or not. That's what you deserve.'

'I don't know, does it ever really work like that?'

'Of course it does. Daniel says he likes his work, but I know there's days where he'd rather chuck it all in, most days probably, but he sticks at it because he knows I'm worth it. And he knows if he ever tried anything on, like Christian's pulled on you, I'd be off like a shot.'

'That's easy to say, Lottie, but would you really do it, if you still loved him?'

'Love isn't unconditional, darling. If Daniel took a year off, burned a whole fucking year of earnings on writing some fucking book, it would mean he didn't respect me. How could I be with someone who doesn't respect me?'

'I don't think it means Christian doesn't respect me, it's just his passion.'

'Waxing the car on the weekend is a passion. Golf is a passion.'

'Well, all right, it's his dream then. Shouldn't we follow our dreams?'

'Of course not. This is real life. Putting your future in jeopardy to chase a fantasy, I can't think of anything more selfish.'

Beatrice looked down. 'Christian says the world would be a better place if more people tried to follow their dreams.'

'Well, Daniel says if everyone did what Christian is doing, nothing would get done. The wheels would shoot off the economy, the cost of living would go through the roof. The Porsche, the pool, the boat, the villa – none of it would be possible. It would be like Poland, fucking Poland, darling.'

Beatrice said nothing and tried to refocus on the fashions. She sized up a pencil dress she couldn't afford or get away with. She was still in two minds whether to share the real news.

A member of staff came over but said nothing. Lottie looked her up and down. Mid-fifties, grey hair, dowdy. This wouldn't go well.

'We're not going to buy anything with you standing over us, dearie,' said Lottie.

The woman seemed thrown, but stood her ground.

'Go and do your mark-downs,' said Lottie, pointing to the sales desk. She held the glare and soon the woman was off adjusting racks on the other side of the shop.

'There's something else, Lottie,' said Beatrice, 'it's not just the writing any more, it's his new friend, that woman.'

'You already know what I think of that,' said Lottie. 'That's fucked up, that's what that is.'

'Well, now she's paying him to keep writing, instead of him going back to work.'

'She's paying him?'

'Yes, she thinks it's a guaranteed winner. And she's wealthy, so I suppose she can afford it.'

'Might be wealthy but she seems pretty dumb if you ask me.'

'Well … yes,' said Beatrice.

'And you put up with this?'

'What can I do? It's a free country. He has to make his own decisions.'

'But it's not a free country. He has commitments to you. Even if he's not been man enough to put a ring on your finger, you are his wife, he owes you.'

'Maybe, yes, maybe you're right. But what can I do?'

'Only one thing you can do girl – draw a line in the sand.'

'An ultimatum?'

'Ultimatum? No, of course not an ultimatum, this isn't the cubic missile crisis. No, you're just making your needs clear and letting him make his choice.'

'I don't think I can do it. It's not me.'

'Well, it's your life, darling, but I can't believe what you're letting him get away with at the moment. You need to make a stand.'

Charlotte held up a Prada cocktail dress.

'Gorgeous,' said Beatrice.

'It is, isn't it.' She did a quick check for staff and cameras, before slipping it into her bag.

'Lottie,' whispered Beatrice.

'What, darling?'

Chapter Twelve

3,159 miles to the west of Bracknell, sunrise was still an hour away. The sea was calm, the moon full, but there were storm clouds ahead and a thick bank of fog on the horizon. Two blue-green figures were making their way east across the tips of the waves. Out front was a slim figure of average height and purposeful gait, dressed in a superbly tailored once-fashionable business suit and wearing a bucket on his head. Behind, a rounder, shorter, more couched figure was struggling to keep up, now mentally as well as physically.

'Please, please, man, I can't go any further,' said Foz, 'I need to stop, I need to sleep.'

Mitch didn't break stride. 'I told you to sleep when we stopped in the park.'

'I'm sorry, man, Mitch, dude, but can't we sleep now? If we can even sleep here. We should stop. Look at those fuckin' clouds, man.'

'While we have the stars, we press on.'

'Can we at least rest up a while? I'm just, I'm outta shape, man ... I need to sit down.'

'You are sitting down.'

'You see, I got me a fitness station, you know, one of the Buck Minglestein ones, but I didn't get a shot at using it. If you'd come in a few weeks' time ...'

'Look, buddy,' said Mitch, 'you only think you're unfit. You're dead.

Fitness is only in your mind now.'

'Easy for you to say, dude, you ain't luggin' the couch.'

'But it's not a couch.'

'Sure feels like a couch.'

'Well we all have our crosses to bear, ay.'

'Look, I sure don't wanna piss you off, dude,' said Foz, 'but please, man, I'm on the edge here, I'm begging ya, please.'

Mitch slowed and then stopped.

'Just five minutes, man,' said Foz.

Mitch looked out to the dark clouds and the fog on the horizon. He turned to Foz. 'Five minutes,' he said.

Foz sank back into his seat cushion. 'I just ... I gotta get my head straight, y'know, I'm having like a total mind-fuck.'

'It will all make sense in time.' Mitch remained standing, checking the stars.

'How,' said Foz, his voice fracturing, 'how the fuck can we be walking on water? That ain't right.' He stared into the black waves, unwisely contemplating the depths below.

'How many times,' said Mitch, 'you're dead. You're a ghost. You think ghosts need boats?'

'But I don't wanna be dead. Can you help me, man? Please, please, I don't wanna be dead.'

'Well you are, buddy-boy, so get used to it.'

'So what does that make you? Come on, level with me, man, I can take it. If I'm dead, then what are you, who are you ... Are you Jesus?'

'Jesus? *Jesus*? Oh yeah, 'cos that totally stacks up, ay.'

'I thought, y'know, with the walking on the water thing ...'

'So are you Jesus too then? Front-room Jesus? Lay-Z-Boy Jesus?'

'Oh holy shit,' said Foz, his eyes flicking low, 'are you Death? Are you him, man, are you the reaper?'

'No.'

'Some sort of fucked-up angel then?'

'Stop, okay, just stop. I'm not Jesus, I'm not Death, I'm not an angel. I'm not Santa Claus or Sasquatch. I'm not the Tooth Fairy. Like you, I am a ghost, and for my sins I am your guide, got it?'

Foz lifted his eyes. 'You're not like me, you're nothing like me. What happened to you, man ... Your fuckin' head, man, your–'

'Right. Enough rest.'

'Hey, hey, no, you said five minutes.'

'You've had long enough.'

'Come on, you *said*.' Foz's voice was breaking. 'Well, fuck you, I'm not coming, you hear me? I'm not coming.'

'Do you want me to get the chains and drag you?'

Foz shook his head and his lips tensed. 'I don't fuckin' care, man, I'm spent.'

'No. No, why should I drag you,' said Mitch. He looked out on the open water they had already put behind them. 'Look, do you know the way back to shore?'

Foz looked round. They'd long since lost sight of land. 'No. No, I have no fuckin' idea,' he said, panic in his voice.

'Yeah, I figured.' Mitch resumed the journey.

'Stop,' shouted Foz, 'you gotta stop.'

His guide strode on.

'Oh fuck, oh fuck,' said Foz. He leaned forward and started scuttling after his guide. 'I'm coming, I'm coming,' he said, his casters spinning for all he was worth.

Half an hour later, Foz was still whining but Mitch had stopped responding. He'd had difficult cargo in the past, of course, and knew more talk mostly made things worse. At least they were moving, even if the speed was slow.

As they ploughed on, a star appeared, brighter than the others, dead ahead and low in the sky. Mitch broke his stride as he noticed it, before pressing on, but when it began tracking down towards the horizon, he stopped. He watched the star continue its descent, moving in and out of vision against the cloud cover until it disappeared from view into the fog bank.

Foz had now caught up. 'Pretty weird shooting star,' he said, with a snivel.

'It's not a shooting star,' said Mitch.

The light came back into view on the horizon, blue-green, diffuse and dimmed.

'What is it then?'

Mitch stayed silent as the light began moving towards them, returning to bright focus as it emerged from the fog. An outline began to appear, a figure – caped, perhaps.

'Are those ...' said Foz. 'Is that ...'

'Close your eyes,' said Mitch.

'... Holy Mary mother of Jesus.'

Mitch stepped across Foz's line of sight and turned to face him. 'Close them now or I'll close them for you.'

'Whatever you say, man,' said Foz, and he closed his eyes.

'Now put your fingers in your ears and sing – loudly.'

'But–'

'Do it. Do it now.'

Foz obliged and stuttered into a surprisingly tuneful rendition of Foo Fighters' 'Learn to Fly'.

'Long time no see,' said a well-spoken voice behind Mitch.

It sounded about six feet away. 'Fuck you,' said Mitch, clamping his left hand over his helmet's eyeholes before turning to face the voice.

'Gone all shy, have we?' said the voice, maintaining its distance.

'Don't fuck with me, Hotswap.'

'How about a hug then?'

Mitch felt eight small digits on his hips, causing him to flinch and bat away bony forearms.

'I said don't fuck with me.'

'Would I ever?'

'Put it on.'

'Come off it, Langers ...'

'Put. It. On.'

'All right, all right,' said the voice. 'Always by the book with you, isn't it?'

'You damn well know it is.'

'So fucking uncuntlewade,' said the voice, followed by complaints and mutterings that lasted a full minute.

'Are you done?' said Mitch.

'Hold your horses,' said the voice, 'right ... all clear.'

'Don't fuck with me. Is it on?'

'*Yes.*'

Mitch lowered his hand from his helmet's eyeholes.

Hotswap – the 'a' pronounced as an 'o' – was five foot nine with a waffle-wave blonde comb-over, though like the rest of him, and like Mitch and Foz, it was currently a uniform blue-green, as was the full-length cat-skin fur coat that now shrouded him down to his knees. The outfit's false arms were not entirely unconvincing, but Mitch had seen the trick too many times to be taken in, triggering unresolved angst. He tried not to think about it. That was always the best policy.

'You just don't care, do you?' said Mitch.

'Why should I care? I'm not ashamed,' said Hotswap.

'It's not about being ashamed, it's about being seen.'

'How many times, Langers, that doesn't matter.'

'Rimreach says it does, so does Wiffinpitch.'

'Well, whatever.'

Foz had now reached the chorus and was getting into his stride.

'He seems like fun,' said Hotswap.

'He isn't,' said Mitch.

'Such a shame it's the wrong one.'

'What do you mean wrong one?'

'I mean it's the wrong one.'

Mitch looked at Foz and then back to Hotswap.

'Not possible, no way,' said Mitch.

'Yes way. There's been a mistake.'

'No, no mistake. I got there straight away. Point of fact, Hots, I was there when the poor bastard was still alive … I saw him die, this is your man.'

'No, Langers, I know this is the one who had the little accident, but what I'm saying is, the accident should have been someone else's.'

'What?'

'Yes, it seems the forms went over to the–'

'Hots. I don't want to know.'

'Of course, Langers, very wise. Anyway, well, let's just say there was a fuck-up. Red faces all round, but well, what can you do? C'est la vie.'

'C'est la vie? That's all you've got to say?'

'Yes. That's it.'

'Look, I can't say I've warmed to the fella,' said Mitch, looking back at Foz, 'but Jesus, Hots.'

'What?' said the angel.

'I give up, I give up,' said Mitch. 'All right, so where's the real one?'

'Sorry, what did you say?'

Foz was now bellowing out the chorus again, giving it all he had.

'I said,' said Mitch, 'where's the … I said … oh hang on a second.' Mitch turned to Foz. 'You can stop now … Hey, I said you can stop.' Foz wasn't responding, so Mitch made his way over.

.   .   .

Foz felt hands pulling his fingers from his ears. He opened his eyes, stopped singing, and stared in confusion at Hotswap. 'Who ... what ...'

'Hello down there,' said Hotswap, beaming. 'Don't get up.'

Foz looked up to the sky and then back at Hotswap. 'Was that ... you?'

'It sure was, cowboy.'

'I saw wings, you had–'

'Foz,' said Mitch, 'don't ask questions, don't think about it, you didn't see anything.'

'That's right,' said Hotswap, with a smile, 'you must have imagined it.' His fur coat lifted a little behind his shoulders.

'A miracle, a miracle, an angel!'

Foz threw himself forward to his knees, his couch tipping up behind him. 'My saviour,' said Foz, 'you are an angel, aren't you?'

'In the flesh,' said Hotswap, his eyes ablaze.

'Help me, please,' said Foz, crawling forward and grabbing Hotswap's legs. 'I've been kidnapped. I'm here against my will.'

'Deary me,' said Hotswap. He bent down and pushed Foz back onto his casters. 'Such soft upholstery, I do love that distressed worn-in feel. You just can't get that upstairs.'

'Help me, please help me,' said Foz, 'please, pl ...' His voice trailed off as close up he noticed a pair of black iron rods emerging from the torso of the angel's coat and re-entering at the cuffs. Now he noticed the lack of movement in the angel's hands.

'Oh, looks like someone needs a hug,' said Hotswap. He sat down on the couch, close to Foz, and puppeteered the false arms in to embrace him.

'Oh for pity's sake,' said Mitch.

Foz froze. It was still an angel, he told himself. Through gritted teeth, Foz returned the hug, flinching as he reached behind to make contact with the angel's oversized shoulders, gnarled and knotted even through the cat fur.

'There, there, Uncle Hots'll make it better,' said Hotswap. He released the armrods and slid his clawhands down inside his coat, out and over Foz's sizeable love handles and down onto his buttocks as far as the bonds with the cushion would allow.

'Woah, woah there, mister angel, sir,' said Foz, in pain as Hotswap squeezed hard with both clawhands.

'I'm only saying hello,' said Hotswap, 'it's how angels do it. Now, how about a better hello?'

'No, no, get off,' said Foz, craning his neck backwards to avoid the angel's probing lips.

'Hots,' said Mitch, 'Hots, stop goofing around.'

'Who's goofing? I've been stuck out here since Tuesday waiting for you boys. Hots wants his tot of rum.'

'Please get off,' said Foz, as the angel's clawhand scampered its way to the back of his head, where it briefly cradled him before gripping his hair tight, painfully so, holding him in position as the angel eyed his lips. Foz winced.

'Well why did you make me drag him all the way out here?' said Mitch. 'Why didn't you just come to the death site?'

'Thought you'd already be on your way,' said Hotswap, still trying to plant a smacker. 'Even out here, I was beginning to think I'd missed you.'

'Look, put him down.'

'Put him down? But he's got me,' said Hotswap and he swung his legs up onto Foz's lap. 'Come on, cowboy, you know you want to.'

'No, no, let go of me you … fuckin' angel fag,' said Foz.

'Oh yes, I love that dirty talk,' said Hotswap, pulling Foz even closer, 'you know you're asking for a spanking.'

'Hots,' said Mitch, in frustration.

'Oh all right, suit yourselves,' said the angel and he dismounted.

Foz trundled the few yards back to Mitch, tipped himself up like a hermit crab and tried to gather himself.

'Anyway, it's Bracknell,' said Hotswap.

'What is?' said Mitch.

'You asked where the real cargo is and I'm telling you, it's in Bracknell.'

'Where's Bracknell?'

'England.'

'Doesn't ring a bell.'

'Come on, Langers, grey new town west of London, you'll have passed it plenty of times.'

'You don't mean, what's it called, Braisingstoat?'

'No. Bracknell.'

'And the real cargo, has it had an accident too then?'

'Not yet. Well, maybe. You see nothing had been decided when I left. The Pansies will–'

'Stop. I don't need to know any more.' Mitch tapped the sides of his helmet with his palms. 'All right,' he said.

'All right what?'

'All right, let's get going.'

'Oomlah's sweaty balls,' said Hotswap, and he puppeteered his false hands to his hips. 'I knew you'd be like this.'

'Like what?'

'Just let it go, Langers. They'll have already sent a local, probably several – lots of keen young talent working the South East these days.'

'No way, this one's mine.'

'Come off it, all the way over there, why bother?'

'Because this is a big one, Hots, this is a big fish. You can't tell me it won't be enough to get what I want.'

'None of that's my decision, Langers, you know that.'

'I was promised. You know I was, that was the deal.'

'Well I'm sure it still is, but it's not like we can slap a reserved sign on him, is it? I'm sure it's first come, first served.'

'I don't know why I do business with you people,' said Mitch.

'Oh, I think you do,' said Hotswap. For a moment nothing was said as the angel stared at the eye slots in Mitch's headgear. 'Look, bide your time, there'll be other jobs.'

'I'm sick of biding my time,' said Mitch, 'this is my chance, I'm not waiting for another.'

'Well, knock yourself out, no down off my armwings.'

'Enough,' said Mitch, pointing a finger. 'Enough of that, I'm not kidding.'

Foz tipped his couch back a fraction, popped his head out like a nervous turtle and crawled forward. 'I'm sorry about calling you a fag, mister angel,' he said, grabbing Hotswap's feet again. 'Please help me. Can you help me? I don't wanna be dead, I just don't wanna be dead.'

'Shut up,' said Mitch, slapping Foz on his frame and shooing him away. 'Right then,' continued Mitch, 'let's make tracks. You can give me the rundown on the way, unless you have other business?'

'No, my work here is done. Three days hovering over the ocean and all for what, a quick grope with someone who's half upholstered. Not much of a perk, is it? You try to tell people it's not glamorous getting overdimensions business travel but do they listen?'

'How many times, I don't want to know.'

'Yes, yes.'

They turned to the horizon to head off, but Mitch paused. 'Hang on,' he said and pointed to the whining couch-tortoise behind them, 'what about him?'

'What do you mean?' said Hotswap.

'Can't just leave him here.'

'Well he's not coming with us.'

'Hell no, I couldn't take any more of his moaning.'

'So what do you have in mind? We can't exactly put him back.'

'True, true,' said Mitch. He drummed his fingers on the sides of his helmet before turning and stepping back towards his former cargo.

'Oh come on, Langers, he'll work it out, he'll be fine.'

As Foz listened, he heard Mitch's voice get closer.

'I'll just be a second. Right, buddy ... Foz.'

Foz felt his frame being lifted and a moment later he was back on his casters.

'We're going that way,' said Mitch, pointing east, 'so probably best if you trundle back home.'

'Please help me, man, I'm sorry about before, please.'

'I'm afraid there's nothing we can do. All a big mistake, it seems.'

'A mistake? So what, so I'm not dead?' For the first time there was hope in Foz's eyes.

'No, you are dead,' said Mitch, 'though seems you weren't supposed to be. Er, bad luck. Anyway, best thing for you is to head home and forget you ever met me. Probably best to forget about Hotswap too.' Mitch gripped Foz by his couch-back and spun him round to face west. 'There ... you ... go. Now, just keep straight ahead, you'll be there in no time.'

'But the fog, the storm?'

'Well you're in luck there – you're dead, so they won't trouble you in the slightest. You see? There's always a silver lining.'

'But I won't be able to see the stars?'

'Well do you know how to read them?'

'No,' said Foz, looking even more worried.

'Well no loss then. Now, keep heading that way and sooner or later you'll see the Nauset Light or the Chatham Light. You remember the light-houses from the way out?'

'No ...'

'Good, good.'

'Langers, come on, let's go,' said Hotswap, already drifting eastward.

'Oh and read your leaflet,' said Mitch, 'it's all in the leaflet.'

Foz pulled the leaflet from down the side of his cushions.

'Well obviously not now,' said Mitch, 'put it away, save it for later.'

'But what if I have questions it can't answer?'

'Oh you will.'

'But who'll answer them?'

'Well no one, hopefully, remember what I said? Questions good, answers bad.'

'I don't understand.'

'There, you see, you do remember. Okay, buddy, now off you roll.' He gave Foz a hefty shove and turned to catch up with Hotswap.

'But I can't see land,' said Foz, craning back, 'and the fog? What if I get lost?'

'Look, if you miss the cape, just keep going until you sight land,' said Mitch over his shoulder. 'It's not like you've gotta be at work tomorrow.'

'But ...'

'Done?' said Hotswap.

'Done,' said Mitch.

'Right, finally.'

They set off east, immediately trebling Mitch and Foz's previous top speed.

'Wait,' said Foz, spinning back and trot-trundling after them, but they were already opening up a large gap. 'Wait. You gotta wait,' he shouted, struggling and failing to keep up. 'Wait, you fuckers.' But they were already moving in and out of sight behind the swell of the waves being whipped higher by the strengthening winds. Foz slowed, stopped and then watched as Mitch and the angel disappeared into the approaching storm.

Chapter Thirteen

Christian was braced for more frostiness on Sunday morning, but when Beatrice returned she was bright and chatty. It was good, it was great, but it didn't normally happen before they'd had a chance to go through the standard reconciliation process:

1. Tentative exchange of olive branches
2. Awkward reestablishment of diplomatic relations
3. Heartfelt discussion
4. Resolution
5. Perfunctory make-up sex
6. Full reinstatement of all privileges.

This time Beatrice seemed to have jumped straight to stage six. His emotional journey had been bypassed, as had his physical one.

He was no wiser by the time she left for church. But matters became clear when she returned.

'Tony can see us on Thursday morning,' she said, 'eight thirty.'

Christian paused in thought to apply the ridiculous adjustment that was required whenever Beatrice gave him the time of an appointment. The maths was easy. The tricky bit was keeping up with the required offset. Four hours at the moment, he reckoned. So eight thirty a.m. would be twelve thirty p.m. 'Alright,' he said, 'but couldn't we do it Saturday or Sunday?'

'No, we can't. I've booked a half day off work so I'm sure you can take an hour or two off from the magnum opus. But then again, perhaps you're not bothered?'

'What do you mean?'

'Well, maybe all that matters now is your writing. Maybe I – we – don't mean anything?'

'Don't be like that, of course we do.'

'Excellent. Friday at the vicarage then.'

'Well, well all right then.'

'Good.'

'Um, what's it about, exactly?'

'We're going to help Tony choose a new cassock.'

'Seriously? Surely he has people for that, specialists with–'

'For heaven's sake, Christian, we're going to fix a date for our wedding.'

'Oh. Well, um, don't I get a say in this?'

'Of course. You get to say if you'll turn up or not turn up.'

'What's that supposed to mean?'

'Look, I'm not asking you to give up the book, I'm not even asking you to give up your dear patron, all I'm asking is for you to make this commitment.'

'But–'

'No buts, no excuses. This is it. Take it or leave it.'

On Monday morning, Nikki's car drew up at eight thirty. Christian was still irked he'd be spending the day at her place – and not just because the earlier start meant missing out on the rest of the breakfast news and his fifteen minutes with Elmo and Grover.

A toot from the horn. She wasn't even going to come to the door.

He made his way out.

'Morning.'

'Morning.'

That was the limit of the conversation. But as Christian swum around in his thoughts, he became less bothered about missing *Sesame Street* and began to yield to the earthy nose of the Beamer's leather, the cosseted ride and the purr of the V12. Material goods didn't matter. Of course they didn't. Not a bit.

It took them less than thirty minutes to get to Virginia Water.

As the automatic security gates opened, Christian realised he hadn't given the slightest thought to Nikki's house. His embarrassment grew as they cruised up the winding drive and morphed into inadequacy when the main residence came into view. Why hadn't she said something? Dropped a hint? Even a hint at a hint? Humiliation as he recalled all those mornings he'd hosted her at the pebbledash mud hut, his pride in showcasing his surround-sound system and the muffin maker, all the while having not the slightest concept of what she cruised home to.

He shouldn't have been surprised. He knew she was successful, he knew she'd have a spacious house, but somehow he'd pictured something not so different from 22 Vestments – two extra bedrooms perhaps, detached of course, perhaps a double garage, garden big enough for a small pool, but never had he imaged what was now before him. It was a bona fide mansion. He felt the weight of the hard work and relentless drive it represented – the self-made woman – and realised, for good or ill, this force of nature had now been turned on him.

A tour of the residence followed. Behind the oversized front door lay a wide and inviting hallway, tastefully carpeted and adorned with inoffensive accessories – a large distressed timber frame mirror; matching side tables; Greek urns garnished with the most expensive twigs money can buy. He followed her into the cavernous main living room. He estimated that this space alone had a square footage comparable to Beatrice's entire house. It contained far more furniture than two people could get reasonable use out of, but then Christian supposed that with a space like this, you'd have to fill it with something.

Several large paintings dominated two of the walls. Christian dismissed the works as *anonymous modern*, grander versions of what you might find in the waiting room of a good dentist, though in fact they were valuable Jane Lafarge Hamill and Marlene Dumas originals.

The furniture was obviously expensive and top quality, yet had a corporate coldness about it, all brushed aluminium, glass and black leather.

'Kevin's at work I suppose?' said Christian, running his hand across the black marble expanse of the bar top.

'I don't know.'

'You don't know?'

'We've split up. I left him – well, metaphorically at least. He did the actual leaving – I have excellent lawyers.'

'Oh, oh I'm so sorry, Nik.'

'Don't be. Second happiest day of my life. I've wanted to do it for years.'

'I had no idea. So when was this?'

'I'm not sure, six weeks ago, maybe.'

'Six weeks? Will of Ockham, why didn't you mention it?'

'It wasn't important.'

'Really? But you were married for what, seven years?'

'Nine.'

'And that's not important?'

'I never loved him.'

'Jeez. How sad.'

'Not really. Just the way it goes. You gotta do what you gotta do, in this life, Christian.'

She caught his eye with a half smile he didn't understand.

'Yes ... yes, I suppose so,' he said.

The tour continued. They exited the main living room at the far end and made their way down a short corridor.

'And, here's the home gym,' said Nikki, opening some double doors. 'Home gym' was a sizeable understatement, contrasting with Christian's sizeable overstatement when using the same term to refer to his dusty dumbbells, foam mat and Buck Minglestein exercise station. This wasn't a home gym, it was a gym. Fourteen pieces of equipment, all looked top of the line and in perfect order. The only things missing were ten sweaty red-faced patrons and a sprinkling of bored and incredibly fit employees. Even Christian, with his lamentable track record of barely used memberships, couldn't fail to feel a primal urge to burn some calories.

Next came the swimming pool. By now Christian was revising his expectations upward, but was still undercooking things. What he expected to be a sculpted medium-sized hole in the back lawn was indoors, heated, four lanes wide and twenty-five metres in length. To the side there was a Jacuzzi and a sauna bigger than Bea's bathroom.

The remainder of the downstairs leg of the tour took in another smaller lounge, two bathrooms, a large drawing room, an even larger dining room, and a room Nikki referred to as the snug, despite it being large enough to comfortably accommodate a home cinema and two full recliner suites.

'Now, what would you like to order for lunch?' asked Nikki. 'Jean Claude can whip up just about anything.'

'You've got a cook?'

'A chef.'

'A French chef?'

'He's from Dundee.'

'Oh, right. I didn't think people had staff any more. Do you have a butler too?'

'No, just a chef. It makes economic sense, once you cost your own time. So what would you like?'

'I'm not sure.'

'Well, he does an awesome lightly seared fresh Tuna salad. Not too heavy and good for the brain.'

'Okay, yes, that sounds fine,' said Christian, still in a daze of opulence.

For more than one reason, Nikki omitted to show Christian the basement rumpus room, the door to which was now locked, so they proceeded upstairs. The astonishment kept coming. Christian counted six bedrooms, all doubles, all en suite, with even the smallest bigger than the 'master bedroom' in Beatrice's house. Much of the furniture in the last bedroom had been stacked against the wall to make way for a large office desk, Mac Pro, additional monitors and other office equipment.

'I've moved into here,' said Nikki. 'I'm giving you the home office. It's all yours.'

'Really? I don't want to be any trouble.'

'Your work is far more important than mine, Christian.'

He could tell she was serious. It made him nervous.

'So, the office,' she said, 'would you like to see?'

'Oh, well, yes, sure.'

They made their way back across the landing to the room at the end and entered.

Christian was unprepared for what he found inside. The room itself was huge – semicircular with full-length wall-to-wall glass looking out onto the rear gardens, a star field recessed spot-lit ceiling, with central lightbox, and all furnished to a standard far higher than most office-offices, certainly the blue and grey flat-pack ones Christian was used to. In the centre stood the main work area – designer modern furniture, wide and deep black glass desk, phone, lamp, PC. To the left stood a top-end, high-output, combination printer-scanner. To the right stood Christian's former chemistry teacher, Mr Hargreaves.

Christian was unable to prevent himself executing a ridiculous double take.

The old man smiled and gave a nod. Christian just stared blankly back at him.

Hargreaves stepped forward and offered a warm handshake.

'Christian, lad, wonderful to see you again.'

'Mr Hargreaves?' said Christian.

'I think you're safe to call me Stuart, now,' said Hargreaves.

Having been in his late forties when he taught Christian, he'd now taken on a whiff of Mr Chips – pullover, slacks and supermarket shoes – yet he appeared not to have added much girth to his waistline or lost the zeal from his eyes, though now they sat behind rimless specs. The voice, too, was unchanged: the practical and purposeful tones of Sheffield sending Christian back to afternoons at chemistry benches and occasional rugby practice. Also unchanged was the man's legendary facial hair. The colour was now a mottled grey but the bizarre style was just as it had been – a full beard, trimmed short, but with a clean-shaven rectangle around his mouth, exposing all of his top lip and about the width of a thumb either side and below his mouth. Christian remembered the debates between his classmates over the rationale for the style, the consensus being it was the result of a compromise domestic deal – the woman in his life conceding the beard; him conceding to smooth hairless lips for kissing and other activities.

'Stuart's here to help you,' said Nikki.

'What? I mean … why?' said Christian. He pointed at Hargreaves. 'How did you even … find?'

'Stuart's here now, here to help,' said Nikki, 'nothing else matters.'

Christian requested a moment in private with Nikki. They stepped out onto the landing and closed the door.

'I have no need for a chemistry teacher,' said Christian, in a hushed tone, 'there's very little chemistry in the afterlife.'

'Well I know that, but he's not here for his chemistry, he's here to make you more productive. I know he was your most effective teacher at school, the one who got the most out of you.'

'You don't think I'm productive?'

'Oh come on, Christian, you barely get out of first gear. We've been at this two months now and you've done what, the introduction, "Death" chapter three, "Death" five, and some bits and pieces?'

'"Walk the Earth" sixteen B is more than bits and pieces, and I've started ... seven, nine, oh, and twenty-one.'

'Christian, you don't have any focus, there's no discipline or structure to your work.'

He didn't reply.

'Now Stuart's only here to help. Here to gently place his foot on top of yours and increase the revs, get into second, third and beyond.'

'I know you mean well, Nik, but I can't see this helping.'

'It will. Trust me.'

No reply.

'You do trust me, Christian?'

'Of course I do, but I still don't–'

'Good. Just try it, then. Try it for me.'

Twenty seconds later, he returned to the office and the company of his former teacher.

'Ah, Christian, lad. All sorted?'

'I suppose so.'

'Good good,' said Hargreaves. His eyes flicked to the door. 'She's a bit tasty, eh? Are you, er?'

'No, *no*,' said Christian.

'Right, I just thought, you know ...'

'I have a partner, a girlfriend.'

'Right, right, excellent, good for you.'

'Yes, it is.'

'So you won't mind if I, er' – his eyes flicked back to the door – 'later on?'

'She's married, Stuart.'

'Yes, yes, exactly,' said Hargreaves, appearing lost in his thoughts. 'Anyway, to business. I'm so excited about the project, lad. The boys are back together. Just like old times, eh?' He thrust forward a fist of bonding.

'Er, yes,' said Christian, offering a somewhat limper fist to meet the old man's, hoping this wouldn't be a precursor to free-form motivational rapping.

They spent fifteen minutes catching up, followed by another fifteen on the project – Hargreaves voicing his keenness to understand Christian's vision 'from the foundations'. And, for this at least, Christian was a willing party. Talking about writing was so much easier than writing. But when Hargreaves delivered his final nod, brought his hands together in a single clap and said, 'excellent, let's get started,' Christian began hunting for excuses. And he didn't have any. All he managed was a request for a 'kick-start coffee', which yielded little more than a walk to the windows once Hargreaves pointed to a tray of cups and two freshly prepped flasks. And so they began.

'Right, well sit yourself down,' said Hargreaves, leading Christian to the breakout area, 'and we'll take it from the top.'

Christian sat but Hargreaves remained standing.

'Now,' he said, 'according to Woody Allen, eighty per cent of success is showing up. Wise words, but I like to think it's nearer to ninety-five.'

'This has a familiar ring to it,' said Christian, 'your old "Hard work gets results" speech?'

'Tried and trusted,' said Hargreaves, with a wink.

'Really?'

'Of course. Remember what I told you at the start of your GCSEs?'

Christian smiled. 'You said until now some of us will have got away with being smart, but for the GCSE, being smart wasn't enough, we had to work hard too. If we tried to wing it, to cut corners and cruise through, we would be found out.'

'Well remembered, lad, full marks.'

'Yes. Thing is, I didn't work at my GCSEs at all and I still aced them. Well, apart from Religious Studies, of course.'

'Well yes, all right, maybe you could get away with it at GCSE, but at A-level, that was a different matter. It was a B, wasn't it, for chemistry. Hard earned.'

'Not really.'

'Point proved then. If you'd have worked harder, you might have got an A.'

'Which would have made no difference. The B along with my two Cs was enough to get me into Bristol, my first choice, so I did exactly the right amount of work. Working harder would have been for nothing.'

'But you'd have got an A.'

'And still ended up at the same university. And it would've meant giving up all those weekend sleep-ins, a lot less time for having fun, I'd have never finished *Grand Theft Auto Three*.'

'But what about the actual learning? The knowledge?'

'Well, I'd have forgotten it all by now anyway, just like all of my A-level material.'

'You've retained nothing?'

'Well, bits and pieces, odd details. I remember you telling us beer has benzene in it. I remember copper sulphate solution is green.'

'Blue.'

'There you go, you see, all forgotten.'

Hargreaves sat down. 'Well all right,' he said, 'maybe you could get away with it at A-level, but I bet when it came to university, you had no choice then. You can't cruise your way through university.'

'I did.'

'Really?'

'That was easier than A-levels actually. There's far fewer controls, you see, and well, they just don't expect people to game the system. They're academics, they assume everyone is as deeply into the subject as they are.'

'Dear God. So how exactly did you "game the system"?'

'Well, before any exam I would get all the previous year's papers out of the library, spot patterns and make some educated guesses at what would come up.'

'Well, that's not so unusual,' said Hargreaves, 'and you'd still have to know your subjects.'

'I suppose ...' said Christian.

'There you go,' said Hargreaves and got back to his feet. 'Now–'

'... but the exams were just part of it,' said Christian. 'My real triumph was the telecoms project in the final year. We had to design and build a digital phone, from base components. Professor Valboss set up a communications network around the lab so we'd be able to plug in and talk to each other through the phones we'd made.'

'Sounds like a fascinating project.'

'Oh it was.'

'So how did you do?'

'Great. My project report scored a first, top in the year.'

'What's your point then?'

'That it was the report that did well, not the phone. You see, I spotted early on that you'd never have to demonstrate your phone working.'

'What?'

'Yes, it was crazy. The report was the only thing that got assessed. So, as soon as I cobbled together a design that looked plausible, I stopped work on the phone itself and put all my effort into writing up a knock 'em dead report. I never actually built the phone. Well, I built a phone substitute – a bit of electronics breadboard with a selection of chips, a keypad for dialling, a little digital display, a speaker for the ringtone, and a handset for talking, all garnished with a spaghetti of random wires, resisters and capacitors. Only took half an hour. It was beautiful.'

Hargreaves sat down and swallowed.

'So, whereas most students spent twenty-seven and a half of the twenty-eight weeks of the project struggling to build, test, debug and refine a working phone, and a few days and nights frantically failing to write it all up, I spent forty minutes on the design, thirty on the build, and twenty-seven weeks writing a perfectly crafted report.'

'I don't believe it,' said Hargreaves, holding his chest. 'Could you, er, get me a glass of water, please?'

Christian strode the ten yards to the water cooler and obliged as he continued the horror story. 'Well, I say twenty-seven weeks on the report, but it was more like twenty-four weeks off, and three weeks writing up, but it was still enough to trump even the most impressive of the working designs.'

'But that's ... that's ...'

'I know. It is a bit of a scandal, isn't it?' said Christian. 'And I'm not proud of what I did ... though I have to say I did do a real number on it, I really went to town. Obviously I made up a comprehensive assessment of the performance of the phone in action, but I also included customer satisfaction surveys from the other students I claimed I'd talked to over the lab network, their identities of course kept anonymous for reasons of eliciting full and frank disclosure.' He chuckled. 'You know, I got extra marks for that. It was crazy really, I even included some magazine ad mock-ups and sales tag-lines for if the phone went on sale. Like I say, I'm not proud ... and yet, I can't deny, it was a masterpiece.'

'But an insult to your professor. An insult to the subject,' said Hargreaves.

Christian handed over the water but did not sit. 'Well perhaps to that professor and that subject, but to the subjects of marketing, advertising, public relations, it was a triumph!'

'This is what's wrong with modern Britain,' said Hargreaves, and he took a large gulp of water. 'Brunel would never have stood for it.'

'Look, I don't like it any more than you but you have to get real.'

'Well–'

'The lesson here, Stuart,' said Christian, wagging his finger, 'is it doesn't matter how good anything is, it won't fly if it's badly presented.'

'No ... no–'

'And of course we mustn't forget the converse. That people will buy anything if it's dressed up the right way, with a nice pink ribbon.'

The old teacher reached into his pocket and withdrew some white tablets.

'Heart pills?' asked Christian.

'Gaviscon,' said Hargreaves, wheezing, and he popped one in his mouth. 'Well all right,' said the old man, 'maybe you can fake university, but real life? You can't fake that.'

'Well, funnily enough, you can,' said Christian, 'especially in something like IT. The managers don't understand what's going on, you see, so it's not hard. You still have to know your stuff, but I reckon most days would only need two or three hours of actual work, less on a good day. So that's sort of faking, I suppose?'

'Well. All right,' said Hargreaves, after gulping down the rest of the water, 'all right, so you can fake real life, so it seems, real corporate life anyway, but this is where the buck stops, lad. You're writing a book now, you can't tell me you can fake that.'

'Well no, no, I think you've got me there. That wouldn't make any sense, would it? Faking writing my own book?'

Christian sat.

'Exactly,' said Hargreaves, a little substance returning to his voice. He took a moment before rising back to his feet. 'Now, what we need is a proper work timetable, with specific periods for–'

'Got it.'

'Got what?'

'Faking writing the book.'

'What?'

'Yes. Yes, I don't want to fake it, as such, but the tools of my method can still be used. Cutting corners, thinking smart, gaming the system.'

'Explain.'

'Well I'm already doing it, now I think about it. Instead of wasting time with a creative writing course, I skimmed through a *how to write a novel* book. Instead of spending six months analysing the techniques of the masters, I searched online for novel writing titbits. And I bypassed the standard apprenticeship of writing thirty or forty short stories and just launched straight into a novel.'

'But–'

'And when I struggled with settings, plot and characters, instead of blowing months working through the difficulties, I took on Nik's ideas of turning it into an afterlife guidebook which made all those problems go away. You see, it still holds' – Christian brought his hands together above his head – 'the method still holds.'

Hargreaves sat down again, motioning for Christian to refill his water. Christian obliged again, a spring in his step.

Hargreaves took three large gulps the moment Christian handed him the water.

'So it looks like fake-and-cruise is still on track, wouldn't you say, Stu?'

'Enough,' said Hargreaves, wheezing again. 'I need a break.'

'No problem, I'll be in the snug.'

Chapter Fourteen

The next morning Christian's spirits were in a deep trough, which is where they'd been since Nikki had driven him home the previous evening. The rest of the previous day had gone well enough, having followed the pattern of the initial confrontation, with Christian keeping his old master off balance, shamefully doing anything to avoid writing. Hargreaves had manfully maintained his straight-bat defence and had even started to make headway mid-morning, getting Christian to run through what he'd written so far, but when Christian hit upon his Achilles heel, chemistry, the old man had succumbed. It had been years since he'd had an opportunity to teach his lifelong passion to a willing student. And this time Christian really was willing. At school he'd learned the facts but never saw the wonder. Now older, he found himself genuinely interested, which Hargreaves sensed like a pig on the trail of a truffle. They'd spent the rest of the morning on the periodic table, exploring atomic weight and atomic number and discussing the grey areas between metals and non-metals. After lunch they touched on acids and bases, before popping into town for a junior chemistry set. It wasn't until the end of the day that Hargreaves realised Christian hadn't produced any new writing, not one word.

But Christian's high hadn't lasted. As soon as he was in the car, Nikki made it clear that the arrangement would be continuing, and though he protested, he knew there was little he could do about it. He'd won the battle, but Hargreaves would be there again tomorrow and the day after and the day after that. The war was already lost.

And Christian's mood was to take a surprise dive lower still when Nikki dropped him off. He'd never minded living at 22 Vestments before, well, not after the first five years anyway, but the return to the old grey shack after a day at Nikki's mansion shocked him. He might not have felt so bad if the little house hadn't looked so pleased to see him, its punch-drunk Quasimodo smile welcoming him home like a senile Labrador. And it was an empty house, too, Beatrice only returning much later after having spent the evening at her father's.

He checked the clock. Eight fifteen. Soon he was going to have to do it all again.

Eight twenty. He finished his toast, brushed his teeth and clutched at some straws. Perhaps she'd realise it wasn't the right strategy after all? Perhaps she'd picked up on his discomfort? Perhaps she wouldn't show? But outside, right on time, there was the car.

Okay, he thought. Okay.

He used the journey to steel himself, to prepare for battle. One day at a time, he told himself.

On arrival at Tooting Towers, his heavy steps took him straight up the stairs to the office, where he found a depressingly animated Hargreaves putting some finishing touches to a marker pen diagram on a large portable whiteboard in the breakout area.

'Good morning,' said Hargreaves, 'how are we today?'

'Fine,' said Christian, 'did you get the Liebig condenser?'

'Yesterday was fun, lad, it really was, but today we're going to put rubber to the road. Take a seat.'

Christian sat.

'Now, what we've got here is the results of my author survey.'

'Okay ...'

'This will be our reference point – a means of assessment and some targets to push for.'

'Right ...'

The diagram featured a vertical scale with various points marked off and arrows to blank Post-it notes. On top of the scale, in large neat letters, were the words 'Hargreaves' Author Productivity Scale', with a small 'TM' at its top right-hand corner.

'What we have here is a way to objectively compare authors based on aggregated weighted scores for published work. Now, I've kept it simple, with points for novels, short story collections and standalone short stories. Only published works count and we exclude posthumous publications.'

'Stuart, have you actually trademarked this?'

'What? Oh yes. Posted the forms this morning. Early bird and all that.'

Hargreaves took Christian through the scale, removing the blank Post-it notes as he went – a reworking of his old trick to illuminate the periodic table – revealing some two dozen authors he'd weighed and measured. Starting at 'Bone idle', he called out several one-novel wonders like J. D. Salinger and Margaret Mitchell. At 'Surprisingly sluggish', he named and shamed a whole batch of authors including J. R. R. Tolkien and J. K. Rowling. Six at 'Fair' included Henry James, Terry Pratchett and Agatha Christie, but the numbers thinned out as the ascent got serious, with only Isaac Asimov making 'Productive' and Barbara Cartland making 'Star performer'. And at the summit, Hargreaves revealed the 'Untouchable' Corín Tellado, the Spanish romance author who, so Hargreaves claimed, squeezed out a novel every six days.

'Okay, now, back to Max Trenchard,' said Hargreaves, pointing at the board. 'As we've established, he scores a lowly two hundred points, but we must remember he's always had fingers in many pies, so only spends part of his time in the role of a writer. So, he could warrant some further analysis.'

'Really?' said Christian, with disdain.

'Yes. Turns out he's a man after my own heart, at least when it comes to his focus. You see he has immense discipline. He wakes at five in the morning and gets straight down to business, working in strict two-hour blocks, four blocks a day. He even has an hourglass on his desk to make sure he works every minute of every session. This allows him to generate prose at the rate of an industrial sausage machine. I think he should be our model.'

'Oh no, come on,' said Christian, 'can't we pick someone else? How about Douglas Adams?'

'Adams? No, no, no, he was always missing deadlines, famous for it. No, trust me, Trenchard's our man.'

Hargreaves reached back behind the bench seat and retrieved an hourglass the size of a fire extinguisher.

'What the …'

'So. Shall we?' said Hargreaves, with a wink.

'What, now?'

'No time like the present.' He gestured towards the black glass desk.

'But ...'

'No buts. Session one. Two hours. Let's see if you can't finish "Walk the Earth" sixteen B.'

Christian found himself rising, walking to the desk and sitting down. 'But I need my files, sixteen B, it's on my laptop.'

'Fair point,' said Hargreaves and ruffled his beard. 'Let's not waste time getting them now though, we'll do that during your break. For now you can start something new. So, let's see ... "Death" chapter one, you've not started that one, have you?'

'Well no, but ...'

'But what?'

'But how about, how about instead I sketch out what chapters I may need for Heaven and Hell, you know, get a feel for the road ahead.'

'No, no, no, far too vague. This is much better – a specific measurable goal.'

He spun Christian round to face the screen and touched the mouse to bring the computer out of power save.

Word was already waiting for him, open at a blank document.

'"Death" chapter one,' said Hargreaves. With the silent confidence of an executioner, he turned the hourglass over and placed it on the desk.

Christian stared at the blank screen, his old enemy, the evil eye of the cursor winking at him, mocking him. 'I, well ... okay, okay I'll give it a try,' said Christian. 'Um, I suppose I'll see you in two hours then.'

'Oh no,' said Hargreaves, shaking his head and pointing to the seating area, 'I'll be right here. Can't have you going through this all alone, can we now?'

The next two hours were torture for Christian. He tried all his old tricks but Hargreaves was a step ahead at every turn. The moment Christian began to rise from his chair, or paused too long between keystrokes, Hargreaves was over in a shot, fetching Christian water, coffee, whatever he needed. Christian's sole modest victory was spinning out a toilet break to seven minutes. He knew it was seven minutes because Hargreaves stood outside the bathroom and timed him, calling out each time the second hand hit vertical. Even when Christian claimed he felt sick and was about to throw up, Hargreaves produced a masterfully anticipated bucket and merely suggested Christian hurl between sentences. There was no escape; he just had to get on with it.

And even when Christian was typing, he felt the old man's omniscience: always watching from the seating area; occasionally standing and walking a few measured paces. He was like an expectant father. The only thing missing was him holding Christian's hand and telling him he loved him while being repeatedly told to fuck off.

With the session finally ticking down, Hargreaves announced, with unbridled relish, 'You have five minutes remaining. I repeat, you have five minutes remaining,' and then, when the last grains tumbled from the top bulb, he followed with the iconic 'Stop writing now.'

Christian left the room and went straight to the bathroom across the landing. He felt an overwhelming desire to take a shower. Under the Trenchard model, he would be entitled to a two-hour break, but because of the late start, Hargreaves trimmed it back to thirty minutes plus thirty for lunch. And then, under some protest, Christian was obliged to return to the desk. The second break period was also restricted to an hour, and he only ended up getting forty minutes of that to himself because the remainder was taken up by the Hargreaves 'Healthy body, healthy mind' lecture, which culminated with the old man presenting Christian with a personalised diet and exercise programme. And then it was back to the keyboard once more.

By the end of the day he had produced 3,452 words, obliterating his previous one-day record of 449. Yes, he had delivered, but he felt dirty and used.

In the car on the way home, he tried to protest but got little sympathy from Nikki. All she could see was that in one day Christian had written as many words as the previous six weeks combined. It was a revelation. She kept referring to Christian and Hargreaves as the dream team and going on about how everything was now in place.

He knew he'd get no solace from Beatrice either, not that she would get the chance to offer any. For one, they'd hardly exchanged a word in days, but more to the point he knew there was no way he could share this problem with her, his anguish at doing exactly what he'd asked heaven and earth be moved for in the first place.

Chapter Fifteen

In the power corridors of Limbo, Dexter had made an early start to his day. He had a lot to get through and yet when he arrived at his office, just after five a.m., Gordon had already been and gone. On the desk were more articles torn from transcriptions of *The Financial Times*, this time profiling British companies likely to seek an initial public offering. Over each was written 'the boy?' with various sentences underlined.

On top was a handwritten note:

SEE ARTICLES ENCLOSED. ONE OF
THESE IS THE BOY, I KNOW IT. FEEL
IT IN MY BONES. GET ON IT, THEN
SEE ME.

G.

P.S. YOU NEED TO RUN A TIGHTER
SHIP. I WAS HERE AT 5:47 AM.
FUCKING GHOST TOWN.

P.P.S. YOU WERE RIGHT ABOUT THE
PANTIES. PICKED OUT A PURPLE
COTTON PAIR LAST NIGHT.
SNUGLY SOFT YET SUPPORTIVE.
HOW WRONG IVE BEEN ALL THESE
YEARS.

Christian's alarm sounded.

It couldn't be morning already. Surely not.

He'd spent much of the night in the nightmare world of the previous day, the highlights reel on infinite loop, garnished with an exuberant Erdy-grot perched on the printer-scanner, pausing his laughter only to photocopy his arse.

Now faced with the prospect of a second day's fiction milking, he did the only thing he could. He took a deep breath, summoned up his courage, and called in sick.

At first Nikki seemed more understanding than he'd anticipated. Perhaps the cough and strain in his voice was convincing after all? But in concluding the brief conversation, she brought him back to earth: 'That's fine, Christian, we all get sick, we all need one day off now and again.'

One day. Of course she'd seen through him, and now he was on notice.

But at least he did now have today. He resolved to spend it coming up with a plan.

After four episodes of *Seinfeld* and one of *Come Dine with Me*, which he didn't even like, his battle plan was still a blank page. Whichever way he looked at it, he had little choice but to return to the mansion. She was paying his wages – if he pushed things too hard, he'd find himself without a patron, without an income.

He turned over to the news and let it run in the background as he made himself some lunch.

And we can now go back live to the incident in Virginia Water. Hugh Watson is on the scene. Hugh, can you give us an update?

Christian ferreted about in the cupboard for something to put in a sandwich. He pulled out a tin. *Tuna chunks in Virginia Water* flitted across his mind. Hardly freshly seared, but it'll do.

Well it's a scene of devastation and confusion here, Jenny, something, something airborne, has crashed into the residence behind me, the building has partly collapsed and as you can see there is smoke and debris all around.

Do we know what impacted with the property?

There have been unconfirmed reports of a small aircraft, perhaps a private jet, in difficulty nearby, and there is growing speculation that this may have been what crashed into the building.

And can you give us a feel for the mood, Hugh?

Well, the residents tell us this is normally such a quiet suburb, and as you can imagine, they've never seen anything quite like it. Everyone is shocked and the mood is pretty sombre as we wait for reports on any casualties.

Sombre mood. It was consoling when the mood of the news reflected his own.

Christian popped his head round the door to glance at the report, multitasking with a turn of the tin opener. All these mansions looked the same. This one looked like Nikki's place, at least the half of it he could still see did. Oh sure, she had a mansion, but it was the same as the one next door and the one next door to that. And imagine the heating bills.

He returned to the kitchen to forage for mayonnaise.

He finished making his sandwich and took it through to the living room. A large red banner headline was now plastered over the lower quarter of the screen: 'BREAKING NEWS: Pope's Plane Missing.'

Who would steal the pope's plane?

He turned over in time to catch the opening titles of *The Ten Commandments*. Okay, he'd watch the film and then really get down to some hard strategising.

Half an hour in, his phone rang. It was Nikki. Maybe she wasn't okay with his mental health day after all? His finger hovered over the red cancel button but he couldn't remember if that indicated to the caller that the call had not connected or that you'd pressed the red cancel button. It kept ringing. He kept leaving it. Give it another minute, he thought, she'll soon get tired. But still it rang, so he braced himself, muted the TV and accepted the call.

'Nik, hi, sorry, I was in the bath,' he said. 'They're good when you're not well.'

'Christian. Are you okay?'

'Still a bit groggy.' He coughed. 'Hopefully be fine for tomorrow, but then you never know with these viruses.'

'But nothing's happened? You're alright?'

'I am ill. I am, honestly.'

'Yes, yes, but not injured?'

'No. Why would I be?'

'No reason … Look, sorry, I'm a bit shaken up.'

'Why? What's happened?'

'You don't know?'

'Know what?'

'It's been all over the news, there was an incident at the house.'

'What sort of incident?'

'Stuart's dead.'

'Dead?'

'Yes. He was hit by the pope.'

'What? Why? Had he offended him or something?'

'No, I mean he was hit by the pope's plane. It hit my house, Christian, flattened half of it.'

'Will of Ockham, that was your house?' He switched back to the news and watched the pictures as they talked. 'I saw it on the news, but I didn't think ... Stuart, he's really dead?'

'Yes. Lucky you skived off or you'd be dead too.'

'This is just dreadful.'

'The whole back end of the house was taken out. Stuart was in the office, right at the point of impact. He was working on something for you, kept going on about a revolutionary five-session day or something, he was so excited. Jean Claude and I only survived because we were down in the sauna. Anyway, I just wanted to check you were okay?'

'Yes, fine. But why wouldn't I be?'

'Um, no reason. Look, stay inside today, keep your head down, and tomorrow I'll pick you up as normal, okay?'

'Okay ... sure ... but what about your house? Where will you stay?'

'It's just a house. Don't worry. Oh, and I've had an idea, an easier way to move things along with the book. I can now see that Stuart's methods were making you uncomfortable.'

'Jeez, poor Stuart. I feel terrible now. He was only trying to help.'

'Yes, it's a tragedy. But it can't be helped. He would want you to continue though, Christian, to finish. So let's do it for him, okay?'

'Well, yes ... I suppose so.'

Nikki was saying all the right things, but something seemed odd about the timing, something to do with all the right things being squeezed into fifteen seconds instead of spread over a fortnight.

'Anyway, my idea,' she said. 'There's an expert, a friend of mine who can help us.'

'Right. Really? What, um, in what way?'

'Look, I'll tell you about it tomorrow, on the drive in. He's had a cancellation.'

'Tomorrow?'

'Yes, in London. I'll pick you up at half past eight.'

'Okay, and we'll be back by lunchtime?'

'No, we'll be there all day.'

'That won't work then. Remember, I've got that thing with Bea at the church. But we could see your friend on Friday, or next week maybe. Or, well, the whole month after that is totally free at the moment.'

'Just reschedule.'

'I can't, Bea's insisting.'

'You'll have to, Christian. My friend is impossible to get hold of. Tomorrow's our only shot. You can see the damned vicar any time.'

'Well, yes, in theory, but Bea's a real livewire right now, she'll flip if I back out.'

'So do I mean that little to you? Is this the thanks I get after everything I've done?'

'No, no, of course not, why would you say that? What you've done for me is, well, amazing.'

'And all I'm asking for in return is that you attend this meeting, this one meeting.'

'But–'

'We have to be there, Christian, you and me, tomorrow.'

'Look, all right. I'll talk to Bea.'

'Good. Now, one more thing, on the book, did you ever think about that appendix idea?'

'Not really, no.'

'Well …' There was a pause. 'Well maybe give it some more thought, okay? Today?'

'Okay. Sure.'

'All right then, all right. Well, look after yourself, keep your head down and I'll see you tomorrow. Half past eight.'

Christian ended the call and sat back into the sofa. He tried not to think what he knew he was about to think – he was better than this, he was – but the thought had already entered his head: relief. Stuart was dead. His problem had been solved.

Then he felt guilty.

Then he felt wretched.

He returned his attention to the TV, to the rolling news coverage of the house, the fire crews still damping down the flames. He watched for a while before making himself another coffee and going upstairs to fetch the laptop. He knew guilt was the motivator but pressed on anyway: 'Death' chapter four, all to a background of continuing coverage of the incident … interspersed with *Brief Encounter* and the snooker.

He worked on through the afternoon, until Beatrice came home and he could relay the sad news.

'Stuart's dead,' said Christian.

'Stuart? My God. Are you sure?'

Christian nodded.

'What happened?'

'Freak accident.'

'Well what about Carl? Is he okay?'

'Who's Carl?'

'Stuart's partner.'

'Partner? What, as in business partner?'

'As in life partner.'

'Stuart was gay?'

'Of course.'

'Jeez, he kept that quiet. But then so did Liberace ...'

'Stuart's never hidden anything.'

'... though that does explain the beard.'

Christian mentally added a leather cap, rubber vest and a light lisp. It was all making sense.

'Stuart doesn't have a beard,' said Beatrice.

'Well he did yesterday.'

'Darling, do you think maybe there are two Stuarts?'

'Well, I suppose it's possible. Which one are you talking about?'

'Stuart Deacon.'

'Stuart Deacon?'

'My friend from work, he came to the barbecue with Carl.'

'I don't remember, but yes, that's definitely a different Stuart.'

Beatrice relaxed her stance. 'Oh, well I'm glad he's not dead. They've just booked a holiday. So anyway, which Stuart are you talking about?'

'Stuart Hargreaves.'

'Stuart Hargreaves?'

'My old chemistry teacher.'

'Oh. And your point is?'

'My point is he's dead. He was in Nikki's house.'

Beatrice looked blank.

'Nikki's house,' said Christian, 'it was the one that got hit by the pope.'

'You're not making any sense.'

'But it's been all over the news.'

'I've been at work, darling. You remember work?'

'The pope's plane crashed into Nikki's house. Stuart was there. He's dead.'

'What about Nikki?'

'She's fine. She was in the sauna with Jean Claude.'

'Who's Jean Claude?'

'A chef. He's from Dundee. Look, that doesn't matter.'

'So your old chemistry teacher was in Nikki's house and now he's dead?'

'Yes.'

'What was he doing at her house? Is she organising your school reunions as well now?'

'He was motivating me. Sorry, I thought I mentioned it?'

'No.'

'Oh.'

Christian went on to fill in the details and segue, eventually, into why he wouldn't be able to make the meeting with Tony.

'Why should I change,' said Beatrice, 'why can't you have her oh-so-important meeting on another day?'

'Nikki says it's our only chance. He's a busy man.'

'Who is?'

'The person we're going to meet.'

'And who's he?'

'I don't know.'

'Well what does he do?'

Christian shrugged.

'So you're telling me we have to change the meeting with Tony, the meeting where we're going to put our future into a concrete footing, the meeting where we're going to set a date for our wedding, Christian, and in doing so prove our commitment to each other ... because you have a conflicting appointment that's more important, even though you don't know who it's with, what they do, or why you need to see them?'

'Well, okay, I know it doesn't sound great, put like that, but have some heart. Nikki's had half her house destroyed, she's in a terrible state, my former chemistry teacher's dead. Look, I do still want to meet with Tony, I really do, and I am committed, all I'm saying is can we just do it another day?'

'No, we can't. That's the whole point.'

'But–'

'No. No buts. All you see is the sodding book, that sodding woman ...'

'Her name's Nikki.'

'... I'm tired of being an afterthought so it ends here. You either come to the meeting or ...'

'Or what?'

'Or that's it.'

'It?'

'Yes. It.'

'You're giving me an ultimatum?'

'No. I'm just making my needs clear and letting you make your choice. For God's sake, I'm asking you to come to one meeting, I'm not looking for the earth.'

'But–'

'I don't want to discuss it any further.'

'Look, all right, I'll call Nikki, I'm sure we can sort something out.'

Beatrice picked up Christian's phone from the kitchen counter and held it out to him.

'What, now?' he said.

She held eye contact and continued to hold out the phone

Christian shook his head but then held up his hands and took the phone.

Beatrice stood and watched, arms folded, as Christian placed the call.

'Nikki. It's Christian.'

'What's wrong? Are you okay?'

'Nothing's wrong, I'm fine. Look, I'm sorry but I can't make the meeting tomorrow. I know it's important, and this guy, this person, is mega busy, but–'

'No. I told you, we only get this one shot. You have to move the other meeting.'

'No, look, listen, Nikki, just listen, it's too hard. The meeting with Bea at the church, it's my whole future, my whole fucking future. I have to put that first.'

'Christian, can I remind you who's paying your wages.'

'Yes, I know, and I'm very grateful, and look I'm still totally committed to the project, and the meeting, whatever it's about. We'll do it as soon as you can get another appointment, just don't ask me to be there tomorrow.'

'Christian, you listen and you listen good, you will be at this meeting, and–'

He hung up.

He turned off the phone.

Beatrice put her arms around him and held him tight. 'Thank you,' she said, tears now streaming down her cheeks.

They held each other.

'We'll be all right now, won't we,' said Beatrice.

'Of course we will. Of course we will.'

It was evening in the Pirate Lounge. *Queen Anne's Revenge* was in port, moored to the jetty, as ever – for though the east and west shores of Port Royal and the settlement of Port Henderson on the opposite shore hinted at a gateway to adventure, they were mere paintings on the lounge walls, little more than 150 feet across the water.

Two figures sat talking on the poop deck. It was only minutes since Gabriel had been piped aboard, yet already the merriment had ceased. The platter of fish-fingers had been tossed overboard, the not-so-youthful-looking all-cabin-boy crew sent off on surprise shore leave, and God was now rolling a cigarette to go with the one already in his mouth.

'Stop, stop right there,' said God. He lifted his eye patch. 'Now, from the top. How, exactly, did we miss him *again*? How many of him are there?'

'Oh no, this time we targeted the right one, the English one,' said Gabriel, 'but regrettably he wasn't where he was supposed to be.'

'Right …'

'Took the day off sick, it seems.'

'Great …'

'By the time we found out, well, the pieces were already moving.'

God removed the hook from his hand and ruffled his hair.

'Look, it's not an exact science, Tel, never has been.'

'Well perhaps if they'd picked a simpler plan?'

'Well–'

'And I thought I asked for discretion? The Bible-basher TV satellite was bad enough but hitting him with the bloody pope, that's about as subtle as a nuclear strike.'

'Well, yes, the Pansies did perhaps get a little carried away, but they really wanted to make up for the mistake with the American Bootstrap, so when we went back and said could they have another go, well, they rather went to town.'

'Went to town?' said God, hopping to his foot and comedy peg-leg.

'They're gonna get us rumbled, Gabe. Evidence. If they've left any trace of interference and it links to us, well that's as bad as the book getting out. It's worse.'

'Now I know it looks bad, but they are professionals, we can trust them.'

God shook his head as he hobbled back and forth. 'This technology,' he said, 'it works both ways, you know. This is the age of science and reason, these things get investigated, you've seen the TV shows.'

'I know, I know.'

'Well I hope you bloody do, Gabe.' God retook his seat and grabbed a handful of weevily biscuits.

'Still, it's not a total disaster,' said Gabriel.

'How, exactly?' asked God.

'Well, we got the pope.'

'So what? They'll only appoint another one. There's no silver lining here.'

'No. No, I suppose you're right,' said Gabriel. 'Still, third time lucky.'

'Oh you really know how to inspire confidence.' God troughed the biscuits and started rolling a third cigarette. 'Right,' he continued, 'dare I ask, what's the plan now then? When are we finally gonna nail him?'

'Soon. We've had intel. He'll be in London tomorrow. The Pansies say it's ripe for a strike, a keyhole relocation they say, no loose ends, no nasty coincidences. Not this time.'

Christian was helping Beatrice unpack the takeaway she'd insisted on buying to celebrate and cement their new beginning.

Curry.

Stylish? No.

Romantic? No.

Traditional makeup glue? No.

Guaranteed to appeal to Christian? Absolutely.

The doorbell rang.

Christian went to answer but as he approached he could already see the frosted svelte outline through the glass. He opened the door and slipped outside.

'Not good timing, Nik. You need to leave.'

'You have to come with me tomorrow,' she said.

'I've already told you, I can't.'

'You must.'

'I can't. Don't you get it? Bea will leave me.'

'Oh get real, she's just saying that to pull you away from me, from our success.'

'That's not fair.'

'I disagree. But it makes no odds. We're out of time, Christian. We only have tomorrow.'

'What utter rubbish.'

'It's not rubbish.'

'It is rubbish and I'm not listening,' he said and began to turn his back.

'You don't understand,' said Nikki, stepping in and grabbing his arm, 'this is it, this is our one shot, our final shot.'

He stopped, surprised at the strength of her grip.

She held on.

'Explain then,' he said, 'because you're right, I don't understand.'

'I can't explain. You just have to believe me.'

'But I don't believe you.'

'You have to. You have no choice.'

'What's that supposed to mean?' He placed his hand on her wrist and, with some effort, forced her to release her grip.

'It means cards on the table,' she said, 'you either come with me tomorrow, or it's all off.'

'What?'

'You can kiss goodbye to my support and my funding. No more wages. And you can pay me back for the last month too.'

'But, Nikki, be reasonable.'

'No, Christian, I've had it up to here with being reasonable. Tolerating your laziness, your nonchalance, your delusion. Either you commit or it ends here. Because make no mistake, you walk away from me, you walk away from your book.'

'Well, well maybe I'll go back to doing it myself.'

'Oh right, and who's going to cover your costs then? Beatrice? I don't think so.'

'I can't believe you're doing this.'

'Well, believe, Christian, believe.'

The front door opened and Beatrice emerged armed with a chicken bhuna.

'Get off my property, you home wrecker.'

'I'm not a home wrecker,' said Nikki. 'I'm just trying to help Christian make something of himself. Unlike you, I don't want him to stay being someone he isn't.'

'I said, get off my property.'

'Oh yes, and what are you going to do if I don't?'

'I'm warning you. I'm not messing around.'

'What, so you're gonna assault me with a takeaway, oh I'm quaking.'

'I'll do it.'

'Oh really? I'd like to–'

Beatrice hurled the hot bhuna bomb. Her oven gloves made aiming awkward, but the wide spread, characteristic of sauce-based weapons, assured Nikki caught the brunt of a full portion, a stream of hot ghee scalding her left hand and neck, and a chicken chunk hitting her left eye dead centre.

'You fucking bitch,' screamed Nikki, 'that's red hot.'

'I warned you,' said Beatrice, 'now get off my property.'

'Get inside,' yelled Christian, and he bundled Beatrice back into the house. 'Stay inside before you do something stupid. I'm dealing with this.' He shut the door and turned back to Nikki, who was picking onion shrapnel from her hair. 'Are you okay?'

'I'm fine.'

Christian stepped in to wipe the sauce from her leather jacket.

She batted his hand away. 'I said I'm fine.'

Christian took a step back. 'Okay, okay. Look, you need to go. Bea may have gone to reload. There's still a lamb jalfrezi back there.'

'It's not too late,' said Nikki, 'I'll be here in the morning. Eight thirty sharp. If you still want to do this, if you still want to become a rich respected author instead of a fucking nobody, then come out to the car. If not, good luck with the rest of your life.' She turned and left.

Christian went back inside, locked the door, and returned to Beatrice.

'What did you do that for?' he asked.

'She had to be told,' said Beatrice. 'That woman is mental, it's like *Fatal Attraction*.'

'You can't go around throwing curry at people. You've only made it worse.'

'How could it get worse?'

'She's going to withdraw support.'

'So?'

'That's my funding.'

'And?'

'And that's the book.'

Beatrice said nothing.

Christian relaxed his hands and opened his palms. 'Look, couldn't we ...'

'Don't you dare,' said Beatrice, stepping back, tears erupting, 'don't you fucking dare.'

'What?'

'Try to get me to move the meeting.'

Christian said nothing.

'Whatever she said,' said Beatrice, 'it changes nothing. So it's up to you.'

More silence.

'I'm going to bed,' said Beatrice, eventually, 'you can sleep in the spare room.'

He didn't try to stop her.

Half an hour later, he took up a plate of what remained of the curry, but she refused to let him into the bedroom. So he sat the tray down on the landing and went back downstairs.

He spent the rest of the evening trying to work out what he would do the next day. There was no way out. Neither of the women in his life were ready to give an inch or listen to reason. He knew of only two ways to be in two places at once and he didn't have a time machine or a twin brother.

Time passed. He kept thinking but kept getting nowhere. Okay, so he wasn't trapped on Everest with fading light and no oxygen, or deep behind enemy lines and out of ammo, but for Christian, these were his darkest hours. He did not ask for miracles. He did not pray. That was never going to happen. But he did slip out of the house for a midnight walk to the petrol station where he invested in a pork pie and £175 worth of scratch cards.

He went to the spare room on his return, but couldn't sleep. He tried telling himself that whatever would happen tomorrow wouldn't get any easier if he was tired, but that just made it worse. At half past one he gave up, got up and went back downstairs, instinctively taking the duvet and pillows with him. For some time he just sat on the sofa and stared at the TV. He tried again to find a solution, but his mind just went around and around the same loop. It seemed one part of his world was destined to fall apart the next day and all he could do was choose which.

Far away, two companions were passing the southern tip of Newfoundland and with it the last sight of land for the next 2,000 miles. On they went, into the wind and out across the open ocean.

Chapter Sixteen

They knocked again, much louder this time. Still nothing.

'Gird your loins,' said Gabriel, 'we're going in.' He waited for Harold to act. 'Well, go on then.'

Harold gingerly took hold of the handles and opened the double doors.

If the air was any thicker it would have refracted light. It was as if the room had just finished hosting an oversubscribed kipper and cabbage festival.

'Here,' said Gabriel. He handed Harold a sunstone torch from the wall.

With the torch in one hand and his mouth and nose in the other, Harold peered in.

Gabriel took a measured step back, placed a foot on Harold's backside and shoved him in, sending him falling forward onto the floor of the bedroom.

Gabriel closed the doors on Harold and held the handles tight.

Harold spluttered and coughed from the other side, before trying the handles, banging on the doors and begging for mercy.

'You'll get used to it in a minute,' shouted Gabriel, 'don't fight it.'

The banging and rattling made its way down the back of the door and died away.

'Are you still conscious?' asked Gabriel, placing his ear to the door.

There was a long pause followed by a weak 'Yes.'

'Excellent. Now, can you see him? Is he decent?'

Another long pause. 'He's asleep,' said Harold, hoarsely.

'Wake him.'

'Will he mind?'

'Yes, I expect so.'

'Perhaps we should wait then?'

'Absolutely not. There's no time. Shake him, shake him hard, and ...'

'And what?'

'And, well, stand back.'

The silence that followed was broken by bellowing, light screaming, confused shouting and the tinkle of fragile things hitting stone walls. Then the *clack* of wall sliders as pea-green peridot light slunk under the door.

Gabriel pulled open the doors and stood back.

'Tel, Tel,' said Gabriel, through clenched nostrils, his voice sounding like a baritone duck as he peered into the gaudy green-lit boudoir.

'What the fuck is going on?' said God from a tangle of bedclothes.

'We need to talk.'

'It's the middle of the fuckin' night.'

'It's an emergency.'

A long pause.

'Wait there,' said God.

Gabriel retreated to one of the sofas at the back of the large antechamber.

God emerged, a few moments later, bleary-eyed and stark naked. It had been some centuries since Gabriel had seen his boss in this condition, and he'd forgotten how mightily hairy the Almighty was.

'Oh, can you please put something on?' said Gabriel, armwing shielding his eyes.

'I thought you said it was an emergency,' said God.

'Well it is, but even so.'

'Okay, okay,' muttered God and he shuffled back into the room.

Harold emerged on his hands and knees, moaning.

'Good work, Harold,' said Gabriel.

Harold crawled over to one of the easy chairs and dragged himself up onto it.

Finally, God returned, this time sporting a short silver Playboy-print silk dressing gown and black suede slippers.

Gabriel looked his boss up and down.

'What now?' said God.

'Doesn't matter, doesn't matter. Look, Tel, there's been another development with the monkey, a big development.'

'I thought you said it wouldn't be until tomorrow?'

'What wouldn't?'

'The relocation.'

'It won't be.'

'So he's still alive then?'

'I assume so.'

'You've woken me up to tell me you assume he's still alive?'

'We've woken you up to tell you something else, something far worse.'

'How can it be worse?'

'Well. I think you'd better take a look at this.'

Gabriel passed a transcript to God. It was open at the fourth page.

'And?' said God.

'Well don't you see,' said Gabriel, 'it's the master codes.'

God looked again. 'Yeah. You may be right.'

'I am right.'

'Well very nice, Gabe, now can I go back to bed?'

'No, Tel, it's the monkey. This is the latest transcript. He's started to write out the master codes.'

'What? But, bloody hell fire, when?'

'Tonight, an hour ago. Five pages worth and they all match.'

'How the hell …' God sat down and looked at the pages again. 'They're not in the second edition, they're not in any edition.'

'We know that,' said Gabriel.

'So …' said God. There was a short awkward silence. 'Why are you looking at me like that?'

'Who did you tell, Tel? Who's been watching? Where did you write it down?'

'Fuck off, this is nothing to do with me.'

'It must have been you. You must know how these got leaked.'

'Why? Why's it always me?'

Gabriel raised his browfeathers.

God's beard frizzed like bellowed embers. 'The bloody nerve. The bloody–'

You have to have a good reason to interrupt the Almighty. You have to be very confident indeed. You have to be certain.

'Turn back a few pages,' said Gabriel.

God held his stare for a moment but did as Gabriel asked. 'You trying to be funny?' said God, after glancing at the page.

Gabriel craned his neck to see.

By now Harold had picked himself up and was looking over God's shoulder at the page. It was filled with cartoon sketches of male genitalia, along with some scrawled writing at the bottom which Harold could just make out.

'There was a young lady called Eve, who was created rather naive ...'

'*Harold*,' said Gabriel, 'honestly' – the archangel peered over to check the page – 'not that one, the one before, Tel.'

God turned back a further page.

Gabriel peered over again, and this time sat back.

'This is your ...' He left just the right pause. '... *artwork*, isn't it, Tel?'

The page contained brief notes for a couple of early lounge designs but was mostly filled with cartoon portraits of Gabriel. Though flawed, they captured key elements of the archangel's facial features: the ever earnest expression; the slight tensile asymmetry in his mouth; and the way everything seemed to be under gravitational pull towards a point six inches in front of his nose. And if anyone was in any doubt, the large central cartoon sported a badge on the subject's chest saying 'Name: Gabriel. Title: Chief Tosser'. And though this was a transcribed copy, in fact a copy of a copy, to Gabriel, the hand was without doubt that of Terry, for this was not the first time he'd happened upon a page of his boss's doodles.

'Oh fuck,' said God, flicking forward a few pages.

'You don't have to apologise, Tel, but we need to know–'

'I wasn't about to, Gabe. It's oh fuck because I know where these are. I'm talkin' about the originals, lads.'

'What? Where ...?'

'Follow me.'

In the early hours of the morning, a trio hurried across the manimoon-lit central courtyard of the Deital Palace, the chill breeze lifting the shorter, hairier one's Playboy-print dressing gown. It was their fourth trek across the white marble flags that night, having spent most of the last hour at the mercy of God's memory. But then Gabriel couldn't remember where his boss's much-neglected office was either, and they only now strode out with confidence because God had finally agreed to consult the palace archives.

They soon arrived in lounge 679, the Brighton Pavilion Lounge, which had been built some two centuries ago inside the then out of favour Blenheim Palace Lounge, itself built inside the long-obsolete Witch Trial Activity Lounge.

They made their way down the wide central corridor and into the banqueting room. From the three sets of blueprints they'd brought from the records office, they established that their goal was, in theory, sitting behind a timber and plaster facade in an alcove at the back, a facade they now saw was decorated with what Gabriel identified as a unique and priceless example of early True Jerusalem printed wallpaper – a delicate chinoiserie design in crimson, gold and black. God ordered it ripped down. The regency-attired aides, still in shock at seeing their boss for the first time since 1875, were unsure quite how to, but with encouragement soon started inflicting impressive damage with their bare hands, buckled shoes and inventive use of a porcelain lampstand. Soon the facade was down, only to expose a further facade behind, this time an immense Baroque oak panel adorned with intricate layered lime wood carvings of trumpeting cherubim set within Garden of Eden fruits and foliage. This too was soon decorating the floor. To general relief, there was no third facade, the hacked out space revealing only a dark void in front of the heavy studded iron doors of their goal: God's office.

With a grinding metal-on-metal screech that could uncurdle Heaven's cream, they forced the doors open wide enough for access. God called for a sunstone torch and led the group into the stale darkness. Aides followed and opened all the sliders, illuminating the dingy hollow for the first time in five centuries, the thin light revealing towers of documents, numerous rolled-up blueprints, several globes and other bric-a-brac. God made straight for the large primitive safe behind his old chair.

A final delay was thrust upon them as God struggled and failed to remember what he'd done with the safe key, a problem that only resolved itself when Harold tried the handle anyway, at which point God remembered he'd not locked it in the first place, in order to cater for this very eventuality.

God reached inside and withdrew various chunky blue manuals, some reference cards, half a dozen wallets stuffed with documents and finally a small tower of black A4-ish numbered journals.

Gabriel told the aides to wait outside.

God started running his finger along the spines of the journals. 'It's in here,' he said, 'we need to find the last one.'

'What exactly are these, Tel?' asked Gabriel, taking one off the stack.

'What's it look like? These are my old notebooks. This, lads, is the book.'

'My oh my ... the original manuscripts,' said Gabriel. 'I've not seen these in, well, a very long time.'

'And the extras for the second edition,' said God, pointing out the yellow circles on some of the spines.

Harold picked up one of the blue manuals – it was glossy, spiral bound, and quite unlike any other written material you would encounter in Heaven. '*World Builder Pro, Mega-Annum Edition, Quick-Start Guide,*' he said.

'Never mind about that,' said God, snatching it. He returned it to the safe, along with the other manuals and the reference cards.

They set to work searching the stack of notebooks.

'May I ask what are we looking for then?' said Harold.

'The end,' said God, 'the last journal, back half'll be blank pages.'

They found it towards the bottom of the stack. God cleared some space on his old desk and laid out the journal. The majority of it was indeed blank. At the front they found the final pages of the final section of the final chapter of the book, followed by a single blank page, and then the page with the cartoons of Gabriel.

Harold picked up the transcript and flicked to the same page. He placed it next to the original. The works were identical.

'What are your cartoons doing in there with the book then?' asked Gabriel.

'Well, I'd barely used this last one,' said God, 'and you know me, can't stand waste, so I used the pages at the end for critical notes, details of state business, you know.'

Gabriel turned the page in the journal. Harold did the same in the transcript. Two pages of cocks. Each a match down to the last hair on the last ballsack.

God gazed at the page with a proud smile.

The next page contained some brief notes, perfectly matching the content of the transcript page. And then the start of the code sequence, block after block of tightly packed hexadecimal. In the journal they had been written in another, tidier, hand, on separate sheets, and glued in, scrapbook style. But once again, the transcript page matched exactly.

The transcription ended after the fifth page of codes. Gabriel flicked on in the journal. Six, seven, eight, nine, ten ... twenty-five pages in total. 'Is that, is that the full sequence?'

'It is,' said God, 'it is. Oh this is bad, this is very fuckin' bad. If our monkey keeps writing ...' God slumped down on his old chair, the shrivelled leather crumbling under him.

'Beg pardon, but what are these master codes?' asked Harold. 'Why are they dangerous?'

'It's, well, a sort of key to the genome for a living planet,' said Gabriel, 'coded parameters for making an entire world, this world.'

'Twenty-five pages? Doesn't seem like much.'

'Well no, but it's like the codes for the grottos, and for the judgement rules. Every element interacts with every other element. And in this case, the possible combinations exceed the number of atoms in Sweden, so I'm told. Even now, even with our best minds, we don't really understand it. But if someone was to crack it, well, it would lead them to ... certain truths.'

'Expose the boot-up thing,' said God. He put his hands to his cheeks and gripped his beard.

'The kick-start signature,' said Gabriel.

'Beg pardon, you're losing me,' said Harold.

'The kick-start,' said Gabriel, 'it's well ... bear with me a moment.' He went to the safe, withdrew the Quick-Start manual and flicked through to the introduction. '*Six quadrillion megatonnes of matter inflated in minutes. Hundreds of thousands of ecosystems, plants and animals from the smallest virus to the largest ocean behemoth. Systems of ecosystems, global interdependencies, all summoned into being and set into perfect balance in a matter of hours, including apparent deep long-term evolved histories and flawed designs, backed up by surface crust impregnated with matched fossil records, multiple sets of apparent corroborating dating evidence from tree rings to radioactivity, from meteor impacts to moon-planet history.*'

'Extraordinary,' said Harold. He picked up the journal as Gabriel put the manual back in the safe. 'And you're saying these codes tell you how to do this?'

'Well they're just the parameters, as far as we can tell,' said Gabriel, 'but yes, in principle, if they could be understood, it would set science down a dark path. And being science, the path would be followed, deeper and deeper down the rabbit hole, until they reach the truth – that all this, the world, the transit zones, the afterlife realms, and all living things, was created in a little under a week.'

'Extraordinary' said Harold, again, now holding the journal with greater reverence, 'extraordinary ... it's just ... well ... extraordinary.'

'Impressive, eh, lad?' said God, leaning back in his old chair, hands behind his head.

'But there's no real danger then?' said Harold. 'Even if Mr Bootstrap does write it all out, it won't make any sense.'

'Not to him, from what we can tell,' said Gabriel, 'but if it got into the hands of someone intelligent, you know, proper engineers, proper scientists, things could unravel.'

'But if we can't work it out, why can they?' asked Harold.

'Because it's not an intellectual challenge, as I understand it,' said Gabriel, 'it's a computational one. We have the finest dead scientists. They have the finest living scientists, but they also have computers.'

'And we don't?' asked Harold.

'We've literally got a big bank of abacuses,' said Gabriel.

'Hey, we're not so backward,' said God. 'What about Babbsy?'

'It's not the same, Tel.'

'Yes, it is, he's built a mechanical brain, Harry, him and his floozy.'

'My word, really?' said Harold.

'It's not a brain,' said Gabriel. 'Look, all right, so they've managed to get some processing going, they can run programs on it, but it is *not* a brain.'

'Well it still sounds most impressive,' said Harold.

'It is,' said God.

'It's not,' said Gabriel. '*Shallow Thought*, they call it. All cogs and levers, size of a house and keeps the neighbours up at night. I'm told it can almost match a ZX81, whatever that is.'

'He's improving it all the time, though,' said God.

'All right, but even so, we're still decades, tens of decades behind ... and anyway, our capability's not the problem, is it? The problem is mortal computing, and we know how advanced that is ...'

God screwed his nose up.

'... no, with modern computers and modern science, well, if it got into the wrong hands, in the mortal realm, they'd rip through it in no time.'

'My goodness, so this is rather hot stuff then,' said Harold, looking down at the journal.

'It's creationist kryptonite, son,' said God.

'Well quite, Tel,' said Gabriel. He turned to face God. 'Which brings us back to the point. What the devil is it doing in your journal?'

'Hey, don't blame me.'

'Well this is clearly where he's getting his inspiration,' said Gabriel, placing his clawhand on the pages, 'so what is the code sequence doing in here?'

'I stuck it in there for a meeting.'

'A meeting?' said Gabriel, his browfeathers furrowing.

'Yes, a meeting. I wanted to go prepared.'

'Oh come off it,' said Gabriel.

'O ye of little faith,' said God. He flicked the pages of the journal back to the notes on the page before the start of the master codes. 'There you go,' he said, 'realm heads meeting, last one we ever had, before we disabled the portals, Tuesday August the twenty-fourth, Two forty-five.'

'p.m.?' asked Harold.

'VE,' said Gabriel, leaning in to take a look.

'VE?'

'Vulgar Era.'

Harold still looked puzzled.

'Anno Domini,' said Gabriel, in frustration, 'AD. Two forty-five AD.'

'Oh, right, well I never,' said Harold. 'And the realm heads?'

'Oh do try to keep up,' said Gabriel, 'Tel runs this place, Gordon runs the middle place, Stan runs the lowest place.' Gabriel studied the meeting details. 'Two forty-five,' he said. 'That's when we changed the judgement rules. So that was the purpose of the meeting, to let them know?'

'Yes,' said God.

'But that only affected the judgement codes,' said Gabriel.

'Yeah.'

'So what's that got to do with the master codes?'

'Nothing.'

'So why take them to the meeting?'

'For credibility, o'course. I'm the guy in charge, people expect it.'

'But you don't understand the codes.'

'Yes but they didn't know that.'

'I bet they did ...'

'Hey,' said God, pointing a finger, 'you're getting right cheeky, Gabe.'

Gabriel was lost in thought. He began pacing. 'But of all the things, Tel, you know how dangerous those codes are.'

'They only saw the first page, where's the harm?'

'Even so, Tel, even so,' said Gabriel, shaking his head.

'Anyway, can we get back to the point?' said God.

'Which is what?' asked Gabriel.

'That the monkey is on the verge of getting the full sequence, all twenty-whatever pages.'

'Right, yes ... yes.'

'So what I'd like to know is,' said God, 'how's this monkey got my journal into his head, when it's been sitting in my safe, my ... unlocked safe.'

He turned to the doorway and shouted, 'Oi.'

Moments later, the heads of two aides appeared nervously round the doorframe.

'Who's been in this room?' bellowed God. 'Who?'

The aides looked at each other and dropped to their knees. 'We don't know, Lord, no one, Lord.'

God stood. His beard began to spark. 'I will not ask again,' he said, and took a stride towards the men.

'Tel, get real,' said Gabriel, 'no one's been in this room for centuries.' He waved the aides away.

'Well how's he got it then?' asked God.

'Is it possible he's accessing the book remotely?' ventured Harold.

Gabriel and God looked at each other. They both knew Harold was right.

'Fuckin' 'ell, we're wasting time,' said God, and he started hopping around the room, fresh sparks in his beard. 'He could still be writing, he could be writing this minute. He's only a handful of pages to go, we gotta stop him.'

'Well the Pansies are–'

'Fuck the Pansies, Gabe, fuck the Pansies, we need to stop him now, fuckin' right now.'

'All right, all right, keep calm, we need to think smart here,' said Gabriel, and he began pacing again. 'If we can't stop *him* now, how about we stop his *access* now?'

'Could we create some sort of disruption?' said Harold. 'Block his signal?'

'I suppose we could line the safe with moist linens,' said Gabriel.

'You lads think too much,' barked God, already ripping pages from the journal. 'Come on, help me. Come on.'

'Yes ... yes, this solves everything,' said Harold, reaching in and grabbing a handful of pages.

God bellowed out to the main lounge, 'Lads, get in here.'

The two aides rushed back in.

'Destroy this journal, now,' said God.

Again they looked at each other, but a moment later joined the frenzied tearing.

'And these,' said God, pushing the other journals off the desk into a pile on the floor, 'it's all gotta go.'

'We'll have to make the bits very small,' said Harold, dropping to the floor.

'You,' said God, addressing the aides, 'start eating the bits.'

The aides again hesitated, but then began tucking in.

'Gabe, Gabe, come on,' said God, 'help us, there's no time.'

Tiny pieces of papyrus were now flying everywhere as the crack team tore into the journals like an industrial wood chipper.

'Eat faster,' shouted God. He scampered round to the pile and began stuffing handfuls of papyrus confetti into the aides' mouths.

'Stop,' said Gabriel. 'Stop.'

The others looked up, but didn't stop ripping, shredding and eating.

'I said *stop*.'

They all froze and looked at Gabriel.

'That,' said Gabriel, pointing to the remains of the journals, several already stripped to their spines, 'is not the book he tapped into.'

'Yes it is,' said God, 'of course it is.'

Harold nodded in agreement. The aides soon nodded too.

'I mean it's not these physical pages,' said Gabriel.

'How can it not be,' said God, 'he got it all word for word.'

'No, Tel, it's the version of these pages inside your brain,' said Gabriel. He tapped Terry on the temple. 'Think about it. You make psychic connections with a living mind, not a bunch of papyrus.'

'It can't be,' said God. 'Look, I don't remember the book, not half of it. And the numbers, the master codes, I couldn't tell you what was top of the first page, let alone bottom of the twenty-third.'

Gabriel was shaking his head. 'Not you, Tel, your brain.'

'What's the difference?'

'All the difference in the world. Tel, the mind, especially your mind, only occupies a tiny corner of the brain. I know *you* can't recall all of these details, any of them even, that would be asking way, way, too much. But your brain, well, that's another matter.'

'Actually, I have heard this,' said Harold, 'what is it, we only use ten per cent?'

'Some of us a lot less,' said Gabriel, glancing at his boss. 'Look, of course you don't know this stuff, Tel, you haven't got a clue. But your brain does, trust me, *it* is right on the money.'

'But the codes? I only took a quick squiz as I glued each page in.'

'A scan past the eyes, that's all it would take.'

'Bugger me. Well I never knew I was so smart.'

'Well … quite.'

'All right,' said God, 'so the crafty bugger's got inside my head.'

'In a manner of speaking,' said Gabriel.

'But how? How the hell did he do it?' said God, thumping his skull.

'Well isn't it obvious?' said Gabriel.

It was God's and Harold's turn to look at each other.

'He's a foresayer, Tel, channelling the book like it's scripture. It's the only way. We've been watching him for weeks now, writing out the book and yet no one's ever seen him with a source text. This would explain why.'

God raised his eyebrows and screwed up his nose again.

'Think back to Moses,' said Gabriel, 'this is exactly how we did it. You'd say what you want, we'd get it translated, you'd copy it out, he'd start spouting it.'

'But he got it all wrong, went off on his own agenda.'

'Yes, but the point is the mechanism was the same.'

'But we haven't created a sayer,' said God, 'not for centuries.'

'Well, yes.'

'Are we certain?' asked Harold.

'Absolutely,' said Gabriel, 'Terry banned them after the Galileo debacle.'

'Well, could there be any other explanation?' asked Harold.

'I can't think of one,' said Gabriel.

'Look,' said God, 'forget about how he came to be, there'll be time for that later, the question now is how do we stop him? How do we stop him gettin' in between me ears?' God clamped his arms around his head.

'We proceed as before,' said Gabriel, 'relocate, collect. Foresayer or not, once he's here with us, he can't do any more damage.'

'Agreed. But bloody when?' said God. 'We've got to act.'

'I'm told the Pansies are likely to strike tomorrow, in London. So we're talking hours only.'

'Likely? Likely?' said God, jumping to his feet and throwing up his hands. 'We need certainty.' He slammed his fist onto the desk, cleaving it in two, the shock sending Harold and the aides cowering for cover.

'All right,' said Gabriel, standing calm and opening his armwings a little. 'I'll get onto Pringle and get an update. All the details, where and when, then we can watch it all on a window box, yes?'

God relaxed his stance a fraction. 'Yeah, yeah, okay,' he said. 'Just the cabinet, mind, not the section heads.'

'Of course, Tel, we'll keep it small, discreet, just a select few.'

'Right ... right ... good,' said God. His eyes dropped to look sheepishly at the desk halves. 'You'll let me know the moment there's news?'

'The moment,' said Gabriel.

God now turned his attention to the snowdrift of page fragments. 'So we didn't need to tear this up then?'

'Well, no ...'

God turned to the aides. 'I'd appreciate those pages back, lads, if you wouldn't mind.'

Chapter Seventeen

Christian woke on the sofa to the sound of the toaster popping. Beatrice was already dressed and ready, her mascara heavier than normal. She didn't say anything. She didn't offer Christian a coffee. Ten minutes later she was picking up her bag and heading for the door. 'I hope … I hope to see you later,' she said and was gone.

Christian made himself a large strong coffee. He skipped breakfast, he couldn't face food.

8:00. Half an hour to go. Still no plan.

He took a shower. Showers are good for thinking.

8:15. Still no plan.

He got dressed, he waited.

8:25.

8:26.

8:27. He looked out of the window. No sign of Nikki. No car. No plan.

8:28.

8:29. No car. No plan.

8:30. No car. No plan.

Car. The BMW outside. A silhouette in the tint. The engine running.

How long would she wait? Two minutes? Three? Maybe four?

He looked at the second hand on the hall clock. He watched it jerk through one revolution, remarking to himself what a short period of time a minute really is. Were they normally that short? Still no plan.

Car. No plan.
Car. No plan.
Car. No plan.
Car. No plan.
Car. No plan.
He watched the hands tick round another semicircle.
'Fuck it.' He picked up his wallet, coat and keys, and left the house.
'Good morning, Christian,' said Nikki, as he got into the car.
He didn't reply.
She flicked the central locking. 'London. Can't be too careful.'

In the compact and underused formal dining room close to God's bedroom, two mid-sized portable privets had been set up on the main table, which itself had been pushed up against the far wall. At the first box sat William McDougal, one of the senior operators from Blotchley Hall. He was tracking Nikki's car, maintaining an overhead helicopter view as it sped out of Bracknell. At the other box sat Gabriel and Harold, who were scouting out a view of London streets.

'It's not going to be ideal,' said Gabriel, zooming out to a wide shot, 'but then you can't have everything.'

'What would be ideal?' asked Harold, flatly.

'Large open space. No one watching. An area prone to natural disasters. Active warzones are always good.'

'Not what springs to mind when you're looking at Westminster.'

'Quite.'

'How's that, sir?' said one of the aides behind them.

Gabriel turned to survey the rearrangement of the furniture, additional seating and assembled refreshments. 'That's satisfactory. You can go.'

As the aides left the room, a runner entered.

'I bring news from Dr Pringle of the HFP,' he said, referring to a parchment note, '*Address established. Twenty-seven Soho Square. At this stage we are a go. Repeat we are a go.* Message ends.'

'Very good,' said Gabriel, 'we saw it too. Tell Pringle to proceed. He has the call.'

The runner took out his pencil and a fresh page, and scribbled down the message.

'One moment,' said Harold, as the runner was about to leave.

'Harold?' said Gabriel.

'Surely there's another way. If we can only think of–'

'Harold. We've been through this. Nothing's changed.'

Harold's head dipped.

Gabriel released the runner. 'This is much bigger than it seems, Harold. I can't tell you why, but you have to trust me when I say there is far more at stake than you imagine, even after everything you learned last night. We have no choice.'

Harold said nothing.

'Anyway,' said Gabriel, 'I think it's time to wake Terry.'

'I suppose we must,' said Harold.

'Off you go then.'

They'd driven in silence for the first twenty minutes as they made their way out of Bracknell and onto the M4.

'I know it wasn't easy,' said Nikki, 'I do appreciate this commitment, coming with me today.'

Christian maintained his intense interest in the uninteresting view out of the passenger window.

'It's all going to be all right,' said Nikki, 'Bea will come around. She just needs time.'

'Will you stop saying that,' said Christian. 'Look, please, don't mention Beatrice. Don't mention her ever again.'

He wanted to know where they were going, but didn't want to talk. He still didn't know if he was doing the right thing. And regardless, Nikki didn't deserve absolution from him. An ultimatum. He would never do that to anyone.

They continued in silence.

The M4 soon became the A4 as they continued into West London. Hammersmith, Earl's Court, Knightsbridge, through Piccadilly Circus to Dean Street and finally into Soho Square where Nikki stopped the car outside number twenty-seven. Inside, Ted Binge, of reception security, was on his way down to the basement boiler room, having smelled gas.

'So this is the mystery location then,' said Christian, coldly.

'No, this is a little detour. We're just here for a quick look.'

'At what?'

'At your publishing house.'

'What are you talking about? I don't even have a book yet.'

'But you've got a publisher.' She pointed to the higher floors of the building. 'May look a bit anonymous, but this lot have some of the biggest names in the business. Their next project is your book.'

'What? But. How?'

'It's not what you know, Christian ...'

He didn't know what to say.

'So, feeling better now?' said Nikki.

A pause before Christian replied. 'But ... but what if they, what if they don't like it?'

'Trust me, they will love it. But even if for some reason they don't, it won't matter anyway, because I bought the company last week.'

Christian turned his head to the passenger window, unable to suppress a shameful grin. 'So is this supposed to impress me?' he said.

'Yes. It is.'

'Okay, all right, that is quite impressive,' he said, still looking out of the window, 'but it doesn't excuse you for putting me in the position you put me in last night, for putting everything at risk.'

'I know. And I am sorry. But I want you to know how much I appreciate the commitment you made today. And to show you what my commitment means in return. So, do you trust me?'

He made eye contact for the first time that day. 'Don't push it.'

'Okay, fair enough,' she said, 'onward,' and they moved back out into the London traffic.

Gasps and then everyone was on their feet in God's dining room.

'Why didn't they go in?' said God, hopping about like he'd trodden on Lego bricks. 'That was the address, Gabe, you said that was the address.'

'It was,' said Gabriel, 'but look–'

'They're bloody onto us,' said God. 'Fuckin' useless Pansies.'

'Tel, please, if–'

'If you want something doing ...' said God, glaring into the flames, both privet boxes now tracking Nikki's car. He closed his eyes. He thrust his head back and held out his arms in tension. Time slowed. As he began to lift his hands and stretch his fingers, the walls of the dining room appeared to bow inwards and the chairs and tables began to vibrate to a loud low-frequency hum.

'Please, no,' said Gabriel, rushing in behind and gripping God at the shoulders.

The rumble in the room intensified. In the image in the flames, pedestrians in Soho Square stopped mid-stride and looked up. A string of vehicles impacted nose to tail. Alarms sounded everywhere.

Gabriel tightened his grip. 'Cool, wet grass,' he said.

In the flames, roof tiles and masonry were now falling from buildings and people were running for cover.

'Cool, wet grass, Terrence, cool, wet grass.'

God's whole body tensed and his fingers closed into fists. Everyone had now backed away to the walls. Some had closed their eyes. Some were cowering. But then God's arms relaxed and his fingers opened. The noise and vibrations faded.

'What?' said God, opening his eyes.

Relief in the room.

Gabriel sat down, flexed his armwings, and composed himself. 'Setting off an earthquake in central London isn't going to go unnoticed, Tel.'

God held up his hands. 'Okay, my bad.'

'We just need to hold our nerve,' said Gabriel. 'Pringle has lots of pieces in the field this time. All is not lost.'

Silence had descended on the car once again, but it didn't last. Christian wanted to stay mad but it wasn't possible. She'd bought him a publishing house! Wait till he told Beatrice!

'So,' he said, 'who exactly are we here to see?'

She looked across before answering. 'Blondeldark,' she said.

'Blondel what?'

'Blondeldark.'

'Blondeldark who?'

'Just Blondeldark.'

'Who's that then?'

'You've not heard of him?'

'Should I have?'

'Of course. The hypnotherapist. Lots of celebrity clients.'

'You're taking me to see a hypnotist?'

'Hypnotherapist.'

'Hey, look, I don't want some crank messing with my head.'

'He's not a crank, he's a professional, best there is. What are you afraid of?'

'That he'll make me take my clothes off and eat a raw onion.'

'Listen, will you, hypnotherapist, not hypnotist. He's not going to make a fool of you, he's going to help you.'

'What the hell with?'

She didn't reply.

He looked across at her.

'Well what do you think?' she said.

'I don't know. You tell me.'

'Your focus, Christian.'

He folded his arms. She might as well have brought him to see a faith healer. He'd risked Beatrice for this?

He should end this sideshow, of course he should. But, he reminded himself, it wouldn't be in anyone's interest to upset the publishing house apple cart.

Fresh indecision brought him back to the meeting at the vicarage. For the first time he realised he was still operating in the moment, as he had been since the previous evening. Despite all the thinking, he still had no strategy, none whatsoever.

Beatrice. Should he text her? At least then she'd know he wouldn't be there. Put an end to the false hope she'd surely have been nursing since breakfast, save her the embarrassment of turning up at the vicarage only to endure just sitting there with Tony, her faith ebbing away to the tick of the clock. But if he texted her, that was final, that was a decision – he wouldn't be there and he'd have to accept that he wouldn't be there, accept that he'd decided not to be there. As things stood, despite physics having already ruled it all but impossible for him to now make the meeting, the decision was still somehow not yet made and therefore there was still hope. It was Schrödinger's cat gone wrong: the cyanide had already been released – logically the cat was dead and he knew it, yet part of him still insisted it wasn't an absolute goner until the box was opened.

They crossed Fitzrovia, the traffic flowing at little above walking pace, before cutting down New Cavendish and looping round into Harley Street.

'So I suppose we lost all the work from Tuesday?' asked Christian.

'You didn't take a copy?' There was a strange lack of concern in her voice.

'No,' said Christian, now queasy at the thought of the rewriting. He tried not to think about it, turning his gaze to the Georgian architecture.

'So how did you get on yesterday?' asked Nikki.

'Not so good. I was a bit distracted, you know.'

'Fair enough.'

'Did a bit more last night though.'

'Right.'

'Couldn't sleep.'

'Understandable,' she said, softly.

'Yes, I ended up having a stab at that appendix idea.'

Nikki stamped on the brakes, stopping the car dead.

'What the fuck,' said Christian, his seat belt digging tight into his chest.

Car horns blared from behind.

He looked across to Nikki. She was staring straight ahead, her hands gripping the wheel tight.

'Sorry,' she said.

'Are you okay?'

'I thought … sorry, I don't know what I thought.'

Another car horn sounded.

She took her foot off the brake and they resumed progress up Harley Street.

'Perhaps we should stop,' said Christian.

'We're stopping anyway,' she said, 'we're here.'

They drove another forty yards and pulled into a parking space.

She turned off the engine. 'Look, why didn't you tell me all this earlier?'

'Tell you all what?'

'The appendix.'

'I didn't think it was important. And besides, I wasn't exactly in the mood.'

'Yes. Right. Sorry. So tell me about it now.'

'There's nothing to tell.'

'I don't follow.'

'Well, let's just say it wasn't my best work. It all felt a bit weird.'

'Why?'

'Mostly I just doodled.'

'Doodles. What of?'

'Just … doodles.'

'What's weird about that?'

'The timing, mostly. You see I doodle, sometimes, but only before I'm in the zone, or when I'm trying to get back into the zone, but this time I was doodling from within the zone.'

'But it was only doodles?'

'Well, I got down to some writing eventually, though not much, just a few sentences, and no real continuity, just fragments that read like meeting notes, and then I got it into my head that what it really needed at this stage was big blocks of hex numbers, sorry, hexadecimal, that's base–'

'Sixteen. Yes, I know.'

'Oh … right. Well, anyway, I wrote pages and pages of them. Barmy, eh? I think maybe I went a bit, you know, "here's Johnny." I dunno, maybe it was the shock of the accident, of Stuart, you know.'

'Who's Johnny?'

'No, *here's* Johnny.'

'No, really, who is Johnny? Tell me.'

'*The Shining*. Jack Nicholson? Look, it doesn't matter, forget it. Anyway, in summary, not my best night's work.'

'No. No, you've done well, really well.' She looked at her watch. 'Look, you didn't delete it, did you? You kept it?'

'Yes.'

'And do you have it with you?'

'No, no I left the laptop at home. Sorry, should I have brought it?'

She looked at her watch again. 'No, don't worry about it.'

'Look, are you all right, Nik?'

'Yes, yes I'm fine. I'm fine.' She turned to him, smiled, and gestured to the street outside the car. 'Well, shall we?'

'Get 'em, get 'em now,' yelled God.

'Tel, please,' said Gabriel. 'Pringle will choose the right moment. Trust me.'

The increasingly animated dining room collective watched as Christian and Nikki were allowed to enter the building unencumbered.

'It'll be a surgical strike,' said Gabriel, 'just you see.'

The tick of the wall clock was the only sound in the waiting room, despite the volume of the wallpaper.

For the second time that day, Christian watched a second hand mark out a minute.

Tick.

Tick.

Tick.

Ten twenty-four a.m.

Ten thirty, the receptionist had said, six minutes until they would see this crank.

He got to his feet.

'Where are you going?' asked Nikki.

'I need to use the rest room,' he said, and left the room.

He needed space. He needed to think.

Why had he called it a rest room? So American.

What was he going to do when he got there? What could he do with six minutes?

It just felt wrong to call it a toilet in such plush surroundings.

It was too late. He couldn't change course now.

But why, just because it's in a posh place? It's still a toilet. People still go to the toilet in it, people still shit in it.

All too late, way too late.

He hurried down the corridor, still looking for the toilets, and into reception where he executed a simultaneous double take and emergency stop on his toes. It took him a moment to place the face, but with the mental addition of five inches and an infomercial backdrop of buff men in tight shorts, he recognised the individual as Ultimate Fighter and fitness equipment endorser Buck Minglestein.

Everyone shits, even Terry Wogan and the Archbishop of Canterbury. Buck shits. Probably big American super-sized ones.

'Look, missy,' said Buck, 'no one cancels me. I cancel them. If there's cancelling to be done, I'm the dude who does it, comprende?'

'It's a postponement, Mr Minglestein, not a cancellation. We did try to let you know.'

'I ain't leaving till I get seen. I got stuff to get out. Big stuff.'

'Well, you're welcome to wait, Mr Minglestein, but the earliest B can see you now is Tuesday.'

Should he take Buck to task over his exercise station? How the brackets had bent and how it just wasn't up to the task. No. No, this was not the time, not really. Also, Buck appeared to have been using his exercise station a lot more than Christian had been using his, so perhaps a customer service challenge to an already frustrated Minglestein would not be the wisest move at this stage, so Christian hurried past and finally found the toilet.

Inside, the decor jarred just as much as in the other rooms, with bronze diamond over lemon wallpaper mixing it with gold and marble fittings. There was artwork, too: a series of black-and-white fish-eye photos looking down from the tops of iconic buildings. The floor was still tiled though. Somehow he'd expected plush carpet, but realised there was no reason why rich people would have better aim than anyone else. He went into a cubicle and locked the door. Safe, sort of, at least for the moment.

What would Buck call it? The *John*. No, the *can*.

Look, forget what it's called, forget Buck.

Fuck Buck.

Think.

Concentrate, and think.

Ten twenty-four – ten twenty-five now. Two hours and five minutes before the meeting. The meeting. Beatrice. He left the cubicle and went to a basin. He turned the cold tap and splashed some water on his face. He looked in the mirror. What was he doing? He went back to his cubicle and watched his mind chase its tail for another sixty seconds, and then another, before reluctantly returning to the waiting room. What else was there do to? It was all too late.

'Everything okay?' asked Nikki.

'Yes, why wouldn't it be?'

'You seemed to take a while, that's all.'

'Just a little anxious.'

'Relax. He's a professional. There's nothing to worry about.'

The receptionist put her head round the door.

'Ms Tooting, B will see you now.'

Nikki and Christian got up from their seats.

'If you could just wait here, Mr Bootstrap.'

'Oh, okay,' said Christian, and he sat down.

The decor in Blondeldark's sanctum was not, at first glance, highly worked. But then that was the trick. The ten-parts-to-one emulsion of professionalism and mysticism: barrister's chambers spiced with Bhutan monastery. The same was true of the host himself: balding hair cut earnestly short; titanium frame Bugatti glasses; minimalist tailored suit with leanings to the East. Moccasins.

'Sorry about the short notice,' said Nikki.

'Think nothing of it,' said Blondeldark, his voice clear and deliberate. 'Now, what are we dealing with here? Would I be right in thinking it's a biggie?'

'Not just a biggie. *The* biggie, the ...' For a moment her mouth and chin trembled.

Blondeldark said nothing but gave a small nod of acknowledgement.

She composed herself. 'The biggest,' she said.

'And he's here?' asked Blondeldark. 'That's who you've brought with you?'

'Yes.'

'My, oh my.' Blondeldark leaned back in his chair and placed his hands in semi-prayer pose. 'I never thought we'd see the day.'

'We don't have much time,' said Nikki. 'We've been compromised.'

'Oh my. That is ... unfortunate.' He sat forward. 'Let us waste no more then. How can I help?'

'Okay. Christian believes you're going to work with him on his focus. He can write, you see, or rather, he can receive. He's the real deal, Ian, word for word, but it comes out at a snail's pace.'

'But that's not why you're here?'

Nikki shook her head.

Blondeldark leaned closer. 'Then I can only assume you want me to extract it directly?'

'Can you?'

'Well, you know it has risks. Primarily to the information itself, of course. Even if we're careful, anything we extract may not be reliable. Interference you see.'

'Yes, yes I know, but we're out of options.'

'Well, if the stakes are already high, there are some extra measures we could look at.'

'Go on.'

'What's his emotional state like?'

'Placid, rational – usually.'

'Usually?'

'He's had a rough couple of days. I've patched him up this morning, but he's still fragile.'

'And would you describe him as naturally open- or closed-minded?'

'Closed. Dead locks. Double bolts.'

'I see. And therefore I presume he doesn't know who he is?'

'He hasn't a clue.'

'Okay. Well, that's going to make things harder. But if we adjust the approach, and by that I mean take a lump hammer to it, I think we could still get a result.'

'Go on.'

'Well, once our friend is under, we tap into the unconscious at a much lower level, force a more intense connection, go right to the receiver nodes, dissolve any host resistance with some accelerators.' He leaned back and brought his fingertips together. 'It would substantially reduce the risk of damage to the information ...'

'Okay.'

'... but substantially increase the risk of damage to the patient.'

'What sort of damage?'

'Hard to say. It's uncharted waters. This wouldn't be psychological keyhole surgery, more like going in with an ice cream scoop. Could be limited to some mild personality changes, some minor neural rerouting. He could start calling sausages bananas, that kind of thing. But it could extend to paranoid delusions, schizophrenia, major neural trauma, perhaps a permanent disconnection from reality.'

'And the chances?'

Blondeldark took a moment. 'I'd say an eighty per cent chance of permanent damage, of some sort.'

'And this damage, it would be to his mind, not just his body?'

'Well, that's probably an open question, in my field, but in my view, yes, mind as much as body, perhaps more so.'

Nikki paused in thought. She understood sacrifice more than most. Hers had been the greatest, but also the easiest. And forcing it on others wasn't so hard, if they deserved it. But so far she'd been untested on those that didn't.

'Would you like me to proceed?' asked Blondeldark. 'It would appear time is of the essence.'

'Just give me a moment.' She had to remember the big picture, remember what this was all for. There was no alternative. They would swat him soon anyway, there was no way to prevent that now.

'Nikki?' said Blondeldark.

'Do it,' she said.

'You're sure?'

'Positive.'

'All right then.'

'One final thing,' she said, 'the information, you know what it is? You know it's the book, right, the codes beyond the last chapter?'

Blondeldark nodded. 'I assumed as much.'

'Well, won't that leave you compromised? Won't it mean you gain prohibited knowledge?'

'Yes, it will. There's no way of avoiding that, I'm afraid. But then no one knows the criteria for sure, right? And anyway, I already know there is such a thing as prohibited knowledge, even if I don't yet know what that knowledge is. Simply knowing it exists may in itself be regarded as prohibited knowledge, so it's possible I'll be no worse off than I already am, if you follow my logic.'

Nikki leaned across and put her hand on his. It was a gesture of comfort and acknowledgement but she watched Blondeldark's eyes lift to meet hers. She saw the love, pure and unconditional. She'd always known, of course, and had been careful not to offer encouragement over the years. But she allowed him this moment, this one time, before withdrawing her hand.

His gaze dropped and he gave a small nod. 'Okay,' he said, 'let's make a start. No sense keeping the poor fellow waiting. And just think, I could be the first man to be damned for all eternity for successful removal of a man's appendix.'

Nikki forced a half smile.

Blondeldark pressed the intercom.

'Emily, would you show in Mr Bootstrap, please.'

'I'm sorry, B, he's gone.'

Christian was sprinting up Weymouth Street. He had to find transport and quick.

Bus? Don't be stupid. Train? That could work. Bracknell was well connected but how frequent were the trains? And did he need Paddington or Waterloo? Fuck. Why did he never pay attention to stuff like that? Ewan would have known. Ewan would have known the station, departure times, and the best awayday saver specials. Taxi? Get a taxi, ask the driver. No, get a taxi, call Ewan. No, just get a taxi. Get a fucking taxi to Bracknell. There was time. Fuck the cost. Get a taxi, job done.

But he still needed to find one and so far there were none in sight.

He was gifted a green man as he approached the junction with Portland Place. Mid-stride glances revealed no taxis left or right, so he decided to keep running and cross, but a second reflex glance to his right caused him to pull up sharp, up on his tiptoes as a speeding police car bore down on the junction.

He caught a glimpse of the officer wrestling with the wheel as the car shot by.

'Hey,' shouted Christian, 'put your fucking siren on.'

No time, no time.

He resumed his sprint up Weymouth, on until he emerged onto Great Portland Street. He stopped, allowing his already burning lungs a few seconds of respite as he weighed up the options.

Right nothing; left nothing – fuck. He headed left, his sprint now beaten down to a stitchy jog.

The street seemed so quiet. It was London on a weekday. Why was it so quiet?

Up ahead he saw a line of people queuing at a bus stop and he briefly considered a change of strategy, but decided to press on. There will be a taxi, there will.

As soon as he'd passed the queue, there was an audible gasp. He assumed it was directed at him, so, mid-stride, he looked back but instead saw shocked faces turning the other way. In an instant, the collective gasp was overtaken by shouts and screams. Still moving up the street, he craned his neck further to see the bus queue scattering and being scattered as an approaching double-decker ploughed into the stop, ripping and shredding the shelter as if it were a combine harvester attacking wheat, before being brought to a halt just yards behind him by the much less easily harvested Portland Hospital.

'Ooohhhhhhhhh.'

By now, everyone was back on their feet in God's dining room, arms whipping the air and clawhands clasping foreheads at the second near miss.

'Couldn't hit a fuckin' barn door,' shouted God, 'that's none from two. Don't they train, don't they practise?'

'Pringle says there's no point,' said Gabriel, 'says you can't replicate the tension of doing it for real. They'll get him though, mark my words.'

McDougal zoomed one of the privet boxes in on Christian's face, capturing his confused panting as he stood, hands on knees, looking back at the crash scene, before pulling back to a wide tracking shot as their target turned and resumed his leggy jog.

'Keep still, you bugger,' shouted God.

He should have stopped. He knew he should. But then no one had actually gone under the bus; they'd all got out of the way, hadn't they? It was an insurance matter, that's all, and they'd have lots of better witnesses anyway, especially the ones that weren't under the bus. He'd only be filler next to their more visceral testimony.

He pressed on, pushing the nugget of guilt to the back of his mind, along with his breathlessness and his stitch.

Great Portland tube station was now in view and again he was tempted.

No. Stick with the plan, there will be a taxi, there will. Come on, come on, where are you, you fuckers?

As he reached Marylebone Road, he saw it – a black cab pulling up on the slip road at the other side of the junction. One, two, three business types got out, the first soon moving to the passenger window to lean in to pay.

How much time?

The westbound traffic was heavy and moving steadily. No green man at the crossing to his right. No time to wait. Fuck it.

He stepped off the kerb.

It was like playing Frogger on his PlayStation retro collection. He didn't need a big gap, it's all in the timing.

He took his chance and darted across to the thin halfway island, incurring nothing more than a couple of horn blasts and a 'Wanker!' from a cycle courier. Across at the cab, the woman settling the fare was now putting away her purse and on her way back to the others. There was no more time. The traffic was heavier and faster flowing on the other side, but he was nearly there.

He looked back to the cab. Its light was on.

'Taxi,' he shouted. 'Hey, mate, taxi.'

He saw the indicator start to blink; he saw the driver check his mirror.

A gap, a gap, my kingdom for a gap.

His feet were off the kerb, he was on a hair trigger, flinching at demi-gaps, causing some cars to slow, but not enough to let him commit.

Still no gap.

The cab's wheels were beginning to roll.

He shouted again, as loud as he could, and frantically waved both arms in a wide arc. Finally he made eye contact. 'Taxi,' he mouthed, with an expectant nod. The driver raised a lethargic thumb and turned off his light. Relief, sweet breathless relief. It was all going to be okay. The green man appeared across the junction, stopping the traffic, and Christian jogged out into the lanes of the far side. As he did, there was a loud and continual blast of a horn. The three business types that had arrived in the cab were now all staring, open-mouthed, in his direction. Christian got a dreadful sense he'd not done something, something important. But he *had* done everything. The traffic to his left was stationary. He had the green man.

And then he glanced to his right.

That's not supposed to be there. That's on the wrong side. What's more, that's coming very fast. Why was that coming so fast? They're not supposed to be on this side and they're not supposed to go that fast.

The room erupted.

'Gotcha,' shouted God as he pumped his fist in the air.

Amid the cheering, a nod from Gabriel triggered the popping of Jeragne corks at the back of the room.

Angels hugged immortals. Aides hugged operators.

A chorally thin but spirited chant sprang up.

Easy! Easy! Easy!

Only Harold wasn't joining in. When everyone else had jumped up, he'd felt his core give way. His eyes were now closed, his hands clasped behind his head, forearms tight over his ears.

The chanting tapered off as attention returned to the images in the flames. Everyone wanted to be sure.

McDougal hovered and probed for a good angle, while the other viewer held a wide shot.

Bravado met caution in the chatter of the lounge.

'Is he?'

'I think so.'

'Course he is.'

'He'll not be getting up from that.'

'They could burn him too. They should make sure. Why don't they burn him?'

Blondeldark returned from the southern end of Harley Street. Nikki was waiting for him.

'Nothing,' he said, out of breath.

'Same. Fuck. I thought he was okay.'

'We should check the side streets.'

She shook her head. 'Maybe he'll talk though.'

She took out her phone.

Christian began to become aware of himself again. His everyday senses were offline, somewhere way behind him. The only thing he felt was awareness of himself, that he occupied a space.

He tried to open his eyes, but observed no image. Were his eyes open but not working, or working but not open? Where was he? He started to hear noise, indiscernible sounds, faint at first, but then louder, rising in an arc around and in front of him. It was as if he was on his back on the bottom of a swimming pool, being shouted at through five metres of over-chlorinated sticking-plaster-infested water. On his back. Yes, he was on his back. The road? *The road*, yes, the road, the junction. Something must have hit him. How long had he been out? He didn't know, his internal clock just flashing unhelpful big red zeros.

Soon the awareness of the road at his back began to fade and slip away. He couldn't feel his legs; he couldn't feel anything at all. A mental gulp as explanations flashed before him. Shock? Paralysis? Both? He dared not investigate further, terrified that if he tried to move, he could find himself unable to. He put all his concentration into not moving anything, not so much as a toe (especially not a toe – the doctor's standard paralysis test, according to what he remembered from *Casualty*, anyway), and keeping his eyes tight shut – even if he wasn't paralysed, the sight couldn't be good.

Stay calm and wait.

Stay calm and wait.

Stay calm and wait.

No pain though? A blessing, but surely not a good sign. Though again, it could just be the shock. He'd heard about the drugs the brain has available for desperate times.

He started to make sense of the noise around him. Blended anonymous traffic drone combining with car and bus engines idling nearby. A phone was ringing – his phone. There was more sound, too, less familiar, more guttural. It sounded an awful lot like synchronised vomiting with occasional breaks for gasping. He could make out some words, too.

'That's not good.'

'Oh, you think?'

'His phone's ringing. Hey, mate, your phone's ringing.'

'I don't think he can hear you. Besides, he's in no condition to answer.'

'Should we answer?'

'No, just leave it. We need to call for an ambulance, has anyone called for an ambulance?'

'What's the point?'

'I think you have to anyway, you know, they have all the right forms.'

'Be easier to pop him straight in the back of this, wouldn't it?'

'I think they've got one in the back already, see?'

'Oh yes …'

'Stand back, there's nothing to see.'

'Yes there is, look at that.'

He summoned up the courage to try to open his eyes again. An image formed. He found he was looking down on a scene, a crowd of people, individuals pushing closer to see, a few trying to help, but most trying to get better angles for videoing with their phones. He noted and lamented how many were recording in portrait orientation.

Christian believed in out-of-body experiences but didn't believe there was anything supernatural about them – *It's just the brain going a bit haywire when the body is in crisis* – and he held to this now. But it did mean the situation was serious, perhaps grave. How could this have happened? He'd done nothing wrong. He'd had the green man.

He looked down again on the scene. Through the semicircle of leaning heads, he could see a ghastly and disturbing sight. Ghastly and disturbing even though he knew it was just a vision created by his impressively vivid imagination. Limbs were flexed in novel directions, there was some unnatural twisting, and some things were visible that were normally not – blood, bone, brain. A holy trinity of things you are thankful to own but rarely pleased to see. This was … well … this wasn't good.

His senses began to desert him. The scene melted away.

Nikki let it ring for a full minute.

'He's not answering. Fuck.' She cancelled the call.

'All right, what can I do?' asked Blondeldark.

'There's nothing you can do,' said Nikki. 'I need to think.'

'Do you know where he would go?'

'That's just it. I know exactly where he's going, he's already told me, I just don't know where *where* is.'

'I don't follow.'

'He's going to a church. But I don't know which one.'

'Look, I'm here when you need me,' said Blondeldark, 'day, night, call me when you've found him.'

'Okay. Thanks, Ian. Really, thanks. Right, I need to move.'

Chapter Eighteen

'Hello, sir,' said the old man.

The voice was drab and donnish, and yet against the vast interstellar silence, it was compelling. The silence? How long had Christian been hearing it? And what purity, what perfection. There was no sound. Nothing. This was aural absolute zero.

'Hello, sir,' said the old man, again.

'I'm sorry?' said Christian, his own voice now embarrassingly commanding.

'I said, "Hello, sir." Twice, now thrice.'

'No, before that.'

'That's the first thing I said, sir.'

'No, no, we were talking about, you know, um, you were telling me about the, oh, the' – Christian clicked his fingers – 'oh, don't you just hate that, when you lose your ... train of whatsit ...'

'Oh yes, sir, most frustrating.'

'Well not to worry, cheerio then, don't let me keep you.'

'But I'm not going anywhere, sir.'

'I thought you were catching a bus?'

'No, sir, I've been waiting for you.'

'Really? Oh. Did I keep you long?'

'But a blink, sir,' said the old man and gave a wink.

'That's a relief, I'm sometimes a bit late for appointments, you see. Be late for my own funeral, me.'

'Oh, very good, sir.' The old man chuckled. 'Now, there are a few formalities, if you'll just bear with me.'

Christian's senses begin to return for the second time that day – actually, the third, but like most people on most days, he didn't count or even acknowledge the first one. He found himself in an environment of complete darkness, save for a doorway and the old man standing next to him. The door was closed inside its frame, but brilliant-white light was escaping all around the edges, surging through the gaps. The door itself was nothing unusual – panelled with a brass handle. There were two unusual details though. First, it said 'THIS WAY' in large authoritative gold letters on the front. Second, and more significantly, there didn't appear to be anywhere for the door to lead to: it was just hanging in space (as for that matter were Christian and the old man) – no walls around its frame, no floor beneath or ceiling above. Christian peered round the back, and saw, perhaps not surprisingly, the back of the door. It was much like the front, only it said 'NO ENTRY, WRONG WAY, GO BACK' this time in large authoritative red letters.

Despite the surreal nature of the environment, Christian was filled with a vague sense of familiarity. He tried to place it, but his mind felt stretched and incomplete, like he'd accidentally left two-thirds of it wherever he'd been half an hour ago.

'As I was saying, sir, just a few formalities. Now here's your soul card.'

The old man handed Christian a small white rectangular card.

'Christian Joshua Bootstrap,' said Christian. 'Seventy-seven. *Seventy-seven?*'

'Your soul number, sir. Allocated at birth.'

'With ... nine leading zeros.'

'Indeed, sir.'

'Bit on the low side, isn't it?'

'Is it, sir?'

'Well, seventy-seven. There must have been more than seventy-six people born before me, quite a lot more.'

'Perhaps they're filling in some gaps, sir.'

'Yes,' said Christian, still looking at the card, 'easy to remember though.'

'That's the spirit, sir.'

The old man began flicking through some parchment forms on a wooden clipboard, making occasional ticks and notes with a small quill.

'Odd that I don't recognise you though,' said Christian.

'Is it, sir?'

'Well, I would have thought you'd be someone I know. They're the people I tend to meet in my dreams.'

'Really, sir, well not to worry.'

'I suppose I must have met you, somewhere, and forgotten. It's amazing what the brain records and tucks away without us even knowing. You could be someone who advised me on air filter selection at Halfords, or perhaps you came to read my gas meter?'

'I don't ever recall working for the gas board, sir.'

'Or perhaps you were asleep and dribbling in a chair when I last visited my grandfather?'

'Delightful, sir,' said the old man, ticking a few boxes. 'Now, I think we're all done, if you could sign here, and here.'

'And what exactly am I signing up for?'

'It's a standard death acknowledgement form.'

'But I'm not dead. This is just a dream.'

'Then there's no danger in signing the forms, is there, sir?'

'I'm not signing anything.'

The old man seemed unperturbed by Christian's protest.

'I'm ... I'm going for a walk,' said Christian. 'Um, can I do that?'

'Of course, sir, feel free, you have all the time in the world.' He gave a small but warm smile.

Christian turned and put one foot in front of the other. He found he could walk with ease, despite there being no ground on which to propel himself. He felt no gravity, yet felt no weightlessness either (not that he could say quite what that should feel like). It should have been a disturbing and distressing sensation, yet he felt calm, at peace, even. And when this serenity gave way, as he left the old man and the door behind him, it was only to a sensation of slight discomfort. Not bed of nails discomfort, or standing up all day at a festival discomfort, it was more like the mild curtailment of freedom discomfort that comes with wearing an inexpensive suit. He looked down to find that this was because he was wearing an inexpensive suit – his inexpensive suit, the suit he'd not worn since his last day at work, almost a year ago. It triggered a Pavlovian response, a sensation that was the bedfellow to his low-level physical discomfort – it was the low-level psychological discomfort felt by someone who knows they are not quite where they belong, in Christian's case the sensation having been learned and burned into his neural pathways by extended exposure to the bowels of a large retail organisation's head office.

He decided to take off the jacket but found himself unable to do so. It wasn't buttoned, and he was able to open it as far as his inside pocket, but no further. It was the same story at the lapels and cuffs: the suit was seemingly fused to him. He began wrenching at it, as a rising panic took hold. But each time he pulled at the limits, he was met first with resistance and then searing pain, like he was trying to take off his own skin. On closer examination, there didn't appear to be any obvious join or interface, leaving him unable to work out quite where he stopped and the suit started. In effect, a new layer of skin, a 70% polyester epidermis, by Gustavo Bandini, dry clean only, warm iron. Now Christian noticed what he was wearing underneath his jacket. Instead of an office shirt, he was wearing his ragged old AC/DC T-shirt, a relic from the *Stiff Upper Lip* tour of 2003. Coupled with the suit, and what appeared to be a pair of once-white but now shabby-shit high-top trainers from his teenage years, it created a rather unfortunate ensemble, missing only cigarette and super-strength lager accessories to really complete the look; if Christian had met anyone else coming the other way, it would have given them ample cause to have crossed over to the other side of the infinite nothingness to avoid him.

It's just a dream, it doesn't matter.

He moved on, walking deeper and deeper into the nothingness, every step taking him farther from the old man and the door. And then it hit him – the source of the familiarity. This was 'Death' chapter three, 'Passing Through'. The infinite nothingness, the door or tunnel of light: a perfect adaptation of his writing. He remembered that the chapter was only half finished, half started if he was honest, and this surely explained why he hadn't recognised his sage host. Having written next to nothing about him, his unconscious must have filled the gap with the archetype of the wise old man. Just typical – his mind could have given him an audience with Mr Miyagi, Obi-Wan Kenobi or Albus Dumbledore, but instead had offered up someone who looked like an extra from *Last of the Summer Wine*. He remembered he'd given the man a name though. Something common, something normal. Smith? Jones? No, too obvious. It was common but not obviously common. Robinson, perhaps?

He looked out ahead of him as he walked, marvelling at the endless void. He looked down at his feet and watched as they moved him forward, propelling him no closer to anything, because there wasn't anything to get closer to. But a glance over the shoulder confirmed he was still getting further away from the door and the old man, both now small in his field of view. What was the man's name? Johnson? No, it was something faster.

He returned his attention to the bigger picture, deciding that, though startling, the quality of the match didn't necessarily signify anything special – this whole environment was something he had conjured in his mind, when writing the book, so it would be a candidate for inclusion in a dream just like anything else from his memory. But as he began to think further on his observations, he began to notice troubling differences. Not with the book, but with the normal aesthetic of his dreams. Here, now, there was clarity – despite the sensory limitations of an infinite empty space, he really felt like he was *here*. So far there was none of the incongruence and annoyance of normal dreams either – the random incursions of Darth Great-Aunt Pauline just as your *Star Wars* epic is getting interesting, the sudden change of venue to the set of *The IT Crowd* midway through your Booker Prize acceptance speech, and of course the waking up the moment after Cleopatra gives you that look and asks if you would like to join her in her banana milk bath. This dream was different. It was stable. So far there had been no sudden changes in scene, narrative or cast. So what did this mean? Perhaps this particular kind of stability, this purity, depth, and clarity, was something one only experienced in a coma?

Coma.

Holy fucking fuck. He tried to find a bright side. There wasn't one. The best he could do was tell himself that at least this meant he was still alive. *I think, therefore I am.* He was still alive; there was still hope. Snippets of the potential life ahead of him passed across his mind, post recovery, perhaps severely physically disabled, perhaps mentally disabled – perhaps that was what he was now already experiencing? He didn't want to think about it.

He'd now been walking for some time, or at least he felt he had. Turning round, all he could now see of the door and the old man was a white dot next to a beige dot, two stars in an otherwise empty but perfect night sky. He stood for a while, taking in the wonder of the nothingness, before heading back.

The stability of the dream continued to hold for Christian's return leg. The same thought returned. Was this a coma? And then something new, something darker: was this worse than a coma? Was there anything worse than a coma?

He recalled Kirk in *Star Trek V: The Final Frontier*: 'What does God need with a starship?'

Reason. Yes, reason had always been Christian's shield, barometer and flask of hot chocolate. Why desert it now? Okay. This would appear to be a sparse yet stable dream, based on a partly written chapter of the book. It felt real. But of course it felt real, all dreams do at the time, giving you a new normal while you are in them, however objectively strange the temporary normal might be. Of course it seems crazy when you wake up in the morning, but at the time you never think to question, you just accept – you really do believe with all your heart that your performing bird show is the only thing capable of melting the hearts of the Lizard King and the Lord of the Loafers, and avert all kingdoms being dashed into the folds of the great pudding. Insane. And yet in the moment you believe with all your heart. That's how dreams work.

But there was another difference, thought Christian, which was he was analysing the dream from a point mentally outside it – and he had been since he started his walk. On previous rare occasions when Christian had realised he was in a dream, it normally brought about its swift end – universe-hatingly frustratingly so in his almost-erotic adventure at the palace in Alexandria.

So in realising he was in a dream now, why hadn't he woken up? Could this be the icy reality of a coma, the dream from which one can never wake? Or could he really be dead?

Dead.

For the first time in his life, he felt *it*, existence after death, was possible. He didn't know why he felt this now, having never felt it before, he just knew in this moment, he believed. But then his intellect countered, challenging his credulity on the basis that if he really was dead, that would mean the environment he was now in was real, and therefore 'Death' chapter three, 'Passing Through', was in fact a pretty decent description of the real passage to the afterlife, which seemed pretty damned unlikely, given he'd made it up. Though, retorted his infant belief, perhaps the nature of this environment is different for everyone and is based on the subconscious of the individual, and so of course for Christian it would be the 'Passing Through' setting from his book. But, countered his intellect again, it's possible to believe anything in a dream: if in a dream you can believe you are Tot Hornpipe, of Hornpipe and Sons Amazing Duck

Circus, in principle at least you can certainly believe you are dead, and therefore however strongly you *believe*, it counts for nothing. But, retorted the upstart belief once again, would you persist with the belief you were Tot Hornpipe once you had realised it was a dream? Christian's intellect thought about this for a moment before telling his upstart belief that he had been around an awful lot longer and so it could go and shove its newfangled unhelpful opinion up its arse.

Christian's mind twisted in on itself several more times before arriving in a knotted bundle back in the company of the door and the old man.

'Had a good look around, sir?'

'Yes, I suppose.'

'Plenty to see, isn't there?'

'There's nothing to see.'

'Exactly, sir, and an awful lot of it. Now, if you'll just–'

'Williams. Your name is Williams.'

The old man seemed surprised, but stayed on message. 'If you wouldn't mind just signing–'

'The keeper of the door,' said Christian, 'administering the passage of every soul, every human life since Adam.'

The old man did not reply and instead again presented the quill and clipboard.

'Well?' said Christian.

'Well what, sir?'

'Are you him? Are you Thorndike Williams?'

'No, sir.'

'Oh.'

This was the first detail that didn't match. He tried to work out how this affected the death/dream balance of probabilities, and decided it made death the slight favourite.

'Thorndike Williams is my father,' said the old man. 'I am Wycliffe Williams, the second keeper of the door.'

'And ... your father?'

'Retired.'

Now Christian was more confused than ever. Perhaps the retirement of Williams senior could have been hiding in the unwritten bits of the chapter, but it was a bit of a stretch.

'And you've been here how long?'

'Questions of time are not always terribly meaningful, here, sir. But if you pressed me, I'd say some time this morning.'

'I'm sorry, are you telling me this is your first day?'

'Yes, as far as I can tell.'

'Right, right ...' Further unresolved problems resurfaced in Christian's mind, chief of which was the one of fashion. 'Why am I wearing these clothes?'

The old man lowered his clipboard. 'It's the rules, sir.'

'It's the rules that everyone has to wear a cheap suit, trainers and an AC/DC T-shirt?'

'No, it's the rules that everyone gets to wear their favourite clothes.'

'Yes ... *yes* ... I remember.' And he did. He'd only sketched them out, but Christian had decided it would be funny to dress the dead in their favourite clothes, such that the mechanism doing the dressing would misfire in a modern context, interpreting a wig as a hat, so long-time wig-wearers would have to spend eternity with their hairpieces bonded to their heads.

'So why, then, am I wearing these things?' asked Christian. 'These aren't my favourite clothes ... well, the T-shirt was, once, I suppose, as were the trainers, possibly, but not the suit, definitely not the suit.'

'But you wore each of these garments more than any other, sir, during daylight hours, so they must have been your favourites.'

'Well what sort of rule is that?'

'How else would you define favourite, sir?'

'Well can't you just sort of ... tell?'

The old man smiled and shook his head. 'I'm afraid we're not mind readers, sir.'

'But ... just look at me.'

'Believe me, I have seen far worse,' said the old man. 'And though there's the occasional anomaly these days, the system has worked well for us down the millennia.'

'Look, forget the favourite clothes thing, why not have people wear what they died in?'

'Oh that would never do, sir. Just think, what if you died in the shower? You might have to spend eternity making do with a face flannel. That would hardly seem fair.'

'Well ... why not let people choose what they wear?'

'We're not a gentleman's outfitters, sir.'

'Well ... well how long do I have to keep it on for?'

The old man did not reply straight away. 'Sir, my advice to you would be not to look too far ahead.'

'What, for ever? But I can't. I hate it, I can't wear this for ever.'

'Then why did you spend so much time in it when you were alive, sir?'

'I had no choice.'

'Ah, so you were forced to wear it?'

'Well, no, not exactly. I had to wear it for work. The suit, that is.'

'You must have loved your work then, sir?'

'Well, no, I hated it.'

'Oh, so you were forced to attend?'

'Well, not forced, as such.'

'So why did you go then?'

'Because ... because everyone else did.'

'"Because everyone else did"? Dear me, with respect, what sort of answer is that, sir?'

'Hey, now look, I'm not a bad person, why should I be punished? My only crime was to go with the flow, is that so bad?'

'Well, it's not for me to say, sir.'

'But it's for someone to say?'

'I'm sorry but can't divulge anything further.'

Christian kicked the door in frustration. It seemed surprisingly solid for something hanging in empty space.

'So what's through here then?'

'The afterlife, sir, or at least your journey towards it.'

'You really think I'm dead then?'

The old man nodded.

'Look, are you *sure*?'

'We're always thorough, sir.' He referred to his documents. '*Horribly mangled and squashed*, it says here.'

'But I don't believe in life after death.'

'Well, I'm afraid that's not terribly relevant. One can choose not to believe in the French, but that doesn't mean they're going to go away now, does it, sir?'

'But my ... my affairs aren't in order.'

'Affairs?'

'I hadn't finished my book. I hadn't finished switching our broadband provider.'

'Try not to worry.'

'But we'll have no internet.'

'Trust me, sir, such things matter little, now. Here, this should help answer any questions.' The old man handed Christian a folded papyrus leaflet.

'So I really am dead?'

'Indeed you are, sir. But don't worry, it often takes a bit of getting used to, you know, like getting divorced or starting a new job.'

'As traumatic as that?' said Christian.

'Oh yes. Now if I could have that signature?' said the old man, presenting the clipboard yet again.

'So what awaits me through there?' asked Christian as he signed. 'God, judgement?'

'I really can't say, sir.'

'Can't or won't?'

'Won't, sir.'

And with that, Christian opened the door and stepped through.

Chapter Nineteen

Christian's senses were coming back online. Once again, sound was the first messenger and once again it was the background sounds of London blended with nearby distressed voices. But this time he was aware of a chronological disorientation, a diffuse and sickening assertion from deep in his gut that he had woken from a sort of anti-sleep – a sense he'd been experiencing a block of time that the rest of the world had not.

There was smell now, too, that familiar dirty fumy urban fug, but now with coppery high notes.

'It's weird, isn't it? You can't look, but you can't look away either.'

'Well you could try.'

'Do you think we should try the kiss of life?'

'Um, no. Besides, you'd need to find a mouth to kiss first.'

'Yes, that whole area's a bit squashed. What about a tractorotomy ...'

'Tracheotomy.'

'... I've got my old Swiss Army knife. The blades are blunt, but the corkscrew's dead sharp.'

Vision was next to return. He could see clouds, bordered by a crescent of grimaced faces, some looking at him, some looking at their phones looking at him, plus one wide-eyed excited smile, peering in.

He was lying on the road at the scene of ...

And then he remembered. He remembered the thumb of approval from the taxi driver. He remembered crossing in front of the traffic and then the blast of the horn, turning to see the final moments of the hearse bearing down on him, the driver's expression of helpless horror.

He sat up. He sat up before he realised it might not have been a good idea to sit up. But he felt okay, a bit groggy, a bit smacked about, but no worse than a bad hangover. He shifted forward and got up. While not entirely stable, he'd managed it and felt a wave of relief. He felt insubstantial, definitely not all there, but at least he was in no pain, all in one piece, and up and about. A lucky escape, a minor miracle. He left through a gap in the crowd before glancing back at the scene of the accident. Then he stopped. The bloody, meaty mess was horrific enough, but Christian was doubly shocked because he hadn't realised someone else had been crossing as well. If it hadn't been for that poor soul, he'd surely have taken the full brunt of the hearse's impact.

'Don't move him,' said one of the onlookers.

'Has someone called an ambulance?' said Christian.

Everyone was either voyeuring, videoing or vomiting. No one seemed to be listening.

'Well I'm fine, anyway. Really, no need to worry.'

Christian turned to the hearse, which was sitting a couple of metres back from the impact site, its front dented, steam and fluids leaking. The driver was now being helped and videoed by his own gaggle of bystanders. Christian wanted to give him a large piece of his mind, until he realised the driver had already given a large piece of his to the windscreen.

Anyway, he needed to get moving. He needed to get to Bracknell. He looked over towards the black cab and was relieved to find it still there on the slip road, north of the junction. The driver was looking his way, too, staring blankly through him at the scene of the accident.

'Be right with you,' shouted Christian.

But again he stopped himself. Should he wait? He should probably give a statement. This was no simple insurance job; the poor lanky chap still lying on the road wasn't going to get away with a bump on the head and a few scratches: they'd be scraping him up with a spatula. There would be police. There would be an investigation. But he didn't have time to get involved, not today, not now. So he decided to slip away, assuring himself he could always make a statement later.

He struggled the few yards towards the cab. His progression was uncertain – unsteady and numb, like his legs had gone to sleep. Perhaps he'd been more badly injured than he thought? Dislocation? Fractures perhaps? Fuck it, he could worry about that in the cab. Okay, so it may get a bit painful when the endorphins wear off but that wasn't going to happen straight away. That was the new plan then: get to the church, set a date, head to the hospital. Sorted. A short hospital stay might not be so bad, in fact. Might help him focus on the writing, and surely it would buy him some brownie points with Bea. *Hero Braves Injury for Love*. Okay, don't get ahead of yourself. Focus. First off, get this cab.

With his growing suspicion of lower leg injuries and persistent sense of instability, he decided the best approach would be to prop himself against the black cab's large rear window, gather himself, and then open the door from there. But when he went to lean against the cab, he instead found himself falling mostly inside it and half inside the back seat.

What the fuck?

Had he opened the door? No, no it was closed. It was definitely closed. It was, wasn't it? Or was it open? Wide open and he'd fallen through? How could he not know? Concussion? Perhaps. That could be serious. Should he go straight to hospital? No. *No.*

'Bracknell please,' he said. 'Quick as you can.'

The driver continued to stare at the scene of the accident.

'Look, I'm in a hurry. I'm going to be late. Bracknell. A4, then M4.'

He tried to pull himself up out of the seat but was unable to get a hold of anything, like he was trying to grasp a projection. As he struggled, the opposite passenger door opened and a man poked his head in.

'You free, mate?'

'Yes, boss,' said the driver, snapping out of his trance.

'Hey, this is my cab,' said Christian, 'I was here first.'

'Greenwich, please,' said the man, getting in.

'No, that's the wrong way,' said Christian. 'Hey. *Hey.*'

The man stepped across, leaving the near-side seat for his female companion.

'Fucking hey,' shouted Christian.

The man sat down into the half of Christian that wasn't inside the seat.

Christian felt like he was going to be sick. Being inside a seat was bad enough, but now he was inside another man.

'This is my fucking cab,' yelled Christian, from between the man's lungs.

The driver indicated and shifted into drive.

As cab, driver, passenger and companion moved forward, Christian didn't. Instead, he found himself slipping out through the rear right corner of the cab as it sped off.

Now on the slip road, he got up and then got run over for the second time that morning, this time by a double-decker bus. Or rather he was run through, passing into the engine and gearbox, before taking a conveyor belt horror ride down the aisle, the feet of oblivious passengers skimming past his ears. Christian failed to react. He failed to shout. He failed to scream. He failed to get out of the way before being run through by two cars, a transit van of builders, and finally a Tesco home delivery van, before the traffic stopped.

His intellect grasped that none of the vehicles, or anything in them, appeared to be harming him, but that made it all the more terrifying because this sort of thing wasn't supposed to happen. The universe didn't work like this. But as he sat there in the road, in between the Tesco van and a Renault Espace, an even greater terror registered, the kind of mono-lithic terror that's powered by a surfacing truth that your unconscious has already accepted – for with each non-impact, the one reaction Christian had managed was to instinctively raise his hands in a futile attempt to protect himself and yet they had not obscured his vision. The hairs on his neck rose to spines as he held up his trembling hands. All he saw was the space they weren't in – thin air right through to the insects in the grille of the Espace. He traced back from the space where his hands weren't, to the space where his arms weren't, to the space where his chest and torso weren't, to the space where his legs weren't. And it all rang horribly true. A single penny made the longest of drops as he realised that the drivers of the cars, the transit van of builders, the driver of the Tesco van, not one of them had tried to stop, or even slow down; they hadn't seemed bothered at all; they hadn't even noticed, running him through to yawny indiffer-ence, idle chatter, or a wailing serenade snippet from 'Eye of the Tiger'.

Now he screamed. Long and loud. He held it. How he was able to scream with an apparent absence of lungs, or vocal cords, or all the other normally rather essential apparatus around the lungs and vocal cords? And how he was able to hear the scream? It was possible he did still have ears, he supposed, but then with no hands there was no way to check. Was he really screaming? He varied the pitch and volume. It certainly sounded so. He carried on for a while longer, looking up to the Espace driver, then over to the people at the accident scene, at the blocked lanes. He upped the volume. He hunted for eye contact. There were two dozen people only metres away. No reaction.

He stopped screaming. As the traffic began to move again, exiting up the slip road, he got to his feet. Or rather, he decided to get to his feet, which resulted in his point of view moving upwards, via a sort of forward and then rear moving arc, to a point roughly commensurate with where it would have been had he still had a body and had he decided to make that body stand up.

The traffic flowed through him again, but this time he didn't raise his non-hands; he didn't scream; he didn't get out of the way. He didn't know why, but he just stood there, letting himself get run through. Cars, another bus, more cars, and then, as the traffic slowed, a Shell petrol tanker, its brakes hissing and popping as it came to a stop around him. A snap of panic and he instinctively tried to close his non-lungs as the toxic bouquet of 95 RON enveloped him. He could hear the fluid sloshing at the tops of the baffles, in the absolute darkness, but felt nothing as it surely inundated the space he used to occupy. And with it came a cold realisation that something had gone terribly wrong with reality. Scrambling, he ducked his point of view down and out under the tanker and made his way to the pavement. He sat his point of view down, a torso and head's height above the kerb, to catch his breath, still not realising he had none to catch.

For a long while, he just sat there.

This is not real. This is not possible.

Soon his space was being invaded again, as a crocodile of teenage school children approached and passed through him, exposing Christian to snippets of chatter: Nelson and the Houses of Parliament, Buckingham Palace and West End shopping, reality TV and labiaplasty.

Revolted, he reversed his point of view back into the mouth of the small cobbled alleyway that ran between the railed terraced gardens that bordered the pavement. He was dreaming, that's what it was. He just needed to snap out of it. Perhaps if he closed his eyes, took a long moment, he would wake up from whatever this was. But much as he tried, he could not close his eyes, because he had no eyelids to close, or eyes for them to close over. So his point of view just hovered there, staring at the accident scene and the backed-up traffic, but taking none of it in.

He hadn't the faintest idea what to do.

Back in God's dining room, the gathering was beginning to break up. Tension had turned to satisfaction as they'd watched Christian first stop breathing and then stop twitching, all to a pool-of-blood backdrop oozing ever outward. There'd been a flutter of concern when the paramedics arrived, but when their brief focused efforts turned to exchanged micro-shakes of heads, everyone knew it was over. Cheers had broken out again, softer than before, and then a ripple of applause, which God accepted with a raised thumb held high in the air.

Twenty minutes later, half the guests had gone and the rest would soon follow.

'You'll keep me posted, yeah?' said God through his cigar-clenched teeth as he put an arm around Gabriel. 'Great result today, great result, knew we'd get him. I'm off for a bit of bowling with the lads. You'll be off to wait in Arrivals, yeah?'

'Yes,' said Gabriel, somewhat affronted but not altogether surprised. 'I suppose I will.'

'Great. Let me know the minute they bring him in, the minute.' God gave another thumbs up, winked and left the room. Moments later, the muffled sound of another chorus of 'We Are the Champions' reverberated through the wall.

Gabriel sloped over to the corner of the room where a shell-shocked Harold was still staring across at the crash scene still filling the flames of the window boxes. 'What's done is done,' said the archangel, placing a clawhand as softly as he could on Harold's shoulder. Gabriel wasn't sure if he'd been heard, but then Harold slowly turned his head and looked up.

'So what happens now?' asked Harold.

'Now the shepherds bring him in,' said Gabriel.

Harold turned back to the window boxes, for all like he was expecting to see them in the image in the flames.

'So do you want to help me collect him,' said Gabriel, 'from Arrivals?'

'Yes ... yes, I think I'd like that.'

'Good.'

'Would it be all right if I spoke to him first?'

'Absolutely not,' said Gabriel, 'he's still a dangerous rogue element, we're not out of the woods yet.'

'He's just another poor victim of circumstance. Like all of us,' said Harold.

'That doesn't make him any less dangerous,' said Gabriel, before turning towards the door. 'Anyway, shall we?'

'Beg pardon, now?'

'Of course,' said Gabriel. He pointed to the crash scene in the flames. 'He can't be more than a couple of miles from the Gate. They'll have him there in no time, which means we'll have him here in no time.'

'But the queuing time?'

'Well yes, that will add a bit extra, I suppose.'

'A good deal more than a bit.'

'Not really.'

'But it takes decades.'

'No,' said Gabriel, with a dismissive shake of the head, but then he stopped. 'Oh, I see what you mean, no, no, he won't have to worry about that at all.'

'But they'll never let him push in. I've seen what happens.'

'He won't have to push in. We're fast-tracking him. It's a separate queue.'

'Beg pardon?'

'There's a fast-track entrance, round the other side. Angels and approved guests only, of course.'

'You mean like first class?'

'If you like.'

'And it's faster I suppose.'

'Well yes, a fair bit. Can still take a good while though, when it's busy. Best part of forty minutes sometimes.'

'*Forty minutes?*'

'Well we're trying to do something about it, put on some more staff, but you know how difficult it is to make things happen around here.'

'Gabriel. Do you have any idea how long I queued for?' said Harold, his eyes wide. 'Out there in the Zone, day after day, year after year …'

'And what a good job you did. You'd still be out there otherwise.'

'I … I … unbelievable …'

'Anyway, let's get down there,' said Gabriel. 'A lot of people want to have a word with this Bootstrap fellow, myself included.'

By now Nikki was back in her car and holding off a rising urge to begin ramming the clogged London traffic.

Stay calm. He wouldn't have left if he didn't think he could make the meeting with Beatrice. So that must be an hour away, at least, plus he'd have to find transport. There was time. First thing, get back to Bracknell. The church must be near there, surely.

Navigate to – Point of Interest – Point of Interest in City – Bracknell.

… Parking Lot … Pharmacy … Place of Worship.

Fuck.

Even discounting the non-Christian entries, the candidates ran to two screens.

Christian's point of view was still in the cobbled alleyway. The only movement was the arrival of a slight back and forth rocking motion as what he still presumed to be his mind went around in circles. Was he still here? Or did he just think so? Was he still him? Or did he just think so?

He noticed something familiar in his field of vision, so familiar he was unsure how long it had been there. Skin-tone translucent curves, left and right, framing the continued defocused developments at the accident scene. As he looked down, the ghosts of his nasal flanks went with him like a head-up display. He saw knees in full frame. And as he saw, he realised for the first time since he'd been run over that he was in contact with a solid object: himself. He could feel his arms around his shins, his thighs pressing at his chest. He released his hands and held them out in front of him. Solid, undamaged, and what's more, they were connected to his arms, which were connected to his torso. With some trepidation, he brought his hands up and back, palms open to each other above his shoulders, like he was about to take a throw-in with his head. He began to bring his hands together, millimetre by millimetre, until, to his immense relief, he touched ears, hair, skull under skin. And then he was up on his feet, running his hands all over his head, face and neck, before executing a pat-down that would make Heathrow proud: genitals, torso, genitals, arms, genitals, legs, genitals. Everything was present; he wasn't in pain; nothing seemed to be in the wrong place or at the wrong angle; he wasn't pierced or leaking; everything felt solid, everything felt like him. He still felt woozy and had an inexplicable sense of being slightly shorter, but he didn't care, none of that mattered, because he was back – he was he once more.

He re-ran a less frenzied version of the pat-down, for reassurance more than anything else. But on checking his hips, a new flavour of panic shot through him – where was his wallet?

How? But … wait. Those fuckers, those fucking thieving onlookers …

He checked again, only for wallet-displacement panic to itself be gazumped by another new panic, a panic that stemmed from a far less familiar but far more disturbing realisation, the kind of discovery that leads to wild speculation of the darkest kind: in checking again for his wallet, he'd found polyester cotton blend instead of denim. His mind went fishing straight for long-shot explanations, there being no short ones with which to start.

Who would do this? Who changes the trousers of accident victims?

It didn't seem like a service the paramedics would offer, even if his jeans were bloodied beyond a boil-wash.

He scratched his beard, only to find it wasn't there.

What, but ... how?

Not only had someone taken his wallet and changed his trousers, but they'd clean-shaved him too.

What sort of wacko shaves accident victims? That was sick, sick and twisted.

And then he realised it wasn't just his trousers, it was all his clothes, and these new clothes were his old clothes, or at least the suit was – his old suit, last seen hanging on a poorly assembled flat-pack clothes rack in Bracknell. Was he still concussed? Had he put the suit on that morning for the trip to London? He was sure he hadn't. Plus, though he was no fashion guru, there's no way he'd have married it up with his old AC/DC T-shirt and grubby trainers – trainers he no longer even owned.

Even longer shots now came to mind. Could someone be playing an elaborate practical joke on him – fetching his suit from Bracknell, running him over, then changing his clothes and shaving him while he was unconscious, bleeding and mangled in the road? No, no that was beyond ridiculous.

Bleeding and mangled in the road.

Horribly mangled and squashed.

And then he realised. It was him, it was his body lying in the road. There was no second pedestrian. But then he was here. The guy in the road was over there, still over there somewhere in the middle of the crowd, wasn't he?

He stepped forward and then realised why he'd felt slightly shorter. He was ankle deep in pavement.

Oh fuck, oh fuck, oh fuck.

He stepped back with a sense of disgust, like he was escaping from twin cow pats, leaving him standing on – in fact slightly in – the cobbled surface of the alleyway.

He emitted a thin anguished cry.

He lifted each foot in turn. He could sense the uneven surface permeating his feet but it was more like balls of wire wool than stone. He bent down and lowered his right hand, his left clamping straight to his mouth as his fingers passed through the cobbled surface like it wasn't there. Yet he felt the lightly abrasive texture, its solid form, solid yet empty. He remembered his physics. All matter, even a solid block of lead, is almost entirely empty space. It didn't explain anything and yet somehow it rung horribly true.

More cries and then a thin whimper.

He stepped forward from the cobbles, at once unstable and revolted as he made his way back onto the pavement, pavement his feet were convinced had now been surfaced with three inches of good-quality candy floss.

An old woman approached with a Scottie dog.

'Excuse me, excuse me,' said Christian.

She continued towards him.

'Hello? Please, hello?'

Still no reaction.

'Please,' he said, moving across her path.

Faint prods and slices from her skeleton as she passed through him, and on down the street.

He dry retched, hands on knees, and then sat down, two blocks of candy floss pavement invading his buttocks.

Don't lose it. Do not lose it. There will be an explanation.

At least he was he, again. Yes, he was back, even if reality wasn't. Maybe reality would catch up later, just as he'd caught up later? Yes, there was no need to panic. Reality could catch up later.

Later.

Later.

Beatrice – the meeting, the vicarage. Could he still make it?

Think, think, think …

He needed transport, and quick.

Okay, this could be tricky: no wallet. No money. Possibly separated from reality.

What about hitching?

He stepped back into the road and made his way out between the cars of the stationary eastbound traffic. Once halfway, he waited for the westbound traffic to slow and stop. He braced himself before slowly dipping his arm and then his whole top half through the window of a spotless but ancient beige Volvo. After a quick scan, he stepped through the body shell into the unoccupied rear.

'... Ruth said if he painted it, she'd just paint over the top,' said Mrs Foley in the passenger seat, 'and guess what happened then?'

Mr Foley's eyes didn't shift from the road ahead.

'That's right, he painted it duck egg blue. Well, turns out Ruth quite likes duck egg blue, so kept her brush dry. They're still not talking though ...'

Christian thought back to the traffic running through him, how he'd not been able to stay in the taxi. But now he had his body back, now it might be different. He could feel the car, or at least its shadow – he just needed it to feel him.

Maximise the contact area ...

He pushed himself forward through the gap between the front seats and placed his feet on the rear seatbacks. Gritting his teeth, he extended his arms out perpendicular to his body, skewering the couple, to leave him in a prone crucifix position.

The engine note of the truck in front dropped. Christian braced himself, taking the gear knob into his mouth in a final desperate and degrading attempt to gain extra purchase.

The traffic started to move off. Mr Foley dabbed the accelerator. For a gentle chauffeur, Christian could not have chosen better. In the middle years of his marriage, Mr Foley's crown-green-bowls driving speed had been the only thing that allowed him sufficient time to counter the frequent impulses to steer him and his wife into oncoming traffic. And the plan seemed to be working as Christian felt himself edge forward with the car, but then even Mr Foley's wispy acceleration was soon enough to send Christian slipping back through the rear of the car, still in crucifix pose, as if a waterslide stage had been added to the stations of the cross. Once again he landed on and in the road, before getting run through by another train of vehicles, this time each dragging him a little, until the traffic stopped again.

He stepped out through a community minibus and made his way to the pavement.

All right. All right. Fuck it. Fuck it, fuck it, fuck it.

Fuck it.

He started running west along Marylebone Road.

Chapter Twenty

Half an hour later, Nikki was still driving the car hard as she approached the southern housing estates of Bracknell. She'd decided to switch strategy from the meeting to the step beyond the meeting. It was a gamble, but a better one than trawling random churches. At least this way she could be sure of crossing his path, assuming he'd make it alive, and it would buy her some thinking time, too.

Nearly there, nearly there.

She turned into Vestments and drove slowly but not too slowly past the little house and its empty driveway. She turned the car around and parked up, only to find herself immediately reversing back another thirty metres. She wanted to be closer but didn't want to risk Christian spotting her and doing a runner.

Okay. Relax. Breathe. Wait. Wait and think.

She still had no plan for what would follow. He'd made his choice; he'd called her bluff. So what now? Heavier persuasion, really lay on the eye contact and the lashes? Maybe it was even time to go all in. But what if he came back with Beatrice? That was a given, she thought, if Christian managed to make it to the church in time.

But then perhaps it was too late for the soft sell anyway, too late even for the hard sell. She placed her hands on the wheel and dug her nails into the leather. Many unsavoury options crossed her mind, most involving chloroform, drugs and duct tape; guns, knives and scenes from *Casino*. She would do what she had to do, of course, but where to even start with that kind of operation? She didn't move in those circles, she didn't even move in the circles that intersected those circles. She berated herself. It was always possible it would come to this. She should have been better prepared.

Christian had started in frustration and sheer unwillingness to accept the situation, but as he found himself making quick progress, he'd soon started to convince himself it might be possible. And at least now he was doing something, at least he had something to focus on.

He tried to picture the journey ahead. He thought perhaps it wasn't as far as it might first appear, and on foot he'd have no delays from traffic jams. What was the distance? Thirty miles? No, less, perhaps twenty-five. Wasn't that the length of a marathon? What was the marathon world record? He had no idea. He tried to think back to watching the London Marathon over his cornflakes, but never getting up early enough to see the elite athletes, all he could picture was everyday people in fancy dress on the verge of cardiac arrest.

As he passed the edge of Regent's Park and Park Crescent, the sight of a tourist map sign post made him realise he'd soon have to do some navigating. Christian was someone who knew routes instead of maps. He didn't know the quickest way from Marylebone Road to Bracknell – he didn't know any way from Marylebone Road to Bracknell – but he did know if he could find the A4, it would get him there. So he checked the map and picked a route south. It was only now he realised he was standing at the top end of Harley Street, metres from where he'd done his runner from Nikki. He thought about going back, about asking for help. But then there was no reason to think she could, or would.

Okay, then, new plan, next junction, then south on ... Baker Street ... yes, then ... then look for another map.

No time to rest. Off again, back up on the toes.

To begin with, he'd made efforts to duck and weave to avoid the drag, distress and disgust of passing through the general public. Likewise he'd taken care at the first junctions to avoid contact with traffic. He'd accepted that, for now at least, no physical harm would come from a collision, but that hardly made it all right. Plus with traffic there was now what he saw as the added risk of being caught inside it when reality returned, a prospect that brought to mind a Routemaster version of Jeff Goldblum's closing scenes in *The Fly*. But caution was slowing him down, burning seconds he didn't have. And so in no time at all he was passing through everything. His heart still sprang up to his tonsils every time he shared space with a vehicle, but he decided he could at least spare himself the terror of seeing them coming if he kept his eyes low to the pavement. So as Christian approached the junction with Baker Street, he only noticed the people queuing across it when he collided with them.

He bounced off and fell back, over and slightly into the pavement. Meanwhile, the impact sent shockwaves of quick shuffles through the packed ranks. Several people fell and one was forced out and over into the asphalt, close to Christian.

A storm of shouts and condemnation erupted.

'What do you think you are doing?' said the young woman. She spoke with what Christian recognised as an African accent, but didn't recognise as Nigerian. His assessment of her clothing was equally insightful, managing only *tribal traditional*.

'I'm so sorry,' said Christian, dazed but relieved at least part of reality was receiving him again. He now saw that the people were queuing right through the junction, despite the traffic flowing straight through them. 'You can see me?' he said, the statement emerging as a question.

'Of course we can fucking see you,' said a twenty-something chef a few metres up the queue. He spoke with a Dutch accent. 'Why don't you look where you're going?'

Christian got to his feet. 'Sorry, I didn't, er … I didn't … I just didn't.'

'Well you just watch yourself.'

Christian turned to help the woman as she was getting back to her feet. She was already being helped by others – though they all seemed to be more concerned with keeping their place – but he held out his hand and took her arm all the same. He was duty bound to assist, but in truth also wanted to check he could touch her, that she could feel him.

'Please take your hands off,' she said.

The woman's companions shouted to Christian to stay away and began gesticulating at him. They again seemed reluctant to move too far from the queue, and after pulling the woman back into the line they closed ranks.

'I didn't mean any harm,' said Christian, and he took half a step towards the queue.

'Get back,' said the chef.

A ripple of twitches ran down the queue, as in unison the whole formation took a step sideways towards Christian, and then back.

'He was trying to push in,' said the woman.

'I'm not trying to push in. I don't even know what you're queuing for.'

Titters of sarcastic laughter.

'Come on, boy, do you think we joined up yesterday?' said a young man in a tatty beige overcoat.

'Yeah, get to the back,' said the chef. 'Lousy freeloader.'

'Look, I don't want to join your queue,' said Christian, 'I just need to get past.'

'Fuck off,' said the chef, 'you're not getting in.'

'Perhaps he does just want to pass?' asked a young woman, standing near the chef. She looked and sounded Spanish, as far as Christian could tell.

'Yes, really, I just want to get through. I need to get to Bracknell.'

More laughter.

'Please, I must get past.'

'Why doesn't he go over the top?' came a voice from the back.

'Or underneath?' said another. 'Yes, he can go underneath.'

Everyone stopped talking. It was as if something heinous had been suggested. Only the low background drone of London remained.

'Through the ground?' asked Christian.

'What you frightened of, boy,' said the man in the overcoat. 'Or don't you want to get to Bracknell?'

All eyes were now on him.

'Let us be reasonable,' said the Spanish woman. 'He only wants to make his way. Have some heart.'

'No, he can go underneath, or he can fuck off,' said the chef.

'Okay, people, that's enough,' said a voice from farther up the queue, 'let him through.' The man had a convincing New York accent and was dressed in vintage American cop gear reminiscent of that worn by Sean Connery at the start of *The Untouchables*.

'What has it got to do with you?' said the chef. 'Always fucking interfering.'

'Sir, let the man through,' said the cop.

'Sir? *Sir*? For the millionth time, you're not a fucking cop any more, *Paul*, you're the same as the rest of us.'

'I still got this badge, buddy.'

'It's a picture of a badge, it doesn't mean anything any more, you fucking bonehead.'

'Don't mean I can't come back there and teach you some manners.'

'Oh yes, and lose your place? I don't think so, *Paul.*'

'Boys, boys,' said the man in the overcoat, 'let's let him by and be done with it.'

'I do not trust him,' said the Nigerian woman.

'Well I don't trust him either, but at least it'll move him on.'

'Let the man pass,' said the cop.

They all looked at the chef.

'You know what, do what you like,' he said. 'But don't say I didn't warn you.'

'Right, back up, people,' said the cop, 'let's make some room here.'

Several layers of the queue shuffled back and out, in a remarkably coordinated fashion, allowing a thin channel to form.

Christian could see a developing agitation in the rear of the queue. Heads were bobbing; entire segments seemed to have woken up and were now pushing back and forth. Closer to him, he could see feet nervously tapping and fierce glares burning into him.

The chef executed a sarcastic grand, wide sweep of his arm to indicate the path was clear.

Christian hesitated.

By now those ahead in the queue, off to his right, had turned and were now watching him, every face in the line, all the way up to where it curved through the junction and disappeared into Madame Tussauds.

'Come on then, boy, best make it quick,' said the man in the overcoat.

'Are you coming through or not, son?' said the cop.

Christian stepped forward and into the channel. He kept his gaze low, trying to avoid eye contact, but this only served to reveal more strangeness. For one, the Spanish woman was, like the man dressed as a cop, in fancy dress – a simple but impressive lace-edged burgundy gown. Stranger still was that the man in the overcoat appeared to have three legs. Like Jake the Peg, the man had his hands deep in the pockets of his coat, presumably to operate the additional appendage, but unlike Jake the Peg, leg three was making a poor attempt to blend in, matching neither appearance nor behaviour of its peers. While they were relatively static in their beige slacks and sheepskin slippers, the rogue leg was adorned with grey cotton trackpant and a Nike trainer, and was constantly fidgeting and shifting its position, as if it was itching to go for a hop.

As soon as Christian was halfway, he sensed the gap closing behind him like the returning Red Sea. He quickened his step but a stride later he felt a boot in the small of his back, then a blow to the base of his neck sent him headlong out the other side, sprawling onto the road and into the traffic flowing through the far side of the junction.

Before he could get up, the queue flicked at him, slamming into his backside and hurling him another five metres.

Shouts and abuse.

'Enjoy Bracknell,' a lone voice shouted, before letting slip more sarcastic laughter.

Christian picked himself up and turned back to the queue. Its ranks had re-formed and most of its members seemed to have gone back to their business, checking their places or up on their toes looking for movement ahead. The Spanish woman was looking his way though.

'Are you all right?' she called.

'I'm fine,' said Christian. He took a step towards her.

'That's close enough, boy,' said the man in the overcoat, as the queue twitched and flicked at Christian again.

'Yeah, you're going to Bracknell,' said the chef, 'so ... fuck off.'

The cop said nothing but was staring at Christian, arms folded.

'Thank you,' said Christian to the Spanish woman, before turning his back and resuming his journey.

He was shaken, confused and angry, but his immediate desire was to try to put the altercation out of his mind, to bury it. He was unhurt, he told himself – it was nothing, he'd had worse assaults during rugby at school. Besides, he didn't have time to do anything about it. What was there to do anyway? File a report with the splintered reality police?

The journey. Get out of London. Get to the vicarage. Recover his sanity on the way. His brain had other ideas, of course, and forced him to churn it over and over in his mind as he jogged on.

He found another tourist map sign post at the next junction and realised he'd overshot Baker Street. It didn't matter. Okay, next left, then straight down.

Gloucester Place was posh and professional, lined with puffed-up mini poplars, taking him back to his dash from Harley Street. That seemed a lifetime ago now. What he would give to be back there. What he would give to have not stepped into the car with Nikki that morning.

Spilled milk. Forget it. Focus.

Five minutes later he was approaching Oxford Street. His intention was to go straight on, farther south, but as he approached he saw another queue, again running across his path.

They were as tightly packed as before, groups of people from numerous races and cultures, with another sprinkling of eclectic outfits, their number this time boasting an airline pilot, several Angus Young impersonators, and a large group of Second World War recreation enthusiasts in Wehrmacht garb. As before, the traffic and other pedestrians moved freely through them, oblivious to their presence.

Not dead. Something else. Not dead. Something else.

He crept in for a closer look, hoping to spot a gap, hoping to find a way round. Looking left, the queue made its way as far up Oxford Street as he could see, gradually crabbing across to his side of the road, mashing in with the traffic, up onto the pavement and into the walls of the buildings. To the right it seemed to stretch out just as far, but here there was a channel between it and the buildings, the queue mostly occupying the far lanes of the road. Looking to the distance, the channel appeared to open out, too, as presumably the queue either curved away to the left or ended. He didn't want another confrontation, so the channel to the right was the only choice.

Get past, get around, then cut south.

Immediate claustrophobia as he made his way into the channel, the opening at the end of the street seeming to fall away as he realised it was farther than he thought. And as he made his way, he felt the queue's menace, its packed ranks ever-present in his peripheral vision, enveloping the standing traffic like Yorkshire pudding around sausages.

He shifted up a gear into a power-walk, but no faster.

Don't hang about. But don't stand out.

Head down, don't make eye contact, do *not* make eye contact.

And then a shout from the queue. 'Hey, hey, over there.'

He realised his mistake: he'd passed clean through a mungle of teenagers on the pavement.

'That's him, the tramp, he wants to push in.'

'Watch him.'

'He's gonna push in.'

And then he was running.

'We've had word, laddie, we've got your number.'

Shouts started coming at him from farther ahead as he ran along the queue's length; all eyes – all already facing his way – were now fixing on him as word spread faster than he could run. To his horror, he began to see agitation and movement ahead as swathes of the queue's members began stepping across in unison, over into the inside lane of traffic, close to him, wave fronts forming and flicking onto the pavement up ahead.

Faster, faster, got to move faster.

He tried to accelerate but it was like his clutch was slipping – he just couldn't translate his faster leg movements into greater speed.

The queue was now alive, no longer a line of shuffling individuals, but an unpredictable wrathful serpent, rippling waves shooting up and down its length.

And then it swiped at him.

A hard *thwap* on his ankles sent his weight forward and he almost fell, stretching his arms wide to catch his balance.

He was now hard over on the pavement, the queue having moved across to occupy the whole inside lane of the road.

Up ahead the channel was closing. He wasn't going to make it.

As he tried again to find an extra gear, a sledgehammer blow on his whole left side sent him flying from the pavement through the window of Boots and on into a promotional dental floss stand.

He got to his feet but before he could get his bearings, the queue smacked into him again, carrying him deep into the shop, over towards Foot Care and Plasters, before rushing out away from him like a breaking wave.

Now came a menacing chant:

> *One for the back! One for the back!*
> *One for the back! One for the back!*

He made for the far wall, sprint-staggering right through it, through the thick blackout of the bricks, and out into a shoe shop, and then on again through its wall, into another shoe shop, and then another, before bursting into the temporary daylight of a side street, across into the next building, and into the fat fryers at KFC.

Still the queue attacked, stabbing and flicking, and this time hands stretched out to grab at him, almost hooking his collar, trying to drag him back out with them.

> *One for the back! One for the back!*

One for the back! One for the back!

He kept running, driving on as hard as he could into the next shop, his panic compounded as he ran straight across the cavern of a wide stairwell, on through a bureau de change, and on again, running through people, walls, interiors and anything in his way until he shot out through the wine and spirits section of Sainsbury's and into a side road.

He kept running, belting headlong through the shadow-swipes of the traffic and taking a few swervy strides to edge him back onto the far pavement as he sped farther down Oxford Street, before grabbing a glance over his shoulder, with a second glance confirming he was no longer being pursued. He slowed, stopped and collapsed into the pavement.

The queue, now some forty metres away, was still lithe, still boiling with aggression as waves spiked up and down its length, but now it seemed satisfied with standing its ground, watching him as it flexed back and forth.

He pulled himself up out of the pavement and edged himself back into the wall of the building behind, all the while watching the queue, keeping it in his sights as he tried to gather himself.

The queue calmed as boil turned to simmer, jab to indifferent twitch. It stretched, shook itself down and repositioned itself. Soon all aggression had evaporated. The serpent was once again a simple if bloated queue of shuffling people.

Christian now realised he had emerged at Marble Arch, which he knew to be at the corner of Hyde Park. Before hitting Oxford Street, the queue had come through the arch itself, and through the park, its tail snaking out between the fountains and trees where it disappeared from view.

He considered his navigational options and found he didn't have any. The way south was blocked by the queue, and there was no way he was going to try to get through again. So he gathered himself once more and headed west along the road that bounded the top of the park.

Again he tried to put violence out of his mind and again his mind was having none of it. He told himself he didn't have the time or the desire to try to process what had just happened. Yet still he thought of nothing else as he plodded on. Not just the twin assaults he'd suffered, but the nature of who and what had attacked him: its scale, its bizarre makeup, and most of all, that wherever its members were from, and wherever they got their moral code, it was obvious they were dislocated from reality in the same way he was.

. . .

Bayswater became Notting Hill Gate, Notting Hill Gate became Holland Park Avenue, on and on, through Shepherd's Bush and down into Chiswick. Now more than ever he was aware he was burning time. He wouldn't make the start of the meeting – he had to be realistic. But then she wouldn't give up on him straight away, she'd hang on, she'd wait. And it was quite possible she'd moved to plus four and a half, maybe even plus five. There was still time, he had to believe.

Tony returned with more tea and a packet of Jaffa cakes.

'Still nothing,' said Beatrice, and she put her phone back in her bag.

'Dear me,' said Tony.

He put the tray on the table and retook his seat.

She picked up the deck of cards and began to shuffle them half-heartedly. 'I really thought he would be here,' she said. 'I was wrong. I've been wrong about everything.' She put the cards down and took out a tissue. 'I feel such a fool ...'

'Now let's not be hasty. Perhaps there's a simple explanation, perhaps he's just running late?'

'Oh he's always late. That's why I told him to be here at eight thirty, sharp.'

'You mean twelve thirty, sharp.'

'No, I mean eight thirty, sharp.'

'This evening?'

'This morning.'

'I don't follow. Our appointment was for half past twelve,' said Tony, looking at the wonky wall clock, now showing one twenty-five p.m., 'and that is when you arrived.'

'Sorry, the offset's got a bit out of control.'

'The offset?'

'Christian is always exactly thirty minutes late.'

'Well, everyone's late from time to time.'

'Christian's late all the time.'

'Surely not all the time?'

'Was he late for you, when he came to see you?'

'Well, yes, he was, now I think about it.'

'By thirty minutes?'

'I suppose it could have been …'

'It would have been. It's always thirty minutes. An exact half hour. That's what's so infuriating, he's so punctual in his lateness, like delayed clockwork.'

'I see.'

'It doesn't matter what for – a drink, dinner, job interview, charity fun run, funeral. Add exactly thirty minutes, there he is. There's only one thing in the world he'll never be late for.'

'And that would be?'

'Live comedy. He's terrified of being singled out, you see.'

'Right.'

'And that's why I know it's not a genetic thing, as he claims, because he's proved he can do it if he wants to, because he's never been late for a live comedy show, not once. So he can do it if the appointment is … important enough.' She wiped her eyes. 'Bastard.'

Tony passed the box of tissues and then the Jaffa cakes. 'You know, I'm rather a fan of live comedy myself,' he said. 'And it's funny you should mention the lateness thing.' He took his mug of tea and sat back. 'Now this is rather naughty, but between you and me, I take something of a guilty pleasure in being late for comedy shows. I really do, especially if I've been able to get a seat near the front, somewhere in the middle of the row. Do you know, even if I arrive in good time, I'll wait in the foyer until everyone's gone in and the show's started, and then make my entrance. There's something about the attention. Something about being singled out by the comic as I make my way through, the occasional trampling of toes, my whispered apologies. Yes, it's the attention, but I think piqued by everyone's assumption that it is attention I do not seek. It gives me, well, a rush. Do you think that's wrong?'

'I don't know. I don't really care. Can we please get back to me and Christian?'

'Of course, of course. So you were saying he thought it was a breakfast meeting? Now I don't normally meet parishioners for breakfast, but I suppose I could make an exception, lay on some tea and muesli or something?'

She shook her head as she dabbed her eyes.

'Perhaps a croissant then,' said Tony, 'or actually, the bakery in the shopping centre does these rather nice pain au choco–'

'No, Tony, listen. He's always thirty minutes late. Always. So I started compensating by giving him a time that was thirty minutes before the real appointment time. It was easy, I manage our diary, problem solved. Anyway, eventually he noticed something was up – the lack of glares, the absence of any *what kept you?* comments, prepped excuses never called into service, and once he twigged, he started making an adjustment himself, adding thirty minutes to the time I had given him, to work out the real appointment time and taking us back to Christian being a consistent thirty minutes late.'

'Yes. Um, I still don't see how this gets us to breakfast?'

'It gets us to breakfast, Tony, because I countered. Instead of giving him a time that was thirty minutes early, I'd give him a time that was an hour early, which fixed the problem, but again eventually he twigged, and well, you can fill in the rest.'

'Now I see. A sort of time-management arms race?'

'Exactly.'

'So you're telling me you give Christian appointment times that are, let's see …'

'Four hours before the actual time,' said Beatrice. 'I think he's still on a three and a half hour adjustment, but it's hard to be sure.'

'Why so?'

'Well, it's not like we talk about it.'

'You don't talk about it? How could you not?'

Beatrice shook her head. 'You don't really know anything about relationships, do you?'

'Yes I do. I've done courses.'

'But not much practical experience?'

'Well, I–'

'No, of course not. It's the whole celibate thing, isn't it.'

'That's just the Catholics, Beatrice. I'm not celibate, I'm just single.'

'Oh. Right. So do you have your eye on anyone in the congregation?'

'Not appropriate.'

'Ah, some lady vicars then?'

'Well no, it's not like that.'

'Oh. Male vicars then? Of course there's nothing wrong with–'

'No, it's–'

'Not … oh not the boys, Tony? Please not the boys.'

'No!'

'Oh yes, silly me, that's just the Catholics again, isn't it.'

'Look, I think we're getting off topic,' said Tony as he grabbed a Jaffa cake. 'Now from what you've said, it sounds like he may well still show up, so I think you need to give Christian a final chance.'

'I suppose so,' she whispered through fresh tears.

'Good,' said Tony.

She dried her eyes. 'But are you sure I'm not keeping you from anything?'

'No, no, bit of a free day actually.' He took the cards and gave them a shuffle. 'Now, how about we up the ante. What shall we say, five pounds a round?'

Christian had finally found the not-so-straight-and-narrow path of the A4. And when the A4 gave birth to the M4, the ramp to the raised roadway lifted Christian and his spirits. He put on a fresh burst of speed knowing at least his navigation woes were behind him. There would be fewer little victories now, though. So far, he'd managed to keep himself together by focusing on each tiny bit of progress, each junction passed, each new street or road, and by celebrating the sight of every encouraging road sign. You climb the impossible mountain by focusing on your feet, not the summit. But also integral to his progress had been his decision to resist all temptation to check the time. On some level he knew if he did, he'd have to accept how late it was. So in the miles he'd put under his belt already, he'd not looked at one car dashboard; he'd not popped into a single office, shop or front room. But his irrational discipline was obliterated a short way along the M4, when the dirty-white EMC Tower, and its immense clock face, hove into view. He managed to see it before he saw the time and dipped his head straight to his feet. And he managed to ignore it for a long while as he approached. He knew it well from numerous trips back from London over the years. It took long enough to clear by car, but on foot it would stick in the field of vision for an age. It was like trying to walk past the moon.

Still there …

Still there …

Still there …

In the end he couldn't do it. Before he'd even clenched his fists, his eyes had already flashed up to take in the hands' message.

Two twenty p.m.

Two twenty.

He sped up, rising to a full sprint. He held his pace, arms thrusting, knees pumping.

Two fucking twenty.

And then he slowed.

And then he stopped.

He stood and stared at the clock face, still there, now full in his vision. This wasn't a tower with a clock, it was a tower for a clock, the subordinate roof following the curve of the huge round face to arc out a semicircle. Its sole purpose was to tell the time. There was no bell, but it tolled for Christian all the same.

He moved out of the lane and sat down on and slightly in the thin strip of concrete next to the barriers. Knees up in front of him, he hugged his legs.

It was done.

For a long time, he just stared at the huge numberless face and the Heathrow planes overhead as his mind entered a holding pattern.

He couldn't be dead. He didn't feel dead. It wasn't possible. This was something else, something weird. Perhaps it was to do with dark energy or the Higgs boson.

As he fidgeted with his lapels, he felt a sharp edge on a rough surface inside his jacket. He looked down and saw a folded piece of paper poking out of his inside breast pocket. He gently pulled it, half expecting a surge of pain, though unsure why, but it came free with ease. The paper was grainy, like the cheaper recycled stuff, and it was almost but not quite A4 in size.

He opened it up …

The Afterlife: An Introduxion for the Recently Deceased

1. Death

You have died. Your time in the Mortal Realm has come to an end.

2. The Wandering Spirit Zone

Once you have passed through the Door/Tunnel of Light* you will enter the Wandering Spirit Zone. This realm occupies almost the same space as the Mortal Realm, so things will feel familiar. You may remain in this realm for as long as you wish, though you are advised to proceed to the Gate once you are all present and correct.

3. Contact with the Living

Please do not attempt contact with the living.

Thank you for your co-operaytion.

* Manifestaytions are based on unconscious preference and may vary.

Instant heat through his core, rising up his gullet and out through his cheeks. He needed some air. He needed a clear head.

He stood and began to take off his suit jacket, but as soon as he started, he realised he already knew, somewhere in the back of his mind, it may not be possible. And he was right, déjà vu pain scribing lines down the sides of his chest as he found the limits of freedom.

He was shocked. He told himself so. His jacket was bonded to him; he couldn't take it off – this was an objectively shocking thing.

So why didn't he feel …

How? How had he known?

It was like his unconscious was laughing at him, revelling in a sick private joke.

'This is fucking bullshit.'

He took the leaflet and tore it up, ripping it over and over, before tossing the pieces into the air like homemade confetti. Instead of falling, they hung in space, buoyant as dandelion seeds.

He swiped at them, trying to get them down to the surface of the hard shoulder, trying to instil in them a proper sense of respect for the laws of physics, but the more he thrashed, the more they seemed keen on staying aloft.

'Fucking bits. Get down, fucking get down.'

Eventually he stopped and took a moment before serving them a brief scream.

He turned and resumed his march.

Out in the western Atlantic, two figures were on a journey that dwarfed that of Christian's. After good early progress, they were now hampered by a violent storm, far worse than the one they'd encountered after leaving Foz and his couch. The fishing fleets were long gone. Even the tankers and container ships seemed to have charted safer courses.

'Let's rest up,' said Hotswap.

'We continue,' said Mitch, maintaining his drift.

'Can't even navigate properly.'

'I can,' said Mitch.

They pressed on.

Chapter Twenty-One

Harold and Gabriel had been on the security gantry above the crumbling old amphitheatre for three hours, scanning the zombie conveyor belt that was the never-ending supply of bewildered faces. It was always the same at Arrivals. Souls would materialise to sparks of static at the oak-and-sandstone turnstile, at the western end, each encrusted in brilliant-white blacenta, stumbling and staggering into their new plane of existence. Most would fall to the stony ground after a few heavy steps; none ever managed more than six. Sometimes they would look back to the turnstile, from the ground, and with incredulity to the great wall of jasper, beyond; sometimes they would look forward to the field of white detritus littering the ground before them; some would lift their eyes further to the noisy crowds beyond the bannered barriers, perhaps in search of a familiar face. Distress, disorientation, processing, and everywhere a sweet stale odour that bore through all attempts to mask it with oils and perfumes.

Occasionally, Angel Field Ops agents would come through, materialising at the same turnstile but not breaking stride as they emerged to make their way disdainfully through the human wreckage of the amphitheatre floor and on down to customs. Mostly agents came alone or in pairs, but sometimes they arrived escorting a fast-tracked arrival, raising false alarms for Gabriel and Harold as the call went out for porters.

Regular megaphoned instructions filled the space, momentarily masking the cries and moans of the Kingdom's newest residents as they felt gravity, temperature and matter for the first time in a long time.

Your disorbrianation will pass.

Keep moving, keep moving.

Crawl if it's easier.

This was Harold's first visit since his own arrival. Barely a dozen weeks had passed and yet it had seemed an age ago until today. Harold closed his eyes and allowed that sweet stale odour to register. Now he was back down there, crawling the long stony crawl, stripped of those with whom he'd spent a second lifetime queuing; his clothes transmogrified to a lime-wash white crust, like he'd been dipped in plaster of Paris, his now-white Oxfords and moustache extensions already in pieces on the ground.

For longer than a decent lifetime, he'd longed for his own space, longed to be free of his companions, to be free to set his own course. But in this first moment, cast away here, alone, all he wanted was to have them back. It was made worse by material matter spurning him, too. He'd felt the stony ground under his feet the moment he'd stepped through, but only now, crawling against its face, did its unnatural and callous solidity hit home. For so long he'd enjoyed that special material intimacy of the second age, but now it refused him like a disillusioned lover.

Like many, he tried to get back to his feet, to defy the indignity of the crawl. With effort, he managed to sit up on his knees. He took a moment to gather himself, before lifting and planting his right foot in readiness to stand.

A millstone rumble from behind. A beat and then a shove in the spine sent him back to the ground, this time followed by a second smack as the shover bounced off him, elbows sharp in his shoulder blades. He turned to see a woman lying next to him, clothing as white and stiff as his. Was it Freda? No. There was recognition, though, a face from farther back, a few hundred places, perhaps. Too far to have known but near enough to have exchanged glances at a loop or an info stop.

'Are you all right, madam?' he said.

She turned her face towards him, scraping it along the ground in a way that made him wince.

Her eyes stared out beyond him.

He stretched out a heavy hand to her shoulder. 'Are you hurt, madam?'

Another rumble from the turnstile and then searing pain as what felt like a rhinoceros in stilettoes trod on his calf before falling on top of him, crushing him once more, this time enveloping him, bringing back distant memories of school rugby scrums and more recent dark panic. After a frantic wriggle, this second person dismounted. The man, thickset and cloth-capped, and as whitewashed as the rest of them, didn't acknowledge Harold or the woman and instead just embraced the rocky surface, licking and lapping at it in a manner that lay towards the opposite end of the Kinsey Ground-Greeting Sensuality Scale to where one may find the pope and asphalt.

Harold began to crawl forward, the lower halves of his mummified trousers now drainpipes at his ankles, revealing long-lost knees and legs.

Approaching breathless chatter caused him to lift his head. Four people carrying a sedan chair were careering towards him, but soon passing by.

'Annie, Annie,' they shouted, 'you made it, you made it.'

He looked back to see them help the wide-eyed woman up onto the seat, prop her head with a pillow, and spirit her away.

He struggled on. All the while more arrivals behind, more rescue parties in front. But not for him.

Soon he was slowing.

A few more yards and he could go no further. He stopped, slumped and rolled onto his back.

From behind his eyelids, he sensed a shadow. He lifted his hand and opened his eyes to see a figure in silhouette. Short stature. Light frame. Huge wingspan.

He'd come a long way since then, of course, but not all for the better.

Gabriel glanced at the clock in the window box flames once again. He mumbled some words of discontent before flexing his shoulders and flicking his armwings to half span, startling Harold.

'Is it possible we missed him?' asked Harold.

'No,' said Gabriel, 'not with an escort, and besides, customs and processing have been alerted. There's no escape once he gets here.'

'Well, could he have emerged in one of the other places?'

Gabriel shook his head and turned to lean back on the rail, his armwings spread wide against the wood. 'I know it's already been a long day, but think for a moment, will you. If he came through and went lower, we'd know because his escorts would still have arrived here, empty clawhanded.'

'Oh yes, I see what you mean,' said Harold, 'unless they went to a lower place too.'

'The escorts?' said Gabriel. 'I don't think so.'

'But it is possible, isn't it? You said they're subject to the same rules as everyone else, or does all that get waived in first class?'

'The fast track is just a queue, Harold. Judgement is universal, like the laws of nature. If the plane goes down, being in first class isn't going to save you.'

'Right.'

'Well, actually that's not strictly true,' said Gabriel, rolling his shoulders, 'there are some exceptions.'

'Terry?' said Harold.

'Well yes, the creator gets blanket immunity, naturally. If that wasn't the case, we'd never keep getting his boy back. Still, you can't have everything. But there are some further subtleties.'

'I believe I read something on that in the guide,' said Harold, 'because of the changes after Boot Out the Devout?'

'Well yes, but then even before that there had to be exceptions. You think about it. In those days, if you didn't have faith, well, that was an express ticket downstairs. But if you were to apply that judgement to returning angels, you'd be condemning every single one of them.'

'Why? Surely they'd still have faith?'

'Not at all. They were born in Heaven, they'd seen the evidence. How can you have had a pasty and cigar with the Almighty and still have faith that he exists? You know he exists.'

'So, angels didn't get judged on return?'

'Oh we got judged all right, on all the other stuff. Can't have angels running amok in the Zone, snaffling vases, coveting donkeys and what have you, and then popping back up to Heaven, no questions asked. No, no, we were subjected to the same rules as everyone else, still are, but in those days the requirement for faith was waived if you were a returning resident of Heaven.'

'Ah, I see … and now?'

Gabriel straightened up and stretched his armwings to half span. 'Well of course now we sort of have the same in reverse. As you say, following Boot Out the Devout, the general rule these days is that if you believe in a life beyond the Gate, if you believe in Heaven and in Terry, then you don't get in, *unless you're a returning resident of Heaven.*'

'I see ... because they couldn't very well not believe in him, once they'd met him?'

'Exactly,' said Gabriel. 'Took us a while to work it out though, when we first changed the rules.'

'Really?'

'Oh yes. Sorry episode. Two hundred and forty angels got sent down on return, because of the missing exception clause – sent to another place for belief in Terry. They didn't have a leg to stand on, poor fellows. But then we tweaked the settings a bit more, waited for them to kick in, and well, got it working.'

'So could Bootstrap have tricked them then? Got them to commit a sin, got them sent down on other criteria?'

'Well, all right, I'll grant you it's possible, but he'd have had to get up pretty early in his ethereal body to have caught us out like that. Honestly, what would he have said? "Alright fellows, I'll come quietly, but how about a bit of larceny before we go?" No, no, we're too experienced.'

'But the escorts, they're just guard angels, aren't they? Well, I'm sure they're accomplished at what they do, but perhaps they're, well, not blessed with quick wits?'

'You're clutching at straws, Harold. No, it's something else. In fact, we've given it long enough. It's time to ask some questions.'

Half an hour later, a runner arrived along with the strident Head of the Happy Fluffy Pansies.

'What's this all about then, sir?' asked Pringle. 'You have rather dragged me away from the celebrations.'

'Bootstrap,' said Gabriel. 'He's not here yet.'

'Right. Went to another place did he?'

'No, we've discounted that.'

'Right.'

There was a pause.

'The only explanation,' said Gabriel, 'is that he's not been delivered yet, to the Gate.'

'Okay.'

There was a longer pause.

'You don't seem overly concerned,' said Gabriel.

'Oh I wouldn't say that,' said Pringle. 'Let's see, how would I put it, oh yes, *concerned but not involved.*'

'Not involved?'

'Well no, sir. Our job was to relocate him. And he has been relocated. Comprehensively. The shepherds do the collections.'

'Under your direction.'

'No, under your direction. They don't work for me.'

'But we directed them to your direction,' said Gabriel.

'When?'

'On Tuesday, when we sent two dozen of them to Virginia What-sitsname.'

'In response to us giving you the relocation location ...'

The breast plumage at Gabriel's shirt collar ran pale.

'... just like last night, you'll have moved them into London, I assume?' said Pringle.

'What, but–'

'When I gave you the details of the plan.'

'Now wait just a–'

'And sent you the message with the address detail this morning.'

'No, no,' said Gabriel, 'that was just for our information, so we could watch. You were supposed to update the shepherds.'

'How would we do that?'

'Well, you can talk to Field Ops just as much as I can.'

'Nice try,' said Pringle with a chuckle, 'but you're not getting me on that one, sir.'

'Great Garbok-Glit,' said Gabriel, clenching his clawhands.

'So hold on,' said Pringle, 'you're telling me you've got twenty-four shepherds twiddling their thumbs in Virginia Water and no one at the death site?' He rocked on his heels. 'Oh that is good, that is classic, just wait till I tell the lads.'

'Runner,' shouted Gabriel. He turned to the service desk. 'I need a runner.'

Chapter Twenty-Two

Beatrice had parked up in Vestments having cried most of the way home. She'd waited with Tony for more than three hours. And in all that time he hadn't even let her know he'd made his choice.

Still in the car, she sat looking over at the house, at her house. Now she realised how much there would be to sort out. Shared possessions, shared photos, shared everything. It was finished. It was all over.

Tears welled again.

Oh God, that bastard. Why couldn't he have just turned up? Why did he have to push her into pushing him? She took a handful of tissues and held them to her eyes.

She took a minute to gather herself, before leaving the car and making her way up the drive. Her hand went for the door. And then she stopped. What if he was in inside? Back from London, back from his fucking meeting about his fucking book. No doubt planning to apologise his way out with KFC and Kronenbourg. Okay, whether he was there or not, she'd get in, get some things and get out. No conversation, no scene. What then? Where then? Lottie's. Lottie's or Claire's. Yes.

She tried the handle. Locked. A surge of adrenaline as she realised what she wanted now more than anything was not to see him today, to be out and gone before he got back.

Quick, quick, quick.

She fumbled with her keys, opened the door and stepped inside.

A week. Take enough for a week. No coming back tomorrow or the next day, no way.

She went into the kitchen and pulled her phone charger from the socket, then ducked into the living room. The bedding from the spare room was still on the sofa. Lazy bastard.

She took her iPad and the charger.

Anything else here? No.

She ran upstairs and pulled her luggage from under the bed. She began packing. Bedroom first, then bathroom. Quick, quick, quick.

Nine minutes later she was done. Should she leave him a note? No, fuck him. She lugged the bags to the top of the stairs and began taking them down. On the fifth stair, the doorbell rang. She left the bag and went down to answer. She could see two dark-dressed figures through the frosted glass. She opened the door.

'Beatrice Brinner?'

She nodded.

'Could we come in?'

Nikki opened the car door and leaned out again. Again her stomach muscles contracted and again she braced, but this time she didn't add to the vomit on the kerb.

Only minutes earlier she'd been running through the implications after seeing Beatrice return alone: possibly a good development, possibly a grave one. But when a police car drew up, it meant only one thing.

She returned her forehead to the steering wheel. Purpose had died. Her life had been wasted.

'Will you please tell me what's going on?' said Dexter.

'Nothing. I'm fine,' said Gordon, from the other side of the door.

'You're not fine, Gordon, people who are fine don't break off mid-sentence to flee for paperclips.'

There was no reply.

Dexter took hold of the handles again, but hesitated.

'I just needed a minute,' said Gordon, eventually.

'You've been in there ten.'

A pause.

'Well it's a nice cupboard,' said Gordon.

'I don't doubt it, Gordon, but you'd be a lot better off out here. Come on, whatever it is, let's talk it over.'

No reply.

'Look, I'm coming in,' said Dexter.

Still no reply.

'I'm coming in. Okay?'

He waited another ten seconds and opened the door. And then he stopped. Momentary vertigo as his eyes revised their expectations for the dimensions of the space beyond the frame. They found the far wall and located left and right with flicks of the head. Then they looked up, then up, then up.

He'd been meeting Gordon in his office for more than thirty years, and he'd often seen Gordon nip into the cupboard for some papyrus or a pack of pencils, but he'd never ventured in himself, he'd never needed to. And besides, what was there to see? It was a stationery cupboard. Walk-in, yes, but then so were the ones in any of Limbo's larger offices. But then there's walk-in and there's *walk-in*. This was hold-a-major-tennis-tournament-in. It was immense, many times larger than the office it was connected to, and Gordon's office was big. Dexter ran his eyes along the perimeter of the space, mentally picturing the rooms and corridors that must logically be on the other sides, realising they were spaces he knew well and feeling stupid that he'd never once questioned what should have been obvious as an enormous unaccounted for void sitting within the structure of the building. Unaccounted for, but far from empty: multilevel, multi-row, shelf after shelf, packed with every conceivable stationery item. Inkwells, ink, quills; pencils, rubbers and rulers; drawing pins, corkboards and paperclips; envelopes in every size; foolscap folders, dividers and binders; carton after carton of correction fluid; and of course papyrus, boxes and boxes of the stuff in endless weights, shades and sizes, piled to the ceiling in great columns. And, just in from the entrance, a small grey free-standing shelf with a little of everything.

Dexter was in such awe it took him a moment to remember what he'd come in for.

'Gordon? Gordon?'

Silence.

But then came a thin 'here' from just inside the door.

He turned to find Gordon on his hands and knees, caftaned buttocks up to the heavens as he hugged the last reams of a stack of A4 210 gsm.

'What's this all about, Gordon?'

Dexter bent down and carefully prised his boss's hands away from the stack.

'Mine,' said Gordon.

'I'm not here to take your pappy,' said Dexter, 'it's me, I'm here to help, whatever the problem is, just tell me.'

Gordon looked up. His vacant eyes, partly obscured by a matted curl that had come free from his daffodil hair slide, eventually gave way to recognition. He slowly turned round, edged over and sat down on the carpet tiles, his back to the wall.

'Why did you run away and hide?' asked Dexter.

'A leader must project calmness and control at all times.'

'You're only human,' said Dexter, without thinking, 'Sorry, I–'

'Doesn't matter,' said Gordon. 'Nothing matters.'

Dexter sat down next to his boss.

'I saw things as they really are,' said Gordon, 'just for a moment.'

'What do you mean?'

'A cold flash of reality.'

'And?'

'And it's all hopeless.'

'What is?'

'Everything.'

'Everything?'

'Everything.'

'There's no meaning to any of it,' continued Gordon. 'We're doomed. Doomed not to be doomed. Same thing every day. Meet our targets, set some new ones, meet our targets, set some new ones. We get up, we plan, we work, we host or attend networking events, we work, we allocate six or seven minutes' quality time to our loved ones, we work, we go to bed. Then we do it all again. And again, and again, for ever and ever …'

'We all get jaded, from time to time,' said Dexter, 'and you have been hitting the office extra hard lately.'

'You don't understand,' said Gordon, digging his thumbs into his cheekbones, 'you can't understand, you've only been here a blink.'

'I've been here nearly forty years, Gordon, forty years is still–'

'A blink.'

Dexter said nothing.

'But then I've only been here a blink too,' said Gordon. 'That's the rub, you see ... and I've been here since the beginning.'

'I don't follow,' said Dexter.

'Listen,' said Gordon. He pointed to six long empty shelves. 'Look, look over there, you know what those spaces are for?'

'No.'

'Toner cartridges.'

'But ...'

'Exactly. I know what you're thinking, you're thinking we don't have toner cartridges here, because we don't have photocopiers in here.'

'Well what about–'

'Not some wooden crate holding six sweaty scribes, I mean real photocopiers, like the mortals have.'

'Well no then.'

'But we will.'

'Well hang on, we've barely got our printing press working, we don't have electricity, we don't have proper tools and manuf–'

'That's precisely the point. It's a long, long way off, but it will happen. One day we will have all those things, and one day we will have photocopiers, we will have laser printers, we will have combination printer-fax-scanners.'

'But that'll be a good thing,' said Dexter. 'Think of the efficiency.'

'Of course it'll be good, it'll be fucking Disneyland, but that's not the problem, is it?'

'And what is the problem?'

'That there will be something else to take its place, something else to try to make, to strive for. There is no escape. There is no end.'

'Well, no, I suppose not.'

'At least the mortals get to die,' said Gordon. 'Only you don't, do you, not really.' He turned to Dexter. 'Was it at least delicious to retire? To stop?'

'I never got anywhere near.'

'Is that right?'

'I died when I was twenty-six.'

'Really? I didn't know. I suppose I never asked.'

'Doesn't matter. It was a long time ago.'

'Well what about death then? Was the illusion of death sweet while it lasted?'

'It wasn't an illusion. I still died.'

'Yes, yes, I mean an end, the prospect of oblivion, while you were a mortal?'

'Death seems an awful long way off when you're twenty-six, Gordon. I never spent much time thinking about it.'

'Balls, man. You savoured it and you loved it.'

'I didn't.'

'You did. Admit it.'

'No. I–'

'Imagine … just imagine getting to say it.'

'Say what?'

'Getting to say, "I'm done".' Gordon raised his arms aloft. 'I'm done.'

'Look, Gordon–'

'But we can't, can we? Not now, not ever. We're trapped, Dex, bogged in this infinite cavern in an infinite universe until the end of time, and even then there's no guarantees, is there? Maybe there is no end of time, maybe it just goes on and on and on and on … and on and on and on and on …' Gordon stared up into the ceiling of the cupboard, far above them. 'You know the old joke about eternity?' he asked.

'No, no I don't think I do,' said Dexter.

'Well, it's…' Gordon followed with what seemed like an infinitely long half word, 'loh.' He held its tail in one continuous tone, his posture, expression and gaze frozen, as if his system had glitched. He held and held and held, continuing the tone for a full minute, before releasing with a gentle slide into a brief 'ong'. *Eternity. Was. Long.* He looked at Dexter and released a long bellowing laugh that trailed off into a sort of high whinny.

'Let's go back into the office,' said Dexter, 'back where it's comfortable.'

'Yes. Yes, in a minute. I just need a minute.'

'Of course, Gordon.'

'A minute on the carpet tiles.'

'No problem.'

'They're more woollard than you'd think.'

'Well. Yes.'

'I have them in my bedroom, you know.'

'Um, good for you, Gordon, good for you.'

As they sat in silence, taking in the magnificence of the structure, Dexter found himself beginning to see why his boss might venerate this space. Now they were sitting quietly, he found it fostered an unexpected calm. This place housed the fuel of work, the tools of toil, and yet it was all so still. The soft scent of long-stored papyrus, the sandalwood of the shelves, the subtle spice of rubber that registered high in the nostrils.

'It's a good cupboard, isn't it?' said Gordon, eventually.

'Indeed it is,' said Dexter. 'I've never seen anything like it.'

'Do you know,' said Gordon, 'I've got one hundred and thirty-four thousand years' worth of staples on those shelves, give or take.'

Dexter glanced up at the rows and rows and rows of little boxes. 'I never thought I could be impressed by stationery,' he said.

'You better believe it,' said Gordon. 'I ordered seventeen thousand cases at the start.'

'My oh my, that's a staggering amount for one person.'

'Not when you'll be around for ever.'

'Fair point.'

'I've barely dented it, but believe me, one day it'll all be gone. One day I'll run out. That's why I don't bother messing around with small orders.'

'That's perfectly sensible, it's … business efficiency.'

'But then there is no order that isn't too small. That's the problem …'

'Gordon, really can we–'

'I could have ordered a million cases, a billion. Would make no odds, I'd still get through them eventually.' Gordon stood. In silence, he ran his eyes along and up the rows.

'Come on, we're going back into the office,' said Dexter, standing.

'All this stationery, it's laughing at me, Dex.'

'Oh I don't–'

'Would you like some? You'd be helping me out. Consumption is the only language it understands.'

'Um.'

'Come on, what are you short of?'

'Nothing, Gordon, I–'

'What about envelopes?' Gordon picked up a large box of them and forced it on Dexter.

'I'm already well stocked,' said Dexter.

Gordon piled on another.

'Really, that's enough,' said Dexter, struggling with the weight.

'Don't be such a girl, plenty more where that came from,' said Gordon, and he went for another.

'Really, no, look, stop, Gordon, please, stop – stop.'

Gordon stopped.

'I don't need any more,' said Dexter.

'Really? You don't need this one?' said Gordon, flicking his eyes to the box in his hands. 'Neither do I.'

He put the box down, ripped it open, grabbed two armfuls of envelopes and hurled them up with a cheer, sending them showering down over Dexter.

'Right, what else do you need?' asked Gordon, turning to another shelf.

'Gordon, really, I–'

'Paperclips. Yes. Paperclips.'

'I don't want any, Gordon.'

Gordon reached into an open box, took a single paperclip and held it out. 'Here,' he said, 'you can have this one,' and laughed hard.

'I'm not in the mood, Gordon,' said Dexter, and he put down his boxes.

'All right, I'll be serious. You can have two.' He laughed again.

Dexter didn't.

'Take some paperclips, Dex.'

'I don't need any.'

'Everyone needs paperclips ...' Gordon picked up a large handful. 'Take my paperclips,' he said, thrusting them out.

Dexter was about to suggest, once again, that they should return to Gordon's office, but before he could get the first syllable out, he was struck by a hailstorm of tiny bits of hand-bent metal, stinging his face and eyes.

'Take my paperclips,' blasted Gordon, as he began to rain down handful after handful onto his assistant.

'Gordon, what the fuck are you–'

Next came a volley of liquid-clay highlighters and mini notepads, before things got serious with Gordon launching metal-edged dividers, spinning and whipping them in hard as they chopped into Dexter's hands and forehead. All he could do was curl into a ball and try to wait it out.

'Now what did I do with those experimental typewriters?' said Gordon.

Dexter braced and waited.

And waited.

And waited.

But the attack did not resume.

And then a cannonade laugh from Gordon, a little farther away now, interspersed with sounds of straining.

Dexter opened his eyes to see Gordon braced against one of the huge columns of papyrus, his shoulder into it and his hands down low like he was about to toss a caber.

'No,' shouted Dexter, 'Gordon, please, no!'

One big heave and it was teetering, rocking back and forth like a giant metronome. Gordon watched it complete two cycles, and then when it next passed the midpoint, he gave it a further almighty shove, sending it crashing over into the next column, and the next, and the next, and then into the rows of shelves, a domino topple that rippled a swathe of destruction, ploughing a twenty-metre-wide strip down the entire length of the cupboard.

'Come on,' cheered Gordon, standing tall, arms in a 'v' above his head.

They both watched as ten thousand airborne pages fluttered down over the path of destruction. And then Gordon's head tipped forward and his hands dropped to his hips. Three seconds later and he was crouching, a steadying hand dipping to the floor. And then there was sobbing.

Many impotent minutes had passed as Nikki sat motionless in the car, head still bowed to the bonnet. What now? What should she do with the rest of the day? What should she do with the rest of her life? How does anyone begin to answer that? Even the first step, who should she ... where should she ... what should she?

But then she sat up. There was still one final mortal chance: Christian's draft of the appendix. What was it he'd told her that morning ... *pages and pages?* Maybe enough pages. It was her last shot. And it was within reach – all she needed was the laptop. Everything else in her life melted away. Her reason for being, now her only reason for being, was the contents of Christian's hard drive. She felt energy and purpose return. Though she knew destiny was now in the balance, a hair's breadth between Shangri-La and oblivion, she embraced the quietness of mind afforded by a single all-or-nothing focus.

But how to get it? This was hardly the time for popping into Beatrice's on the pretext of a social call, especially given the curry incident the previous evening, not to mention the reasons for Christian being in London in the first place. But if she waited, the place could soon be crawling with friends and relatives.

Perhaps she should hang on until the small hours and then break in, but she knew even less about that than she did about kidnap.

Maybe she should grasp the nettle. Just stride up and knock on the door. What would happen? Think, think. Okay, two possible reactions:

One – violence. Could even get nasty. She was stronger and fitter than Beatrice, no question there, but Beatrice would be in an unpredictable state: the wounded, cornered tabby.

Two – capitulation. She breaks down at the sight of a familiar face, even this one.

She went through her options three more times, and three more times she could see no other possibilities, no other outcomes.

Two minutes later and the police were leaving.

Right. If it was to be today, it had to be now.

She left the car and made her way along the road and up the path to the house. She rang the bell.

After a while, a figure came to the door but waited behind the frosted glass.

And then the clunk of the latch. The door opened a few inches.

'Beatrice, I …'

Beatrice said nothing, but left the way open as she went back inside.

Elation as Nikki stepped inside and closed the door. She went into the living room, telling herself to keep calm.

Beatrice was standing at the mantelpiece, her faced turned away. 'Were you there?' she asked, without turning, her voice thin yet direct.

'Was I where? What's happened?'

'Don't lie to me. He must have been with you. How else do you know?'

'We were in London, on our way to the meeting, but he said he'd made a terrible mistake and had to get back, to meet you at the church. He said he wanted to make his own way and that was the last I saw' – *almost true, actually* – 'I came round to apologise and then I saw the police just now. Please, tell me what's happened.'

Beatrice turned to Nikki and began crying. 'He's gone, he's dead,' said Beatrice, struggling through the tears.

'But how? When? Oh I'm so sorry, Beatrice.'

Should she go for the hug? Will she buy it? Nikki stepped forward and put her arms around her. Beatrice hugged her back. Yes! This was in the bag.

'I'm sorry I threw curry at you,' said Beatrice.

'It's okay, I deserved it. I'm so sorry.'

'We were getting married.'

'Yes, I know you were.'

'But now he's gone.'

'The police, did they say what happened?'

'He got run over by a hearse.'

'By a ... well, well I suppose he must just have been in the wrong place at the wrong time.'

'That's what they said.'

'Look, you poor thing, can I make you a cup of tea?'

Beatrice shook her head.

'I think it would help, Bea, really.'

Nikki released her embrace and went to the kitchen. She filled the kettle.

'Have you called anyone?' she said on her return. 'You shouldn't be here on your own. I can stay if you like?'

Beatrice mumbled that a friend was coming over.

Shit. How soon? How much time did she have? 'Oh, that's good.'

'I ... I suppose I'll have to call Christian's parents.'

'One step at a time, try not to think too far ahead,' said Nikki. 'Sorry, could I just use the loo?' She didn't wait for a reply. She left the room and climbed the stairs, trying not to run, looking back to check Beatrice was staying put.

She slipped into the box room. Desk, monitor, keyboard, mouse, CDs ... no laptop. Shit.

She looked harder, scanning the chipboard shelves, cardboard boxes, plastic storage bins, washing, ring binders, stacks of books and DVDs, a dusty Buck Minglestein exercise station and a fully assembled game of Mousetrap. She hadn't realised how untidy Christian was. Still nothing. Fuck.

She started going through the boxes and storage bins, but was soon pushing the upper limits of acceptable time for a toilet trip. She admitted defeat, for now, and went back downstairs.

Beatrice had made her own tea and had a tight grip on the cup as she stared out of the kitchen window.

'Sorry, just a bit of shock, I think,' said Nikki.

Beatrice turned to Nikki, but said nothing.

'Why I took so long in the loo,' said Nikki.

Beatrice turned back to the window. 'What do I do,' she said, 'I don't know what to do.'

Forty-five minutes later, Nikki was still at the house, now on the sofa, comforting Beatrice. She'd been to the toilet three times and was now having to cite cystitis as well as shock. Still no laptop. The frustration was growing, as was the sense of urgency – how long before the friend got here? What then?

She had to stay calm. The laptop was here, it had to be here, somewhere. It would reveal itself eventually. And anyway, what else was there to do? Her life's to-do list now read:

1. Find Christian's laptop
[End of list]

Of course, other tasks would follow, many complex and expansive activities to extrapolate this new unfinished mathematical gospel and bring it to a gloriously ready world. But that utopia would not be rendered real until the sacred computer – sacred tablet, ha – could be found.

There was something else gnawing away at her too, though, or rather some*one*. Nikki was here playing the role of comforter to the person who had cost her the information, perhaps cost her her life's work. If Beatrice hadn't laid down her ultimatum, Christian would have stayed, gone under at Blondeldark's, and Pandora's box would now be wide open.

And Nikki didn't have the malevolent nullifying power of grief to dissolve away her animosity. She had to sit on hers while it stuck skewers in her legs, not daring to let it show for even a moment.

She told herself to stay strong, to focus on the goal. She was close, so close.

'Beatrice,' said Nikki, 'I'm so sorry. I never meant anything like this to happen.'

'It's not your fault.'

'I never wanted to drive you apart. I just saw something wonderful in Christian's words, and I wanted to help.'

Beatrice didn't say anything.

'Look, don't take this the wrong way,' said Nikki, 'but you weren't a big fan of the writing, were you?'

Beatrice's eyes began to well up again.

'It's okay,' said Nikki, 'really.'

Beatrice's head dipped forward into her hands. 'I feel terrible. I'm a terrible person. He would never let me read it, he said he'd show me when it was finished. But I did read it, some of it. I found a page in the bin, and I took it. I took it, I hid it and I read it.'

'Don't blame yourself.'

'He trusted me, and I betrayed that trust.'

'You're only human. I'm sure it didn't do any harm.'

'But it did. The writing, it didn't make any sense, it was rubbish, clichéd rubbish. But I couldn't talk to him because I couldn't tell him how I knew. He never let me in, he never let me try to understand. And when I saw him sharing it so freely with you, I hated him for that, I really did. And now I can't put it right.' She buried her head into Nikki's shoulder as the tears flowed again.

Nikki scanned the living room. It's a laptop, you don't have to work at your desk, that's the whole point. Maybe it's not upstairs, maybe it's downstairs, maybe it's ...

'What are you looking for?' asked Beatrice.

'Nothing.'

'Yes you were, I saw you. You were looking for something.'

'I was just staring into space, I was thinking about, well, you know.'

'No, no you weren't,' said Beatrice. She sat up. She held eye contact.

'All right,' said Nikki, 'so, I was just wondering if Christian's laptop was here.'

'His laptop?'

'Yes.'

'Why?'

'Well ... okay, now don't take this the wrong way–'

'The book. You're still on about the fucking book, aren't you?'

'If you'll just let me–'

'My God. You don't care about Christian at all, do you? You never did. How dare you. How fucking dare you.'

'Stop, listen, I'm on your side. I just thought we could still publish the writing, you know, as a tribute. We could self-publish, for you and me, for family and friends.'

'He's only been dead four hours, four fucking hours. Oh my God, I don't believe it. I let you in, I thought you cared. You don't care at all, you're cold and you're empty.'

'I do, I do care.'

'Get out.'

'But Beatrice.'

'Get out of my house.'

'Beatrice, it's the grief talking, don't do this.'

'Get. Out.'

Chapter Twenty-Three

By the time Christian had passed beyond the M25, the sun was low in the sky and he'd needed his hand as a shade as he tracked ever westward.

Having given up on his hope of making the meeting, a new hope had refuelled his progress – hope of being able to talk to Beatrice, to explain what had happened, to beg for forgiveness. But now he'd had time to pick that illusion apart, too. What could he say that would be heard? And even if he could be heard, what could he say that would now make any difference? Even if she did forgive him and believe the sincerity of his late change of heart, he was fairly sure the living and the dead should not be cohabiting.

Not dead. Something else.

Not dead. Something else.

Not dead. Something else.

He stopped.

He walked over and sat down in the grass verge next to the hard shoulder. Opposite, a large advertising board promised not to increase his gas prices for the next eighteen months.

And as he sat there, he wept.

So he could still cry. Great.

Once he started, he couldn't stop. And there he was thinking he'd been holding it together, thinking his rationality was carrying him through. Who had he been kidding? The only consolation was that the tears made him feel human, which then fed back into more tears, as it served to underscore what he was beginning to accept he may have lost.

He could still cry but so much else was now missing. He was solid enough but nothing else was. He was unable to assert his form on the world, to render it in his hands. And it wasn't the thought of the sugar-rush tactile pleasures that came to mind. It was the honest and dirty crude matter – the rough, cold surface of the road, the unloved foliage on the verge, the piece of shredded truck tyre. He wanted to stride over the motorway lanes in fear and wipe the condensation off the Armco. In all his years on Earth, in all those lost hours in stagnant traffic, he'd never once stopped to think he'd miss being able to caress an unloved metal crash barrier. Now he studied it, noting its imperfections, the utilitarian repairs it had accumulated over the years. Had anyone ever regarded this piece of Armco, or anything else in this anonymous scene, as he did now?

Temperature too was apparently now gone. It was a cold late-March evening. By now, he should have been shivering in just suit and T-shirt, yet he felt no chill at all. Thinking on it now, he knew he'd felt no warmth either. No ember embrace from the afternoon sun and, more starkly, not so much as a hint of a burn or scald as he'd passed through all those hot engine blocks.

He looked to his right, tracking the Armco past his shoulder and out to the horizon, back over the path travelled. And as he did, he noticed a small sapling. It was close to him, about halfway up the verge. It stood alone, distinct from the Berkshire jungle on the top of the incline and would be doomed next time they brought the mowers in. And yet there it stood. It was young and proud, all height and no body, and it cast a clean shadow. And then he realised something wasn't right. Something was missing from the scene.

He shot to his feet, scanning the grass all around him, waving his hands and moving his head from side to side, hoping to prove to himself it was there, merely faint and indistinct. But there was no trace, not the slightest change in the tone or hue of the grass. He studied the rest of the scene. They were everywhere, clear as you like – a skewed ladder from the Armco and its posts; a great long spike from the advertising board; fast mobile blocks behind the cars as they passed.

He sat down again.

And then he thought about something he'd not thought about in more than twenty-five years. He thought about Harry Haddow, the boy with no shadow from *Did I Ever Tell You How Lucky You Are?* He remembered how much the poem and its stark illustration had disturbed him. He remembered asking his mother whether they could help Harry. He remembered his mother laughing and telling him not to worry, that it was just a story, but also, on occasion, telling him the same thing would happen to him if he didn't clear up his room, if he didn't say his prayers.

Christian hugged himself again. Partly because a hug is what he needed, partly because he just wanted to touch something and he was the only thing available.

Now he sat without regard for time. He watched the traffic fall away from its rush-hour peak. He watched the overhead lights flicker into life. He watched the last light of day fade and die. And as the street lighting gradually took the baton from the sun, defending this long strip from the darkness, he was presented with nature's final surprise of the day – a nocturnal blue-green luminous hue. It didn't do much for his mood. He already felt lost. He already felt beaten. Now he felt ridiculous. It was too much, so much so he laughed out loud. It was cheesy. A cliché, right out of *Star Wars*. He looked like a Jedi Tramp.

'To Obi Hobo-Gin you must listen,' he said, followed by a thin, cold chuckle.

He thought of Beatrice. She would be horrified to see him like this. Wearing a suit with trainers was bad enough, but add in the all-over blue-green wash, well, she'd never have let him out of the house. He tried to console himself that at least he had *some* colour, even if it wasn't particularly natural. He didn't think he'd be able to cope with grey: dead bodies were grey, or so he'd heard.

Not dead. Something else.

Not dead. Something else.

The traffic had begun to slow, and in the westbound lanes, his lanes, it was now stationary and backed up as far as he could see. It hadn't bothered him when it was moving – then it was leaving him alone, which is how he wanted it. But now it had stopped, he felt exposed.

They're not looking. No one can see; he would know about it if they could. But that is what it felt like. Vacant stares settling on him, mocking him: everyone tucked up in their carcoons, heaters and radios on, caught up in the usual trivial frustrations of being in a traffic jam, not one of them thinking for one moment how fucking amazing it is to be alive and how reassuring it is that there are others in the same world with a common purpose, even if it is just to get to Chipping Sodbury. They were separate of course, absolute strangers to one another, yet to Christian they were together, all playing their little part in the bigger jam. All together. All the same.

He got to his feet once again. He didn't want to go any further, but there was nothing else to do.

Beatrice held onto the handrail as she came down the stairs, carefully placing each step like a frail old woman, unsure of the world she had taken for granted only hours earlier. Everything around her was now somehow disconnected, somehow no longer for her.

She caught herself in the mirror on the landing – she looked hollow and washed out, the only colours the pinks and reds in her puffed eyes.

She found Charlotte washing up in the kitchen.

'How are you doing?' said Charlotte. 'Better for a bath?'

Beatrice shook her head.

'I did a tidy up,' said Charlotte, 'hope you don't mind?'

'I'm sorry. I didn't even realise ... I–'

'Don't apologise, darling, it's fine.'

'Thank you,' whispered Beatrice.

'Like I said, you don't have to worry about a thing. I'm going to stay for as long as you need me. I'm your personal assistant, cook, cleaner, shopper, whatever you like.'

Beatrice burst into tears.

'Oh, darling,' said Charlotte, putting her arms around her, 'it'll be okay.'

Beatrice held on tight and cried into her friend's shoulder. 'I'm sorry, it's just, I think that's the kindest thing anyone's ever said to me.'

'Well that's a tragedy, my girl.' Charlotte held on for a moment before breaking off. 'Now, you go and sit down, and I'll make you a cup of tea.'

'Thank you.'

'And then I'm going to insist on you having several large stiff ones.'

'I'm not sure there's much in,' said Beatrice. 'There might be some Baileys somewhere.'

Beatrice trudged through into the living room.

'Don't worry,' said Charlotte, from the kitchen, 'I brought a small selection, well, actually an absolutely massive selection. We're going to drown this day.'

'Where's the bedding?'

'Upstairs,' said Charlotte, 'I guessed it was from the spare room.'

Beatrice tried not to start crying again. She was relieved Charlotte had dealt with it. The last place Christian had slept in the house – not next to her, but alone on the sofa.

'Where was the laptop?' asked Beatrice, noticing Christian's computer sitting on the coffee table.

'Under the duvet,' said Charlotte. 'Is it Christian's?'

'Yes,' said Beatrice, then after a pause, 'Nikki was looking for it.'

'Who?' said Charlotte, coming through to the living room.

'Nikki. The woman who was paying for him … for him to write.'

'When?'

'Today. She came right after the police.'

'And you let her in?'

'Oh God, I know, I wasn't thinking straight.'

'And she wanted his laptop?'

'Yes. She was kind, and everything, to begin with, but then she started going on about the writing.'

'The fucking nerve. Who says that? On the fucking day, the actual fucking day.'

'Exactly. I threw her out.'

'I don't blame you, surprised you didn't punch her lights out.'

'Well, yes.'

'Anyway, it's time for alcohol. Vodka I think. Now shall we start with a triple or quadruple?'

The last leg of Christian's journey had been a return to the format of the first. Endless featureless motorway traded back for a stream of little wins. Windsor, Winkfield and Warfield. Not that he now took any heart from ticking off the milestones. He had long since passed into a zoned-out, trudging zombie-like state, his mind quietly dismantling itself somewhere near the back of his skull as autopilot plodded him on through cycles of sodium-lit suburbs and pitch-black B roads.

The walking dead. That had almost made him laugh.

It was after ten when he finally reached the churchyard, according to the clock on the tower. He had no reason to doubt it.

So, only nine hours late.

The wire-covered windows of the church itself were dark, but there were signs of life at the vicarage. He knew Beatrice was long gone, no one waits nine hours for anything, but a last ember of hope propelled him towards the building anyway.

He thought about drifting straight in, but decided he should at least try to observe basic manners, to maintain standards – good for morale, good for holding onto ... things. He was sure that's what Shackleton would have done, right before eating his shoes.

He attempted to knock on the door but, as he expected, his fist slipped into the oak, making no sound at all, like he was trying to knock on a chocolate waterfall.

He half walked, half drifted through the fibrous grain of the door, into the small reception area.

The sound of the TV from the living room.

He mustered a greeting. Of course there was no reply, but again it seemed wrong to barge in without at least an attempt at an introduction.

He drifted on into the living room with some trepidation, even in his exhausted state responding to his long-held general suspicion of what goes on behind closed doors, but especially when those doors belonged to a man of the cloth.

Tony was sitting in an easy chair with his feet up, plate of cheese on his lap, watching an old episode of *The Two Ronnies*. The cat was asleep in its basket, next to the hearth.

'I'm, er, sorry I'm late, Tony,' said Christian.

No response.

'I suppose Beatrice left hours ago? I did want to be here, I really did. But you see, I think I might be dead and no one's explained the transport options.'

He stopped and stood perfectly still. It was the first time he'd referred to himself as dead. It sounded ridiculous. How could anyone announce they were dead?

'Well, not dead, obviously, but something else. I'm, just, not myself, really, really not myself.'

Tony scratched an eyebrow.

A sign? No, of course not a sign. Don't be stupid.

'I don't suppose you can see me or hear me?'

He stepped over in front of the TV, blocking Tony's view.

Tony didn't seem to suffer the slightest inconvenience or hint at even the mildest degradation of picture quality from watching the programme through Christian.

'Thought maybe you being a vicar, you know, it might be different for you. But I suppose it doesn't work like that, does it? It's just, I don't know what to do. Will this pass? Will I ever be me again?'

Tony reached for the cream crackers.

'Look, would you mind if I sat down? Of course you wouldn't fucking mind, you can't hear me, you can't see me, can you?'

Christian stepped in close, bent over, and lowered his mouth to within five centimetres of Tony's left ear.

'Can you hear me?' shouted Christian.

Tony yawned, stretched for the remote, and began flicking through the channels.

Christian retreated and slumped down onto and mostly into the near-nothingness of the sofa.

He didn't appreciate how exhausted he was.

He didn't appreciate that ghosts could get exhausted.

Within fifteen seconds, he was asleep.

Chapter Twenty-Four

Beatrice was exhausted but wide awake. It was five a.m. She didn't want to be awake. She wanted to be unconscious but her brainstem wouldn't let her. It knew something was up. There was no mistaking the chemical signals: stress, fear, shock. The last thing to do in this condition was sleep, thought the stem – no, we need to be wide awake and alert to the danger. Beatrice had tried her hardest to get drunk the night before. She'd matched Lottie drink for drink, and then some, but no matter what her blood alcohol had said, she'd remained horribly sober throughout. Now, after four hours of fitful sleep, she was wide awake with nothing but a long nuclear winter of a day stretching out in front of her, a day she wished she could fast-forward through.

She went downstairs, turned on the TV and slumped into the sofa. She'd always hated TV in the mornings, only eventually tolerating it through years of living with Christian. But now it was what she wanted: anything not to have to remain in the purgatory of her own thoughts. She flicked through the channels. Who watches TV at five a.m.? Insomniacs and the early-stage bereaved. Several channels were showing forgotten noughties comedies. She hadn't been a fan first time around, but oh how she was not in the mood now. She flicked on through TV shopping, TV casinos, TV sex lines, before settling on the BBC News Channel. She knew it wouldn't be enough, so she got up and went over to the TV unit. She tried not to acknowledge Christian's *Star Trek: The Next Generation* box set, but it was too late. Why hadn't she given it more of a chance? Several discs and four of the cases were sitting on top of the incorrectly-arranged remainder. She reverently put the discs back in their cases and put the cases back in order. She went back along the line, adjusting and nudging here and there, until every case was in perfect alignment. She sat back on her legs to double-check everything was now in place, before reaching to the side of the TV unit to unplug the iPad from the charger.

In the middle realm, Dexter had been up early, churning over the events of the previous day. With Gordon in no fit state for state business following the stationery blitz, the working evening had been written off, and now Dexter was contemplating the uncertain prospect of a longer hiatus. He was used to volatility in his boss, more than the odd bout of bitterness, and plenty of recrimination, but the depths of this current trough were uncharted, and it was the first time in all the years Dexter had known Gordon that the boss hadn't put in his usual fourteen hours.

So as Dexter made his way over to the royal chambers, he didn't dare speculate on Gordon's state of mind after what he assumed would have been a long and troubled night. But as he crossed the first-storey landing, he met Gordon coming the other way, accompanied by Hervarðr and Séverin from the board, and Dickie Dinks, a long-time junior from Future Strategy Planning Possibilities.

'Dex,' said Gordon, 'are you joining us?'

Dexter looked them up and down. Plus-fours and knitwear; an overdose of loose-fitting pastels and unnecessary tartan; a green jade visor for Gordon.

'Golf,' said Dexter. 'Seriously?'

'Well we're not off to a fashion show,' said Gordon.

'I think I'll pass.'

'Balls you will.' Gordon turned to the others. 'Dinks, I'm demoting you to caddy.'

Dinks looked like his heart had been scooped from his chest. 'Delighted, Lord,' he said, 'Dexter should of course take my place.'

'Exactly,' said Gordon, then turning to Dexter, 'but we can't have you going like that. Now, I've got some spare pantaloons here somewhere.'

'Really, Gordon, I won't join you.'

'Come on, man, do us both good.'

'I'm sorry, but really, no.'

Gordon stared at Dexter, holding eye contact for what felt like an eternity. 'Well, suit yourself. Gentlemen, shall we?' They continued on their way.

'Gordon,' said Dexter.

His boss stopped mid-stride and turned back to him.

'A quick word?' said Dexter.

Gordon turned to the others. 'I'll meet you there.' They continued on.

Dexter walked the three strides to Gordon.

'I don't get it,' said Dexter. 'Last night you were on your knees.'

'No I wasn't.'

'Yes you were, literally and metaphorically.'

'A blip, Dexter. It happens to men at the top. Sometimes Goebbels would hide in the dumbwaiter at the Berghof. Didn't mean he'd lost it, not for a moment.'

'Look, I'm glad you're feeling positive, but I'm not sure this is a good idea.'

'Balls. You're always saying I need to get out of the office.'

'Well, yes, I suppose. It's just last night–'

'A. Blip. Which we will never speak of again. Now are you sure you won't come?'

'I'm sure. I'm very sure. I'm going to reread the hypnosis transcripts.'

'Dexter, my boy, stop worrying. I feel fine, I feel … free.'

'Free?'

'Yes. Unencumbered.'

Dexter looked Gordon up and down again. 'So free you want to play golf?'

'Yes. Today I'm going to hit a little ball into a little hole, that's it. Now you know that's nuts, and I know that's nuts, but today it feels right. It makes all the sense in the world.'

'You're not well, Gordon.'

'That,' said Gordon, holding up a stiff finger – there was a pause – 'may be true, but sometimes life is about … getting little balls in little holes.'

Christian woke with a sudden empty gasp, his top half springing up through the sofa cushions, panic gripping him as he hunted for breath. His hands shot to his neck, clutching at his throat, and then to his chest as he told his lungs to inflate.

No breath. Nothing.

His fingers snapped to his mouth, probing inside as he opened wide, desperately searching for an obstruction.

Still no breath.

Too long, too long. Breathe. Come on, breathe!

He hit his chest, beating it hard like he was trying to shift a lunged crumb. Still nothing. He tried again, harder still, punching now.

Still no breath.

He checked his heart, palm pressing hard, flat to chest. No beat. *No beat*. Wait, check, give it a chance …

The void was counted out by the yellow *Praise Cheesus!* clock on the mantelpiece.

Tick.

Tick.

Tick.

Oh fuck, oh fuck, oh fuck.

Now his right hand shot to the wrist of his left. He pressed his thumb between the tendons. Wait. Wait.

Come on. Come on, *please*.

His wrist was as inert as his chest as the clock counted him out a second time.

Tick.

Tick.

Tick.

No pulse. No breathing.

But no pain …

No discomfort even …

And still conscious …

And inside a sofa …

Dread washed through him as he subsided into the frame.

Slower now, his hands rose to cradle his face, pulling tight on his skin as he released a grinding pitiful wail. It all came flooding back. The fateful decision, his attempt to reverse it, the accident, each ghastly revelation of loss, the death march to the gaudy sofa which he was now wearing like a floral overcoat.

And now no breath or pulse either. How long? Was it possible he'd not drawn a single breath in the entire journey back? How could he not have noticed. He knew he wasn't always terribly observant, but to not spot a cardiac arrest – your own cardiac arrest – was plain ridiculous.

Replaying the events again, he couldn't recall taking a single breath after the accident. But then he couldn't remember taking one while in the shower that morning either, or while making his coffee, or on the drive into London, yet he was in no doubt that he had. But then he remembered gulping down air on his Harley Street run, hands on knees and burning lungs, when he was short of breath, when he'd had less than he … needed.

He sank lower still.

For a long time, he cowered inside the sofa, legs hiding in the upholstery along with the fluff and the crumbs and the loose change, eyes clamped shut, trying to wish away his new reality, trying to shut out the unrelenting prod of the Cheesus clock.

Tick.

Tick.

Tick.

Eventually, his rational self began to assert some control. His thoughts turned to Beatrice. She would be frantic. He'd never not come home, not once. Whatever had happened to him, he owed her an explanation.

With some difficulty he got himself up and out of the sofa, triggering recall of the new strangeness of his movements, the softening of the traditionally close relationship between what his legs were doing and where he was going.

Where was Tony? What do vicars do first thing on weekday mornings? Who cares. It doesn't matter.

For the first time he noticed the mirror, or rather, for the first time he noticed the lack of himself within it.

Another shock ran through him as he ducked out of the way, out of the mirror's line of sight like it was a paparazzo.

Idiot.

He shuffled over to the wall, keeping his head low, until he was under the frame. He began to stand, slowly bringing his head up in front of the mirror, slowly revealing his absence in the image.

Hold it, hold it, hold it. He had to keep a grip. He couldn't let this beat him.

But he couldn't hold it. He turned and slumped down into the bath foam of the carpet and the Cornish wafer of the wall, and he wished for the oblivion button.

He'd never been suicidal before, not really. Yes, on bad days he'd sometimes crossed the road when the red man was flashing and had once driven into Maidenhead without his seat belt on. And yes, in recent months he had found himself acknowledging that if he were dead, it would at least mean he wouldn't have to finish the book, or go back to work, or get married. But these were mere idle dalliances. Yet he'd always thought suicide would be a handy option to have in the locker – perhaps if he developed some horrific disease, or found himself trapped under-ground with no prospect of rescue. And that had led him to the oblivion button thought experiment: the idea of a button hanging on a cord around his neck, a button that if pressed would end his life, instantly and without pain. And that thought had inevitably led to a question: if he'd had such a button, throughout his life, would he ever have pressed it? Christian had never suffered much sadness, hardship or despair, and nothing even approaching the really grave and nasty surprises of life, yet there were times when he'd thought he'd have pressed it. But it was hard to be sure. Normally he'd never think of the button at the time – the thought would always come later, after the peak pain of England getting knocked out on penalties had eased. And even then, even if he'd thought of it in those low moments, pressing an imaginary button is a whole different kettle of dead fish from pressing a real one. So what about now? Well, that was easy. He made a single prod at his chest with his index finger.

No. No. Fucking no. Wallowing wasn't an option and he couldn't just wish this away. Do something, get a grip and do something, anything. He got to his feet. He slapped his cheeks. He thought again back to Beatrice. Yes, yes that could be the something. He would meet her and try to explain. He checked the clock. Six minutes past nine. He could drop by now, but then she'd always hated him calling in on her at work, especially turning up unannounced. Stay positive. Okay, head over to the house, wait for her there. That would still be something and anything would be better than festering here.

He drifted over to the window and looked out onto the churchyard, to the path out to the street, to the grey, damp day. He moved to drift out through the window and wall, but hesitated. He turned and instead made his way through to the hall, to the front door. A longer route, but, once again, the right thing to do. Civilisation – the last defence against anarchy, the last defence against madness. Women and children first, the tunic top button, taking the door instead of the wall.

He hesitated again at the door itself, forced to accept he'd still have to pass through it if he wanted to leave the vicarage. A check with the hand first and then the rest of him in one big wincing scratchy stride.

It was raining outside – that particular light, almost invisible drizzle that Bracknell and England did so well. Great.

He stepped out from under the small porch but only took four steps before stopping, caught out by the entirely new way of experiencing the entirely humdrum. He turned his eyes to the heavens, stretched out his arms, and took a turn on the spot. He waited, giving it a full minute, but there was no gathering moisture on his hair, no drips on his nose, no trickles tumbling down his collar. Yet he was feeling something. All over his face, shoulders and arms, tiny droplets were passing into him. And under his arms, groin and feet, they were passing out of him. An ever-changing infinity of almost imperceptible points of softness, a new order of magnitude for subtlety of experience. There was nothing in life that had anything on this. The most delicate spec of airborne dust, the most insubstantial of gossamer fibres, even the almost-nothing felt by the hand passing through a breeze was like swimming in porridge compared with this brilliant assertive lightness. It was the first thing since getting run over that wasn't completely and utterly awful, and, though it served as yet another reminder of his separation, it lifted him.

He made his way out through the empty churchyard – its only other occupant being Tony's cat, Welby, stalking something in the undergrowth – and out onto the street, where he began a thankfully much shorter journey than the one that had almost finished him.

He settled on the autopilot route to the house. It wasn't the fastest, but he knew the majority of it well enough from a futile fitness initiative three years earlier. And taking in South Hill Park and Bracknell's other islands of greenery would be at least slightly less depressing than going the whole way via the grey suburban streets.

For most of the journey, Christian's only company was his new friend the rain and the passing traffic. But as he passed Point Royal, the monolithic hexagonal tower-block that was the concrete jewel in Bracknell's architectural crown, while cutting through the cramped and wooded grassy pocket of Caterpillar Park, he saw a few brave souls going about their day – an iPodded jogger, an old couple clutching a brolly as they walked the dog, and two men sitting on one of the park benches in among the oak, sycamore and ash. From the uniforms, one of these men appeared to be a postman and one appeared to be from British Gas. It was a strange enough sight as it was, them sitting there, apparently just staring into space, but in the now more aggressive drizzle, it was even more incongruous. But Christian gave it scant regard, his greater concerns weighing on him as he trudged by.

There'd been no prospect of news for Gabriel while the shepherds were belatedly making their way into London, and little prospect for the first hours of their search, but he'd been unable to sleep all the same.

By sunrise he was at his desk but already knew that no news was bad news. Now, at ten a.m., a runner arrived with a report from Trimbrilly's deputy at Angel Field Ops.

ANGEL FIELD OPS.: REPORT

GROUP	JN7	JOB No. 37623SC
DESC.	S&C CHRISTIAN BOOTSTRAP. SHEP. SUPP.	

ALL ANGELS REPORTED IN.

SHEPHERDS ARRYVED DEATH SITE - CONFIRM: JUNC. GREAT PORTLAND AND MARYLEBONE, LONDON - 18:14.

COMMENCED SEARCH. SPOKE ONE QUARTER MYLE.

SEARCH TERMINAYTION 09:00. TARGET NOT PRESENT.

DIRECTED SEARCHWORK TO RESIDENCE - CONFIRM: 22. YESTMENTS. BRACKNELL, BERKSHIRE.

ENDINGS.

	NAYME	SIGHNED	DAYTE
COMMAND	RIMREACH	*Rimread*	27 MAR 2015
			REV.: 13 JUN 1531/1.1

Barely had the first runner departed when another arrived. God was requesting Gabriel's presence for a celebratory debrief breakfast in the Rouge Lounge, and there was a footnote:

Bring the monkey.

It was eleven fifteen by the time Beatrice heard activity in the bathroom and, some minutes later, slow footsteps coming down the stairs.

Charlotte appeared at the living room door and propped herself against the frame, her eyes only half open.

'What did we drink last night?' she said.

'Everything, I think,' said Beatrice, before going back to solitaire on her iPad.

'Coffee?'

Beatrice didn't look up but nodded.

The TV was still on the news channel.

'What's happening in the world then?' called Lottie, softly, from the kitchen.

'Nothing much.'

'Don't blame you. I never bother with it. Just depresses me.'

'You know what I've been sitting here thinking?'

'What, my love?'

'I thought, please … please let there be a disaster. Let there be a tsunami, let there be a September eleventh.'

Charlotte appeared at the door. 'I'm sorry, darling, but, why?'

'I wanted something, on the news,' said Beatrice, 'something big enough and awful enough to take me away from yesterday.'

'Oh, Bea.'

'I'm a bad person, Lottie.'

'You're still in shock, that's all.'

'But what sort of person thinks that?' said Beatrice, shaking her head. 'I'm a bad, bad person.'

'You can't tear yourself up over this. It's not your fault.'

'No it's your fault, Lottie. If I hadn't set him your stupid ultimatum, he wouldn't have needed to leave his meeting. He wouldn't have been in the road when the hearse was there, he would have been somewhere else.'

Gabriel and Harold had arrived at the Rouge Lounge.

No one was in the mood for bowling.

'Well is he definitely dead?' asked God, spitting globules of scrambled blue eggs.

Gabriel wiped his chin and nodded.

'You're sure?' said God. 'They've not got him on life support or something? They work miracles down there.'

'We've been watching his body since the hit, Tel. Most of it's in a bag at the hospital. The rest got sloshed away with a hose. He's definitely dead.'

'So why no pickup?'

'He must have slipped through the net, before materialisation.'

God screwed up his face. 'How many shepherds did we send?'

'A couple of dozen ...'

'And didn't you say we had a double perimeter?'

'Look, Tel, you can't expect them to even see a disembodied consciousness, let alone get it in shackles. If he made a run for it before his new body appeared, well, a thousand shepherds couldn't have stopped him or even tracked him if he kept his mouth shut.'

'But,' said Harold, 'surely as a spirit, he'd have no mouth to–'

'I'm speaking figuratively,' said Gabriel. 'What I'm saying is if he didn't scream or cry out or try to talk to anyone, he could just drift on by, right through our lines.'

God screwed his face up again.

'It does happen, Tel,' said Gabriel. 'Remember that brain-dead mute marathon runner? We never did find him.'

'Well, all right ... so what's the plan now then?'

'Well the death site's as clean as a whistle,' said Gabriel, 'so we're told, so they're making their way over to the house.'

Gabriel exchanged micro-glances with Harold.

'Okay,' said God, 'well, you make damn sure they all know what's at stake.' He ruffled his hair and tugged on his beard. 'Not out of this one yet.' He stared across at Gabriel and Harold. 'Well don't let me keep ya, lads.'

They rose and backed out. Gabriel closed the doors behind them.

'You–'

'Wait.'

'You–'

'*Wait,*' said Gabriel, holding up his clawhand and keeping it there until they were halfway up the corridor.

'You didn't inform him,' said Harold, 'about the shepherds not being in position at the start.'

'It wasn't important.'

'But–'

'It's just a detail, Harold. Terry's like all men at the top. All he needs is the big picture. In fact, all he needs is the highlights of the summary of the gist of the big picture. You don't want him in your details, believe me.'

At the top of the corridor, they met Trimbrilly, the stuffy and often ridiculous angel who somehow had risen to being responsible for all angelic operations in the Zone, hurrying towards them. Shoulders back and breast puffed, as ever, yet still in something of a flap.

'Ah, Trim, you don't need to disturb him,' said Gabriel, 'I've filled him in on your behalf. Shame Bootstrap wasn't at the death site, but there you go, these things happen.'

'Oh, yes, well–'

'Terry wants you to know he has absolute faith that you'll get our man.'

'Really?' said Trimbrilly. Some colour returned to the breast plumage at his shirt collar and he relaxed his stance. 'Well … thank you.'

'This is Harold by the way,' said Gabriel, opening an armwing, 'he is assisting.'

'Pleased to meet you. Trimbrilly. Angel Field Ops.'

Trimbrilly brought his heels together and offered a clawhand.

'And you, sir,' said Harold and he shook the clammy appendage.

Trimbrilly's eyes flicked down the corridor to the entrance to the Rouge Lounge. Harold took half a step to the side but Gabriel kept still.

'Was there something else?' asked Gabriel.

Again Trimbrilly looked past Gabriel and again Gabriel stood his ground.

'Well, there was one more thing,' said Trimbrilly.

'Go on,' said Gabriel.

'Well, my team reported there was no sign of a body, or even an accident, when they arrived.'

'Is that right?'

'Yes.'

'So quick aren't they, those London emergency services? A modern marvel.'

'Yes, yes I suppose so. I just wondered ...'

'Wondered what?'

'Well, if I should mention it to Terry.'

'Best not,' said Gabriel. He stepped in, placed an armwing on Trimbrilly's shoulder, and turned him round. 'I tend to find he only likes one type of news. Good news.'

'Right, right, and this would be?'

'Well it's no news, isn't it.'

'Yes, I suppose so.'

'And if it's no news, then there's no need to tell him, is there?'

'No, no I suppose not.'

'So anyway, you'll let us know the moment there's news from the field?' asked Gabriel. He raised a clawfinger and smiled. 'Good news, mind.'

'Yes, of course,' said Trimbrilly. 'Well, I'll er, get to it then.'

He nodded twice and left.

Harold turned to Gabriel.

'What?' said Gabriel.

Chapter Twenty-Five

As Christian drifted into Vestments everything seemed so normal, like nothing had changed. Perhaps everything would be okay; perhaps this was where he'd work out how to make it right. But as he approached the house, he slowed and stopped.

Beatrice's car.

She was home. But then of course she was home. She'd have been told about the accident by now. In fact she'd have been told last night.

She's not at work, she's inside. Inside there, sick with worry.

Now he recognised another car, too, beyond the Fiesta. Charlotte's Porsche.

He sat down on and slightly in the kerb. The thought of Beatrice suffering made him want to dash straight inside. But what was he going to say? And was he still going to say it with Charlotte listening in? So he sat there and watched the lack of comings and goings while he tried to work out his options.

An hour later and he was still sitting in the kerb, the only development having been the small bonus of Charlotte's departure. Any way he looked at it, it still came up the same. And short of waiting for a year or two, it wasn't going to get any better by itself.

He stood up and made his way over to the front door. This time he didn't try to knock. Not because it was futile but because this was still his home (even if it had never been, legally speaking, his house). He was still faced with the ignominy of drifting through the door though – there was no getting away from that. He widened his stance, straightened his back, and, as proprietarily as he could, stepped inside.

'Darling ...' He almost couldn't finish the word, his face tightening into a forced high-cheek smile. 'I'm ... h-home.'

He wanted to project an image of relaxed confidence, but already sensed a rip in his right to be there. Now it really was just her house. It made his drift into the living room stiff and stilted.

He found Beatrice curled up on the sofa, iPad in her hands. The coffee table was pulled close – flowers, a mug of tea, lots of tissues. He was relieved to see she wasn't crying though it was obvious she had been. She didn't look worse than he felt, but it was a close contest.

He dropped to his knees.

'Darling, oh darling, I'm here. I'm back. I'm so sorry, I've been an idiot, about ... well ... about everything. I was trying to get back for the meeting, I got there in the end, I did, but I was late. I got a taxi, but I couldn't stay in it.'

No response. The only thing filling the pause after Christian's speech was the weather on the TV. *Cloud continuing to move in across the south.*

He shuffled closer, still on his knees.

'I'm going to fix it,' he said, his voice cracking. 'I'm going to fix everything.'

He was desperate to put his arms around her, but to do so with grace and dignity is a challenge when the object of your affection is ignoring you while she sits on a sofa, absorbed in an iPad, and is mostly residing in different dimensions.

As carefully as he could, he manoeuvred himself on and into the seat next to her, and, starting with a wide arc, brought his arms around her. He broke down as he sucked in the familiar scent of coconut milk moisturising lotion and sensibly priced body spray. More than anything, he wanted to be able to hold her, but he'd amassed enough experience from the previous twenty-four hours to know that to feel his hands pass through her would be heartbreaking. With great care, he began to close the arc of his arms, watching the gaps close, until his hands and forearms were only a centimetre or so away from the sweatshirt of his beloved. He thought about backing out, unsure if he was ready for what he was about to discover, but he kept going, holding his non-breath as he moved his arms in to touch. But as the gap closed to nothing, he felt nothing, almost – just the shadow of what was there, the shadow of Beatrice Brinner. He closed a little further, desperate for contact, but his hands and arms were already passing into her. He flinched and, letting out a gasp, jerked his arms out like he'd brushed into nettles. It felt wrong, like he was damaging her. He got up and drifted over to the corner of the room. He slumped down. Tears began to flow again.

He heard the front door open and close.

'Hi. Got the stuff. Plus a few extras.'

The sound of shopping bags hitting countertops and then Charlotte came into the living room.

'So, how are we?'

'I don't know,' said Beatrice, softly, as she shook her head.

'Ice cream?'

'I'm sorry?'

'I got us some ice cream, most expensive one they had.'

'I don't want anything.'

'Well I'm going to have some.'

Charlotte retreated to the kitchen.

The rustle of plastic bags, kitchen cupboards opening and closing, glassy clinks. And then a long, low pop. Ten seconds later, Lottie emerged with two flutes of champagne.

Christian looked up from his sobbing in the corner and stared.

'What on earth?' said Beatrice.

'Thought you deserved a little treat, darling.'

'My God, it's not, it's not a celebration, Lottie.'

'Of course not, no, but it is a new start, you have to admit. Like it or not, he's not coming back ...'

'I'm right here,' pleaded Christian, before putting his hands over his ears.

'... now there's a guy at Daniel's office, recent promotion, already paid off his mortgage. I've wanted to introduce you for ages, but, you know, there was never quite the right time, what with your old situation.'

'Stop,' said Beatrice, 'Lottie, please, stop. Christian's only ... only just, yesterday, how could you suggest this?'

'Look, I know the timing's not great,' said Charlotte, holding up her hands, 'but I can't guarantee how long this guy'll be available. You snooze, you lose, sister. I don't like it any more than you, but that's how life is these days.'

Beatrice put her head in her hands.

'Too soon? Well, it's your call, of course,' said Charlotte, 'but remember, there's nothing more seductive than a fresh widow, you know, all vulnerable and sensitive and horny and needing all kinds of support.'

'Lottie, I don't want to throw you out, but I will if you don't shut up.'

'As I say, your call,' said Charlotte and she retreated to the kitchen.

Four minutes later, she returned with two large bowls of toffee fudge ice cream with chocolate sauce, marshmallows and chopped nuts. Beatrice looked at the bowl being held in front of her, looked up at Charlotte, looked back at the bowl and then accepted it.

Charlotte sat.

A few minutes of ice-cream-filled silence.

'I've been thinking about the laptop,' said Beatrice.

'And?'

'And is it wrong to want to look?'

'No, of course not,' said Charlotte, 'but are you sure you want to? All you'll find is more pain. It's not like he was Dan Brown.'

'Was?' said Christian, getting to his feet. 'I'm not a was, I'm an am. I am here. ' He strode over and stood between them. 'I am here. I'm right here.'

'Maybe it'll make more sense if I can read more of it,' said Beatrice. 'He didn't want to show me until it was ready, you see.'

'What, it's not even finished?' said Charlotte. 'Really, darling, don't punish yourself.'

'But would I be betraying him if I look now?'

'Of course not. I'd have read it front to back and sideways by now, if I'd wanted to.'

'Mind your own fucking business,' said Christian.

'I just feel like I'd be betraying him even more,' said Beatrice.

'Yes, yes,' said Christian, 'a betrayal – wait, what do you mean *even more?*'

'Well, let's get rid of it then,' said Charlotte. She stood and retrieved the laptop from the shelf under the coffee table.

'Hey,' said Christian, 'put that down.'

'I'm not sure, Lottie. I think maybe I want to know,' said Beatrice. 'I think I'll regret it, at some point, if I don't.'

'Or maybe you'll regret it if you do?' said Charlotte, shaking the laptop at Beatrice.

'Be careful with that,' said Christian, grabbing at it in vain.

'It's just … oh I hate to say it,' said Beatrice, 'but maybe she's right.'

'She?' said Charlotte, 'the fairy godmother?'

It took a moment for Christian to realise they were talking about Nikki.

Beatrice nodded. 'She said we should preserve what he did, what he was working on. Whatever I thought, it meant a lot to him.'

'Yes, preserve it,' said Christian, 'I can't finish it if you don't preserve it.'

'I'm telling you, Bea, that's a bad idea. Don't keep it, don't read it. Bin it.'

'No,' said Christian, turning to Beatrice.

'I do want to see,' said Beatrice.

'You're sure?' said Charlotte.

'My mind's made up.'

'Well. All right then.'

Charlotte sat down, cleared some space on the coffee table and powered up the laptop. Green lights flashed and the hard drive whirred as it spun up.

'Don't do it,' said Christian, 'please, darling, it's not ready.'

'You'd really have looked if it was Daniel's writing?' asked Beatrice.

'Of course I would. I already do. Not writing, obviously, but there's plenty more for me to look at. Credit card bills, his pockets, text messages.'

'You read his text messages?'

'Well of course. How else could I trust him?'

'You do all that and you still say you trust him?'

'It's because I do all that, darling. I'd find out – I'm ruthless and he knows it, which means he never plays around, knows he can't afford to.'

Beatrice didn't reply.

'So you never went through Christian's texts then?'

'No. I trusted him.'

'What, *trusted* trusted? No evidence? No check-ups?'

'That's what trust is, Lottie.'

'Well, maybe in Mr Darcy Willy Wonka land, but this is real life, Bea. Now don't get me wrong, I'm not saying Christian was definitely cheating on you, there's no way to know that for sure …'

'Hey, fuck you,' said Christian.

'… but the girls who get cheated on are always the ones who *trust* trust. But what do they expect? They're as guilty as the men.'

'How, exactly?' said Beatrice.

'Men are weak. They just are. And since they invented Facebook and everything, there's much more opportunity for them. These girls who blindly trust, they're dropping a massive pile of temptation in their men's laps and expecting them to be angels.'

'Christian wasn't like that.'

'Thank you,' said Christian.

'So sure? He was, technically, still a man,' said Charlotte, 'you can't keep a horse and expect it not to shit.'

'Look, just drop the fidelity thing,' said Beatrice. 'I'm just ... you know, not today.'

They looked at the screen. The laptop had almost finished booting.

'Look, are you sure you won't have a sip of champers?' asked Charlotte.

'No.'

'What about a tea or coffee, then?'

'Well, okay, tea then.'

'Good,' said Charlotte, and she went into the kitchen.

The Windows desktop appeared on the laptop screen.

'Please, don't read it, darling,' said Christian, 'can't you just put it away, keep it safe instead?'

Beatrice began her search. All Christian could do was watch. He'd forgotten how untidy his desktop was, the background littered with shortcut icons and files.

'Oh this feels so wrong,' said Beatrice, as she scanned the screen.

She hovered the pointer over a few of the shortcuts.

'Okay, okay, if you really must look, go to the *Thirty Things* folder,' said Christian.

'So, how's it looking?' asked Charlotte, from the kitchen.

'I can't see anything obvious ...'

'There's a shortcut for it right there,' said Christian, his finger in the screen.

'... it's so messy.'

'Well that would be right,' said Charlotte.

Beatrice opened an explorer window and started scrolling the pointer through the folder names. She stopped halfway down the first page. 'I've think I've found it.'

Christian gave a quick shake of his head. Oh no. No, no, no, no, no.

'Fallen Angels,' said Beatrice.

'Not the worst title I've ever heard, actually,' said Charlotte, still in the kitchen, 'so was it sort of *Fifty Shades* meets *Twilight?*'

'I don't know. All I know is it was about the afterlife, so this must be it.'

Christian tried to place himself over the screen in a futile effort to stop where this was going, but in doing so lost his balance and fell into the sofa and partly into Beatrice. 'I'm sorry, I'm so sorry my darling,' he said as he flailed about trying to get out of his girlfriend and the sofa.

'I can't do it, I can't look,' said Beatrice, lifting her hands. 'You look, Lottie. You look for me.'

'No way,' shouted Christian, now just about out of the sofa.

'Okay, if that's what you want,' said Charlotte and she came through.

Beatrice got up and moved to the opposite sofa. 'I can't look,' she said.

'Right,' said Charlotte, taking Bea's place, 'let's see what we've got then.'

Christian spun round, got down on his knees and placed himself inside the coffee table and over the laptop, successfully this time, so much so that the entire screen passed inside his abdomen.

'Okey-dokey,' said Charlotte as she opened the folder.

'Don't, please don't,' said Christian, looking into her eyes, now inches from his.

Inquiry. Puzzlement. Restrained smugness. Less restrained smugness. 'There, er, don't seem to be any *Word* files, Bea darling.'

'Oh?'

'A lot of movie files though.'

'Movies?'

'I don't think this is his writing, my love.' A tiny, naughty, dimpled smile as Charlotte double-clicked a button.

Sound emanated from Christian's hips. Quiet at first, nothing more than the background whir of a video camera, but then voices.

I will not ask you again. Now, confess.

Oh you're right, I admit it, I confess. I'm such a naughty angel. I've been baaaaaaad. You're not going to tell Jesus, are you? I'll do anything if you don't tell.

Beatrice came over.

'It's not what you think,' said Christian as the pornography played inside him, 'the laptop, it got a virus, these pop-ups kept appearing.'

'Oh my God,' said Beatrice, 'I don't ... it can't be.'

'Looks like it is,' said Charlotte.

'No ... no ...' said Christian.

'Seems it's part of a set,' said Charlotte, with a couple more clicks, '*Backdoor Gabriela*. This is clip four.'

Beatrice put her hand to her mouth. 'I don't believe it,' she said, 'I just don't believe it.'

'I know,' said Charlotte, 'she's supposed to be an angel. I thought it would be strictly blow jobs.'

Destructive and traumatic events followed.

Christian begged. He pleaded. But it made no difference.

His beloved Beatrice and her willing accomplice.

They did not flinch. There was no mercy.

An hour later, further unusual events unfolded. Though to anyone in the mortal plane, they went unseen. At the top of Vestments, a troop of some two dozen ethereal figures gathered. For anyone who could see them, they would have made for a strange sight. Among their number: an Asian man with half his right arm missing; a suited white man in a bowler hat; a red-haired woman dressed in overalls and wellies; a man with a red barrel over his head; and, strangest of all, a man wearing a large bronze copper kettle on his shoulders. All had backpacks, of sorts, in varying shapes and sizes.

To the front of the group stood a beaky-featured figure in full-length burgundy robes. He was shorter than the others, but obviously in charge.

'Right then, ladies and gentlemen,' said Rimreach, 'I want to make something absolutely clear. Nothing has changed from last night, nothing. So I repeat, I don't care who snares him. You will all be rewarded equally, all of you. No fights. For one time only you are a team. Now, go get our cargo!'

The shepherds began to move in on number twenty-two, all of them stepping down into the ground as they approached, sinking themselves up to eye level. Some made their way round the back, others to the sides, half a dozen stayed at the front. They closed in on the house and slipped in through the walls.

Chapter Twenty-Six

Nikki drove into Vestments and pulled up. She was still mad at herself over her failure to get the laptop the previous evening, and not wholly confident in the tactics for today.

She took the lilies from the passenger seat. She'd been anxious about what to get. Details mattered. They always mattered.

She walked up to the house and rang the bell.

The door was answered by a thin woman with hair like a yellow toast rack.

Behind her, and unseen to everyone in the mortal realm, several tired ethereal shepherds came out to see if they could learn something, having found no sign of Christian from their search of the house.

'Yes?' said the woman.

'Is Beatrice in?'

Nikki felt the woman look her up and down.

'Fuck off.'

'I … I just wanted to apologise. I'm Nikki.'

'I know who you are. And you've got a fucking nerve coming here after everything you've done. And I won't have you upsetting my friend all over again. So. Fuck. Off.'

'Look, I'm here to say I'm sorry and to ask if there is anything I can do.'

'You're not welcome. That's what fuck off means – fuck off.'

'Lottie, wait,' said a voice from inside, 'wait.'

Beatrice emerged from the hallway.

'Beatrice, I'm so sorry about yesterday,' said Nikki. 'I got you these.'

She handed Beatrice the flowers. Beatrice took them but made no comment.

'You don't have to speak to her, Bea,' said Charlotte, 'and you don't have to take her shitty flowers. I can't believe she had the nerve to show her face here again.'

'No, it's all right, Lottie. Please, go inside.'

Charlotte seemed reluctant to move.

'Lottie. That's an order.'

'Don't upset my friend,' said Charlotte, jabbing an accusing finger at Nikki. 'Just shout if she starts causing trouble, Bea, and I'll come and rip her throat out.'

Charlotte retreated.

Beatrice stepped out, pulling the door closed behind her.

'I'm so sorry, Beatrice,' said Nikki, 'I don't know what I was thinking.'

'Look, perhaps I overreacted,' said Beatrice, 'but I've decided I can't forgive you, so there's nothing more to say. Thank you for the flowers, now can you please leave.'

'Is there really nothing I can do?'

'No.'

'There must be something. Can I help with the funeral expenses?'

'My God, you just don't do tact, do you? Well I don't want your money, I don't want anything from you.'

'I just want to help.'

'You can help by leaving me alone.'

'Beatrice, I know you don't want to hear this, and you're going to hate me even more for bringing it up, but I have to, it's too important not to. The book. Have you thought about what I said?'

'I don't believe my ears, you really don't care who you hurt.'

'It's not what I want, it's what Christian would want. It meant so much to him. Surely we owe him that?'

'I'm not going to listen to you dictate to me what is owed to my late husband-to-be, and what my dead husband-to-be would want. I will be the judge of that. And it's irrelevant now, it's—'

'Bea, Bea,' said Nikki, holding up her hand. She reached into her pocket and withdrew a piece of paper. 'This is a banker's draft. Made out to you. It can't be bounced, it can't be cancelled. It's as good as—'

'I know what a banker's draft is.'

'You'll know I'm serious then. All I want is the laptop. Give me the laptop and you can walk away with one hundred thousand–'

'You're too late.'

'What do you mean?'

'I did think about what you said. And I decided to let the book die with Christian.'

Nikki felt a surge of electricity run through her, the antimatter version of what she'd felt at the dinner table all those weeks ago, when she'd first realised who Christian was.

She stumbled backwards. Beatrice, this time, did not move to help her.

'We've wiped the hard drive,' said Beatrice.

'Wiped?' Nikki's pulse was surging, she was in danger of hyperventilating. But somewhere a cool, calm voice inside her head was gently but firmly telling her to stay calm, reminding her it's possible to recover deleted files from computers.

'And then we took the hard drive out and boiled it ...'

Does boiling destroy data? The cool, calm voice shrugged its shoulders.

'... and then we smashed it up and then we ran it over.'

Another more focused antimatter shockwave hit Nikki. Game over. 'You don't know what you've done,' said Nikki, 'you stupid girl, you petty, jealous, small-minded–'

'Save it. We're done. The book's gone. So, my recommendation for you now is to take your flowers, and, as my friend suggests, fuck off.' She threw the lilies in Nikki's face, stepped back inside and slammed the door.

Nikki felt light-headed. It seemed like this moment was not happening to her, or rather it was, but she was observing it from a distance. She looked down on the broken lilies at her feet and tried to take in the finality of what she'd just learned.

The door opened again. Charlotte came out brandishing a kitchen knife. 'Look, you little book witch, it's over, so fuck off.'

Nikki didn't flinch – she just stood there, staring at the knife.

'I said *fuck off*. Don't think I won't use this.'

Nikki's world collapsed to a singularity. Christian was gone from this world. So was the information. She knew what she had to do. She lurched forward and snatched the knife by the blade, cutting her fingers and forearm in the process.

.   .   .

'Lottie,' screamed Beatrice, before pulling Charlotte back in by her collar. Beatrice slammed the door and flicked the latch. 'Back door,' she shouted, 'lock it, do it now.'

Hands and fingers shaking, Beatrice put the chain on and checked the front door was locked before going to check the windows.

Nikki stood motionless on the step, looking down at the knife in her hand and the blood now flowing. She turned to leave, but stopped. Yes, a final moment for herself, before the return to duty – she owed herself that much. She stepped back to the door and crouched at the letterbox. She flipped it open and stabbed the knife in. 'Little pigs, little pigs,' she said.

'We're calling the police, you mad cow,' said Charlotte.

'Beatrice, dearest little pig,' said Nikki, 'Christian wasn't coming to see you. He was with me. We were going to the meeting when he got run over. He was coming to my meeting, not yours. He wanted me, not you. I thought you'd like to know.'

There was no response from inside the house. She made a couple more thrusting jabs with the knife before allowing the letterbox to slam shut.

She marched to the car, unconcerned about the trail of blood.

She got in, turned the ignition but then paused. Where to start? Here? Maybe. No, come on, be thorough, be methodical. Start at the beginning.

Chapter Twenty-Seven

Christian was sitting motionless in a quiet corner of South Hill Park. His head was in an endless spin cycle of emotions: his inability to make contact with Beatrice, the outing and airing of his private downloads, and the malicious destruction of his writing. And all this on top of what had already been, by anyone's standards, a bit of a rough twenty-four hours.

But the book dominated – not only the ending of his dream, but at Bea's hand. He knew he shouldn't have stayed long enough to be a witness at the execution, but he had to know if they would follow through. Right until the final moments he was convinced Beatrice would see sense and grant a pardon or at least a stay of execution. And when she didn't, all he could do was look on in horror.

The book's death-by-a-thousand-cuts demise had only made it worse: the hard drive ceremonially wiped, before being theatrically ripped from its casing, then hammered, boiled and run over. The ignominious end for traitor data. And there was more. Following the main event Christian was treated to the encore destruction of his numerous USB sticks and portable hard drives, and the burning of his few paper notes, sketches and print-outs. Everything was obliterated in a cold and systematic prose massacre.

Now it was as if the book had never existed. Now it persisted only in his mind.

He'd gone there fixed on making things right, and Beatrice had been the only thing keeping him going on the long march from London. But seeing his writing joyfully razed, along with a lovingly curated and important collection of digital erotica, it was too much. It was still his home, she was still his girlfriend, but how could he stay there now, after what she'd done, after what she'd allowed to happen? He'd had no choice but to leave. So that is what he'd done, drifting out of the house, out of Vestments and back towards the town centre. No plan. Not the slightest idea what to do.

Of course what he didn't know, what he couldn't know, is that these events had been his saving. If he'd stayed only minutes longer, the shepherds would have him and he would now be on his way to the Gate and into the hands of God and whatever his administration had in store.

After a desperate, year-long afternoon zombie-plodding round the park and extracting what distraction he could from the adjacent arts centre – where he read about Oscar Wilde's stay in Bracknell, not that it was news to Christian, it being common knowledge among the town's literati – he'd eventually just sat himself down in the grass.

Now the sun's progress towards the horizon brought him back to the present, and to a new anxiety – where would he spend the night? Back to the house, to their old bed, sleeping next to her? Well, it didn't have to be the bedroom. He could stay in the spare room or living room, perhaps. He could even stay in the garage.

No. No, he wasn't going to skulk. He'd done nothing wrong.

So he turned and headed back towards the town centre, still with no destination in mind, but a sense of urgency as the fading light triggered unwelcome recall of his nocturnal glow from the previous evening.

Chapter Twenty-Eight

Half an hour after her bloody exit from Vestments, Nikki was back on the M4, retracing the previous day's journey into London. Her arm was still bleeding, as were her fingers, but not enough to trouble her, not nearly so. There was an uncertain road ahead, a new chapter, but what little remained of this one was clear and simple. Six quadrillion megatonnes had been lifted from her shoulders and she was riding the moment: racing through the traffic, tripping every speed camera, windows down, stereo up, and though unable to find R.E.M.'s 'It's the End of the World as We Know It', she had found Queen's 'Don't Stop Me Now' and was howling along for all she was worth.

But as the M4 gave way to the A4, she dropped the volume, her high on the wane as she realised this final drive was almost over. Now the reality of what she was about to do hit home. It would be easier for her: she had unnatural certainty when it came to what would follow. But then it would be harder too: she was in her right mind; she would be doing it eyes open, sane and sober.

The minutes ticked down. Hammersmith, Earl's Court, and then – and then butterflies as she realised she didn't know. She hadn't got the details.

Focus, girl, focus. But no matter. She had to make the call anyway.

She pulled over, turned off the engine, and called Bryan Fishguard, her former General Manager at iChemiclast and man she had entrusted to reopen and run the Person of Interest research department.

'Nikki, how are you? Long time no hear.'

'I'm fine. I'm good. Look, Bryan, I don't have much time, so listen carefully. First I need some information.'

'Okay.'

'There was an accident, a fatal one in central London, yesterday between half past ten and ... I don't know, two in the afternoon. I need to know where. I need the street and where on the street.'

'Hang on, we'll take a look.'

While she waited, she held out her arm for inspection. She examined it dispassionately, as if it were not her own, watching as fresh blood continued to flow, crossing earlier paths already now black and congealed.

'Have you got it?'

'Nearly there ...'

'Come on, come on.'

'... okay, I have it. *Man Dies in Collision with Hearse.* Road traffic accident in central London, yesterday ... it was on ... Marylebone Road, the junction with Great Portland Street.'

'You're certain. Marylebone and Great Portland?'

'Yes.'

'And there were no other fatal accidents?'

'Nothing's coming up.'

'Okay. Okay, thanks. Now the other thing, Bryan ...'

'Yes?'

'It's time. Time for what we always talked about. Execute Jonestown.'

There was a short silence.

'Sorry, can you just confirm. Jonestown?'

'Yes. Jonestown.'

Another silence.

'How many?'

'All of them.'

'All?'

'There's been a loss of control. I can't take the risk that we won't need everyone.'

'Look, I know we always said there might come a time for Jonestown, but, well, most of them have families now.'

'Don't go soft on me, Bryan. They all knew the deal.'

'I don't think they did.'

'Well they should. It's implied. Why do they think they get such generous packages?'

'Okay. Okay, well, consider it done, then.'

'One more thing. I need you too, Bryan.'

Another silence.

'I understand.'

'Look, I have to go. I'll see you at the rendezvous.'

She hung up.

She turned the ignition, set the satnav and moved back into traffic.

Thirty minutes later she was approaching the Marylebone and Great Portland junction, joining the long queue of traffic at the lights.

Close enough. She turned off the engine.

She took hold of the knife and gave it the once-over. This would do just fine. Large blade. Sharp. Strong.

She placed the tip of the knife at a point between two of her ribs, midway up the left side of her chest.

The traffic in front moved off.

How high up is the heart?

The car behind gave a blast on its horn.

And what was it she once heard? It's more central than you think? Or it's not as central as you think? Perhaps she should stop and do some research first. Perhaps she should– No. She was already late, already twenty-four hours late. Fuck it, anywhere in the general chest area would do. She tightened her grip on the moulded handle. One thrust is all it would need.

Another blast on the horn from the car behind, this time longer and joined by another from farther back.

Her breath was racing.

Okay. One, two, three … nothing.

'Fuck.' She had to get a grip. It was just mind over matter.

She braced herself again. Okay, again, on three.

One, two, three … nothing.

'Fuck, fuck, fuck, fuck, fuck.' She didn't have time for this.

She was interrupted by a voice just back from her open window.

'What are you stopped for?' asked the man as he approached. 'In case you haven't noticed there's a line of– Holy fuck, what are you doing? Look don't do it, really. Don't–'

A chorus of horn blasts drowned him out.

'She's got a knife,' shouted the man. He turned back to Nikki and moved closer. 'Look, miss, my name's Jerry. I'm sure whatever it is, it's not worth killing yourself over.'

Nikki turned. 'Hi, Jerry. My name's Nikki, and you couldn't be more wrong.'

Another cacophony of horn blasts.

'Shut the fuck up, she's got a knife,' shouted Jerry, 'she's got a knife and she's gonna kill herself.' He called to his girlfriend, still in the passenger seat of his Polo, and gestured to the growing queue of traffic. 'Gem, *Gem*. Tell them, tell them to shut up, we've got a situation here.'

Nikki activated the central locking and closed the windows. She'd found an answer to her mental block. There was now a good hundred metres between her and the truck up ahead, just beyond the junction.

She started the car and took off her seat belt. Jerry tried the handle and banged on the glass but it was too late.

Safe from interference, she braced the handle of the knife on the centre of the steering wheel, and, leaning in, guided the tip of the blade, once again, between two of the ribs midway up the left side of her chest, before whirring her seat forward to pin the weapon in place.

Just like a sticking plaster. One sharp sting and it's all done with.

She put the car into drive, turned to wink at Jerry, and moved off.

She floored the accelerator. Ten, twenty, thirty miles per hour. Already fast enough but she kept her foot planted.

A pulse of fear.

Don't look, just don't look.

She closed her eyes but her instincts forced them open again.

Do not look.

She braced the wheel with her knee and covered her eyes with her hands, pressing down hard. She just had to stay strong. It would only take a moment.

She could feel her heartbeat racing, pounding close to the point of the blade, which was already through her blouse and bra and drawing blood. Her hands shook as she fought with herself. And then a tremor in her leg, a twitch of temptation to hit the brake. She pressed down harder on the gas, tensing her muscles and trying to lock her knee straight, but again she felt it, compelling her to back off. She needed a distraction, and quick, something to keep her self-preservation instinct off balance, but she couldn't think of anything.

It could be anything. Anything at all. Why couldn't she think of anything to use as a distraction? She had a whole lifetime of experiences to draw on, it could be as simple as ... as ... she couldn't even think of examples of things to illustrate to herself how simple the anything could be. Oh this was bad, she needed something, anything to stop herself thinking about–

The bang and slam of an impact, but a glancing blow only, the car lurching to the right with a screech from the tyres. A Honda Jazz being driven by a young man on a driving lesson, which until now had been going rather well, had clipped the back of the BMW. He'd had a green light, he'd mirror-signal-manoeuvred, his hands were at ten-to-two. The only thing he hadn't done was check to see if there was a car about to race through a red light being driven by a maniac with her hands clamped over her eyes. His father had warned him about women drivers, but Oliver was an enlightened young man and had paid no heed to such prejudice.

Nikki hadn't seen the red light because you don't tend to see such details when you're in the midst of a life and death struggle with yourself, especially if you have your hands clamped over your eyes while you're doing it. The impact was not enough to stop her from ploughing into the back of the truck a tenth of a second later, but was enough to make it a forty-five degree plough-in.

And so the V12 suicide missile hit its target. As the steering-wheel airbag deployed, it deflected the knife, but not enough to prevent it piercing Nikki's ribcage and passing several inches into her chest cavity as she was flung forward, slamming into the passenger-side screen pillar, the windscreen and door glass shattering in the process.

Jerry sprinted up to the wreckage. He took only seconds to arrive, but already there was blood all over the car's dashboard. Nikki was slumped on her side, in foetal position, half in the passenger footwell. The car itself was now somewhat shorter, but the structure of the cabin was largely intact. With the glass smashed, Jerry was able to reach in and unlock and open the driver's door. He could see Nikki was still breathing, but there was an awful sharp wheeze about it, like she'd swallowed a tin whistle.

'Holy shit,' he said, seeing the embedded knife and the kitschy pulsing squirt of blood coming from the wound. She had multiple lacerations, too, her neck and face now in ribbons. 'Holy shit, holy shit.'

A moment later, the man's girlfriend, Gemma, arrived at the scene behind him.

'Oh Jesus, this is bad,' she said, holding onto Jerry's shoulders and peering round him. 'Oh my. What do we do?'

'We need to call an ambulance.'

'I shouted to the car behind,' she said. 'They're calling for one.' She took a closer look at Nikki. 'Oh Jesusss.'

'Stay with us, miss,' said Jerry. He leaned into the cabin and took Nikki's hand.

'What are you doing?' asked Gemma.

'What does it look like I'm doing, I'm talking to her.'

'Like on TV?'

'Yes, I suppose. So what?'

'That's TV, poppet, it's not real. You don't know what you're doing. I don't think we should interfere.'

'I know it's not real, but it's authentic. They research these things. And anyway it's our duty to interfere.'

'I don't think we are. What if we get it wrong?'

'No, he's right,' said a stocky man in the small crowd that had already formed behind them, 'we have to help. Hey, anyone know first aid?'

There were no takers.

'Reckon we should get that knife out,' he said, his eyes widening.

'No, I don't think so,' said Jerry, 'I think you're supposed to leave it in there.'

'Did you get that from TV too?' asked Gemma.

'Y'know, your fella's right, now I think about it,' said the stocky man. 'There was this farmer on *Casualty*. They pulled this spike out of him, before the medoes got there, and then he was a goner.'

'What was he doing with a spike?' asked Gemma.

'Well, y'know those farmers, thrill-seekers, always messing about with spikes, ignoring health and safety, can't get enough of it.'

'You'd think they would pay more attention,' said Gemma.

'Ah yeah, but it's the pressure of the lifestyle. He got careless, mind not on the job, all blue at losing his subsidy, and then finds his eldest's a poof and doesn't want the farm, plus then some kids from the village had been–'

'Look, does that matter?' snapped Jerry. 'A woman is seriously injured here.' He turned back to Nikki. 'What's your name, miss? I'm sorry, I can't remember what you said, was it Vicki?'

There was no response.

He asked again and on the third time a weak thin voice replied, 'Nikki. My name's Nikki. Am I dead?'

'Not yet,' said Gemma, with cheer.

Jerry turned back to his girlfriend. 'Gem, can you please be a bit more encouraging.'

'I thought I was.'

'Look, leave the talking to me, will you, I've seen more of the right TV shows.' He turned back to Nikki. 'No one's dying here, miss, you're going to be fine.'

'But isn't that just as unfair,' whispered Gemma, 'just look at that knife, look at all the blood. She may, well, … you know. Is it fair to give her false hope that she won't?'

'Good point, missy,' said the stocky man, grinning. 'I always reckon the ugly truth is best. And this looks pretty ugly.'

'What on earth would be the point,' said Jerry, whispering as loud as he could, 'in telling her the ugly truth?'

'Well, she may need to get her affairs in order,' offered Gemma.

'Affairs in order? Oh yes, well perhaps we should be phoning for a solicitor as well as an ambulance.'

'She could write in blood,' said the stocky man. 'Here, anyone got any paper?'

'Shut up, shut up, both of you,' said Jerry, 'no one is dying.'

'Not on your watch, eh?' said the stocky man, hands in pockets. 'I like your style.'

'I want to die,' croaked Nikki, 'I need to die.'

'Don't you do that. Don't you go saying your goodbyes,' said Jerry.

'That's not TV,' said Gemma.

'What's not?' asked the stocky man.

'That line,' said Gemma. '"Don't you go saying your goodbyes" … it's from a film … oh what's it from? I know it, I know it …'

For a moment there was nothing but the gentle rhythmic sound of pulses of blood hitting the underside of the glovebox.

'Got it. *Titanic*. It's from *Titanic*,' said Gemma.

'Good spot, miss,' said the stocky man.

'All right, so it's from *Titanic*,' said Jerry, 'so what, it's still good.'

'And that's been shown on TV,' said the stocky man, 'so maybe that still counts?'

'So I suppose you're going to tell me *Titanic* was real too?' said Gemma, turning to Jerry.

'Well of course it was fucking real, the fucking boat sank, how much more real could it have got?'

'There you go,' said the stocky man, 'ugly truth, you see. When it's going down, you'd better know it's going down.'

'Well this boat is not going down, no way,' said Jerry.

'I'm sorry about all this,' said Gemma to Nikki, 'he watches a lot of TV.'

There was no response.

'Talk to us,' said Jerry.

Still no response.

'You have so much to live for,' offered Gemma, looking to Jerry for approval.

He nodded.

'No, you fucking morons,' wheezed Nikki, just managing to lift her head, 'I have … so much to … die for.'

'That's it, keep talking. Why do you have so much to die for? Tell us about it,' said Jerry.

'So sleepy,' said Nikki.

'Don't you dare go to sleep,' said Jerry, 'stay with us.'

'Maybe rest is good?' said Gemma, 'I think I'd want a rest, in that condition.'

'No. Sleep means they die,' said Jerry, 'everyone knows that.'

'Thanks for … the … concern,' moaned Nikki, 'but … fuck … off.'

'Charming,' said Gemma.

'I want to … sleep, I want … to … die.'

'Stay with us,' said Jerry.

Nikki's eyes glazed over.

'Stay with us, Nikki.'

'What next then, Dr House?' said Gemma.

'I don't know. They never go to sleep on TV. I imagine it's bad for the ratings. We need to wake her up.'

'How about a coffee?' said Gemma. 'You know, like a double shot.'

'You know, I could fancy a coffee,' said the stocky man.

'Shut up, shut up,' said Jerry. He started slapping Nikki's face, softly at first, then harder. But there was no response.

Nikki's first sensory information was visual. She was in an environment of complete darkness, save for a doorway and an old man who was standing with his back to her.

The door was closed inside its frame, but brilliant-white light was escaping all around the edges, surging through the gaps. The door itself was panelled with a brass handle, and the words 'THIS WAY' painted in large authoritative gold letters on the front. She recognised this environment immediately. She had an instinctive sense of it, but the perfectly matching details were informed from Christian's writing. She raised her hands to her mouth, covering her broad smile. For a brief moment, she was filled with something approaching pride for what her lost student had accomplished, her first ever first-person taste of the evident accuracy of his writing, even if he hadn't quite finished the chapter. Oh, if only, she lamented, if only she could have kept him alive long enough to complete the work, to make the truth not just known in the mortal realm but irrefutable.

But there was still time. All was not yet lost.

Sight was, in fact, the third of Nikki's senses to come back online. She hadn't noticed her sense of smell returning because in the infinite noth-ingness there is nothing to smell – not even the mustiness of a very musty old gentleman – and she hadn't noticed her hearing return because the old gentleman standing with his back to her was keeping very quiet.

'Hello?' said Nikki. 'Hello?'

The old man said nothing and continued to look the other way, despite the other way offering literally nothing to look at.

'Excuse me,' said Nikki, 'I said hello.'

The old man began humming tunelessly.

'Hey, hello,' said Nikki, waving her hands in front of the old man's face.

'If you'd like to wait, miss,' whispered the man.

'Wait, wait for what?'

The old man gestured for Nikki to look behind her.

Nikki turned round to see a large spherical hole, about her height, a short distance away. It was a disorientating sight, not just because of the wisps of silver flame around its circumference, but because there wasn't anything for the hole to be in: it was just floating there, a hole in nothing. And yet a hole is what it was: she could see inside, she could perceive depth within. And what she saw was a visceral scene: the interior of her crashed car, her battered body pumping itself dry of blood, her face lacerated and limp, eyes motionless, pupils high under her lids.

She peered closer but had to shift her weight back as she felt the hole's gravity begin to tug on her.

'What is that, and why do we have to wait for it?' asked Nikki, turning back to the old man.

'Look, I'm sorry, madam, but I'm not supposed to talk to you until we have … until we have resolution.'

'Resolution of what?'

'I said, we're not supposed to talk. I'm not here.'

'We're talking so you are here so will you please tell me what's going on?'

The old man put a finger to his lips and shook his head.

'Am I dead?' asked Nikki. 'Come on, I must be.'

No response.

'I said, am I dead?' screeched Nikki into the ear of the old man, causing him to recoil.

'I'm not deaf, madam.' He took a moment to compose himself before adding, 'you are on the brink, my dear.'

'The brink?'

'Yes, it's all most irregular. Now, I've already said too much, so can you please just wait before we go any further.'

'Look, surely I must be either dead or not?'

'Wait.'

Nikki slapped the old man across his bald scalp, causing him to yelp.

'There's no need for street violence,' he said, 'this is a place of tranquillity.'

'Well if you want it to stay tranquil, you'd better tell me what's going on, pops.'

'All right, madam,' said the old man, holding up his hands, 'normally, yes, you are either alive or dead, but it's not, well, it's not a perfect system, you see.'

'Keep talking.'

'Now and again, well, in truth a little more often than I had been led to expect, people come to me when they're not *quite* dead. Most embarrassing. It's supposed to be a one-way trip, you see, not some sort of try-before-you-buy scheme. It's all rather awkward, to say the least.'

'No, there's nothing embarrassing or awkward in the slightest. Let's get on with it. I'm ready.'

'Ready for what?'

'Death.'

'Really?'

'Yes. Never been more ready. Where do I sign?' She grabbed the old man's clipboard.

'But you may be able to go back,' said the old man, reclaiming the clipboard, 'a little willpower, a fair wind.'

'No, I'd be much happier dead, if it's all the same to you.'

'Now this is most irregular. Given the chance, most people do tend to pop back for an extension. All this' – he gestured to the nothingness – 'and whatever's through there' – he pointed to the door – 'will still be here for you, when you return. You won't be missing a thing.'

'No, my mind's made up. Bring on the death.'

The old man put his clipboard under his arm and looked at Nikki properly for the first time. 'Depression?'

'What?'

'Nothing to live for?'

'Exactly.'

'Come, come, surely you have lots to live for. Let's see.' The old man consulted his papers. 'Yes, young, attractive, wealthy, successful ... *significant* untapped capacity for experiencing pleasure' – he gave a small flick of his eyebrows – 'and aside from a large kitchen knife sticking out of your chest, in perfect health.'

'No, I'd far rather be through there,' said Nikki, pointing to the door.

'Lots of lovely people waiting for you, are there? Is that it?' said the old man.

'No. Well, yes ... I think so ... but then I've never met them. Him.'

'This just isn't right, madam.'

'Well, can't be helped. Let's go. Come on, I haven't got all day.' She took a step towards the door.

'Madam, I am sorry, but we must wait.' The old man again gestured towards the hole in the nothingness behind Nikki.

Nikki brushed past him and gripped the door handle. She tried pulling, pushing, twisting, but the door was stuck fast in its frame.

'I'm afraid it's quite impossible to progress until your mortal situation has been resolved.'

'Well I'm not going back.'

'You may not have a choice, my dear.'

'Is that a threat?'

The old man chuckled. 'Dear me, no, madam. But often things in life, and death, are beyond our control, however strong our desire for a particular outcome.'

'Meaning what?'

'Well, in this case, either the hole will disappear and you will be free to proceed or …'

'Or what?'

'Or it will get, well, larger, and you will … *feel inclined* to return to the world inside it.'

'Oh yes? Well we'll see about that.'

'Yes, my dear. I believe we will.'

'Perhaps we should let her sleep,' said Gemma, 'she's had a busy day. Let her save her strength.'

'No,' said Jerry. He grabbed Nikki's arm and pulled up her sleeve to expose her wrist.

'What now?'

'We must wake her.' Jerry placed his hands around Nikki's wrist and twisted hard.

'What, with a Chinese burn?' said the stocky man, smirking.

'They're deadly when they're done well,' said Jerry.

'You'll bruise her,' said Gemma.

'I'll take that risk,' said Jerry. He tried again, twisting Nikki's wrist harder, but couldn't rouse her.

'We need a stronger stimulus,' he said, 'something to get her attention.'

'Stand aside, children,' said the stocky man, and he barged in. He leaned into the cabin and grabbed the handle of the knife.

'What are you doing?' asked Jerry.

'Getting her attention.'

The man gave the knife a flick. A thick jet of blood spat out from the wound.

'Oh yes, get in there, you fat little chump,' said Nikki, as she watched the scene through the hole, 'yes, yes, twist it.'

'Really, this is most irregular,' said the old man.

'So you keep saying.'

The hole in the nothingness had been getting smaller anyway, but now with the stocky man's intervention, it had dropped to the size of a dinner plate.

'Done deal, I'd say, Grandpa,' said Nikki, 'shall we call that closed then?'

'I'm sorry, we must wait until it has disappeared entirely.'

'Oh, come on.'

The old man folded his arms.

They stood and watched the hole as it continued to shrink. But the rate began to fall away, and by the time it was a mere dot, no bigger than a pea, it seemed to have stopped getting smaller at all.

'Temporary blip?' said Nikki, nervously.

The old man shrugged.

Nikki craned her neck around the hole, but it was now too small to discern any image within.

They continued to watch the dot. A full minute passed.

'So ... you spend all your time here then?' asked Nikki.

'Oh yes,' said the old man, 'all my *time*.' He chuckled to himself.

They watched the dot for another minute.

'Must be ... nice for you,' said Nikki.

'Keeps me busy.'

They watched the dot again.

A pregnant thirty minutes passed with little change. But then in a blink the hole shrank to a point, then expanded to the size of a grape and began flipping from one to the other in rapid succession, pulsating like a flatulent sphincter, before stopping and stabilising, holding firm at the dimensions of a medium-sized red seedless.

'Well,' said the old man, 'I've never seen this before. Though, there was once this strange occasion–'

In an instant, the hole expanded to cover half of Nikki's field of view, before doubling in size, and doubling again, its gravity increasing exponentially, sucking Nikki in with the force of a tidal rip. She grabbed onto the old man's cardigan, stretching the wool as the irresistible gravity of the hole, now the size of a ten-storey office block, pulled her horizontal. The old man and the door were seemingly unaffected, the old man staying nonchalantly in place, despite the immense pull of the gaping void, and despite Nikki hanging on for all her worth to his now drastically misshapen cardigan.

'Please, I've only just received this, madam, it's supposed to last me at least the first two and a half thousand years.'

'I want to die. I need to go through. Please, help me die.'

'I'm sorry, my dear, but it appears it may not be quite your time.'

Nikki glanced back over her shoulder and took in the full-screen Imax image of her lying in a hospital emergency ward, a medical team working on her.

She turned her face back to the old man. 'Did you see anyone come through yesterday?' she shouted, struggling to maintain her grip on the unravelling beige wool. 'Englishman, dark hair, about six foot tall. Possibly a bit sullen.'

'I see quite a lot of people, madam. Now really, I think it's time for you to go.'

'Did any fit that description?' shouted Nikki.

'Several hundred, as I recall.'

'Had any of them died at the junction of Marylebone and Great Portland Street in London?'

'I can't say, madam.'

'Can't or won't?'

'Won't, madam.'

The old man ran a finger over the back of Nikki's left hand. She watched her fingers open and her grip fail. She jolted back hard as she began to be drawn into the void. The old man gave a genial smile and tapped her right hand. Her fingers opened and she was sucked into the abyss, along with one of the tortoiseshell buttons from the old man's cardigan.

'She's stable,' said the doctor.

'I think we've got her.'

'You're gonna be okay, Nikki.'

Dexter was pacing at the foot of Gordon's lounger, out on the executive deck of the clubhouse at Paradigm Palms, Limbo's most exclusive and least ugly golf course.

'And you were lying down at the time?' asked Dr Fleaband. His accent sounded like put-on Polish but was genuine.

'Yes. I was right here, taking a nap after my round,' said Gordon.

'This anxiety, this worry,' said Fleaband, 'I think this is normal for a man of your position, to have the little panic after feeling the pains, yes, this is–'

'No. Anxiety first, then pain,' said Gordon.

'Anxiety first?' said Fleaband, standing back and pursing his lips. 'But napping, this does not seem like the anxious situation?'

'I knew this was a bad idea,' said Dexter. He peered out to the oiled gravels of the fairways and 'greens', the black tar sands of the large bunker at the first. 'You didn't need stress. You needed rest.'

'What do you mean stress?' said Gordon.

'I mean I've seen you play golf before.'

'Meaning?'

'Meaning how many clubs came back this time?'

'All of them.'

'Really. Any a bit bent, any a bit broken? Any a bit inserted into Dinks?'

'None.'

Dexter raised his eyebrows.

'Go and fucking look if you don't believe me,' said Gordon, 'I had a great round, round of my life. I hit a ninety-two, ninety fucking two.'

'So anxiety was the beginning? And then the pains ...' said Fleaband, with a frown.

'Yes,' said Gordon, 'anxiety, pain, beautiful closeness, pain.'

'I'm sorry, *beautiful closeness?*' said Dexter.

'Yes, closeness,' said Gordon, 'a great warmth, like, like hugging puppies.'

'These puppies you see, you have seen them before, yes?' said Fleaband. 'They are here now?' He waved a bobbing hand in front of Gordon.

'For fuck's sake, it was *like* hugging puppies, I didn't actually see puppies, I'm not going nuts, man.'

'I see,' said Fleaband, making a note on his pad.

'It was a tender warmth,' said Gordon, roughly grabbing Dexter's hand, 'a wave of emotional intimacy.'

'Um,' said Dexter.

'Oh come on, don't look at me like that,' said Gordon.

'I'm sorry, Gordo, it's just that, well … you've thrown me,' said Dexter, 'thrown us,' he added, looking to Fleaband.

'Indeed,' said Fleaband, 'but this sexiness, it is gone now?'

'Look, there was no *sexiness*, it wasn't a sexual warmth.'

'But when you talk of the puppies, you mean?'

'I mean puppies. Fucking puppies. Fluffy fucking cuddly innocence, man.'

'I see,' said Fleaband, making another note.

'But you're still in pain, Gordo?'

'Yes,' said Gordon, 'I fucking am.'

'And the pains, you say it is here,' said Fleaband, prodding Gordon in the belly.

'No, here,' said Gordon, pointing to his chest, 'but at first it was all over, all over my entire body. It was like I'd been charged by an elephant, Dexter, a fucking big one.'

The doctor continued to prod. 'Indigestion,' he said.

'Indigestion?' said Gordon. 'I've never had indigestion. I haven't even eaten anything, not in centuries.'

'Indigestion,' said Fleaband, nonchalantly, and he put away his notepad.

Chapter Twenty-Nine

Christian felt a small measure of relief as he arrived at the churchyard. He'd regarded his decision to spend a second night in the vicarage as little more than Hobson's choice, but seeing the glow of the vicarage lights already on, he now recognised it as a sanctuary.

And at least he'd made it back before sunset, too, still with a solid spectrum of colour in his hands and clothing.

As he drifted up the path, something caught his eye, a movement down in the bushes a few paces ahead, near the undergrowth that the cat, Welby, had been staking out that morning. It caused him to do a double take, and then straighten up and stop. Not so much from what the something did, but what it didn't. And what it didn't was make any noise – not a sound, not a whisper, and yet it was inching through the undergrowth all the same.

A sense of dread. Was hearing the latest of his sensory anchor points to come adrift? What would be next? Blindness? He began to contemplate an existence informed only by smell, but then thankfully he acknowledged the background hum of the town centre and the low rumble of traffic from the other side of the church.

As he scanned the bushes, the thing moved silently again, only partly visible, hidden behind leaves and branches. Though it could not be, it looked for all the world like an uncooked joint of meat. A roast of some sort, only lacking rosemary, string and a wire rack.

A hedgehog, maybe? Bald, fat, silent hedgehog …

The thought triggered a shiver, but then this mystery ranked pretty poorly against his other troubles. He resolved not to let it get to him, though looked the other way as he drifted past and on into the vicarage.

As he emerged through the door, BBC Radio 4 greeted him like an old friend, Eddie Mair introducing a piece on the budget deficit. It caught Christian unawares. It told him he was safe; it told him everything was going to be all right. He'd have cried if he'd had any emotional reserves left.

He followed the discussion into the kitchen, where Tony was applying the finishing touches to a steak sandwich that wouldn't have looked out of place in an episode of *Scooby-Doo*.

'Um, evening,' said Christian.

No reply.

The sandwich, coupled with the meat-hog outside in the bushes, turned Christian's thoughts to food for the first time since the accident, only now registering he'd not eaten in a day and a half.

Eating. Based on recent events, it seemed unlikely he'd be able to, in his current state – if cars, walls and people could pass right through him, it seemed unlikely a steak sandwich would not. But at least he felt no hunger. Some small mercy.

He felt something at his legs, something *in* his legs. Faint and delicate, but definitely there and definitely moving. He looked down to see Welby strutting back and forth through his shins, before sitting down in his feet and looking up at him.

'Get off, get off,' said Christian, flicking a foot clean through the animal.

Welby sat there, yawned and looked at him.

'You can see me?' said Christian.

Welby was non-committal, but didn't break his stare.

'Great …' said Christian. 'I don't suppose you can pass on a message to my girlfriend?'

Welby yawned.

'No. Thought not.'

Tony turned off the radio. It caught Christian by surprise and triggered a pang of anguish.

Christian and the cat followed Tony and the sandwich through to the living room. Thankfully Welby went to his basket, and thankfully the reverend turned on the TV, partly restoring psychological life support.

Christian retired to the sofa, where he'd spent the night, and did his best to sit on it rather than in it.

Soon the opening titles to a double bill of old *Inspector Morse* episodes filled the screen. Christian couldn't remember ever having such a thankful reaction to the start of a TV show. Yes, he had problems, yes, he'd had better days, but as they sat and watched, Christian entered middle-aged eighties Oxford and for a while forgot the horrors of his new reality.

As the second episode finished, Christian's mind returned to the room and the sofa. *Lovejoy* was up next, according to the announcer. Christian had never been a fan, but it would do, of course it would do.

But Tony was checking his TV guide.

So, not a *Lovejoy* fan either.

Christian began to speculate on the options for ten p.m. on a Friday, hoping he'd not have to suffer a chat show or, Darwin forbid, a reality show.

Tony turned off the TV. No debate, no announcement.

Then he walked to the door where, with one click, he turned the lights off and Christian on, like he was a Christmas illumination, the teal tint appearing the moment the darkness enveloped the room.

Humiliation.

Exclusion.

Emptiness.

For a while he just sat there in the darkness, clinging to a forlorn hope that Tony might be coming back. But he was not. No more TV tonight. No escape.

He got out of the sofa. He moved to the window and edged his face through the curtains. Clouds had collaborated with the haze of street lights to block out the stars. The churchyard was still, but faint muffled bass proclaimed the glory of life raging against the night, in the town beyond – all the more pointed because Christian had never been one for pubs and clubs. Now he felt more distant than ever from the Homo erectus of Bracknell.

All the same, he thought about heading out. Not everyone would be clubbing, far from it. There would be houses with TVs on, hundreds of them, but the darkness outside seemed somehow more threatening than the darkness inside.

So he returned to the sofa and tried to sleep. But now he was bereft of the previous evening's exhaustion soporific. Now his unconscious was free to engage in wide-scale rumination on everything that had happened as well as speculate on what might follow. He didn't stand a chance and after an hour was still staring at the ceiling. Normally he'd have thrown in the towel, got up and done something constructive, or not so constructive, until he was tired, but now there was nothing he *could* do, constructive or otherwise. But he got up all the same and soon found himself back at the window.

This time, as he scanned the gravestones, he noticed an anomaly, a ground-level spotlight that didn't match the others. Diffuse and dim, with a worryingly familiar blue-green hue, and positioned rather too close to one of the brighter, whiter lights to be one of their number. And then it moved, or at least he thought it did. He held it centre vision, unblinking. Was it moving or were his eyes playing tricks?

The meat-hog? Was that where he'd seen it when he'd returned that evening?

Splintered hedgehog? Splintered meat? Animated splintered meat?

Ridiculous.

Another splintered person then, perhaps with just the head on view? The bald, tanned, meaty head of someone hiding mostly in the under-growth … mostly in the *ground*. Why not? If he could be ankle deep in pavement or cats, why not waist deep in a flower bed, why not neck deep?

He bent down and lowered his right leg into the floorboards. His knee and then his thigh disappeared with disturbing ease.

He pulled himself up and returned his attention to the glow. For the first time, he didn't feel safe here – if it was a person, splintered like him, then the walls and window between them meant nothing.

What did they want?

Were they a threat?

Why hadn't they said something?

Had they seen him?

He pulled his head in. They weren't doing anything. They meant no harm. Leave them be.

He went back to the sofa and tried to sleep, tried to forget what he'd seen, but ten minutes later he was back at the window. This time there was no glow, the ground offering only darkness and spotlights. What's worse than finding a spider in your bedroom? Losing a spider in your bedroom …

He spun round, but there was nothing in the room to surprise him. He made straight for the front door, not allowing himself time to think himself out of it. As soon as he was outside, he saw it, a few paces away, at the base of the hedge. He crouched down and moved closer. 'Hello,' he whispered. 'Hello?' No movement. No reply.

Closer.

'My name is Christian. I mean you no harm.' Closer still, within touching distance now. 'What are you doing down there?' He slowly stretched out an arm. He felt the scratchy shadow of the hedge as his hand passed through the foliage, before making just a fingertip of fleshy contact, the thing apparently as solid as he was.

It launched itself at Christian, hitting him square in the chest and knocking him back into the path.

He screamed and flapped at the thing now clamped to his chest, its footprint tight to his T-shirt, already wriggling in under his jacket lapels. He wanted it off, but couldn't commit, beaten back by his own revulsion at the prospect of touching its alien surface.

With his hands hovering around it, he looked down and saw it was an internal organ. It was a liver, a human liver, moving on him, nuzzling into him.

As he scrambled to his feet, it fell back under its weight, but held its grip, stinging Christian's cotton T-shirt skin.

He screamed again. This time, through gritted teeth, he forced himself to take the thing in his hands and tried to tear it off, finding he could break its hold with ease.

As he held it out in front of him, he entered a temporary state of paralysis, his mind circling in a loop of incredulity only broken when his brainstem took an executive decision to intervene.

Christian released and drop-kicked the AWOL organ, connecting rather well, sending it soaring like a football out of the churchyard for a sixty-yard touchdown somewhere near Pizza-a-GoGo.

Christian stood still, trying to comprehend what had just happened.

Finding some company in this strange parallel place would be heartening, but he had assumed if he did find others like him, he would not have to meet them bit by bit.

Chapter Thirty

Dexter took the final stairs two at a time, nearly flooring two Central Administration civil servants making an early start on trying to manage each other into fixing a loose balustrade, and thrust open the doors of the boardroom of Henry Ford House.

There at the far end, in conversation with three bleary-eyed managers, was a sight he'd not seen in twenty years: his boss standing tall and back in his old grey wolf-skin suit, cream shirt, blue tie and red braces, with his hair tied back into a low ponytail.

'I didn't believe it,' shouted Dexter.

Gordon looked up and beamed a wide smile. 'I thought you'd be pleased.' He waved the managers away and strode down to meet Dexter.

'What happened?' said Dexter. 'When I left you last night, you were out for the count.'

'Best sleep I ever had, Dex. I'm a new man, I tell you.'

'And your chest pains?'

'Gone.'

'Gone?'

'Gone.'

'Well, that's wonderful, that's–'

'Fact is, I've never felt better. I feel strong.' Gordon widened his stance and put his hands on his hips.

'So the ...' Dexter lowered his voice, '... the makeup, the nighties, the stockings?'

'Gone, gone, gone,' said Gordon, stretching both arms in the air, his fists clenched, 'as are the panties.'

'Right ...'

'The panties have been replaced with good old briefs, you understand.'

Dexter nodded and forced a smile.

'I tell you it's a new chapter, Dex. I feel cleansed. My mind is uncluttered. My vision is focused.'

'We've missed you,' said Dexter, 'oh how we've missed you.'

He shook Gordon's hand.

'Bad episode all that,' said Gordon, 'all that ... business.'

'It's fine, Gordon, really. I never judged you.'

'Well you damn well should have,' said Gordon, gripping Dexter's hand tighter. 'King of Limbo prancing about like that, for all that time, it wasn't right. What were you thinking, man?'

'I thought it was something you had to work through,' said Dexter. 'We all did.'

Gordon stepped in close, still maintaining his grip. His eyebrow hairs stood on end. His pupils shrank to ball bearings and his whites and irises flooded with yellows and greens.

'You damn well put me right if you see that again, you hear?' said the Lord of Limbo, his eyes slicing through Dexter's.

Dexter managed a wincing nod and just about held his resolve until his boss broke eye and hand contact and his glare returned to normal.

'Right, free up your diary, Dex. Lots to be done, lots to be put right.'

There was a weak knock at the open door.

'You called, sire?' said the cowering Bipton.

'Over here, Bippy,' said Gordon, pointing to the floor in front of him.

The little man scurried over, tape measure flapping behind him.

'Make me one like his but better,' said Gordon, pointing to Dexter's suit.

Dexter smiled.

'Of course,' said the flustered Bipton, and he started measuring Gordon up.

'Right, first new order of business, Dex – restore the old dress code. Immediate effect. And I want it tighter than before.'

'Tighter?'

'Suit and tie. For men and secretaries.'

'Right. Great.'

'Great indeed, Dex. Great indeed. The cultural revolution is over.'

'It's good to have you back, Gordo.'

Gordon placed a hand on Dexter's shoulder. 'It's good to be back. Now, to business!'

Chapter Thirty-One

The next morning, Christian began to emerge from his fitful Erdygrot-and-sofa-filled sleep to a puppy licking his face. After a rough night it was a comforting sensation, despite taking him back to distant unpleasant memories of Forsyth, his Uncle Frank's Irish Setter. But as Christian drifted back and forth across the line between wake and sleep, his intellect began to voice concerns. First, he didn't own a puppy and neither did Tony. Second, something was amiss with the sensation – though slippery, like the lick of a puppy, the tongue itself felt much too firm and fat. The pleasure centres of Christian's mind dismissed the concerns, bemoaning that couldn't the intellect butt out for once, what was wrong with enjoying a bit of harmless pleasure? But the intellect persisted, pointing out that the movements were unfamiliar: longer and slower than one would expect with a pup. Christian's imagination tried to arbitrate with an alternative theory for the facts, but drew a blank – yes, Tony had a cat, but this was something much stockier, and besides, the cat had been passing right through Christian the evening before. And then Christian's short-term memory got involved. And then a revolting thought entered his mind. Surely not. No, please, anything but that. Christian half opened his eyes. The liver was at his lips. He grasped the organ with both hands, leaped to his feet and hurled it across the room like an over-aggressive pass of a rugby ball, sending it sailing out through the far wall.

He dry retched as his tongue tried to distance itself from his mouth.

He rushed to the curtains to wipe it, only then realising his only option would be his own sleeve.

After extensive wipes, none of which did anything to remove the metallic taste, he tried to take stock. It was six fifty-one a.m., according to the Cheesus clock. The meagre light of morning was barely making it through the gaps in the curtains, suggesting it hadn't had much of a night's sleep either. Christian poked his head through. The gravestones were floating on a sea of mist.

He returned to the sofa to try to work out what he might do with his day.

After twenty minutes of his mind going around in circles, he heard an alarm clock upstairs. And so he decided to start his day by having breakfast with Tony, or rather, start by watching Tony having breakfast. It would, if nothing else, postpone bigger decisions.

Tony was also a long-morning person, so it seemed, and the relaxed pace of buttered bagels and BBC Radio 4's *Today* gave Christian the confidence to tell his host about the liver, in between making optimistic nose dives into the ground coffee Tony had retrieved from the cupboard, which was, as far as Christian could tell, as close as he'd be able to get to his morning latte. The sound of the story, as he listened to his own voice, were the ravings of a madman, and by the end he was relieved Tony hadn't been able to take in a word of it. Christian didn't doubt what had happened, but now he realised it was his problem alone.

By eight a.m., Tony was gone and so was Radio 4. Christian was alone again. Normally he was good on his own, great on his own, but now the first thing he did was count out the hours on his fingers. Seven, eight, nine. Nine hours, perhaps, until Tony would return, assuming he'd be out all day. What do vicars do six days a week? Nine hours until Radio 4, evening telly, and civilisation. And what if he was out in the evening? At a vicar social or something. Okay, so he'd have to be up early for Sunday, but it still meant nine hours could become fourteen, fifteen, sixteen. There was no way Christian could fill that time here. The vicarage was well stocked with books, but none that he could open. All just as unreadable as Tony's *Daily Telegraph*, still sitting on the kitchen table.

He had to get out.

The curtains had been drawn and now it was at least a little brighter outside. But what to do? He couldn't face another afternoon tramping South Hill Park and the arts centre, let alone doing it for a morning as well. Going back to the house was out of the question. And until reality restored itself, he couldn't see anything useful he could be doing. All he could do was wait. And there was nothing to do while he did it. Nothing.

Nothing.

Nothing.

Nothing.

Nothing – though he would rarely admit it, even to himself, he'd always been rather good at doing this so long as there was something else he was supposed to be doing while he did it. But being faced with doing nothing without something to do (or rather not do) while doing it was not something he was at all comfortable with. And then it hit him: not shopping. He hated shopping but had always been rather good at not shopping, or window shopping as amateurs call it, at least when it came to his kind of shop. That was the plan, then.

The shopping centre was just over the road, a mere two-minute drift, but instead Christian took a protracted, looping route. When you have an appointment with nothing, the last thing you want to do is arrive on time.

As he drifted through the cricket ground behind the church, and again when he reached the fields of the leisure centre, he had his usual reaction to observed recreation – his father's voice. *Don't all these people have jobs to go to? It's gone eight thirty – all these joggers aren't going to have time for a shower and a change of clothes before nine. What's this going to do to the economy?*

Christian tried to remind his father's voice that it was the weekend, but it was unrepentant. There was only one day of rest and it wasn't Saturday.

The general level of imposed proxy disgust worsened when he passed Point Royal and drifted on through Caterpillar Park, as he'd done on his route to Vestments the day before. Here he came across the same two men sitting on the same park bench – the idle postman and apparently just as idle British Gas worker. They'd be on weekend rates now, too.

It was still horribly early when he reached the shopping centre. But he headed for the technology stores all the same. It was a well-worn routine, so when he needed to get to the second floor, he stepped onto the escalator. He stood as the steps passed under him, and, a few moments later, two cleaners glided through him as if he was a boiled egg on a wire slicer. He stepped to one side, out through the handrail of the escalator. Idiot. But then he never was completely switched on in the mornings.

He looked again at the escalator. He stepped on again, this time attempting an upward-and-along stepped drift, in time with the escalator steps. But they move faster than you think, and he soon found himself lagging. It was only when he'd reached the top and stepped off to the side by the balcony rail that he realised he no longer needed the escalator at all. Idiot, idiot, idiot. Old idiot. Old fool. Stuck in his ways, trying to refuel his Model T by strapping a bag of oats to the front grille. Time to wake up and get with the programme. He looked around. No one was watching. Of course no one's watching – idiot, again. He looked out beyond the balcony rail into the open atrium. He edged out, drifting through the rail and into the open space. One metre, two metres, three. He was now standing clear of the balcony, standing on nothing at all. He got a rush, the thrill of levitation – real, genuine levitation. He looked down at the empty space below him. He braced himself for *Looney Tunes* late gravity, but it didn't come. He was still nervous, it was hard not to be with all his life experience screaming at him to get back onto the platform, but he didn't give in to it. Instead he moved farther out, enjoying the exhilaration that was growing with every step. The only fear he acknowledged as still rational was the possibility of being up here when reality caught up with him – the same fear he'd had when passing through the London traffic. He was already high enough for it to be lethal. But he was sick of the last two days being a one-way street. He needed to take something back and this was it.

After several minutes of aerial experimentation that took him right up to the roof beams, he came off the physical high and took a virtual escalator back to the balcony of level two and moonwalked over to Currys. But it was still only eight forty-five, and the shop wasn't yet open. He pondered how to kill fifteen minutes, before remembering he no longer had to and drifted through the closed shutter. He cruised up and down the aisles, enjoying the royal privilege of having the store to himself, save for a few yawning staff, and decided this was now the only way to not shop. After browsing the big-screen TVs, cameras, smartphones and tablets, he ended up at the video games.

He stood and stared at the Formula One game on the screen going through its demo sequence. Though Christian still loved video games, he'd found himself playing them less and less in recent years. Partly he'd developed some vague and distant awareness that it might be a bit of a waste of time, but mainly he'd found the experience increasingly disturbing as the realism had improved. A Formula One game of the type in his eight-bit retro collection was far too far removed from reality to ever suspend disbelief. It's just not possible to become fully immersed in a

two-dimensional, overhead, fixed-camera view of the featureless track as
your sixty-four-pixel, bright-pink car bleeps its way into the bright-blue
barriers. You always know you're playing the game.

But for the PlayStation generation, the boundary begins to blur. You
drive from the driver's point of view; the cars look like cars; the tracks
look like tracks; Martin Brundle sounds like Martin Brundle. Your senses
are being fed a lie, but your imagination is a willing collaborator, party to
it, welcoming it, devouring it, paving the way to make it all plausible. So
after just a few minutes of game time, you are immersed. You are a
Formula One driver, pushing for glory. The track, your car, your team, your
rivals, everything as real as you are. The hotels are real. The marina is real.
If winning at Monaco wasn't so vital for your push for the Formula One
World Title, you could pull off the track and explore, cause a stir in the
downtown traffic and cruise the boulevards before squirting the gas as you
head up into the hills. So back on the track, after you've crashed off a few
times, and any chance of winning the World Title in your rookie season
with the worst car on the grid has slipped by, that's what you decide to do.
And then you come up against an invisible barrier that extends right
around the circuit – a huge blunt reminder of the true nature of things.

*Look, there's nothing out here but data and program code, the game is behind
you. We've put a lot of work into this, so please turn round, go back, and
enjoy your time here.*

And then you realise. This is all fake – of course it's all fake. But you're
the only one who knows, and no one else is listening. The other cars keep
going round, committed to the pursuit of victory, podium, or points finish.
Martin is still gripped by the tension of the race. Yes, he's expressed his
exclaim at you coming off the circuit for the fifth time, but that's the limit
of his insight. He's unable to comprehend that you are now spending the
middle portion of the race doing doughnuts at Rascasse or repeatedly
hitting 180 mph the wrong way through the tunnel in an effort to precipi-
tate the worst accident in Grand Prix history. So it should be no surprise
he's not interested in the real news of the day – the earth-shattering revelation that the whole circuit is surrounded by invisible barriers, it's not a
real Grand Prix, it's all fake, it's the conspiracy to end all conspiracies. But
Martin is light years away from being able to understand the concept that
he might not be real, let alone embracing the awful truth that he isn't.
And you realise you're the only real thing in this world, and you feel

terribly alone, trapped and isolated, and so you turn off the game and take a few deep breaths.

Christian stopped staring at the screen and became aware of the shop around him once again. Now he felt worse than ever, seeing his world in a new light. He'd been given the invulnerability, invisibility, anti-gravity and walk-through-walls cheat codes of life but all he wanted to do was hand them back.

As was often the case, Gabriel was starting his day in one of the lounges of the Deital Palace compound. However, today he was not meeting God, members of the cabinet, or any of the other senior figures of Heaven. Today he needed to go unnoticed, which is why he'd slipped into the Who Wants to Be a Millionaire room of the Grand Quiz Lounge. It was still a popular venue for evening entertainment, but was currently closed ahead of a slated refurbishment. No staff, no aides, no ears.

Gabriel was perched on the host's chair and looked uncomfortable in more ways than one.

Opposite sat Edwin Northlock: a former new boy, like Harold; slight and serious, like Harold. And like Harold, Northlock sat outside senior leadership circles and outside the old-coot network of the angels.

Gabriel broke eye contact, paused, then held out a folded note.

Northlock grasped the note, but Gabriel did not release.

'Surveillance,' said Gabriel, 'nothing more.'

Northlock nodded. 'Understood.'

Gabriel released his grip and sat back. 'I just hope I am wrong.'

'You rarely are.'

'That's what I'm afraid of.'

Having exhausted electronics, Christian had now drifted into homewares, and, perhaps, danger. Places of earthly comfort rarely offer true solace for the spirit, disembodied or otherwise. And for Christian, this was doubly true, being the scene of his failure with the cushions.

He stopped when he spotted a black-and-white hatch oversize.

Her special cushion, he thought. The one she wanted.

He looked at it properly now. He took his time. He studied it from a variety of angles. And he saw it would make a fine adornment to a small conservatory. He passed his hand through, wishing he could pick it up and hold it to his face.

He took a step back and bowed low, bringing his face down towards it and turning his cheek into the cotton. But he felt almost nothing at all. Perhaps it was the high thread count.

He was soon back at Currys, trying to will his rapidly failing not-shopping solution back into life. But it was no good. And it was only eleven a.m. It raised immediate concerns about the days that would follow and how he might fill them. It was a sobering thought, having already exhausted Bracknell's cultural and commercial offerings in one afternoon and a morning.

He decided to return to the vicarage, retracing much of his roundabout route, in the thin hope Tony might be back for lunch.

As he drifted through the parks and streets, dog walkers turned his thoughts back to the troubling encounters with the liver. A shiver of disgust as he recalled its slippery texture, its weight and its eagerness as it had sat on his throat. Incredulity, too – it *had* happened, it definitely had, but against the backdrop of a humdrum urban English morning, it seemed incredible; it seemed impossible. And now there was guilt – yes, it was just an organ, and yes its behaviour was probably instinctive, like a dog's delight in retrieving a stick, but it was still a living thing. An innocent living liver. He'd overreacted and he'd been cruel. It's not like it was trying to eat his face off – as far as he could tell, it couldn't do that if it wanted to – it was being affectionate. Christian sighed. The only thing he'd connected with that wasn't hostile and he'd reacted by leathering it for a conversion and hurling it through a solid wall. What sort of person was he? He hung his head and drifted on.

In an effort to lift his mood and shirk his guilt, he returned to experimenting with his new physicality – adopting the long rangy movements of a speed skater as he walked, and pausing outside the post office for a nicely impossible Russian Cossack dance to entertain people as they entered. And when he reached the top of the incline after rounding the tower of Point Royal, he held his trajectory a few extra metres before levelling out to hold a surfer pose, gliding on through Caterpillar Park, a metre or so above the path, past the trees and past the postman and the gasman still sitting on the bench, before returning to ground level.

By the time the church came into view, Christian's mind was back in the here and now. Yet something wasn't right. And despite this coming on top of everything else that wasn't right, which was really quite a lot, he couldn't put it out of his mind. He drifted on a while longer, but at the end of the street, he stopped and turned. The liver was sitting on the pavement, about ten metres behind him.

Christian felt an urge to run, but resisted. 'I'm, sorry, about earlier, you … caught me by surprise.'

The liver said nothing. No surprise. Smalltalk wasn't its thing. Protein synthesis and detoxification of blood was its thing, or rather used to be, not that it knew it.

'Are you all right?' said Christian.

It continued to sit there, motionless apart from an occasional flicker of its portal vein.

'I didn't hurt you, did I?'

He started moving towards the organ, but as he did, it backed off.

Christian stopped. The liver stopped.

'I'm not going to hurt you.'

Christian took another step forward. The liver shuffled back an equal distance.

Christian crouched down and beckoned the liver, but it stayed put.

'Well, fair enough, I suppose. Look, what do you want? Is there anything I can do for you? Is there anyone I can … Is there a message I could …'

The liver just sat there.

'I'm talking to a liver. I must be dreaming. I must be insane.'

He returned to the last hundred yards of his journey.

He arrived at the vicarage to find no one home. He trudged around for a while, before settling in the kitchen where he reread the front page of Tony's *Daily Telegraph* and then reread it again. Anyone else rereading the lead article would have done so because it was shocking – a freak gas discharge at iChemiclast Industries, a Guildford-based rising star in the biotech sector, killing all thirteen layers of its management and office staff – but for Christian he reread it because it didn't register the first time. It was no different now. He tried again and failed again. It just didn't seem to matter. So he returned to the living room to again browse the spines on Tony's books.

Five minutes later he was slumped back in the sofa and contemplating going out again. But he soon noticed movement at the edge of the room. It was the liver, or at least the front half of it, edging through the wall. Christian brought his legs up off the floor, as he would for a large spider.

He'd been looking at the liver and talking to it only five minutes ago, but there was something about seeing it now, halfway through a solid wall, that crystallised quite how unhinged things had become, and how unwise it might be to begin to get used to things that were this unhinged.

The organ inched closer. It was now inside its ten-metre exclusion zone, its confidence perhaps returning.

Christian made a conscious effort to remain calm, his intellect just about maintaining control of his senate.

The liver kept coming. It got to within a metre, then stopped.

Christian and the liver regarded each other for a minute or so.

It was Christian's first chance to properly take in its appearance. Its connective veins were ragged at the ends, and what Christian failed to identify as its gallbladder sack was bloated, but otherwise it looked a picture of health. Not that Christian knew for sure what a healthy liver should look like. But it had a shiny coat, with bright white marbling on its top membrane, and looked a lot healthier than the supermarket 'still fresh' matted grey ones he was more used to seeing.

It means no harm. It's just a liver. It won't bite. It can't bite.

Christian slipped himself down through the sofa and forward onto the carpet. He edged closer and stretched out his hand.

The liver tensed, its little portal vein flapping rapidly, but it did not retreat. Christian extended his hand further, trembling as he brought it gently down to pat the liver on its right lobe. He felt the organ relax and push itself up in response to his movements, nuzzling into his palm. He grimaced as he forced himself to hold his hand in place, only managing to do so by turning his gaze the other away.

Well, at least it wasn't a spider.

He gritted his teeth and slowly returned his eyes towards what he was touching.

'It's okay, it's okay.'

The liver now crept closer, until it was right next to him. It stopped, wiggled its portal vein, and hopped up onto Christian's abdomen.

Christian clenched his fists and thrust his arms out away from his sides, suppressing every impulse to brush the thing away.

The liver positioned itself over the lower right half of his ribcage, wriggled around to make itself comfortable, and then whirled its portal vein contentedly. It was heavier than it looked – or maybe it just seemed heavy, Christian not being used to having a joint of meat strapped to his ribs – and Christian could feel the tension in his chest muscles, on standby for goodness knows what. But slowly he relaxed and soon returned his hand to the top side of the organ and patted it again.

One man and his liver.

One man and his livers.

The man with two livers.

Edwin Northlock was an old hand and had made short work of locating Gabriel's surveillance target. And as an old hand, he anticipated a long wait; he expected indirection and counter-surveillance. He was wrong. Just two hours later, he was reporting back on what he had seen – a meeting in a back room of The Idle Cock, a small nectar hall close to the Deital Palace compound. A dozen or so attendees, all dressed in robes of white linen.

With no prospect of Tony returning until the end of the day, Christian had decided to wander out again, the liver seeming happy to join him, bobbing along a few paces behind.

By the time they found themselves back at Caterpillar Park, several people were walking their dogs in the early afternoon sun and the liver scampered ahead to say hello, apparently unaware and unabashed at his non-canine, non-whole-organism, non-wholly real status. One of the owners, a young woman with two Labradors, let her dogs off the lead and threw a ball. Dogs and liver alike chased after it.

The liver was at a significant disadvantage to the dogs, but more than made up for it with enthusiasm. It was a masterclass in not letting one's disabilities get in the way of having a good time. Quite apart from being a lot slower than his competition, the liver was doubly disadvantaged when it came to retrieving the ball, given a) the few times he did get in range before the dogs, the ball passed straight through him, and b) being a liver, he had no means with which to pick up the ball anyway. It was a heartening display, despite suggesting to Christian his new charge wasn't the brightest kid in the class.

As the eclectic woman–dogs–Christian–liver collective drifted through the centre of the little park, over towards Point Royal, they passed by the bench where, yet again, the postman and the gasman were sitting, still in their uniforms. Christian had never before seen such dedication to skiving.

A chill ran down his spine as the postman made eye contact.

Christian looked down at the path, but three paces later he couldn't help snatch another glance. Now they were both looking at him.

'Nice liver,' said the gasman.

Christian put his head lower still and kept moving.

'I said, nice liver.'

Christian stopped and turned. 'I'm sorry, you're talking to me? You can see me?'

'Could hardly miss you earlier, *dude*,' said the gasman, 'this isn't Bondi beach, y'know.'

'Oh, how does the *Baywatch* theme go?' said the postman, before commencing a patchy rendition of the *Hawaii Five-O* theme tune.

Christian glanced over at the liver. It seemed happy enough, so he drifted the few paces over to the men. Neither made any attempt to get up. Christian leaned in and gripped the gasman's right arm.

'What d'ya think you're doin', pal?' said the gasman.

The arm felt solid, in more ways than one, the gasman having biceps twice the size of Christian's.

Though Christian could tell both men were of a similar age to him, the gasman had that look of someone who had always been more knowing than his peers, the sort of kid who at fourteen is having sex with Miss Babcock instead of worrying about the undercarriage on his Airfix.

'I said, what d'ya think you're doin'?' said the gasman, half brushing, half bashing Christian's arm away.

'Sorry,' said Christian, and he took a step back. 'I ... don't understand.'

'Don't understand what, mate?' said the postman.

The postman was a far less Tarzanic specimen, occupying a larger portion of bench and testing his uniform's ability to keep him decent. The haircut spoke of brutal necessity rather than any particular style, but he had a kind and friendly face, and this was something Christian found instantly reassuring – somehow the mildness peering out over the tops of the smoke-shaded specs told him everything might be all right after all. If this guy could survive here, surely so could Christian.

'Anything,' said Christian, 'I don't understand anything at all. Can you help me?'

'You new, are ya, mate?' said the postman.

'I ... I got run over.'

'You haven't worked it out then?' said the gasman.

'Worked what out?'

'When was it, mate, when you got run over?' asked the postman.

'I ... um, Thursday, I think.'

'Two days?' said the gasman, turning to his friend and laughing. 'Two whole days and he's not worked it out.'

'Worked what out? Please tell me.'

'You're dead, mate,' said the postman.

A chill ran across Christian's shoulders and down his back. 'No,' he said, shaking his head.

'Yes,' said the postman and gasman, nodding theirs.

'No, I'm just having an episode, I'm waiting for reality to catch up.'

'This is reality, pal,' said the gasman.

'Well if I'm dead, what does that make you?' said Christian.

'Same, of course,' said the gasman. 'You think we'd be talking to you otherwise?'

Christian didn't shake his head this time; instead, his chin just jittered up and down.

'Look, we do know what we're talking about, mate,' said the postman. 'Sorry.'

Now closer, Christian saw that the men were sitting slightly in the park bench. His head dropped. 'Look, would you mind if I sat down?'

The gasman shrugged.

'I'm Sol,' said the postman, offering a hand as Christian was mid-sit.

'Christian,' said Christian, and he shook the man's hand. '... and?' said Christian, offering his hand to the gasman.

'This is Tray,' said the postman.

The gasman tensed his arms, while keeping them folded.

'Oh,' said Christian, withdrawing his hand and sitting down on and slightly in the path. 'Tray?'

'Tracy,' said the gasman, 'as in Dick, not Sharon and, okay?'

'Um, okay.'

They sat in silence.

'Can I just say, er, Sol, it felt good to shake someone's hand again,' said Christian.

Sol shifted in his seat.

'You're not a poof, are you?' said Tracy.

'I'm sorry?'

'It's nancy,' said Tracy, 'talking about liking men's handshakes.'

'No, it's just that's the first one I've had in quite a while. It's just, you know, a welcome sign of civilisation, don't you think?'

'Handshakes are a dangerous custom,' said Tracy, looking out into the distance over Christian's head.

'Dangerous?' said Christian.

'Never know what you'll catch. *That*' – he pointed at Christian's hand – 'could have been anywhere.'

Sol pulled a face and wiped his hand.

'It's not been anywhere,' said Christian.

'I bet it's been touching that liver of yours,' said Tracy.

'Well he's not dirty.'

'How d'ya know? Look at him rolling around out there. Could be pickin' up all sorts.'

'Well I'm sure whatever he has can't do me any harm if I'm dead.'

'Oh, so you're an expert are you now? Didn't even know you were dead till we told you.'

'I still may not be …'

'Will you just listen to him?' said Tracy to Sol.

'… but I suppose I can't prove I'm not, so, all right, it's a possibility, I suppose.'

'Oh yeah, *a possibility*. That's what you get from a university education, isn't it? Can't ever accept the bleedin' obvious. You're dead, pal. Anyone with half a brain would have worked that out the moment it happened.'

'Well. I could be dreaming.'

'A dream? Don't gimme that bollocks. When've you ever had a dream like this?'

'Actually,' said Sol, 'I've had some pretty weird dreams m'self, y'know, now and then. Like when I'm painting the white lines at Wembley before the Vase final. Slade full blast over the Tannoy, whole pitch to myself.'

Christian and Tracy both stared at Sol, who himself was now staring out into space, his arms outstretched, gripping the handles of his imaginary white line marker trolley, his feet moving up and down in a motion not at all like real walking.

'How do you even know if I went to university?' said Christian.

'Well did you go to university?' asked Tracy.

'Well okay, so what if I did?'

'So. You're typical university. You can't see what's right in front of you, but at the same time you're an instant expert. You've been dead two days and already you're surfing through the park with a pet liver in tow, like you're David bleedin' Hasselhoff. That's not how we do things here.'

'I'm just trying to work things out. I don't know the rules. It's been a traumatic few days.'

'Oh boo-hoo,' said Tracy. 'Listen, pal, everyone dies. It's the most unoriginal thing you can do. Normal people just get on with it, we don't turn it into a big song and dance.'

'Well, all right then, if you're the real experts, tell me, tell me how it all works.'

'How what works?'

'Everything.'

'What do you mean, *everything*?'

Christian stood. 'All right, well … let's take health. Right, you don't shake hands. You're concerned about picking stuff up. So does that mean we can still get ill?'

'I reckon.'

'What, you don't know?'

'Not for certain. M'self, I've never been ill here, but maybe that's because I don't shake hands.'

'Well what about you, Sol?'

'Perfect health since the day I died.'

Christian smirked, but stopped when the others failed to join him.

'Tenth of May, seventy-five,' said Sol, proudly.

'What of it?' said Christian.

'The day I died.'

'I'm sorry, did you say seventy-five? Nineteen seventy-five?'

'Yes.'

'You're telling me you've been dead, for what, nearly forty years?'

'No. Not forty,' said the postman, 'no, wait, hang on …' He counted out four fingers. 'Yes, I suppose so. Hey, how time flies, eh? Woo hee,' he said, and raised an imaginary champagne flute.

'And you, Tracy?' said Christian.

'Same.'

'Same?'

'We died in the same workplace accident,' said Sol, 'gas leak at the post office. Tray was checkin' it out, I came in to see how it was going, then *booooooom!*'

Tracy rubbed his forehead.

'It was all my fault, you see,' said Sol, beaming, 'not the leak, the explosion.'

'Oh no, you didn't flick a light switch or something, did you?' said

Christian. 'Easily done. Or was it a jolt of static? You all wore a lot of polyester back then, didn't you?'

'No, I was lighting a ciggy.'

'Yeah, you daft prat,' said Tracy.

'He's still a bit sensitive about it,' whispered Sol.

'Forty years though,' said Christian, turning and pacing, 'that's incredible. So where have you been in that time?'

'All over,' said Tracy, focusing out to a distant point behind Christian.

'Wow, what so you've explored other countries?'

'No,' said Sol, before Tracy could answer.

'No?'

'We're still exploring this one,' said Tracy.

'Right. Okay. So what about up?'

'Up?' said Tracy.

'Yeah,' said Christian, pointing skyward, 'how high can we go?'

'Why would we want to do that?' said Tracy. 'There's not going to be anything up there.'

'Call us old-fashioned, but we like it on the ground, Christian,' said Sol.

'Okay … right, but you've been outside the area, outside Bracknell?'

'No,' said Tracy.

'Really?' said Christian, stopping mid-pace.

'Not since we died,' said Sol. 'We tend to stick to the bench.'

'What the … seriously?'

'What's wrong with that?' said Tracy. 'It's a good bench.'

Christian shook his head.

'Then again,' said Tracy, 'we do have a wander down the bottom end, now and then, and we're always in and out of the houses.'

'Only way to keep up with the telly,' said Sol.

'I don't believe what I'm hearing. You could have done anything. You could have gone anywhere, you could have … toured Europe, climbed Everest, seen the wonders of the world, the Pyramids, the Grand Canyon, Machu Picchu.'

'Machu Picchu,' said Tracy, 'that's all you lefties go on about, isn't it? Machu bleedin' Picchu. *Oh, let's all climb Machu Picchu … Oh let's all eat hummus and cashew nuts*. Always full of grand ideas you lot, head in the clouds, never paying any attention to what's going on around you.'

'But come on, forty years in a park?' said Christian, putting his palms to his forehead. 'There's low horizons and then there's just plain staring at your feet.'

'Look 'ere, Michael bleedin' Palin, just because we've not gone swanning off on the beatnik hippy trail doesn't mean we don't know stuff, doesn't mean we don't know what's going on.'

'All right. All right, I'm sorry,' said Christian, and he sat down again. 'Tell me then, please. Really, I want to know. What *is* going on?'

'Well, I don't know if we should share our knowledge,' said Tracy, shaking his head, 'took us a long time to get in tune with it all.'

'Oh, please, there's so much I want to know,' said Christian. 'I'm so lost.'

'Come on, Tray, he seems like a nice enough fella,' said Sol.

'Well, all right. Maybe we can share a bit. But where do we start, Sol lad?'

'Yeah, tricky, Tray, tricky. There's so much to know, isn't there?'

'Well,' said Tracy, 'how about we start with forty-two?'

'Forty-two?' said Christian, recalling *The Hitchhiker's Guide to the Galaxy* and leaping back to his feet. 'What, you're telling me it really is significant? What, is it like a universal constant or something, a key to understanding the higher dimensions?'

'What are you blathering on about?' said Tracy. 'Forty-two. Number forty-two.'

'Yes, the number forty-two,' said Christian.

'Not *the* number forty-two, just number forty-two,' said Tracy.

Christian still didn't follow.

'Forty-two Caterpillar Park,' said Sol, thumb over his shoulder.

Christian looked across past the trees to the houses that bordered this section of the park.

'Now, the Willises used to live there,' said Tracy, 'but last month it was bought by the Joneses. It'll be the death of the neighbourhood, you wait and see.'

'Oh no, they seem all right, Tray,' said Sol.

'Well I don't trust 'em.'

'They're fine once ya get to know 'em. Nice people. That Felix, he's a stockbroker, y'know.'

'That's the bleedin' point,' said Tracy, turning to Sol, 'why can't they stay where they belong, in bleedin' London? Poncing about in their bleedin' pinstripe suits.'

'Oh, give it a rest, Tray,' said Sol.

'All I'm saying is–'

'Stop, stop,' said Christian. 'Look, sorry, but where is this going? I thought you were going to tell me something useful?'

'This is useful,' said Tracy, 'we're giving you the inside track.'

'No, I want the big picture.'

'This is the big picture,' said Tracy, sweeping his arms in a wide arc, Sol repeating the action a moment later. 'You see, the Joneses only got into forty-two 'cos they know the Portmans. Now, the Portmans are at thirty-six–'

'No, please, stop,' said Christian, 'I want the *big*, big picture.'

'What d'ya mean?' said Sol.

'Well,' said Christian, 'take your big picture, and then ask yourself, what's the big picture around that?'

'Wycombe Wanderers?' said Sol, looking puzzled.

'No, you spanner,' said Tracy, 'he's talking about the town planners. Here, have you got friends at the council?'

'For crying out loud, of course I'm not talking about the town planners or Wycombe Wanderers, think bigger.'

'Football itself?' said Sol. 'Oh that is deep ...'

'No, I want to understand the big, big, big, big, *big* picture, you know, why are we here, the afterlife, what it means, and all that.'

Tracy and Sol looked at each other.

'What for?' said Tracy.

'What for? *What for?* Because if you're right, then we're living proof of life after death. Isn't that amazing? Doesn't that raise about a thousand questions in your minds?'

'Such as?'

'Well, does this mean we have souls? Does this mean that we *are* souls?'

'Arseholes,' said Sol, with a chuckle.

'... is there a god? Is there Heaven and Hell? Is there–'

'Hey, hey, slow down there, pal. You're not at university now. Send you nuts thinking about all that bollocks. And all the while you're ignoring what's right in front of you.'

'And that would be?'

'Real life. Real people. The real stuff that's going on locally.'

'And that's interesting?' said Christian.

'Now you're getting it,' said Sol.

'I ... I don't know what to say,' said Christian. He rolled his shoulders.

He wanted to scream. They were fools. They were a waste of consciousness. They were the smallest of small-minded bumpkins. But then he
stopped himself and tried to look at it another way. At least they'd given
him some information, even if it wasn't useful. And at least they were
friendly small-minded bumpkins. Or at least Sol was, anyway.

'Look, I'm sorry, gents, I have to go.'

'Already?' said Sol.

Christian turned to locate the liver, which was now snuffling around
the birch trees near the community centre.

'Given you too much to think about have we, professor?' said Tracy.

'You couldn't be more right,' said Christian, 'well, it was nice to meet
you.'

'Doesn't sound like it,' said Tracy.

'Well, all right, it was nice to meet you, Sol. It wasn't nice to meet you,
Tracy. But all the same, it's, well, still nice to know I'm not alone.'

'You're sounding nancy again,' said Tracy.

'No, I'm just saying, it's nice, you know, to have some company.'

'That sounds really nancy,' said Tracy.

'Thanks for offering, Christian,' said Sol, 'but we're not really into all
that.'

Chapter Thirty-Two

After completing three layers of security checks, Harold had arrived at the surprisingly dank inner sanctum of the fortress of the garden of the tree of life. He was fifteen minutes early and thought he had the place to himself. But after only moments staring at the strange and underwhelming centre-piece, he felt a clawhand at his shoulder.

He turned to find Gabriel standing much closer than he'd expected.

'Quite a sight, isn't it?' said the archangel.

'It certainly is,' said Harold.

They stood in silence looking across to the caged shrub on the little island at the centre of the circular room. Even for a desert perennial, it was a wizened and withered specimen, lopsided with peeling grey bark, and accessorised only with a scattering of indiscernible shrivelled pinkish-brown fruit.

'Doesn't quite live up to the billing,' said Harold, eventually.

Gabriel half smiled.

'I feel rather foolish,' said Harold, 'I'd heard tales of a mighty sequoia, three hundred feet tall, laden with every fruit imaginable, ruby-red apples, golden ripe bananas, watermelons set to burst, and all on the one tree.'

'The tree that offers forth every fruit of creation,' said Gabriel.

Harold nodded. 'I was told it even had fruits that don't exist in the mortal realm.'

'Well, I suppose that part may have some truth – did you ever see anything quite like those little dried up dumplings down on Earth?'

Harold shook his head.

'No, I thought not.'

'So did it once produce all the other fruits, as the people claim?'

'As I've told you before, Harold, don't believe everything you hear.'

'No variety at all?'

'Well, it's been known to squeeze out a limp quince, from time to time, but pretty much all this tree puts out, all it's ever put out, is what you see before you. A few shrivelled crab apples.'

'So not that special then.'

'Not special at all.'

'So why bother to guard it?'

'Well, Terry's always been strangely fond of it. And the fruit is his, and his alone.'

'I suppose it must taste better than it looks.'

'Tastes worse than it looks. Like little acid balls, even sharper than Terry's sambuca scotch eggs.'

'That bad?'

'Yes, that bad.'

'Yet people still covet it?'

'Of course, why do you think we need the fortress?'

'Not very logical.'

'In my experience, logic has little to do with human motivation.'

'But still, there must be some reason?'

'Well there's the old many-fruits myth, as you've heard, plus some say if you – humans, that is – do eat the fruit, it grants eternal life.'

'But surely we're already immortal, are we not, once we've died?'

'Exactly, you'd have thought that would be enough for anyone.'

'It's ridiculous then. A fairy tale.'

'Indeed it is.'

'So why the razor wire, the security guards, the high walls?'

'Natural escalation.'

'Meaning?'

The archangel flexed his armwings. 'Long ago people started taking the fruit, Terry got a bit upset, so placed it under guard. That generated interest, so more people came, wanting to see what was being guarded, wanting to try the fruit for themselves. So then we built a little perimeter wall, and then a building, and that created even more interest, and bigger crowds, and so sooner than you think we ended up with this, this stupid fortress right in the middle of town, just because people can't accept that a tree may just be a tree, and there may be no other reason to build a great big fortress around it other than to protect it from people's superstition, greed and paranoia.'

'Right,' said Harold.

'Right,' said Gabriel, with a small nod.

'Right ...'

They looked on at the tree again in silence.

'Then again,' said Harold, 'it's unfortunate it's called *the tree of life.*'

'Well, yes. That does tend to stoke the expectations.'

More silence.

'So, we understand each other then?' said Gabriel.

'Um, yes,' said Harold, 'why would we not?'

'Exactly, Harold. Say no more,' said Gabriel, with a tap of his nose.

'Right ...' said Harold, 'so, shall we move on to business?'

'I don't follow.'

'The reason we are here. You said there was business.'

'We've just discussed it.'

'Have we?'

'Of course.'

'I don't believe we have.'

'Yes we have, the tree.'

'The tree?'

'Yes.'

'Right. So ... we're ... done, then?'

'Apparently not,' said Gabriel, ruffling his feathers, 'what I was saying, about the tree, I was using it as a metaphor.'

'I don't think you were.'

'Yes, I was. Look. This tree is just a tree.'

'And ...'

Gabriel rolled his eyes. 'And people can't accept that some things are as they are, and can only ever be as they are, however much they would like them to be otherwise.'

'Okay,' said Harold, 'I'm still not quite–'

'That however much you want a bitter crab apple to be a rich ripe mango, there is nothing you can do to make it a rich ripe mango. A bitter crab apple will always be a bitter crab apple.'

Harold rubbed his chin.

'Oh for goodness' sake, Harold, your associations, I'm talking about the company you've been keeping.'

'What do you mean?'

'The dirty dozen. I know you've met with them, and I'll wager more than once.'

'And I was supposed to get that from the tree?'

'Well obviously. And to be frank, I'd hoped you'd be a bit more contrite about it.'

'It may help if I knew what I was supposed to be contrite about.'

'Meeting with them. Having contact. Those people inhabit dangerous circles, Harold.'

'I met them in my own time.'

'It makes no difference.'

Harold broke eye contact.

'Now,' said Gabriel, 'what did you tell them?'

'I told them nothing.'

'What did they tell you?'

'Nothing.'

'Well you must have discussed something.'

'Of course.'

'Well?'

'Carpentry and mass catering.'

'Very funny,' said Gabriel. He took a step closer. 'Can't you see I'm trying to help you?'

'All right, do you really want to know? Do you really want to know what they told me?'

'I don't want to know. I need to know.'

'They told me the truth.'

'Regarding?'

'Boot Out the Devout.'

'What? Is that it?' said Gabriel. He stepped back and relaxed his stance. 'You already knew that truth.'

'I knew the what and the why, but not the how. I wonder why you skipped those details.'

Gabriel did not reply straight away. 'It was a long time ago,' he said, 'we did our best under difficult circumstances.'

'But you did deceive them, didn't you? When you made them all go through the portal, back into the Zone?'

'We did.'

'You told them they were going on a field trip to the Holy Land?'

'Well that is where we sent them. They went willingly.'

'But you didn't tell them it was a one-way trip, that they'd be turned away at the fast-track queue when they attempted to return.'

Gabriel said nothing.

Harold shook his head. 'Did you really call that part of the operation "No Room at the Inn"?'

Gabriel lifted a clawfinger. 'That was not my idea.'

'I was told they all joined the Queue, the Great Queue,' said Harold, 'every last one of them.'

Gabriel nodded. 'Anything to return to his kingdom,' he said, softly.

'But that's monstrous,' said Harold. He turned away from Gabriel and stared vacantly back to the tree. 'Can you picture the despair, at the end of it all, after a second time in the Queue, to step through the Gate only to emerge in a much darker arena, the darkest, for some of them.'

'The postscript was unfortunate, and unforeseen.'

'Unforeseen?' said Harold, turning sharply. 'How could that be unforeseen?'

'Look, no one expected them to try to get back in. They should have worked out what was happening, seen that Heaven had moved on.'

'Why didn't you just tell them the rules had changed?'

'Think for a moment, Harold, how could we tell them and not risk them telling others?'

Harold shook his head.

'Look, we did our best,' said Gabriel, 'there never was going to be a neat solution.'

'A solution to a problem that didn't exist. You didn't have to boot them out in the first place.'

'It was Terry's will.'

'That's not an excuse, that's–'

'*It was Terry's will.*'

Silence.

Gabriel flexed his shoulder muscles. 'Look, as I said, it was all a long time ago.'

'That's no excuse either.'

'So sure? Did your new friends tell you quite how long ago it was?'

Harold didn't answer.

'No, I thought not,' said Gabriel. 'Boot Out the Devout was conceived and executed eighteen hundred years ago. The world was a different place back then. You can't judge the morals of antiquity by the niceties of today.'

Again, Harold did not reply.

'Come on,' said Gabriel, 'you know Terry, you've worked for him. He's a reformed deity. He's kept his nose clean for centuries.'

'Until now.'

'No, Harold. The Bootstrap situation is totally different. I've already told you, there is far more to it than you know, and this time there is more to the solution than whim or even Terry's will. You must trust me on this.'

'But–'

'Look, it is what it is. What's done is done. And whatever you think, the reality is you can't turn Heaven into a utopia any more than you can turn a crab apple into a mango. Others have gone down that path, none have returned. My advice to you is to keep your feet in the real world, keep your head down, and well … learn to live with the crab apple.'

Chapter Thirty-Three

The muffled sound of Tony's alarm clock from upstairs signalled a gasping panic sofa-spring-filled start to Christian's third morning at the vicarage. Thankfully, the pattern of the previous day soon rescued him: Tony making breakfast. Tony eating breakfast. Christian watching while holding tight to Radio 4. But today the reverend didn't leave. He had another piece of organic rye; he hung around. To Christian's embarrassment, it was only when he heard voices outside, and saw several small groups gathering in the churchyard, that he twigged what was going on.

But despite now living in a vicarage, with a vicar, he found the idea of attending morning worship uncomfortable – not least because there was a fair chance Beatrice would be there, she having rarely missed a Sunday service. Either way, he wasn't keen on sticking around. So as soon as everyone had entered the church, he and the liver headed out for a long walk that eventually brought them to the park, where they found the bench occupied as usual.

'Aye aye, it's Bamber Gascoigne,' said Tracy.

'Morning, gentlemen,' said Christian, and he sat down.

'How do,' said Sol.

'So you worked out yer big picture yet then?' asked Tracy.

'No. How's the park been so far today, any more stockbrokers moved in this morning?'

'No, we're very vigilant,' said Sol.

'Thought we might not see you again,' said Tracy, 'thought you'd be halfway to Tokyo by now.'

Christian said nothing.

'So,' Tracy continued, 'staying here's not so bad after all?'

'I just,' said Christian, 'I just have things to sort out.'

'Hello, boy,' said Sol, bending down to pat the liver, 'you're a fine fella, aren't you?'

The liver revelled in the affection, nuzzling into Sol's hand and wagging his portal vein.

'Does he have a name?' asked Sol.

'He hasn't mentioned one,' said Christian.

'No, I mean have you given him one?'

'No.'

'Let's call him Leslie.'

'Leslie the liver?'

'Yeah.'

'I'll think about it.'

'You not worried, then?' asked Tracy.

'About what?' said Christian.

'About what people are gonna say?'

'Why, what are they gonna say?'

'They're gonna say, "Have you seen that bloke taking his liver for a walk?"'

'So?'

'So you're a bleedin' laughing stock. One step off having him on a lead.'

'That's not a bad idea, actually,' said Christian.

'You're not getting it,' said Tracy, 'you can't get him a lead, you can't take him for walks.'

'Why?'

'Because he's an internal organ, pal. Now if he was a foot, different story.'

'Oh yeah,' said Sol, 'I love foots, I do, I'm a real foots person.'

'What?' said Christian. 'You're telling me a pet foot is okay, but a pet liver is ridiculous?'

'No,' said Tracy, 'pet liver's alright. Still comes off all la-di-da, you know, sort of pet you put in a handbag. No, the stupid thing is taking it for a bleedin' walk. Organs, they're their own boss. They do their own thing. They go for walks, they don't get taken for walks.'

'Why not?'

'They just don't.'

'And feet do?'

'Course. Fat Larry, he's got seven of 'em.'

'Seven feet?'

'Nine, including his own,' said Sol.

'You've not seen him then?' said Tracy.

'No,' said Christian.

'Really?' said Sol. 'Can't miss Fats. He's always here, taking them foots for walkies.'

'No, Sol, if I'd seen someone taking seven feet for a walk, I think I'd have remembered.'

———————————————

To almost all, but not quite all, of the living, the idea of befriending bits of people will seem distasteful. However, with closer examination it is possible to understand why many of the dead see things differently. As is often the case, the source of the distaste is made up of a) a reaction to the unfamiliar (I don't want to eat a sheep's eyeball, because I'm not used to eating sheep's eyeballs) and b) practical reasoning (I don't want to eat your sheep's eyeball because I don't know where it's been). In the case of dead people befriending bits of people, the reaction to the unfamiliar component of the distaste is understandable, because unless your parents were extremely theologically astute or extremely dangerous, you are unlikely to have spent your formative years playing with discarded bits of people. But when we consider the logical practical component, the drivers of the distaste begin to break down, for they are not bits of people, they are ethereal bits of people, mere shadows of their former selves, yet shadows alive with animation.

And of course pet bit-of-person ownership is far cheaper and easier than earthly pet ownership. There are no vets' bills, no food bills. You don't have to pick up their poop. They don't urinate all over your new Italian leather sofa. The only downside, as with earthly pet ownership, is death – not the demise of the bit of the person, but the demise of what remains of its original earthly owner, which usually triggers the end of the relationship, or at least an uphill custody battle.

All this behaviour would, of course, be quite a different matter in the mortal realm, where putting little collars on bits of people, naming them and dragging them behind you when nipping out to the shops will almost always be a precursor to intervention by the mental health authorities. Quite apart from the total lack of animation, which tends to render bits of people poor companions in mortal life, there is the unpleasant tendency for flesh left at room temperature to decay as well as pick up gravel, chewing gum, leaves and dog shit when dragged behind you on all but the briefest stroll. And we haven't even considered the smell or the flies. If you remain unconvinced, give it a go and see what it does for your social standing.

Yet despite the ubiquity of animated semi-conscious bits of people in the Zone, and a widespread willingness to embrace them, few of the dead ever stop to question how this phenomenon came about. And for those seeking understanding, this is a missed opportunity, for it is perhaps the starkest example of the latent design flaws in the earth and the heavens, and conveys much about those responsible.

In the early days of this world, the anomaly didn't present much of a problem. Most stray bits of people were never separated from the whole for long: if you lost a foot in ancient times, the rest of you would usually follow along soon after, hot on your heel. The occasional ear or eyeball might linger for an extended period, as would stray tonsils, adenoids and foreskins, but all being small and timid they went largely unnoticed. Hence in those early millennia, the Heavenly authorities regarded these aberrations as nothing more than a niggle.

Then man began to discover the ability to cauterise wounds. Lost limbs would keep turning up as usual, but now they could hang around for decades before the arrival of their masters. And what with many dead people missing the experience of pet ownership (there being no dead animals in the Zone to pet), a natural symbiosis began to form. Dead pet-lovers filled their void by adopting bits of people; dead bits of people readily accepted becoming pets as a substitute for being part of a larger organism. And in the eyes of Heaven, a niggle became an annoyance.

In the late nineteenth century, appendixes began to arrive, but like the other small bits of people, they were never any bother. However, in the mid-twentieth century, complex internal organs started to appear and soon became the exotic part-of-someone-pet for the wandering spirit wanting to make a statement. And thus an annoyance became an embarrassment. It's one thing to have someone walking around with a spare leg, or a couple of extra arms, but when people started parading about with lungs peeping out of handbags, Heaven decided it could ignore the problem no longer. However, the flaws in the mechanisms that caused the anomaly were hard-wired into the fabric of creation, making it impossible to do anything about it without starting all over again. So Heaven did what any disreputable organisation would do in such a position – it would put its principles to one side and quietly move the goalposts by pretending it was part of the grand plan all along. A quick update to the welcome-to-death leaflet with a suspiciously nonchalant passing reference, plus a reworking of a few chapters in *Terry's Field Guide To the Afterlife* to make it all sound perfectly normal. Then sit back and brazen it out until the end of the world, and try to get it right next time.

———————————————

'Anyway, an arm, a leg, a hand, a foot, that's normal,' said Tracy, 'all loyal bits of people, those.'

'Especially foots,' said Sol, 'man's best friend. Faithful to the end, are foots.'

'Yeah, all right, Sol,' said Tracy.

'But not organs?' said Christian.

'No,' said Tracy.

'What about heads?' asked Christian.

'Heads?' said Tracy.

'Yes. Are they faithful?'

'Are heads faithful?'

'Yes.'

'What, are you thick or something? How's a head ever gonna get here on its own?'

'I don't know, maybe if someone got decapitated?'

'What, and their body decided to give it a go living on without them? We're not fuckin' chickens, pal.'

'Oh. Oh yes, I see what you mean.'

'Maybe you're not so smart after all then, professor?' continued Tracy.

Christian did not reply.

They watched as the liver scampered off to examine a collection of McDonald's litter over by the ash trees.

'Maybe Leslie thinks he's a foot?' said Sol.

'What?' said Christian.

'Well, that could explain a thing or two,' said Tracy.

'I must be mad. I don't want to be, but it's the only explanation.'

'For what?' said Tracy.

'For sitting here, in the grass, talking to two ghosts about whether my pet liver thinks he's a foot.'

Sol thrust his hands to his cheeks and began emitting an intermittent *beep* noise, suggesting he was about to reverse.

'Ay, pal, do you mind if you don't use the g-word?' said Tracy.

'What, God?' said Christian. 'Oh, *ghosts*.'

Sol clamped his hands on his ears and started singing 'You'll Never Walk Alone'.

'Hey. I said not to use it, pal,' said Tracy.

'Sorry. Sorry, I wasn't thinking,' said Christian.

'Our Sol gets a bit frightened sometimes.'

'Of g-words? But, but hang on, if we're dead, then isn't that what we are?'

Tracy nodded.

'So why isn't he scared of us?' asked Christian. 'Why isn't he scared of himself?'

'Well, we're just us, mate. We're just people, aren't we? And you, you're a bit *University Challenge*, a bit full of yourself, bit of a tosser, but you're still just a person. Technically, yeah, okay, we're g-words, granted, but we don't go prowling around graveyards at night, moaning and groaning under white sheets, do we now?'

'Well, no. But does that mean there are g-words who do that?'

'No, course not, don't be stupid.'

'So what's Sol's problem then?'

'Well, it's a fear, isn't it, a phobia.'

'Oh dear,' said Christian. 'Poor Sol. Well anyway, I won't mention it again.'

'Good,' said Tracy, before turning to the postman, and, after a brief struggle, pulling his hands from his ears. 'Sol, Sol, it's safe to come out now.'

'Oh good, how are we doing fellas?'

Sitting next to Beatrice, on her sofa, Kevin Tooting now felt awkward, disappointed and stupid all at the same time. It was quite a feat of emotional dexterity, especially for Kevin. He always hated being the last to know and on this occasion what he hadn't known had been quite a lot.

In the hours after Nikki's condition had stabilised, Kevin had tried to piece together what had driven his estranged wife to attempt to take her own life. But he had little to go on. Nikki had not yet regained consciousness, plus, she'd been keeping him well beyond arm's length since the breakup anyway, letting him see her just once, and even then, to his bewilderment, only wanting to discuss Christian's former school teachers. He's tried other lines of inquiry, but he'd come up against brick walls at every turn, and even when he did get answers, they only served to raise further questions. The police could offer no insights, other than to insist, like everyone else, that with the incident coming so soon after the horrific industrial accident at iChemiclast, it was a rare but clear case of despair brought on by guilt and potential corporate manslaughter charges; Kevin, of course, wasn't buying that for a moment. The police had been able to tell him that the man who died when the pope's plane hit the house was called Stuart Hargreaves. After asking them to repeat this information, with a couple of clarifications, Kevin was able to inform them that this man was his former chemistry teacher. The revelation didn't invigorate their investigation as much as Kevin had hoped.

Forced to proceed alone, Kevin had developed a theory that Nikki had become embroiled in some sort of reverse sugar daddy situation, perhaps seduced by the famously exotic Hargreaves facial hair. But from there the trail had gone cold. He'd tried to lean on Jean Claude, but he'd maintained his enigmatic eternal loyalty to Nikki, saying nothing other than to complain about losing his livelihood and to ask Kevin if he knew of any women who needed a twenty-four-year-old, live-in chef in peak physical condition.

Kevin called Nikki's few friends, but no one seemed to have heard from her for months or were even aware of the breakup. iChemiclast was literally a dead end – he learned that Nikki had stepped back from the business, but as no one senior had survived the accident, no one could tell him why.

There wasn't a living soul, so it seemed, who had any idea what Nikki had been doing with the last two months of her life.

Kevin never suspected that Beatrice was the key. He'd only gone round to see her because he'd heard about Christian's death. Kevin wasn't decent enough to visit out of duty, but he was indecent enough to visit out of having the hots for Beatrice. She was now an attractive and single woman in need of consolation, support and a good seeing to.

He knew *people* would think this predatory, but that was just people and they were all hypocrites anyway. Their disgust didn't mean they wouldn't do the same in his position. Life is short; he who dares wins. Okay, so this wasn't how Superman or The Equalizer would behave, but they weren't real people, were they? Fred West and Jimmy Savile – they were real people. They wouldn't waste a second moving in on Beatrice, and with far worse intentions, so was he so bad? No, he was just a normal human being, as flawed as the next. And anyway, this was all just in his head. So long as it stayed in his head, *people* would never get to know anyway. And if he could snare Beatrice, he knew he would love and care for her, or at least he probably would, so the ends justified the means. He could certainly be a far better partner than Christian ever was. So it would be in her interests too, in the long term. Yes, he would do it for her.

All fine in theory, but in practice it had been heavy going. He'd got her in his arms easily enough, but the constant tears, wailing and burying her face in his shoulder made going in for a kiss a logistical nightmare. His angles were all wrong. Every time he'd tried to look her in the eye, all he'd got was the top of her head. And he knew he couldn't use conventional weapons to bring the situation around – no, the mood wasn't quite right for *any* form of wise crack or smooth line. So he'd deployed his dirty bomb, telling Beatrice about Nikki's suicide bid, how Nikki was now in a coma, and how it had rocked him to his core. It had an immediate effect. She'd stopped snivelling; she'd sat back; the angles had instantly got better. But then it was Beatrice's turn to drop the bombshell, telling Kevin not just of the fight on the day of her suicide bid, but spilling the details of her involvement with Christian, the book and her patronage, tracing it all back to the fateful dinner party.

Now he didn't know what to think. Now he had answers, but still no understanding.

'But why? Why on earth would she try to kill herself?' said Beatrice.

'Well ...' said Kevin, coming back to his senses.

This could still work. These angles are okay. What about ... yes, worth a try.

'... do you think perhaps there was more going on? Do you think they were ...' He made a ring with his right thumb and index finger and pushed his left index finger through.

'Oh no,' said Beatrice, with a shudder.

'Oh yes,' said Kevin, with a nod.

'So you're saying she couldn't go on without him?'

Kevin nodded again.

'But,' said Beatrice, 'but she didn't even look upset when I told her. She seemed more interested in the book.'

'Well, sometimes people don't show it, do they. Nick Nack especially. Hard-nosed businesswoman you know, spent a lifetime boiling and pickling her emotions. I thought she loved me, right up to the moment when she gave me the boot. That's how wrong I was, so who knows?'

'So she loved him?' said Beatrice.

Is this working? The angles are still doable. Yes, yes go for it. 'And broke my heart in the process,' said Kevin.

'And he loved her?'

'What, er ... well ...'

The tears and wailing started again, as Beatrice turned away and buried her head into the sofa cushions.

Fuckin' great. These angles were the worst yet.

Most of the dozen unseen frustrated, bored, voyeuristic shepherds who'd been watching sighed, jeered and threw screwed-up P16 collection forms into Kevin.

Back in the park, the three ghosts were still in conference.

'Sol,' said Christian, 'yesterday you said those stockbrokers–'

'The Joneses?'

'Yes, the Joneses, you said they were okay once you got to know them.'

'Yes, they are.'

'They are not,' said Tracy.

'Oh they are,' said Sol.

'Are not.'

'Stop, stop,' said Christian, 'put aside whether they're okay or not, my question is ... what I want to know is ... how have you communicated with them?'

Sol and Tracy looked at each other and then spluttered into laughter.

'What?' said Christian.

'We haven't,' said Tracy.

'Haven't what?'

'Haven't communicated with them.'

'Have you learned nothing, Christian?' said Sol, shaking his head.

'Well how've you got to know them then?'

'Well how d'ya think, pal?' said Tracy. 'We go and sit in their front room on an evening.'

'Just 'cos they can't get to know us, doesn't mean we can't get to know them,' said Sol.

'Oh. Right ...' Christian's head dropped. Why had he got his hopes up? He already knew it was one-way traffic, of course it was.

'We've struck gold, when you think about it,' said Tracy. 'There was so much goin' on here when we were alive, but now we get the inside track, too. Like Kylie at number thirty-eight and Joan at thirty-two, they're civil enough in the park, but at home Joan says Kylie's a little tramp and Kylie says Joan's a turkey-necked gossip-monger.'

'Isn't that a bit disrespectful?' said Christian.

'It's just their opinions, Christian,' said Sol.

'No, I mean aren't you being disrespectful, invading their privacy?'

'On no, we're very discreet,' said Sol, 'you see, they can't see us.'

'Yes, but–'

'Look,' said Tracy, 'it's not like we can do any harm, can we? It's not like we can pass anything on, well, apart from in the g-word world, but that's, y'know, totally separate.'

'But it's still an invasion,' said Christian.

'Well maybe people should be more careful,' said Tracy, 'it's like they say, everywhere has ears.'

'Walls,' said Christian.

'Walls?' said Tracy.

'Yes,' said Christian, 'you know, *walls have ears.*'

'Do they?' said Sol, and he looked with suspicion across towards the houses before coving his ears.

'Point is,' said Tracy, 'if people choose to live here, in the world, they've got to expect this.'

'How? How can they possibly expect to be observed by g-words,' said Christian.

'Well, how can they not? They all say they believe in life after death 'n that. Can't then act all surprised when they find out g-words might have been looking in on them now and again, joining them for *Strictly* on a Saturday. They can't have it both ways.'

'They choose to live in the public eye,' said Sol.

'The public eye?' said Christian.

'Yeah, we're members of the public,' said Tracy.

'And we've got eyes,' said Sol, leaning forward to flick his pupils left and right.

'But not everyone should expect to be observed,' said Christian. 'What about atheists?'

'Them lot? They deny we even bleedin' exist,' said Tracy. 'Trust me, we've 'eard 'em. They'll do it right while we're sitting there, right next to 'em, like we're a draught from under the door. Arrogant bastards. So yeah, too right we invade their privacy, and we don't feel too guilty about it, I can tell you.'

'So you cosy up to whoever you like and listen in to the most intimate personal conversations?'

'Yes, on a good day,' said Sol.

Christian shook his head.

'You know today could be a good one,' said Sol. 'Mrs Patterson's getting her test results. You can come with us to the docs, if you like?'

'No,' said Tracy, 'he's not–'

'I'm sorry,' said Christian, 'you're going to sit in on someone getting medical test results?'

'We find it's best to get the details from the horse's mouth,' said Sol.

'You'd use that for entertainment?'

'Course it's not entertainment,' said Tracy, 'we're being bleedin' supportive. No one else'll be there with her. And it won't be long before she's sitting on the grass right where you are, only now we'll have the info, be able to be all tactful and that.'

'We're very caring,' said Sol.

'And I'll tell you one thing,' said Tracy, 'when she is here, she won't be going on about Machu bleedin' Picchu.'

Christian shook his head.

'You see, local affairs, local community,' said Tracy.

'No, no,' said Christian. He got to his feet.

'This is where it's at, pal,' said Tracy, 'this is your answer.'

'He's right, mate,' said Sol, 'just give it a chance.'

The little park seemed to tighten and close in. The packed trees in full leaf, the perimeter of semis and, as he turned, Point Royal casting its shadow over all of them.

Christian started walking. He turned his head to the liver, which was still snuffling about in the grass over towards the community centre. The organ stopped what it was doing and for a moment sat stiff and still, stretching its portal vein towards Christian, but then it began to follow.

Christian broke out into a jog.

'Can't stand the heat, eh, Bamber?' shouted Tracy. 'Same time tomorrow then?'

He started running.

Now he caught sight of a heavyset man on the path up ahead. Despite having seen a lot of odd things over the last few days, and despite explicit advance notice of the odd thing now central in his vision, once again his new reality exposed him as unprepared. Though the rotund man was some distance away, there could be no doubt he had a gaggle of shoes, boots and one bare foot jumping and scampering around him, and what appeared to be a wicker ball on a rope, stretching out from his side.

Fat Larry.

Not today. Not now.

Christian put his head down and cut an exit via the gardens of the semis on the edge of the park, the liver following on but barely keeping up.

He was soon clear of the park, clear of Fat Larry, clear of Sol and Tracy, but he didn't stop, and as he ran, liver in pursuit, a single thought came knocking on the door of his mind. He didn't want to think it, he tried to keep it out, but by the time he approached the churchyard, it had wormed its way in. *This ... isn't ... going ... to ... work.*

It wasn't going to work for the rest of the day, let alone the rest of the week. And what then? What about in a month? A year? What then? What if reality never returned?

And then another thought – a possible solution. He stopped, turned and bolted back across the dual carriageway towards the nearby houses, meeting and passing the liver on the way.

Could it be enough? It had been the other night, but how about now, in the cold light of day? And for how long?

He ran into the first house he saw. No one home. The next was empty, too. The third had its set on, but its owners were engrossed in a daytime soap, which was worse than nothing. The next house was showing coverage of an indoor bowls match – no way, absolutely no way.

He was halfway to the next when, in the alleyway in between, he stopped, again. Another thought, an improvement – it was so obvious, how could he not have thought of it sooner? He ran out into the street, back over the dual carriageway, back through the churchyard and on into the shopping centre, passing through cars, people, children and anything in his way, his eyes only on the middle distance, and all the while the liver chasing after him, desperate to catch up. He didn't stop until he was at the other side of the town centre and zipping up the path of the escalator that led into the main floor of the Bracknell Picture House cinema.

He raced through the list of titles and times.

A film, a film, my kingdom for a film …

But then a calmness washed through him. He slowed himself down. He reread the titles, he took in the start times. He made an informed choice.

His hand moved to his pocket and he almost smiled before drifting past the ticket counter and on down to screen three, passing right through the man checking tickets. This was the first aspect of life, with the possible exception of being caught in the rain without a brolly, that was now better than before. All the usual pleasures were still there – huge screen, great sound, latest releases, but now he didn't have to pay, didn't have to queue, didn't have to fill himself up with overpriced high-calorie snacks. And unlike all other media, it wasn't dependent on other people's whims – it didn't matter whether they would keep reading or listening; whether they would change channels before the dénouement; whether they turned the pages too fast or too slow. Now he had scheduled start times. He had films that would play all the way through without interruption, even to an empty house.

Yes.

Yes.

Yes.

Chapter Thirty-Four

It was Kevin's second visit to the hospital. His first had been soon after Nikki had been stabilised, when she was still in intensive care and most of her face was covered in bandages. That visit had been an autopilot decision, as much a given as breathing or having breakfast. And the reality of the situation had only hit him once he was perched on the chair beside her bed, sitting there like a lemon, just staring at her and all the equipment. He'd looked at the visitors at other beds. Okay, so they probably felt anxious and helpless and worried, but at least they could do something, at least they could say some soothing words, or read the poor sod another chapter from *Wind in the Willows*. What was he supposed to do? He was the last person she'd want to see. Well at least the feeling was now mutual, having had the time to convert his dejection into far more satisfying spite.

'Get well soon, my old ice-queen,' he'd muttered on exit from that first visit, before failing to stifle a snigger that attracted stony glances.

His detachment had been compounded by him not even being Nikki's first visitor, several items already marking out the territory: a large but sparsely signed get well card from her remaining staff at iChemiclast, one from Jean Claude, and a CD player. Kevin hadn't brought anything, except *What Car?* and a packet of Polos. Well, it wasn't like there was going to be much conversation.

This visit, his second visit, was different though. Now he'd made an active choice to come, albeit a reluctant one. He was here because his solicitor thought it prudent – a husband deserting his wife in the midst of a life-threatening crisis being unlikely to play well at a divorce hearing.

He exhaled, sat back in the chair, and looked down at his watch. Three minutes. Surely it had been more than three minutes? He'd have to stretch it to ten at least. A brief but committed daily visit – just enough to keep her lawyers muzzled.

He took another look at the junk cluttering her bedside table. He was pleased to see that the CD player had followed her from intensive care, as had the cards. And now there was a silver helium balloon and a bowl of fruit. *Fruit?* How moronic.

He looked at his watch again. Three minutes and twenty seconds.

Why hadn't he brought his magazine? What was he thinking? Perhaps if he thought of the magazine, it would be almost as good as the magazine. Anything would be better than staring at his stagnant wife. Yes, still his, for the moment at least. Bruised, swollen and scarred. Disfigured, perhaps? Yes. Perhaps.

'So what was it all about then?' he said, finally, his voice low but measured. 'You still haven't given me a proper reason, … any reason.'

Nikki said nothing. Not an unexpected move, but even so he couldn't help wonder whether the lawyers had already been coaching her.

'No, no, wouldn't want to prejudice the case, would we now?'

Still nothing.

'I gave you everything,' he said. 'You wanted to get together, we got together. You wanted to get married, we got married. You wanted all that stupid furniture, we got it, all of it.'

He looked around. No one seemed to be watching.

'I gave you everything,' he said, leaning in. 'All my jokes, my stories, my goss, the names I came up with for your friends. For what, ten, no, eleven years of being at your side, never once resenting how you earned thirty-five times what I did. How many husbands would have put up with that? I suffered the Mercs, the Astons, the Beamers, the houses, the boat, the ski trips, the cruises. And what did I get in return? A poxy eight hundred grand and a fuck off from your lawyers.'

He realised, in his enthusiasm, he was spitting. A small globule sat glistening on the stitches in Nikki's left cheek. He took a tissue and wiped the saliva away. Then he stopped. He looked around again. No one was looking. He stood and leaned over until his mouth was directly above her head. He mustered a large specimen of sputum and, with relish, ejected it from his lips, watching it descend a mucus bungee into her hair.

He sat down.

Another one in the mouth? No, no, he wasn't a monster.

As he clock-watched, his mind drifted back to their breakup conversation. How calm she'd been when she told him he would be moving out as a precursor to them getting a divorce; how he could accept the situation and get a generous payoff or fight it and get nothing. It wasn't what she'd said that had hurt, it was how she'd said it. No tears, no bile, no Villeroy & Boch hurled at the walls. She was relaxed, she was rational, she was smiling for chrissake. And the one meeting since, where she'd asked all the questions about Christian's teachers, acting surprised when he tried to turn the conversation back to their marriage. She'd humiliated him and she knew it.

But nothing was official yet. Preliminary actions had been taken by Nikki's lawyers, letters of intent, letters of *Don't you even think about making this difficult or you'll get nothing*, but legally, so he'd been told, they amounted to little more than pre-fight posturing.

The thought crossed his mind again. It couldn't not. But thinking it, that didn't make him a bad person. Of course he wanted Nikki to wake up just as she was, with all her faculties intact, with full use of her writing hand and ability to quickly and easily digest and sign legal documents, so did everyone. But what if, tragically, she didn't? He had to face facts, like the concerned visitors at the other beds, that the worst could well happen. Life's not fair sometimes.

He ejected the CD – Macy McClane, *Distillations of Liberty*. He tossed it into the bin and replaced it with the *Nikki's Special Favourites* compilation he'd put together the night before. It opened with 'This is the End' by The Doors, then Beck's 'Lost Cause', before heading off into a cheery wilderness of Radiohead, Joy Division, Morrissey and Leonard Cohen.

He pressed repeat-loop play, checked her headphones were well seated, and, with a spring in his step, left the ward.

Out in the middle of the North Atlantic, two figures were standing just above the waves as they checked the stars now fading into the dawn. With a final course correction, they would soon resume their journey.

No rest for the wicked.

Not yet.

Chapter Thirty-Five

1. Thankful departure of Erdygrot
2. Floating inside upholstery
3. Terror
4. Recollection
5. Despair
6. Embarrassment – the cliché of realising, yet again, that what he was waking up to had not been a dream, and, a week into his nightmare, the final stage of what had become Christian's morning boot-up sequence.

His early days of breakfast with Tony were now gone, Christian's wake-up time having now drifted past nine. So now he normally woke to silence. But today there were voices outside. They seemed similar in number to Sunday, but their tone was more measured. He could almost sense the respectful stooped stances. He sat up and peered through the windows. He saw people clustered in groups, as there had been on Sunday, though now there seemed to be more unity. The sprinkling of black removed any remaining doubt over the reason for the gathering.

In life he would have paid no further attention, other than perhaps sparing a passing uncomfortable yet indifferent thought on the mortality of his parents, always assuming their demise would be faced before his own.

Being an atheist, he thought there was at least an outside chance of not having to face his own mortality at all, his hope being for good health until a ripe old age, and then an in-absentia death in his sleep taking him straight to oblivion, with facing oblivion being a piece of cake so long as you didn't have to do it before you got there.

'After death comes oblivion.' He'd often wondered why so many people felt such unease with this position, eventually concluding *oblivion* was the problem, because *oblivion* is a word, which has a definition, and so still means something, even if that something is nothing. It's then only a small step to start asking yourself what oblivion might be like, even though it's impossible to be like anything, or even be anything. And before you can shut the gate, off your imagination gallops, ... *Hmm, eternal nothingness, I don't like the sound of that, sounds all cold, dark and dreadfully long-winded.* 'After death comes nothing' is no better, for the same reason. Christian had always thought 'After death comes ' was the right way to think of it. He'd even sent it in to the British Humanist Association in 2004, offering it to them as their new motto, but never received a reply.

But in his present state, the events outside stirred interest. And for the first time he pondered his own funeral. He wasn't sure why it hadn't come to mind sooner. Perhaps it was because he didn't feel particularly dead, because despite no longer being quite the man he was, he was still a whole lot more than oblivion / nothing / '', if only because he was able to make this assertion.

He decided to take a closer look, but first turned to check on the liver. It was partly visible, asleep in the cat, which was asleep in the cat basket. He decided to let it be – an excitable yappy liver was the last thing the bereaved would want to contend with.

He drifted through to the kitchen and out through the door into the churchyard.

As he approached the mourners, he felt a ripple of guilt and slowed his drift. He made his way respectfully around the groups, picking up bits and pieces of information. He heard talk of a long and happy life, of every day being lived to the full, and of release. He also heard how house prices were really on the move in Winnersh. But then really, what did Tony know?

A hearse drew up and after Tony made a few remarks in reassuring tones, pallbearers delivered the coffin into the church, and the mourners began to file in. Christian hung around at the back. He wasn't sure if he wanted to go in, and even if he did, he certainly didn't feel entitled to be jostling for the best pews.

Another mourner hung back. She didn't seem to fit in with the others at all – three-quarter length tie-dye lace dress; blue sandals; hemp sling bag over the shoulder; part-plaited brunette hair with the rest flowing free. At least he'd bothered with a suit, even if it did come with grubby trainers and an AC/DC T-shirt.

He guessed she was twenty-five-ish, but could be three or four years either side. She was slim and attractive, though not model-beautiful, being devoid of a certain something he eventually identified as a total lack of vacancy in the eyes. The life in her eyes was at the other end of the scale; she was really *looking* – taking in the overcast sky and underwhelming shrubbery like she'd spent her whole life inside a shipping container, and yet, after each micro-stare, always returning her gaze to the ground at her feet, like she was embarrassed. Even with his hapless sense for female emotion, Christian could not miss a suppressed smile, a concealed joy that she was presumably trying to keep a lid on because of the occasion – you can't beam at a funeral, however keen you are to get to the will.

So strong was her radiance it clashed with her clothes, which was saying something given how much they were already clashing with each other. Why wasn't she wearing black? She could really wear black.

He followed her into the church and made sure he got an adjacent pew.

Christian soon discovered the service was for a Catherine Whysocky, who'd died just short of her one hundredth birthday. Close but no telegram, he thought. The proceedings ran much to the format he remembered, though it had been more than fifteen years since his last one, for Great-Aunt Margaret.

Many would say Christian had been lucky to reach thirty without losing anyone from his immediate family, but Christian was indifferent to it. Yes, he could imagine the rip-your-heart-out-while-it's-still-beating brutality of losing someone close, but apart from Beatrice, Christian didn't have anyone close. Blood is thicker than water, but in Christian's family, they'd been popping the warfarin for decades. He'd never had a problem with this, but in recent times he'd started to resent what he was missing out on. He was a writer now, and writers need intense experience. Furthermore, his subject was death, or at least the silly ideas humanity has hung onto regarding what might come after, so it was doubly lamentable. *Write about what you know.* He'd heard the novelist Howard Jacobson say he could only write about sorrow after his father had passed away. It was all so unfair. Why couldn't Christian's father get on and do the same, then Christian could write about it too. All he'd got from Great-Aunt Margaret's departure was an afternoon off from swimming and chemistry. Useless. There were other options of course – Beatrice had suggested he could get involved in grief counselling or volunteer at a hospice. They were good ideas, really good ideas, but in the end he'd opted for buying the director's cut of *Ghost* on DVD.

This service already seemed far more intimate than Great-Aunt Margaret's. For a start, most of the people looked like they actually wanted to pay their respects. Christian remembered thinking that, given the chance, Great-Aunt Margaret's immediate family would have preferred to dispense with the funeral altogether and just put her out with the recycling.

There were still some reluctant attendees here, of course: buttoned-up schoolboys; put-upon partners, but the overall impression was one of warmth and love. Several people stood to speak – memories; thoughts; a poem, all of which seemed heartfelt.

Christian looked across again to the funeral-crashing girl. The spark was now absent from her eyes, her chin was lower and she was playing with the knuckle of her ring finger. Perhaps she wasn't feeling so clever now, perhaps now finally realising that today wasn't about her. But he soon found that thought slipping away. The more he watched, the more vulnerable she seemed. Perhaps he'd jumped to conclusions. How did he know Mrs Werwhatshername didn't instruct the mourners to come dressed like it was a gay pride parade, and this girl was the only one brave enough to honour her wishes and was now paying the price for doing so?

As the service progressed, he further pondered the potential requests of the deceased. Lots of people have themed weddings, why not themed funerals? You are invited to the *Priscilla Queen of the Desert* funeral and cele-bration of the life of Catherine Werwhatshername. No feathers.

After Tony's closing remarks, the pallbearers gathered at the coffin and the mourners began to file out. Once more Christian thought back to Great-Aunt Margaret. She didn't have pallbearers, or at least he couldn't recall there being any. He seemed to think she'd come in on a sort of hostess trolley, but that didn't seem right at all. He definitely remembered the coffin ending up on a black conveyor belt, though, like the ones at supermarket checkouts. And he remembered having to hold off an urge to laugh as she'd passed between the little wooden doors like she was retreating into a cuckoo clock having chimed the hour.

As the last of the mourners filed out, he looked across to the girl once more. She was still seated and seemed to be composing herself.

She rose to leave, as did Christian.

'Thank you for coming,' said the girl as they met in the aisle.

Christian looked behind him. Idiot. 'Oh, um, not at all,' he found himself saying, 'least I could do. Sorry, I didn't realise you were a g-word?'

'A *g-word*?'

'Sorry, a ... I mean, I didn't realise you were ... I mean, I thought you were alive.'

'You know, I'm not quite sure how to answer that ...' she said. A little of the joy seemed to return to her face. '... but really, thanks for coming. It's nice to have someone to talk to. I thought there might be a few more spirits here, but I suppose it was quite short notice.'

'Right.'

'And I imagine for many it wouldn't be possible to make the journey.'

'Yes, well, that's public transport for you.'

They emerged into the light and fell in with the general milling about as the other mourners waited for the coffin.

'So, um, did you know Miss Whatshoey well?' asked Christian.

'Wysocki.'

'Sorry, Whysocky.'

'Well, yes, I'd got to know her rather well,' she said, smiling. 'Did you?'

'Er, no, not very well. Actually, not at all.'

'No, I thought not,' she said, studying Christian. 'So do you make a habit of attending stranger's funerals then?'

'No, no, I ... I drifted in. I'm a bit new to all this, you see, thought I might learn something.'

'Well snap. I'm rather new to it myself.'

'Really? How long have you been ... um ...'

'I passed on Sunday morning, early hours. So that's what, five and a bit days.'

'Oh yes, that is new. I've been around just a bit longer. About a week now, I suppose. All been a bit of a shock.'

'Really? Oh dear, I'm so sorry to hear that. But I'm sure you'll get used to it.'

'That's not been your experience then?'

'Well no, it's all been rather fun, actually.'

'Fun?'

'Well, yes. Obviously not so much this morning, though, seeing everyone sad and mournful.'

'No, no of course.'

'But overall, yes, it has been fun. Strange as well, though. I'm still me, but now I'm so much more than I was, beyond words. I think it's going to take some getting used to.'

This wasn't what Christian needed. Though he hated himself for it, he wanted to hear that she was struggling, that she too was lost and alone. But no, here she was, dead three days and loving it.

'But it is amazing, isn't it?' she said.

'What is?'

'This,' she said, spinning round, stretching her arms out to the finger tips, gesturing to everything around her.

'Yes, it is quite a nice churchyard, I suppose. I like the way the flower beds–'

'Not the churchyard, silly – life, eternal life!'

'Um ...'

'You don't agree?' she said, stopping her spin.

'Well, to be honest, I'm struggling to come to terms with it all,' said Christian. 'I didn't believe in an afterlife, you see. I'm not even sure I do now.'

'Ah, so you were agnostic?'

'Atheist, well, as near as damn it, a sort of six point nine on the Dawkins scale.'

'Oh I am sorry.'

'What for?'

'Well, this must all be quite a shock then, you poor thing.'

He laughed.

'What's funny?'

'I don't know,' said Christian, 'perhaps I've just got too many questions, too many unknowns.'

'Well. I'm sure all will become clear.'

He gave a nod, not knowing what else to do. 'So you were religious then?' he asked.

'I was, in a broad sense. I prefer ... should it be prefer or preferred? It doesn't seem right to be talking about oneself in the past tense, does it? But the present tense then seems to deny we've passed. No one prepares you for these problems, do they, these little details? Anyway, I preferred and prefer to think of myself as spiritual.'

'But you believed, *believe* in an afterlife?'

'Oh yes. I always knew there was something more, there had to be. So for me, waking up after I passed was, well, it was as expected as waking up in the morning, actually, more so these last few months.'

Christian turned to see the pallbearers loading the coffin. Catherine Werwhatshername's final journey. Next stop the cemetery and six feet under. It wasn't like she'd be pulling in for an ice cream.

'So when are you heading off?' asked the woman.

'I don't know,' said Christian, turning back, 'probably wait for the hearse to leave.'

'I don't mean here, silly, I mean the Gate. When are you going to set out?'

'What gate?'

'Look.' She reached into her bag and withdrew a leaflet.

'Oh yes, I've got one of those,' said Christian, 'or at least I did have.'

'Right, so have you worked out where it is?'

'I've not given it much thought.'

'Really? Why not?'

'Well, I'm still trying to work everything else out. It's only been a week. Besides, the stuff in the leaflet didn't seem too helpful.'

'But it's the instructions.'

'For what?'

'For our final judgement, for the entrance to Heaven.'

'How do you know?'

'Well it's obvious.'

'Is it?'

'Of course, listen,' she said, and unfolded the leaflet. '*You are advised to proceed to the Gate once you are all present and correct.* It has to be for judgement, for passage to the afterlife.'

'But if we're dead, then surely this is the afterlife?'

'No, no, I think it's just the first stage, I think it's purgatory.'

'Well I'm with you there.'

'No, I mean this is literally purgatory, you know, the struggle to purify us before the glory of the Kingdom.'

'I'm not convinced.'

'Well this can't be all there is. There must be more. For starters, where's the Almighty? Where are my friends and relatives who have passed?'

'Where's Elvis, where's Lord Lucan?'

'Well there's no need to mock.'

'Sorry, but really, what if there is no Almighty? Perhaps this is it, and we have to make the best of it here.'

'So who made the leaflets, why are we being told to pass through a gate? What else can that be for if it's not the gateway to Heaven?'

'Well I don't know. Perhaps it's a marketing scam.'

'A marketing scam? Whatever for?'

'I don't know, one of those golf sales, or a timeshare scheme. You know it's all hard sell once they get you through the door.'

'Well there's only one way to find out.'

'Well, it's your funeral.'

'No, this is my funeral.'

'I'm sorry?'

'Catherine, pleased to meet you.'

'What. No,' said Christian, shaking his head, 'no, Tony said Miss Whatsocky was–'

'Wysocki.'

'Whysocky, was nearly a hundred.'

'Yes, I was ninety-nine.'

Christian took another look at her. 'Well I have to say, you look … fabulous.'

'Well I didn't look like this at the start of the week.'

'Oh. Wow. *Wow*. So you looked …'

'Like I was ninety-nine. Though I liked to think I could pass for mid-eighties.'

'Well, well I don't know what to say.'

She smiled.

'But how do you explain your transformation?' he asked.

'Well how do we explain any of this? We can't. It's all just part of the magic.' She went into another spin, slower this time, her hands crossing her chest. 'And I don't care how it works,' she said. 'It's wonderful. I'm young again, I have a young body, I can move without pain, without restriction. I can see, hear and think clearly. I'm full of energy and every-thing feels so fast and fresh.' She clicked her fingers at him in quick succession.

'Seriously, you're not fooling around here. You're telling me you're ninety-nine and we've just been to your funeral?'

'Yes.'

'I think I'm going to need a moment to process that.'

He thought back to the other ghosts he'd met, to Sol and Tracy. Were they older than they looked? Where they younger?

As they drifted towards the lower end of the front of the churchyard, Catherine took Christian by the arm.

'Have a look down here,' she said, and she led Christian down one of the grass aisles and over to a hole in the turf, about half a metre square, close to the flower beds.

'What do you think?'

'About what?'

She smiled, seemed to wait for something, and then turned to look at Bracknell. 'Nice vista?' she asked, opening her arms to the multi-storey car park.

'Um, yes ... though not exactly Sydney Opera House,' said Christian.

The boot lid closed on the hearse, causing them to turn. Soon the engine was running and the hearse was making its way out of the churchyard.

'So, er, looks like you're ... off,' said Christian.

'Yes.'

'Which, er, which cemetery?' It was another stupid question. But then he didn't know what else to say. The perils of funereal small talk.

She shook her head. 'Crematorium.'

'What, they're going to ...'

'Well, my body, yes.'

Christian's face tensed.

'It's all right,' she said with a smile. 'I don't need it any more. And it was on its last legs anyway.'

'It's just, that's so final ... you, you can't undo that, can you.'

'Really it's fine. We always have to move forward, as my grandmother used to say.'

'Good advice.'

'Well, it's the only option, really, when you think about it.'

'Yes, yes I suppose so.'

The mourners began to drift off to their cars.

'So you're not, er, not going along for the next bit then?' asked Christian.

'I think I'm safe to give that part a miss.'

'Yes, yes of course, very wise.'

'It'll be back tomorrow anyway.'

'I'm sorry?'

She smiled and pointed to the hole in the turf.

'Oh you mean?'

'Yes.'

'Really?'

'Yes.'

'Bit small, isn't it?'

'Well there won't be a great deal left, will there.'

'Oh no, no I suppose not.'

'Dear me, you're really not taking this well, are you?' she said.

He forced a smile.

The final mourners were now gone, leaving Christian and Catherine alone in the churchyard.

'So, where are you staying now then?' asked Christian.

'At my home.' She seemed puzzled by the question. 'Where else would I be staying?'

He looked down at the little hole in the turf. 'No, no, of course. Sorry.'

'But I'm only staying a few more nights,' she said. 'I just want to say my last goodbyes, you know.'

'You're serious then, you're going to look for this gate?'

'Of course.'

'Right …'

'For me it– oh dear God, what is that?'

'What's what?' asked Christian.

'That,' cried Catherine, pointing to the exuberant bundle of human tissue joy scampering towards them.

'Oh, it's just a liver. My liver …'

The little organ went straight for Catherine, leaping onto her sandaled feet and playfully nudging and bumping her ankles. She froze.

'Urgh,' she said, closing her eyes tight and clenching her fists.

'… well, obviously it's not *my* liver.'

'Please, please, get it off me.'

'Don't worry, he's quite harmless.'

'Oh get it off, get it off, please get it off.'

Catherine snapped out of her paralysis, flicked the liver off her foot, and ran behind Christian, using him as a shield, holding on tight to his upper arms. Christian could feel her body press into his back. The sensation took him by surprise, the bliss of personal contact once again, to be held again, even if it was only as a dead pensioner's liver shield.

'Keep it away,' said Catherine.

'You're not good with pets then?' asked Christian.

'This is your *pet?*'

'Well, yes, it seems so.'

'But it's moving for heaven's sake, it's alive.'

'That's what I struggled with, at first. But he really grows on you. Look at him wagging his little top vein, he likes you.'

'But it's not right, it's unnatural.'

'Well, it's certainly unusual, but I don't know about unnatural.'

Christian decided it wasn't fair to leave Catherine suffering just to prolong his small pleasure, so he bent down and patted the liver and tried to calm it down. The liver responded to Christian's touch, nuzzling into his hand.

'Go on, boy,' said Christian, pointing at the vicarage, 'go back to bed. Go back to bed, boy.'

The liver spun twice on the spot, before scampering off to chase the leaves blowing in the breeze.

'I'm afraid he's not that smart,' said Christian.

'Is it possessed?' asked Catherine.

'I don't think so. What would be the point?'

'Well how does it move then?'

'I don't know. All part of the magic I suppose,' said Christian, with a wink.

'Is it dangerous?'

'No, no, he's quite harmless. It's not like he could bite anyone if he wanted to. He's just a bit excitable, that's all. I'm sure he'll be great with the ghosts of children, that kind of thing.'

Chapter Thirty-Six

The next morning, Christian woke to find Welby purring in his chest and the curtains still closed.

Ten fifteen.

Bugger.

He hurried over to the window and poked his head through. The gates were deserted, as was the entire churchyard, save for a man unloading a small mechanical digger from a trailer at the far left end, across from the gates.

Bugger ...

'Why didn't you wake me?' he said, turning to the liver, which was spinning end over end in the cat basket, chasing its portal vein.

Christian had ended up spending most of the previous day with Catherine. They'd drifted up to Warfield, where Catherine had grown up, and spent a pleasant afternoon touring some of her new haunts. And they'd parted with Christian offering to show Catherine some of his the next day – today. But agreeing to meet at nine thirty – what was he thinking? It wasn't like he could request an alarm call. It was all the worse because for the first time in a long time, he'd had an appointment he'd wanted to turn up for. In fact, the previous night had been the first time since his death that Christian had gone to sleep with only medium-level dread of waking up in the morning.

He fetched the liver and made his way outside to stand and wait at the gates. Perhaps she was running late too?

As the minutes passed, he watched the man with the digger set up and then begin his work, preparing what Christian assumed to be a grave next to where they'd be burying Catherine's ashes. He felt foolish at his surprise that despite it being the twenty-first century, this wasn't being done by two cloth-capped chipper cockney types with shovels. Did people even get buried these days? Wasn't it all cremation and composting? Then again, perhaps this man was here to fix the drains.

Eventually he accepted he'd missed Catherine. He cursed himself, before he and the liver drifted off to the park. He'd mentioned it to her in conversation the previous day, so it was worth a shot.

Of course she wouldn't be there, he'd tried to tell himself, as he busied through the streets, liver in tow, but as soon as he strode into the park, and Point Royal and the benches came into view, there she was, her brightly dressed form sitting on Sol's and Tracy's bench, next to the more matted form of Sol, with Tracy sitting in the grass. This was the first time Christian had seen Sol and Tracy allow someone else to sit on their bench, apart from the occasional mortal use, of course, which they were power-less to prevent.

'Morning,' said Christian. 'Sorry I wasn't at the gates. Something came up.'

As soon as the words left his lips, he wondered why he hadn't used the truth as his excuse, the truth being a reasonable one for once, but was then thankful he hadn't, realising saying he slept in because his live-in vicar hadn't opened the curtains might take some explaining or at least sound a bit precious.

'Not a problem,' said Catherine. She got up and kissed Christian on the cheek, while keeping an eye on the liver. 'Solomon and Tracy have been entertaining me.'

'*Solomon*,' said Christian, 'that's your name?'

'Yes,' said Sol.

Christian chuckled.

They all looked at him.

'What's so funny?' said Tracy.

'Well it's just, you know, Solomon.'

'Yes.'

'In the Bible.'

'And?'

Christian didn't have an answer and was thankful when Tracy broke the silence, even if it was with an insult.

'So how come a lovely girl like this is hanging out with a waste of space like you?'

'Aren't I lucky to have such great friends, Catherine?'

She smiled.

'So,' said Christian, 'still up for the grand tour?'

She nodded.

'Not taking you away from us, is he, Cath?' said Tracy.

'Just for a while,' she said.

'You mind she comes back in one piece, fella,' said Tracy to Christian.

'Sol,' said Christian, continuing to ignore Tracy, 'would you mind looking after the liver?'

'Can I?' said Sol, his face lighting up.

'Oh, you don't have to on my account,' said Catherine, 'I'm sure I'll be okay.'

'No, it's fine, they get on very well,' said Christian.

'Brilliant,' said Sol, before getting up, slapping his thighs and doing a dance.

'Come on then, Leslie,' he said, splash-diving into the grass and commencing what would be an extended roll around with the organ.

'Hope you weren't too bored chatting with Sol and Tracy,' said Christian, once they were out of earshot.

'No, not at all, they're fascinating.'

Christian laughed.

'They are,' said Catherine.

'Really?'

'Yes, the changes they've seen in the area over the years.'

'What, the Japanese garden at number thirty and the various replacements of their bench?'

'Now come on, don't be a meany.'

'Well I don't want to sound ungrateful. They have been kind to me. Well, Sol has, but I find their world so small, so claustrophobic.'

'I didn't. I liked their stories.'

'Maybe they told you more interesting ones. Yesterday they spent half an hour telling me about some missing leeks.'

'Well I thought it was interesting.'

'They told you too?'

'It's just a matter of empathy for their perspective. If you'd known Mrs Fosbury for thirty-five years, you'd be concerned about her leeks too.'

'I don't think I would. And anyway I thought it was Mrs Willoughby's leeks?'

'No, Mrs Willoughby is at number twenty-nine, she's the one with different size feet.'

'Oh ... yes.'

'You know, Christian, the funny thing is, Solomon and Tracy feel the same way about you.'

'What do you mean?'

'Well, before you arrived, they were apologising for you.'

'*What?*'

'Yes. Now don't tell them I told you, but they said they felt sorry for me having to spend a day with you. They said you'd chatter on and on about your love of holding men's hands, new-age travelling and a big picture.'

'The traitors, how dare they.'

She smiled. 'Oh I quite like you when you're angry.'

They walked on through the park.

As they approached Point Royal's moat-like perimeter road, a heavyset man in an ill-fitting brown suit plodded into view. He had a wicker ball on a rope, stretching horizontally away from him at waist height, and six or seven boots, shoes and one bare foot excitedly bouncing around his ankles.

'Ah,' said Christian, lowering his voice, 'now this is a bit of a local legend, this is–'

'Hi, Larry,' shouted Catherine.

'Hello Sparkles,' said Larry, booming warmly and ignoring Christian with equal enthusiasm, 'told you the sun would get out.'

'And you were right,' she said.

Larry's feet ran ahead of him, up to Catherine and Christian, where they began jumping up and nudging and bumping into their ankles. Apart from one tanned lefty, all were encased in a shoe or boot, though no two styles or sizes appeared to match.

'Down, Foot!' growled Larry, trotting to catch up, 'get down, I said. Hattersley, heel. I said heel. No *my* heel.'

'They really are a lively bunch,' said Catherine, nervously.

'Sorry, Sparkles,' said Larry, 'they really like you. *Stop it, Callaghan.* So where you off to?'

'Oh just taking the air. It's turned into such a lovely day for the time of year.'

'Sure has my dear. *Kinnock!*'

Christian made no attempt to engage with the man, partly because Larry hadn't given him so much as a glance, and partly because Christian was transfixed by the all-out bizarreness of the spectacle. What did the free feet make of attached feet, the strange stalks growing up out of their ankles, up and then down to a conjoined twin? Was all the leaping and nudging and bumping an attempt at inciting a revolt, a mass bid for freedom? And over time had they given up on freeing Larry's feet?

He edged round to sneak a look at the strange wicker ball arrangement – the same accessory he'd noticed on his first brief sighting of Larry. Up close, Christian could now see it was crudely fashioned, yet sturdy, and contained a single sandaled foot, apparently straining to escape, toes stretching and pointing permanently towards somewhere out beyond Point Royal, and this, he assumed, was why the rope was under tension. It was a peculiar sight, especially its apparent independence from Larry's orientation, causing Christian to think it could serve well as a combined personal compass and artificial horizon.

He realised Larry was now staring at him – staring at him as he stared at his wickerballed foot.

'I, er ...'

Larry turned to Catherine. 'Well, look after yourself,' he said before briefly glaring at Christian.

Larry and the feet moved on and Christian and Catherine resumed their drift.

'You know him?' whispered Christian.

'Oh I think I'm going to be sick,' said Catherine.

'Yes, he's no looker, is he.'

'Not Larry, the feet. This bits of people thing, it's all wrong.'

'Oh yes, I see what you mean. Look, don't worry, you'll get used to it, trust me. But really, how do you know Fat Larry?'

'I met him this morning.'

'He's not given me so much as a glance. Well until just now, and even then I think he was only working out which fist he'd most like to pound me with.'

'Well maybe if you didn't call him Fat Larry.'

'I don't call him Fat Larry, Sol and Tracy do.'

'Well, you must have done something to get his back up. He's really very friendly.'

'So it seems. So is Sparkles your nickname then?'

'No, he just started calling me that.'

'You met him only this morning and he's already calling you Sparkles?'

'Is that odd?'

'Well, yes, I think it is.'

They took a left and drifted up along Rainforest Walk and on through the fields behind, Christian deciding the first stop on the tour would be his old primary school. At the dual carriageway, he took her hand.

'What are you doing?' she asked.

'It's a busy road.'

'And?'

'And well, you're ... it's just–'

'Oh my. You're helping me across, aren't you? I'm the old biddy and you're the kind young gentleman?'

'No, no ... it's–'

'Christian, I'm not a pensioner any more.'

'Sorry.'

'Does it mean you're seeing me differently now?'

'What do you mean?'

'From how you first looked at me at the church?'

Christian tried to look like he hadn't understood what she meant.

'Oh come on,' she said, 'it may have been a good while ago but I have lived.'

'Well, all right, but can you blame me? You're a good-looking ghost.'

'I'm not complaining, Christian. It was most welcome. It's been a long time since anyone looked at me like that,' she said. 'Well, there was Mr Boyd, but he looked at everyone like that, even the men. Even some of the furniture, actually. He had a thing going on with his old blue chaise. They had to get rid of it in the end.'

Christian looked into her eyes as she talked. He had to hand it to Fat Larry – 'Sparkles' was bang on. Was it wrong to find her attractive? She was ninety-nine years old. Last week she'd have been smelling of stale urine and having her food put through a blender. But then now she wasn't ninety-nine, she was twenty-five-ish, younger than him, sort of. But then again her mind, her consciousness, was surely still ninety-nine? It wasn't like they'd wiped the last seven decades of her memory.

'And another thing,' she said, 'you're twice silly because it's not like we can get run over anyway. It doesn't matter if the road is busy.' She drifted out into the traffic, several cars passing through her. 'You see, they can't hurt you.'

'Yes, I know. I don't like being run through, that's all. It's so undignified.'

She made her way to the far pavement and turned back to face him. 'Will you give me a straight answer to a straight question?' she shouted.

'Possibly,' he shouted back. He spotted a gap and crossed to join her.

'Okay,' she said, 'how old do I look now?'

'Oh no, that's not fair. That's always a no-win question. You may as well ask me if I think you look fat in that dress.'

'Christian, I'm ninety-nine years old, or at least I was at the start of the week, I doubt you could offend me even if you tried.'

'Well, all right. I've never been good at guessing ages, but I'd say twenty-five-ish?'

'Really? Golly, twenty-five ... *twenty-five*.'

'You didn't know?'

'I guessed it was somewhere a lot younger than I was, just from the look of the rest of me. And from the feel, see ...' She took his hand and ran it over her cheek, causing Christian to briefly forget his name and address. '... but I wasn't certain, you know, with not being able to see myself.'

'I'm sorry?'

'No reflection,' she said.

'Oh yes, I see. You know, er, that really disturbed me, at first. It still does. All a bit Bram Stoker.'

'Really?'

'Well, yes,' he said. 'Obviously not because of anything as stupid as a belief in vampires, no, it's that sudden reality check – or rather un-reality check. It's like the universe smacking you round the head with a cricket bat to remind you of what you're not.'

'I don't follow.'

'Well, okay, here we are, two people chatting, taking a stroll, it's not weird, is it, not in the slightest, and we could continue the conversation and head up to the town centre, all still fine, but then you find yourself glancing into a shop window, seeing the scene behind you reflected, but you're not in it. And then your heart sinks all over again.'

'So not seeing yourself in a mirror reminds you that you've passed?'

'Well, it certainly reminds me I'm not what I was.'

'And walking through doors and walls doesn't?'

'Yes, of course,' he said, 'but the reflection thing catches you by surprise, it's the reality-rug being pulled from under you. If I walk through a wall, at least I've chosen to do it. I can grit my teeth and be ready for it.'

'So what are you doing about it?'

'About what?'

'Well it sounds like you have a psychological problem. You need to tackle it.'

'No, I just work around it.'

'How?'

'By avoiding reflections.'

'But that's not dealing with it.'

'It's working fine so far. And I find most problems go away if you leave them long enough.'

They walked on.

'So I take it you're totally fine with it then,' said Christian, 'the whole lack of reflections thing?'

'Well, no, actually, but for different reasons,' said Catherine. 'Rather shallow ones, I'm ashamed to say. I didn't regard myself as vain in life, well, no more than the next person, but I always took pride in my appearance. And after a lifetime of doing so, it is rather rough to have that taken away from you, don't you find?'

'Um, yes. I suppose I've just been, well, coping with it as best I can.'

'Well good for you,' she said, 'but for me there's more, and I can't deny it's even more shallow.'

'Go on. I promise I won't judge.'

'Well, when I was young, I used to look at the old ladies, wrinkled and grey, and I would ask myself why do they still get their hair done, why do they still put their makeup on? Don't they realise it isn't going to make the blindest bit of difference now.'

'Like trying to paint a rotten fence.'

'Well, yes ... But of course eventually the girl becomes the old lady. And what do you do? You get your hair done, you put your makeup on. I suppose you become the old lady in such small steps. Time kills your body so very slowly. So there never is a point where you think it's not worth it, because it was always worth it yesterday.'

'Yes, yes I suppose so.'

'Anyway, when I was a child, I used to think what if I went to sleep for a hundred years, like Sleeping Beauty, but with my body ageing while I slept. So I'd go to sleep in a young body and wake in an old one. Would I want to die, having got there in one leap? Or would I want to keep living, despite the horror? But now, the reverse has happened, and it's not a Grimms' fairy tale, it's real. I've been transported back into my young body, in one leap. The feeling is beyond words.' She looked at Christian. 'Now this part is going to sound rather shallow, because it is rather shallow. The tragedy is, the miracle has happened, but I can't see it, and I suppose I never will.'

'Well, yes, that is a tragedy of sorts. Still, not a bad deal, as deals go?' said Christian. 'Fountain of youth, but you don't get to see your face. I mean, would you swap it for looking ninety-nine again but being able to see yourself?'

'Not a chance,' replied Catherine, allowing herself a smile. 'I may be old but I'm not stupid. But I would so love to see myself just once, now I am young again.'

'Yes, you don't know what you're missing,' said Christian, making the most of an excuse to take a good long look at her. 'Oh but hang on,' he said, peering at her mouth.

'What?'

'I think you've got a piece of food in your teeth.' He took her face in his hands. 'It's a big piece of spinach,' he said. 'I can't believe I didn't see it before.'

'Oh no,' said Catherine, trying to remove it with her fingers, 'that won't do. Is it gone?'

'No.'

She tried again. 'Now?' she said.

'No,' said Christian, looking concerned. 'Oh, do you think perhaps you're stuck with it, like we're stuck with these clothes?'

'You mean it's going to be there for ever?'

'Well it certainly looks that way. It's no problem though, just keep your lips permanently oder your teech,' said Christian, looking and sounding like he was auditioning for *Gurning Idol*.

'Dear, no. I've only just got them back. We must be able to get it out.' She started frantically picking at her mouth.

'Hey, hey stop. I was only joking,' said Christian, taking her hands, 'there's nothing there.'

'Oh, you swine, you monster. That's not funny.'

'It was quite funny.'

'Meany.'

'Just a little joke. No, I can't see anyone having to spend eternity with food stuck in their teeth. Surely even God wouldn't be that cruel.'

Chapter Thirty-Seven

Dexter had been summoned to meet Gordon on the central landing of the third floor of Henry Ford House. Ostensibly it was to review Gordon's new suit, but, given the location, he suspected there may be something else on the agenda. He didn't want to speculate quite what – Gordon was more Gordon than ever, these days.

'Not bad, eh?' said Gordon, taking a turn, as a haggard Bipton looked on at his creation – a slate-blue, single-breasted, classic cut – or at least his closest approximation.

'It's all right,' said Dexter, 'you're starting to look the part again.'

'You don't sound convinced,' said Gordon. 'Come on, out with it. Bippy will make the changes.'

Bipton gave Dexter a desperate look.

Dexter stepped closer. 'Well, these days everything's going one size too small, Gordo. Here, you see, I'd have the sleeves a good inch shorter, show some cuff, sculpt the shoulders more, lose some slack from the trousers.'

Gordon smiled and took off the jacket.

'But, sire,' said Bipton, 'to make these changes, this is not straightforward, this will–'

'Just start again,' said Gordon. He held out the jacket. 'You've got until lunchtime. You can do the pants this afternoon.'

A trembling Bipton took the jacket but just stood there, panic pouring through his face.

'Shoo,' said Gordon.

Bipton scuttled off.

Gordon turned to Dexter and flashed a smile. 'There's something else,' he said.

'I thought there might be,' said Dexter.

Gordon led the way over to the entrance to the north wing. 'Tell me what you think of this,' he said, and he thrust open the doors to reveal a cavernous graphite-grey empty shell.

'Wow. Where's all the furniture? Where's, well, everything?'

'Gone. We've ripped it out, the whole damned lot.'

'Um, why, exactly?'

'Too spacious. Too relaxed. Too open. There were fucking pot plants in here, Dex. Big ones.'

'Right, right. So what's the plan?'

'We're going old-school, subdividing the lot, then subdividing again, then subdividing again. I want cramped little spaces in battleship grey, everyone on top of each other, getting on each other's nerves, generate some stress, some tension, some pressure.'

'Okay, well, that's quite a vision.'

Gordon's eyes widened, orange flame sparking in his nostril hair. 'Project Battery Hen's just the start,' he said. 'I want to look at everything. I want to ratchet up the dress code–'

'Again?'

'Yes, Dex. Again.'

Silence.

'And it's time for another purge.'

'Gordon, the first two were very thorough, more than thorough, but–'

'Bullshit.'

'Look, it's great to have you back to your best, it really is, but we have all the time in the world. Why not space this out, let the first changes settle.'

'Bullshit, again, Dexter. We've got eighteen years of slacking-off to undo, as you well know.'

He looked Dexter in the eye, then continued, 'I have clarity for the first time in decades. All this dead wood, this is why we've not found the boy. So no, we don't have all the time in the world. We need to move faster.'

'Faster?'

A longer silence.

'I hope I've not misplaced my faith in you, Dex?'

Dexter put his hands on his hips. 'I can't believe you feel the need to ask. I'm with you one hundred per cent, Gordon, as I always have been.'

Chapter Thirty-Eight

After a tour of the school, Christian and Catherine headed back towards town, Christian talking up the splendour of the arts centre as a potential excursion for the afternoon, while offering up other pieces of sage advice from his slightly longer experience of being dead in Bracknell. But again Catherine put him to shame. As they passed the leisure centre, she pointed out three sporty types working on their drift speed at the running track and insisted on introducing Christian.

Once they resumed their walk, Christian confessed he'd seen them before, but as with Sol and Tracy, hadn't realised they were ghosts. He admitted it was embarrassing, but maintained it was inevitable when Bracknell's living population did so little to distinguish itself from its dead.

When they reached the top end of South Hill Park, it happened again.

'Oh there's Toby and Jenny,' said Catherine, 'now they're lovely.'

'Oh not more,' said Christian, 'please, can't we just–'

'No, you'll love Toby, he's rather witty.'

'No, look, he's wearing a Barbour jacket. I can already tell we won't have anything in common.'

'Well you're both dead, so that should get you started.'

'Toby, Jenny,' shouted Catherine, running over to them, 'hello again, this is my friend Christian …'

Part one of the ethereal *Let's pretend we find each other interesting* ritual now played out, which Christian found as hollow as he had in life. How had you died? How old were you when you died? What had you done for a living before you died? What sort of car had you been driving before you died?

Eventually they moved to part two of the ritual, but here, to Christian's relief, it proved far less awkward than its real-life equivalent: 'Well it would be great to stay in touch, such a pity there's no post, or phones, or internet, but hey, I'm sure we'll bump into each other.'

They continued on through the park.

'Who were they again?' asked Christian.

'Toby and Jenny,' said Catherine. 'Honestly, you're hopeless.'

'Let me guess, you met them this morning?'

'Last night actually, lovely couple.'

'I think I might have seen them before, too. I'm not sure. Either way, maybe you should be giving me the tour?'

'You just have to open your eyes, Christian.'

'I thought I was. Tell me, is life, um, *death*, always like this for you?'

'Like what?'

'Like meeting people and instantly connecting.'

'Well, I suppose so. Isn't that normal?'

'No.'

'Ooh, shall we head over to the swimming baths? It's not far from here. I met this delightful Spanish couple this morning, they may still be there.'

'No, please, no more of the social scene today.'

'Oh. Would you like me to leave?'

'No, no I don't mean you.'

'Good,' said Catherine with a smile.

'How about a film?' said Christian. 'Do you like films?'

'I do, but perhaps not in the middle of the afternoon. Come on, it's such a lovely day.'

'All right then. Something else, something else … I know.'

'What?'

'It's a surprise.'

'Well, all right then, sir,' said Catherine, stopping on the path, 'surprise me.'

'Okay. Come over here.' He led her off the path onto an open area of grass. 'This'll do fine,' he said. 'Now close your eyes.'

'Okay,' she said, and obliged.

'Are they closed tight?'

'Yes.'

'Good, now, I need you to sit down.'

'Here in the grass?'

'Yes, here in the grass.'

'Okay,' she said, and did as he asked.

'Now, I need you to stand up again, but you need to do it slowly. You'll feel a little pressure on your shoulders.'

'Why?'

'It's part of the surprise. Trust me. And keep your eyes closed.'

'Okay.'

Catherine stood, keeping her movements slow and gradual, as instructed.

'Now, take my hand,' he said.

'Okay,' said Catherine, obliging again, 'can I open my eyes now?'

'No, keep them tight closed until I say.'

'Okay.'

'Now, we're going for a walk.'

'A walk?'

'Yes, well a drift. Now, do you trust me?'

'I trust you.'

'All right then, off we go.'

They took a pace forward, Catherine holding tight onto Christian's hand.

They continued on for a minute or two, the gentle sounds of the park gradually growing faint.

'Okay, I think this is far enough.'

'So can I open my eyes?' asked Catherine.

'Yes,' said Christian, 'no, wait.'

'What?'

'Um, do you suffer from vertigo?'

'Why?'

'Oh no reason, but do you?'

'No.'

'Good.'

'What's going on?'

'Open your eyes.'

Catherine opened her eyes to find her entire field of view filled with blue sky and clouds. 'Wooooh,' she shouted, grabbing onto Christian like he was Superman as she spun round to see they were lying down in mid-air over the park, high above the treetops. 'Oh my Lord, what have you done? We're up in the air.'

'Cool eh?' said Christian, once again enjoying being held.

'How have we got here?'

'We walked.'

'But–'

'We went up instead of along. When you sat up, I rotated you, that light pressure at your shoulders?'

'Dear God. Is it safe?'

'Yes, it seems so.'

'Seems so? Don't you know so?'

'It's fine, really. I did a test run in the shopping centre.'

She didn't reply.

'You know,' he said, 'I don't believe we could fall even if we wanted to, and anyway, if we really are dead, then surely we can't come to too much harm?'

'Well no, no I suppose not,' said Catherine, relaxing her grip a little. 'It's … it's incredible.'

'Isn't it just? I think it's safe to say the old laws of physics no longer apply. We're sticking two fingers up to Isaac Newton, we're mooning Einstein.'

'In a funny way, I knew we could do this,' she said. 'Several times yesterday I found myself wading through the pavement rather than walking on it, but I didn't take the thought to the next stage.'

'And I think we could go further,' said Christian, 'to the edge of space … perhaps even into space itself.'

'How far is space?'

'I don't know. Be a fair old stroll I should think.'

'Yes, one for another day perhaps.'

'It's a date.'

'Um, yes.'

Christian sank into the awkwardness he'd created. Why had he used the d-word? It had all been going so well, and now he'd curdled the milk, made all the worse because they were holding onto each other. Had Catherine loosened her grip a little just then? Had he just tightened his?

'Let's sit up, shall we?' said Christian.

'How?'

'Just sit up. Don't think about it, just do it.'

Catherine released her grip and sat up.

'Oh yes, easy.'

They sat there saying nothing for a minute or two. It was serene. The world at ground level, and all its troubles, was far below, their only company up here wisps of cloud and the shadow of the breeze flowing through them.

'Still nervous?' said Christian. Catherine was playing with the knuckle of her ring finger, as she had at her funeral.

'A little,' she said.

'Why the finger?'

'Excuse me?'

'You play with your finger now and then,' he said, mimicking the action.

Catherine stopped and folded her arms.

'Sorry, I didn't mean to pry,' said Christian.

'Oh it's okay.' There was a long pause. 'It's my wedding ring, you see.'

'But you don't have a wedding ring?'

'Exactly.'

'You don't have one … but you'd like to have one?'

'I used to have one, but not any more.'

'Oh. So it didn't work out?'

'No, I mean I had one in life, almost all my life, but I don't have it now. It's gone. Well, no, it's not gone, it's just not come with me, if you see what I mean. I know exactly where it is. It's at home in my best jewellery box.'

'Ah.'

'And it's not as if I can just go and collect it.'

'Ah, no …'

'It didn't stop me trying, but well, that was never going to work, was it?'

'I'm so sorry,' said Christian, 'that must be hard to accept.'

'Do you think that's worse than losing it?' asked Catherine. 'Knowing where it is but knowing I'll never again be able to pick it up, roll it around in my hand, put it on?'

'Oh yes, I see. Well, I don't know, I don't really have a parallel. Well, apart from my *Star Trek Next Gen* DVD collection. It's the limited edition box set and everything. But, well, I suppose that's not quite the same.'

Catherine looked down, focusing not on the distant ground but somewhere in the empty space beneath them. 'It's strange what you come to rely on,' she said, 'what you fall back on, without even realising it. It isn't even as if I wore it much, but it was always with me in life. It would always make me feel better, no matter what had happened. Silly really.'

'No, I don't think so.'

'So there was really nothing for you,' she said, 'no keepsake?'

'Dunno. I suppose I've not thought about it, what with this all still being a bit new. It's a sobering thought, isn't it, though, every single one of our possessions is now out of reach. I suppose they'll soon be someone else's, shared out, given away, or just chucked in the bin.'

'Yes, you really can't take it with you, or at least not much of it anyway.'

'Actually, now I think about it, there is one thing I will miss. My grandpa's watch. It didn't have much of a story behind it. It's not like it spent three years up his best friend's bottom or anything' – Christian was lost in his thoughts and it didn't cross his mind that Catherine may not have seen *Pulp Fiction* – 'but it was his, and he left it to me. So it would've been nice if I'd have been able to bring it with me. Maybe I'd have been able to give it back to him, or at least let him see me wearing it.'

'That's not it then?' said Catherine, pointing to Christian's watch.

'Oh no, this is a piece of junk. A fake a friend of mine picked up in Hong Kong. Never kept good time from the day he gave it to me.'

'But you kept it?'

'Well I liked the look of it, and I could never justify the cost of a real one.'

'A real watch?'

'A real Omega.'

'Ah.'

'And it didn't matter that it didn't keep good time, because I never really needed a watch anyway.'

'No?'

He nodded. 'I always know what the time is. I have an innate sense for it.'

'Really?'

'Oh yes.'

Catherine smiled. 'So you got to bring a watch but not the one you wanted?' she said.

'Yes. Now you put it like that, it doesn't seem fair, does it?'

'No, and that's what I don't understand about the ring,' she said. 'It was the one little object I cared about, so why didn't they let me have it?

Now if I'd wanted to bring garden furniture, or a sewing machine or a holiday cottage in the Cairngorms, I could understand, they'd have to make inquiries. But it's just a ring. You've got your watch, or at least a watch, so it's not like there can be a ban on jewellery or anything.'

'True. True. But then even though I have the watch, it's not like it's real.'

'Yes, you said it's a fake.'

'No, what I mean is it's also a fake. It's a fake fake.'

'I don't follow.'

'Here,' he said, holding up the watch, 'if you look closely, you'll understand.'

'Oh yes, the hands aren't moving.'

'It's worse than that.' He tilted the watch. 'You see, they aren't even distinct from the face, it's like they're painted on.'

'Oh dear me, your friend must have been rather gullible. That wouldn't fool anyone.'

'No, they weren't like that on my fake, but they are on this one.'

'Oh, oh yes, I see what you mean. And the little clocks, too, they look like stickers.'

'Actually they did look like that on my fake too.'

'Oh.'

'Yes, well, like I say, it wasn't a great copy. I always had to stop anyone getting a close look. I suppose James Bond never had to contend with that.'

'James Bond?'

'Yes, he always had an Omega. Though I expect he could afford the genuine article, or at least a really top-notch copy that kept good time and where the little clocks weren't stickers. But anyway, do you see what I'm saying, this watch here on my wrist now is like an image of my old watch, an impression, a bad copy. The watch itself is still, well, actually, I don't know where the watch is, but this suit I'm wearing, for example, this suit is still hanging in the box room at my house, I know it is, I've seen it. So I reckon even if you had your ring here, you wouldn't really have it here, you'd have an image of it here, a copy, if you get my logic.'

'I see what you mean.'

'Does that make it any better?'

'No.'

Chapter Thirty-Nine

In the upper realm of the afterlife, Gabriel was reluctantly making his way to Terry's latest meet and greet, this time being held in the finally finished *Heaven's Got Talent* Audition Lounge. It wasn't a business meeting – Terry barely did them in the week, and the idea of one on a Saturday afternoon was unthinkable – but Gabriel knew Terry and he knew the subject of Christian Bootstrap would come up all the same. There was no good news and the only news he did have was worse than no news at all, the latest update from Trimbrilly confirming there was still no sign at the house, despite a weeklong stakeout, and that he was now directing the shepherds to sweep Christian's former workplace and the wrecked house in Virginia Water, before another pass of the death site in London.

So Gabriel held his head low as he trudged past the lentil plants and burned wooden half-statues of Diagoras Plaza. And his mood would worsen when he came across Harold, sporting a white linen smock instead of his angelwear, in conversation with a short, earnest-looking man in cream robes at one of the chess benches.

The conversation broke off as Gabriel approached. The short man got to his feet and started walking.

'Archangel,' said the man, as he passed.

'Matthew,' said Gabriel.

Gabriel stopped and waited for the man to leave the courtyard before turning to complete the last steps over to Harold and taking the vacant seat.

'What do you think you're doing?' said Gabriel.

'I was saying hello,' said Harold.

Gabriel shook his head.

'Is there a problem?' said Harold.

'You sat with him, Harold, in a public place.'

'There isn't a law against it.'

'There doesn't have to be.'

Harold gave no reply.

'So, the waistcoat's out of favour now, is it?' said Gabriel.

'It's a warm day.'

'No warmer than all the others.'

Again, Harold gave no reply.

Gabriel leaned in. 'What have you told him?'

'Nothing.'

'The truth, Harold.'

'I swear I told him nothing.'

Gabriel pursed his thin lips, then casually looked down at his right clawhand and tapped his clawthumb to each clawfinger in turn. 'I really *really* wouldn't recommend this path, young man.'

A pause.

'All right,' said Harold. 'All right, Matthew says Jesus is worried.'

'Oh is he indeed?'

'Yes. About Terry.'

'Really ...'

'Well, he is his father, it's only natural.'

'Terry is his father, but also him as well,' said Gabriel. 'Believe me, there's nothing natural about their relationship.'

Harold looked away for a moment before restoring eye contact. 'Look, I think they know,' he said.

'Know what?'

'Nothing specific, but they know there's something going on, something they're not being told about.'

'Which is how it always is,' said Gabriel. He sat up straight. 'Cabinet never publishes its business, why do they think we have a cabinet?'

'But are matters not exceptional in this case? Shouldn't Jesus be included at least?'

'Harold, I don't know where this is going, but I advise you, again, to be circumspect in your actions and your associations. There's a fine balance to the politics, here, and keeping Jezza out of the picture is central to it.'

'But doesn't he have a right? He is the heir.'

'Heir? Heir to what? This isn't a monarchy.'

'Indeed. It's more like a dictatorship ...'

'Yes, that's exactly what it is. And it works.'

'But it doesn't,' said Harold. 'He's ordered assassinations, we've witnessed it, you and I.'

The archangel leaned in. 'You will show some respect and you will lower your voice.'

'Beg pardon, apologies. But you do know I'm right.'

'No, I don't. We've been through this. Terry had no choice. Bootstrap forced our hand. Sometimes these things are necessary.'

Harold shook his head.

'All right, I'll tell you,' said Gabriel, 'I'll tell you why this is bigger than you can imagine, why we had no choice.'

'I'm listening,' said Harold.

'Bootstrap was going to publish the master codes,' said Gabriel. 'In weeks, perhaps even days, humankind would have had verifiable evidence of creation. In a heartbeat, we'd have a world of believers down there, meaning no more new souls in Heaven.'

'And so what? So Terry doesn't get any new artists and writers, or those exotic performers he's so keen on, is that such a price to pay?'

'I told you, you don't know the full story. The true situation is much more grave ...' Gabriel glanced left and right before leaning in again. 'We have been the number one realm right from the start, from day one, but that status is not cast in stone. And one thing it depends on is a regular supply of souls. We don't need many, but we do need some. Now Terry likes it that he gets the free-thinkers, these days, he really does, but it's not like we had a choice. Opening our doors to them was a necessity if we were to close our doors to the devout.'

'And?'

'And what?'

'And what would happen if no one comes up here any more?'

'The whole system would become unstable and would quickly reset. Number one status would automatically go to the realm with the most souls, simple majority.'

'And we'd be?'

'A distant third. We've been selective for far too long, we just wouldn't have the numbers.'

'So what? So Terry loses a bit of face, loses out on the bragging rights, loses–'

'Harold, Heaven would fall.'

'Meaning?'

'Meaning the skies would darken, then harden.'

'Harden?'

'We would become an underworld realm.'

'No,' said Harold, shaking his head.

'No, what do you mean no?'

'I mean you could have avoided this, you could have restored the original codes, start admitting believers again. It would have had other benefits too, it still could, just think–'

'Oh please. Come on, Harold, you know that was never going to happen. And besides, I told you, changes to the codes take months to kick in, months to take effect. If Bootstrap had published, we'd have weeks only, perhaps just days, before the well would run dry.'

'No,' said Harold, 'no, there's all the people in the Queue, hundreds of thousands, they'd still ...'

The archangel was shaking his head. 'They can see everything in the mortal realm. I'm sure you kept up with mortal news when you queued? Anything to help with the boredom, yes?'

Harold said nothing.

'No, they'd all become believers too,' said Gabriel, 'and just as quick.'

Silence.

'Now you see why you've been naïve,' said Gabriel. 'It's not so easy to hold onto those principles when you're confronted with reality, is it?' Gabriel sat back and flexed his shoulder muscles before leaning in again. 'Now, you will break off your ties with your new friends, you will refocus your loyalties, and you will not speak of this to–'

'It's still not right,' said Harold.

'What?'

'Even if that does happen, it doesn't justify killing Mr Bootstrap, killing anyone.'

'I don't believe what I'm hearing.'

'Open your eyes, Gabriel, can't you see? This confirms what is already plain.'

'And that is?'

'That this place is an ethereal Sodom and Gomorrah. And its destiny is clear.'

'*What?*'

'The corrupt realm. Its renewed depravity. Its inevitable fall.'

'That's just a story, Harold, and besides, its ending might have been different if God was head of the Sodom and Gomorrah district council and running the whole show from the start, don't you think?'

'No, I don't think,' said Harold, folding his arms.

Gabriel flexed his armwings, stretched his clawfingers and gripped the edges of the bench. 'So what are you proposing then?' he asked.

'I'm not proposing anything.'

'Oh no?'

Harold said nothing.

'Come on, let's hear it.'

A stare-filled silence.

Harold blinked first. 'Well, all right, what if Terry was to … retire?'

'Retire?' said Gabriel. 'He's eternal. He's never started, what makes you think he'll finish?'

'But what if he could be persuaded?'

'Are you out of your mind? He's the supreme being, he's the only one who does any persuading around here.'

'But Jesus is also a supreme being, isn't he, as you say, the same supreme being, in a way, so he must be as powerful as Terry?'

'Harold, do not utter another word. I am warning you, if you mention this again, or meet with Jezza's people again, your role here will be terminated and far worse besides. Do I make myself clear?'

Chapter Forty

High above Bracknell, Christian and Catherine had decided to resume
their drift and make their way back to the park, retracing their route, only
this time at eighty metres above ground level, giving them a whole new
perspective on the area. The roof of Point Royal and the trees above the
benches eventually came into view, and with some trial and error they
found a line of sight to Tracy, Sol and the liver.

'Hey, Sol, Tracy,' shouted Christian. 'Hey … I've found the big picture.'

Tracy looked up and soon spotted them, and then shook his head in
disapproval. Sol looked all around but not up, seeming unsure where the
distant voices were coming from.

'I say, I've found the big picture,' shouted Christian.

Tracy put his hand to his ear and shrugged, before folding his arms and
breaking eye contact. Sol just kept looking around in bewilderment,
making Christian think it might have been better not to have said anything.

They thought about descending, but decided instead to drift on,
reasoning there was no telling what it might do for Sol's sanity were he to
witness it.

'Okay, so you were married but didn't wear your ring,' said Christian,
'so was it a sort of open relationship or something?'

'Oh no, nothing like that,' said Catherine, laughing, before pausing.
'He died.'

'Oh, oh no, I'm so sorry.'

'It's all right. It was long ago, and I came to terms with it long ago. I got on with my life, as they say. But it's strange, you know, looking back to when I was married, I can still remember every detail, and yet now it's like a different life, like it was someone else's. That's what time does to you, I suppose. It slowly turns you into a succession of different people, different yet, in all the important ways, still the same ...'

'Like Doctor Who,' said Christian, instantly regretting it.

'... but now it's stranger, now it's all become relevant again. Six months seventy years ago, that's all it was, and yet it's been on my mind ever since I passed.'

'Really? You were only together six months?'

'There was a war on, and back then, life was short. I suppose it still is, but then it was really short.'

'Yes, I suppose there just wasn't time for living together for fifteen years to see how it feels first?'

'Well ... no.'

'So you were married, your husband passed away, you now pass away, so where does that put you now, if you don't mind me asking?'

'To be honest, I'm not sure. I took my marriage seriously, I took my vows seriously. But once you've passed, they don't really help you much, do they?'

'How so?'

'Well, I signed up to *Till death us do part*. But what then? It only ever talks about the first death in the marriage, not the second. Is it *Till death us do part, then we take a break, till second death does rejoin?* Or is it *Till death us do part, then that's it and second death shall make it awkward at afterlife social gatherings?*'

'Yes, yes, I see what you mean,' said Christian. 'Well, do you think perhaps they left it hanging because of the elephant in the room?'

'Which is?'

'That one party goes to Heaven but the other goes downstairs. And long-distance relationships, they never work, do they? Um, not that I'm suggesting for a second that your husband might be downstairs.'

'That's all right, I know he's in Heaven. He was a good man, it couldn't be any other way.'

'Well,' said Christian, 'perhaps whether a marriage continues again or not is just down to how you feel?'

'Yes … thank you, that's what I've been telling myself. And you know, the truth is, I don't think I'll know until I get there, until I find him.'

'Really?'

'Yes. You see, I can doubt too, sometimes.'

He half smiled.

'And there's other factors, too,' she said.

'Such as?'

'Well, though I never remarried, I had many relationships and lovers after Marek departed.'

Christian raised his eyebrows.

'Don't look so surprised,' said Catherine, 'anyway, I'm sure he'd have done the same, and it's quite possible he's met someone else in Heaven.'

'Do you think that's possible? The dead getting married?'

'Well I don't see why not.'

'Consummation might be a little tricky. There's getting the clothes off for a start.'

'Just wide-scale dry humping then,' said Catherine.

Christian tried not to look shocked.

'Will you stop looking so surprised,' she said. 'Why is it every generation thinks they invented sex?'

'So you weren't a sweet innocent old lady then?'

'Well as I say, I honoured my marriage vows, but life was for living.'

'Was?'

'Well, it feels different now. Don't you think?'

'In what way?'

'Well I'm not sure the *live every day as if it's your last* approach works now. In life there were no tomorrows, especially when I was with Marek, but now all we have is tomorrows, don't you think?'

Christian didn't answer.

They soon stopped and sat again, taking in the wide vistas. A flock of birds passed beneath them, just metres from their feet.

'It's incredible though, isn't it, to think someone made all this,' said Catherine.

'Yes. I surprise even myself sometimes,' said Christian.

Catherine laughed, but Christian didn't join in.

She took a long look at him. 'You're not joking, are you? Not completely?'

'Of course I am.'

'No, you weren't, you meant that.'

'Well, all right, maybe a little.'

'Really?'

'Really,' said Christian.

'What, so you're God? God is a mild-mannered young man from Bracknell?'

'Well possibly. But even then only from a certain point of view.'

'My word, you are serious. But come on, you didn't build all this, Christian, don't be silly.'

'Oh but I did, or at least I may have. Well, actually, I definitely did in one sense.'

'I think the altitude has affected your mind.'

'I'm perfectly rational.'

'You built all this?'

'In a way.'

'Have you any idea how arrogant that sounds?'

'Well, it's not such a stretch … if it turns out it's all going on inside my head.'

'You're serious?'

'Yes. You see, I think I may be dreaming, or in a coma or something, living inside that world, in my mind. I can't be sure, but it's a possibility.'

'That's crazy. And I suspect not original.'

'I know it sounds crazy, but is it any crazier than the alternative? That there is life after death and we're all ghosts? Even if that does turn out to be true, you've got to admit it's also high on the insanity stakes.'

'No, not at all. Of course there's life after death.'

'Why?'

'There just is, it's obvious. We're living proof.'

'Exactly. All we have is our own personal sensory experience, there's just no way to be certain.'

'So I'm just a figment of your imagination?'

'Well, possibly … but a rather nice figment.'

'Oh, well thank you very much, that makes all the difference.'

'Sorry. That's why I've not mentioned it before. I thought you might not take to the idea too well.'

'Well can you blame me?'

'No, but what can I do if it turns out to be the truth?'

'Well, you could get me my wedding ring.'

'Ah, I wish it were that simple, but I suspect making all this isn't the same as controlling it.'

'Convenient.'

'No, not in the slightest.'

'Convenient in that you can't be called upon to prove your theory.'

'Oh yes, yes I take your point there. But there's something else though, something specific to me. You see I was writing a book, a fantasy guide to the afterlife.'

'Really?'

'Yes.'

'And?'

'And so if it's a dream, it's no surprise I'd dream about a made-up after-life, my made-up afterlife.'

'Sounds like you've got it all worked out.'

'Oh no, not at all. Like I say, it's just a possibility.'

'Oh come on, Christian, you can't claim you're God one minute and then backtrack straight into not being sure.'

'Why not?'

'Because you must have a view.'

'I have possibilities. That's all.'

'But–'

'Look, I do accept there's a chance you're right, that we are dead. But I also think it really could be a dream in my head, or maybe something else again.'

'Something else? What else?'

'Well, I don't know. But everything still seems so real, it all seems exactly as it was. And though we can't interact with it, we're still real' – he touched her on the shoulder – 'see, definitely real.'

'So?'

'So maybe we've just shifted a little, there's been a sort of schism, you know, like the Catholic and Protestant Churches. Exactly the same in every way that matters, yet somehow completely incompatible.'

'What, all of us? You, me, Solomon, Tracy, Larry, your liver?'

'I said it was just a possibility.'

'I think you think too much.'

'I think most people don't think enough.'

'Oh come on, Christian, you're dead. Of course you are, we all are.'

'But how can we know for sure?'

'It's just ... obvious, it's common sense, it ... it says so in the leaflet.'

Christian chuckled. 'With respect, if I decide to believe I'm dead, it won't be because I read about it in a leaflet.'

Chapter Forty-One

Sunday started much the same way as Saturday. Christian had agreed to meet Catherine again, but for today she had suggested the benches in the park, perhaps assuming she might have some waiting to do. But she needn't have worried, because for once Christian was on time. Well, nearly.

When Christian arrived, he could see Sol and Tracy already there as usual and, once again, Catherine was waiting there with them.

'Morning.'

'Good morning,' said Catherine.

'Aye,' said Tracy.

'Morning, Christian,' said Sol.

Christian stood and waited to get into the conversation, but none arrived.

'What?' said Christian.

'We weren't talking about you, mate,' said Sol.

'Who said you were?' said Christian.

'No one,' said Catherine.

Everyone looked at each other.

'You were, weren't you, you were bloody talking about me,' said Christian.

'We've got better things to talk about than you, sunbeam,' said Tracy.

'Look, all right, I have a problem with punctuality,' said Christian. 'But

I was only just late today, I think that deserves some credit. It's not easy, you know, there's no bloody alarm clock, he's a law unto himself' – he pointed to the liver – 'and Tony doesn't draw the curtains half the time.'

'Who's Tony?' asked Sol.

Eventually they got away, and their day was spent in much the same way as the previous one, the same route through the park, a much longer upward drift and even longer existential chats high in the clouds, this time occasionally interrupted by the odd jet liner on final approach. Catherine seemed to enjoy herself, and they agreed to do it all again the next day. And though Catherine had again spoken of her plan to leave for the Gate, Christian had already got used to hoping she might stay.

He was sleeping better; he was feeling better. Things weren't exactly looking up, but at least for the moment they'd stopped looking down. But what he didn't know, what he couldn't know, was that a blasé angel and a bucket-headed ghost on a manhunt had crossed the Isles of Scilly that afternoon and were now making landfall at Penzance. Fourteen days with little sleep, with little rest, and still they pressed on, now moving faster than ever. They would soon be at their destination.

Chapter Forty-Two

On Monday morning, Christian and the liver made their way out to the park to meet Catherine once again, and once again they arrived late.

'Morning.'

'Good morning,' said Catherine.

'Sorry to leave you waiting alone, I thought Norm and Cliff would be here.'

'Norm and Cliff?'

'Sol and Tracy. The dynamic duo.'

'Yes, I've not seen them today.'

'I didn't think they could escape the gravitational pull of the bench.'

'Well, yes,' said Catherine. 'Anyway, are you in the mood for a stroll?'

'You read my mind, though it looks like the little fellow will have to come with us today,' said Christian, with a nod to the liver. 'Hope that's okay?'

'That's fine, don't worry, I'm getting used to him.'

'So, the usual circuit?'

'Let's try somewhere different today,' said Catherine.

'Okay. What do you have in mind?'

'I thought we might walk out towards Popeswood and do a loop, it's quite rural out there. There's a lovely golf course, too.'

'Dunno, how's that going to work? Was never really my game, you know, and that was when I could hold the club.'

'Not to play, silly, just for a walk around. It's pretty with the kept grass and all the little ponds.'

Two hours later they'd completed a tour of the back nine, having been played through a couple of times, and made their return via Binfield Manor, Long Copse and the string of parks and sports grounds that lay to the north of the town. Christian only now realised they were about to pass by the church. He wondered if this was a good time to tell Catherine that this was where he was living, perhaps interspersed with some of his expanding knowledge on the building's history. But Catherine beat him to the punch.

'Would you mind if we popped into the churchyard?' she asked. 'We could see if there's any flowers on my grave.'

She made it sound like the most normal thing in the world.

On entering the churchyard, Christian and Catherine found groups of people milling about. As they moved closer, Christian began to recognise some of the mourners, in fact, most of the mourners: Jack, Steve, some former work colleagues, and now he saw Kevin Tooting, who looked to be comforting someone … Beatrice. There were members of her family here, too.

'Catherine,' said Christian, his voice dry, 'I'm not sure how to say this, so I think I'll just say it.'

'Say what?'

'I think this is my funeral.'

'Really? Are you sure.'

There was no other explanation. And it was only now he realised he'd barely given it a thought. Even when getting the prompt while attending Catherine's a few days earlier, he'd given it short shrift. His funeral. The idea was preposterous. And yet, so it seemed, here it was.

'Why would they even hold it here?' he said.

'Isn't this your church?'

'I don't have a church. I'm an atheist.' He drifted forward a few paces. 'How dare they. How could they?'

'Oh dear,' said Catherine, 'look, I'm sure they think they're doing the right thing. Perhaps it'll be a secular service? They're most accommodating these days.'

'Oh, yes … well, yes, I suppose it could be.'

He looked on. Was this it? Fifteen, maybe twenty people. Perhaps there were more coming, perhaps they were struggling to find parking spaces.

Several meaty protocol questions scrummed down in his mind: should he stay? If he stayed, should he ask Catherine to stay? Was it acceptable to bring a date to a funeral – your own funeral – when your girlfriend is also in attendance? If the women lived in different realities, was that still two-timing?

A hulking number-eight question piled in behind and squashed the others: was Uncle Frank here?

'Um, I'm not sure what to do,' said Christian. 'I think perhaps we should leave.'

'No, let's stay,' said Catherine, 'it may help.'

'Really?'

'Yes,' she said, and took his hand.

'And you're okay to stay?' he asked.

'Yes, I want to. And besides, it only seems fair. After all, you came to mine.'

'You know my, um, my partner, Beatrice, is here.'

'Well of course she is, this is your big day.'

They edged towards the mourners. One of their number, a small squirrel-like man with a beard to his belly, was trotting around, circling the others, doing military aircraft impressions that featured occasional side missions to strafe the stragglers.

'Who's that?' asked Catherine.

'I have absolutely no idea,' said Christian.

'Surprise,' yelled Sol, as he leaped up from behind a gravestone.

'Sol, you dingbat,' said Tracy, appearing from the hedgerow, 'how many times, this is not a surprise party.'

'Course it is, we're here for Christian, he didn't know about it, it's a surprise party.'

The postman puffed out an imaginary party blower, his right thumb and forefinger pinched to his lips while he thrust his left hand to within an inch of Christian's face. '*Bllllluuuuurrrrrppp.*' The action was more like a wonky trombone, but the effect was just as annoying. 'No hats or cake though,' said Sol, shaking his head, 'sorry, mate.'

'You knew about this?' said Christian, turning to Catherine.

'Guilty,' said Catherine.

'… of course, of course, *let's try somewhere different today.*'

'Sorry.'

'We were going to tell you,' said Tracy, 'but we decided not to.'

'We thought a surprise would be loads more fun,' said Sol. '*Bllluuuuur-rrr-ppppuuuuppp.*'

'No,' said Catherine, 'no, that wasn't it at all.' She took Christian's hand again. 'We just thought you might not come along if you had a chance to think about it.'

'Attending your own funeral can be psychologically traumatic,' said Sol, raising a finger of warning.

'I don't doubt it,' said Christian.

'So we're the boys to cheer you up,' said Sol, with joy, 'we're the clowns to keep away the frowns.'

'No, Sol,' said Tracy, 'we're not.'

'Oh yes we are,' said Sol. The postman dropped to one knee, widened his arms and launched into the cheery theme song from *It Ain't Half Hot Mum*, but he only managed a couple of lines before Tracy put him in a headlock.

The postman did his best to continue, despite also having to contend with the attentions of the liver, who was now scampering around him and jumping on and off him every few seconds.

'Just shut it,' said Tracy, tightening the headlock, 'we're here to support him, not fuckin' entertain him.'

'Sorry, Tray,' said Sol, sounding like he was speaking through a kazoo, 'but don't worry, we'll blow the roof off in the second half.'

'I can't believe this,' said Christian. 'How did you all find out about this and I didn't?'

'It was in the paper,' said Tracy.

'Local affairs, Christian,' squeaked a barely audible Sol.

'But why've you done this? What's it to you?'

'We thought it would help,' said Catherine.

'How?'

'With your big picture,' said Tracy.

'With acceptance,' said Catherine.

'With you still thinking you're not dead, mate,' said Sol.

'Wait a minute, hang on, hang on, are you telling me this is an *intervention*?'

'No, no,' said Catherine, 'well, all right, yes, in a way. We just think you'll start doing a lot better once you've accepted you've passed. And we're here for you. Everyone is.'

'Oh this is rich, the boys who haven't left the park in forty years and the girl who's loving death more than life are worried I'm not getting real. Well thank you for the concern, but I think the best thing, the thing that would help me most of all, would be for you all to just sod off.'

Silence.

'Oh that's charming, isn't it,' said Tracy, 'here we are trying to help, outside the park, too, and you throw it back in our faces.'

'I can't do this,' said Christian, shaking his head. He looked at Catherine. 'I'm sorry. I know you're all trying to help, but just … just leave me alone.' He turned to leave, lazily clicking his fingers for the liver to follow. 'Come on then.'

The liver jumped up onto Sol's head and spun round to face Christian.

'Oh you too? Well. Suit yourself.'

And with that Christian drifted away from the scene.

'I'll go after him,' said Sol.

'No,' said Catherine and Tracy at the same time.

'I'll go,' said Catherine.

'All right,' said Sol, 'we'll brush up on the can-can, see if we can recruit some others.'

Christian had sat down under the willow tree, beyond the war memorial in the corner of the far side of the churchyard. A moment of contemplation next to the A3095 and the Hodgkiss Business Centre.

'I'm sorry,' he said, as Catherine approached. 'I shouldn't have said those things.'

'Don't worry, we all say things in the heat of the moment.'

'No, it was wrong. This isn't easy for any of us, is it?'

'Well, no.'

She sat down next to him.

She told him how helpful her own funeral had been, how it was cathartic, and how she knew it would be for him, too. And she told him how grateful she'd been for him being there for hers.

'Won't you come back?' she asked. 'They're all there for you, you know. We'll have to go now or we'll miss it.'

'I don't think I can face it.'

'I know it's hard but it's a once-in-an-eternity event. You think about it. Even Elizabeth Taylor only got one funeral.'

He didn't reply.

'Look,' she said, 'even if you are right, and this is all a dream, aren't you curious to see what people have to say?'

'That makes me even less inclined to want to go back.'

'Really? Oh come on, how bad can it be.'

'You don't know my family,' he said.

A few miles away, a pair of weary travellers had arrived at 22 Vestments, Bracknell.

'No one upstairs either,' said Mitch, as he returned to the living room.

'Just look at their curtains ...' said Hotswap, still in his fur coat, as he idly strolled back and forth through the coffee table.

'I'm gonna sweep the area,' said Mitch.

'... what were they thinking? And with those sofas ...'

'I said I'm gonna sweep the area.'

'Cool your boots, Columbo. Have you not seen these?' Hotswap puppeteered a false hand to point out the condolence cards on the mantelpiece.

'Oh ... fuck,' said Mitch, smacking the sides of his helmet.

'May have missed the boat on this one,' said Hotswap.

'How long've they been there, d'ya think?' said Mitch, approaching the mantelpiece.

'Hard to know. It's not like people date them, is it?'

Mitch undid the buckles at his helmet's front anchor points, and then, reaching behind, the single one at the back. Placing hands either side, he lifted off his helmet. The sting of light made him wince, trillions of photons all trying to talk at once as he swapped silk-screened coin slots for the widest of widescreen panoramas. He pushed the headgear to Hotswap then raised a hand to shield his vision until the moment passed and his senses recalibrated.

He leaned forward and peered inside the cards, scanning all along the row. An abundance of awkward, bland, supportive comments, recommendations to be strong, to trust to time, and to have faith in the care of the Lord, but nothing even hinting at the timing or circumstances of the cargo's demise.

He pulled back and straightened up. He stretched his arms and cracked his knuckles. All those days and nights at sea. All that energy; all that effort.

His gaze lingered on the scene in the mirror. A sad blessing. Mitch was one of a handful in the ethereal plane who didn't lament the absence of their reflection. It hadn't always been the case. Some people, lucky blessed types, have a certain something, an exceptional physical characteristic that asserts itself before any other, something that takes root in the mind of the observer, for ever anchoring the character regardless of the conduct that follows: an irrepressibly reassuring yet sincere smile; blue eyes and a jaw-line that would grace a Greek vase; a svelte figure with legs that go up to eleven; a massive pair of tits. For these people, while their blessing doesn't guarantee an easy ride through life, it does buy a lot of free upgrades. Doors are opened; lies believed; sins forgiven. Mitch used to be one of these lucky few and he knew it, oh how he knew it. But that was then, and then was a long time ago.

'What the fuck are you looking at?' he said to Hotswap.

'Funny, isn't it,' said Hotswap, as he continued to stare, 'it doesn't matter how many times you see it, you never quite get used to it.'

'Fuckin' tell me about it,' yelled Mitch.

'Oh come on, don't be so sensitive.'

'I fuckin' needed this one,' said Mitch, 'you know I did.'

'May not be a done deal. Look, you've come this far, why not hang around for a while, see what you can find out?'

Mitch gripped his shoulders tight, let out a grinding moan, and then dropped his hands to his hips. 'Yeah … yeah, all right,' he said, 'but later, much later.' He turned to head upstairs. 'You've got first watch.'

'Well where are you going?'

'Where d'ya think? To find somewhere dark and quiet.'

Back at the churchyard, Catherine had persuaded Christian to return to his funeral. He apologised to Sol and Tracy, and, with Catherine at his side, drifted forward to take a closer look at who had come to pay their last respects.

In the background, Christian could see the little beardy man still trotting about doing his aeroplane impressions, running reconnaissance on the latest arrivals, and again drew a complete blank as to who he was.

Christian pointed out Beatrice.

'She looks dignified,' said Catherine.

'Yes. She never did like black, though. Always thought she was too pale for it. Said it made her look like she was in The Cure.'

'So who's that with her?'

'Kevin Tooting. A former friend of mine.'

'Former friend?'

'Yes, he's a total pain in the backside. So far that's been one of my few positives – I don't have to worry about bumping into him any more.'

'Well it looks like he's a bit of a brick, I'd say, comforting Beatrice. Maybe you've got him wrong?'

'He's probably trying to get it on with her.'

'Oh, Christian.'

'Well all right, it does seem like he's doing the right thing, I suppose. I am glad to see Bea's not alone in this. Must be, well, just the worst thing to have to get through.'

Christian spotted other friends. Some he'd seen quite recently, but some he'd not seen in years, which made him feel guilty, even more so when he realised how few of their funerals he reckoned he'd have attended should roles have been reversed.

He continued to scan the faces, providing a commentary to Catherine, and as he did, it became clear to both of them that his early prediction of a parental no-show was right on the money. Assuming illness, infirmity or perhaps great distance, Catherine said it was sad they weren't here, but she soon revised it to 'beyond disgusting' when he told her they were alive and well and enjoying a golden retirement in Worthing. But he told her not to get upset about it, because all he was feeling was relief. He'd never connected with them, even as a child, adding that they'd got off on the wrong foot and grown apart from there.

And his parents weren't the only family absence Christian was crossing his fingers for. One guest-fear still loomed larger than any other. But when Christian spotted Uncle Geoffrey walking through the gates, alone, he thought he might have got away with it – his uncle's down-the-nose disdain of a C-of-E send-off and video camera to record the day would be a mere shadow of the horrors that could have beset the event.

But as Christian turned to Catherine to point out the sole representative of his family, he heard gasps behind him. By the time he turned, everyone, ghosts and mortals alike, were staring open-mouthed at another latecomer, on the other side of the churchyard, a man who was orders of magnitude ahead of Uncle Geoffrey in the poor-taste stakes, and far more shocking. At least people assumed it was a man, it not being possible to be certain due to the full face mask. To really carry off this look, you need to be six foot six, with a good physique and a strong imposing stance, not five foot eight with a forty-six-inch waist and splayed feet.

'That's an odd outfit for a funeral,' said Catherine, 'looks like they're expecting chemical warfare.'

It had to be. There could be no doubt. Quite apart from the tell-tale body shape, who else would come to a funeral dressed as Darth Vader?

'Uncle Frank,' said Christian.

Uncle Frank had been the deciding factor in Christian's long-held conviction that he would never be able to get married. Of course there was all the usual doubt, uncertainty, absence of religious faith, absence of faith in marriage, absence of faith in himself, but Uncle Frank was the straw that broke the nuptial-camel's back – the prospect of Uncle Frank in all the photos dressed as Hermann Göring, a pantomime dame or a desperately out-of-shape Batman was too much.

Frank had an impact on every event he attended. On this occasion, the effect of the attendance of the Dark Lord of the Sith at the funeral was to split the mourners into two camps: the majority, which included Beatrice and her family, were incredulous, horrified and disgusted; the rest, which included Kevin – when Beatrice wasn't looking – were all for it, generally seeing it as a stroke of genius. As Christian and Catherine drifted around the mourners, they heard more than one person remark how it was a breath of fresh air, because funerals were normally 'such depressing occasions'.

'That's the bloody point,' snapped Christian.

Catherine just held his hand, not knowing what else to do.

'Christian, Christian lad,' called a voice from behind him – a familiar voice, a stoic Sheffield accent.

Christian turned and, for the second time in two weeks, was surprised to see his old chemistry teacher standing before him. But old no more. No crow's feet, no glasses, no grey. Pullover, slacks and slip-ons swapped for grey worsted three-piece and polished brown brogues. The unusually styled facial hair was ever-present, but cut shorter and, like the thick hair on his scalp, was now a bright copper red.

He thrust out a hand. As in the previous surprise meeting, Christian just looked at it.

'Stuart?' he said, with a few micro-shakes of the head.

'Tremendous to see you again, lad, shame about the circumstances. Tragic, quite tragic.'

Hargreaves's hand was still hanging out for a shake. Christian obliged, finding it as real and solid as his.

'Stuart Hargreaves,' said the now not so old man, turning to Catherine, 'at your service.'

'What? Oh, sorry,' said Christian, 'Stuart, this is Catherine, a friend of mine, Catherine, this is Stuart, my former chemistry teacher.'

'And personal motivator,' added Hargreaves and offered his hand.

'Really?' said Catherine, shaking his hand. 'Well it's lovely to meet you.'

'The pleasure's all mine, madam,' said Hargreaves. He bowed and kissed her hand.

'Delightful,' said Catherine. 'Well, I'll go and check on the proceedings. Give you boys a chance to catch up.' She smiled and drifted off.

'Not taken you long to get yourself sorted then?' said Hargreaves as he checked out Catherine's peachy rear-end and gave Christian a wink.

'It's, er, it's not like that,' said Christian.

'What, again? Come off it, lad, you can tell me, we're men of the ...' His voice trailed off as he continued to stare.

'She's ninety-nine, Stuart.'

'Ninety-nine what?'

'Years old.'

'Never,' said Hargreaves. He brought his focus back to Christian. 'You're winding me up?'

'Nope.'

'Well. Talk about the older woman.'

'So how ... how is it you're here?' asked Christian. 'I thought you died?'

'Well exactly.'

'Oh. Oh yes, of course. I'm so sorry, how stupid, um, how are you coping?'

'Good, actually. The first day was a bit rough, but I'm doing fine now.'

'So you found your feet?'

'Yes. How did you know?'

'Know what?'

'That I had to find my feet?'

'Well don't we all?'

'Oh yes, I see what you mean,' said Hargreaves, 'no, it's just I literally had to find my feet. They got severed when the plane hit the house. I gritted my teeth and hung on for an extra hour or so before carking it. Bad move, in hindsight, can't say I'd recommend it, but then you have to try, don't you? Anyway, so the old feet got a bit of a head start on me.'

'Oh jeez, that must have been dreadful.'

'Was a bit of a trial, I don't mind saying. The pope's pilot helped me out though, finding the feet, awfully nice chap, amazing how they always stay calm in a crisis, even their own.'

'Yes. Right. I suppose it's the training. So what about the pope then? Didn't try to wash your feet, did he, after you found them? Or before you found them, for that matter?'

'I didn't see him. No, it seems he and his entourage fled the scene before I appeared. The pilot said they all seemed rather surprised at their continued existence.'

'Well anyway,' said Christian, 'you look, great, really great.'

'Yeah, about thirty years knocked off, I reckon.'

'Time off for good behaviour.'

'Well, perhaps,' he said, chuckling. 'Hey, I've brought a friend with me, hope you don't mind?'

'Oh, no, not at all,' said Christian, looking round.

'He's the chap running around pretending to be a Lancaster bomber. Sorry. Derek, *Derek,* come here.'

The little man executed a course correction and headed towards them. '*Rrrreeeeeooooooooowwww,*' he shouted as he cruised past and saluted from his cockpit window.

'Derek,' said Hargreaves, with disapproval, but the little man ignored him. 'We'll get him on the next pass,' said Hargreaves.

The circling man made for an unusual sight, even against the stiff competition of the day so far. His trotting action was that of someone unaccustomed to jogging or running of any kind: it was all high knees, with each foot going limp on the rise, like the prancing of a Shetland Lipizzaner. And his stale attire didn't complement the choreography at all well, but then the only things it could have complemented would have been research libraries or excrement – from his tie to his shoes, every item of clothing was a sickly sun-faded brown or beige.

'So, why is your friend pretending to be an aeroplane?' asked Christian.

'Yes, sorry, long story, he's not quite himself at the moment. In hindsight, I shouldn't have brought him. The trip's got him overstimulated.'

The little man executed a steep banked turn and came back, his hands forming fists to grip a machine gun. '*Duh duh duh duh duh duh duh duh.*'

'Derek,' shouted Hargreaves, again.

'You will address me as Professor Collier,' shouted the little man as he passed by.

'So he thinks he's a professor as well as a pilot?' asked Christian.

'Oh no, he really is a professor,' said Hargreaves, 'theoretical physics.'

'Really?'

'Oh yes. One of the top men in the field, apparently. He's just having trouble adjusting.'

'Jeez. And I thought I was struggling.'

'Still, it's good for him to get out,' said Hargreaves, 'good to let off some steam.'

'Steam?' said Professor Collier, bailing out of his plane and using his beard as a parachute. 'Why didn't you say so? The four fifteen to Brigadoon is about to depart.' He began shunting himself in and out of various sidings between the gravestones. '*Chuff chuff chuff chuff chuff chuff.*' He stopped to pull with frenzied vigour at his trousers, before giving up and resuming his duties. '*Chuff chuff chuff chuff ... wooooooooo woooooooooooo.*'

'I'm quite relieved the clothes don't come off,' said Hargreaves. 'I've an awful suspicion it'd be like baboons at the zoo. He keeps trying though. Determined little fellow, I'll say that for him.'

'Trains,' shouted Sol, hurrying over, '*chuff chuff chuff.*'

'*Chuff chuff chuff?*' said the professor.

'*Chuff chuff!*' said Sol. He hitched up to the back of the professor and they chugged off around the churchyard.

'Who's this fella then?' said Hargreaves. 'He a physicist too?'

'No. He's a postman.'

'Oh. Right. You looking after him then?'

'Again, no. Surprising as it sounds, he and his friend have been looking after me.'

The liver came scampering over, circling Christian and Hargreaves before chasing around the feet of Sol and the professor.

'That yours too?' asked Hargreaves.

'Yes, sort of. You don't seem surprised?'

'I've seen a few people with them,' said Hargreaves, 'not livers exactly, mostly legs and feet.'

'Bizarre phenomena, eh?'

'Undoubtedly,' said Hargreaves, looking intently at the liver. 'You know, they've got some theories on it at the school.'

'The school?'

'Yes,' he said, and gave a broad smile, 'I'm teaching again.'

'Will of Ockham, you really have found your feet.'

'Yes, it's a pretty good silver lining, I have to say. And not much danger of being pensioned off this time.'

'No, I suppose not. But, well, who do you teach?'

'Children, of course, you know, ghosts of.'

'Of course, of course. And that's at some ghost school I suppose?'

'No, at St Benedict's.'

'Our St Benedict's?'

'Yes.'

'And they're okay with that?'

'Well they don't know, do they. How could they?'

'No, well, right, of course.'

'We sort of piggyback. It's become a common model actually, more than a hundred British secondaries have ethereal attachments now.'

'Sounds very organised.'

'It's just practical. They have the books and kit, you see. But it's good, it's important work. Lot of neglected young ghosts out there.'

'Yes, well I suppose there must be.'

They watched Sol and the professor switch from trains to hide-and-seek, taking cover inside mourners and then popping out to surprise the liver.

'I have to say, lad,' said Hargreaves, 'fair play for attending today. Must admit, I couldn't face my own.'

'Thanks, but you've got it all wrong. My associates got me here under false pretences.'

'Ah.'

'So you're not part of this intervention then?' said Christian.

'Intervention?'

'Yes. They were worried about me not accepting the truth.'

'About what?'

'That I'm dead.'

'And you don't accept that?'

'Well, no ...'

Sol and the professor broke off from hide-and-seek and began circling Hargreaves and Christian, making bird calls.

'Sounds like an intervention was a bloody good idea then,' said Hargreaves. 'Got to keep a grip on reality, lad.'

Professor Collier approached and reached up to place his hands on their shoulders. '"Luminous beings are we,"' he said, in a poor but recognisable Yoda voice, '"not this crude matter."' He pinched Christian on the arm and made a few Yoda yelps and cackles before collapsing into manic laughter, sinking to the grass and rolling around, only to stop moments later to commence another frenzied assault on his trousers.

'You'll never get them off,' said Sol, shaking his head.

Catherine returned along with Tracy. 'Christian, sorry to barge in,' she said, 'but I think you're about to arrive.'

'I'm sorry?' said Christian.

The mourners stepped back from the driveway as a hearse reversed in.

Christian froze.

She took his hand.

'I'm in there?' he said.

'Yes,' said Catherine.

'In there, and out here, but in there.'

Tony appeared and was immediately accosted by Beatrice. Christian couldn't hear what was being said, but he could see her pointing at Uncle Frank and struggling to maintain her composure. From the body language, it seemed Tony either couldn't see what the fuss was about or didn't feel able to do much about it.

The boot lid of the hearse was now up, and unknown men dressed in black were unloading the coffin.

'They're using a trolley,' said Christian. 'How dare they? I'm not a piece of meat.'

'Well, you kind of are now, when you think about it,' said Tracy.

'And you'll be well past yer eat by date,' said Sol, chipping in.

'Solomon, no one's going to be eating anyone,' said Catherine.

'What about the little worms?' said Sol. 'But I suppose they don't care about eat by dates. They're not fussy, are they?'

'*Solomon*,' said Catherine.

'I want to see,' said Christian.

'See what?' asked Catherine.

'The worms?' said Sol.

'Inside,' said Christian, 'I want to see inside.'

'That's not going to help, lad,' said Hargreaves. 'Besides, you won't see anything. The coffin's closed, you've no way to open it, and there's no light inside.'

'Yes, it's not a fridge,' said Sol.

'But what if … what if I'm okay,' said Christian, 'what if I'm in there but not dead?'

'Oh yeah, I'm sure you're just having one of your lie-ins,' said Tracy.

'They make mistakes,' said Christian, 'they do. You hear about it all the time.'

'Not after a week, lad,' said Hargreaves. 'Your body will have been … prepared. Trust me, you don't want to go there.'

'Well … well, I suppose you're right … of course you're right,' said Christian, staring at the coffin. 'Not after a week.'

Tony began ushering the mourners to gather.

'Looks like kick-off's approaching, lad,' said Hargreaves. 'I'd better get Derek.'

'All set then?' said Catherine.

'I don't know. I don't think so,' said Christian. 'Look, do you mind if we sit at the back, like we did for yours? I don't fancy a front-row seat.'

'Not at all. Besides, I don't think we have much choice unless you want to get sat in,' she said.

He couldn't force even a fraction of a smile.

The ghosts hung back until the living were all inside.

'Good luck, pal,' said Tracy.

'It's gonna be the best funeral ever,' said Sol, giving Christian a double thumbs up.

'Um, thanks, guys.'

They filed in, the liver following at Sol's heels.

'I always forget, is it left or right for the groom?' said Sol.

'It doesn't matter,' said Tracy, 'it's all fuckin' groom.'

Hargreaves returned with Professor Collier in a half nelson.

'Nervous, lad?'

'Very,' said Christian.

'You'll be fine. You don't even need to say "I do" for this one. So, stiff upper lip. We'll talk more afterwards.'

Professor Collier cleared his throat and offered some Dickens: '"Where we hope to go, and all to meet each other after we are dead, and there be happy always together."' He broke into a snigger before being bundled into the church.

Catherine and Christian hung back a little longer.

'Come on then,' said Catherine, 'soon be over.' She took his hand again and they drifted in.

The other ghosts had filled the back pew, leading Christian to suspect it was a planned move in case he tried to make a run for it, but the thought was quickly superseded when he took in the whole scene, stopping him mid-stride. Everyone was here for him. Everyone was now seated and waiting, the coffin – his coffin – front and centre.

'Here,' said Catherine, pulling gently on his arm. She led him to the pew just in front of the others.

A hand on his shoulder after he sat. 'Good luck,' said Hargreaves.

Tony entered the small pulpit. The congregation fell silent. 'I am the resurrection and the life. He who believes in me will live, even though he dies, says the Lord.'

'Or even if he doesn't believe in me, so it seems,' said Christian.

Catherine squeezed his hand.

'Be good if we had some popcorn, eh?' said Sol.

'What are you talking about, you spanner,' said Tracy.

'You know, for atmosphere. Hey, or what about some Matchmakers? Remember Matchmakers?'

Catherine turned round. 'It's time for quiet, boys.'

They stood for the first hymn, 'All Things Bright and Beautiful'. The ghosts were mostly fine with the first verse but unsure thereafter and had to resort to mumbling through, being unable to open or hold the order of service booklets.

At first, Christian thought the choice of hymn a reasonable one, recalling the tune from primary school and seeming to remember it not being heavy on the dogma, but as it progressed, he grew more and more indignant at its Intelligent Design subtext.

'I wonder if they sang this at Darwin's funeral?' he said to Catherine.

'Well I think it's nice,' she said, 'it's joyful.'

Tony proceeded with his introductory words, but soon broke from the standard patter. 'Often, on these occasions, I have only been able to know the departed through the love of the bereaved. But today I can say I knew the deceased personally. Christian was kind and thoughtful. Above all, I think he was a man who questioned. And we should not fear this nature. No, it is to be embraced.'

'Well, I suppose that's okay,' said Christian.

'For to question is not to turn one's back on the Lord. The Lord wants us to question, for did Matthew not say, "Keep on asking, and it will be given; keep on seeking, and you will find; keep on knocking, and it will be opened, for everyone asking receives, and everyone seeking finds."'

'Not so sure about that bit,' said Christian.

'And I am sure our dear departed friend would want me to share something with you. For Christian had recently come to see me, to talk about his questions, to share his concerns ...'

'I thought you were an atheist?' said Catherine.

'I was,' said Christian, '*I am*. He's taking my visit out of context.'

'... and was in the process of returning to the faith.'

'Straight out lie,' said Christian, 'that's– Why am I whispering?' 'That is a lie,' he shouted, rising to his feet. 'I am an unbeliever,' he declared, 'I am an infidel.'

'Ay, quieten down in front, mate,' said Tracy, 'we're trying to hear about your return to the flock.'

'But I didn't return,' said Christian, turning round.

'That's not what the vicar says,' said Sol.

'I was just doing research,' said Christian.

'That's what Gary Glitter said,' said Tracy.

The professor let out a guffaw.

'But I was.'

Sol grinned and began chanting the opening rallying call lines to Gary Glitter's 'Leader of the Gang (I Am)'.

The professor joined in, and they began clapping, goading Christian.

'Shut up,' said Christian, 'just shut up.'

He watched them fall silent and sink into their pews, smirking at each other like naughty schoolboys.

'What was I thinking,' said Christian, turning to face front and shaking his head, 'this was a terrible idea.' He took a step towards the aisle.

Catherine stood and took his hand, tugging him back. 'No, stay,' she said, 'please, sit.'

Hargreaves stood and placed a hand on Christian's shoulder. 'She's right, lad, stick with it, we've barely got started.'

In the commotion, no one noticed the professor exchanging nods with Sol, edging off the pew and trotting up the aisle towards Tony, quietly muttering the 'Leader of the Gang (I Am)' lines as he went.

'Oh, all right,' said Christian, and he sat back into the pew.

'Good decision, lad, good decision,' said Hargreaves. 'You know, I always say it takes a big, a big ...' He looked round. 'Shit, where's Derek?'

The professor was now up front, standing inside Tony with his face poking out of the reverend's thorax.

The professor stretched out his right arm from Tony's chest and traced out a flat arc of recruitment as he addressed the congregation with more lines from the song, asking if they would like to join his gang.

'Oh yeah,' shouted Sol, slapping his thighs.

'This isn't a funeral,' said Tracy, 'it's a bleedin' circus.'

Christian and Catherine both stared open-mouthed at the attempted hijacking of minister and ceremony.

'You know, I never saw Gary's songs as religious,' said Sol, 'but this is really speaking to me.'

The professor strutted forward out of Tony, left arm aloft, right arm holding an imaginary microphone, and proclaimed his leadership with more lines from the song.

He did a couple of spins, flicked his beard back, and then lost focus as he tried and failed to turn up the collar on his corduroy jacket.

Hargreaves rugby-tackled the professor and after a brief scuffle in the altar, brought him to heel with a couple of slaps and another half nelson.

Christian began to stand again, but Catherine held him down. 'It's okay, it's okay,' she said, 'look, Stuart's got him, Stuart's got him.'

Despite the wash-cycle of thoughts spinning in Christian's mind, he again took comfort in Catherine holding onto him. She was now hugging his entire left arm and the sensation permeated his entire body.

Hargreaves marched the professor back down the aisle, pushed him back into his pew and whispered an apology to Christian.

The service proceeded through a reading of 'They Are Not Dead' from Uncle Frank – his numerous sniggered *Netherworld* additions producing gasps and even heckling at one point – a muted 'Immortal Invisible', and prayers and closing words before Tony led the coffin procession and the mourners outside, with the ghosts following on.

When Christian emerged, he found the hearse gone and the mourners instead following his coffin down through the churchyard. It wasn't until they approached the grave – the hole he'd seen being dug so matter-of-factly two days earlier – that he realised. This was his grave. He was about to be buried.

All energy left him.

His legs felt like they were made of dark matter.

Everything came crashing down as his world came into sharp focus: they were going to put him in the ground. They were going to put him in the ground, and they were going to fill in the hole, and they were going to walk away. And who was behind this? The people he loved and trusted most in the world.

In his mind, he was eleven years old again, being held down on the operating table. Green sterile fabric covered his face, save for an opening to expose his right eye. His breathing was quick and shallow as he peered up at the bright lights and the masked men. Injections to anaesthetise and paralyse his eyeball, disabling blinking and feeling but not seeing – seeing the clamps and the swabs, seeing the scalpel come down to cut the blood vessel from his cornea. Despite the fear, the thoughts that had dominated his mind were of the deceit and the conspiracy that had been perpetrated: his parents' promise of a general anaesthetic so he would 'sleep soundly through the whole thing'; the charade of having a case packed for the non-existent overnight stay; the resolute and unapologetic post-op position that the ends had justified the means.

Everyone gathered at the graveside.

'Look, wait,' said Christian.

'We're all with you,' said Catherine.

'Just, hang on ... let's wait a minute, please ... *stop*.' He lurched forward towards the coffin.

Tracy managed to grab his right arm, but Hargreaves was caught off guard, allowing Christian to get close and extend his left arm out into the coffin. He felt almost nothing, but enough to sense when his hand passed from the outside air into wood and silk, inside air and then into what felt like an especially delicate vulcanised rubber soufflé. He let out a gasp as left hand passed through left arm and then torso, before an enforced flash retreat through air, silk and wood, and outside air again as he was hauled back.

'Not a good move, lad,' said Hargreaves.

'What d'ya think you're doing?' said Tracy.

He tried to lunge again, but their grip held.

'Have you got him?' shouted Tracy.

'Yes,' said Hargreaves, straining.

'I don't think you realise the sacrifice I'm making here, mate,' said Tracy, right in Christian's ear. 'If I catch some bleedin' disease off you, you're a dead man.'

Sol weighed in, grabbing Christian's left leg, hugging it like a tree trunk. The liver joined the fun, too, sitting on Christian's right foot.

They shuffled him back a few metres.

'Oh come away, Christian,' said Catherine.

'No,' said Tracy, 'he needs to see.'

'It's too much for him,' said Catherine.

'No, he's right,' said Hargreaves, 'the lad needs to see this.'

'I'm in there,' said Christian, pointing to the coffin, and laughing slightly.

'Yes, Christian, that's why we're all here,' said Catherine, 'we're here for you, it's not so bad, really, and look, look, you'll be next to me, see, we're neighbours now.'

The professor, now free from restraint once more, wasted no time. He skipped forward, stepped into the coffin and lay down inside it. A moment later, he sat bolt upright, and with a manic smile declared, 'I am feeling better.'

'Derek,' shouted Hargreaves, 'you little monster. Lads, lads, have you got Christian?'

'Yes,' said Sol and Tracy in unison.

Hargreaves let go of Christian and went for the professor.

'I'm sorry, I'm sorry,' said the professor, flinching as Hargreaves grabbed him.

'Enough,' said Hargreaves, marching the professor off by his ears.

Christian struggled, but Tracy and Sol held firm.

'Oh dear,' said Catherine, 'just hold on, it's nearly over.'

The coffin was now over the grave. Beatrice stepped forward and placed a rose on the lid. Tony gave a nod and the men in black suits began lowering the coffin.

Tony gave the committal. 'We now commit his body to the ground; earth to earth, ashes to ashes, dust to dust: in the sure and certain hope of the resurrection to eternal life.'

'No, please ... no,' said Christian.

Uncle Geoffrey leaned down and dropped in a crucifix, a rosary bead chain and a photograph of the late pope.

Frank stepped up and tossed in a Luke Skywalker toy figure, revelling in his opportunity for an enthusiastic over-acted cry of 'Nooooooo' after it bounced off the coffin lid and down into the gap.

'Hey, it's a Luke,' said Sol. He released his grip and moved forward to peer into the grave. 'Cool.'

Christian broke free and rushed forward. In a futile act of desperation, he tried to pull on the ropes to halt the coffin's descent. 'Stop, stop,' he cried.

'Christian, no,' shouted Catherine. She tried to step forward to help, but Tracy held her back.

'He won't listen to reason. Let's just let him be.'

The coffin was now almost at the bottom. Christian descended into the hole, sinking up to his waist in wood, silk and himself, trying and failing to grip the underside and halt the last few centimetres of its slow drop.

'Bea,' he yelled, 'Beasy darling, don't let them do this. Geoffrey, Frank, stop them, please. They're going to bury me. There's been a mistake. I'm right here. This is my body, I still need it.'

The coffin hit the floor of the grave. The ropes were pulled free.

'Oh, Christian,' said Catherine. She sat down and put her hands to her cheeks.

He decided there was only one thing left to do. It was crazy, properly insane, but he was desperate. He took a tight hold of his fear. He closed his eyes and lay down inside the blackness of the coffin, placing himself inside his lifeless body. He was overcome by the unnaturally thick stillness of his corpse; it was now just a slab of old meat, a cadaver. But whatever passed for ethereal adrenaline fought back his disgust and horror for one last effort.

'Move,' he shouted as he tried to will his lifeless limbs back into service. 'Come on, move, you fucker, move.'

He kept trying, over and over, despite not the merest hint of success, repeatedly turning the ignition key on the long-dead battery and seized engine, flogging it over and over in the vain hope of one last spark of life.

It was some time before he stopped and emerged from the trench.

Chapter Forty-Three

Afternoon had turned to evening; evening had turned to night. But Christian would not leave his graveside. The mourners had long since left for the buffet, back in Vestments, and would now be long gone, back to their own warm, fulfilling, fully rendered lives. Sol and the professor had been having such a good time at the funeral that they'd followed the living on to the house, too, along with Tracy, but Hargreaves and Catherine had stayed behind, deciding Christian shouldn't be left alone.

At first they'd sat close to him, occasionally trying to persuade him to leave the graveside, but he kept finding excuses to stay. First he'd insisted on waiting until all the mourners had left. Then he had to wait to watch the grave get filled in by the man in his digger – who seemed to find the task about as emotional as building a patio – and after that he insisted on staying for no reason at all. Hargreaves and Catherine eventually accepted it was something Christian had to deal with himself and so were now observing from a discreet distance.

Mitch woke in the darkness of the loft, following his first chance at proper rest in three weeks. For Mitch, absolute darkness was his only sure-fire way of getting proper sleep, but it carried a risk of sleeping long.

How long this time? Many hours. Too many hours?

He descended through the floor and onto the landing where he froze at the sound of the TV downstairs. Hotswap couldn't have turned it on any more than he could. It had to have been someone else, someone mortal. Lights were on, too. He carefully made his way down.

He spotted the clock on the wall. Just after eleven. From the hallway he could see into the kitchen. He saw his knapsack. It was open, his papers strewn everywhere.

Oh shit ... oh shit.

Laughter now from the living room.

He edged forward. The living room door was open. He leaned in.

Hotswap and an unknown woman were on the sofa, watching the TV. Hotswap was stretched out lengthways, with the woman curled up in his torso, box of tissues next to her. She was attractive, but washed out, like someone had turned her colour settings all the way down.

'What the fuck are you doing?' said Mitch.

'Finally,' said Hotswap, turning his head, 'thought I'd have to get a prince to kiss you.'

'I said what the fuck are you doing?'

'Keeping watch, like you said.'

'Who's this?' asked Mitch, pointing to Beatrice.

'Widow,' said Hotswap, stroking a false hand through her head.

'You sure?'

'Photos,' said Hotswap, directing the hand to the mantelpiece.

'And what's so funny?' said Mitch.

'*Touched by an Angel*,' said Hotswap, nodding to the TV, 'honestly, it's fucking hilarious.'

'Right. So what's happened?'

'What do you mean?'

'My stuff, my knapsack, the documents.'

'Yes, that is curious.'

'You don't know what happened?'

'I was out.'

'Out?'

'Scouting the area. Helping you look for your cargo, thank you very much.'

'You were supposed to be here, on watch.'

'Yes, well I got a little bored. There was nothing happening.'

Mitch grabbed the angel by the lapels of his fur coat and lifted him up into the wall.

'Not a good idea, Langers,' said the angel, from within the plasterboard.

'What do you know about this, you little fairy?'

'Is that the best you've got?' said Hotswap. 'Squeeze me harder ...'

Mitch felt fumbling near his stomach and then clawhands low on his back.

'... come on, big boy, you know you want to.'

Mitch tightened his grip and hurled the angel through the wall into the kitchen, before striding through after him.

Hotswap had landed in the cupboard under the sink and barely had a chance to pull himself free when Mitch grabbed him by the throat and lifted him up again.

'All right, so I left my post for a bit of an afternoon cruise,' said the angel, 'you have me there, but on the boss's eternal existence, I don't know anything about this.'

Mitch looked back at the strewn papers. Some on the floor; some in the floor; some floating at knee height. Was there a good reason why it would be Hotswap? He couldn't think of one.

He released his grip.

'We've been raided,' said Mitch.

'Really?'

'We've been fuckin' raided. Caught with our pants down and fucked in the ass.'

'Come off it, Langers, who by?'

'By those British shepherds, that's who. *One Man and His Foot* ... flat-cap ... lung-fuckers.'

'More likely a pack of stray hands, I'd say. They're like magpies, those little beggars.'

'Oh shit ...'

'What now.'

'My headgear, where is it? Fuck, oh fuck, this is all I need.'

'Hang on,' said Hotswap, extending a false hand to showcase the kitchen counter – empty bottles, dirty plates, half-eaten sandwiches and screwed up serviettes. 'I think we've missed something.'

'Oh flamin' fuckin' shitsticks,' said Mitch, hands to his shoulders. 'Okay, this is what's gonna happen. First off you're gonna help me find all my stuff, then we're gonna work out what's the hell's gone down.'

· · ·

They searched the entire house, managing to recover most of the loose pages, the quill and inkpot, and finally the book, which they found in the bowl of the downstairs toilet. There was no sign of Mitch's helmet, though, or much of the other equipment from his knapsack. Mitch decided they should split up and do a wider pass.

Fifteen minutes later, Mitch returned from checking the garden and the rest of Vestments.

'Any luck?' said Hotswap, staring at the TV, which was now on the BBC News Channel.

'Couple more forms, that's it. Fuckers must be miles away by now. You?'

'Pope's dead.'

'What?'

'The news. Says the pope died. Couple of weeks ago. Near here too.'

'And?'

'They've announced an inquiry.'

'And?'

'I'm saying, the pope's dead. That's big news.'

'Why? Do you need him collecting?'

'Shouldn't think so,' said Hotswap.

'Well it's not big news then.'

Mitch awaited Hotswap's update on his detective work in the living room, but the angel just kept staring at the TV.

'So what have you found out?' said Mitch.

'Well, Chelsea are seven points clear with a game in hand.'

'I'm not in the mood, Hotswap.'

'Only kidding, Langers. All right, well, I can't imagine she'd be in the mood for a house party' – Hotswap gestured to Beatrice, who was still on the sofa but now back on her iPad – 'so if you ask me, what we missed here was the wake, or you know, whatever the Bracknell equivalent is.'

'So he died within, what, the last week?'

'Be thereabouts.'

'Okay. Okay, not great. But then those local shepherds still felt the need to raid us, so maybe he's not been picked up yet, ay?'

'That's possible,' said Hotswap, with a nod.

'Only thing is, why didn't they take the book and my papers?'

'Who knows, who knows – hey, wait, hang on.'

'Yes? What?'

Hotswap pointed to the TV. 'The weather's up next.'

The silence of the churchyard was broken by distant discordant singing and cheery voices.

'Stop, wait, I have to get me hat on. Okay ... no, wait ... okay, right, sorted.'

Sol and then the professor broke into 'Show Me the Way to Go Home' as they marched into the churchyard, near to where Hargreaves and Catherine were keeping watch.

'Quiet,' said Tracy, drifting wearily behind, 'folks'll be sleeping.'

The now blue-green-hued revellers had acquired the ethereal equivalent of traffic cones: the professor was dragging some primitive handcuffs on the end of long chains, while Sol was wearing a bucket on his head, slots cut for eyeholes and leather straps dangling from the front and back.

'What the ...' said Hargreaves.

'Jesus, he's still there?' said Tracy, spying Christian.

'I'm afraid so,' said Catherine.

'And you've been watching him all this time?' said Tracy.

She nodded. 'We're a little worried he may go for the coffin again. He could get disoriented.'

'He's a sad case,' said Tracy.

'Well, some of us take it harder than others,' said Hargreaves.

'Anyway,' said Tracy, 'I've brought your birdbrain friend back. Reckon he's ready for his bed.'

'I'm not tired,' said the professor.

'Anyway, we're not stopping,' said Tracy.

'No, let's stay,' said Sol, 'I'm not tired either.'

'Come on, Captain Nemo,' shouted the professor, and he started trotting down towards Christian.

'Nanu Nanu,' said Sol, lifting his helmet to orientate himself, before replacing it and following on.

'Where do they get their energy from?' said Hargreaves, getting to his feet. 'And where in all of creation did they find that junk?'

'Beats me,' said Tracy. He shouted after Sol, 'Right, you've got five minutes.'

The professor, still dragging his chains, started doing a zombie walk, rocking from side to side, arms stretched out as he approached the still motionless Christian to offer more Dickens: '"Listen to me, Ebenezer. I wear the chain I forged in life. I made it link by link and yard by yard. I gartered it on of my own free will."' The professor broke off into a snigger. 'Free will,' he said, before just about completing the quote, '"and by my own free will I wore it,"' and letting out more sputtered laughter.

Christian turned his head and stared at him. He no longer cared, numb to the silliness from a super-saturation of it throughout the day.

'Derek,' shouted Hargreaves. He marched over and grabbed the professor by his collar. 'Sorry, lad,' said Hargreaves to Christian. He waited for a reaction that didn't come, then dragged the professor away.

A few moments later, Sol completed his stumbled drift to the grave-side. 'Hey, Christian, Christian, you'll love this, look, look … it's the return of the Cybermen. *Bleep, bleep, bleep.*'

No reaction.

'*Bleep. Bleep.*'

Still nothing.

'*Bleep?*'

Sol lifted his helmet, looked around, and scuttled off behind Hargreaves and the professor to rejoin the others.

Chapter Forty-Four

Late the following morning, Christian was slipping fitfully in and out of sleep in Tony's armchair, the sofa having been taken by an exhausted but now absent Professor Collier in the early hours. Soft-spoken voices from the kitchen mashed incoherently with visions of Uncle Frank struggling to hurl a grumbling but largely indifferent Erdygrot into a reactor shaft. But gradually whatever passed for reality asserted itself on his mind and he woke. He felt hungover, but couldn't remember drinking anything, before reminding himself how that wouldn't have been possible anyway.

As he sat up and surveyed the room, he started to recall scattered events from the previous day, and then the whole shebang, scene by scene, in horrific detail. He sunk back into the chair, deep into the upholstery, and asked for it to consume him.

His thoughts turned to the dark hours alone at the end. How long had he sat by the graveside in his vigil for himself? He recalled Hargreaves eventually persuading him, forcing him, to call it a night, and that it had been late, very late.

He pushed his head up through the cushion of the seatback. The Cheesus clock said eleven fifty. He looked around. No sign of Tony, Hargreaves, the professor, the cat or the liver. But again he heard the voices in the kitchen, only now realising they weren't part of his dream. He hauled himself out of the chair and made his way across the room, but stopped at the door when recognition hit.

'Do you think we should check the patient again?'

It was Catherine.

'I think he's still sleeping,' came Hargreaves's voice in reply, 'he'll be exhausted.'

'And, um, how are you doing in that regard?' she said.

There was no reply.

'Oh dear, I didn't push you too hard, did I?' she said.

'No, not a bit of it,' said Hargreaves.

'Good. Good,' she said. 'So ... how long are you staying?'

'Not long I'm afraid, got to get Derek back, and I've got my commitments at the school. We'll make a move once Christian's up. Just want to check he's okay, you know.'

'Yes of course. Don't we all.'

'And what are your plans?' said Hargreaves.

'I'll be making a move, too,' she said, 'the Gate, you know.'

'Ah, yes.'

Silence.

'Look, about last night,' said Hargreaves, 'about, well, you know.'

'It's fine.'

'I know this is the king of clichés, but it's never happened to me before, honestly.'

'It's fine, really.'

'I wanted to. Boy did I want to, but–'

She chuckled. 'It's funny how men are always more bothered by that than women. I'm quite used to it. Seriously, it's been thirty years since I had a man in my life who could get a reliable erection ...'

'Do we have to be so clinical about it?'

'... well, apart from Mr Boyd. But then, though I was often randy, I was never desperate. But anyway, it's hardly your fault, we're not machines.'

Christian clenched his fists. How could they? And of all days – his funeral day. What had happened to common decency? Did they think so little of him?

'Well, I'd better go and track down Derek,' said Hargreaves, 'see if he's finished playing with that postman.'

'All right, I'll check next door,' said Catherine.

'Now you won't go without saying goodbye, will you?'

'Of course not,' she said, her voice softening. Christian couldn't help but picture her easy smile, the lean in, the lingering kiss on the weird beard.

He turned. He thought about doing a runner through the far wall, but there wasn't time. Besides, why should he run?

He retraced the few steps to the chair and sat down.

Catherine emerged through the door. 'Oh, you're up and about,' she said.

'So it seems.' He sat down.

'How are you feeling?' she said, in a concerned tone, kneeling by the chair as if checking on a poorly nephew.

'How am I feeling?' He offered no eye contact. 'A little shocked, and, well, pretty empty I'd say. Yes, empty.'

'That's to be expected, I suppose.'

'Oh is that right?'

'Yes. It was quite a day yesterday.'

'Indeed. Quite a night too, it would seem.'

'I'm sorry?'

'Oh please, don't tell me you're embarrassed?'

'About what?'

'Sweet nothings are supposed to be whispered, Catherine, not broadcast to the parish.'

She paused before answering. 'That was a private conversation,' she said.

'Well, it wasn't like I had to hold a glass up to the wall.'

'I thought you were sleeping.'

'I wasn't.'

'Well, I'm sorry if I offended your sensibilities. But I haven't done anything wrong.'

'Yes you have. You did it, with Mr Hargreaves.'

'Who's Mr Hargreaves?'

'Stuart.'

'Look, not that it's any of your business, but we didn't do anything. Much.'

'Doesn't sound like it was for the want of trying.'

'I'm sorry but what is your point, Christian? Yes I stayed up most of the night trying to have sex with Stuart, is that a crime?'

'He's my chemistry teacher.'

'And?'

'And it's wrong.'

'How?'

'You're old enough to be his mother.'

'So what? I'm old enough to be your grandmother. None of that matters any more. Actually, none of that ever mattered. So what if I'm older.'

'Look, I just thought, you know, maybe we had something.'

'We do.'

'You know that's not what I mean.'

'Christian, I have a husband.'

'Didn't seem to be a problem for you last night.'

'That was different. It was the heat of the moment, spontaneous. It'd been a stressful day, we were all on edge ... What am I even saying? I don't have to justify myself to you.'

'No, you're right, you don't.'

'Good.'

'Good.'

'Good.'

There was a short pause, followed by a slightly longer one.

'Oh, come on, let's not fight about it,' she said, 'it's so silly.'

'Yes. Silly.'

'Look, shall we go for a walk?' she said.

'No. We won't, but I will,' he said, and stood.

'Suit yourself then,' she said, offering no eye contact.

Christian took the shortest exit available, out through the wall and into the churchyard.

He was immediately bowled a bouncer by the sight of his grave. Now, in the light of day, it looked so anonymous and insignificant. No headstone yet, of course, and if it wasn't for the fresh flowers, anyone might think it was nothing more than Tony having had some new turf laid in preparation for his annual boules tournament. He thought about sitting down by the graveside again, but resisted, and instead drifted on through the gates, out onto his standard walking route. He tried to think of other things, other times, but couldn't shift the thought of Catherine with Hargreaves or displace the standard questions: where had they done it? How many times had they done it? And of course the daddy of them all: was it any good?

As he reached the road leading to the park, he saw Hargreaves coming the other way with Professor Collier in a head lock.

'We were only playing mountaineers,' said the professor, to Hargreaves.

'Why were you hanging off his ears then?' said Hargreaves.

'He was the mountain,' said the professor.

Hargreaves spotted Christian. 'Ah, good to see you up and about, lad. How are you feeling?'

'Oh like all of a sudden you care about my welfare,' said Christian.

'What?'

'Feeling guilty I suppose?'

'About what?'

Christian looked Hargreaves up and down. It was all so easy for him, with his systems and his direct northern ways and his sex beard.

'Derek,' said Hargreaves, 'go on ahead to the church. I'll meet you there shortly.'

The professor gave an unconvincingly innocent smile from under Hargreaves's arm.

'Go straight there, mind, no messing about, okay?'

'No messing about,' said the professor.

Hargreaves released him, but the professor immediately spun round and headed back into the park.

'The hills are alive, with the sound of music,' he sang as he made a twirling exit.

Hargreaves closed his eyes and rubbed his temples.

'Right then,' he said, 'maybe you can tell me what I'm supposed to have done?'

'I trusted you,' said Christian, 'I thought you were on my side.'

'I am.'

'Funny way of showing it.'

'Hey, I stayed up half the bloody night looking after you.'

'And the other half looking after Catherine? Although not "up" exactly?'

'You cheeky little toad.'

Hargreaves hit Christian with a jab, hard on the bridge of the nose, sending Christian toppling back and into the pavement.

'You hit me. You fucking bastard, you hit me.'

'Yes.'

'That really hurt.'

'Don't be so wet, I barely touched you,' said Hargreaves, and he let loose a few more punches into the air in front of him.

'There was no need for that,' said Christian, feeling his nose.

'Yes, there was. You, my lad, were out of order.'

'I think you broke my nose.'

'Nice to know some things still work though,' said Hargreaves, looking with admiration at his fists and clenching them tighter.

'I said I think you broke my nose.'

'Oh don't be ridiculous, you're a ghost, I couldn't break your nose if I had a sledge hammer.'

'Still hurt.'

'Never joke about a man's tackle,' said Hargreaves. 'Didn't I teach you anything at school?'

'You didn't teach me that,' said Christian, getting to his feet.

'Well consider yourself taught now then,' said Hargreaves, shadow-boxing despite having no shadow to box with. 'I reckon the joke's on you, though,' he continued, 'because I'm pretty sure it's not just the late great Bomber Hargreaves that can't get it up any more, it's all of us. So you're just as buggered as me, lad.'

Christian stood there, keeping his distance, watching his old chemistry teacher go through a Bruce Lee montage of martial arts moves and wondering why only northerners can be intelligent *and* a bit handy.

'Come on, hit me,' said Hargreaves.

'What?'

'Hit me.'

'Why would I want to hit you?'

'Do it.'

'But–'

'I said do it. Just–'

Christian stepped forward and slapped Hargreaves across the chops.

'Not slap me, you big girl, I said hit me.'

Christian clenched his fist, hesitated and then bopped Hargreaves on the nose.

'For the love of god, I don't want a kiss, I want you to hit me.'

Christian put his shoulder into it this time and connected with Hargreaves's left cheek.

'Better. Again.'

Christian obliged. Left cheek again.

'Harder.'

'All right,' said Christian, and he started to bob around. He attempted an Ali shuffle and then let fly another blow, this time connecting with Hargreaves's windpipe.

'What are you doing?' said Hargreaves, with a splutter. He put his hands to his throat. 'You don't hit people in the bloody throat.'

'Sorry.'

'Now stop prancing about and hit me as hard as you can.'

Hargreaves stood still and adopted a forward lean and open stance to present his face as the easiest possible target.

Christian wound up and unleashed a sort of spin bowler's haymaker and connected hard below the right eye, causing Hargreaves to stumble back a pace.

'That's more like it,' said Hargreaves, and he punched Christian hard in the stomach, doubling him over.

'Hey, I didn't say you could hit me back.'

'Sorry,' said Hargreaves and punched Christian again, a hammerfist blow hard on the top of the head, sending him into the pavement up to his waist.

'Stop!'

'There. I'm done.' Hargreaves offered Christian his hand.

'I don't believe you,' said Christian, cowering.

Hargreaves laughed. 'I said I'm done.'

Christian waited, then took Hargreaves's hand and dragged himself up out of the asphalt.

Somewhere in the back of his mind, Christian was aware he'd just had his first fight. Not his first ethereal fight, his first fight full stop. A street brawl with a no-nonsense northern chemistry teacher. It felt exhilarating. It felt real. The stuff of Hemmingway.

They sat down side by side in the pavement.

'You know, I suspected as much anyway,' said Hargreaves, 'even before last night.'

'Suspected what?'

'Widespread erectile dysfunction in ghosts.'

'Oh.'

'Have you had an erection since you got here?'

Christian stopped feeling like Hemmingway and started feeling uncomfortable. Hemmingway wouldn't have been uncomfortable. He'd have talked freely about erections, no question; he'd have upped the ante and got out the tape measure. Instead, Christian felt like he was back at school. It had been Hargreaves who'd delivered the facts of life classes, and without the slightest hint of embarrassment on his part.

'I'd rather not talk about it,' said Christian.

'Exactly. Neither have I,' said Hargreaves, 'thirteen days now without a boner.'

'Look, that's really too much information,' said Christian.

'My previous record was twelve hours.'

'Twelve hours? You're not serious?'

'Hey, look, I was going through a bad patch.'

'Will of Ockham, no, I mean *only* twelve hours. You're seriously telling me you've never gone longer than half a day between …'

'I am,' said Hargreaves, 'and mostly a lot less. Caused the odd awkward moment at work, I can tell you. If there's one thing they won't tolerate in pretty much any school, it's a teacher with an erection. Well, at least that's something I don't have to worry about now.'

'No, I suppose not,' said Christian. He only now noticed that their pavement seating position was uncomfortably close to a fresh dog turd and wondered why it still bothered him.

'Still,' said Hargreaves, 'I imagine there's plenty of folks here who get pretty damned pissed off about it. All those terrorist suicide bombers getting rewarded with their seventy-two virgins, but all the while they can't get it up. Eternity with those sexy fillies, floating around you playfully, wanting you to sort them out, begging you to, and all you can do is make friends with them and be interested in their thoughts and opinions, and then watch as they get it on with, well, I dunno, angels or something. That's actually a pretty good definition of Hell if you ask me.'

'Well, yes, I suppose so,' said Christian. 'You know, the thing I never understood with that one was what on earth the seventy-two virgins had done to have to spend eternity as a terrorist's personal sex harem. That's pretty harsh punishment, isn't it? They must have been really evil virgins. And where would Heaven get them from? Where do you find even one evil innocent girl, let alone seventy-two?'

'Well,' said Hargreaves, 'I'm not sure there's anything that says the virgins are necessarily female. Think on that for a second. You've done your bombing, you and the target are all blown to bits, it's been a good day. You show up in the afterlife to claim your prize and bada-bing, you're thrown into a big tent with a barrel of cider and seventy-two pale-faced curious boys. Then you'd be pretty thankful for not being able to get it up, I reckon.'

'Unless you were gay,' added Christian.

'Well, yes, good point. But then you'd be in Hell anyway, which means you'd be there for punishment … so in that case, again, I reckon being flaccid would be an appropriate torment.'

'So if you're a suicide bomber, you'll be damned either way,' said Christian.

'Well, there's justice in that, I suppose.'

They watched a businessman hurry through their legs before losing traction on the dog turd, arms flapping as he extended its influence along the pavement.

'Do you think it's different if you die with an erection?' asked Hargreaves, putting his hand to his crotch.

'What, a suicide bomber?' said Christian. 'I can't see that happening. It's not an erotic act, is it? I suppose he could die with someone else's erection, you know, if he blew up a brothel or something?'

'No, I mean in general, what if you had an erection when you died?'

'Your own erection?'

'Yes.'

'Is that possible?'

'Oh yes. It's quite common, actually.'

'So what, you mean lots of men die … on the job?'

'No, well, I dunno actually, maybe,' said Hargreaves, 'but not what I was getting at. No, it's if you die lying face down or standing up. Any orientation that lets the blood pool in the lower half of your body. It's just physics. Eventually your lower half fills up and where does the blood go next? It inflates your sergeant major and hey presto you're giving a final salute. Angel lust, they call it.'

'You're having me on.'

'No, it's true. It's a common side effect from hanging.'

'Really?'

'Oh yes. They even ejaculate sometimes.'

'Well I never,' said Christian. 'I guess it would pay not to be in the front row then.'

'Makes you think though, doesn't it? Do they feel that last wave of pleasure, with the agony? Sort of like the lemon and the salt with a shot of tequila.'

'Don't you die immediately, in hanging?'

'If it's done right, I suppose,' said Hargreaves, 'but if something goes wrong, well you could be there for a good few minutes. What a way to go eh?'

'So what about crucifixion?' said Christian. 'You die standing up in crucifixion, no doubt about that.'

'True.'

'So does that mean Jesus could have ...'

'Well. It's a possibility,' said Hargreaves, raising his eyebrows.

'Imagine that,' said Christian. 'An unwanted erection is embarrassing at the best of times, but imagine if he's got one up there on the cross, right at the moment where he's trying to look all spiritual and holy, and what with his dad watching.'

'Well it would only be after he died.'

'Yes, yes, of course. But even so, they left the poor wretches up there for a while, didn't they?'

'I believe they did,' said Hargreaves.

'Oh, imagine if you were a member of the audience. You think it's all over, and then it's like, wait, hang on, I think I saw some movement ... Praise be! He has risen!'

'Well, it could have happened,' said Hargreaves.

'Not something you see on the average crucifix, is it though? Jesus with a boner.'

'No.'

'Be a bit of a health and safety hazard, I suppose, or at least would lead to a lot of snagged cardies.'

'Well, yes.'

'But you don't see it in paintings, either,' said Christian. 'They're missing a trick there, aren't they? New line of saucy postcards in the Vatican gift shop. They'd clean up.'

'Well, though you jest, there were depictions of just that during the Renaissance, but the Catholic Church suppressed them. Father Colby was always on about it, actually little else, now I think about it.'

'Astonishing. No surprise they were hushed.'

'Well no. I imagine they were worried about the rise of a sexualised Easter.'

'It would fit nicely with the bunny theme, though,' said Christian.

'That's an old pagan thing, lad.'

'I know. I'm joking, I'm joking.'

'Oh, yes. Very funny.'

'I wonder if you could still get them at the time though,' said Christian, 'the banned paintings, I mean. If you went to the right places, maybe Catholic newsagents? You know, simple frame, kept under the counter, brown paper bag, no questions asked.'

'I don't think the devout see it that way,' said Hargreaves.

'No?'

'It's more about Christ as a man. Man has a cock, Jesus is a man, Jesus has a cock.'

'You seem to know a lot about this, Stuart?'

'Well I'm a teacher.'

'A chemistry teacher.'

'Well you have to read around your subject.'

'Yes, I suppose. That is quite a long way around though.'

'No such thing as useless knowledge, lad.'

Mitch was standing in the kitchen, watching an autopilot Beatrice reach for the teabags to the sound of the kettle boiling and, upstairs, bath taps running. Twenty-four hours on from his arrival, he was well rested but had made little progress regarding Christian.

'So what have we learned then?' said Mitch.

'I've already told you, nothing new,' said Hotswap. The angel was sitting on and slightly in the kitchen counter, his legs swinging in and out of the cereals cupboard, clipping the Sugar Puffs.

'Yeah, but nothing can be something, ay,' said Mitch. 'The wake, the raid, but no sign of the cargo. What are we missing?'

Beatrice plodded through Mitch into the hall and up the stairs.

'Well, if he's not loitering around here, he must still be at the death site,' said Hotswap.

'Possibly,' said Mitch.

'What d'you mean possibly? Of course he'll be there.'

'It's not always that simple.'

'Yes it is. It's exactly that simple, you're always telling me. Ninety-nine times out of a hundred, it's either the home or the death site.'

'All right then, where's the death site?' asked Mitch.

'No idea,' said Hotswap.

'Oh whoop-de-doo, pretty much got this nailed then.'

'Well, it's really none of my business,' said Hotswap, getting down from the counter and drifting through to the hall. 'My work is done. I'm off.'

'You're just gonna leave me to it? Thanks a fuckin' million.'

Hotswap turned to Mitch and gave a shrug. 'You're the shepherd.'

'Well you can at least find out where the death site is for me.'

The angel shook his head.

'Don't gimme that,' said Mitch, 'you're going back anyway. So ask around.'

The kettle switch clicked as the water boiled.

'It's more than asking around,' said Hotswap, 'I'd have to make another trip down to tell you. I'd need clearance.'

'I don't care. This is all your fault. You fuckin' owe me.'

'Langers ...'

They heard the bath taps being turned off upstairs.

'Bring me some new kit, and new headgear too,' said Mitch.

'Get your own headgear.'

'I had my own headgear.'

'You had a bucket.'

'Well get me a bucket then, and make sure there's eyeholes.'

A now naked Beatrice came back down the stairs, through Mitch and Hotswap and on into the kitchen, where she filled her cup of camomile.

'Look, I'll see what I can do,' said Hotswap, 'but no promises.'

'Okay ...' said Mitch, his eyes now on Beatrice. She took her cup and came back through them and on up the stairs.

'I said I'll see what I can do, but no promises.'

'Right ...' said Mitch.

'Nothing more you want? You seem so grateful for these favours.'

'No, no ...' said Mitch, his eyes rising to the landing.

Hotswap just shook his head and drifted out through the front door.

Mitch heard the cup being placed on the side of the bath. A pause. A small splash and then another.

He drifted upstairs.

Christian and Hargreaves had decided to head back into the park to see if they could find the wayward professor.

'So anyway, getting back to the point,' said Hargreaves, as they drifted, 'I was wondering if you die with an erection, do you get to keep it as a ghost?'

'Which would, presumably, stay for eternity?' said Christian.

'Like taking an everlasting erectile pill.'

'Yes, Willy Wonka style. That's quite a thought isn't it.'

'It certainly is,' said Hargreaves. 'Sure, it sounds great ...'

'Does it?'

'... a permanent boner, ever ready for the call to an eternity of duty, but would it really be great, to have one all the time? Take me, I'd never be able to teach again, no way.'

'You'd be lucky to make it through the interview,' said Christian.

'No, no, despite the massive upside, so to speak, it would be a disaster. Just imagine meeting God. It's a solemn moment, he's the Lord of all creation, naturally, you're trying to think noble, pure thoughts, and there you are, with wood. He's bound to notice, isn't he?'

'Well he's omniscient, it's impossible for him not to. But maybe he'd be okay with it. After all, if he created man, he knows what men are like. So maybe he'd see it as a compliment, you know, sort of paying homage?'

'I don't think that's a road you'd want to go down,' said Hargreaves. 'No, no, on balance we're best off flaccid. Jesus Christ, that's something I never thought I'd hear myself say.'

On arrival at the park, they soon spotted the professor in the area of grass between Point Royal and the bench. He was standing on Sol's shoulders, the chain from the previous night slung under Sol's nose, like a bridle, for support.

'We climb him because he is there,' shouted the professor, when he spotted Christian and Hargreaves approaching.

'Give me strength,' said Hargreaves.

The liver came scurrying over to greet Christian, circling him three times. And Christian found himself pleased to see him. Though undeniably bizarre, their relationship was pure and uncomplicated.

'Hope he wasn't too much trouble, Sol,' said Christian, bending down to pat the organ.

'I'm just glad he couldn't find any crampons,' said Sol.

'No, I meant this fellow,' said Christian, nodding to the liver.

'Oh right, yeah, no problemo. Hey, he's a bit tired, I think. He's been a Sherpa all morning.'

'Derek,' said Hargreaves, 'that's enough. Come down.'

'Sorry, sir,' said Sol.

'What? Oh it's not your fault, lad,' said Hargreaves, 'Derek's the troublemaker.'

The professor unhooked the chain and jumped down, kicking off against the postman's forehead and bombing into the grass, disappearing into the ground before popping his head up out through the blades. 'Come on in, the soil is lovely. Turf's up!'

Sol looked wide-eyed at Hargreaves. 'Can I, sir? Can I?'

'You don't have to ask my permission, lad,' said Hargreaves.

'Thanks, sir, you're the best.' Sol belly-flopped into the ground to join the professor.

Hargreaves and Christian sat down in the bench. The liver followed and settled at Christian's feet.

'Look, lad, I'm sorry about all the disruption yesterday,' said Hargreaves, 'I shouldn't have brought Derek. He's not ready.'

'Oh, no harm done,' said Christian. 'It's not like he was the craziest act there.'

'Can you do this?' said the professor to Sol, before diving forward head first, to leave his legs poking out of the ground towards the sky. He held the position, like an artistic swimmer, then let himself sink from view before emerging back in the vertical.

'Hey,' shouted Hargreaves.

'I don't like putting my head under,' said Sol, doggy-paddling round the professor.

'Hey,' shouted Hargreaves again, 'you lads play safe, you both stay on the surface, you hear?'

'So what's the story with your professor then?' said Christian. 'I never did get to ask what he's doing with you.'

'I've got him on a trial release,' said Hargreaves, looking on with some concern, 'we're trying to rehabilitate them, get them out into the community ...'

The professor started circling Sol, while making tug-boat toots.

'... it's not a very successful programme.'

'So there's more like him?'

'Oh yes, they've got two hundred of 'em in a barn in St Albans. Total chaos as you can imagine.'

'And they're all nuts?'

'Oh, Derek's not nuts, not really. He's just uninhibited.'

'Is there a reason?'

'Indeed there is. Physics, lad.'

'Physics?'

'Second law of thermodynamics, to be specific.'

Christian hadn't been good at physics. Quite apart from approaching the subject from the *Let's pass a physics exam* angle, instead of the more fruitful *Let's learn about physics* angle, he always suspected there was something they weren't telling him, a sort of physics equivalent of *Look, let's just tell them it literally was created in seven days. The important thing for now is we get them onside. We'll have plenty of time to convert it all to metaphor when they're old enough to understand what a metaphor is.*

'You're gonna have to refresh my memory,' said Christian.

'You don't remember the second law of thermodynamics?'

'No ...'

'Entropy?'

'Rings a bell ...'

'Honestly, I don't know why we bothered with you. All right, it's all about the universe's arrow of time – in a closed system, things always tend towards greater disorder. Heat always flows from a hot thing to a cold thing, it's why an ice cube cools your tea down.'

'Why would I put an ice cube in my tea?'

'Forget why, the point is the cube will melt and the tea will cool. You'll never see the cube get colder and the tea get hotter, not unless you reversed the direction of time.'

'Oh yes, yes, I remember.'

'Good. So you see how that applies to Derek's state of mind?'

'Not really ...'

Hargreaves rolled his eyes. 'Living things are more ordered than dead things. On the face of it, this goes against the second law – everything should move towards disorder, over time. Life only manages to pull off the trick of existence by constantly taking in an external source of energy, usually food or sunlight, to overcome the deficit. And if that's removed, then the second law asserts itself pretty damn quick – death, decay, disorder. Now ghosts and spirits don't have a source of energy. You don't see them chowing down at Burger King, you don't see them out photosynthesising on sunny days. They expend energy – moving, talking, thinking, running around doing aeroplane impressions – but they don't take any in, which vomits all over the second law of thermodynamics. And that's the most immutable law in nature. It's the daddy. As near as science gets to infallible. So all this makes it nigh on impossible for Derek to believe in himself.'

'So what does he believe? Surely he still has to account for himself?'

'Indeed he does. He believes he's dreaming. And he believes it with absolute certainty.'

'Poor fellow.'

'And that's what spawns this mode of behaviour. He's convinced it's a dream. You can do what you like in a dream, of course, and well, being a theoretical physicist he didn't get out much when he was alive, so it's no surprise you get a bit of a reaction.'

'Well I have to admit I have some sympathy for his position. I'm not yet convinced myself it's not a dream, or perhaps a coma.'

'Yes, you said as much yesterday. Bit of a worry if you ask me.'

'I only think it might be a dream. I can't say for sure.'

'Well I'd keep hold of that doubt, if I were you. Probably all that's stopping you becoming a Spitfire.'

'Spitfires,' shouted the professor, with delight.

'Oh Buddha,' said Hargreaves, 'no, look, you did Spitfires yesterday.'

'Not so. I was a Lancaster bomber yesterday,' said the professor.

'Well it doesn't matter, we're heading off soon. Playtime's over.'

'No,' said the professor.

'Derek. Come here.'

The professor stood still.

'I said come here.'

The professor looked down at his shoes.

'*Derek.*'

He shuffled over. Hargreaves stood and took him by the shoulders.

'Now you remember what we said, Derek?'

The professor smirked.

'Come on,' said Hargreaves, 'I'm not joking, give me your serious face. Come on.'

The professor struggled and after some effort managed to suppress most of his smirk.

'Now, once again,' said Hargreaves, 'the second law of thermodynamics isn't wrong …'

'The second law of thermodynamics,' said the professor, the corner of his mouth beginning to twitch.

'Derek,' said Hargreaves, 'the second law of thermodynamics isn't wrong, it is, perhaps …'

The professor's whole mouth began to quiver. He tensed the muscles in his face to compensate.

'… it is perhaps just incomplete,' said Hargreaves.

'Phhhhumpuuuuuuuuu, pip pip pip phhhhumpuuuuu,' said the professor.

'Focus, Derek.'

The professor exploded with laughter, bending over, dropping to his knees and then rolling over onto his back to kick his legs in the air.

'Derek.'

'I am not Derek, I am Professor ... Peter Pan, Peter Rabbit, Professor Peter-Pan-Pammy Rabbit, the first forever young Playboy bunny.' He wrenched at his trousers. 'Bunnies don't have trousers,' he told his trousers, 'only little jackets.'

He got back to his feet and hopped off, with Sol in pursuit.

'It's a labour of love,' said Hargreaves, returning to the bench.

'But hang on, you understand all the science,' said Christian, 'so what's your excuse for staying sane?'

'Well, yes, I do understand it, and I still believe it, but I'm open to bending it, too. No, I think the problem is I never understood it to the depth that someone like Derek would have, so it was easier for me to wrestle with, it wasn't much bigger than me, I could get it off balance, kick it in the nuts if I had to. Whereas for Derek, well, he's trying to wrestle a proud and quarrelsome elephant.'

'Ah.'

'It's always a no-contest for him. He starts to give it some thought, he's up on his toes looking for a new angle on the problem, second law of thermodynamics squashes him flat.'

'Poor fellow.'

'Indeed.'

'All right, so if you don't think it's a dream, what do you believe?' asked Christian. 'What's your account for all this?'

'Well I believe I'm dead, of course. Let's face it, we're here, aren't we?'

'But you weren't a believer before? In life?'

'Oh I was always a Christian,' said Hargreaves, 'I believed in the overall message, I just regarded all the miracles and supernatural stuff as metaphor.'

'So no divine creator?'

'I wouldn't go as far as that,' said Hargreaves, 'but not one who cares about us, and not an afterlife where the sun's always shining and all your pets are there and no one ever argues. It seemed too easy, too much like wishful thinking.'

'But you believe now?'

'Of course.'

'So you've thrown a lifetime's scepticism out of the window?'

'No, I've revised my thinking, based on the evidence. That's what science is.'

'But is it evidence, really? What about "I think therefore I am"?'

'Well, yes,' said Hargreaves, 'fine in theory, fine in a textbook, but look …' He rabbit-punched Christian on the shoulder.

'Ow,' said Christian, coiling back and lifting his hands, 'what was that for?'

'Don't panic, I was just making a point.'

'You've given me a dead arm,' said Christian, 'well, a deader arm.'

'The point,' said Hargreaves, 'is though this is just my personal experience, it's pretty damn clear and convincing personal experience. So I think the most likely explanation is that it's real.'

'So why can't the professor take that journey too?' asked Christian, rubbing his shoulder.

'Well, like I say, he was a devout non-believer. It's too deeply rooted in him.'

'But he's still rational, he's a scientist. What's happened to him?'

'Well, nothing really. That's why he believes what he believes. From his point of view, believing it's a dream is rational. It explains his personal experience, and leaves the second law of thermodynamics happily ripping up trees and smashing them over the heads of the meek.'

'But obviously we know it's bunkum, his theory, I mean,' said Christian.

'Of course. And do you know why?'

'Because … we're observing from outside his head, so this can't all be his dream.'

'Well done, lad, that's right. But for the same reason, his theory does still hold from the perspective of being within his head.'

'Just like it would from within our heads.'

'Exactly.'

'That's a tricky one, isn't it.'

'Certainly is. Does lead to tension at the barn, I can tell you. Lots of fights, all these professors telling each other to get out of each other's dreams. It's crazy. Even if it is a dream, only one of them can be right, but will they listen? No chance.'

'Must be awful.'

'Well, it's not too bad. Mostly they're having too much of a good time to bother fighting.'

'So what's the prognosis then, for someone like Derek?'

'Hard to say. I'm told some of them eventually drop the dream idea and move on to thinking it's all a simulation – the whole world, the universe, not just the Zone. A small step, but at least it gets them to be a bit less selfish, bit less uninhibited.'

'So we're all bits and bytes in some alien kid's laptop?'

'Well, I'm sure the alien kid would be a scientist, or teacher of some sort, from some super-intelligent species, and the computer would be a machine of almost infinite power. You could picture that better than me. But from what I'm told, it's perfectly possible, which like the dream thing is why it gets adopted as an explanation by the physicists.'

'And that there really is an afterlife doesn't?'

'No. That would break the second law of thermodynamics. That would be ridiculous.'

———————————

There has been much debate in afterlife realms on what to do about the problem of the incredulous physicists, ever since they began appearing towards the end of the nineteenth century, when the full implications of the second law were beginning to sink in. Before this, most physicists, having found no ironclad reasons to discount the viability of an afterlife, tended to take their death with good grace. But the power of the second law is so strong that for those who study it, once internalised it inevitably leads to an afterlifetime of scepticism and disbelief. Seeing fellow ghosts in this perpetually deluded dream state is troubling for many, and the short history of the incredulous physicists has been accompanied by a lamentable parallel history of failed intervention. Many approaches have been tried, including a handful of rational arguments, such as the argument from time (how can a dream last years?), the argument from detail (how can a dream produce such clarity and richness?) and the argument from recursion (how can you have dreams within dreams?), but though rational, all are like new-born lambs in comparison to the omnipotent second law.

The truth is that the power of the second law of thermodynamics is so strong, so founded in diamond-tipped evidence, that rational argument rapidly becomes pointless. Hence many have said the path may lie in irrational arguments, and this has indeed formed the bulk of recent attempts, including, but not limited to, the argument from majority opinion; the argument from ancestral opinion; the argument from trusting obscure documents; the argument from using semantics to bypass the problem; the argument from a pig-headed refusal to look facts in the face; the argument from waking up on a sunny day and knowing everything's all right with the world; the argument from that funny feeling you get when you look at a nice painting; the argument from that funny feeling you get when you look at a nice person; the argument from *I was thinking about my friend the other day and then when I went out I bumped into my friend and you can't tell me that's just a coincidence even though I live quite near my friend and tend to forget all the times when I thought of my friend but didn't bump into her later that day and don't understand or accept basic probability*; and of course the argument from *but wouldn't it be nice if it was true?*

Though irrational, these arguments are occasionally not without their ingenuity – the argument from imaginary numbers being the best example. However, none of the many irrational attempts to date have resulted in so much as a single successful 'awakening', leading some to suggest that challenging a rational belief with an irrational argument is as futile as challenging an irrational belief with a rational argument.

In recent times then, the arguments have become more sophisticated. The in-vogue approach has been to embrace the guerrilla tactic of hiding an irrational argument inside a rational one, by attempting to frame the second law of thermodynamics not as wrong, but merely incomplete, in the same way that Newton's laws of motion can be viewed as incomplete with regard to not including a role for relativity, or the theory of evolution being incomplete with regard to not including a role for God. The track record of the approach is, at best, poor, mainly because no one can offer anything even approaching a credible explanation for the bits that are missing, or even reach agreement on which bits are missing, or what they look like, none of which is made easier by the fact that the people best placed to work on the problem are the ones preferring instead to spend all day playing Spitfires.

And then there are those who say the physicists should be left alone, pointing out they are far happier because of their delusion, far happier than all the people who have to cope with the inescapable horror and angst of being dead coupled with the prospect of having to do it for an awfully long time to come.

The professor and Sol drifted back into view, both now singing 'Run Rabbit Run'.

'So why are you bothering with Derek then? If it's all so futile?' asked Christian.

'Well, you have to try,' said Hargreaves, 'some might have said it was just as futile trying to get you to properly understand the material in your A-levels.'

'Mrs Spassky did say that,' said Christian, 'and let's be honest, she was half right.'

'Yes, but that's beside the point. Glory comes from seeking glory, not from being sure you'll get it.'

'Dunno. Sounds like a recipe for frustration to me.'

Hargreaves sighed. 'Same old Christian,' he said.

'I'm just being honest.'

'So am I.'

The professor and Sol came in for a couple of tight passes round them, before drifting back out to the open grass once again.

'I am glad you're teaching again though,' said Christian.

'Thanks. Yeah, it feels good,' said Hargreaves.

'So what about the Gate?'

'What of it?'

'You're not going for it?'

'No. Not yet, anyway.'

'You're not curious?'

'Oh, of course I'm curious, that's why I teach science. But you know, what can it offer that I don't have here?'

'But if you're a Christian, don't you feel obliged to go to the Gate, to receive your reward?'

'Well, yes, that's a view. But, and this is going to sound a bit Frank Capra, maybe I have my reward right here.'

'Yes. Very Frank Capra.'

'I'm serious though. I love teaching. Here I can teach, maybe for ever, so I reckon that'll do me fine.'

'But you're not worried about incurring God's wrath, for not offering yourself up for judgement?'

'If he's the sort of God I imagine, then he'd be happy with my choice, I'm sure.'

'What if he's not the sort of God you imagine?'

'Well, then I suppose I'll have to take my chances.'

They sat in silence, looking out to Point Royal. Sol and the professor were still playing, running around and through mortals and their dogs out enjoying the sunshine. The liver had now calmed and seemed happy to sit at Christian's feet.

'So what's next for you then, lad?' asked Hargreaves. 'What's your plan?'

'I haven't got one,' said Christian.

'Really? Well do you at least have a plan for a plan?'

'No. But then I didn't think I needed one until I got run over, you know, being an atheist and that. So I suppose I'm still working it out.'

Hargreaves shook his head. 'And you've had a whole week? Come on, where's your structure? Where are your goals? Where's your five-year plan? I've got my teaching, I've got my research interests, I've got my community work with Physicists In Need. Now what have you got?'

'I, well … look, I don't know, and I don't want to be hassled about it.'

'Keep your hair on, I'm on your side, lad. Look, let's step back and think this through. Okay, are you going to go for the Gate, like Catherine?'

'I'm not sure.'

'Okay. Are you going to continue your book?'

'No.'

'Why?'

'Lots of reasons. It's all gone, for one.'

'Gone?'

'Destroyed. Bea didn't like the idea of preserving my legacy.'

'I'm sorry to hear that. Must have been a body blow.'

'Well, yes. But then I realised it's made no difference, really. If she'd kept it, it's not like I could just pop over, boot up the laptop and crack on with the next chapter.'

'No, no I suppose not,' said Hargreaves, 'so why not rewrite it? Start again?'

'Who for?'

'There are dead readers, millions of them, and not many books. Least not ones we can hold.'

'No point. It worked as a funny idea for the living to read, but who wants a tongue-in-cheek guide to the afterlife once they're actually in it?'

'It might work.'

'Trust me, it won't. The jokes work when the reader knows it's nonsense. It'd be torture if they knew it was real.'

'Oh, I dunno.'

'It would. Imagine Alice reading *Alice In Wonderland* while she's in Wonderland. She wouldn't find it whimsically charming, she'd be terrified. No, the whole thing's dead in the water, unless I'm dreaming.'

'Hey, now watch it with the dream talk.'

'Well you say that, but if I am dreaming, then you actually have a point. The book would be viable again, it would still exist, out there in the real world. And I'll have all this great new material. Only trouble will be remembering it.'

'Well, though I can't condone the dream theory, if it gets you motivated why not continue on that assumption? Write down all your experiences. It's better than nothing.'

'But if I am dreaming, then what good will it do me writing it down here? Soon as I wake up, it'll be right, where's my notes … oh.'

'Ah, yes. I see your point.' Hargreaves got up off the bench and took a few paces. 'All right,' he said, 'well how about going back to the more positive assumption that you are dead, and write a new book, one that would appeal to dead people?'

'Well, I could do, I suppose, but I'm a bit short on ideas. Besides, what would I write with?'

'I thought you might say that,' said Hargreaves, with a wink. He reached into his jacket pocket and handed Christian a large poorly made pencil, a small blade, and a wrinkled pad of beige papyrus bound at the top with some thin twine. 'Now, don't say I never do anything for you.'

'Oh, er, thanks. But you know I'm really more of a laptop man,' said Christian, and he offered the items back.

'Christian, do you know how hard it was to get just this? Material, all material is rare here. You're only getting these because I snuck them out from the supplies store.'

'No laptop's there then?'

'We don't even have textbooks, lad, not ones we can touch.'

'Well again, thanks, but I'm not sure,' said Christian, 'not sure it's worth it.' He tried again to return the items.

'I'm not taking them back, lad. You do with them as you see fit.'

'Well, all right,' said Christian, and put them in his pockets, 'thanks.'

'Always the shortcut with you, isn't it?' said Hargreaves, hands on hips. 'If it's a little bit hard, it's not worth doing.'

'Look, I'm sorry, but I don't think I've got it in me any more. I don't want to get your hopes up.'

'Well, you'd better work something out sooner or later. Don't want to end up like that postman and his mate.'

'There's no way that's going to happen.'

'Well, I dunno,' said Hargreaves, 'remember what I used to tell you? You blink and a year's gone. Ten blinks, ten years. Twenty, thirty, forty, you're done. It'll happen before you know it.'

'It won't happen to me. I'm feeling better actually. Really. Yesterday, it got me thinking. It's like death was the wake-up call I needed. Now I just need a bit of time to work it out, to put the pieces together.'

'Sounds an awful lot like the old Christian to me.'

There was no reply.

Hargreaves sat down. 'Okay, maybe you were right,' he said. 'Maybe you can fake your way through school, through university, through work, life and novel writing, but you can't fake your way through the afterlife, no way. Eternity. That's the killer. Seems to me faking's only ever good for getting you to the next island, and okay maybe it does that pretty well, but what if there are no more islands to get to?'

'Stuart, I'll be fine, really.'

'Look, this may sound a bit off the wall, but why don't you come back with me, to the school? I reckon you've got it in you to teach.'

'What? Me? I couldn't teach. I don't know anything.'

'Well you could teach art, maybe?'

'That's your afterlife, Stuart, it's not mine.'

Hargreaves paused. 'Well, it's your choice, of course.'

They again sat in silence for a few minutes. Sol and the professor were now sitting in the grass, their energy spent.

'Well. I think it's time,' said Hargreaves. He got to his feet. 'Derek ... *Derek*.'

The professor begrudgingly got up and started making his way over. Sol followed.

Christian stood.

'Derek and I'll head back to the church and say goodbye to Catherine, before heading off,' said Hargreaves. 'You joining us?'

Christian was big enough for building bridges, but not two in the same place at once. 'You know, I think I'll do my own thing for the afternoon,' he said. 'Will you wish Catherine all the best from me?'

'Sure, no problem.'

'And, um, sorry about earlier.'

'Water under the bridge, lad, water under the bridge.'

Chapter Forty-Five

Christian watched the credits roll on the second film of the afternoon, safe in his digital surround-sound man cave. He'd left the liver to look after Sol, who on being asked if he was okay to be left alone replied he was a grown man and was quite capable of playing trains unsupervised.

Christian decided it was now safe to head back to the vicarage.

He was calm enough on leaving the cinema, but as he emerged into the dusk of evening, he soon found himself hurrying, only now realising he didn't want her to leave without saying goodbye.

As he passed through the churchyard gate, he met Tracy coming the other way.

The gasman gave a grunt of acknowledgement, barely raising his eyes from the path.

'Oh not you too,' said Christian, looking him up and down. 'I know she's making up for lost time, but jeez, I thought she'd have some standards.'

'What?'

'Sex.'

'Sex?'

'Come on, don't deny it. That's what you've been doing in there, isn't it?'

'No.'

'Why the long face then?'

No reply.

Christian broke into a chuckle. 'Of course. You can't get it up either?'

'You looking for a smack in the mouth, pal?'

'Maybe I am. Come on, take a shot, gasman. Do your worst. I'm experienced. Come on, let's rumble.' Christian put up his fists.

Tracy shot out an arm, grabbed Christian by the collar and pushed him back and over into the rose bushes, before resuming his drift out of the churchyard. 'We were talking,' he shouted over his shoulder.

Christian pulled himself out of the bushes, decided he'd lost his footing, and drifted on into the vicarage.

The kitchen was empty, but as he entered the living room, he found Catherine sitting in the sofa.

'Finally,' she said, standing, 'you took your time.'

'Yes. Sorry.'

'How's your day been?' she asked.

'Bit of a rollercoaster,' said Christian. 'Seems to have levelled out now though. I think.'

He wanted to sit next to her on the sofa. She'd left a space, but this was a clear-the-air session. You can finish a clear-the-air session on the sofa, but you can't start one on it.

He sat in the armchair he'd spent the previous night in.

'Are you okay?' she asked. 'Stu mentioned you'd had a bit of a scuffle.'

'More than a scuffle, it was more like the Rumble in ... Binfield. But yes, I'm fine.'

'Well it's flattering to have men fighting over me.'

Christian didn't know what to say.

'But anyway,' she said, 'I'm glad you sorted it out.'

'Me too,' said Christian. He looked at her and then turned his gaze away. 'So have they gone?'

'Yes, left a couple of hours ago.'

'And, er, Tracy?'

'You've just missed him,' said Catherine.

'Yes, I saw him outside. Said he came round for a ... chat.'

Catherine said nothing, but looked Christian in the eye.

'What?' he said.

'Just wondering if you're going to make an outright accusation or stick with going around the houses.'

'I'm not accusing you of anything. And anyway, as we've established, it's none of my business.'

'Oh dear, not off to a good start, are we?'

'No.'

'Look, Christian, it really was just a chat, it's important you know this.'

'It's okay,' said Christian, 'really, it's okay.' Was she telling the truth? But then, what did it matter now anyway – she did it with Stuart, with *Hargreaves*, she *did it* with *Hargreaves*. So what if you add in Tracy, so what if you add in Sol, Fat Larry and the liver for that matter? One big ghost gang-bang. It made no difference now.

'And you're next I suppose?' he asked. 'Next to be leaving?'

'Well, yes, that's still the plan.'

'When?'

'Tomorrow. First thing.'

Christian said nothing. What was there to say? They were done.

'Look, are you sure you won't come along?' she said.

'I'm sure.'

'You don't have to worry about my husband, you'd like him. And I'm sure he'd like you.'

'I really don't think that would work, but that's not the reason.'

'No?'

'No. Going to the Gate – it's not for me, not yet anyway.'

'So what are you going to do?'

'Stuart was asking me that. I'm not sure.'

'Yes, he said as much.'

'But I'm okay that I don't know, that's at least something I can be certain about.'

Catherine shook her head. 'I feel for you, Christian, I really do. If you can't make a leap of faith now, when will you? Do you need God to come down and appear to you personally?'

'You know, I'm not sure that would change anything.'

'Well then, I fear you are lost.'

Chapter Forty-Six

In the days that followed, normal service, such as it was, resumed. Each morning Christian took the liver for a drift in the park, where they met Sol and Tracy. And each morning Christian's heart sank when he failed to find Catherine waiting there with them. There was no reason for her to be there, but it didn't stop him hoping. But gradually he accepted she'd simply done what she said she was going to do, and he would probably never see her again.

He still thought about her though. He wanted to talk about her, too, but found trying to do so with Tracy and Sol eternally frustrating, never getting beyond their assertion that she was a classy lady and the sun would have to shine in hell before she would become romantically interested in Christian.

So he kept his thoughts to himself, only occasionally verbalising them to the liver or Tony, when he felt sure no one was listening. She had a husband, a husband she was committed to finding in death. He told himself that this alone meant further speculation was pointless, but he couldn't stop his mind drifting back to the subject all the same. Would it have mattered that there was a sixty-nine year age gap? He'd dated older women before, but then there's older and there's *older*. And what about her being far more social than he was, would he be able to handle an inevitable and never-ending stream of spectral soirees? But the thought that gave him most angst was whether it would have mattered that she was a believer – a thought all the more unsettling because it had never been a problem when it came to Beatrice.

On the fourth day of waking up with Catherine still in his thoughts, he decided enough was enough. He had to get real, he had to stop dreaming about something that would never happen. And so he swore to banish her from his thoughts and make a promise to himself to move on.

As he drifted through to the park, he wondered whether he should declare his new resolve to Sol and Tracy. But it turned out they had a bombshell of their own.

'But why now?' said Christian.

'Well, we're not getting any younger,' said Sol.

'Or older. So why rush into a decision?'

'We're not rushing it,' said Tracy, 'we've given it lots of thought.'

'That's right,' said Sol, 'Tray's thought long and hard about this.'

'I still don't get it. Forty years in a park, and now all of a sudden you're going to up sticks and go in search of this mythical gate?'

'There's nothing mythical about it,' said Tracy.

'No, Catherine told us so,' said Sol.

'Catherine? Of course, of course, so she put you up to this?'

'Yes,' said Sol.

'No,' said Tracy, 'okay, so maybe we got the idea from Cath, but we're doing this because we want to.'

'Yes, she was very clear on that,' said Sol.

'I don't believe it,' said Christian, 'just on her say so, you're going to leave, throw away everything you have here?'

'Well excuse me, but that's what you said we should do,' said Tracy. '"Get out and see the world," you said.'

'Well, yes, okay, but do it because you want to, not because someone tells you to.'

'You told us to, pal.'

'But that's completely different.'

'How?'

'Well I knew you wouldn't listen.'

'Well you were right there.'

'Why don't you come along?' asked Sol.

'Sol, he's not coming,' said Tracy.

'I'm not ready,' said Christian.

'See, he's not ready,' said Tracy, 'stop pushing him.'

'The world's bigger than the park, Christian,' said Sol.

'I bloody told you that,' said Christian.

'And they were wise words,' said Sol, nodding sagely.

'Anyway, two's company,' said Tracy, 'best if you stay here, pal, hold the fort.'

'Well, the offer's always open,' said Sol.

'No it's not,' said Tracy. 'To be absolutely clear,' he said, turning to Christian, 'the offer's not open. It's closed, padlocked and buried in a secret location, and always has been. Nothing personal, you understand.'

'I just think you're both making a big mistake,' said Christian.

'Well, only one way to find out,' said Tracy, 'we've made our minds up. So look after yourself, and we won't see you around.'

Christian didn't believe a word of it. He went along with it, of course, but he knew when he'd amble over to the benches the next day, they'd be sitting there. Some sort of delay, not a cancellation, of course, just a post-ponement. They'd still be adamant, but a few more days and the idea would be forgotten and they'd be back to the mystery of the missing leeks.

Even so, he found himself up earlier than usual the next day and wasted no time in getting over to the park. But he slowed and stopped as the sincerity of their intentions came into view.

He slowly made his way over and sat down on their empty bench.

Now the thick tower of Point Royal was not at his back, but looming large in front of him.

'Looks like it's just you and me then, boy,' he said, looking down at the liver as it examined a Snickers wrapper. 'We'll be fine ... we'll be fine.'

Chapter Forty-Seven

Gabriel was back in the Who Wants to Be a Millionaire room of the Grand Quiz Lounge. Edwin Northlock, the slight and serious former new boy who had been tasked with monitoring Harold, was again sitting across from him.

The archangel put down the pages and drew his clawfingertips together. 'And he was with them?'

Northlock gave a nod.

'Every time?'

'Every time,' said Northlock.

Gabriel turned away before hitting the host's plinth, almost knocking it over.

'I'm onto something big here, aren't I?' said Northlock.

'Possibly,' said the archangel.

'So what now? Are we going to move in?'

'Move in? Of course we're not going to move in, this isn't *T J Hooker*.'

'But–'

'You are onto something, Edwin, but this was never a something that would lead to a frastication.'

'Well then, with respect, why did you ask me to investigate?'

Gabriel picked up the pages and passed them through his clawhands, before sitting back in his chair. 'I needed to know. I just needed to know.'

'But we have the evidence, surely–'

'What did I teach you, Edwin? It's not a matter of evidence, it never is, it's a matter of context. Jesus and his entourage are always talking like this. If we acted every time something like this came along, well, no good would come of it, and we'd have total chaos ...'

Northlock sank back into his seat.

'... no, no, I have a feeling this will all blow over.'

'Well, whatever you say,' said Northlock. 'So for now, we'll just keep watching, keep building the picture?'

'Oh no,' said Gabriel, 'this investigation ends here.'

Chapter Forty-Eight

Dexter was sitting in Gordon's office, the ketone hangover of the fresh paint masking the last of the lavender. No pastels. No art. No breakout area. Now it was battleship-grey walls and back to black.

The man himself – now once again Lord Swan to all but the most inner of his inner circle – was standing imperious, his hair now trimmed, waxed and swept high and back, once again into an imposing full-Gekko.

'I thought this got dumped years ago,' said Dexter, eyeing the old swivel business throne, now once again installed behind the imposing desk.

'Merely stored,' said Gordon, eyebrows twitching, eyes wide and unblinking.

'Look, Gordo, are you–'

'So,' said Gordon, with a raised index finger, 'the results of round three then.'

Dexter paused. 'You really want them?'

'That's why you're here,' said Gordon.

Dexter referred to his notes and began reading through the long list of casualties. As he read, his mind began to ruminate over the speed and severity of recent events. Since Gordon's 'resurrection', as people were calling it, Gordon had embraced his old self with ever-increasing zeal. It had been little more than two weeks, yet already he'd enforced three purges – condemning en masse for long hair, earrings and beards, as well as filtering for other unacceptable traits such as homosexual tendencies or being female. These were dangerous developments. Not for what they were, but for where they came from and where they could lead.

'... thirteen hundred and twenty from level eight,' said Dexter, 'and, finally, three thousand one hundred and two from level nine.'

'Excellent. The service will be lean and mean, once again.'

'Well. Certainly lean.'

'Too damned right, especially after the next one.'

'Next one? Oh come on, Gordon.'

Gordon held up his hand. 'I'm still seeing salmon shirts, Dex, I'm seeing under-polished shoes, I'm seeing over-polished shoes. This is the moment to be strong, this is the moment not to flinch.'

'Well–'

'Save it, Dex. I've already signed the order.'

Dexter motioned to speak but in the end just shook his head.

'Now,' said Gordon, raising an index finger again, 'you know what I want next?'

Dexter put down his pen. 'Honestly, Gordo, I have no idea and that worries me.'

Gordon walked over to the hedgerow, showing the skyline over the financial district of Sydney. 'Special General Meeting.'

'What? Really? The annual is only, what, six weeks away.'

'Exactly. Last thing they'll expect. Shake things up a bit.'

'We've already shaken things up a bit,' said Dexter, 'we've shaken things up a lot.'

'Balls, man,' said Gordon, 'we're only just getting started, we're only just ... just ...'

There was a brief flare of flame in his nostrils, but it snuffed to a tiny puff of smoke as Gordon's eyes glazed and defocused as he appeared to stare out to an unknown point beyond the walls.

'Gordon?'

The Lord of Limbo's stance relaxed. His right hand rose gracefully to the back of his neck and he began to play with his hair.

Dexter rushed forward. 'Are you all right, Gordo?'

'Mmm ...' said Gordon, his head taking on a slight tilt.

Dexter took his boss by the shoulders. 'Gordon? Gordon?'

His boss half sang, half spoke, *'The end of the road, the final throw ...'*

Dexter looked Gordon in the eyes. He saw nothing but a relaxed wistfulness. But in a blink there was steel; there was focus.

'What are you doing, man?' asked Gordon.

'Sorry,' said Dexter, 'I thought …'

Gordon was now staring at Dexter's right ear. 'Is that a piercing hole?'

'What?'

'I might purge that,' said Gordon. 'Lobe holes. Think about it. Each an obvious Achilles heel, only a matter of time before you give in to weakness, before a stud pops back in. And then where are we? Hairbands and goatees, that's where.'

'Gordon. It's a chickenpox scar. And in any case, you can't afford to purge me too.'

A pause.

'You're right,' said Gordon, 'at least not today.' He gave a vulpine grin. He held it before winking and then extending his arm out towards the doors.

Dexter turned and began to make his way out.

'Special General Meeting, Dex. Set it up. Set it up for tomorrow.'

'Tomorrow?' said Dexter, turning back. 'Gordon that'll be very disrup–'

'To – fucking – morrow.'

Chapter Forty-Nine

An awareness without form. Without context or continuity. Just a staccato sense of something.

Nothing.

Something.

Nothing.

Something. Was this something the same as the first something? Had there even been a first something or was it imagined? What about before that? This something was different though – this something had melody.

My heart is broken.
And all is taken …

And this something stayed, there was recognition, there was scaffolding.

And you say let's go …
But under this skin …
The phoenix within …

And the something morphed into something else, something recognisable – herself.

I will rise ...

She was thinking. She was she again. She was back.

She tried to think back to the last thing she remembered. What had she been doing before now? A knife, a big one, in a strange place. The sauna? The living room? The car – yes, and, her chest – yes. With her right hand, she returned spatiality to her consciousness. Her body, or at least the top part of it. No knife, just chest. Good. So – mind, Macy McClane, arm, chest. What else? She tried to open her eyes, but her lids were having none of it. She touched her left forearm and traced a line up to her shoulder, neck and face. Something odd under her nose, *in* her nose – tubes. Not good – ghosts don't need tubes. She could feel something below her now, too, and became aware of her orientation, that she was lying on her back. A mattress.

No. No no no no.

How much time had she lost? It must be hours at least, perhaps days, even. Oh how stupid. How very stupid.

Her eyes felt heavier than ever.

Heavy.

Heavy.

Heavy.

Chapter Fifty

The next day seemed like Christian's longest since the long march from London. He forced himself to make a token effort towards conversation with the faces he recognised in the park, and on the streets, but having failed to follow up on Catherine's introductions, he knew they saw right through him, and so soon he retired to the bench and sat alone.

It didn't matter. He still had the liver, faithful as ever. But come the afternoon the organ seemed pensive. Gone was the carefree mingling with canines, the snuffling in the long grass, the spinning inanely on the spot. The liver was tense, portal vein pricked, and constantly stopping to turn and face north-east. Christian tried to settle him with a few laps of Point Royal, but it didn't seem interested. And as soon as Christian returned to the bench and sat down, it leaped up to him and hugged tight to his liver, as it had done during their kitchen armistice all those weeks ago. Though this time there was no kneading and prodding, no making itself comfortable, there was only a flat, calm embrace. Christian wasn't sure what was happening, but he knew this was not a hello. He gave it a pat and felt the organ lift to meet his hand.

For a few minutes, they did nothing more than enjoy each other's presence. But then, as Christian was thinking he was worrying over nothing, the organ was off, hopping down into the grass and speeding away from him.

Christian shot to his feet.

'What's the matter? Where are you going?'

About a hundred yards away, it stopped and turned. But after a brief wiggle of its portal vein, it turned back and made off across the park, its pace determined, its course straight as a javelin.

Christian briefly followed but soon stopped. He knew it wasn't coming back.

'Good luck, Leslie,' he said.

He watched until it disappeared from view.

He was alone.

Chapter Fifty-One

Thirty-five miles and a world away, the Princess was lost in a better place. A familiar world, even though she'd never bustled through its carpet-tiled corridors, networked around its manicured golf courses, or paid insufficient attention to its ornamental fountains. It was a home she'd never visited, yet knew one day she would, and when she did she would stay for ever. Yet this was no utopia. She saw the fading of the grandeur, the stagnating growth rates, the regurgitated outmoded paradigms. She saw the calcified King unable to see that his time had passed, that all could not be made good by tripling the level of reporting and extending the working day yet again.

But it had been a great land, and it would be great again. For today a phoenix would rise. The King had seen sense. Finally, tragically, stumbling aside to make way, to make way. A queen, *the* Queen, a new age, a new corporate philosophy.

The coronation crowds would cheer her on. *Tear down these cubes!* And she would. She would sweep them aside for bright open-plan spaces in crisp secondary colours. And much more besides.

So many thoughts and possibilities had passed through her head as she sat in her dressing room, the excitement and emotion overcoming protocol as she'd confided radical matrix management theories with her chambermaids, showing a quite immodest degree of familiarity.

And then there she goes again, the junior chambermaid, wanting to know whether the senior chambermaid is going to replace the microwave oven. Who cares? It's the day of the coronation. And yet the junior chambermaid persists, she's getting quite tetchy about it. The oven still works, but you can turn it on with the door open – a clear breach of palace health and safety guidelines. The senior chambermaid stands her ground, saying they don't have money to throw about willy-nilly. She'd missed the point here, surely, thought Nikki. The Queen can buy a new microwave. The Queen can buy microwaves for all!

And then she became aware of voices, or rather she became aware that the voices she'd been listening to had changed their tone, moved from inside her head to about four metres to her left, and were now talking about microwaves more than ever. *Microwave ovens* – it was a strange development, because Nikki knew, with absolute certainty, that the palace did not have microwave ovens. The incongruity took root and began to sprout and branch – she noticed how clinically clean the chambers smelled; she sensed discomfort in her nose and a tightness in her chest; she realised her eyes were closed. And then the palace melted away as she slid back to reality.

'So the oven still works then?'

'Well, yes, but that's not the point.'

'I think it's exactly the point. You want me to spend money we don't have on a new working microwave, to replace the old working microwave.'

'But it's not safe.'

'Does it heat your food?'

'That's not the point.'

'Yes or no, Sarah, does it heat your food?'

'Well, yes, but–'

'No buts. It heats your food, therefore we don't need a new one.'

'But, Karen, come on, they're only thirty quid at Argos.'

'Thirty quid? This is the NHS, Sarah. We don't have that kind of money sloshing around, and besides, it's thirty quid more than the other option.'

'Which is?'

'You spend five minutes printing a notice to stick above the microwave, warning people not to use it with the door open, and adding a note to the health and safety file.'

'But it's no longer idiot-proof.'

'It doesn't need to be. We're trained medical professionals, Sarah, we don't employ idiots.'

'What about Jodie?'

'With the exception of Jodie.'

'So can we get a new–'

'No. Tell Jodie yourself. Be clear, make sure she understands. Everyone else can just read the sign.'

As far as Nikki could tell, the nurses hadn't realised she was awake and could hear every word.

To have regained something approaching full consciousness undetected was unusual. But then the expectations of the doctors and nurses, the prescribed drug dosage, and the configuration of monitoring equipment were all tuned towards people who were 100% human, because, apart from the odd advertising executive, 100% human was the type of person they tended to have in for treatment.

Nikki continued to drift in and out of consciousness as she desperately tried to regain her faculties.

Despite the boardroom taking up the entire top floor of Henry Ford House, it was standing room only for most at the Special General Meeting. Gordon had everyone there – his most trusted advisors, all executive and non-executive board members, every section head, plus the top tiers of Central Administration. And over at the doors, Tokugawa and his security service cronies, with enough staff outside to arrest the whole room should Gordon be in the mood. And Dexter knew he might be. But then so did everyone. During his eighteen-year pink period, few had ever followed him into mascara and experimental hosiery; however, many at the top had taken advantage of the softer culture in less overt ways, principally polo necks, sports jackets and chinos. At one point there had even been a grass-roots dress-down last-Friday-of-the-year movement. But not any more. Only the incongruous figure of Spitback, the fallen angel, had resisted the scrambled return to conformity. For that, if nothing else, Dexter acknowledged a grudging respect. But then it was classic Spitback: The Pigeon, as he was also known, had more staying power than a vindaloo stain. There, posed for an imagined mirror, chest out like a peacock in burgundy satin angelwear-cut suit and black opal accessories, sat a creature who had promised heaven and delivered nothing. And yet, despite everything Dexter had achieved, bullshit still had mileage in Limbo. Did Spitback know Dexter saw through him? That was what always rankled.

For everyone else, once more it was dark suits, cream shirts and blue ties; top buttons done, single Windsors all round. Many now had even left rings and necklaces at home. And they were wise to do so. The purges had been so thorough Dexter was beginning to wonder how they'd backfill all the vacancies. Several in the room had already been promoted twice that week, and some of those had been in Limbo itself little more than a year. So what was about to happen would, in time, be regarded by many as something of a blessing.

The meeting had been going well enough, Gordon having announced a fifth purge under the working title 'Impediments, Stammers and Twitches', but then Dexter began to notice a change in Gordon's seating position. His previously stair-rod straight back had developed a gentle concave curve; he'd edged his position on the seat forward to a front perch with backward-thrusting buttocks. His head, too, had now taken on a slight tilt to the left.

'Are you all right?' mouthed Dexter, silently.

Gordon nodded, before starting to play with his hair.

Dexter looked across to Spitback and Grímsson, but neither made eye contact. Fucking typical.

'So we are in agreement then?' asked Janssen, the head of internal affairs.

Everyone nodded. A few voiced an over-alpha 'yes' before looking to Gordon for approval.

'Lord Swan?' said Janssen.

Gordon smiled. He licked his lips. 'You know what, gentlemen,' said Gordon, 'I feel gooooooooooood.'

Silence.

Most of those sitting at the long black table remained composed, though some swapped nervous glances. Those standing mostly shifted their weight or began studying the ceiling.

'I think we could all do with a break,' said Dexter, 'shall we take five?'

'Five? Why yes, that's a fabulous idea,' said Gordon. 'I could, perhaps, slip into something ...' He took his pen and brought it to his lips.

Janssen held up his hand. 'If we could just make the fast run through these last items,' he said.

Gordon sat back and carefully, teasingly, crossed one leg over the other. 'No, Willem,' he said, 'it's breaky-break time. Because, I think we're all far too stiff in these buttoned-up collars, aren't we?' He flicked the clasp on one of his braces, sending it twanging back over his shoulder.

'Gordon,' said Dexter.

'Dexter,' said Gordon.

Dexter leaned in. 'You remember when you said if there was ever a reoccurrence, of ...'

'I don't care what I said, I–'

'But Gordon–'

'But nothing,' boomed Gordon, his nostrils sparking flame and embers like a red-hot brazier.

A brief but thick silence.

'I don't ... care what I said. Because. *Because* ... I want my panties.'

Nikki was awake. This time her change in state had been sudden, an adrenaline-fuelled instant snap. She had clarity, a return of absolute focus and purpose. She opened her eyes. Ceiling tiles, pink and silver balloon oscillating with the air-con. She looked lower. The bed, hand sanitiser on the rail at her feet. Chair, table, a large window to her left, more stacked chairs, doorway and an empty bed to her right.

Voices outside the room.

She shut her eyes. She lay still.

Use the time. Plan A? Yes. It was viable – risky, but viable. Any other options? Any better options?

Sanitiser? No.

Balloon? Helium. Long shot.

The voices died away. She opened her eyes again. The window – that could work, if she was high enough, but then she saw the security locks and no sign of a key. Okay, what else. Table, chairs – useless. Side table with cards, fruit, CD player – CD player with about three rolls of gaffer tape wrapped around the loading mechanism and a handwritten label saying 'DO NOT CHANGE'. Monitoring equipment, lots of it, drip and paraphernalia behind her – plugged into her. Nothing obvious, nothing easy. What about the fruit? Maybe that could work. Grape up each nostril. Banana down the throat? Unlikely – she'd never quite got the knack.

Movement in her peripheral vision. She snapped her eyes shut and again lay still. She listened to the person approach, decoding their soft steps, tracking them around the room. Her heart was racing, its beat surely visible to the naked eye. The steps moved to the right, then stopped. A cupboard opened then closed, then silence. More steps, closer this time, coming right up to the bed. Then silence again. They had to be standing right there, right next to her. Had they seen something? Had they noticed something on the monitors? Surely it would now be just dumb luck whether the person would glance at the right screen. One double take and the game would be up. She'd heard the conversations ... *deliberate self-harm*. What would follow? Closer observation? Sedation? Restraint? A padded cell? Did they still have those? Her only chance would be to act now, to finish it before they realised.

Still the person lingered.

Nikki focused on steadying her breath, resisting the burning urge to breathe more deeply. And then the steps again, moving away and out of the room.

She opened her eyes and breathed more freely again, filling her lungs. There was pain, and not just from restraining her breathing. But it didn't matter. Soon none of this would matter. She took in the scene again. A final check for other options. Nothing – no convenient wall-mounted racks of scalpels, no multiple preloaded morphine syringes. Plan A it was then. She knew it was close, having heard it from her bed more than once. She'd only need a minute or so, she reckoned, then it would all be over.

She winced as she pulled the tubes from her nose and the drip line from her wrist. She shuffled towards the edge of the bed and in doing so realised, with a sense of invasion and revulsion, there was something else to remove. She gave the catheter a sharp tug. An instant searing burn doubled her over and forced her eyes tight shut. She clenched her teeth – she couldn't afford to make a sound, let alone scream. No choice but to hold it in and swallow it down to her stomach. Such pain, and yet the thing wasn't out. No time, no time. She took a few deep breaths and gripped the tube again, this time tight with both hands. She gritted her teeth.

One, two, three.

She pulled as hard as she could. A wall of pain passed through her as the device gave up its grip. She doubled over again and buried her head in the pillow. It was just pain. It was just sensation. It didn't matter. Soon nothing would matter. She had to get a grip and focus.

She swung her legs round. She tried to stand, but fell hard to the lino, knees impacting first, then elbows and ribs, but again she sucked in the pain, her only concern whether anyone had heard. She lay there motionless as she listened for approaching footsteps. But there was only silence.

She pushed down on the pain and crawled forward, the weakness in her legs now apparent.

It took her almost a minute to get across the floor, but she was getting her strength back and now had a view out into the corridor. She could see an open doorway into a side room opposite, a small kitchen or break room, perhaps. She edged farther forward, and, once at the door, struggled to her feet, bracing against the frame. She looked across into the room – tables, chairs, noticeboard, and, hurrah, there it was, complete with sticky-taped warning notice. She shuffled a pace forward and leaned out, just enough to get a line of sight down the corridor. It was clear. She held her breath and stumbled across into the little kitchen. As she crossed, she glanced down to the far end of the ward, to what appeared to be the reception area, spotting a man at the desk. Oh shit, oh shit, had he seen? Quick, quick, quick, no time, no time.

She hobbled over to the microwave, opened the door and hit the power button. Nothing.

Fuck. Fuck.

Then she spotted the timer dial. She gave it a twist and the old beast came to life with a familiar light-industrial whir. The light was on, the plinth was rotating. She took a couple of quick breaths and thrust her head inside. How long? How long to cook a head?

Chapter Fifty-Two

Mitch checked the bedside clock – three thirteen p.m. – and again noticed his fingers drumming out the same beat on the back of the book, his copy of *Terry's Field Guide To the Afterlife*.

He got out of the bed and drifted over to the window. He checked the garden. It looked exactly as it had at two thirty. Exactly as it had all week.

He turned, stretched and surveyed the bedroom. Clothes strewn on the carpet, a pair of knickers hedging the lip of the linen basket, unwashed mugs on the bedside table.

He took another glance at the garden and returned to bed.

The first few days had been tolerable enough – proper rest had been a godsend after the marathon journey, and he'd enjoyed watching Beatrice in the shower, as well as in the bath, as well as getting undressed, getting dressed, or just making cups of tea. And he'd enjoyed sleeping in her too, but it was hardly filling his days. He'd already collated, sorted and updated all his forms and loose pages. He'd already gone through what remained of his kit and equipment. He'd already twice repeated his search of the local area for his headgear and the other missing items, now given up for lost. Trawling the other houses on the estate for voyeuristic entertainment didn't make much of a difference either. Sure, he was spoiled for choice for an hour each weekday morning, but what about the rest of the day? Who takes a bath during office hours? And of those who do, how many are female, svelte and under sixty?

All he was doing now was waiting. But what else could he do? He couldn't go to the death site, because he didn't know where it was, and if he strayed too far out of Vestments, he might miss Hotswap returning with news and replacement kit. He'd thought about leaving a note, but concluded it would be too hit and miss – where could he leave one that Hotswap would find but a shepherd would not? Damn it all to hell. He just had to suck it up and wait.

And all the while, the temptation of the book. He never had trouble leaving the back section buckled when he had a mission in hand, when he was busy. But with nothing but the prospect of an endless line of empty hours to pass, punctuated only by occasional voyeuristic distractions, it had become unbearable. Forbidden knowledge – the original temptation, the juiciest of apples, right there in front of him, right there in his lap. And the only thing protecting himself from himself was his belief that it was forbidden for a good reason. And this was the real act of faith, because though he had some theories, he didn't actually know what that good reason was. The knowledge was so dangerous, so potent, that knowledge of the reason why it was so dangerous was dangerous in itself … apparently … probably … possibly.

He clenched his fists.

He stretched his fingers.

He cracked his knuckles.

But temptation lingered.

He released the clasp and opened the book to the bound back section, then gently ran his finger along the leather strap, sensing both its softness and its strength. He paused at the buckle, before tracing out its brass box perimeter, then up and over the prong that penetrated the hole. He allowed himself to contemplate what lay inside. Pages and pages of secrets: dangerous, deadly, and almost certainly very cool and very sexy. He gripped the free end of the strap, eased it back through the retaining loop, and pushed it halfway through the frame of the buckle. He slipped his finger under and pulled gently, the strap coming through the frame with only token resistance. It was half open. He gripped the strap and tugged it firmly back on itself, forcing it to yield to still higher tension. The prong came free. He eased it aside and released the tension on the strap, allowing it to pass through the buckle, before pulling it free. All was now laid bare. All he had to do was turn the page.

Chapter Fifty-Three

'So she's awake then?' said Shadblot, as he approached the bed. 'Or then again not?'

'We've sedated her,' said Holt, the duty doctor.

'Why for heaven's sake? I thought we'd only just got her conscious again?'

'Well she–'

'Psychotic episode,' said the sister.

'She just went mental,' added Jodie.

'... following self-inflicted radiation exposure,' added Holt.

'Radiation? How on earth did she get down to X-ray?' asked Shadblot.

'She didn't, she microwaved 'er 'ed,' said Jodie.

'What? Don't be ridiculous,' said Shadblot. He turned back to Holt. 'Tell me what happened?'

'She's right,' said Holt, 'that is what happened.'

Shadblot turned to the sister.

'It was the one in the kitchenette, John,' she said, 'you know, with the dodgy door?'

'Oh ... oh yes ... dear, dear.'

'D'ya think it'll make the Christmas party top ten?' asked Jodie.

'Quiet, Jodie,' said the sister.

'Won't win though,' said Jodie, 'that bloke who'd been riding his bike with no saddle, he's gonna win for sure.'

'*Jodie.*'

'I was just sayin'.'

Shadblot cleared his throat and turned to Holt. 'And your assessment is?'

'She's a little red in the cheeks, but no signs of trauma.'

'Right, good. And when did this happen then, this microwaving?'

'About forty minutes ago,' said Holt.

'And how long did she have her head in there?'

Holt looked to the sister.

'Well, we, er–'

'Be about three minutes, wouldn't it,' said Jodie.

'On what basis?' asked Shadblot.

'We 'eard it go ping,' said Jodie.

'And?'

'Well, that's how long you cook your stuff for, innit? Bung it in, three mins, ping.'

'I'm sorry,' said Shadblot, 'are you telling me she was able to complete a full cooking cycle?'

'Well we don't know for sure, John,' said the sister.

'I don't see how that's possible,' said Shadblot, 'I don't see how she could survive.'

'It, um, seems it was set to defrost,' said Holt.

'Defrost? Oh right, well I suppose that would make a difference. Probably got away with just a light brain warming. Good, good, lucky escape then, it seems. Wouldn't have been a pretty way to go, eh?'

'Go where?' asked Jodie.

'To die, Jodie,' whispered the sister.

'What, you think she was trying to kill herself?' asked Jodie.

'Of course,' said Shadblot, turning to the young nurse, 'what possible other reason would someone have for putting their head into a microwave oven?'

'Maybe she was trying to dry her hair?'

'Can we please be serious, Jodie,' said the sister.

'I am. My flatmate Bev tried it once, she was in a rush y'see, but we couldn't get ours to come on with the door open.'

'Jodie …'

'I was just sayin–'

'Enough,' said the sister.

'Dr Shadblot,' said Holt, 'do you, um, do you think she'll make a complaint?'

'Possibly,' said Shadblot, 'but I think, on balance, not. Anyway, let's keep a close eye on her, yes? And perhaps some restraints while I see if we can't rustle up a psych evaluation.'

'So are we going to get a new microwave?' asked Jodie.

'Not now, Jodie ...'

'But are we?'

'Yes,' said the sister.

'Can I take the old one home then?'

'You know what, Jodie, I'm going to give that serious consideration.'

Chapter Fifty-Four

Come the evening, Mitch was slumped in the armchair in the living room, continuing his descent into the seventh circle of boredom. But at least Beatrice was proving to be an able companion and guide in this grey land, helping to keep his head above the rising waters. Though the nature of her malaise was different, its derivation yielded the same despair and lethargy, now their common bond.

And the black-dog TV backdrop to the water-treading was making its own substantial contribution to the gloom: the grand final of some godforsaken talent show, and somehow the producers would have to find a way to shoehorn it all into a mere two hours of solid bronze middle-of-the-seat television. Mitch didn't fancy his chances of going the distance. It was only twenty minutes in and already he was wishing he could still harm himself. He sank back into the chair, merging with it. Its arms were his arms; its back was his back. He looked down at the book sitting innocently on his lap, its strap wide open once again, the pages laid bare, the exotica of the second section but one turn away. He'd managed to resist the forbidden fruit thus far, but his resolve was cracking and he knew it. He'd taken the foreplay to its limit. Consummation was all that remained, and it had taken all of what little discipline he possessed to resist. Now he was running on empty. Where the hell was Hotswap? No doubt dropped in on the London zonal club scene before heading back upstairs, the flaky little fairy.

He slammed the book shut and held it up in front of him, clamping it between his hands.

Would it be okay to see a little? Surely there was some leeway, first offence and that.

He put the book down on his lap again, allowing it to fall open. He took a tentative glance. It had opened at the beginning of the second section. He closed the book and opened it again, and again it fell open in the same place. Of course it was always going to open there, after all this time clamped down, and yet it was as if it was teasing him, flaunting itself in front of him.

Mitch took the whole second section in his left hand, and raising his right hand to block his vision, he riffled the pages. He listened to the sound of each one release off his thumb. He stopped halfway and laid the pages flat. With his right hand still blocking his view, he placed his left hand on the forbidden text. What was the ink under his hand saying? What could really be so bad as to be too dangerous to know? He eased the fingers of his right hand apart just a crack, a series of pinholes allowing him blurry access to the clean white of the page. A micron further and he'd be able to perceive the text.

His fingers twitched. He felt them begin to open.

And then he caught sight of a blue-green glow in the darkness outside the window. He froze. But then he carefully sank himself further into the seat, so he disappeared from view altogether. He focused on the glow. It was a person – a man at the window, peering in. It was the man from the photos on the mantelpiece, the face now pasty and sheepish, but it was him, his target, the cargo, it was the real Christian Bootstrap!

Part Three

Salivation

Chapter One

It was now late April. Birdsong and bluebells filled the churchyard. Two weeks had passed since Tracy and Sol, and then the liver, had left, two weeks since Christian had even tried to hold a conversation with anyone who could offer a reply. Occasional awkward nods to Fat Larry, all unreturned, were now his only connection to the ethereal world, as he increasingly spent more time in the cinema and now every evening back at Beatrice's. Life had become a broadcast, the position of the camera his only influence. Yet Christian wasn't suffering. His morning terrors were gone and he was sleeping soundly through the night once more – Erdygrot was still there, as ever, but now back to being an extra, or off stage altogether, skulking in the wings.

And Christian had become less preoccupied about quite when reality would return, now he'd found a workable routine. He'd start his days much as before, in the quiet of the vicarage, but now he'd managed to reintegrate TV into his day – various islands of predictable pensioners in the houses close to the church providing vital stepping stones of *Frasier*, *Sky News* and *Bargain Hunt* to get him through to early afternoon. Then the drift through the shopping centre in time for the first proper film of the day. In the evening he'd drift on over to the house, steering clear of the park these days, preferring the anonymous streets instead.

And his path to reconciliation with Beatrice had been less winding than he'd expected. He'd still not forgiven her for the destruction of the book, but had found a way forward by acquitting her on the grounds of grief-induced temporary insanity. Even so, he never slept over at the house, preferring instead to depart when she went to bed, and drift back to the vicarage – these days blasé about his blue-green glow – to hopefully catch *Newsnight* or a late film with Tony. Christian liked it this way – he got to spend time with Beatrice, yet retained his independence. In fact, it had begun to dawn on him that his new life was working out far better than he could have imagined. Death, it seemed, was underrated. For starters, the day-to-day aspects of his relationship with Beatrice had improved no end. She no longer complained about him not listening; he no longer had to pretend to listen. He was able to rant on about the growing proportion of air time devoted to ever more empty reality TV and the associated decline in quality drama; she never got frustrated or angry that he'd made her miss whether it was Billy-Bob or Zorbar who'd won double immunity. They never fought; they never argued. And that they never had sex any more was no longer a source of tension.

There was of course one tiny niggle – Beatrice wasn't actually aware she was still in a relationship. This did trouble Christian, at times, but not enough to stop him coming over. There's no such thing as a perfect situation, he told himself, and besides, he knew other couples with far bigger problems who stayed together, so why shouldn't he and Beatrice?

His newfound stability had also given him the mental space to reflect on other positive aspects of being separate from the messy complications of mortal life – there were no money worries any more, no mortgage contributions, no credit card bills, no expensive presents to buy for other people's weddings, and no crappy job needed to pay for it all. And, based on the evidence, it seemed unlikely he'd now get any older or fatter. He'd never go bald. He'd never go grey. Best of all, he no longer heard so much as a peep from that nagging all-pervasive voice inside his head: *Life is short. Come on, it's a nice day, let's go outside. A couple of hours jogging, then later we can get stuck into those Italian courses, repaint the kitchen, make a start on that tax return, and then relax with a few chapters of* War and Peace.

Carpe Diem. That insatiable lofty ideal had been jabbing at Christian's shoulder throughout his life, always clear, always audible, yet always that fraction weaker than: *Sure, right after* The Simpsons.

But now, Carpe Diem was no more. It had died with honour though, not to mention a fair degree of plain old pig-headed stupidity. Remaining true to its blind idealistic character, and despite its lamentable track record, it had still backed itself when Procrastination turned up for the latest scrap with a new friend in tow: the towering muscle-rippled booming bellow of Eternity. Carpe Diem had stood its ground, looking to defend from the off, dig deep and go the distance for a gritty points victory, only to have its head blown clean off by Eternity's Smith & Wesson Model 29 before there was even a shake of hands. As the pimp of Procrastination, Eternity is omnipotent, invincible and it plays dirty.

Of course there were negatives, too. Christian could no longer eat, touch things properly, remove his clothes to have sex, have sex, or even have sex with himself. He couldn't talk to the living. He couldn't play video games. He couldn't watch his *Star Trek Next Gen* box set – at least not in a way that was entertaining.

Some things, though, were just as they were. He still felt a lift when it was a sunny day; he still liked to lie in in the mornings; he still liked to keep up with news, current affairs and sport. And, most of all, within himself, he was still he. Reality had changed around him, his body had changed around him, but he was still Christian Joshua Bootstrap.

But what surprised him more than anything was that though most things were as they were, or as they were but from a different point of view, a few of them were now an awful lot bigger. That the earth would one day be engulfed by the sun now seemed a bit more relevant; of some concern, too, was the broader issue of the eventual heat death of the universe. But what weighed on him now more than ever was when England would win another World Cup. This had been a troubling enough prospect when he was alive, projecting forward a few multiples of four, but in the context of eternity it took on an altogether more disturbing dimension. In fact, this one scenario seemed to Christian to embody the all-enveloping malevolence of eternity far more chillingly than any rational attempt to internalise its meaning and implications. He pictured the dreadful suicidal songs he may one day have to witness, the once optimistic 'Three Lions' crushed to a funeral march, thirty thousand years of hurt, Jules Rimet *still* gleaming. The terrifying nuclear winter cloud of despair that would descend on the country every four years, each time that little bit worse than before, 1966 that little bit further away, the situation that little bit more hopeless.

However, these remained rare wobbles – like most of the newly dead, Christian had spent the vast majority of his existence in a mortal context, and thus found eternity hard to grasp even when he thought about it really hard, which in turn offered its own protection, at least in the short term. The shield of naivety, the cloak of ignorance. And so, in the main, Christian was able to put these disturbing thoughts to the back of his mind and enjoy his afternoons at the cinema relatively unencumbered.

There was one other problem Christian could not ignore though, because it was manifest in his day-to-day life: in the last couple of weeks, he'd started seeing things, or rather he'd started seeing something. On several occasions now, out of the corner of his eye, he'd glimpsed a figure lurking in the shadows. That he might be being watched was bad enough, but the nature of what appeared to be doing the watching made it all the more disturbing. This figure, this thing, had a palpable eeriness about it, something not at all right, something terrifyingly wrong in an old-school Mary Shelley, Edgar Allan Poe, Scooby-Doo kind of way. And though he'd now encountered the apparition several times, he remained unable to put his finger on quite why it was so chilling. This was partly due to its tendency to quickly disappear from view, but mainly it was because the reptilian reflex part of Christian's ethereal mind always made an early executive decision to look away the moment the thing entered his peripheral vision, and his ethereal visual cortex and unconscious conspired to then deny having seen anything much in the first place, creating a cover-up of governmental proportions. Christian was left knowing only that he'd seen something, something bad, and that it was probably not in his interests to ask any more questions. And so the terror was born of what might be, which, of course, has always been far worse than what is.

Christian had first experienced the apparition in the churchyard on his way back from the cinema. Afterwards, shaken, all he was certain of was that it carried an unmistakable blue-green glow. It had made him wonder whether Sol had had good reason for his fear of g-words. Though the jagged edge of terror was blunted, somewhat, when next Christian spotted the creature squatting behind the recycling bins at Sainsbury's in the cheery light of a warm Thursday afternoon.

As usual, Christian tried to rationalise it out. He couldn't use the Scrooge defence, cheese and underdone potato now sadly beyond him, but he could still remind himself of his overactive imagination, having had a solid history of it getting him into trouble in the past, like the time he momentarily converted to a devotee of the paranormal while watching the bonus materials on his *Ghostbusters* twentieth-anniversary edition DVD. It also occurred to him that this supernatural stalker would be a good fit for the Professor Collier defence, it being possible evidence that Christian's entire present reality existed only in his own mind. Though he didn't relish the implication that the dream could at any point begin to crack, crumble and become a nightmare. Especially as he still had no idea how to get out of it.

Chapter Two

Nikki had been in her new surroundings for a week now, and her own private purgatory for a lot longer. Four days after her attempt to break one of the last remaining catering taboos, she had been deemed fit enough to be moved to a different hospital, only this one had swipe-card security, twenty-four-seven CCTV, and a noticeable absence of anything pointy. After successive suicide attempts, the sectioning had been as straightforward as it gets. Kevin had readily accepted the role of nearest relative and was in strong agreement. Furthermore, despite the fully-funded option to move Nikki to the New Horizons private clinic in Highgate, Kevin decided staying within the bosom of the NHS would be 'far more up her street'.

The King George Unit was not actually an NHS facility, but a private concern taking advantage of NHS trusts in difficult circumstances. It was a depressing place, but not quite as bad as it had been. Though still retaining an air of the iron curtain, it had benefitted from a recent renovation. Gone was the tired, matted, old dandelion yellow, swept aside with shiny new dandelion yellow. Furthermore, the television could now receive BBC Four, and the ward now had a jigsaw with nearly the required number of pieces.

Nikki was sitting on her bed, staring into space. Most of her fellow patients spent much of their days doing the same, though some chose to stare at the walls instead, especially recently, what with all the new paint. Nikki wasn't sure if all the staring time afforded by those running the unit was part of the treatment or just another symptom of inadequate funding. Either way, it was the only thing she had going for her at the moment – the time to think, to plan, to find a way out. Except she wasn't thinking and planning and finding a way out, she was beating herself up, once again, over botching the two previous attempts to kill herself. She knew she had to let it go and focus on the present and the immediate future, but time and again she couldn't resist going back to pick over the bones. Her first attempt, in particular, hung heavy on her mind. Why hadn't she researched suicide first? An hour or two online would have been all she'd have needed to come up with something fool-proof. *Failing to plan is planning to fail* – all the worse because that had been one of her mantras for her team at iChemiclast.

And her if-only demons got bigger still when she contemplated the full consequences. She'd been in the coma for nineteen days, so she'd been told, and a further ten days had now passed – a month, give or take. A month since Christian had died. What of him now? How would he have handled 'the change'? Would he still be hanging around in London? Would he have gone back to Bracknell, or somewhere else? He could be anywhere. Worst of all, she knew it was possible hostile forces had already found him. After all, his death had been no accident. Hope was fading.

She tried to snap out of it. She couldn't change what's done. She had to focus on now. What was she doing *now*?

She looked around the ward. She still couldn't believe this was her present reality – banged up with a bunch of nutcases, and not even her kind of nutcase. The ward was long and wide, with a high ceiling that looked like it would play havoc with the heating bills. Apart from the nurses' office-cum-watchtower, near the entrance, it was open plan, though each bed sat in its own shallow alcove against the wall. The only segregation in evidence was by sex, women on the left wall, men on the right, like a bed-bound teenage disco. So those with personality disorders rubbed shoulders with bipolar sufferers who rubbed shoulders with paranoid schizophrenics. It was a heady brew and changing all the time. New patients could be admitted at any hour, in any condition; it was commonplace for arrivals to be bleeding, handcuffed, in distress, or all of the above. The undercurrent of unpredictable violence would be a constant concern to most patients, but it had been an early source of hope for Nikki. If she could just place herself in the wrong place at the wrong time, she'd thought, or just annoy the right patient in the right way, it might be enough. But this initial burst of optimism had soon given way to a more balanced assessment: yes, she could probably get herself injured easily enough, but getting herself killed seemed like a stretch. The whole place was geared up to prevent harm, or at least enough of it for anyone to die from – ward veteran Milos said it always generated too much paperwork.

There was the hope of eventual release, of course – they couldn't keep her locked up for ever. And she'd resolved to project calm, reflective sanity to maximise those chances. But getting out this way was still her worst-case scenario – she just didn't have the time. There were other reasons for playing it cool, though, principally less chance of increased meds and less chance of increased supervision.

If she couldn't kill herself inside, and couldn't wait for release outside, her only option was escape. So she'd turned her attention to the routine, which is what the King George, like all institutions, ran on. With enough observation, she would find and exploit a weakness in the system. All fine in *Ocean's Eleven*, but here on the ward it had been heavy going. She'd understood the routine easily enough: breakfast and drugs; laying on of hands; lunch and drugs; afternoon sermon; dinner and drugs; sleep/screaming; repeat. These were processes, just like in business. She should have been able to find a chink in the armour by now, but she had nothing. Maybe it was the drugs? Nikki, so she was told, was on diazepam, with the occasional clorazepate chaser – a popular choice, so it seemed, from comparing notes with her fellow patients; Kendo was on the same, as was Milos, as were two of the Jesuses.

But then maybe she was just losing her edge.

No. Not now. Not after getting so close. There would be a way.

Chapter Three

Monday. And just as Christian thought he was getting a grip on his new life – with the possible exception of his fears about the wraith that was stalking him – he started to feel it slip through his fingers. Beatrice hadn't come home the previous night. Rationally, he'd decided it was nothing to worry about, probably just a relapse, struck down by another wave of grief. She'd have gone to Charlotte's for vodka and sympathy, had a few too many and stayed over. Still, he didn't sleep well at the vicarage that night, and this morning he'd broken with routine to go straight over to the house. He was relieved to find her there, safe and sound, but surprised that she was singing in the shower. Actually *singing*. And then there was the shock of the new hairstyle – her first since the infamous 'Sarah Palin' of 2008. She was now a dirty-blonde and her trusty bob had been buzzed back at the sides and blended to short rough swirls on top, creating a sort of Marilyn Monroe-after-three-weeks-at-Guantanamo look.

His poor girl.

Had she asked Lottie to have a hack at it? Or was it the conclusion of a hairdresser's vendetta?

She eventually left for work: late (she was never late) and unstressed (she was never unstressed, even when she wasn't late).

As usual, Christian didn't like being in the house on his own, so once she'd left, he began his usual rounds of TV-trawling and tried to forget about these developments.

.   .   .

Someone else had taken note of Beatrice's absence, though, and her new haircut, her return early that morning, her singing in the shower, her casual approach to workplace punctuality. And much more besides. And the someone wasn't surprised like Christian was. For them, this was the confirmation they needed, the underbelly exposed. It was time.

When evening came, Christian decided not to go back to the house, instead staying at the cinema for another film, despite having seen most of what was on offer four times already, and it was late when he returned to the vicarage. The lights were out, but Tony hadn't closed the living room curtains, so at least Christian had the orange rays of the sodium street lights to partially illuminate the room.

He wasn't ready to sleep, so stood a while at the window. He looked out onto the churchyard, at the graves, many of the inscriptions now known to him. His eyes rested on Catherine's grave – now with headstone – and then at his own. The burden and the privilege of living within sight of his earthly remains.

'Hey there, friend,' called a voice from the back of the room.

Christian spun round to see the cat sitting on the top of its scratch pole and looking his way.

'Welby?'

'Who's Welby?'

'You can hear me?'

'Well sure I can hear you.'

A talking cat. American, too. A … talking … cat.

Welby jumped down from the pole and wandered over. Christian flinched as he approached.

'Anyway, how ya doing?' said the voice, still at the back of the room.

'Tony?' said Christian, now peering past the cat.

'Who's Tony?'

'The vicar.'

'He a dead vicar?'

'No. At least he wasn't this morning,' said Christian.

'I guess I'm not Tony then, ay,' said the voice.

'Who are you then?' asked Christian, edging to the middle of the room. 'What are you doing here?'

'Mitch Langford, at your service. Just passing through.' A chuckle. 'Passing through? Get it?'

'In the middle of the night?'

'Ah it's only ten thirty, hardly middle of the night.'

'Well, it's still late.'

'Well yeah, I guess. Sometimes the day kinda gets away from you, ay? Anyway, I thought I could bunk down here for the night, if that's good with you?'

'Here? Look, I'm sorry but this isn't a hotel, it's a … vicarage.'

'So?'

'So vicars only.'

'Are you a vicar then?'

'Maybe.'

'You don't look like a vicar.'

'I'm a guest of a vicar.'

'Well … good for you, good for you. Look, I'm only after a place to sleep, I'll be no trouble.'

'No, I'm sorry, it's out of the question.'

'But it's late, you said so yourself. You're not gonna kick me out into the night, are you?'

'I'm sorry, but yes I am. I don't know you from Adam.'

'Well get to know me then.'

'What, now?'

'Yeah, why not?'

'Because I'm tired, and because … look, can you please come out where I can see you?'

'That wouldn't be constructive.'

'Why not?'

'Just trust me on this one.'

Christian paused. 'Okay, so let me recap,' he said. 'You want to spend the night here, where I live, even though you're not a vicar or a guest of a vicar, and I've only just met you, at ten thirty at night. You ask me to trust you, yet you won't even come out of … where exactly are you hiding?' Christian took a step towards the wall, towards the voice.

'I will come out, just not yet.'

'Why? What are you hiding?' said Christian, moving closer.

'Look, can't we just shoot the breeze a while first?'

'No. We can't.'

'Why?'

'Because it would be weird. I don't want to chat to men I don't know late at night in shady spaces. This isn't a cruising zone, you know.'

'Hey, no, you got me all wrong. It's nothing fruity, straight up. I just don't want to freak you out, that's all.'

'And why would I be freaked out?'

'Well, I look kinda unusual.'

'You've nothing to worry about there,' said Christian. 'The things I've seen recently, well, you can't imagine.' He was now only a few paces from the wall.

'Hey now, just stop right there, buddy.'

The voice seemed to be coming from the crucifix on the wall. Yet not for one moment did Christian believe he was being addressed by the son of God. One thing he knew for sure was that the son of God wasn't an American.

'Come on,' said Christian, 'you can hardly expect me to let you stay here if I can't even see you.'

'You're not ready.'

'This is ridiculous. Come out.' Christian was now at the wall.

'Really, buddy, not a good idea.'

'Now,' demanded Christian. He stretched out a hand towards the crucifix.

'All right, all right,' said the voice.

'Come on then.'

'I said all right. Now you promise me you won't freak out?'

'Yes, I won't freak out. Now can we please get on with this.'

'Back up a few steps there.'

'Oh come on.'

'Back up and I'll come out.'

'Okay,' said Christian and he obliged.

'Right. Here I come.' Glowing hands and arms emerged from the wall, palms up and held low.

Christian backed up another step, almost stumbling over himself.

'Easy there, fella,' said the voice. The hands rotated for Christian's approval. 'See, nothing funny here,' said the voice, 'just a regular guy.'

Aside from the blue-green glow, and that they were emerging from a solid wall, the hands and arms looked normal. Eight fingers; two thumbs. Ring. Wristwatch. Suit. Good suit.

The arms retreated as a leg emerged, suit-trousered and booted. It showcased itself, articulating in the usual places, before it too retreated.

'Doing fine so far?'

'Well of course. I have seen other people like me, you know.'

'Not like me, I'll wager.'

'Look can we get on with this?'

'Okay. Now don't freak out.'

The figure began to emerge from the wall.

'So what is it then?' said Christian. 'Some really tasteless tie? Eternal bad hair day, or a wig, maybe? I can't imagine what could be so bad that you had to hide yourself in brickwork, and I'm not someone who gets shocked easily. It's like when Derek Wilkie chopped off the top of his finger in home economics, some of the other kids threw up, but not me, I gave him some Fruit Pastilles and went to fetch Mrs Troughton, I was totally fine, I was *eeeeeeaarrgggghhhh*.'

Christian fled the vicarage in terror, exiting through the front wall and setting a drift speed personal best in the process. This time there was no getting away from accepting what he'd seen.

No head. Just empty space from the neck up. It had *no head*. But it had spoken to him. They had chatted. It had been relatively pleasant.

No head. No head. No head. *No head*.

As he reached the edge of the churchyard, he glanced back, only to see the headless figure of Mitch Langford just metres behind and gaining. Christian tried and failed to find a higher gear. His pursuer sped past, stopped and turned to face Christian.

'Hey,' said the empty space above Mitch's shoulders.

Christian doubled back towards the vicarage. Mitch sped past again, and again blocked Christian's path. Again Christian turned, and again Mitch blocked.

'Hey, calm down, buddy, I don't mean you any harm. See, I knew you'd freak out.'

There was no escape. His only option was enthusiastic cowering. The place he chose to do it was behind the gravestone of Mrs Betty Margaret Wilson – 1855 to 1948 'Step softly, a dream lies buried here.'

He thought back to his fight with Hargreaves, considering whether to take this thing on, but decided little of that experience could be applied here. Head punches would be useless for a start.

'Are you the headless horseman?' asked Christian.

'The headless horseman?' said Mitch. 'The headless horseman is American.'

'You're not American?' said Christian, quivering.

'I'm Canadian,' snapped Mitch, 'why does everyone here always think I'm a damned Yank?'

'Well, um, limited exposure to the Canadian accent, combined with a tendency for Canadian actors and musicians to work in America and therefore be mistaken for Americans.'

Mitch paused, chuckled a little, and sat down next to Christian. 'Yeah, I reckon that's about right, ay.'

'Please don't take my head,' said Christian.

'Look, I'm not the headless horseman, okay?'

'Are you a modern version of the headless horseman?'

'What, the headless limo driver?'

'Um ...'

'No, I'm not the headless limo driver, I'm not the headless bus driver. I'm not the headless anything. Well, I am headless, but that's it. Just headless.'

'Please don't hurt me.'

'Look, buddy, I'm not going to hurt you. Just 'cos a guy has no head, it doesn't mean he's someone who goes around hurting people. I'm a regular guy, okay, just like you, I just happen not to have a head, okay?'

'And you really don't want mine?'

'No, I don't,' said Mitch, 'anyways, it doesn't work like that. The only head I can have is my own. I just have to wait for it to arrive.'

Christian pondered this but couldn't come up with a single plausible circumstance where a man's head would say to his body, 'you go on ahead, I'll catch you up.'

'Did it get lost?' he said.

'No. Look, I don't have a head, because I died. My body died, but my head didn't. Until my head dies over there, I have no head over here, okay?'

'Okay. Yes, I understand,' said Christian, not understanding and not daring to lift his eyes away from the acorns on the ground in front of him that he was now surveying so intently.

'You can look, buddy, it's okay.'

'Um, yes, sorry.'

'Really, it's totally fine.'

Christian snatched a glance, but the vision was too disturbing. Not having a head was worth a double take on a mannequin, but in something animated, something alive, it was terrifying.

'I won't just now,' he said, 'if it's all the same with you.'

'Well, please yourself. No big deal, I'm quite used to it.'

'I'm sorry. Just I thought you didn't like people staring. So this is me, not staring.'

'Well, no, I guess I don't like people staring. But I don't recall telling you that?'

'I meant you as in people like you, I mean, um ...'

'Ah. You mean freaks? Freaks like me?'

'No, no, not at all, it's just, I can never remember the right terms, er, cranially challenged? No. Cranially absent? Absent-minded?'

'I'm gonna let those go, buddy, but I'd say "people like me" dislike people overtly not looking just as much as the folks who can't stop.'

'Yes, of course, sorry,' said Christian. He forced a glance while trying his utmost to disguise the revulsion his face seemed so intent on expressing. 'And what did you say your name was?'

'Mitch. Mitch Langford.'

'Oh, yes,' said Christian, returning his focus to the safety of the acorns.

'You know, in case you hadn't worked it out, the customs of introduction are pretty much the same in the afterlife, buddy. I'm Mitch Langford, so you now follow with ...'

'Sorry, again ... Christian Bootstrap,' said Christian.

'There you see? Nice and civil, ay. Good to meet you, Christian.'

Christian calmed a little, but stayed crouched low and close to the gravestone, his feet well inside the ground above what remained of Mrs Wilson. 'How can I be hearing you when you've got no head?' he said, unsure if he was challenging Mitch, the fabric of the universe, or his own sanity.

'Oh come on, you telling me you've still not worked this stuff out? Despite your friend with the feet?'

'You know Fat Larry?'

'No, but I've seen you two passing the time o'day.'

'I think I've seen you too,' said Christian, 'are you the thing that's been following me?'

'Following you? No. Why would I wanna do that? And do you mind not referring to me as a "thing". I'm a person, you know, a person with a name, and feelings and everything.'

'Yes, sorry ... Mitch,' said Christian, embarrassed at having to apologise yet again, but relieved at remembering the thing's name, 'but it is you, isn't it? I've seen you hiding in the bushes at the park, here at the church, in that lingerie window display in town, and wasn't it you inside the popcorn machine at the Picture House?'

'Look, I hate to burst your bubble, fella, but it's not all about you. You think I get to stroll around in the park without a care in the world when I look like this?'

'Well don't you? If you're a ghost, what does it matter?'

'Seems you don't know much about people,' said Mitch, his tone hardening. 'Listen, buddy, they don't change. Not when they're alive, not when they're dead. If they're not staring in shock, or pretending you're invisible, they're treating you like you're street theatre, they're calling their buddies over, "Hey, Chuck, get a load of this guy," then they're hitting you with the same dumb questions, and you can't get away till you answer, "Yeah, that's right, I don't have a head. No, it doesn't mean I'm evil. No, I didn't die in the French Revolution, do you think they had suits like this in the French Revolution?"'

'Oh, oh yes, I see ...'

'And that's just for starters, then it's, "Yeah, I can still see and hear and talk, as should now be plain. Yeah, I do miss being able to wear hats. Yeah, you'd think it's lucky I didn't need to wear glasses, but turns out it makes no difference."'

'Jeez, that must get you down.'

'Well ...' He took a pause. 'I'm used to it, but it doesn't get any less frustrating.'

'You've really not been stalking me?'

'No, buddy, I've not been stalking you.' Mitch stood. 'Look, d'ya mind if we head back inside? Like I say, I don't enjoy being out in the open.'

'Oh, yes, yes of course.'

Christian got up. As they drifted back towards the vicarage, he felt a rising sense of guilt. His visitor was disabled, and not a little bit, but really quite a lot. Christian had always hated himself for not being totally and utterly comfortable with disability, berating himself for anything forced or conscious in his reaction, or lack of reaction, to anyone who looked or acted a bit different, but that was nothing compared with what he'd done now. He'd screamed and run away, treated this poor man like a monster.

But Christian had little time to digest his guilt before it was joined by a huge side serving of awkwardness. What to say? What do you say to a new headless acquaintance, an acquaintance you have insulted in a deep and inexcusable way, as you drift back towards the residence you just refused him refuge in, the sort of residence no one should be refused refuge in?

'So, um, well, what brings a Canadian to Bracknell then?'

'This place,' said Mitch, nodding to the church, getting no reaction and then pointing to the church.

'So what, you're an overseas vicar or something?'

'Me? No, not my thing. No, I'm on a tour, you see. Researching the family history, finding out where I came from. And well, the churches still have all the records.'

They returned to the front room of the vicarage, this time via the front door and the hallway.

They chatted on for a while, and Christian found his remaining concerns at the idea of Mitch staying over begin to ease. Body language was a bit limited, the man not having a head, but he seemed genuine enough. And even if Christian still didn't have his measure, what was the worst that could happen? It wasn't like he could make off with the silver.

Chapter Four

Unlike general wards, the patients in the King George Unit ate their meals communally, in the Rothko room – a large multipurpose common room across from the ward. Once again, Nikki was unsure whether this was part of the treatment or just another cost-saving measure.

'Why the wrists every time?' asked Nikki, looking at Vivian's bandages. 'You've not thought about trying pills or a rope or something?'

Vivian was the youngest on the ward, waiflike, with straggly pink hair and sharp features. She flicked a nervy glance but said nothing.

Nikki tapped her teeth with the plastic runcible spoon before trying again to butter her toast. A prohibition on metal was fair enough, she thought, but to have no knives at all, not even child-safe plastic ones, was demeaning.

'It's just that, if it's your fifth time,' she continued, 'well, doesn't that say the wrists aren't working for you, that they're not your thing?'

Vivian bent her head lower and kept her focus on her cornflakes.

'I'm interested, you see,' said Nikki.

'Don't want to talk about it,' said Vivian, to her cornflakes.

'No tips? Tricks of the trade?'

No response.

'Come on, you must be an expert by now. I bet you could, even in here … I bet you'd know how to do it right, and be sure, if you really wanted to?'

Vivian took her bowl of cornflakes in her hands and shook her head.

'Or perhaps it's too hard, even for you,' said Nikki holding up her runcible spoon, 'perhaps it's–'

Vivian tipped up the bowl over Nikki's head. Whoops and cheers followed.

'Go away,' shouted Vivian, 'go away, *Nigella*, go away, go away, go away.'

Everyone was watching.

Nikki sat there as trails of milk ran down her back and clods of sodden cornflakes dropped onto her shoulders.

A nurse walked over. Nikki made an attempt to stand but was met with a hand on her shoulder.

'Finish your breakfast, Mrs Tooting.'

The daily laying on of hands was soon under way. They always started before people finished eating. Nikki assumed this was so they could catch a lot of troubled souls all in one place before people started to drift off outside for a smoke or return to their beds for the mid-morning stare.

Wee Jesus and Barry Jesus did at least look the part, even if Wee Jesus was on the short side. Barry was pale with shallow features and looked to be in his late thirties. Wee was at least ten years older, with darker skin and a strong chin. Both had long hair and trimmed beards, and the shoe-less white-pyjama *Messiah at breakfast* look worked a treat, despite it being standard issue for all the unit's patients, not just its living deities.

'You are healed, my son,' said Wee Jesus, and he removed his palm from the patient's forehead.

'Now you are healed, my son,' said Barry Jesus, following on and applying his hand to the same patient.

'I've just done that one,' said Wee Jesus.

'Well now I've done him,' said Barry Jesus, rolling his eyes to the patient.

'But you don't have the gift,' said Wee Jesus.

'No, *you* don't have the gift,' said Barry Jesus, and he brushed past up the line.

'Now you're healed,' whispered Wee Jesus, as he laid his hand on the same patient, yet again.

'Stop it, stop healing me,' said the patient, 'I can't t-take the pressure.'

'Yes, sorry about the extra one,' said Wee Jesus, pointing to his rival, 'only he doesn't wash his hands.' He scurried after Barry Jesus. 'Look, I'm serious, you don't have the gift, but I forgive you for your false representation, you know no better. Now go in peace, my son.'

'Don't you "my son" me, my son,' said Barry Jesus, stopping and turning, 'you fucking go in peace, you're buggering up my healing.'

It was the same every morning. The practice wasn't officially mandated, at least Nikki assumed it wasn't, but then again there didn't seem to be any great willingness to intervene, either. Some of the patients recoiled or rebuffed the attention with an insult, but most seemed content to let the Jesuses get on with it, be it through apathy, bewilderment, compassion, or a genuine eagerness to finally be receiving some sort of treatment, however alternative.

By now the theological skirmish had mutated into a physical one, duty to their flock forgotten as they handbagged each other for undisputed ward dominion. But they stopped, mid-grapple, when they realised Autumn Jesus – older, slower, balder, fatter – had the other end of the room to himself and was doing brisk trade. They hurried over.

'You are healed.'

'No. Now you are healed.'

'No ... *now* you're healed.'

'Look, if she gets better, that was down to me.'

'No it wasn't.'

'You're both wrong, I healed her, she's mine.'

'Mine.'

'*Mine.*'

Chapter Five

Christian woke early, having not slept well, but found Mitch already up, sitting at the kitchen table going through some papers. Christian barely registered that his guest was holding the pages in his hands, because that particular observation was some way down the pecking order. Top of the order was that a headless man was sitting at the kitchen table. It had seemed okay last night, eventually. But not now.

'S-so … so you're a morning person then?' said Christian.

'Ah, good morning, sir,' said Mitch as he collected his papers and tucked them away, 'yup, always have been.'

'That. That …' said Christian. He stopped and tried again. 'Is that your family history stuff then?'

There was a pause. 'Sure is,' said Mitch, 'can't do it justice without taking on a lot of paperwork.'

'This. This is probably a silly question, but how do you look at the records?'

'I thought we covered this last night,' said Mitch. 'Just 'cos I don't have a head, doesn't mean I can't see.'

'No, I mean how do you get at the information in the church, the parish registers, when you can't hold them, when you can't open them up and turn the pages?'

'That's a good question,' said Mitch, smiling an unseen smile, 'well, I just have to be patient.'

'What, you mean you just ... wait?'

'Yep.'

'You wait for someone else, someone living, to come to the church and request access to the parish records, and then just hope they're interested in the same page of the same ledger that you're interested in?'

'Yes,' said Mitch, after a pause, 'that's exactly what I'm saying.'

'Jeez. There's patience, and then there's patience.'

'You better believe it. Tower of Hanoi has nothing on this.'

'No, no I suppose not.' Christian fished around in his mind for what came next, it only now dawning on him just how many of the morning hospitality protocols become redundant once you and your guests are dead. There was no tea, coffee, orange juice or toast – or need for tea, coffee, orange juice or toast – and so nothing with which to bridge to bath or showers and getting dressed, themselves now absent and redundant and so removing the subsequent bridge to a second tea or coffee, itself a vehicle for the slightly awkward conversation about when the guest would be leaving. This last stage was still perfectly viable of course. There seemed no reason why two ghosts couldn't have a slightly awkward conversation about when the one without a head would be leaving, but it didn't seem polite to launch straight into it. But Christian didn't know what else to do. It wasn't like Tony was going to get rid of him – he'd have him stay all week. So in the end Christian came right out with it. Sort of.

'So I assume you'll be keen to get back to the records then?'

'Normally, yeah, but maybe not today. Gets pretty slow midweek.'

'Right ...'

'And sometimes it's good to take a break.'

'Yes ...'

'Not good to spend too much time on your own.'

'No ...'

'So how 'bout we hang out?'

'What? Um ...' Christian wasn't in the mood for hanging out, especially with someone who had a name for it and felt comfortable asking other men if they would like to do it. Why did Americans, and now Canadians, it seemed, have to manufacture unnecessary awkwardness by giving things a name which are better off without one?

'Well, I, er, I have plans,' said Christian.

'Oh yeah? What ya up to?'

'Oh this and that, you know.'

'No, I don't,' said Mitch, 'I'm interested. Tell me.'

'Boring stuff. Going out for walks.'

'Yeah, of course. Good to get out of the house, good to get some exercise, ay? Sounds good to me.'

'Right, well, anyway it was nice to meet you.'

'No, I mean I'll come along.'

'Oh. Right.'

Chapter Six

It was late morning. Nikki was sitting on the visitor's chair in Kendo's room, twisting her hair around her fingers, auto-piloting through what had become a regular session of draughts and relatively sane conversation.

Kendo (Ken to everyone else) was the only patient who had his own room. This wasn't for his benefit, or the result of some private health plan, but because he'd been deemed a security risk. In his eyes, he'd done nothing to deserve this familiar label, but as usual he took it in his stride – old enough and wise enough to have long since stopped expecting people to see past their first impression. People judged others by what they saw on the surface. And people didn't like his surface. They didn't like its bald head or its tattoos; they didn't like its piercing stare or the way it liked to relax by cracking its knuckles; they didn't like the way it was the size of a static caravan. *They* saw what *they* wanted to see. His model behaviour, placid nature and impeccable manners since using a sarcastic afroed orderly as a toilet brush had to cut no ice. 'But that's the nature of prejudice,' Kendo would say, 'it's not rational, so why fight it?' Not that he was complaining. The TV in his room had always been able to get BBC Four.

And he'd taken an immediate liking to Nikki, though she had no idea why.

'Call me Kendo, girl,' he'd said, on their first meeting. No one called him Kendo, not any more.

Nikki had found herself drawn to him too, though the reasons why had changed over the days. Unfortunately, it turned out he was quite a bit less homicidal than he'd first appeared, once you got to know him. Now she just enjoyed his company, which was quite unusual for Nikki, though her original motivation for getting within grasping range was never far from the surface.

'Kendo ...'

'Yeah.'

'I ...'

'You're not going to ask me again, are you?'

Nikki said nothing.

'You were, weren't you?' He laughed. 'You crack me up, girl.'

'It's not a joke.'

His eyes returned to the draughts board. 'Still your move,' he said.

'I'm deadly serious.'

He looked up from the game and made eye contact.

He was the first to look away. He chortled and shook his head. 'How do you do it, girl, that poker face, like you really mean it.'

'But I do.'

He laughed.

She didn't.

There was a brief silence. 'I like you, girl, I really do. I like you making me chuckle, but you shouldn't make fun of me ... The docs, I expect them to patronise me, but not you.'

'I can't win, can I? I'm not playing games here. What can I do to make you see I'm not joking?'

'Maybe we should drop it then, 'cos I couldn't do that, even if you wanted me to. What do you take me for?'

She looked down. 'I know it's a dreadful thing to ask, but it's something I need, more than anything.'

He shook his head.

She said nothing.

Another silence. 'But, I would say this, girl. If I was up for it, I'd do it nice and clean, quick-smart and clean as a whistle.' He stood and walked round behind her. 'I'd take your lovely head' – he placed his huge hands either side of Nikki's skull, like it was a child's football – 'and I'd ...'

She felt an increase in the pressure of his grip. She closed her eyes and held her breath.

'… twist and snap.'

He held on for a moment before removing his hands.

Nikki exhaled and opened her eyes.

'You wouldn't feel a thing, girl,' he said, returning to his seat, grinning.

Chapter Seven

Christian had found himself back in the park for the first time in weeks. As he sat in the bench, he felt like a fraud – the stranger in his own town, thankful, so far, at not having seen anyone he recognised. Though if any dead observers were drifting through the park, Christian would have made for a sad sight, another ghost driven mad by taking too many long hard looks at eternity – with afterlife technology centuries away from cassette tape players, let alone Bluetooth headsets, there was no other explanation for the sight of an ethereal grown man talking to himself.

'So you're not going?' said Mitch, from the middle of the holly bush.

'No,' said Christian.

'May I ask why?'

'I don't see any reason to. I'm happy enough marking time here for now. Besides, the summer blockbusters will be out soon.'

'No other reason?'

'Just the obvious – it's an old wives' tale.'

'So, a non-believer, ay?'

'I prefer sceptical.'

'Well, it's not just hearsay, you know, there is evidence.'

'Oh yes?'

'It is written,' said Mitch, with reverence.

'Written where?' said Christian. 'Apart from on a promotional pamphlet?'

A pause.

'It's still written.'

'Seriously,' said Christian, turning to the holly bush, 'that's the best you've got? The welcome-to-death leaflet?'

'That's just the start,' said Mitch, 'the main reason I believe is the best reason of all. My own observations.'

'What, so you've actually seen this gate, have you?'

'Maybe.'

'I thought as much.'

'I've seen its effects. The mark it's made on the Zone. You could see them too, if you bothered to open your eyes, my friend.'

'Go on.'

'You really wanna know?'

'Try me.'

'Okay,' said Mitch, 'you've been dead, what, three weeks? Four weeks, tops.'

'I, er, well, yes, I suppose it is about four weeks, I think. How did you know?'

'It's in your behaviour. Anyone can see it. You're a newbie. Mentally you're still in the land of the living.'

'Well. It's been a big shock.'

'Yeah, yeah, yeah, now, tell me, how many other ghosts have you met so far?'

'I'm not sure, ten, a dozen, maybe.'

'And most died in recent times, yeah?'

'No, I wouldn't say that at all. I met two of them who died more than forty years ago.'

'That's exactly what I mean, buddy. Your head's still in a mortal mindset.'

'Meaning?'

'Meaning over here, eighteen hundred is recent, so forty years back is like last week.'

'Oh, right,' said Christian.

'So ...'

'So what?'

'So ain't that strange, all the ghosts being recent arrivals?' said Mitch. 'Where are the ghosts of the ancient Brits?' Mitch thrust his arms out from the holly bush. 'Where's all the dead Roman legions? Where's the folks from Shakespeare's time?'

Christian thought about it but had nothing to say in reply.

'It's the Gate,' said Mitch, 'has to be. Eventually everyone goes through, y'see.'

'That's conjecture. There could be other explanations.'

'Such as?'

'Well, maybe you die. When you reach a hundred say?'

'Ghosts dying? Come on …'

'Well that was just off the top of my head. No offence.'

'None taken,' said Mitch, wearily.

'Well,' said Christian, 'maybe they've … gone on holiday?'

'On holiday?'

'Or emigrated.'

'Oh come on, buddy.'

'Hear me out. Maybe they've got bored here and gone to the Bahamas, or Costa Rica maybe, or maybe they've gone to see Machu Picchu.'

'What, all of them?'

'It could happen.'

'I don't think so, my friend.'

'All right,' said Christian, 'let's say you're right. Let's say there are no older ghosts here because they all went through this gate. It still doesn't explain why. Why would everyone go through? You haven't gone through.'

'True, but I'm sure I will, someday.'

'Even though you have no idea what's on the other side? You have no idea what you'd be drifting into, good, bad or ugly?'

'My friend, it's *because* people have no idea what's on the other side. That's the kicker, y'see. Curiosity and eternity equals inevitability. Sooner or later, everyone has to go take a look.'

'Well, that could make sense, I suppose,' said Christian.

'That's it? I lay my grand theory on you and that's all I get?'

'Well what do you want?'

'How about a little amazement, a little stunned awe at the revelation.'

'Woo,' said Christian, half waving his arms.

Mitch didn't reply.

In the afternoon they headed out of Bracknell and went for a drift along the grass verge of the A329M. It was a noisy and soulless setting, but it made for a much reduced chance of running into other ghosts, meaning Mitch was more comfortable with being out in plain sight.

It took Christian back to his lowest ebb on the long march out of London. It wasn't this piece of anonymous motorway, but it might as well have been. Still, having company made it easier to put it to the back of his mind.

'Mitch, could I ask you something?'

'Sure.'

'It's about your head.'

'Okay,' said Mitch, after a pause.

'Tell me if it's not appropriate.'

'No, it's fine,' said Mitch, after a pause only slightly shorter than the previous one.

'Okay, you said you died, but your head didn't.'

'Yup.'

'I don't get it. How's that possible? How can a head stay alive without a body?'

'I never said my head was alive. I said it wasn't dead.'

'Right, right,' said Christian, 'I'm no doctor, but doesn't *not dead* equal *alive*?'

'There are some grey areas.'

'Really?'

'Cryonics, my friend.'

'What's that, artificial tears or something? Like they gave Steve Austin?'

'No. Cryonics is freezing people after death.'

'Oh, you mean cryogenics?'

'No, I mean cryonics.'

'Oh, okay. But wow, wait a minute, that's what happened then, you got frozen?'

'Well my head did. Cheaper you see.'

'Jeez. So they cut off your head? Or should that be cut off your body ...'

'They got no choice, that's how it works.'

'So ... so, what did they do with your body?'

'Well what d'ya think they did with it, had it stuffed and mounted? They cremated it.'

'Right, yes of course, of course.'

They walked a few paces in silence.

'So was there a funeral then?' asked Christian.

'There was kind of half a funeral.'

'What, just for your body?'

Mitch laughed. 'No, I mean some of my friends and family believed in the power of cryonics, like me, so they didn't think I'd died. And the rest pretty much didn't, so they thought I did.'

'And what about your estate, your money?'

'It's all in trust for when I wake up.'

'Oh.'

'Yeah,' said Mitch, with an unseen smile, 'kind of a bummer for my beneficiaries, ay.'

As they drifted on, Christian tried not to stare at the ragged flesh at the top of Mitch's neck. He thought it poor the cryonics people hadn't made a neater job of it, given the presumably significant costs involved, and wondered if Mitch had ever felt like asking for his money back, or at least requesting a cut-price trim. And to leave it open and uncovered, that didn't seem right at all. Couldn't they have topped it off with something? If only to keep the rain out. It wouldn't have been expensive – the plastic lid from an 800 g tub of McDooley's Gold Roast would have done the job just fine. And they could have had a coffee afterwards.

Christian took another short look, and then another longer look. Soon he was staring, but it was hard not to – from soles to shoulders, Christian was an inch shorter than Mitch, but the circumstantial height advantage of having a head meant Christian towered over his new acquaintance. So it was hard not to peer into the neck cavity now and again, especially as he'd always thought it civil to look at someone when you're talking to them. He tried to tell himself to keep eye contact instead, but it was a near-impossible task, his subject having no eyes to keep contact with.

'So ... and say if you mind me asking,' said Christian, 'what's it actually like, not having your head?'

'Ahh, look, I'm not sure you wanna get into that,' said Mitch. 'I've had a long time to get used to it, but trust me, you wouldn't want to be in my shoes ... People's judgements, reactions. Truth is, mostly people just stare ...'

'Honestly, some people,' said Christian, glancing away.

'... and then like I said last night, there's the ones who ask all the dumb questions, but sometimes it's worse.'

'Worse?'

'You bet. I've had plenty of abuse off strangers, they even get violent sometimes, it's the same wherever I go.'

'How on earth do you cope?'

'Well it's way worse when I'm exposed, like now. See, normally I have a helmet.'

'What, to protect you from the violence?'

'Course not, I've got nothing to protect. No, I have it for cover, for disguise.'

'And it works?'

'Pretty much. Still get lots of looks. A ghost with a full face helmet is still pretty weird, but not as weird as having no head, ay.'

'Yes, yes I suppose so,' said Christian. 'But presumably you find yourself forgetting about it, at least, when you're on your own?'

'No, I don't. See I can always feel it, it never ever goes away. That's the kicker.'

'What, so it's more like it's invisible then, rather than not there at all?'

'No, that's not what I mean. It most definitely is not on my shoulders … here, look.'

Mitch stopped and grabbed Christian's hand.

'What are you doing?'

'It's okay, I'm not going to freak you out, just trust me for a second.' He took Christian's hand and passed it six inches above his neck, from one side to the other. 'You feel anything?'

Christian shook his head.

'There you go then,' said Mitch, releasing Christian's hand.

'But you said you can feel it?' said Christian.

'I can. Okay, now this *may* freak you out. I can feel it, but not here. I feel it where it lies, where it is now, way over the Atlantic, over at Cyber.'

'What?'

'It doesn't feel like a head, it's more like a weight on a fishing line. A sort of constant tug. I can feel it now. I can always feel it.'

'All right, yes, that is freaking me out.'

'Well imagine how I feel, buddy. So now you see. Now you see I can never really forget about it.'

They drifted on.

'All right, my turn,' said Mitch, 'you're not a believer, ay?'

'We've discussed this.'

'Not the Gate, your living arrangements. You're a non-believer but you live with a priest. Now I heard of believers going to churches when they die, 'cos I guess that's where they think they need to be, but what's your story? You reckon you backed the wrong horse? You tryin' to get with the programme?'

'Not at all.'

'So why a church then?'

'Well, I didn't choose it,' said Christian, 'I ended up there through circumstance. But it's worked out all right. It feels safe, it's calm. Tony's easy company, well, apart from the Ronnie Corbett impressions.'

'Who's Ronnie Corbett?'

'It doesn't matter.'

'So why aren't you living at your old place then?'

'I'm sort of working back to it, possibly. But I don't feel ready just yet. There was, well, there was an incident. Several, actually.'

'Really?'

'It's … well … it's not felt like my home recently.' There was a contraction in Christian's stomach as he spoke the words aloud.

'And where is it?' asked Mitch.

'It's here, in Bracknell.'

'Right. Down on, what's it called, Ringpriest?'

'I'm sorry? How …'

'Vestments, ay?'

Christian stopped. 'How do you know that?'

Mitch stopped a stride ahead. 'I saw you over there. Bunch of times.'

'And what were you doing there?'

'Often ask myself the same question. Reckon I've walked every street in this town.'

'Again, why?'

'Like I said, it's a slow business with those records, and this place has a lot of churches.'

'Oh yes. Right.'

'That your girl then? The one at number twenty-two, yes?'

'What …' said Christian, slowly.

'Nice,' said Mitch, 'real shame.'

'What's a shame?'

'Well, you being dead 'n all.'

'Well … yes.'

'Sweet girl though.'

'Meaning?'

'Meaning sweet girl,' said Mitch, 'classy …'

Christian waited. It felt like further elaboration was coming, but Mitch just stood there. What Christian couldn't know was that the pause was being filled by Mitch sticking out his non-tongue and flicked it around, lapping and salivating like he was a sex-starved pervert, an action which came quite naturally. This was one of Mitch's small pleasures, a tiny gossamer-thin silver lining in the cloud of having no head.

'... oh yeah,' said Mitch, 'real classy.'

On reaching signs for the M4, they decided to turn and retrace their steps. On the return journey, Christian noticed there had been a change in Mitch's neck muscles, a persistent twist, a certain tension, but failed to realise that this was because Mitch's non-head was turned towards him, studying every aspect of him.

'Buddy, could I make an observation?' asked Mitch.

'Um, okay.'

'Don't you think it's time to move on with your afterlife?'

'Excuse me?'

'Living at the church, your old life, looking in on your girl. Don't you think it's time to let it all go?'

'I'm sorry, but that's none of your business.'

'Only trying to help.'

'Well don't.'

'Easier for a stranger to see things, and say things as they are, ay.'

'Oh is that right?'

'And you gotta remember, I've seen all this before, lots of times. I know you don't want to hear this, and that's okay, that's totally normal.'

'Normal? What does normal have to do with anything around here?'

'It's not possible, you know. The thing you want most of all. Just not possible.'

Christian stopped and faced Mitch, looking him square in the space above his neck. 'Okay then, what do I want? You tell me. What do I want?'

'You want to contact your girl, tell her you're still here, get back with her.'

Christian moved off again, quickening his pace. Mitch matched him stride for stride.

'Don't you think you maybe need to let her move on?'

'No,' said Christian, with force, 'we can be happy, I know we can. We will be happy.'

'All right, well, has it crossed your mind that maybe she thinks it's time to move on?'

'No. It hasn't. Look, you don't know her, you only met me yesterday. So keep your ... just keep out of my business.'

They continued in silence.

They still hadn't exchanged a word by the time they reached St Cuthbert's Secondary Modern, a mile or two from the church. The light of day had begun to fade and the more determined stars were beginning to assert themselves. One in particular caught Mitch's eye. It was brighter than the others, dead ahead, low to the horizon, and almost as soon as he'd noticed it, it began to descend and had soon disappeared from view below the Bracknell skyline.

'Did you see that?' asked Christian, stopping and staring out to the horizon.

'What?' said Mitch.

'A shooting star.'

'No.'

'You must have, it was right in front of us.'

'Nope. Ah well, there you go.'

'It seemed to slow down.'

'Really? Amazing. Anyway, what about a treat?'

'I'm sorry?'

'A treat. You know, by way of an apology.'

'What do you have in mind?'

'Well,' said Mitch, 'take a look over there.' Mitch gestured towards the school.

'And?' said Christian.

'And what do you see?' said Mitch.

'A school.'

'And ...'

'And a hockey game.'

'And playing in the hockey game?'

'School girls.'

'Oh yeah, that's what I'm talking about.'

'So ... ?'

'So, they'll be finished soon, and then it'll be' – Mitch clicked his fingers – 'shower time.'

'Oh no ... you're not serious?'

'Come off it, you can't tell me you don't do a bit of looky-looky?'

'No, I don't.'

'Straight up?'

'Straight up.'

'Not even once?'

'Not even once.'

'Well I'll be.'

'And you have, I suppose?'

'Whenever I get the chance,' said Mitch. 'I may be dead but I'm still a dude.'

'How, how can you be so brazen about it?'

'I got nothing to hide. Bitta beaver's the only thing that keeps me going some days.'

'But they're young girls, Mitch.'

'Come off it, they're high-schoolers, gotta be what, seventeen, eighteen?'

Christian raised his eyebrows.

'Don't look at me like that,' said Mitch, 'it's not like I hang around the elementaries.'

'They're still innocent girls,' said Christian. 'It's not right to take advantage.'

'Innocent? You're the innocent one if you think they're sweet little virgin angels. You should hear the things they come out with. Not like it was in my day, I can tell you. And anyway, whatever innocence they do have is all nice and safe, how can it not be? They have no idea I'm there, they have no way of ever knowing.'

'Well. It's still not right.'

'Why?'

'It's just not. What about our self-respect? What about what going to watch would do to us, psychologically?'

'It doesn't do anything to us. I've been doing it all my death, what harm has it done me?' Mitch wiggled his non-tongue in the direction of the school.

'Look,' said Christian, 'maybe we should be getting back.'

Mitch laughed. 'Come off it, who are you kidding? Admit it, you want a front-row seat just as much as me.'

'No, Mitch, I don't.'

'Well, you be a monk if you like, but the afterlife is for living, my friend, and I'm not going to pass this one up.' Mitch turned and headed into the school.

'Well I don't want any part of it,' said Christian, standing still.

'Fine, fine, see you later then,' said Mitch, without looking back.

Christian resumed his drift.

The diversion had worked perfectly. Mitch was pretty sure Christian would be too uptight to be up for perving on the girls, or at least too much of a hypocrite to admit it.

Once he was sure Christian was gone, he raced over to Beatrice's house.

He drifted through the front door and found almost but not quite what he was expecting, sitting on the stairs, idly swinging its legs back and forth through the carpet and staircase.

'Who are you?' asked Mitch.

'Ah, Mr Langford, I presume?' said the slight figure, jumping up and overextending a gloved false hand.

'I said who are you.'

'Dwheeblebridge, sir, at your service.'

'How do you know who I am?'

'Hotswap said you'd be the one without a head,' said Dwheeblebridge, chuckling.

'Where's Hotswap?'

'He couldn't make it.'

Mitch looked young Dwheeblebridge up and down. Short, even for an angel; ink-black side-parted hair with rogue rear tuft standing to attention; huge false moustache; spotless black leather trench coat, so long in the torso and arms he looked like he'd suffered a double amputation at the knees.

'Suppose they told you you'd grow into it?' said Mitch.

'I'm sorry?'

'First assignment, son?'

'No way, that was eleven days ago!'

'Really? That long. Well that's a relief, I'd hate for Hots to have sent me someone inexperienced.'

'Oh no, I'm very experienced. I've been–'

'Good for you, son, good for you. Now you got something for me?'

'I sure do, sir. Hotswap asked me to give you this.' The angel retrieved a small wicker waste paper basket from within the stairs.

'What's this?'

'Your new bin, Mr Langford.'

'It's ... a fuckin' bin.'

'Yes,' said Dwheeblebridge, 'and a particularly nice example. Nanny has one in the same style, lovely detailing with the gold cherubim on the lavender edging, contrasting with the wicker.'

Mitch snatched the bin. 'It hasn't got any eyeholes.'

'Eyeholes?'

'To see through.'

'Why would anyone want to see through a bin?' said Dwheeblebridge, with a snorty chortle.

'Because, I'm going to put it over my head,' said Mitch.

'But you don't have a head,' said Dwheeblebridge, laughing even harder.

Mitch put the bin to one side, grabbed Dwheeblebridge by the lapels, and pulled him close. 'And that makes me stand out almost as much as you in your sweet little Seven Dwarves Gestapo outfit ...'

'I see, I see,' said Dwheeblebridge, gawping into Mitch's neck cavity.

'... and I'm not here on some jolly-good-teatime daytrip,' continued Mitch. 'I have to live here, so I have to take precautions, I have to cover up. Get it?'

'Oh yes, yes I see now, sir,' said Dwheeblebridge, his brow furrowing as he nodded. He stretched up and puppeteered a consoling false arm around Mitch's shoulder. 'Hotswap didn't say what you wanted it for.'

'Well what did you think I wanted it for?'

'I assumed you wanted to tidy up.'

Mitch pulled the angel closer still. 'Don't push me, sonny. Now what else have you brought for me?'

'I've brought news, Mr Langford.'

'News?'

'The location of the death site. Hotswap said you wanted to know?'

'Oh, yeah,' said Mitch. He released the angel.

'Mr Bootstrap died on Marylebone Road,' said Dwheeblebridge.

'Okay.'

'That's in London!'

'Thanks.'

'Just where it joins up with Great Portland Street, quite near the tube station.'

'I got it.'

'That's what they call the underground railway here, you know.'

'Yeah, thank you, I have actually been to London before.'

'Really? Well, good for you, Mr Langford,' said Dwheeblebridge, serving up another furrowed brow smile. 'Anyway, that's where all the other shepherds are looking.'

'Right, right,' said Mitch, 'so I guess they already checked here, ay?'

'Oh yes. They were here almost a week.'

'No kidding? Well it pays to be thorough.'

'Oh yes, we're being thorough, Mr Langford. But it's got everyone stumped.'

'Yeah, well, that figures.'

'Actually we were hoping he might have turned up here.'

'We?'

'Me and Hotswap.'

'Just you and Hotswap?'

'Well, me and Hotswap and Hotswap's boss.'

'Ah, right. So it's not just news then, you're here to check up on me too?'

'That's right, I need to check you've not seen him.'

'Well, you can tell them I've not seen a thing in two weeks. Reckon it's a million to one he rocks up now, ay.'

'I'll be sure to tell them, Mr Langford.'

Mitch studied the young angel. Was this all an act? His gut said not; his gut said this kid was as green as a Granny Smith.

'So, son, did they tell you why they wanted you to check I've not seen him?'

Dwheeblebridge pursed his lips. 'I'm, er, supposed to stick to whether or not you've seen him, I do hope you understand.'

'Right, right, but they did tell you why?'

The angel nodded.

'And?'

'I'm not supposed to say.'

'Sure, I know, but that's just 'cos they're going by the book, standard procedure with beginners, but we're both experienced professionals, right?'

'Right.'

'So this is a frank exchange between equals, right?'

'Right.'

'And we trust each other, right?'

'Right.'

'So,' said Mitch, putting an arm around the angel's shoulder, 'level with me.'

'Well … um, okay,' said the angel, 'just between you and me, Hotswap's boss thought if you found Mr Bootstrap, you might try to bring him in on your own.'

'What, and not share the credit with the locals? Who do they think I am?'

'That's what I said, Mr Langford! "We're all on the same team," I told him.'

'Well, now you can put his mind at rest.'

'I will do, and thanks, Mr Langford.' He removed a tiny notebook from his top pocket and made a mark with a small pencil. 'This job is now complete, so I had better be getting back.'

'Hold your horses there, Dweeby, you're not quite done, where's the rest of the kit?'

'Rest of?'

'The new shackles, the chains.'

'Oh yes,' said Dwheeblebridge, 'oh now you're not going to believe this, Mr Langford, but they got confiscated at customs.'

'What?' Mitch smashed a fist through the wispy hint of balsa wood that was the banister rail, causing Dwheeblebridge to step back.

'Yes, I gave them the cover story, from Hotswap,' said the angel, 'about them being items for use in my personal life, for use with my sexual partner or partners, but they just laughed and took them away.'

Mitch gripped his own shoulders hard. 'Son, they were way more important than the bin. How am I gonna deliver the cargo now if I can't get it to come quietly?'

'But, but you said you hadn't seen him?'

'Yes. I know,' said Mitch, gripping his shoulders even tighter, 'and I haven't. But if I do see him, and he won't come quietly, then I'm stuck. We're stuck. Remember it's your department I'm doing all this for anyway.'

'Okay, Mr Langford, I'll speak to Hotswap.'

'Good. No wait, just wait. What are you going to say to Hots. Tell me exactly.'

'I'll tell him you need chains and shackles to bring in the cargo by force.'

'No. You're going to say I need chains and shackles *in case* I find the cargo, *in case* I need to bring him in by force.'

'I understand.'

'You're sure?'

'Absolutely-loo.'

'Okay. Well, off you trot then.'

'Aren't you coming too?'

'Why, you need me to hold your hand crossing the street?'

'No way! Crossing the street's not dangerous for me here,' said Dwheeblebridge. 'No, I just thought you'd be travelling into London to join the search, so we could drift in together? I could point out some landmarks for you.'

'No, no, you've got it all covered. I'll stay here, I'll be your insurance policy. There's always that million to one shot he might show, ay.'

'Well thank you, Mr Langford,' said Dwheeblebridge, with a nod.

Mitch took the angel by the shoulders and turned him to the door.

'Now you go straight to the Gate and don't talk to any strange ghosts on the way now, you hear?'

'I won–'

Mitch gave him a push through the door but at the last moment pulled him back. 'One more thing,' he said, 'before I arrived, you had a good look around the house?'

'Yes.'

'You checked everything? All rooms, the garden, the garage?'

'Yes, everything.'

'So you satisfied yourself the cargo's not here?'

'Yes. What's your point, Mr Langford?'

'Just wanted to make sure your mission was a big success. Now, off you trot, mustn't keep nanny waiting.' He pushed the angel out through the door.

Mitch drifted into the front room and over to the sofas to think. Now he'd need to speed things along. Even if this kid got his lines right, there was gonna be more attention. And now he had no backup plan either – a delivery by force was pretty much impossible without chains, shackles or similar.

He got up and checked every room in the house. Beatrice wasn't home.

That was good, so long as she was where he thought she was. The plan was still on then.

There was still the problem of timing, though. The following week would be better, or even the week after that – more time to work on the cargo, more time to cement the setup. But he couldn't risk waiting, not now. He needed to bring things to the boil. Maybe go straight for the big guns? Go for it and hope his luck held?

He went into the kitchen to recheck Beatrice's calendar. So far she'd been like clockwork. If she kept to the pattern, his next window was the day after tomorrow. Miss that and he'd be into the weekend.

And then there was still the problem of getting to the Gate undetected. Mitch had already quizzed Christian on his death, so Dwheeblebridge's information only confirmed what he already knew (that Christian had died in London, close to the Gate) and already suspected (that the death site was now the focus of the search). The Gate would be inside the search area, so their path to it would be crawling with shepherds, perhaps angels, too. But he couldn't wait. He'd just have to solve those problems once the wheels were in motion. It was settled then. D-day in two days.

Mitch returned to the vicarage to find Christian and Tony watching an episode of *Midsomer Murders*.

'Hey,' said Christian, with a sheepish glance.

'Hey,' said Mitch.

'You made the most of it then?'

'Pardon me?'

'Been almost two hours,' said Christian, pointing to the Cheesus clock.

'Yeah, I went for a bit of a stroll afterwards.'

'Oh, please tell me you didn't follow any of them home.'

'Don't look at me like that. I just needed some air.' Mitch drifted over and sat down. 'Hey, sorry about earlier, buddy,' he said, 'about, you know, hassling you.'

'Ah, no harm done,' said Christian. He spied the basket. 'What have you got there?'

'Oh yeah,' said Mitch, 'I found it while I was out.'

'A waste paper basket?'

'Yep.'

'Where was it?'

'In the street.'

Christian turned to Mitch. 'You found a waste paper basket, one you can pick up, just lying about in the street?'

'Who'd have thought it, ay?' said Mitch. 'My foot just kicked into it. Anyway, figured maybe I could use it as headgear.'

'Really? But won't it look ridiculous?'

'Yes,' said Mitch, 'I guess it will.'

'Are those *cherubs* on the edging?' said Christian, looking more closely.

'I believe they are.'

'No eyeholes either.'

'No.'

'You've got to have eyeholes, right?'

'Yes, buddy, you're right. Again.'

'Not really thought it through, have you?' said Christian.

'No. I'm obviously a total retard.'

'Well, no, let's not be hasty. Maybe we can modify it? Perhaps we could make some eyeholes.'

'Oh yes, sure. Our friend with the collar has an ethereal knife in his kitchen, I suppose?'

'It's wicker, perhaps we don't need a knife.'

'So what, you're gonna gnaw through it for me?'

'Well,' said Christian, taking the basket, 'maybe we can tug at it a bit.'

'No, I don't think–'

'That's the beauty of wicker. It's semi-transparent already, if you get the right angle.' Christian held the basket up and rotated and tilted it until Mitch saw at least some of Christian through the cracks. 'Now if we tweak it a little here ...'

'Hey, no, Christian, it's gonna unravel.'

Mitch tried to reclaim the basket, but Christian swept it away.

'Just give me a sec,' said Christian. He tugged hard on the edges. Gaps formed easily enough while he held it under tension but closed up as soon as he let go. 'Need a bit more force ...' He ripped at it like he was a seventies strongman with a phone book, but still he made no lasting impression.

'Buddy ...' said Mitch, wearily.

'Hang on, I know.' Christian sat down and put his foot in the basket. He clenched his fingers tight around the rim and heaved. The wicker began to creak and stretch as the largest gaps yet began to open up between the strands. 'It's working,' said Christian, 'now if I push just a little harder.'

'Stop,' shouted Mitch, but it was too late.

A tight cluster of snaps accompanied the passage of Christian's foot through the base of the basket.

'Oooh,' said Christian.

'You stupid fuck. I fuckin' told you.'

'It's fine, don't worry.' Christian removed the disembowelled basket from his thigh. 'We can fix that, no problem.' He held up the remains for inspection. The basket was now twice as tall as it had been. He placed it over his head and peered at Mitch through the now generous gaps in its sides. 'What did I tell you. Now you can see through it easily.'

'And?'

'And what?'

'And so can everyone else, which makes it fuckin' useless as headgear, you doofus. Why d'ya think I need one in the first place? For fuckin' health and safety?'

'Oh, yes,' said Christian, taking it off, 'well, maybe we could line it with tissue paper?'

'Oh yeah, some nice scented lilac stuff, complement the fuckin' cherubs.'

'Look I'm only trying to help.'

Mitch stood up, clamped his hands to his shoulders and counted to ten. 'Do you have any tissue paper?' he asked.

'No.'

'Great.'

Chapter Eight

Mitch woke the next morning feeling no better than when he'd gone to sleep. However, on entering the living room, he soon found that Christian had been up early and had been busy.

After a brief greeting, Christian reached into the sofa. 'Ta-dah,' he said, as he withdrew the basket like it was a prize gateau. It was now lined in a patchwork of little papyrus pages, Christian having stripped the notepad he'd been given by Hargreaves and painstakingly attached the sheets.

'So what do you think?' he asked, turning it round.

'Great,' said Mitch, flatly, and he sat down in the armchair.

'It wasn't easy doing this without glue, you know,' said Christian. 'I had to make little strings out of some of the pages – tore them into strips and rolled them up, and I had a limited supply to work with.'

'Like I say … great.'

'I don't know why I bothered,' said Christian.

He put the basket down next to him on the sofa and folded his arms.

Mitch gripped his shoulders, gave them a pat, and turned to take a proper look at Christian's handiwork. It was still just as tall, and just as ridiculous, but it did now look workable. The gaps had been closed, save for two thin eyeholes at the front. It was better than nothing.

'Look um … thanks,' said Mitch.

'You're welcome, mate, you're welcome.'

Christian unfolded his arms and tweaked one of the sheets on the

Colton Lazars

basket. 'Hey, hey, I've got something else to show you,' he said, getting up. 'Look what I found in my ticket pocket this morning.' He dipped a hand into his jacket and produced a small white rectangular card.

'What's a ticket pocket?' asked Mitch.

'It's, you know, the little pocket, above ... here, look.' Christian showcased the left front side of his suit jacket and lifted the flap that covered the extra pocket.

'Right. Cool,' said Mitch, looking first at the pocket and then at the card.

'Is that all you have to say?'

'What do you want me to say?'

'Well what does it mean?' asked Christian, waving the card. 'It's not mine but it's got my name on it.'

'It's your soul card, buddy. Everyone has one.'

'But I don't remember getting it?'

'People rarely do.'

'Oh ... right.'

'Perfectly normal, perf–'

'What's up?' asked Christian.

'Let me see it,' said Mitch.

Christian handed it over.

'*Christian Joshua Bootstrap*,' said Mitch. '*Seventy-seven*.'

'Yes, what does that mean? And all those leading zeros, too.'

Seventy-seven. That was wrong, very wrong. Not just a bit odd, but way out there. In twenty years he'd never seen anything lower than twenty-six billion. And here's this guy with seventy-seven. What the hell did– He stopped the thought. *Think of something else, think of something else, think of something else.* He thrashed his arms around in the space where his head wasn't, like he was trying to clear dandruff.

'What on earth are you doing?' asked Christian.

'Nothing, I'm fine. You just tuck that away now.' He handed the card back.

'Why? What does the number mean?'

'Nothing, forget about it.'

'Oh come on, I saw your reaction. Tell me.'

'Look, just trust me on this.'

'But–'

'Let it go. Okay?'

'Okay,' said Christian, and he put the card back in his pocket.

'Good,' said Mitch, and he got to his feet. 'Now, let's get a proper look at this hat.'

'What?'

'I didn't really take it in, just now. Great job, buddy, great job. Now tell me about how you did it. I want all the details.'

For the next ten minutes they executed a thorough but to Christian's eyes strangely disconnected masterclass on his basket repair techniques. Mitch then suggested they take the radical new headgear for a test drift, so that's what they did.

Despite Mitch having to hold it in place with one hand, to begin with, and despite it now being not so much helmet as experimental sculpture, it served its purpose. Mitch even offered some more sincere thanks. In addition, they'd observed a strange phenomenon on the test run: apparent deference in the eyes and body language of some of the ghosts they'd breezed past, the basket's impressive height perhaps triggering a long latent genetic deference to tall headwear in the British dead. Christian called it the top-hat effect, and suggested it could be enhanced further with a brim and a pair of wicker spats. Mitch said he'd think about it.

Chapter Nine

It was another endless knotted morning for Nikki. More meds. More madness. More nothing. Even the reluctant game of draughts was suspended while Kendo was receiving the benefit of his latest consultation with Teasdale, the consultant psychiatrist.

'Nikki Tooting,' bellowed Jean from the corridor, as Kendo returned to the room.

Kendo took a bow. 'Kendo five, pinhead nil,' he said.

'What did you go with?' asked Nikki.

'Today, the pull across the table.'

She managed half a smile.

'Yeah. Lapels,' said Kendo, stretching his arms out to the jacket of an imaginary Teasdale, 'pull, flip, pile-driver, splash.' He chanted, 'Easy, easy, easy,' and clasped his hands above his head, before sitting down next to her. 'Would not be good for my case if I did it though, girl,' he said. 'That's the thing with the trick. You gotta remember to keep it between yer ears.'

'Nikki Tooting,' bellowed Jean, again. And then her form appeared in the doorway, filling most of it. Jean was one of the staff who had been hired not so much for her mastery of nursing as for her mastery of half nelsons. The first thing anyone ever noticed about her was her centre of gravity, an impressive three-quarters of her body weight being below her waist, and there was nothing that hairstyle, makeup or clothing could do about it. But she didn't care. She was strong, she was fearless, she was resolute, and no one had put her down yet.

'Do you want me to carry you there?' said Jean. 'Because I will.'

Nikki slowly got to her feet.

Jean looked disappointed.

'Remember what I told you,' said Kendo, 'don't tell him nothing, don't even give him an outline.'

Chapter Ten

Dexter watched as Gordon waited for the whispers to die. It was the Lord of Limbo's first public appearance in months. And there were a lot of whispers, even from those who'd missed the fleeting return to full alpha and were coming at this from the closer and more familiar island of hairclips, popsocks and blusher. Now their leader stood before them in a long-sleeve black horsehair evening dress and heels; hair dyed black and tied into a bun; blackberry lipstick; black eyeliner. He looked around, connecting with the thousands of faces, seeming to take care to catch as many eyes as he could. All witnesses to his example, his change, his repentance. He clopped forward from the group of senior dignitaries, his movements made awkward by the heels and the tightness of the dress. He laid the wreath at the base of the monolith, then stepped back, head bowed.

'Are you quite done?' whispered Dexter.

Gordon lifted his veil. 'I'd appreciate it if you'd show some respect.'

This solemn opening ceremony for the Wall of Remembrance in the new Productivity Through Diversity Garden Complex would have taken place sooner, but it had taken New Limbinian's closest approximation to craftsmen two weeks to scratch out an epitaph without shattering a dolostone slab. The rest of the expansive bowled 'garden' had taken time to assemble, too, the huge clumps of black spinifex the product of many days of many suits sent foraging deep into the outlands.

After yet another minute's silence, Manners did his best to sound the last post on his portable glockenspiel. The senior ranks then filed out past Gordon, Dexter and the board, and the other dignitaries, to bring the ceremony to a close.

Half an hour later, Gordon and Dexter were back in Gordon's office. The space had just been redecorated after just being redecorated, and was now pretty much back to how it was a month earlier, the only difference being a move from mustard to strawberry pink.

'And how's the corporate wellness initiative going,' said Gordon, still in his horsehair dress, though now in stocking feet, 'are we getting any ideas yet?'

'Nope,' said Dexter.

'Well what does Rothschild think about it?'

'I'm pretty sure he doesn't know about it.'

'That was a top-level memo, what the blazes is going on, man?'

'Well I'm sure he would have read it, had he not been purged.'

'Oh ... yes. Kalonymus then? I assume his lot picked up the pieces?'

'Well again, doubtless he would have, had he not been purged in the round before.'

'Viktorov?'

'Went in the first wave.'

'Cromwell?'

Dexter just raised his eyebrows.

Gordon shook his head. 'So many fine servants of Limbo. If only there were something we could do.'

'Well we can't exactly unpurge them, Gordo.'

'Don't malwang, Dexter. They were valued members of our corporate family, our diverse community.'

'Not so diverse now though, eh.'

'True. So how's the recruitment drive going?'

'Not good,' said Dexter. 'Look, I'm sure they'll come round eventually, but it's too soon, too soon since they saw you back in the suit and spitting flame. Right now they're all nominating each other for the promotions. You've never seen so many people scrambling away from avalanches of glowing references.'

'That is regrettable.'

'It is, Gordon. It really is.'

The King of Limbo scratched his ribs as his gaze drifted to the stationery cupboard.

'How's the horsehair?' asked Dexter.

'Itchy,' said Gordon. 'Had to get Bippy to run me up a linen union suit.'

'Doesn't that rather erode the gesture?'

'It's the thought that counts.'

Dexter smiled.

'What?' said Gordon.

'A glimmer of the old Gordon.'

'Meaning?'

Dexter put his hands on his head. 'Meaning you were back,' he said, 'for three weeks we had you kicking arse and putting the fear of retirement into the eyes of everyone.'

'I didn't recognise myself.'

'Well I did. You were magnificent. Fire and brimstone, old time wrath of Limbo.'

'No,' shouted Gordon and he slammed his fist down onto his new shabby-chic lilac coffee table, splintering the dogwood. He stood up. 'That was not the real me,' he said, 'that was, it was, just ...'

'Just what?'

'Just an episode. A turn.'

'Well I wish we knew why,' said Dexter.

'I don't want to know why,' said Gordon, 'and if you see me acting like that again, you put me right, you hear?'

Dexter studied his boss, hoping to catch that lupine flash he'd seen last time Gordon spoke those words, but this time there was no sign. 'Look, it may be a bit out there as theories go,' said Dexter, 'but perhaps the suit does play a part? A policeman isn't a policeman without the uniform and truncheon.'

'Drop it, Dex.'

Gordon retook his seat.

'Just try it,' said Dexter, 'bring back the braces for one more day, get out the hair wax, see if you can channel your inner Gekko?'

'You're not listening. I don't want to go back to the old me. Why do you think we've been laying a fucking wreath today, why do you think I had a wall of fucking remembrance commissioned anyway?'

'There are always casualties, Gordon, you taught me that.'

'Such senseless waste,' said Gordon, eyes to his feet, 'innocents all of them.'

'Oh come on, not innocent, not one of them. They'd been taking advantage for years. If they were reckless enough to go around with two-tone shoes and hemp bracelets then they have themselves to blame.'

Gordon shook his head. 'Where was the love, where was the compassion?'.

'This is business, Gordon. No sentiment. No compassion. No exceptions.'

'There's always room for compassion.'

'You're not yourself, Gordon, you don't know what you're saying.'

'I am myself. This is the real me. Balanced, considerate, open to my emotions. All I want now is for everything else to get back to normal.'

Dexter did not reply.

Chapter Eleven

Nikki entered the side room that doubled as Teasdale's office for his consultancy sessions. She'd seen two of the unit's junior doctors since her arrival, but this was the first with the head honcho.

Teasdale was seated in a vinyl swivel chair with his back to her, behind a table. Nikki saw a clean, bald scalp bordered by a crescent of unfashionably long grey sprouts – not quite mad professor, more soon-to-retire maths teacher.

She sat on the single plastic chair set close to her side of the table.

'Mrs Tooting,' said Teasdale, still with his back to her, 'I have been so looking forward to meeting you.' His voice had a patronising overpronounced quality about it, none of his words ever bleeding into each other, as if Nikki was to receive council from a satnav.

'Really,' said Nikki.

He rotated to face her. 'Oh yes …' He hesitated. '… yes, a most welcome surprise in my in-tray. I do hope we can help each other.'

'Well I hope so too,' said Nikki.

'So how are we feeling?' he asked.

'Much better.'

'Injuries on the mend?'

She nodded.

He leaned forward and looked her in the eyes before commencing an unhurried survey of her face. 'Do not worry about the scars. They enrich the character. Especially on a woman.'

She did not reply.

He leaned back in his chair. 'And in yourself?'

'I'm fine. I feel good.'

'Really?'

'Yes. I feel I'm back to normal.'

Teasdale allowed a smile to form, enjoying it unashamedly. 'Remarkable. So we have gone from double para-suicide to healthy member of society in' – he looked at his notes – 'a little over a week.'

'Yes, I'm so relieved.'

'Indeed you must be.'

'So can you sign me off?'

'Dear no,' he said, with a chuckle.

'No?' she said, calmly.

'No,' said Teasdale, with a slow shake of his head.

'I don't seem okay to you?' asked Nikki.

He smiled again. 'Well, perhaps if I had just met you, perhaps if, let us say, that you had come in for a job interview … then yes, I do not suppose I would have any reason to suspect otherwise … but, if I was to look further and under general comments, hobbies and interests it said attempted suicide twice in the last calendar month, well, then I would have to think again, would I not?'

She felt the blood pumping, the cortisol rising. But she kept a lid on it, her breathing slow, her muscles loose. 'But,' she said, 'what if I'd just had a freak episode. That happens doesn't it, sometimes? Temporary insanity?'

'Perhaps on some rather low-rate American television show that just runs and runs, written by people who have had no professional experience with the mentally ill … but in the real world, people do not try to kill themselves, twice, for no reason.'

Nikki said nothing.

'So,' said Teasdale, leaning forward, 'tell me what happened.'

'I've already told the other doctors. I'm sure you've read their notes.'

'I have. But if you wouldn't mind, I would like to hear it for myself.'

'There's little to tell. I was under a lot of stress at work, my husband had left me, it all got too much.'

He smiled again. 'Come, come, Mrs Tooting. Stan and Ollie out there may have bought that, but this is not my first week in the job. So please give me a little credit and tell me the truth.'

'It is the truth.'

'I assure you, you can confide in me.'

'There's nothing more to tell.'

'Please. Do not play games, Mrs Tooting. Your story does not fit the facts.'

'What facts?'

'You are not suicidal. Any fool can see that. And yet that is what you attempted. And this makes me curious, very curious indeed.' He leaned in closer still.

'I attempted suicide,' she said, 'therefore I was suicidal.'

'No, no, I do not think so, Mrs Tooting. Far from it.'

Nikki exhaled. 'I don't know what you want me to say.'

'Well. Let us start with the theme, shall we?'

'Theme?'

'The knife. The microwave. Kitchens, catering … food.'

'They were just what was to hand.'

'Oh come, come, it is a clear metaphor.'

'For what?'

'Consumption, digestion, transformation.'

Nikki said nothing.

'So tell me,' said Teasdale, his eyes low, 'how many are we talking?'

'How many what?'

'People. How many people have you eaten?'

'What? I haven't eaten anyone.'

'Well what about a bit of someone?'

'No, absolutely not.'

'I'm not saying they had to die, Mrs Tooting. Perhaps you had a toe or a finger or a foreskin? Cooked up crispy, like a pork scratching.'

'No.'

'Slice of buttock? Wafer thin?'

'No!'

'Earlobe?'

Nikki said nothing and folded her arms.

'Hair off the barber's floor?'

'This is ridiculous. I'm not a cannibal, I'm just a normal person who let life's pressures get too much, that's all.'

Teasdale stared at her. 'I am not sure there is any point in us meeting, Mrs Tooting, if you refuse to be open with me.'

'I've already told you everything.'

'Well, in that case,' said Teasdale, fixing on Nikki's pupils, 'I will have to hold on to you. Indefinitely.'

Nikki took a deep mental breath.

'How does that make you feel?' said Teasdale.

She dug her nails into her thighs under the table. 'A little disappointed.'

'Is that right?' said Teasdale. 'Well thank you so much for your candour. So nothing worse? Not feeling frustrated, are we? Not feeling like jumping over the table and trying to strangle me with my tie?' He leaned forward and dangled his frayed fade-to-beige. He pushed its tip forward across the table, within Nikki's reach.

She thought about it. Would she have the strength to throttle him with it? Of course she would. Would she have the time to then remove it and throttle herself with it, before the nurses rushed in? Is it possible to throttle someone with a tie? Is it possible to throttle *yourself* with a tie?

'No,' said Nikki, 'you're the expert, I trust your judgement. I know you know best.'

'Oh come off it,' said Teasdale, springing to his feet, 'you are seething. You are ready to burst. I can feel it.' He paced round the desk and stood behind her. 'Come on,' he whispered hotly in her ear, spitting on her lobe, 'tell me.'

'I have told you.'

'Come on,' he said again, taunting her, flicking the end of his tie in her face, 'it is burning you up, is it not? You are under the grill, you are in the pressure cooker, you are inches from the whirling blender. You need to tell someone, you must tell someone. You must.' He eyeballed her and waited.

'I have already told you everything,' said Nikki, and she placed her hands on the table.

Teasdale gave Nikki a few more tie flicks, before straightening up and taking a pace back. 'You are lying, Mrs Tooting, like all the others.' He turned to study a notice on the wall advertising a forthcoming quiz night. 'No one tells us the truth any more.'

'Yes they do, of course they do. I'm telling you the truth right now. Barry Jesus tells you the truth, they all do.'

'Oh yes yes,' said Teasdale, turning back towards her, 'your run-of-the-mill Jesus, they cannot stop telling the truth, never shut up about it, spreading the damned word, preaching the damned gospels, they're obliged to, aren't they, but that hardly counts for anything, does it?'

'I'm sorry, hardly counts for what?'

'For anything interesting. Long-haired hippy saying he is Jesus. Sandals, sermons, yawn, yawn, yawn. Hollywood has seen it all before.'

'Hollywood?'

Teasdale returned to his chair and leaned back. 'I get it,' he said, 'I am not stupid. You think because I am mature, because I am stuck in here, that I do not watch the films that the younger people do.'

'I don't follow.'

'Films,' said Teasdale in an accusing tone, '*The Terminator*, to be specific. You have seen *The Terminator*?'

'What are you talking about? No I haven't seen *The Terminator*.'

Teasdale looked away. 'It has never been the same since that film. No one tells us anything of substance any more.'

'I don't follow?'

'No, no, of course you don't … *you have not seen it*.'

'No. And anyway, I *have* told you everything.'

'So you keep saying, Mrs Tooting, so you keep saying …'

Chapter Twelve

The following day, Christian found Mitch keen to do another walk, though this time he insisted on a change of route, and a mid-afternoon start, saying there were some 'sweet local sights' he wanted to show Christian. So this time they drifted east, Mitch dictating a steady pace, seemingly lost in thought.

The lack of conversation meant Christian was soon staring again. Mitch could now keep the basket in place with just small movements of his shoulders, leaving his hands free, but it still wobbled now and then, and when it did Christian would get a glimpse into Mitch's neck cavity.

'Mitch,' said Christian, 'I've been thinking further about your head.'

'Oh.'

'Sorry, is it getting annoying?'

'No ... no, carry on.'

'Well, they have your head in a chest freezer, yes?'

'Pretty much.'

'And you can't get a head here ...' Christian thought about making a joke, but let it go. '... until the flesh thaws out and dies.'

'Yep.'

'Well, those companies, their whole business model is based on them keeping your head frozen until the technology is invented to grow you a new body and bring you back to life.'

'Yep.'

'And they take your money and invest it so they will always be able to pay the electricity bill for the freezer.'

'Well, pretty much, yeah.'

'Even if it takes hundreds or even thousands of years?'

'That's right. They will always be able to pay the bills.'

'But, let's suppose we're dead, and I'm not saying we are, but let's just suppose. Well, if you're dead and your consciousness has already left your head and seems to be making a real go of it without your head, doesn't that sort of suggest they never will discover a technology to bring your head back to life, grow a new body and get you back in there?'

Mitch stopped drifting. 'That's right, buddy, I don't believe they will.'

'And do you think you're dead?'

'I do.'

'And stuck without a head, for ever.'

'Well, maybe not for ever, but yeah, for the foreseeable future. I hold out hope that one day they'll screw up. You know, forget to plug the freezer back in after doing the vacuuming ...' Mitch gave Christian a knowing smile, which Christian failed to notice on account of Mitch having no head. '... or longer term there's always a chance some director will embezzle from the trust fund and they'll go out of business, or there'll be a third world war, or hell some other sort of situation that results in the end of civilisation. It's sure to happen eventually.'

'So there's reasons to positive.'

'I guess. It's not good for your soul though, buddy, praying for Armageddon. But then again, I wouldn't be the first, ay.'

'Is there no way you can go and unplug the freezer yourself?' asked Christian. 'I don't know how, but–'

'You don't think I've tried?'

'Sorry. Yes of course you would've.'

'Two years straight before I gave up.'

'Wow. So no way at all?'

'No.'

'But–'

'There are no buts.'

'But–'

'Christian,' said Mitch, stopping, 'I know you're trying to help, but there's nothing that can be done, so please, just drop it.'

Chapter Thirteen

True Jerusalem was a place where things never changed much, and even when they did, the pace was geological. This was in large part due to the all-pervasive influence of eternity. *Why do today what you can put off until tomorrow?* That phrase, graffitied onto many of the walls, bridges and gatehouses across the sun-baked metropolis, is greeted by many new arrivals as symbolic of the sheer laziness of the administration – partly for its literal message, but mostly because no one ever gets around to cleaning it up.

But soon a powerful subtext emerges. Because putting off today what you can do tomorrow at least means you'll have something to do tomorrow. Because if you don't have something to do tomorrow, you might start thinking about the problem of all the other tomorrows to come. Weeks, months, years, decades, centuries and on. And most people tend to overestimate their ability to cope:

'A thousand years? Yeah, I reckon I can do that.'

'Ten thousand? No sweat, just think of all those books I could read.'

But on an infinite scale, everyone finds their Waterloo somewhere:

'A hundred thousand, well, now then ...'

'A million? *Ten million*, you say? Now hold on, hold on a second ...'

Ten million years with nothing to do. And then another ten million after that. For many, it's enough to begin the short, straight path to insanity. So it pays to take every opportunity to leave things until tomorrow.

But then, when it comes to eternity, there are an awful lot of tomorrows to fill.

Procrastination at this high-octane level can rapidly become demanding and stressful, and this has been a driver for some to propose other coping mechanisms. The technique of Sports Neural Misdirection, invented by Professor Frank Funchess in the nineteen fifties, is now hugely popular, at least in the upper realm, and is one of the easiest techniques to understand. Followers simply spend all their waking hours in the Kingdom's window box viewing bars and nectar halls watching live sport, thus enabling them to block all other thoughts or activities, which of course includes the hideous mind-bending contemplation of eternity. Not only does SNM prevent the brain drifting off into dangerous existential pondering, but it also has the considerable added advantage of removing the endless trouble and worry over finding things to do (or not do, as it were) that can plague the lives of others. These days it's easy to fill entire days with live sport, remote viewing over to the golf after the Grand Prix, then over to the football, then on to the NASCAR in the late evening. And of course it's a breeze during big multi-week events like the Olympics or the World Cup. But, even nowadays, there are still gaps. Forty-five minutes here, an hour or two there. The followers of SNM tend to counter this problem by banding together in small clumps, at such times, and discussing sport intensely until the danger has passed. According to Professor Funchess, once perfected, this technique can be called upon to fill several consecutive days – more than enough to cover even the longest of twenty-first century *sports gaps*.

To date, the practice, and the movement it spawned, has been remarkably successful, but as Funchess's critics have pointed out, there is one nagging problem – the eventual demise of human civilisation. Even if humanity beats expectations and lasts for another few thousand years, it is inevitable it will one day fail, and die, and, of course, take live sport with it. The problem then, for the SNM disciple, is not that sport will be gone for ever – for it is also inevitable that a new dominant species will emerge from the ashes – no, the problem is how to fill the mega-gap in between, which by anyone's measure is going to be a long one. It's not like the cockroaches are going to invent football straight away, and it'll take them even longer to achieve the administrative, cultural, economic and political sophistication necessary to organise World Cups and Champions Leagues, and longer still to introduce pundits and goal-line technology. Which is why Sports Neural Misdirection is dismissed by many of

Heaven's philosophers as nothing more than a quick-fix, sticking-plaster solution.

And it's hard to argue otherwise. So what Funchess and his followers tend to do is what most people do when presented with an inconvenient truth – they turn up the volume. And that means really *really* getting into their sport, and really *really* talking about it an awful lot.

There was, of course, one resident of Heaven who never had such problems. He couldn't see what all the fuss was about. But then he was lucky, because, uniquely, he had natural existential balance – being eternal, his infinite past stretched out as far as his infinite future. Furthermore, it had always been like that, and always would be. So for him, and him alone, eternity was not a concern, and he tended to regard everyone else's obsession with the passage of time with bemused indifference. But though it meant he was the most grounded person in the universe when it came to the big, big, big, big, *big* picture of time, it often created problems with the day to day.

God had called an emergency meeting in the Beatrix Potter Lounge. It was a sanctuary of purity, simplicity and innocence. It always put him in a foul mood, so for today it was the obvious choice.

God had his feet up next to an untouched plate of Pig-wig pork crackling gingerbread on a little wooden tea table. His arms were folded, his eyes fixed on the empty little wooden chair opposite and the barn doors beyond. Gabriel, looking tense, had squeezed himself into the chair to God's left. To the right sat a large stuffed Mrs Tiggy-Winkle doll, for meeting balance.

'It's just you didn't seem bothered about it last week,' said Gabriel.

'I hadn't looked back through my notes last week,' said God, stubbing out his cigarette on a little pottery saucer.

'You keep notes?' said Gabriel.

'Well of course I keep notes.'

Gabriel raised his eyebrows.

'I'm a busy man, Gabe, in case you hadn't realised. The world doesn't run itself, you know.'

'Actually, I thought pretty much it did?'

'Don't get smart with me, Gabe. Not today.'

Gabriel did not reply.

'Where is he then?' asked God.

'I'm assured he's on his way,' said Gabriel.

God turned and socked Mrs Tiggy-Winkle with an uppercut to the chin, tipping up the chair and sending her flying into the wall.

Another silence.

'So, what about Harry,' said God, 'where's he these days? Couldn't separate you two when he started.'

'I'm not sure,' said Gabriel, 'other assignments, I assume.'

Finally there was a confident knock on the barn doors. Trimbrilly, of Angel Field Ops, entered, followed by two of his subordinate angels. They all stopped when they saw Terry.

Trimbrilly composed himself and bowed, as did his subordinates, before returning to his perfect straight-back posture.

'Ah,' said Gabriel, 'come in, take a seat.'

The archangel gestured to the empty little wooden chair facing God.

As Trimbrilly stepped forward and squeezed himself in, God looked past him and his subordinates, out into the corridor, and gave a nod. Four burly aides dressed as the Flopsy Bunnies stepped in and stood just inside the door.

'So, Brillo,' said God, 'you're running the hunt for our monkey?'

'I'm sorry, the monkey?' said Trimbrilly.

'Bootstrap,' said Gabriel.

'Ah, indeed,' said Trimbrilly, doing his best to relax into the tight chair, 'yes, we're on the case.'

'Is that right?' said God.

'Oh yes, we're making every effort. No sign of him yet, of course.'

'You checked the house, his home?'

'Why yes, we staked it out for a while, a good while.'

'Really?'

'Oh yes.'

'How?'

'I'm sorry?'

'How, exactly, did you stake it out?' asked God. 'How many angels, how many shepherds, how long for?'

'Tel, these are details,' said Gabriel, 'these are–'

'I'm interested in details,' said God, turning to the archangel, 'I'm a details person.' He held the stare for a few seconds before turning back to Trimbrilly. 'Continue.'

'W-well, we had blanket coverage,' said Trimbrilly, 'we sent twenty-three, twenty-four shepherds, plus several of our agents, we saturated.

Blanket coverage for a whole week, and we've done a field angel follow-up since.'

'And the death site?' said God.

'Departure point,' whispered Gabriel.

God's eyes widened and his beard sparked as he glared at Gabriel. 'As I was saying, the *death site*, where we *killed him*, have you checked that?'

'Th-that's the focus of our search now,' said Trimbrilly. 'We're sweeping the entire area, my Lord, we–'

'You can address him as Terry,' said Gabriel, 'you don't have–'

'No, Gabe,' said God. 'Today I think we'll stick with Lord. That is if you don't mind?'

Gabriel's thin lips tightened as he slid into a small, seated bow.

'You were saying?' said God.

'Yes, w-well, we've put all our resources back into London,' said Trimbrilly, 'the house was clean, and so was his workplace, as were his friends' houses, therefore he must be in the vicinity of the death site.'

'But you already searched the death site?'

'Indeed, that's where we started, but we felt it was right to go back. We only searched the immediate area, so now we're widening the search.'

'And why would he be in the wider area?'

'Sightseeing, Lord.'

'Sightseeing?'

'Oh yes,' said Trimbrilly, 'the capital has something for everyone. Theatres, palaces, the National Gallery. And of course once you're dead it's *all* free, not just the museums. And you can walk around all those little private areas. And it's pretty as a picture in springtime. I was there for my holidays last year, we–'

'Oh, how nice for you,' said God, 'but you've not been since?'

'Well … no.'

'Not thought about seeing how the operation's going for yourself? First clawhand, so to speak?'

'No, no, it's best I oversee things from here, Lord. Command and control, you understand.'

'Oh I understand.'

'Though Bobkins and I are hoping to go back there next year, for our holidays, we liked it so much last time, you see, and well, I suppose I could always pop in and see our chaps in the field then? That is if we've not found him by then … of course.'

Gabriel was shaking his head.

'How very decent of you, Trimo,' said God.

'Thank you, Lord.'

God looked beyond Trimbrilly and gave a quick single nod.

The Flopsy Bunny aides marched forward, barging past Trimbrilly's subordinates. The first two bunnies lifted Trimbrilly up by his armwings, the little wooden chair going with him.

'Hey, hey, get off me,' yelled the angel, 'get off me, you brutes.'

The third bunny stepped in behind and forced a thick metal ring, holes in opposite sides, over the angel's clawhands, clamping them together behind his back.

One of the subordinate angels took a step to intervene, but stopped after his colleague gave a vigorous and desperate shake of the head.

A fourth bunny produced a nail the size of a tent peg and sledgehammer.

A single stroke and the nail was in through one hole and out the other, piercing the wrists of Trimbrilly's armwings.

The angel cried out in shock and pain. He struggled but was held firm.

'Thanks for your efforts, son,' said God, 'that'll be all.'

The bunnies turned for the exit with their payload, Trimbrilly's legs thrashing in mid-air, the little wooden chair finally coming free in the process.

'Help. Stop,' said the angel in panic and desperation, 'where are you taking me?'

'You're being resettled, son,' said God, calling after them. 'That is the right word, isn't it, Gabe?'

The room fell silent. It had been many centuries since anyone had been exiled from Heaven, and even then it was reserved for the most heinous crimes, like blasphemy and glee club singing.

The bewildered subordinate angels just stood there, staring at each other.

Gabriel dismissed them with a sorry flick of his clawhand and they were gone.

'Right, time to get this ship back on course,' said God.

'May I ask, what do you have in mind?' said Gabriel.

'Send in the bulldog.'

'Oh you're not serious?'

'Deadly.'

'But I thought you said we needed to be careful, keep this all on a low profile?'

'I never said that. You said that. No, no, we'll send in Slacks. Stir things up a bit.'

'We don't want to stir things up, Tel, this isn't a James Bond film.'

'Hey. Enough,' said God, raising a finger to within an inch of Gabriel's nose, 'my mind's made up. We're sending in Slacks. Okay?'

There was no reply.

'Okay?' said God.

'Whatever you say. Lord.'

'Good. He's all set,' said God, 'you can go and give him the nod.'

'I'm sorry?'

'Over in departures. He's already prepped. And not because he's going there on 'is fuckin' holidays.'

Chapter Fourteen

An hour later, Christian and Mitch were still on their walk.

'Why did we have to come here?' said Christian, increasingly aware there was something Mitch wasn't telling him. 'We're nearly in Ascot. I hate Ascot.'

'Quit whining,' said Mitch, 'we're almost there.'

'Almost where? Will you tell me what we're doing here?'

'Another five minutes and I can show you.'

Mitch led the way into a residential estate, the houses as anonymous as Beatrice's, though several pages on in the brochure.

Several other people, mostly men, were also walking into the estate, in ones and twos, all apparently heading the same way.

'Here we are,' said Mitch, after they turned a corner.

Everyone was converging on the detached house up ahead, a house that already had sixty or seventy men outside, some milling about on its front lawn, some standing in a queue running from the front door to the pavement.

'All those people, what are they doing?'

'Yeah, there's a few more than I expected,' said Mitch, 'must be quite an appetite in these parts.'

'Appetite? For what?'

As they got closer, it became clear the queue wasn't one line of people, but two, forming a sort of guard of honour each side of the garden path.

'Wait here,' said Mitch, diverting Christian to the front porch of the house to their right, number seven, two doors up from the action.

'Why? Why can't I come along?'

'Just do this for me, okay? Your future depends on it, and I'm not kidding.'

Mitch drifted over to the crowd and the twin lines. 'Hey there, friends,' Christian heard him say, before his voice faded into the background chatter. Christian only now realised these people, all these people, were ghosts. He'd never seen so many in one place before, and it unnerved him. He looked on, watching Mitch talk to the men. From the body language it seemed friendly enough, despite plenty of recoils and backward shuffles at the sight of Mitch's wicker headgear.

After a minute or so, Mitch returned. 'We're right on time,' he said.

'On time for what? What did you mean about my future depending on it?'

'You'll see soon enough.'

'Will you stop saying that. I don't like where this is going.'

'Relax, will you. Now, let's head round the back.'

'Why?'

'Be quieter.' He put a hand on Christian's shoulder and they turned to head into number seven.

The sound of an approaching car followed by cheers from the crowd caused Christian to turn back. The men were all rushing towards the pavement.

'Come on,' said Mitch, again taking Christian by the shoulder.

'No, I want to see.'

Their view was obscured by the crowds, but from the movement of the people it was clear the car had pulled up and stopped outside the house. The pavement end of the guard of honour shuffled over a few metres and then settled as the engine was turned off.

The sound of the driver's door opening triggered another cheer and the entire crowd seemed to rise up and come alive as its members jostled for positions.

'What is going on?' asked Christian, unable to see beyond the bodies. 'Is it someone famous?'

'Local celebrity, you might say,' said Mitch, and again he tried to usher Christian away.

'I didn't think they had celebrities in Ascot,' said Christian. 'I suppose Prince Charles would count, when the horse racing is on ...'

They heard the clunk of the driver's door closing and the central locking firing. Moments later a wave of applause and cheering rolled up the length of the twin lines, culminating with a ring of the doorbell.

'This way,' said Mitch, moving towards number seven.

'Wait,' said Christian, standing his ground.

After the front door opened and closed, the men all began to make their way into the house, passing in through the door, walls and windows.

Finally Christian relented and Mitch led him into number seven. They passed through the hall, living room and dining room – as well as several members of a family sitting down to dinner – before exiting via the far wall out into the back garden. There they cut left, through the neighbouring back garden and into the back garden of the house at the centre of all the activity.

'Now what?' said Christian.

'Now we give them a few minutes.'

'Now we give who a few minutes?'

'You'll see very soon.'

'And why do they need a few minutes?'

'To complete a few ... preparations,' said Mitch.

Christian continued to probe, and Mitch continued to stonewall, saying it wouldn't be right to spoil things. Eventually, Mitch called time and they headed in.

'Now, keep quiet and stick close to me,' said Mitch, and they drifted through the back door.

As soon as they were inside it was standing room only. Christian soon realised the sprawling mass of men before them was in fact a winding, coiled queue, the head of which appeared to be somewhere up the stairs. No one was making a sound, or at least no one downstairs was. All eyes were to the ceiling, to the upstairs – vibrations, voices, squeaks, gasps, moans, cheers, shouts and a familiar sound Christian couldn't place. He couldn't place it because it was geographically, chronologically and aurally out of context: geographically because he wasn't used to hearing it in a strange house in Ascot; chronologically because he hadn't heard it in quite some time; and aurally because he wasn't used to hearing it accompanied by the sounds of a small but passionate crowd, grunting, cheering and ooing – in fact, it *was* on occasion accompanied by the sounds of a small but passionate crowd grunting, cheering and ooing, but at the time, Christian, like most of the living, had been entirely unable to perceive this.

Mitch strode forward with Christian in tow and they began drifting up the stairs, barging through, to shouts of derision from the queuing men.

'Special business, special business, comin' through,' said Mitch, flashing what Christian suspected was just a random piece of card.

It soon became heavy going, so Mitch began lifting his basket every few metres, quelling objections and parting the crowd as if armed with a cattle prod. Even so, the horde was getting more densely packed as they climbed higher, and its members more reluctant to relinquish their places, despite the mild terror of being mosh-pit-close to a man with no head.

By the time they reached the top landing, people couldn't make way even if they wanted to.

'Right,' said Mitch, 'follow me.'

He started climbing, laddering up above the crowd, through the landing ceiling and into the gloom of the loft, the fading daylight having to work hard through the single skylight.

'I'm sure I know that sound, that whimper,' said Christian, following on.

The loft was almost empty and provided thankful relief from the claustrophobia of the seething mass below.

'Why don't the others come this way?' asked Christian, as he followed Mitch across the loft floor.

'Sub-optimal point of view,' said Mitch. He removed his basket. 'These men are obsessives, you understand, dedicated to their pastime in death. It's got to be the right point of view or none at all.'

'What do you mean point of view?'

'You'll see.'

'When?'

'Now.' Mitch got down and lay prone in the chipboard of the loft floor. 'Come on,' he said, gesturing for Christian to do the same.

'Okay ...' said Christian, and he got down next to Mitch.

Mitch placed a firm hand on Christian's shoulder. 'Christian, my friend, this will not be easy. What you are about to witness is gonna freak you out, but believe me, it is in your interests to see this. Sometimes painful drugs are required to fix the patient.'

Mitch pointed to the floor. A second later his shoulders and torso dropped and passed inside, with only his legs and hips remaining above the chipboard. Christian followed suit, ducking his head into the bubble bath foam nothingness of the flooring and out through the meringue of the ceiling below.

Christian looked down on the scene. It appeared Mitch had brought him to some sort of suburban sex show. Christian had heard of swinging, of course, but it hadn't occurred to him it might be going on in his present plane of existence, even less it might be going on in the Thames Valley. Also, he was sure swinging was a participatory activity, but the dense throng of people below was largely made up of spectators. The decor seemed odd for a sex den, too: soothing peach walls, which sported a couple of framed pop-art prints; a shelf of books and CDs; cream curtains, built-in wardrobes and a large cheery-faced teddy bear sitting on a chair in the corner. The rest of the furniture, including the double bed, was largely obscured by the baying crowd of wide-eyed male ghosts, heads all craning for a better view. They were packed into every corner of the room, right up to and even into the couple at the centre of it all, a couple who were clearly mortal – a zombie-movie wall of hands flailing and groping in vain for impossible contact, finding it only in each other.

Christian could only see one of the performers – the pale back and bare backside of the large sweaty mass on top, obscuring whoever or whatever it was humping.

As the stroke length increased, tousled curls of dirty-blonde hair and then Beatrice's face flashed into view.

And again.

And again.

And again.

Christian felt all energy drain from him. His head drooped forward. For a moment he thought he was about to fall from his perch and plunge down into the centre of the action.

And now he recognised the other person too. 'Oh no, please no ...'

'I'm sorry, buddy,' said Mitch, now virtually a disembodied voice, with only the tip of his neck breaching the Artex.

Christian tried to look away, but it drew him in like an internet car crash compilation. Disbelief allied with wretched curiosity, as he stared unblinking at Kevin Tooting thrusting away at his special girl. Her face was flushed, eyes half closed, her breathing heavy. And she was shouting and moaning in exactly the kind of way she'd never quite done with Christian.

'Oh yes, oh yes ... yeeeeeeaaaaaaas.'

He looked down at the faces in the crowd, the eyes of the dead alive with desire amid the constant jostling for positions, the pushing and shouting, a feeding frenzy for the red-hot show his girlfriend was giving them – his quiet, decent, girl-next-door girlfriend.

'I've seen enough,' said Christian, almost to himself, and then with more purpose. He shut his eyes and began to lift himself back out to the safety of the loft, but he felt a hand on the back of his head, forcing him back down.

'You gotta see more,' said Mitch.

'Hey. Get off me.'

'Open your eyes,' said Mitch, tightening his grip on Christian's hair and pushing hard.

'I can't.'

'Open them!'

Christian gulped and took another long look, repressing a guttural desire to vomit down into the spectacle.

'I'm ready, darling,' said Beatrice.

Kevin completed a few more strokes, then slowed, then stopped.

The crowd hushed. The jostling stopped. Silence.

'Will of Ockham,' said Christian, his voice thin, 'ready for what? What the hell is next if this is just the warm-up?'

'Yes,' chirped Kevin, 'time for Big Ted to decorate the spare room.'

'Yesssss,' said Beatrice, 'time for Big Ted's meaty roller.'

'No ... please no,' said Christian.

Kevin sat up on his knees and allowed Beatrice to turn over, before adjusting his position and remounting.

'Gently,' she said.

'You can always trust Big Ted,' said Kevin.

The crowd let out an awed '*oooooh*' and some light applause, the cultured kind you find at a cricket match, suggesting they were witnessing something special, at least for the M3 corridor.

Gradually Kevin upped the cadence, responding to Beatrice's encouragement, grabbing what he could of her hair.

'Yes, take a good look,' said Mitch, 'take it all in.'

Christian had nothing to say.

'Oh yeah,' Kevin told the room, his voice even squeakier than normal, 'oh yeah, oh yeah ...'

And then the encouragement started.

'Go on fatty.'

'Give it to 'er.'

'Come on, boy.'

More shouts from the crowd as the onlookers whipped themselves up into a frenzy, shouting and cheering him on like a long-shot dobbin on Derby day.

'Enough,' said Christian. He wrestled himself free and lifted himself back up into the loft. He threw himself into a stack of books and cardboard boxes, and lay there, palms clamped to his temples.

Mitch followed a moment later and was immediately up on his feet. 'Get back there,' he said, pointing to the floor as he stood over Christian, 'we'll miss the big finish.'

'Fuck you, you fucking snake.'

'Hey, don't shoot the messenger, buddy, it's not me you wanna be pissed at.'

Christian shook his head. 'You didn't need to bring me here.'

Mitch took a step back. 'You needed to know,' he said, 'that's all I thought when I found out. My friend needs to know.' He sat down in the floor opposite Christian.

'So?' said Mitch.

'So what?' said Christian.

'So what do you make of it?'

'Well what do you think I make of it?' shouted Christian. He put his hands over his eyes and shook his head.

'Pretty full on, eh?' said Mitch.

'She was … she was …'

'Go on,' said Mitch, 'let it out.'

'She was taking it …' Christian looked up to the loft skylight window, '… she was taking it … up the … up *there*. She was taking it up *there*.'

'She sure was,' said Mitch, with a mellow unseen nod.

A muffled '*ooooaaaaahhhh*' floated up through the chipboard, followed by more applause.

'… but she never took anything there … never, not even once.'

'What a girl, ay?' said Mitch, lifting his hand to the space where his lips would be and blowing her a kiss through the floor.

Christian stood and took a step towards the skylight.

'What are you doing?' asked Mitch.

'Leaving,' said Christian.

'You're not staying for the second half?'

'There's a second half?'

'Sure is. They'll have another go in twenty minutes, after they've had a cup of tea and a biscuit.'

'But, but that was our thing,' he said. 'Hobnobs. Sometimes two each.'

'Well it sure seems to perk her up,' said Mitch, 'him too. Credit where it's due, they go for a lot longer after the break, and well, you know, she keeps takin' it, and takin' it, and he keeps giv'n her, and giv'n her ...' Mitch got up onto his knees and began to thrust his pelvis back and forth.

'I don't want to know, Mitch,' said Christian, turning away.

'And then she does this great thing, kind of a little trick where she–'

'Mitch,' said Christian, with real rancour, 'I don't want to know.'

'Whatever you say,' said Mitch, 'whatever you say,' and he sat back down.

'Come on, let's go,' said Christian.

'Really?'

'I can't stay here another second.'

'Right, cool,' said Mitch, making no effort to stand up, 'it's just, that, you know, it's like I said, the first half, that's really just her preshow.'

'So fucking what?' said Christian. 'You've made your point, now let's go.'

'Yeah, but, you know, we've come all this way. It feels disrespectful to her and the fat dude, you know, not to stay for the full show, ay.'

'They're not performers, Mitch, they don't even know you're there.'

'I know. I know they won't notice, but you know, even if it's dark at the back of the stalls, does that make it okay to leave a regular sex show at half time? No, sir.'

'I'm not listening any more,' said Christian. He began stepping up through the roof. 'Come on.'

'Yeah, sure, I'll catch you up, yeah?'

Christian turned to flash a *don't even think about it* glare, but Mitch was already kneeling down and ducking his shoulders through the floor like he was bobbing for apples.

'Fuck you,' said Christian, and resumed his climb.

Chapter Fifteen

Christian was staring out to the horizon. The rooftop was a fine vantage point for what was turning into a sunset that would delight the most demanding of shepherds. Fucking sunset. Fucking Bea. Fucking Kevin. Fucking Mitch. Fucking afterlife. But mainly it was fucking Bea. How could she.

He sat there, straddling the apex, losing all sense of time, turning the horror over and over in his mind, replaying the details, again and again, and every time totally failing to come to terms with any of it. He tried to lead his mind elsewhere, to numb the pain. He thought of Saturday's football fixtures, he thought again of the summer blockbusters that would soon be at the cinema, he thought of Tracy, Sol, the liver, and he thought of Catherine. But regardless of the subject, fifteen seconds was the best he could manage. Fifteen seconds before his mind found a way to turn his thoughts back to Beatrice's betrayal, back to the spectacle, and back to Mitch duping him into attending.

It was almost an hour later when Christian noticed movement in the street below – punters leaving the house, ones and twos sneaking off at first, no doubt trying to avoid the rush at the final whistle, but soon there were more and more, until they were streaming out of every wall, off into the approaching night.

Mitch's neck and then the rest of him emerged from the roof tiles, basket in hand. 'How you doin', my friend?'

'Friend? You're no friend of mine, you bastard. You could have just told me what was going on. Why did you make me watch?'

'You wouldn't have believed me,' said Mitch, returning the basket to his shoulders.

'You don't know that,' said Christian.

'Yes I do. Look, even if I got you to believe she was seeing the fat dude, you'd have made excuses, *they're just friends, it's a one-time thing, it's not like she's enjoying it.*'

'Well, maybe she wasn't ...'

'Oh you gotta be kidding.'

'... maybe she was doing what she thought he wanted, that's what women do.'

'Dude, you were there. No one screams like that if they're not waaaaaaaaaaaay into it.'

'Leave it,' said Christian.

Mitch began gyrating his hips and doing an imitation of Beatrice's moans, 'oh, oh yeah, oh Big Teddy, fuck me harder, Big Teddy.'

Christian swung a punch and connected with Mitch's basket, sending several pages of the notepad lining cartwheeling free as it tumbled across to the other end of the roof and into the chimney stack.

'Hey. Watch the wicker,' said Mitch, before turning to go and retrieve the basket.

'Fuck you,' said Christian.

Mitch checked the basket for damage, taking his time before turning and drifting back to Christian.

'Look,' he said, 'I know it stings now, but one day you'll thank me.'

'Yeah, right.'

Mitch put his hands on his hips and waited, before sitting down next to Christian.

They looked out over the estate and the town beyond as the last light of day was gradually consumed by the night.

No words were spoken for some time. When they were, they came from Christian. 'How did you find out?' he said. 'How did you even know?'

'The grapevine,' said Mitch, 'they were creating quite a buzz.'

'What?'

'Voyeurism. It's huge here, in the Zone. And it's the same in every town. When someone stumbles across a new local hot show, especially at a regular time slot, word gets out. No, this one wasn't gonna stay secret for long.'

'But those men, there were just … so many.' Christian put his head in his hands. 'It's all gone wrong.'

'You wanna know the worst?' said Mitch.

'How can it get any worse?'

'Maybe they weren't the only ones watching.'

'What do you mean?'

'Some say others can watch the mortal realm too,' said Mitch.

'Others?' said Christian.

'Yep, others.'

'What kind of others?'

'I don't know.'

'Well how many?'

Mitch shrugged. 'Hundreds, maybe.'

'Really?'

'No.'

Christian felt a grain of relief.

'Probably more like thousands,' said Mitch.

'Thousands?' said Christian. He put his hands to the crown of his head and tried to think of FA Cup winners this century, but he couldn't get the sex show image out of his mind, and it was now taking on grander proportions. His Bea, his sweet Beasy-Bea, now the latest afterlife reality porn sensation.

'Then again it could be tens of thousands.'

'Tens of …'

'Look, your girl,' said Mitch, 'okay she's no fillet steak, but she is one spicy meatball. Plus the fat dude, well that's the masterstroke, he's like the underdog every Joe can root for. So yeah, they'd be pretty popular, I reckon.'

'She was never a spicy meatball with me,' said Christian, 'least not lately. More like a cold turkey rissole.' He shook his head. 'Jeez, Mitch, she was like a different person back there.'

'That's what I've been saying, buddy. Face it, she's not the girl you knew.'

'No. No, she is the girl I knew, the girl I know … she's just, well … lost.'

'Oh come on, buddy, wake up. Can't you see? She's not hangin' around. She's moved on and so must you.'

'I don't want to move on. It's all too raw. It was bad enough before but now it feels like I've lost her all over again.'

'Okay, reality check, my friend,' said Mitch, snapping his fingers in Christian's face. 'One, you're dead. Two, she's alive. Three, she's getting fucked in the ass by a fat dude and loving it. It's time to see the writing on the wall, it's time to wake up and smell the mega bucket of coffee. This part of your life is over.'

'No, no, you don't know her,' said Christian, shaking his head again, 'this is, this is a cry for help.'

'*What?*'

'Now she needs me more than ever.'

Christian got up, walked off the roof, and began stepping his way down to ground level.

'Well where the hell are you going?' asked Mitch.

'Where do you think?'

Christian was still striding on out front by the time they entered Vestments.

Mitch, following on, had been unable to make him see reason. He'd seen this sort of thing before, of course, but he was still concerned.

'Look, she's not even home,' Mitch said, as the empty driveway came into view.

'But I'll be here for her when she returns,' said Christian. He strode on, but as he reached the house, he stopped. 'Who the hell's that?' he said, nodding to the living room window.

Through the glass they could see a stout toad-like man wearing a large but still stretched boiler suit, rolls of neck fat spilling out onto the collar. He was standing with his back to them, apparently studying the photographs in the clip frame montage on the wall.

'Surely she's not doing this guy too?' said Christian, not registering the implications of the colours in the scene: the only source of illumination was the yellowed monochrome light from the street lamps, yet the figure in the living room had a distinctive blue-green glow.

'Move,' said Mitch, pushing Christian forward and through to the wheelie bin enclosure on the opposite side of the front door.

'What's your problem?'

'Quiet,' said Mitch. He whipped off his basket and edged his non-head round the wall to look into the living room.

'Perhaps she had a thing for fat men all along?' said Christian. He slumped down into the concrete, with his back to the bin. 'Why didn't she say so? I could have gained a kilo or two, shoved a pillow up my shirt in the bedroom. If she'd only given me a chance.'

'I said quiet,' whispered Mitch, 'look, I know this guy. He's a ghost … he's bad news.'

'Whatever,' said Christian.

'You're going to have to do exactly as I say,' said Mitch. He considered the options. 'Right, get in there,' he said, pointing to the wheelie bin.

'In there?' said Christian, turning to look.

'Yes.'

'Why?'

'No time for questions,' said Mitch, and he shoved Christian, still in his seated position, backwards like he was on a camera dolly, back through the plastic wall of the bin.

'Hey … *hey*,' said Christian. He made a half-hearted struggle, but was held in position. 'All right, all right,' he said, with resignation.

Mitch released his grip.

'It stinks in here I'll have you know,' said Christian.

'It can't harm you.'

'It's not even empty.'

'It's only until I get rid of this guy. You're gonna have to trust me.'

Silence.

Mitch made sure nothing of Christian was showing through the back and sides of the bin.

'Do you trust me?' asked Mitch.

Christian's hand appeared through the plastic, middle finger raised.

'Cool. I won't be long.'

Mitch replaced his basket, paused, took it off again, paused, then finally placed it back on his shoulders before drifting in through the front door, into the hallway, and on through into the living room.

'Hello, Slacks,' he said.

The figure turned and fixed Mitch with his wide eyes. 'Mitchell Langford,' he said. The angel's sad gormless expression and lugubrious tone belied not the merest hint of recognition, let alone any modest pleasure in meeting an old acquaintance, 'I was beginning to think you'd moved on.'

Candleslack's skin was smooth, but everything sagged, like a waxwork left too near a radiator. The baseball cap and stringy black wig wasn't even close to masking his late middle-aged looks, but then Mitch wondered if maybe Candleslack just couldn't give a rat's. But then why? Why wouldn't he give a rat's? Maybe– Mitch stopped himself. He didn't do whys. Whys were worse than whats and led to dangerous places.

'Hotswap send you, did he?' said Mitch. He ambled towards the patio doors, reasoning it would be sensible to put some extra distance between the conversation and the wheelie bin.

'I don't get sent anywhere, Mitchell. You should know that.' Candleslack made his way over to Mitch and then stepped in close. 'Nice basket,' said the angel, flatly.

Mitch half watched through the wicker as the internal buttons on the angel's boiler suit came undone, one after the other from top to bottom, before a naked clawhand appeared and reached up to the basket, its digits caressing the decorative edging. Mitch flicked his eyes upwards, gluing them to the top of his basket, cursing himself for not doing it sooner.

'Cherubs?' said Candleslack.

'Serves a purpose,' said Mitch.

'Oh, and I like what you've done with the lining,' said Candleslack. He stepped closer still, his gut pressing into the tops of Mitch's thighs. 'Clever … no, resourceful. Any situation, any cargo, you find the way, you get your man. That's you, isn't it, Mitchell.' The clawhand disappeared back inside the suit but the angel did not step back.

Mitch removed the basket and pushed it into Candleslack's chest. 'Take a closer look if you like.'

Candleslack's eyes widened as they flicked to Mitch's neck cavity, but the angel stood his ground and it was Mitch who took a step back.

This time Candleslack expertly took the basket in his puppeteered false hands. He glanced down and flipped the basket round. 'You've got a few gaps at the back,' he said. 'Hope you're not losing your touch.' He passed the basket back to Mitch.

'So what are you doing here, then?' asked Mitch, as casually as he could.

The angel took his time to reply. 'I got curious.'

'Oh yeah?'

'Yeah. I heard about the trail going cold on this Bootstrap fella.'

'So he's still not been found then?'

'Well. You tell me.'

Again Candleslack's poker face revealed nothing. Mitch had always been good at that game too, though of course it was considerably easier to hide his tells these days, what with not having a head.

'I got nothing,' said Mitch, taking care to keep his thyroid casual.

'Really.'

'Zip.'

'No leads?'

'Nope.'

'You're telling me you've been here a month and you've got nothing at all?'

'Well obviously not totally nothing,' said Mitch. 'I heard a couple of rumours, but that's it.'

'Rumours, eh? Well let's hear 'em then.'

'They're just rumours.'

'No, Mitchell. I like rumours. Smoke. Fire. You know how it is.'

'Well ... okay then ... I heard he's in London.'

'Really? London. And where did you hear that then?'

'Some local wannabes. They went looking for him.'

'Did they? After a bounty, I suppose?'

'I guess.'

'So there's rumours he's in London. Yet the great Mitchell Langford is still here. Now that strikes me as strange.'

'Well, like I say, they're just rumours. Anyway, if he is in London, the locals will pick him up. Stands to reason.'

'Come off it, you're not gonna give up that easily,' said Candleslack, 'not after what Hots has promised you.'

'There'll be other jobs, I'm in no rush.'

'Really? Never had you down as the ... philosophical type.'

Mitch could feel Candleslack looking him straight in the eyes. Even though Mitch knew the angel couldn't be certain where Mitch's eyes were. It was unnerving. No one ever looked at him like this.

'You sure there's nothing you're not telling me?' said Candleslack.

'Nothing,' said Mitch.

A long stare-filled silence.

'Okay, Mitchell,' said Candleslack, 'okay.' He stepped back. 'One thing, though,' he said, 'why are you still here?'

'He may still show up,' said Mitch, 'it's a long shot but it happens.'

The angel looked Mitch up and down. 'If I find you've been holding out on me,' he said, 'you'll have a lot more to worry about than when you can start wearing hats again.'

They stared at each other, neither moving a muscle.

'Well. I'll be seeing you round, Mitchell,' said Candleslack, 'do look after yourself.'

'I'll try,' said Mitch, before mouthing 'fuck off' with his non-lips.

'I'm sorry?' said Candleslack.

'What?' said Mitch.

'Thought maybe you said something else.'

'No,' said Mitch, before mouthing 'fuck off, you fat hoser.'

Candleslack stepped close. 'I'm watching you, Mitchell.'

Having made sure Candleslack was really gone – silently and secretly following the angel at neck level out to the edge of Vestments – Mitch was back in the living room trying to work out what had gone wrong earlier and, more importantly, what his next move was.

He just didn't get it. Operation Ping Pong had gone off without a hitch and yet its result was the exact opposite of what he'd intended. Now it seemed Christian was more tied to Beatrice and Bracknell than ever. What now? Maybe he should just come out with it, tell Christian the truth? But who was he kidding, that was never going to work – *Hey, Christian, I'm really a shepherd, and my job is to deliver you to the sacred Gate of Judgement any way I can. Sorry for all the bullshit, but often it's the only way. So now that's clear, let's make tracks.*

His thoughts turned to where he'd left Christian. Still in the bin. Should he give him the all-clear? No, he could ferment a while longer.

But footsteps on the drive and a key in the door triggered Christian to authorise his own parole.

Even after two decades of collections, Mitch couldn't fail to feel some pity over the spectacle that followed. But he didn't try to intervene – in part because letting Christian go through this could help the situation, and it would certainly be unlikely to make it worse, but mainly because once a piece of cargo was in this state of mind, they never listened to reason anyway. All you can do is let the events play out. So he retired to the garden, making only occasional glances through the living room window to check on progress.

Christian tried everything. Soft whispers, barked instructions, singing, poetry, mime. He even took a shot at experimental telepathy by, with gritted teeth, placing his head inside Beatrice's while visualising the details of their trip to the Cotswolds in the spring of 2009. Nothing. Then the concern, the pacing, the ever louder knock of reality at the door. Then the rage, the shouting and the screaming; his best swearing; hitting things that couldn't be hit; hitting himself because he could be hit. All that remained was the inevitable descent into the pleading, wailing and incoherent jabbering.

It was the early hours of the morning before Christian emerged, a freshly broken man, the washed-up boxer after his latest comeback fight. He didn't utter a word as they began the slow plod back to the vicarage. Mitch's spirits were almost as low. Not so much because of what he'd just witnessed – yes, he did feel for Christian, it never being easy to see cargo feed itself through an emotional mangle – but because he was running out of time. Too many eyebrows were being raised, too many questions were being asked, and Christian was tied to this place more than ever. He would have to find a new way. And quick.

Chapter Sixteen

Christian opened his eyes. Light was streaming through the bedroom windows.

He didn't understand.

He blinked. He blinked again.

He still didn't understand.

He'd gone to sleep in the sofa as usual, at the vicarage, as usual. He definitely had. So how had he found his way back to the house, back to his bedroom at number twenty-two? He'd never so much as sleepwalked into the bathroom before, let alone right across Bracknell.

His back felt strange. A warm closeness. A closeness on his front, too, though much softer. It was contact, proper contact with the mattress and the duvet.

He got out of bed and his feet found the carpet. The floor took his weight.

A muffled shout from the hall. Beatrice's voice, 'We're going to be late.'

He ran downstairs and into the kitchen. There she was. Ash-brown bob, slight scowl, air of mild irritation.

He picked her off her feet and spun her round, hugging her tight.

'Hey. Hey, what's got into you?' she said.

'I'm back. I'm back! It was … it was …'

'It was what?' she said. 'Actually, what was what?'

He had to sit down. 'I can't believe I'm going to say this ...'

'Say what?'

He cleared his throat and said, 'It was all a dream.'

'Well you were tossing and turning an awful lot,' she said.

He felt his lungs draw breath. He felt his heart beating in his chest. And then he was up, up and running around the kitchen slapping every cupboard door, leaping between strides, opening and closing the fridge, then the oven, then the breadbin, then attempting a juggle of the apples in the fruit bowl as Beatrice watched on with a combination of delight and bewilderment.

And then he stopped. He looked down at the cat basket. The liver was a sickly pale grey. What's more, it wasn't moving. Christian watched and waited, looking for a sign, a movement from the portal vein, a shuffle, anything.

Nothing.

It just lay there on the blood-stained butcher's paper that served as his bedding.

'What's wrong?' asked Beatrice.

'The liver, it's not moving,' said Christian, bending down, 'we've got to do something.'

'Why would it be moving?' said Beatrice. 'It's a liver, a piece of meat.'

'How can you be so cruel? You're talking about Leslie.' He turned to his old pal. 'Leslie. *Leslie.*'

He stretched out a hand. The liver was stone cold.

He took the organ in his arms and ran.

Running.

Running.

Running.

Running to save Leslie.

He burst through the swing doors of A and E.

'Help,' he shouted, 'please, can anyone help?'

Nikki looked up from the reception desk.

'You want some help?'

'Yes, please, help.'

'He wants us to help,' said Nikki, as two nurses appeared.

'Then we should think about helping,' they said.

'What do I do? Where do I go?' asked Christian.

'Yes, we should help.'

'We should.'

'Yes, we *should.*'

More nurses arrived. Soon Christian was surrounded.

'Fucking help then,' he said. He held out the organ, his hands now covered in blood. 'Take him, please, if you say you can help, then help.'

They said nothing, but began to step back, forming a human corridor to another set of swing doors at the back of the reception area.

'The doctor will see you now,' said one of the nurses.

Christian ran up the lines to the doors and pushed them open, leading him into a kitchen.

A figure in a gravy-stained white tunic and chef's hat was standing with his back to Christian behind a large table by the rear hobs. He was whistling. Smoke was billowing up from the hobs and under the ceiling, and there was an acrid smell, possibly coming from the mouldy onions the man was frying off.

The man turned round.

'Finally,' said Erdygrot, cigarette bobbing on his bottom lip. He picked up a meat cleaver from the table. 'Let's have him then, I'm fuckin' starving.'

Christian opened his eyes.

He was alone. Alone in the front room at the vicarage. Alone in the nothingness of the sofa. The tick of the Cheesus clock on the mantelpiece.

Relief.

And then horror at the relief.

And then sadness.

Chapter Seventeen

Nikki was outside in the high-walled atrium garden, having a smoke with the Jesuses.

After staring at walls or empty space, smoking was the next most popular activity-cum-therapy. Everyone did it. Given enough time, even lifelong non-smokers would become packet-a-day stalwarts. It was a perfect fit: aside from the usual addictive qualities, it gave your hands something to do, it calmed you down, you could chat to others while you did it, and it was something they had to let you do outside. And, for some, the known health risks gave them something else to worry about, providing welcome relief from their bigger concerns. Though not Nikki. She didn't lament what it did to your health, at least not in the way everyone else did.

Barry and Wee motioned to speak, but in the end did not comment.

'That's not how it works, my dear,' said Autumn Jesus.

'I know that's not how it works,' said Nikki, 'that's my point. It's a law without logic. If someone wants it to end, and they make this decision calmly, rationally, under no duress, under no external source of pressure, debt, guilt, whatever it may be, and they have no responsibilities to anyone else, then it should be their decision. Their life is theirs and no one else's. They wish it to end, this is all that should be required.'

Vivian came over to the group. 'You've got a visitor,' she said to Nikki.

Nikki took a final drag on her cigarette.

'Do I look all right?' she said. That morning she'd washed her hair, brushed it, and tied it back. She'd been in two minds as to what to do about the scars on her face. She wouldn't be able to hide them completely, especially given the limited toiletries available. But then there was an argument not to try to – it could play either way. In the end, she'd decided to tidy them up as best she could. Empathy not sympathy, that was the strategy. There was nothing she could do about the pyjamas, of course, but she at least made sure she had a fresh pair to put on.

'Pretty as a picture, my dear,' said Autumn Jesus.

Barry and Wee nodded.

She turned to leave.

Vivian followed and, once out of earshot of the Jesuses, tugged on Nikki's sleeve. 'You have to go up the vein, not across,' she whispered.

'Right. Thanks.'

Chapter Eighteen

'Look, how about we take a break from all this?' said Mitch, gazing out of the window, as Christian browsed the newsagent's shelves. Mitch had hoped the cold light of day would bring Christian to his senses. Not a bit of it.

'What?' said Christian.

'You know, get away from it, take a vacation.'

'A holiday? Are you insane?'

'Could be just what you need. We could go anywhere. How about London?'

'London?' said Christian, not looking up from the shelves. 'Have you ever been to London? It's about as relaxing as DIY dentistry.'

'Come on, it'll be fun. London Dungeon, Buckingham Palace, that wheel thing, you know. And we could do it properly, we could stay with the Queen, watch the Prime Minister getting laid, anything you like.'

'Do you think they do occult women's lifestyle magazines?' asked Christian.

'What are you talking about?'

'Something that covers communication problems in your relationship, but you know, maybe with a Ouija board or voodoo angle?'

'You're clutching at straws, buddy. I don't wanna twist the knife, but didn't last night tell you anything?'

'It told me I have to keep trying, that there has to be a way.'

'Yeah, so you keep sayin,' said Mitch. Again he checked the street outside for anyone who looked out of place for Bracknell on a Tuesday morning.

'*Seven Ways To Bridge Dimensions,*' said Christian, still scanning the magazines, 'maybe that could be useful.'

'I don't think so,' said Mitch, glancing back, 'besides, how you gonna read it?'

'Same as your church records, we wait till someone buys one, then we follow them home and wait for them to read it.'

'Sure sounds like a fun way to spend the next two weeks.'

Mitch drifted back in from the window and looked up at the top-shelf magazines. Having no head, he was able to look as much as he liked with no one noticing, not that he'd been fazed in life. But then it was no less frustrating than Christian's viewing experience, only being able to inspect the front covers, and even then, front covers shrouded in grey plastic.

He turned to look at Christian, who by now was going back to covers he'd already checked. And then, finally, Mitch gave in. The problem was also the solution and he'd known as much since the previous evening. It was the quickest, dirtiest, lowest trick in the business, and in twenty years he'd never played it. He was better than that. It was what kept him above all the others, his apology for the smaller deceptions he was forced to pull. But he was out of options and out of time.

'Look, are you insistent on this?' he said. 'Making contact with your girl. Is this what you really want, above all else?'

'Yes, absolutely,' said Christian, 'haven't you been listening?'

'And what would you do to make it possible?'

'Anything.'

'Okay.'

'Why do you ask?'

'No reason.'

'Come on, why?'

'Well, it's only what I heard ...'

'What? Come on, tell me.'

'Well, maybe there is something, or rather someone, who can help. An expert.'

'Really? Why the hell didn't you say so?'

'Well, I'm saying so now.'

'But when I asked you earlier you dismissed it out of hand.'

'I don't think I did.'

'Yes, you did, you said it was absolutely totally impossible to contact the living.'

'Nah. Maybe I said unlikely, but not impossible.'

'You did. And even just now you said I was wasting my time.'

'Well like I say, it's only what I heard,' said Mitch. 'I didn't want you to get your hopes up. Hope can lead you to dark places here, y'know.'

'So it's not absolutely totally impossible?'

'No.'

'Well let's go and see them then.'

'What, now?'

'Yes, now,' said Christian.

'So you're not bothered about the summer blockbusters then?'

'I'm sure they have cinemas wherever we're going, so let's go.'

'Well okay then.'

'So where are we going?'

'London, my friend. We are going to London.'

'Oh,' said Christian, flatly.

'Yes,' said Mitch, a little deflated.

'Well. Let's get to it then.'

After returning to the vicarage for Mitch's knapsack, they were on their way. And for once Mitch wasn't having to take on the motivator role, his cargo showing unheard-of eagerness. Christian had suggested, for navigational simplicity and minimisation of planning time, they take the back road to Windsor and then follow the M4 into central London, retracing his death march in reverse. Mitch agreed, his only stipulation being that they walk next to the road, in the adjacent fields, to keep a low profile, ostensibly because of the unwanted attention his basket, or lack of basket, tended to generate. Christian agreed.

Before long, Christian began to reflect on the last time he'd walked this sorry route. This time it couldn't be more different – now he had hope. The sun was shining, everything was, perhaps, going to be okay. He had company this time, too, and the time passed easily as they talked and drifted, Christian regularly turning to the topic of who they were going to see, and Mitch regularly turning away from it, preferring instead to quiz Christian on his beliefs, family background, employment history and, to Christian's bafflement, on whether he'd ever turned out for a pub darts team.

Chapter Nineteen

Nikki sat on the hospital bed, looking at Kevin – looking at him for the first time since she'd sought him out for information on Christian's teachers, and only the second time since she'd kicked him out and unleashed the lawyers.

He looked clean, unusually smartly dressed, and appeared to be revelling in his sanity as he gawped at the only other patients present, Edgar and Roach, sitting on their beds on the other side of the ward. The weeble-like nurse Jean was also present, sitting on a chair between the windows at the far end, ostensibly doing some paperwork, but obviously eavesdropping.

'Why have you been wanting to see me?' asked Nikki.

'Why've your lawyers been stopping me?' asked Kevin.

'You first.'

Kevin smirked. 'Can't a concerned and loving husband visit his troubled wife?' he said.

She repeated the question.

Kevin leaned back in the visitor's chair. 'Lots of reasons,' he said.

She looked him in the eye, but he made no further response. 'Why are you keeping me here?' she said.

He shook his head and chuckled. 'When did you get so paranoid, love?'

'But you are, aren't you?'

'You're keeping yourself here, my sweetest, after what you did, after what I'm *told* you did.'

She felt him look her up and down, sizing her up, undoubtedly pleased with her unvarnished appearance, and, perhaps, with the scars.

'Can you get me out?' she said.

'Straight to business as ever, eh, love?'

'Well?'

'Quick pro crow, Clarice, quick pro crow,' said Kevin, sounding like Hannibal Lecter's embarrassing Blackpudlian cousin.

'What do you want?' asked Nikki.

'Why don't you start by telling me why.'

'Why what?'

'Why everything,' said Kevin, 'why you kicked me out, why you've tried to top yourself. A proper explanation.'

A pause.

'I don't know why,' she said.

'Come on, love, let's not play games.'

Another pause.

She wanted to make a smart reply, to flex her distaste at seeing him again, her distaste for him in general, but that wasn't going to get her anywhere. 'If you must know, I suppose things just got too much,' she said.

Kevin shook his head. 'No. That's not it. Tell me the truth.'

'I have told you.'

He shook his head again. 'Do you want me to help you or not, love?'

'I can't tell you,' she said, after a pause.

'Can't or won't?'

'Can't.'

'Why can't?'

'I can't tell you.'

'Can't or won't?'

'Can't.'

'So you can't tell me and you can't tell me why you can't tell me, but you still want me to help you?'

'Yes.'

'Right. Well I'll be off then.' He got up from the chair.

'Wait,' said Nikki, 'what if I give you something else?'

'Go on,' said Kevin, staying on his feet.

'Well, how about we discuss the terms? Who gets what, the houses, the cars, the boat, the stock.'

'But I thought I'd already been given a "generous and final settlement"?'

'That can be changed.'

Kevin pursed his lips.

Nikki continued, 'Come on, let's cut the crap, a new deal, that is what you're after, isn't it?'

'Maybe.'

'Well let's talk turkey then. Just you and me. Right now.'

Kevin seemed to hesitate, but retook his seat. 'Okay,' he said, 'half. I want half, including half the equity in the business.'

'Done.'

'Done? What do you mean, done?'

'I mean done. I agree. You get half.'

'Sixty forty, in my favour.'

'I thought you wanted half?'

'I've changed my mind. Sixty forty.'

'Okay, sixty forty then. Done.'

He looked puzzled. 'Seventy thirty, that's my final offer.'

'Offer accepted.'

'All right, wait. Eighty twenty, in my favour. Final, final offer.'

'All right,' she said.

Silence.

'What's your game?' asked Kevin.

'You really don't get it, do you?' she said. 'You have no idea what's going on, even now, after all this time.'

'Ninety ten or I walk away.'

'I don't want any of it, dearest. I don't need it. You can have it all, one hundred per cent, lock stock.'

'So what's in it for you then?'

'I need one thing. To be out of here.'

'That's it?'

'That's it. My sole condition,' she said. 'Soul condition,' she added, turning away.

Kevin sat back and rubbed his chin. 'And that's why you wanted to see me?'

'Don't overthink this, Einstein. Your ship has come in, so draw up the papers and tell me where to sign.'

'I don't believe you. You'll sign and then your lawyers will wriggle you out of it.'

'They won't.'

He laughed. 'In case you hadn't noticed, love, you're in the nut house, I'd say that counts for several lorry loads of wriggle room.'

'Well I'll sign the moment I get out then, I give you my word.'

'Nice try, love.'

'I swear.'

Kevin gave a wry smile and folded his arms.

'Well what can I say to convince you?' she said.

'That's just it, love, there's nothing you can say, it's a legal peat bog sitting at the bottom of a lake of mental health treacle, so my lawyers say.'

'Well if you can't do a deal, then why did you even come?'

'Oh, sorry, love, I thought that was obvious.'

'It isn't.'

'I'm here to help with the case.'

'The case?'

'Yeah, I don't know the proper terms, but it's a sort of reverse divorce I'm filing on you, gazumping your one. So I just popped in to get some dirt, anything that could help, you know how these lawyers are, they're like Rottweilers, sink their teeth into anything. Plus even just a visit looks good, especially after you keeping me away. Helps cement our roles, you know.'

'Our roles?'

'Yeah, apparently I'm the Andy Garcia character from *When a Man Loves a Woman*, and you're that mad rabbit-boiling bint out of *Fatal Attraction*.'

She wanted to poke his eyes out. She'd given him a life of luxury that he never deserved; she'd given her body to him; she *had* given him a generous and final settlement; and here he was, eating into her for more. But it didn't matter; no matter how angry he made her, it didn't matter. Focus, girl, focus.

'So you won't even need my agreement,' she said, 'you'll get what you want anyway. So help me out of here. Do this one thing and I won't stand in your way.'

'Can't risk it, love. Every day you stay in here strengthens the case. You know how it is. Nothing personal, just business.' He grinned. 'Obviously we'll be pushing hard for a long-term extension, but still, I'm sure you'll get out eventually.'

Nikki wasn't listening; she was in deep, desperate thought, flailing for a contingency plan that wasn't there.

Kevin got to his feet once again. 'Good luck with the release,' he said with a wink, and turned to leave.

'Wait. *Wait.*'

He stopped and turned back to her.

Jean looked up from the end of the ward and made eye contact with Nikki and then Kevin. She seemed to shift her weight to stand, but then her eyes returned to her forms.

Nikki stretched out her feet, pushing them under the blanket, and curled her toes. 'Look,' she said, 'what if I put something else on the table, something priceless?'

Kevin waited, then took a single step closer. 'Let's hear it then,' he said.

'Sit down.'

He started to turn back to the door.

'Okay, okay,' she said, 'look, what if I call off my lawyers, you call off yours ...'

'And?'

She held back a primeval instinct to dry retch. 'And we try again..'

'What?' said Kevin, almost laughing.

'You heard.'

Kevin retook his seat. 'Tell me again,' he said, tapping his ear.

'Let's get back together,' she said. 'A fresh start. You see' – she dug her fingernails into her palms – 'I still love you ... Big Ted.'

Kevin laughed. 'Jesus, love, you must take me for a right divvy.'

'I mean it,' she said, 'let's try again, let's put all this behind us, I know we can make it work.' She gave him one of her looks, one of her finest blends: 35% lost puppy; 40% smouldering seductress; 25% naughty schoolgirl keen to explore creative ways out of serving a detention.

'That's not going to work any more,' said Kevin, with a shake of the head.

'Look into my eyes and tell me that,' she said.

He slowly turned his head towards hers and leaned in.

She watched as he took a good long look, adjusting his angles to better appreciate the red ridges of her scars.

He exhaled.

'Really made a mess, that windscreen, eh, love? Reckon you could do a pretty good Mason Verger now. "Goody-goody."'

'I said look into my eyes.'

He smiled and flicked his eyes straight up to hers.

She held onto his gaze, sucking it in, devouring his eyes with hers. She held, and held, and held, but there was no reaction. He just stared right back, even lifting his nose to goad her, flaunting his indifference.

She blinked. She put her hand to her mouth and turned away. A wave of heat flushed through her, her skin suddenly clammy, the bed clothes suddenly itchy under her legs.

'It's over, Nick Nack,' said Kevin, 'you finished it first, but I'm finishing it last.'

'Well. Fuck off then,' said Nikki, turning back to him.

'Fuck off?' said Kevin, chirpily. 'Fuck off? That's all you got? Well, you know what, love, I reckon I will.'

He motioned to get up but she stretched out her arm to his.

'Wait,' she said, 'bring me a knife. Pills, razor blades, anything. Give me the tools and I'll do it.'

'W-what?'

'I'll end it. I'll end it here and you'll get everything.'

'You're, you're serious?'

'Totally.'

A moment of silence.

'You're setting me up,' he said, looking around.

'No. It's just you and me.' She pulled him in close. 'Do it, Kevin, help me end it.'

'Jesus, you really are mad. You're totally fuckin' nuts.'

He got up to leave, but Nikki lunged at him, grabbing him around the waist.

'Help me,' she begged, 'help me end it.'

'Help, help,' yelped Kevin, 'she's gone fuckin' Tonto.'

A hock of ham wrapped itself around Nikki's throat and wrenched her back.

'You don't know how happy you've made me,' said Jean.

'You fucking worm,' said Nikki, as she was pulled away, clawing at Kevin's arms, 'I never loved you, I was using you. From the day we met I was using you.'

'She's drawn blood,' said Kevin, looking down at his arm, 'that's ... that's, hey, hey, have another go, love,' and he dangled his arm back into the melee.

'Maggot,' shouted Nikki, as she tried to take the bait.

'Hey, you're a witness,' said Kevin to Jean, but the nurse was already consumed with closing out the bout. She dropped to the floor, dragging Nikki with her, and rolled, flipping Nikki over and pinning her to the lino.

Jean flexed her massive forearm muscles and in a few seconds Nikki had passed out.

'And a one … and a two … and a three,' Jean whooped, before relaxing and releasing Nikki's limp body.

'Jeano wins again,' said Jean, 'one fall to nothing.'

She stood, bowed to the ward and took the absence of applause.

Chapter Twenty

By early evening, Mitch and Christian had crossed the M25 and were into the outskirts of Greater London. Though the fields were mostly now behind them, they still had some natural cover, walking among the trees and foliage of the motorway verge. But soon three lanes would become two, and soon after that they'd be forced out onto urban streets and pavements, and greater exposure.

Mitch had other concerns, too. He still didn't have a watertight plan for getting in undetected, plus he hadn't yet sorted the paperwork and he needed to do that out of sight of Christian. Worse still, he'd started to feel a rising temptation to just go for it. They were perhaps four hours away. Four hours and it would all be over. Four hours and he could claim his prize. But as they passed signs for the Heathrow terminals, an idea formed. And soon after, across the other lanes and out to the right, a huge white monolith came into view. Yes, that would do fine.

'All right, that's our stop for tonight,' said Mitch, pointing out across the lanes.

'The Ambassador ComfiLodge?'

'What's wrong with an Ambassador ComfiLodge?'

'Well, nothing I suppose, but can't we keep going? Come on, we're nearly there.'

'We're halfway at best. You're gonna need your strength tomorrow and besides, it's going to be dark soon.'

'But–'

'No buts. We're stopping.'

'Oh. All right,' said Christian, 'all right, but if we must stop, can't we at least stay somewhere better?'

'Nothing beats an airport hotel,' said Mitch.

'Everything beats an airport hotel.'

'Explain.'

'They're soulless places with no atmosphere,' said Christian.

'We don't need soul and atmosphere,' said Mitch, 'we need a low profile.'

'I still don't–'

'Think, will you? Ghosts can't fly in airplanes, so ghosts don't need airports, so ghosts don't need airport hotels, so they make a nice safe stopover where we won't be hassled.'

'I don't care,' said Christian, 'I refuse to stay at an Ambassador ComfiLodge.'

'Can we at least get some nice rooms?' said Christian, as they drifted into the reception area.

'Sure, but we only need one,' said Mitch.

'I'm not sharing.'

'Why?'

'Because there's two hundred rooms to choose from and they're all gratis.'

'We stick together.'

'What are you afraid of?'

'What are *you* afraid of?'

The deluxe twin room was comfortable enough, and well fitted out, but any novelty was short-lived due to the depressing though wholly predictable truth of how few of the executive features were relevant for guests who were dead. They could appreciate the little bit of extra space over that of a standard room. They could perhaps detect a tiny degree of greater comfort in the honeycomb nothingness of the beds. And that was it. TV, tea and coffee, shortbread biscuits, bath, mini-bar, Wi-Fi, slippers and top-of-the-line trouser press were all useless. So in only a short while they had returned to practicalities.

'Don't say I never do anything for you,' said Christian, as he pulled the last pages from his notepad.

Mitch looked up from checking his knapsack. 'I didn't ask you to fix it,' he said.

'Half the lining was missing,' said Christian, 'you could see straight in.'

'Well, won't make much difference now.'

'How so?'

'All in good time, my friend.'

Half an hour later and Christian had managed to repair most of the basket's gaps, but it was still looking like something that might attract the sympathy vote at an under-eights craft competition.

'We're a few sheets short,' said Christian, 'you got anything else?'

'Ah, don't sweat it, buddy, it's not worth it. Besides, time to turn in.'

Christian had managed to nod off eventually, but slept fitfully, not being able to stop himself going over everything he was going to say to Beatrice the next day. And it wasn't just the what – it was the how. How exactly would he be able to talk to her? Would the medium pass everything on, word for word, or only a vague approximation? If it was word for word, would that entail Christian borrowing the medium's body for a while? If so, would he be able to hold Beatrice in his arms once again? Would he be able to extend the loan of the body through the weekend? And how would he feel about it if the medium was a woman? Or, for that matter, a man?

Now he was awake again and staring at the ceiling. Most of the room was dark, but the open curtains allowed a weak moonlight-streetlight emulsion to illuminate the central third of the room, enough to prick an unexpected fascination with the topology of the ceiling tiles.

Ten minutes later he'd expanded the survey to include the curtain mechanism and his headboard lamps. But it wasn't working. He mentally exhaled and sat up.

He glanced across to the other bed, but all he saw was shadow. He thought nothing of it, but then his glowing left arm, low in his peripheral vision, reminded him there should be more.

He got up and crossed the room while doing his best to suppress a bud of panic. There would be a rational explanation. Perhaps Mitch hadn't been able to sleep either. Perhaps he'd also got bored with the ceiling tiles and gone looking for international supermodels enjoying competitive room rates and impromptu late-night showers?

Christian drifted out through the door, into the softly lit corridor, and back into technicolour, where he found an immediate answer.

Mitch was sitting on the floor, next to his knapsack, holding a document. In front of him, placed at various levels above the carpet, were a thick leather-bound book, a quill and inkwell, and more documents.

'What are you doing?' said Christian. 'I thought we were supposed to be sleeping?'

'We are,' said Mitch as he began to gather up the documents. 'I was just catchin' up on a few things. Go back to bed.'

'What, you're doing your family tree stuff now?'

'Best cure for insomnia I know.'

'Fair enough.'

'Right, back to sleep, buddy. You'll need your strength tomorrow.'

'Can't sleep. Too excited,' said Christian, and he sat down. 'Good book?' he asked.

'Not really,' said Mitch, and closed it shut.

'Wait a minute, you've got a book.' Christian jumped to his feet. 'A book you can hold and touch. I mean, how did … where did … are they–'

'Buddy, stop. We're not doing twenty questions on this. Yeah, books are pretty rare here, but they do exist. They're all handmade. I got this one off a friend, long time ago, no idea where he got it. That's all I gotta tell.'

'Oh. Right,' said Christian. He sat down again. '*Terry's Field Guide To the Afterlife*,' he said. The title rang a bell somewhere in his mind. It was a small annoying silver bell, like the ones above the doors of old corner-shop newsagents, but the rest of Christian's mind couldn't connect it to anything, so it just hung in the back of his consciousness, tinkling. 'Doesn't sound much like a genealogy book.'

A short pause.

'It's got a genealogy section,' said Mitch.

'So what's the rest of it about then?'

'It's a sort of afterlife guide book,' said Mitch.

'What? Really?'

'Yes, really.'

'Only, I was writing one of those. In life, I mean. That was my book idea, pretty much.'

'Oh yeah?' said Mitch, flatly.

'Yes. Didn't I tell you?'

'Thought you said yours was a novel.'

'It started as a novel, but I converted it, changed it into an afterlife guide.'

'Right … right … fascinating,' said Mitch, turning his attention to his knapsack.

'My unfinished masterpiece. Now lost unfinished masterpiece.'

'Lost?'

'Boiled, smashed and run over.'

'Oh yeah, you did say.'

'Mine was a comic version of course, being a non-believer, so not quite the same.'

Mitch gave no reply.

'So does yours have anything useful in it?' asked Christian.

'Not really,' said Mitch, 'look, it's late, you need to sleep.'

'But surely if it's a guidebook it must have answers, about this place, about this reality? And, hey, what about information on contacting the living?'

'No, there's nothing like that. It's just practical stuff, like, you know, local customs, getting around, good restaurants, that kind of thing.'

'Restaurants?'

'Well obviously not for food, but you know, for atmosphere, hangin' out …'

'Oh right. Still, it's thick, eh?' said Christian, eyeing it again.

'I guess,' said Mitch, and he began to pack up the inkwell, quill and remaining documents.

Christian pinched the book.

'Hey, come on,' said Mitch, 'I'm too tired for games.'

'I only want a quick look,' said Christian.

He'd forgotten what books felt like. He passed it from hand to hand, feeling the weight and running his fingers over the cracked leather, before flipping it face up and releasing the clasp.

'Christian …'

'Odd typeface,' said Christian, having opened the book at a random page, 'and what poor-quality paper.'

'Actually, it's one of the newer ones.'

'Newer? How depressing,' said Christian, his eyes not leaving the page.

Mitch grabbed the book back.

'Hey.'

'Look, it's late, we're both tired ...'

'I'm not tired.'

'Well I am tired, and you should be. And anyway, knowledge can be dangerous.'

'Why's half of it strapped up?' asked Christian.

'You'd know if you paid attention,' said Mitch. He waved the book at Christian and pointed to the back half secured by the leather strap. 'This is Pandora's box. Hazardous knowledge.'

'I don't follow.'

Mitch sighed. 'This is a banned book,' he said, 'well, half-banned.'

'Half-banned? How can a book be half-banned?'

'It just is, okay.'

'But–'

'Look, the first part is all about this world. The Zone. It's what you know already, few more details, no big deal. The second section, the banned part, it describes, or rather may describe, whatever's beyond the Gate. Good places, bad places, how to get in, how to get out, judgement, that kind of thing. Possibly.'

'Really?'

'Yes.'

'Oh come on then, let's read it, honestly it could–'

'No way.'

'But–'

'But nothing,' said Mitch, in frustration. 'Anyway, it's pretty much useless, so I've been told.' He turned to stow the book in his knapsack. 'It's all out of date, inaccurate ... irrelevant.'

'Well can I at least read some of the front bit?'

'I've said no.'

'Come on, please, just the front bit and I won't ask any more questions.'

Mitch gave no reply.

'Or I can just wait until you fall asleep, then read it,' said Christian.

'Don't mess with me on this, buddy. I'm not kidding.'

'Neither am I,' said Christian, with a wink.

A long pause.

'All right ... all right. I'll let you take a real quick look, just while I check our route for tomorrow.'

'Cool.'

'Be no more than a few minutes, you understand.'

'I understand.'

'And you have to promise to then leave it be, until after our meeting tomorrow, okay?'

'Okay, Dad.'

'I'm serious, you have to swear.'

'Okay, I swear.'

Another long pause.

'All right,' said Mitch, 'alright.' He retrieved the book and handed it to Christian, before going back to his knapsack, this time withdrawing some hand-drawn maps from a pouch at the front.

'You've really got the lot in there, eh?' said Christian.

'Well, this ain't my country, buddy, how else am I supposed to find my way?'

'Fair enough,' said Christian. He released the clasp on the book's front cover.

'Anyway, we're going to have to be super careful tomorrow,' said Mitch, as he opened up one of the maps, 'so I'm thinking we get to, I dunno, say, Brent-ford, then we walk the rest of the way under the ground.'

'I thought you said it's super dangerous to go underground, if we get disoriented?' said Christian, as he flipped through the pages.

'Well, you'll be just under the surface, I'll be a little higher, with my neck an inch or two below the pavement. Totally safe, and we can see while not being seen. Neat ay?'

'But how will I see?' said Christian, flipping to the banned section.

'You won't. You'll just follow me.'

'How?'

'I'll lead you on a piece of string.'

'What, like some gypsy's dog?' Christian lifted his eyes to check Mitch wasn't watching, before carefully undoing the brass buckle on the strap that secured the banned section.

'It's like I keep saying,' said Mitch, 'we gotta be careful about security here.'

'Okay, well, how about the underground?' said Christian. 'We could follow the tunnels. Could actually be interesting, too.'

'Yeah ... hey, yeah, that could work,' said Mitch, 'that could ...' He looked up. The forbidden section was open and Christian's eyes were on the text. Mitch launched himself at Christian, sending his shoulder into Christian's head and the book spinning.

'What the hell did you do that for?' yelled Christian, clutching his face.

Mitch scrambled across the floor after the book, grabbing it and slamming it shut. 'Did you see anything?' he said.

'You've hurt my cheekbone.'

'Did you see anything?'

'It really hurts.'

'Don't make me ask you again, did you see anything?'

'No ...'

'I fuckin' hope not.' Mitch sat down, reapplied the strap and closed the book.

'... well not really.'

'Not really? What do you mean not really? Are you saying you saw something?'

'Well, yes, perhaps something,' said Christian.

'Something. What something?' asked Mitch, his body tensing.

'A word.'

'What word?'

'Soup.'

'Soup?'

'Soup.'

'*Soup ...*'

'That's all?' continued Mitch. 'Nothing further?'

'Nothing further.'

Mitch relaxed. 'I think we're okay,' he said, 'can't imagine that doing us much harm. I told you, Christian, I fuckin' told you, the back section is off limits.'

'Oh come on, surely you don't respect nonsense like that?'

'Of course I do, this is deadly serious. I should punch your fuckin' lights out, you Judas.' Mitch tucked the book under his arm and gathered up the map. 'I'll finish this in the morning.'

'Why would a book about the afterlife be concerned with soup?' said Christian.

'Hey, hey, stop that,' said Mitch, 'don't give it another thought, not for a moment.'

'Why ever not?'

'Because a little information, even a scrap, can lead a loose mind to question, to speculate, to become the cat.'

'The cat?'

'*Curiosity*. Christian, knowledge of the afterlife is dangerous, maybe.'

'But it was just one word. One word can't equate to knowledge.'

'You're not listening,' said Mitch, 'it's what that word can lead to. Don't think about it, don't mention it to anyone, especially yourself.'

'But surely there's no harm in just thinking? That wouldn't count, I'd just be working things out for myself?'

'Knowledge is knowledge. Besides, you wouldn't be working things out for yourself, would you? You'll have had soup as a starter. You'll have taken a little piece of truth and expanded it, extrapolated it, embellished it. It's human nature, it's unavoidable, we've been doin' it for millennia. Then you'll go and mention it to someone, disclose the authority of its origin, then they'll want to know more, more about the soup, and its significance, which flavours are holy, which flavours are forbidden, the days you may not eat soup, whether broths are soups and soups are broths, how soup-haters and those indifferent to soup are to be dealt with at meal times. It's a dangerous path, maybe. Leading to crimes even worse than holding knowledge, maybe. The only option is to not think about it, to wipe it from your mind. Never speak or think of it again. Doubt – that should be your watchword.'

'You're seriously telling a lifelong atheist who has recently become a wandering spirit that doubt should still be my watchword?'

'Yes,' said Mitch.

'Well, actually it still is my watchword, come to think of it, but that's not the point.'

'No, the point is reading the banned section is a risk not worth taking.'

'Oh come on,' said Christian, 'what risk? So it's a banned book, what's the worst that can happen? A rap on the knuckles from the afterlife board of censors?'

'All right, you wanna know?' said Mitch. 'You really wanna know?'

'Yes.'

'Well how about eternal damnation?'

'Really? You're serious?'

'Yes. Deadly. Well, maybe. I'm not sure.'

'Oh come off it, how can you say we'd be punished with eternal damnation and then not be sure?'

'Well it'd be in the banned section, which I've not read. So there might not be eternal damnation.'

'This is ridiculous.'

'All I know is knowledge of the afterlife may or may not, well … damage your chances.'

'May or may not damage your chances? Is that the best you can do,' said Christian.

'Yes. Taking a more certain position could be unwise, maybe. Don't you see?'

'No I don't.'

'Well, okay,' said Mitch, 'let's say, for the sake of argument, that knowledge regarding the nature of the afterlife does damage your chances. But knowledge that knowledge regarding the nature of the afterlife damages your chances is in itself knowledge regarding the nature of the afterlife, therefore if it is indeed true that knowledge regarding the nature of the afterlife does damage your chances, then knowing this would damage your chances. So the only option is not to be sure, and even that assertion should be treated with lots of caution.'

'I feel confused.'

'That's great, buddy, we'll make it yet. Hold that thought and you'll be fine. Confusion is the blood brother of uncertainty.'

'But why? Even if it is true, why on earth would this knowledge have you damned?'

'Well I don't know, do I.'

'Why don't you know?'

'I've told you, I haven't read the book.'

'So how do you know?'

'I don't. That's the point.'

'Once again, ridiculous.'

'All right, well why would it be banned if it wasn't dangerous?'

'That's the best reason you've got?'

'It's a good enough reason to not take the chance.'

'Well I think–'

'Well I don't care what you think. You're not reading it. End of.'

Silence.

'Oh come on, there's no harm done,' said Christian, 'let me read a bit more. I promise I'll only look at the front section.'

'Dream on, buddy,' said Mitch, clutching the book to his chest, 'not now, not in a million years now.'

'I'm sorry, okay? Look, I promise, I promise I'll observe the silly rule. I won't read the back section, and I won't walk under any ladders or talk to black cats while I'm doing it.'

'You have some serious growing up to do,' said Mitch. He packed up the maps.

'Hey, Mitch, come on,' said Christian, 'I've said sorry. What about the route? We haven't planned the route yet?'

'We'll do it in the morning. I'm going to bed.'

'Oh don't be like that.'

Mitch disappeared through the room door, taking his knapsack and the book with him.

'Suit yourself,' shouted Christian.

He stayed sitting out in the corridor for a while. He looked at the bland inoffensive decor. He looked at the absence of people and the rows of identical closed doors. He listened to the low whir of the air conditioning. He had to concede that the scene, as a whole, wasn't terribly interesting and the likelihood of something interesting happening within it any time soon was remote. So he too drifted back into the room to try again to get some sleep. It was the sensible thing to do. It would, as Mitch said, be a big day tomorrow.

Chapter Twenty-One

Forty minutes later, Christian was still awake. Why did he feel guilty? It wasn't his fault Mitch couldn't take a joke and actually believed that banned knowledge bunkum. He just hadn't had Mitch pegged as superstitious or religious. Or ethical. Or law abiding, for that matter. If he was serious about his stupid voodoo beliefs, he should have bloody said so.

Christian sat up and looked out of the window, idly wondering if the clouds from earlier had now passed over, and whether he may now be able to distract himself with a view out to the infinity of the universe. They hadn't.

Anyway, there was nothing he could do about it now.

He resolved to stage an apology in the morning. Yes, it would all be fine in the morning. Mitch would see the funny side, and after a few hours cooling off he'd still help Christian contact Beatrice. He would. He definitely would.

He needed to sleep but he couldn't sleep.

He stood and went to the window. A couple of stars were still in denial, their light doing its best to soldier on through the gloom, but by anyone's standards it was a washout. He wondered whether any of the photons from all the stars he couldn't see were disappointed, after having travelled for all those hundreds of thousands of years, to end up hitting a cloud instead of the retina of a living creature capable of experiencing at least some degree of awe for the journey it had undertaken. But then, he thought, even for the lucky few that did make it to a human retina, the best they could realistically hope for would be to make a quantum contribution to, 'oh the stars are nice tonight. I think that's the plough. No, no wait, *that's* the plough.'

His eyes drifted down to explore the more earthly aspects of the scene outside, but there was little to spark interest. Car parks, roads, gardens; strip lights, street lights, headlights; the diffuse glow of the airport. Great. People say do something boring if you can't sleep, but all it ever did for Christian was to make it even easier for his mind to dwell on the source of stress or excitement that was keeping him awake in the first place. No, he needed something diverting yet calming, like ... like something to read.

He drifted over to the other bed. He looked down at the book – still being clutched by the blue-green Mitch. It would, without doubt, be the perfect cure for his adrenaline-fuelled insomnia. But he couldn't take it – Mitch still had it tight in his grasp, and, besides, he wasn't going to risk pissing him off any further.

And then he spotted Mitch's basket. Yes, yes that could work. He'd finish the repair – it would be productive, distracting, meditative, and it would help mend fences in the morning, a win, win, win, *win*.

He took the basket out into the corridor so he could get a better look. He sat down and examined his earlier repair work, then realised he'd need more papyrus to finish the job, so he returned to the room.

He thought the book was the most likely source of material that wouldn't be missed – as Mitch said, it was all out of date anyway – but held to his resolve to leave it alone. And there was still Mitch's knapsack, so he went for a rummage. He soon found the wad of documents Mitch had had out for his genealogy work and took them out into the corridor, hoping he'd be able to find something blank, old or irrelevant.

Once in the light, he saw that the documents were forms of some kind – printed to a poor standard, but neatly filled. Christian still assumed they must be something to do with Mitch's genealogy hobby until he took a closer look at the first one.

A. Smithee & Co. Soul Agency

P16 AUTHORITY TO COLLECT

Shepherd *Mitchell Lanford*   **Lic.** *SHNA246L4*

Cargo { **Family Nayme** *Jones Booth*   **S.N.** *41,094,0*
        Given Nayme *Emily*   *10,813*

Whole [X] **Part** [ ] **List Part(s)** _____

D.O.B. *15/5/37* **O.D.** [N] **Rayce** *Bl Af*   **Height** _____

Sex [F] **Hair** *Various*   **Eyes** *Brown*

L.K.A.   *485 Dufrane Av. Sebastapol CA USA*

Died At   *Palm Drive Hosp. 501 Petaluma Av. Sebastapol CA USA*

Occupaytion *Artist. Post. Imp.*   **Religion** *Christ. Np Nb*

New Fango [∼]	**Faries** [ ]	**Advertising** [ ]
Past Life [ ]	**Majician** [ ]	**Murder** [ ]
Ghosts [ ]	**Estate Ajent** [ ]	**Darts** [ ]
Monsters [ ]	**Danish** [ ]	**Sayles** [ ]
	Theft [ ]	**Preacher** [ ]

Other Info.   *Pet lover. Surivived by daughter (local) and son (Las Vegas) Music – Jazz. Some classical*

For Office Use Only

Reason Code *ARTWT08*   **Job. No.** *132,919*

       Nayme   **Sighned**   **Dayte**

Orthority *Dr JEFFERS*   *Derek Joffers*   *12 JAN 2009*

Delivery *Eastswap*   *Eastswap*   *23 APR 09*

                             Rev.: 24 Mar 1522/2.1

Received

Christian flicked to the second document. The details from 'Cargo' down were different, but it again featured Mitch's name under 'Shepherd'. It was the same on the third, fourth and fifth. Christian skipped the next dozen or so, with growing concern. More forms, all the same, all with Mitch's name, all signed off with a stamp.

Why had he lied?

Who was this guy?

Christian flicked on through the forms. And then he stopped on the last one. His eyes widened.

A. SMITHEE & CO. SOUL AGENCY

P16 AUTHORITY TO COLLECT

SHEPHERD _Mitchell Lanford_   LIC. _SHNA246L4_

CARGO { FAMILY NAYME _Bootstrap_   S.N. ___ 77

        { GIVEN NAYME _Christian_   _Joshua_

WHOLE [X] PART [ ] LIST PART(s) _____

D.O.B. _____ O.D. [N] RAYCE _White_   HEIGHT _5'11'_

SEX [M] HAIR _Short Brown_   EYES _Brown_

L.K.A.   _22 Vestments, Bracknell, Berks, UK_

DIED AT _____

OCCUPAYTION _Unemployed_   RELIGION _Atheist_

NEW FANGO [✓]	FARIES [✓]	ADVERTISING [ ]
PAST LIFE [ ]	MAJICIAN [✓]	MURDER [✓]
GHOSTS [✓]	ESTATE AJENT [✓]	DARTS [ ]
MONSTERS [ ]	DANISH [✓]	SAYLES [ ]
	THEFT [✓]	PREACHER [✓]

OTHER INFO. _Lives with GF, no childen. Query Bracknell Binfield Darts League Division 2, listed 1st reserve for Happy Hurlers? Clear_

FOR OFFICE USE ONLY

REASON CODE _____   JOB. NO. _133 425 (Ver 2)_

	NAYME	SIGHNED	DAYTE
ORTHORITY	_DK JEFFERS_	_Derek Jeffers_	_16 MAR 2015_
DELIVERY			

REV.: 24 MAR 1522/2.1

Instant claustrophobia and a tightness in his chest. Adrenaline of hope and excitement swapped for the adrenaline of grave uncertainty, confusion and fear. Panic would be next, but he told himself to keep calm, keep calm and think it through.

Okay, so Mitch was some sort of serial ethereal human trafficker – that much was obvious. But where to, who to and why?

Don't know, don't know, don't know.

And why Christian? How did they get his address? And who was Mitch working for?

Don't know, don't know, don't know.

Don't know …

Whatever the reasons, they couldn't be good. He thought back to when he'd first met Mitch at the vicarage, how he'd cornered Christian in the churchyard, how he was much faster and stronger.

He had to leave. Right now.

He got to his feet.

His legs felt okay. He was in control. He knew what he had to do. But where? Where would he go? And would Mitch come looking for him? It didn't matter. Anywhere would do for now, anywhere for tonight. He began to drift down the corridor and was about to descend to the lower floors when he stopped. Mitch was still sleeping, it would be an easy escape, and he could hide from Mitch easily enough, too, but what then? Win the battle, lose the war, they say. He could leave now and win an easy battle, but have no idea what the war was about, when it might be over, or even whose side he was on. He put his hands to his head, gathered himself, and turned round. He drifted back towards the room and then passed through the door.

A quick in and out was the plan, but when Christian entered the darkened room, he slowed and stopped. What he was about to do hadn't seemed quite so scary outside in the hint-of-apricot.

He waited for his eyes to adjust back to the half-light. He then drifted the few paces over to the side of Mitch's bed. His former friend was still asleep, or at least Christian presumed as much – it was hard to be sure, there being no eyelids to check.

Christian looked down at the book – Mitch still clutching it tight to his chest – and began to lower his hands. He was only going to get one shot at this …

And then he stopped. Would he be able to do this without waking him? No, no way. So … so he'd need to slow him down.

He turned and went back out into the corridor. He picked up Mitch's basket. Take it with him? No. No he didn't have to. He looked around and then drifted down to the near end of the corridor and placed the basket inside the wall-mounted fire hose, pushing it in until it was obscured from view. He allowed himself a moment to revel in the creativity and fore-thought of this mild vindictiveness; try to take heart from it; use it to summon some guile for what would come next.

He returned to the door and once again waited a moment before step-ping through.

Once inside he returned to his position standing over Mitch.

He slowly lowered his hands. This time he made careful contact with the leather. He probed, flicked, tapped and tugged on the book to get a feel for Mitch's grip, those many hours of Jenga finally paying dividends, but it was not going to budge. He would have to do it the hard way.

He stepped up and over into the space above Mitch and stood just above his chest. He bent down and took firm hold of the book with both hands, and then carefully placed his feet on Mitch's ribcage.

Three.

Two.

One.

In a single swift movement he pulled hard, at the same time kicking down with his feet, ripping the book free, and waking Mitch with a start.

'Eh, what the?'

Christian stamped down into Mitch's stomach, swivelling with his heels, causing Mitch to flinch and wheeze.

With the book now firmly in his right hand, Christian slung his left down into Mitch's neck cavity, then gripped and squeezed as hard as he could.

Mitch screamed the unholy squeal of trying to cry out while someone is digging their nails into your larynx.

Christian screamed the shriek of revulsion at gripping someone's larynx while they are still using it.

Mitch's hands shot to his throat, and Christian's wrist, gripping tightly. Christian thought he would not escape. But he gritted his teeth, and, channelling the anger of betrayal, squeezed even harder, digging his nails into Mitch's neck wall, triggering another gurgling scream from Mitch.

And then Christian brought the weight of the book down hard with his right hand onto Mitch's wrists and hands, breaking their grip on the third blow.

He gave one final sharp squeeze before pulling out and quickly stepping back.

'Fuck you,' shouted Christian, and he disappeared into the wall above the headboard.

As he emerged into the near darkness of the next room, hearing a muffled, croaky, 'Chris, Christian … wait,' behind him, he thrust his shoulders forward, dipping himself forty-five degrees, and drifted as hard as he could on a diagonal towards the lower floors.

Mitch stumbled through the wall and into the room, but there was no sign of Christian. He continued through to the next room, and the next, as fast as he could.

'Christian. Buddy, what the fuck's got into you?' he rasped, but all he found was one sleeping mortal after the next.

At the fifth room, he flipped himself through ninety degrees and sprinted to ground level, before righting himself and exiting the hotel, dropping himself into the ground up to his neck, and continuing out towards the entrance road where he stopped and spun back to face the hotel. He scanned the scene for signs of blue-green glows in a hurry. But there was no movement of any kind, save for a sprinkling of moths dancing at the entrance lights.

This was not Mitch's first case of spooked cargo, and he continued to follow his standard procedure. Another careful scan of the scene, and then, still in the ground, he began to circle the building, rising to a sprint against the drag of the shadows of earth and rock, banking into the curve, and all the while keeping his neck below the surface and his gaze on the building. Because though he'd lost Christian, he knew his man must still be somewhere inside. Christian wasn't fast enough to have got past already, and there was no way he'd have the stomach for an underground drift. A glow would reveal itself sooner or later.

An hour later and Mitch was getting worried. He was tiring, too.

'Christian,' he shouted to the hotel, 'I am the only person who can help you contact your girl. You need me. Come back and I'll explain everything. You have nothing to fear. You have my word.'

No reply.

'Come on, buddy, let's talk about it.'

Still nothing.

'This is a game you can't win, my friend, I have you covered.'

Of course this was a lie. Mitch could drift with the best of them, but he was one man, it was a big hotel and, as far as ghosts were concerned, it had exits everywhere.

'You have to trust me, Christian. You have no choice.'

Nothing. No sound, no signs of blue-green things making a dash for the trees or sneaking about in the darkness.

He did another dozen laps, despite the growing fatigue, before stopping in front of the hotel, concern and frustration rising. He knew the stats better than anyone. If you didn't find AWOL cargo in the first hour, your chances tumbled. He tried to think it through, appealing once again to logic to find his prey. After twenty seconds, he decided logic had had its chance and launched himself forward, letting out a manic war-cry.

He entered the hotel at full sprint, arms outstretched, passing through the lobby, into the kitchens, and out the other side. As soon as he emerged from the far wall, he stopped, did an about-face, and headed back into the hotel a few feet to the side of his first track, like he was mowing a lawn. After a dozen passes, he changed direction, cutting a new trench perpendicular to the first. Nothing. He let out another short scream before heading back outside to resume his perimeter patrol.

And so it went. All night Mitch circled, persuaded, observed and occasionally gave in to speculative trawling of random slices of hotel, but by sunrise Mitch's spirits had taken a beating, and he was fearing the worst.

Christian was sprinting up the hotel's exit road, unable to stay with the acceleration of the bus of the school sports team that had finally given him cover to exit the hotel's reception area.

Sprint. Don't look back.

Sprint. Don't look back.

Sprint. Don't look back.

He crossed the road at the edge of the hotel's grounds, still at full pelt, over into the ploughed fields and made for a dense line of tree cover to the right. Only once in the trees did he stop and finally look back.

Relief. At least for now.

He'd spent most of the night in one of the deeper sofas in a quiet corner of the reception area, waiting for the hotel to wake up and give him cover, waiting for dawn to take away what would be a blue-green beacon were he to step outside while it was dark.

He'd heard Mitch's shouts and rants from time to time, through the night, but they'd only served to fuel his growing anger. He'd believed this man, trusted him, and now he could see it was a deception from the start. The chance meeting at the vicarage, the chipper Canadian doing his genealogy. And he'd fallen for it, like all the others must have. What an idiot. But at least he'd realised in time, in time to get away. Now he had the book, too – perhaps it would have some answers.

He wanted to stop and read, but he needed to be sure. He needed more distance, much more, and so drifted on up through the treeline and on into the fields and suburbs beyond. After several miles, when he hit fields once more, he came across a slope and a hollow that led down to a stream. This would do fine.

As soon as he sat, relief washed through him. He was safe, for now. He released the clasp on the book but tears took over. Last night he thought he had a friend and a path to Beatrice. Now he had nothing.

Chapter Twenty-Two

Twenty-four hours after take-down, Nikki was out of isolation and back on the ward. But her spirits were indifferent to the restoration of relative freedom. She was trying to gather herself, to bring her rational self to bear once again on the situation, but the consequences of the previous day clouded everything. How long now, even with model behaviour? How long now until she would be allowed to walk out?

Jean looked up from the window of the nurses' office as Jim pushed the meds trolley to the last stop on his busy round. He placed a plastic cup of pills on Nikki's table.

'Too many,' she said.

'I'm sorry?' said Jim.

'The blue ones. I only take two.'

'Says six here,' said Jim, checking his sheet.

'I've always just had two.'

'Okey-dokey, I'll check with the doctors,' said Jim.

'What's going on?' said Jean, marching over.

'Just got to check a prescription,' said Jim.

'They've upped her dose,' said Jean, 'help her stay calm.'

'I am calm,' said Nikki.

'You weren't yesterday,' said Jean.

'I want to see a doctor,' said Nikki.

'You can't,' said Jean.

'Well I'm not taking the other four.'

'Perhaps we should get the doctor?' said Jim.

Jean slowly turned to Jim. She folded her arms and stared through his eyes.

Jim shifted his weight and looked at the floor.

'We don't need the doctor,' said Jean, 'the prescription is clear and we have a duty of care to make sure our patients take their meds.' She stepped forward, tipped the pills into her sweaty hand, and pushed them under Nikki's nose. 'Now, Mrs Tooting. Take your meds.'

Nikki slowly raised a hand. She looked into Jean's eyes. She could see the delight, the thrill of another brewing confrontation. Nikki smiled a hollow smile, before slamming her hand into Jean's and sending the pills onto the floor.

Gasps, whoops and quick whispers filled the ward.

Jean took a moment, before leaning in, maintaining eye contact all the time. 'Thank you, Mrs Tooting,' she said, 'thank you very much.' She grabbed Nikki by the collar of her pyjama top, taking two handfuls of hair at the same time, wrenched her out of bed and dropped her onto the floor.

'Hey, now steady on there, Jean,' said Jim.

'You,' said Jean, turning and stabbing a finger to within an inch of Jim's nose, 'you shut the fuck up.'

Jim looked at the floor again.

Two male nurses appeared at the entrance to the ward, but came no closer.

Everyone was now watching. There were cries of protest from some, bursts of manic laughter from others. Barry Jesus and Wee Jesus motioned to get up but then seemed to think better of it.

'Just you try it,' said Jean, turning and scanning the ward, taking care to eyeball every witness, patients and nurses alike, 'any of you, come on, I dare you. I fucking dare you.'

Everyone stayed put.

Jean turned back to Jim and clicked her fingers. 'Gimme another six.'

Jim, wide-eyed, passed her a handful of blue pills.

Jean turned back to Nikki, who was now up on her knees but still dazed. Jean placed a heavy, sensible-shoed foot on Nikki's spine and pressed her to the lino.

'Now, Mrs Tooting, take your meds,' said Jean, and she dropped the pills on the floor next to Nikki's mouth.

'Now, J-J-Jean,' said Jim, 'we can't have her choking, we should at least give her some water.'

Jean turned to the nurse.

'So we should,' she said. She flicked her fingers at him again.

Jim poured a beaker of water, barely managing to control his shaking hands, and passed it across.

Jean held the water out in front of Nikki, making the moment last, before lining it up and pouring it over Nikki's head in a steady stream.

'Now, Mrs Tooting. I won't ask you again. Take. Your. Meds.'

Jean bent over, took Nikki by the scruff of the neck and forced her head over into the pills, now swimming in a pool of water.

There was a loud double slap-crash at the ward entrance, followed by a Mexican wave of gasps.

Jean spun round to see the two male nurses out cold on the floor and Kendo lumbering towards her. She released Nikki, stood up, and edged out into the open space in the middle of the ward.

Kendo closed to within five bed lengths, and stopped. He eyeballed Jean. She eyeballed him.

Both glanced left and right as lines were drawn.

'You've just made my day, fat man,' said Jean.

'This will not help my case,' said Kendo, 'but I'm gonna do it anyway.'

The two behemoths hunkered down, shifting their weight forward like number eights waiting to scrum. Patients in the beds at the midpoint cowered behind pillows or scrambled for cover. Jim half helped, half dragged Nikki to the back of the ward and sat her against the wall.

Kendo began his signature foot stomp for the first time in fourteen years. Jean stood her ground and began to crack her knuckles.

Cheers rang out. Some patients leaped up on their beds, some pulled the bed sheets high over their heads. The Jesuses called for calm and diplomacy, but it was too late, both beasts had committed and were now on a hair trigger.

Jean flinched and then in a heartbeat the mighty beasts were pounding towards each other. Both seemed to feel mass was on their side as the closing speed rose. Five metres, four, three, two, one. And then, just before impact, Kendo lowered his bald head like a battering ram. A moment later, Jean was on her back, out cold, her long-awaited first bout with an actual wrestler having lasted a disappointing two and a half seconds.

Silence.

'Christ in God's holy sidecar,' said Jim. He got to his feet. 'Now ... now everyone let's keep calm. I'll, um, I'll have this all straightened out in no time.' He made a move for the exit, head down, but after one stride found Nikki hanging onto his foot.

'You're not going anywhere,' she said.

His breathing began to race. He flicked out his leg, shaking her free as gently as he could, and turned again for the exit. But this time he found himself bouncing off Kendo and onto the floor.

Kendo picked him up by one ankle and returned him to the back of the ward, oblivious and impervious to the flailing of the now frantic nurse. 'You'd better stay here, fella.'

Back at the hotel, Mitch was still circling, though he now cut a weary figure. His sprint had dropped to a trot, and instead of the hotel, his gaze was now absentmindedly monitoring the grass, road, litter and dog turds passing through the space where his chin should be. The propaganda war was faring no better, Mitch having dropped the frequency of his broadcasts and settled into an unhealthy rut of alternately melancholic and recriminatory tones.

'We should sit tight,' said Edgar, 'we're all nutters, they expect this kind of thing, they'll understand.'

'No, they won't,' said Nikki, 'they will come down on us in great numbers and they will hurt us. A lot. I say again, our only way out is violence.'

'How about peaceful resistance?' said Roach.

'We've started a war,' said Nikki. 'We're the Japanese Imperial Navy and we've just bombed Pearl Harbour. We can't retreat to Tokyo and start making placards.'

'No, *you've* started a war, Nigella,' said Edgar. 'It's nothing to do with the rest of us.'

'Oh, and you think they'll care?' said Nikki. 'If we sit and wait, it's fists in the face and straitjackets all round, snoozy pills on the hour every hour. I promise you this is our fate, unless we riot, unless we give them something bigger to worry about.'

'I'm in,' said Kendo, clenching his fists, 'come on, let's get started.'

'We need everyone,' said Nikki. 'Come on, people, what do you say?'

'What do we do, Jesuses?' asked Roach.

'Yes, yes, what would Jesuses do?' asked Vivian.

Soon there were more voices of support, and then chanting.

Jesus-es! Jesus-es! Jesus-es!

'All right, all right,' said Nikki, waving her arms, 'Barry, Wee, Autumn. Looks like it's your big moment. Tell them, tell them we have to do this.'

Barry Jesus stood to speak. 'We should turn the other cheek,' he said, 'or rather, in this case, first we should turn our first cheeks, I suppose, and then our other cheeks, yes?'

'No. That won't achieve anything,' said Nikki.

'It worked for me last time,' said Autumn, nodding sagely.

'And me,' said Wee and Barry in unison.

'No it didn't,' said Nikki, 'they nailed you to a cross.'

'Well ... yes,' said Autumn, 'apart from that bit.'

'Look, shut up,' said Nikki, 'you're not listening.'

'No, *you're* not listening,' said Roach. 'The Jesuses have spoken.' He scanned the faces. 'Come on, let's get the protest songs going,' he said, and broke into a tuneless rendition of Sting's 'Russians'.

The meeting began to break up as patients started to sing, dance or return to their beds.

'Wait. Jesuses, wait,' said Nikki. 'Stop ... stop!'

The singing stopped, as did at least some of the dancing. Everyone turned.

'You know what your trouble is,' said Nikki, to the Jesuses, 'you've thrown the baby out with the bathwater. Just like last time. So keen to modernise, so keen to get in there with the new broom. You've chucked it all out, and all you've got left is understanding and forgiveness. Well I've got news for you. *It doesn't work.* Reality check, people, you're trapped in here, against your will, day after day, week after week. They're injecting you with whatever they damn well like, and all you do is turn the other butt cheek, and say, "Thank you, sir, may I have another?".'

'There is no other way, not for a true Christian,' said Wee.

'Yes there is, of course there is,' said Nikki, 'there's a whole other Testament. Another way, an older way. Think about it, think back to the early days, would your dad have ever stood for this? He's bothered to give you a second chance, what in all of creation are you going to tell him when you turn up in Heaven after getting crucified, *again*?'

There was a long silence.

'Fuck me, she's right. What's Dad gonna say?' said Wee.

'He will read me the riot act,' said Autumn.

'Boy am I in for it!' said Barry.

'So what do we do?' asked Autumn.

'We unleash the dogs of war,' said Nikki. 'Old Testament, wrath, fire and brimstone. The Law. We lay down your dad's law, like Moses did.'

'She's right, she's so fucking right!' said Wee.

'Let's do it,' said Barry.

'I knew that *love thy neighbour* stuff was a load of old flannel,' said Autumn.

'That's right, I hate my neighbour,' said Wee.

'But I'm your neighbour,' said Barry.

'Exactly.'

'Good point.'

They swapped punches and embraced.

'It's funny, isn't it,' said Autumn, 'sometimes it's, well, right in front of you, but you can't see it. Gee do I feel like a prune.'

'Enough. Let's stop talking and start doing,' said Nikki, 'let's take the ward.'

'Hold on, hold on,' said Milos, stepping forward, 'so we take the ward. What then?'

'Then,' said Wee, 'we take the floor.'

'And then?'

'The building,' said Autumn.

'*And then?*'

'The local health authority?' said Barry.

Milos shook his head.

'Please, come on, there's no time,' said Nikki.

'Wait, wait just a moment there, young Nikki,' said Autumn, 'so what else are you proposing, Mil?'

'Well call me old-fashioned,' said Milos, 'but when we used to have a tear-up back in the old days, we'd make some demands.'

'All right, fine,' said Nikki, 'so what are your demands then?'

'Well, folks,' said Milos, 'what do we want?'

Silence.

'Come on, there must be something,' said Nikki.

'Well, freedom,' said Barry, 'no one should be held against their will.'

'Good,' said Nikki.

'And if we don't want to take our meds, we shouldn't have to,' said Milos.

'Excellent, is that it?'

'We should be able to end our lives if we want,' said Vivian.

'Gets my vote,' said Nikki.

'Be nice if the TV picked up the History Channel,' said Wee, 'and the rest of the free digital ones,' he added.

'Right,' said Nikki, 'freedom, no meds, we can kill ourselves if we want to and the TV stuff.'

'And I demand recognition as the true Messiah,' said Autumn.

'Me too.'

'And me.'

'Okay, okay, and the Jesuses are each recognised as the true Messiah,' said Nikki, 'excellent, right, anything else? No, right then.'

'Paws in the centre, soldiers,' shouted Kendo. He thrust his arm in, and other hands followed.

'Holy war, people, holy war,' said Nikki.

Kendo pounded his chest. 'Let's get ready to ruuuuuuuumble.'

Christian looked again at the shadows of the elms. He'd watched them grow shorter and then longer again as the hours had passed, and still he'd done nothing more than lie curled up in a ball or sit with his hands cradling his head.

But now, finally, he started to listen to what he'd been telling himself all day – that all was not lost. He was safe, at least for now; he had a potential source of answers to some of his questions, and maybe there was still a way to contact Beatrice. He had to try.

He leaned back, opened the book and began to read.

The riot was now in full swing, with patients active on several fronts – mostly fighting staff, but also each other and in some cases themselves. In the main ward, the still unconscious Jean had been hoisted and bound onto a makeshift bed-frame crucifix and was being pelted with various foodstuffs, while nurse Jim, the other members of staff, and any patients unwilling to participate in hostilities had been strapped into beds and were being prescribed doses of varying meds.

Wee Jesus had assumed operational command after early success in breaking out of the ward and had now divided the militia in two: the Popular Army had been dispatched to take the sixth floor, below, and establish a bridgehead at the fifth floor stairwell from which to strike out lower when the order came; the Republican Guard had secured the King George Unit itself and the rest of the seventh floor.

As well as taking eight more members of staff hostage, the taking of the sixth floor had led to the liberation of eighteen patients from the oppression of orthopaedics and special burns treatment. It was hoped the liberated patients would soon join the cause and swell the ranks, and there was much disappointment when they showed limited enthusiasm. Undeterred, Wee declared martial law and brought conscription into effect. Those with reasonable mobility were placed into an infantry division within the Republican Guard, while the remainder were formed into an armaments corps – mostly producing crutch and scalpel bayonet spears and urine bag cluster bombs.

Back on the main ward, Jean had regained consciousness up on her bedframe crucifix and had begun remonstrating with her captors. This was an unwise move and triggered another volley of gammon slices and liver portions, to a rousing cheer from the small crowd of combatants, as well as some of the prisoners, as the gristly missiles hit their target.

'You're absolutely right,' said Barry Jesus, 'it's so much better being in the audience.'

'Exactly, don't know what I was thinking last time,' said Autumn Jesus.

'Yeah, see how you like it,' shouted Barry, pinging an almost fossilised Yorkshire pudding off Jean's forehead.

Nikki was also still on the main ward, but lost in her own world, trying to smash the windows at the far end. She'd been there since slipping away once hostilities had got into full swing, and was now getting desperate. She'd hurled chairs, computer monitors and all manner of medical equipment, but the panes were holding firm.

'Fifth stairwell bridgehead is secure,' said Wee, returning with Kendo from the front.

'They won't break,' said Nikki, barely acknowledging her comrades.

Wee and Kendo looked at each other.

'It's safety glass, girl,' said Kendo, 'tough stuff.'

'Will you try?' asked Nikki.

'Er, sure,' said Kendo. He picked up a chair.

'Why do we need to break the glass?' asked Wee.

Kendo took a powerful but futile swipe.

'Well we … we just do,' said Nikki.

Kendo dropped the chair, stared at the glass, and then retreated the length of the ward. He turned to face the window and began a slow hand clap above his head. The onlookers turned away from Jean and soon started to join with the clapping.

'As I say, the stairwell bridgehead is secure,' said Wee, standing proud.

Nikki was preoccupied with Kendo and the window, but couldn't help notice the newfound confidence in the smaller Jesus. 'You're taking to this new role rather well,' she said.

'Old habits,' said Wee, before leaning in, 'I was in psychic control of the Iraqi military during the early nineties.'

With the onlookers still clapping, Kendo took up a sprint-start stance.

A '*woooooohhhhhh*' rose from the crowd as he pounded down the ward towards the centre window and launched himself at it feet first, only realising mid-flight he would be in a sticky situation should he be successful.

There was a brief silence and then a thick bang as Kendo's feet hit the window. It flexed, but held, causing the rest of Kendo to buckle into his legs before he fell back hard on his shoulders as he hit the floor.

'This isn't going to work,' said Nikki. She turned to Wee Jesus. 'What about the roof?' she said. 'Can we get onto the roof?'

'We need to push on down,' said Wee, 'take more floors, bring more troops under our control. And of course we should set fire to any fossil fuel sources in the building, that's always good.'

Nikki paused. 'Yes, you're right,' she said, 'first idea though, not the second. Carry on. May I have Kendo though?'

Wee looked affronted, but melted when Nikki gave him one of those looks. She still had it.

'By all means, madam,' said Wee, bowing and sweeping his arm as if he were showcasing a recently laid field of land mines.

Nikki smiled and nodded.

'Kendo,' she said, 'come with me.' She strode off with a still dazed Kendo in limping pursuit. As she moved through the ward, Barry and Autumn decided to follow on too. They'd run out of main courses to throw at Jean and felt to progress to the custard desserts would cheapen the majesty of the statement.

Chapter Twenty-Three

Nikki had nearly done it. But not quite. Chains and a large padlock still blocked the door to the roof.

'*Huueerrrrrr,*' roared Kendo.

'Come on, you can do it,' said Nikki.

He adjusted the bed-frame crowbar, pulling it higher to maximise the leverage. '*Huueerrrrrrrrrrrr.*'

There was creaking and plinking as Kendo put the links under greater and greater tension, Barry and Autumn only now deciding to shield themselves at the prospect of fast-flying metal.

'Come on,' said Nikki, 'you are Kendo Dickson, one hundred and forty-eight wins, thirty-five by technical knockout, you have no equal, no cage can hold you.'

'*Heeeeaaaaauueerrrrrggghhh.*'

With a crack and then a bang, the handles came clean away from the doors, still shackled with the chains. Only the basic lock remained. Kendo dropped the bed-frame and put his shoulder to the doors, forcing them open on the first charge.

They rushed out onto the roof.

As they approached the edge they saw what a commotion they'd already caused. Police officers, police vans and cars, reporters, mobile TV units. It seemed the whole of the British media and a fair chunk of the law had come out to meet them.

Nikki peered down over the ledge. Despite all the people and equipment, all that lay directly below was nice hard paving.

A sweet surge of adrenaline. Finally it would be over.

Eyes from below were soon on them.

The high treble of Teasdale's voice through a loudhailer rang through the air. 'Please lay down your weapons. Please come down. Please come down and tell me everything. I am sure we can work something out.'

A short pause.

'How does ten per cent sound? I promise to give you credit and full consultation.'

Everyone on the roof looked at each other. Everyone on the ground looked at each other.

'All right, twenty. I will be sending my agent in, as soon as she arrives. She will be armed only with non-disclosure forms and letters of understanding for an initial synopsis.'

The sound of a scuffle amplified through a loudhailer, before a new voice took over. 'I am Chief Inspector Nigel Cook. There is no need for alarm or further violence. What are your demands?'

Barry Jesus and Autumn Jesus got together, ran through what they remembered of the demands and began shouting them out. Other patients joined in and the list soon became a chant, getting longer each time as they began to remember more terms.

Nikki took Kendo by the shoulder and pulled him back. 'Kendo, will you do something for me?' she asked.

'Depends what it is.'

'Will you go and rejoin Wee Jesus?'

'Why?'

'They need you at the front. I've got the roof, I'm fine now.'

He stared at her, unblinking, and then kissed her on the forehead. 'You look after yourself, girl.'

She shook her head and looked away.

'What?' he said.

'I always do, Kendo, I always do.'

He sloped away.

She took a moment to compose herself, but a moment only. It was time. Amid the increasingly verbose chanting, she stepped forward and up onto the ledge surrounding the roof. Now there was nothing but thin air and gravity between her and her destiny.

The chanting died and stopped, as Barry, Autumn and the others realised where Nikki was now standing.

'What, er, what are you doing?' asked Autumn.

She didn't reply. She didn't look round. She told her legs to take one step forward.

And then she just stood there, her legs deciding a step forward wasn't in their best interests.

'Fuck, fuck, fuck,' she cried out.

'Yeah, fuck, fuck, fuck,' shouted Barry, down to the police.

'Fuck, fuck, fuck,' shouted the others.

She tried again. One small step for Nikki, one giant leap for Limbo.

Nothing.

'Fuck it.'

'Fuck it,' they all shouted.

'Would you, er, would you mind stepping down, my dear?' said Autumn.

Nikki took two deep breaths and turned round. She looked into the faces of her followers. They looked even more worried and confused than normal.

'I'm sorry,' she said, bashing her temples, 'it's, er, a sort of mental block, I think.'

The disciples looked at each other in bewilderment.

'Hang on,' said Nikki, 'what's your favourite type of biscuit?'

'What?' said Autumn.

'Please, do me this one thing. Tell me what your favourite biscuit is.'

'Sweet or savoury?' asked Barry.

'Sweet,' said Nikki.

'Ginger nuts,' said Barry.

'Chocolate digestives,' said Milos.

'I can't eat biscuits,' said Autumn, 'diabetes, you know, but I used to like a rich tea.'

'Jaffa cakes,' said Nikki and she took a step backwards.

Caught by surprise, this time all her legs could do was thrash about in desperation.

As the ledge raced away, so did the faces, but a moment later they reappeared, peering down at her over the edge. And then she saw the unmistakable forms of Barry and Autumn, plus a few other patients, getting up onto the ledge.

'Don't leave us!'

'We need you!'

She watched as first Barry and then Autumn stepped off after her, white pyjamas flapping as they plummeted.

Time slowed.

She was used to devotion, unconditional irrational infantile devotion, but this was the first time she wished it wasn't the case. This was unnecessary; this was regrettable. But what could she do? There are civilian casualties in every war.

A moment later Nikki Tooting embraced the pavement and in doing so left three of the first four dimensions of the universe.

'Right, happy now?' said Nikki.

The old man looked her up and down.

'Well?' she said.

He peered behind her.

She stepped to the side, showcasing the nothingness. No white hole, not so much as a pinprick in the absolute black of the void.

'Just checking,' he said. He handed her a welcome-to-death leaflet and her soul card. 'Now, if you'll bear with me,' he continued, flicking a page or two over on his clipboard.

Nikki grabbed the clipboard and his quill, glanced at the page, and signed.

'Oh, right,' he said as Nikki thrust the clipboard back towards him and strode towards the door. 'Now if you wouldn't mind,' said the old man, 'I've introduced a little feedback survey, only take a moment ...'

But she was already gone.

Nikki found herself looking up at the hospital rooftop once more. The rust stains and the dirty pebbledash; the horrified faces; the clouds in the calm evening sky beyond.

Her point of view sat up, but kept its focus on the roof. Unlike almost everyone who has ever lived, and ever will, Nikki knew exactly what was going on; she precisely understood the transition she'd just made – the permanent metamorphosis that had started and would soon complete, in her case, she estimated, within the next twenty to thirty minutes. But it didn't mean she felt it any less. Perhaps she felt it more. No shroud of confusion, no curtain of denial, only instant and total perspective. Her mortal self was dead. She would endure, and that had to be her focus, but the cold truth was that now there was no going back to her mortal life, or anything else in the mortal realm, as anything other than an observer. No touching ripe wheat in a meadow, no lungfuls of crisp mountain air on a hike, no mornings getting rogered by Jean Claude in the snug.

She knew what was happening, what had happened. And that meant she knew she had to look. The short, sharp shock to force acceptance.

One.

Two.

Three.

She looked down but had to look up again straight away.

She told the spaces where her jaws weren't to bite down on each other. Once again, she counted to three, then forced her point of view to look.

This time she held it, forcing herself to take it in – the double horror of empty space where her new body should be, and through that empty space the sight of where her old mortal body now was. On its back, broken and motionless. Legs twisted, eyes open, skull smashed out into a blood-brain halo on the paving slabs.

She dry retched and brought her non-hand to her non-mouth and so failed to suppress a sharp cry of anguish.

'Nikki,' said the voice of Barry Jesus, 'is that you? Are you there?'

She said nothing.

'Nikki?'

'Baz,' said the voice of Autumn Jesus, 'is that you?'

'Yes,' said Barry, 'are you all right?'

'Yes, I'm all right. I'm not moving, but I feel all right.'

'I'm not moving either, but, I'm not there, I'm here, I don't understand.'

'You don't look well.'

'Neither do you.'

'Hang on, where are you?'

'I'm here.'

'No you're not.'

'Yes I am.'

'Say that again.'

'Yes I am.'

'I can't see you.'

'Well I can't see you. Or me.'

'Shit, I can't see me either.'

'Are we dead?'

'I don't feel dead.'

'I don't want to be dead.'

'Maybe we're just hurt. Can you heal me?'

'Okay, right after you heal me.'

'I asked first.'

By now paramedics were at the bodies. Teasdale was assisting too, his ear close to Nikki's mouth, perhaps in the hope of last words of plot structure and character motivation.

'Hey, hey, help me,' called the voice of Barry, to the paramedics, 'I'm here, I mean I'm there, but I'm here. Please hurry.'

Nikki told herself to focus. The mission was all that mattered now. She got her bearings and looked out towards the exit of the hospital grounds. Her instincts told her to go straight to central London, to the scene of Christian's death, but she'd had a gut full of gut feeling. Now it was going to be as it should be – it was going to be rational, planned and controlled. And that meant not doing anything without backup.

'Nikki will know what to do,' said Autumn, the voice closer now, within touching distance. 'Nikki, are you there, are you there, my dear? What do we do now? Tell us. Tell us and we will follow.'

She remained silent. There was nothing to say. Everyone has to find their own way in death, and the Jesuses were no different. She slipped silently through them, through their consciousnesses, through their thoughts and escalating fears, on and beyond, through the lines of police and media and out.

Dexter sprinted through the Koch Quadrangle, across the atrium, and up the executive escalator – its power plant barely having enough time to adjourn their process improvement review and start pedalling – and along the great long corridor to the recently reopened Meditation, Powernap and Healing Room.

It was full of officials from Central Administration, some of the faces turning to Dexter as he entered. Now he spotted several of the department heads and advisors as well as the unmistakable butterscotch bouffant of Grímsson at the front of the melee. Only the stork-like feathered figure of

Spitback stood apart from the commotion, playing his own game, as ever. He clocked Dexter and gave a slow nod.

Dexter pushed his way through the circles of suits to find Gordon – wearing what appeared to be a lilac chiffon sarong over a cream cotton leotard – stretched out on a daybed.

'Dexter, my boy, great news,' said Gordon, sitting up and straining against the arms of several junior managers.

'Are you all right?' said Dexter.

'Never better. The closeness, my emotional intimacy. It's back, and it's stayed.'

'Please try to relax,' said one of the doctors, and he tried to ease the King of Limbo back down.

'I feel it, Dexter, I feel it, it's right here, right here with me now, my heart is overflowing.' He blew Dexter a double kiss, stretching his arms out wide.

'When did this start?' asked Dexter.

'A short while ago,' said Grímsson.

'Yes,' said Gordon, 'I was reading an excellent article in *Good House-keeping* when all of a sudden it was like someone was slamming my whole body, like before on the golf course, like I was being crushed.'

'Please, you must stay calm,' said another doctor.

'Are you in pain?' asked Dexter.

'No, no I feel fine, in fact, I feel, I feel faaaaaaaantastic.'

A slippery silence.

'Right,' said Dexter, looking around for support and not finding any, 'excellent, excellent ...'

'I do have a theory,' said Grímsson.

More silence.

'And?' said Dexter.

'I believe this intensity of experience can be explained by only one thing. The Lord's connection, to his other self.'

'The boy,' shouted Gordon, 'finally.'

'What?' said Dexter.

'Indeed,' said Grímsson, 'to experience this deep and warm happiness, these sensations of intimacy, where there is no plausible cause for it in the Lord's dutiful life. It can only be his other self. You see, once again we have promised and once again we have delivered.'

'I'm overjoyed,' said Gordon, his lower lip quivering as he clasped a selection of hands, 'thank you, thank you all.'

'But why now?' said Dexter. 'Why not ten years ago, why not twenty?'

'Indeed,' said Grímsson. His comment attracted glances from his team.

'Indeed what?' said Dexter.

'Just indeed.'

'Come on, there's more, isn't there?' said Dexter.

'Well–' He was interrupted by a colleague pulling on his arm, but Grímsson continued. 'I have a theory.'

'Another one?' said Gordon, a measure of authority returning to his voice. 'Come on then, spill it, Grimmy.'

'Well, my Lord, this intensity, from nothing, it can only be a subordinate party multidimensional shift.'

'Meaning?' said Dexter.

'Meaning that you, Lord, that your other self, has, well … died.'

Silence.

'He's dead?' said Gordon. 'My poor darling boy.'

'Yes, passed over, into the Zone,' said Grímsson.

'Wait, wait,' said Dexter, 'let's slow down a minute here. We haven't even found him yet and now you're saying he's dead?'

'As I say, it's theoretical at this stage,' said Grímsson, 'but it fits the facts.'

'Hang on, oh hang on a moment …' said Bhakta, the new head of Future Strategy Planning Possibilities. The room fell silent. '… is everyone thinking what I'm thinking?'

The room stayed silent.

'Isn't it obvious?' He scanned the faces in the room. 'Crucifixion …'

Gasps and murmurs.

'Think about it,' Bhakta continued, 'it was always on the cards, when everything kicked off. I say he's been crucified.'

Gordon crossed his arms over his chest. 'You know I do feel crucifixion,' he said, 'my wrists are tingling and my chakras are just screaming it.'

'Steady on, Gordon,' said Dexter, 'a crucifixion, in Britain, in the twenty-first century? I think we'd have seen that on the news.' Dexter turned to the head of Mortal Intelligence. 'Ken, there hasn't been anything on BBC or CNN, has there? Ritualised executions of CEOs, business leaders, that kind of thing?'

The head of Mortal Intelligence took a moment to exchange a few whispered words with his offsider, before coming back with a shake of the head.

A brief but piercing '*coo-ahh*' from Spitback caused everyone to turn.

He stepped forward and rippled his armwing tips to make some space. 'The question, gentlemen,' he said, 'is not how. The question is why. Why is the son dead.'

'Because he was slain,' said Gordon, 'cut down in his prime.'

'Well, Lord, I'm not so sure,' said Spitback.

'Go on,' said Grímsson.

The fallen angel walked as he talked, head bobbing with every step. 'Well, I think we can assume the son is just like the father,' he said.

'Meaning?' said Gordon.

'Proud, strong, determined, and above all, focused ...'

'Naturally,' said Gordon.

Nods and sounds of agreement.

'... so, we can assume he will have tracked the prophet down.'

'Of course he will have,' said Gordon, 'that's a given.'

'Well, then,' said Spitback. He stopped and turned to Gordon. 'What if the prophet has died?'

'The prophet? Dead too?' said Gordon.

'Conjecture,' said Dexter, shaking his head.

'Foresayers are not made of such steel as deities,' said Spitback, brushing past Dexter, 'and what if Heaven are onto us ...'

Murmurs of disquiet.

'... if they are, they would certainly move to plug the leak.'

'Oh now come on,' said Dexter.

'My dear fellow,' said Spitback, finally turning to face Dexter, 'you forget I know him.'

'Know him?' said Dexter. 'Knew him, more like, and what, eight hundred, nine hundred years ago?'

'People don't change,' said Spitback, 'him especially.'

Murmurs of agreement.

'They would look to eliminate the prophet,' said Tymach, the head of Inter-Realm Affairs, 'they've done it before, when their own go rogue, we all remember Thomas Becket.'

'All right, so the prophet's dead,' said Gordon, 'what's that got to do with the boy?'

'Perhaps he's gone after him, into the Zone,' said Spitback.

'A suicide mission?' said Gordon.

'Bit Hollywood isn't it?' said Dexter.

'Well, Lord, you'd do the same, wouldn't you,' said Spitback, 'if you were in his position? If that is what was required. For the mission, for the glory of Limbo?'

'By jingo, he's right,' said Gordon, 'Spitzy's only got it.'

'Really, Gordo, this is, this is speculation, this is–'

'No,' snapped Gordon, 'this is it. Wow, well I never. But that's my boy, eh?' A tear welled up in his eye. 'That's my boy.'

Chapter Twenty-Four

By the time evening approached, Mitch was still at the hotel. He'd stopped circling and had instead plonked himself down among the ornamental stone balls at the front entrance. He still looked up at the comings and goings, but his comments were now limited to derogatory remarks to guests as they passed, criticising their fashions, their idle chat, and the happy-go-lucky way they flaunted their attached heads.

'I'm such a dipshit,' he said, 'you're not even there any more, are you? Are you?'

Nothing.

'Well I will see you again, my friend. I will find you. And when I do, it's no more Mr Nice Guy. You hear me? You hear me, buddy?'

He trudged over to the entrance, looked up, and then stepped up the outside of the building, floor by floor, almost to the top, and into the room they'd selected the night before, the space now occupied by a lone businessman and a movie that would not be named on his bill.

Mitch gathered up his knapsack, documents and the rest of his kit. Only now did he realise the book was missing. Only now did he realise this must have been what Christian hit him with.

His basket was gone, too.

'Fuuuuuuuck.'

Mitch woke late the following morning in the sofa at the vicarage. After abandoning the hotel, he'd realised he had little choice but to return to Bracknell. It was a long shot, at best, but the only shot he had. It was either that or commence a trial and error search of the rest of creation. Bracknell edged it, just.

When he'd eventually arrived at the vicarage, there was, of course, no sign of Christian. Though Mitch had repeatedly told himself over the long late-evening hours of the drift that he should not get his hopes up, he was still dejected to find nothing more than Tony, another priest and three parishioners in the closing stages of a game of Warhammer 40,000.

Unable to face drawing another blank at 22 Vestments, he'd decided to rest up for the night.

Now, in the morning, matters felt worse, his Bracknell long shot moving into the realms of the ridiculous. But there was nothing else to do. And so he got up and began a slow trudge across town.

On the way he tried to refocus and prepare himself for the long fight ahead. Because, despite everything, Christian would show up eventually – the pull of the known, the pull of Beatrice. It was already strong, and would grow stronger with time, like the pull of the Gate. At some point Christian would return. And until he did, Mitch would just have to do his time and endure the open prison of 22 Vestments. At least this time his days would not be made worse by the unrelenting temptation of the book.

Mitch was soon outside the house. He drifted on past Beatrice's car, up the little path and through the front door. He plodded on through the little square entrance hall, and made his way into the living room.

'You took your time,' said Christian. He was sitting on the sofa reading the book.

Mitch leaped on his cargo, forcing Christian into the floor, before dragging him up and over into the far wall, turning him round and getting both arms up behind his back.

'Get off me, let me go,' said Christian.

'You're not going anywhere,' said Mitch.

'You're hurting me.'

'Yeah, well, you hurt me.'

'Oh yes. Sorry about that.'

'Well, you're not getting away again, not this time.'

'Mitch, get off me, I don't want to get away.'

'Yeah, sure.'

'If you'll just let me explain.'

'You're explaining nothing. You're coming with me to the Gate, I swear to God, even if I have to drag you.'

'Well of course we're going to the Gate, that's what I'm trying to tell you.'

A short pause.

'Pardon me?' said Mitch.

'Well why do you think I came back to the house?' said Christian.

'Because you're an idiot?'

'Because I don't know where the Gate is, do I? I need you to take me there.'

Silence as Mitch thought it over. And then sounds from upstairs, a rhythmic squeaking to a backdrop of muffled moans. 'Who's that?'

'Bea, of course.'

'What's she doing?'

'Well what do you think she's doing? She's having sex with Kevin Tooting. Been at it for a good half hour.'

'And that's okay now?'

'That's what I've been trying to tell you.'

'I don't get it.'

'Look, would you mind letting me out of the wall so we can continue the conversation a bit more civilly.'

Mitch gave it some thought. 'All right,' he said. He pulled Christian out into the middle of the room. 'No sudden moves.' Mitch released his grip.

'I think you sprained it,' said Christian, rubbing his left shoulder. 'Was that really necessary?'

'Yeah, it was.'

Christian didn't reply.

'So let me get this straight,' said Mitch, 'you want to go to the Gate. And you want me to take you there?'

'Yes.'

'Why the change of tune? Who've you been talking to?'

'No one. Well, not unless you count Terry,' said Christian.

'Terry?'

'Yes, Terry,' said Christian, and he reached to pick up the book.

Mitch grabbed it.

'Hey, do you mind?' said Christian.

'Do I mind? It's my damn book,' said Mitch, holding it in front of Christian's nose.

'No, Mitch, it's *my* damn book.'

'Fuck off.'

'No,' said Christian, 'you're not getting it. This is why we have to go to the Gate. It's my book, Mitch, this is the book I was writing before I died.'

Chapter Twenty-Five

Gabriel leaned back in his office chair and looked across at Harold. No angelwear, no office shirt, no slacks. Now Harold wore white linen robes.

The need for updates was long gone – remote viewing having ceased to be of any use the moment Christian had entered the Zone – but still, Gabriel could have found Harold new duties easily enough. He should have. It might have helped. But instead he'd let him drift to a more distant orbit – the weasel way out of the crisis over the company he'd been keeping.

And now here he was before him, in his office. Their first meeting in a month. And it was at Harold's request.

'So?' said Gabriel.

'So they know about Mr Bootstrap,' said Harold.

'Really,' said Gabriel. He chucked his pencil onto the desk.

'They know you're looking for him, that shepherds were dispatched.'

'So what? We pick people up all the time.'

'Yes, but you don't send out shepherds before those people have died.'

Gabriel sat up, retrieved his pencil and began passing it between his digits. 'They don't know anything,' he said, 'they can't prove anything, and even if they could, it wouldn't matter, because around here Terry is judge, jury and executioner.'

'But–'

'But nothing. We've already spoken about this. You know my position.'

'That's why I'm here now,' said Harold. 'Can't you see? You're not like him, you're not like the other angels. I know you had no choice, none of us did, but there is another way.'

'I advise you to tread very carefully,' said Gabriel. 'You are one sentence away from treason.'

'I no longer care. I've come to ask you to join us.'

'Us? *Us?*'

'I'm with the Cause of the Apostles now.'

'I don't believe what I'm hearing.'

'And I don't believe you're like him.'

Gabriel got up from his chair and began pacing, his head bobbing back and forth like a worried hen.

'The only thing necessary for evil to triumph,' said Harold, 'is for good men, good angels, to do nothing.'

'Just listen to you,' said Gabriel.

'You know this place is not what it is supposed to be.'

'Oh get real, Harold. You've been blinded by an impossible ideal. It never could be what it's supposed to be, nothing could. This is real life, not a fairy tale.'

'We can do better.'

'I warned you last time, Harold, I warned you.'

'Perhaps you'd better arrest me then.' Harold held out his hands, wrists together.

Gabriel stopped. 'I should,' he said. 'In fact, I am duty bound to do just that.'

'Well then,' said Harold.

Gabriel turned and retook his seat. 'Now do you see what you've done? For me not to arrest you, right now, puts me at risk, do you see that?'

'So join us.'

'Not another word,' said Gabriel, jabbing out his left armwing at his former charge.

Silence as Harold stared cross-eyed at the gnarled foreclawfinger inches from his nose.

The archangel held position for a moment and then withdrew. He stood. 'I am going to give you one final chance,' he said. 'This reprieve is undeserved, unwarranted and unprecedented, but I grant it to you all the same.' He placed his clawhands on the desk and leaned in, staring into

Harold's eyes. 'Yet even now I see no indication you will yield ...' He waited, but Harold remained silent. '... so I will not ask you if you will turn from your path. But mark my words, Harold, mark my words, you are on the brink. If you ever speak of this again, or if I see or hear further evidence of unwise associations, there will be grave consequences.'

Chapter Twenty-Six

Christian and Mitch were still in the living room, Christian having finally convinced Mitch he wasn't going to try to escape again. But now Mitch had new concerns.

'Straight up, nothing from the banned section?'

'Not yet,' said Christian.

'Well what have you read then?'

'So far just the first few chapters, well, apart from the ones I've already written. No point in reading those.'

'Wait, wait, I don't get it, I thought you said you wrote this?'

'I'm in the process of writing it, back in the real world. I'm only halfway through though … well, a bit less, actually, if I'm honest.'

'Real world? You think this is a dream?'

'I know it is.'

Mitch looked down at the book, then back up at Christian. 'If it's your book, then why are you reading it at all?'

'To fill in the gaps.'

'Why?'

'To remember, of course, for when I wake up.'

'And?'

'And then it's just a matter of, well, dictation I suppose. My productivity will go through the roof. Stuart's gonna be blown away. Oh no, wait, he really is dead, I think. Yes.'

'Who's Stuart?'

'Doesn't matter. Anyway, I have to commit it all to memory, so I remember when I wake up.'

'You're full of shit. Why didn't you tell me this before?'

'I didn't realise before. The title's different, mine was *Thirty Things To Do After You Die.*'

'After you die?'

'Yes.'

'Huh. Not bad, I guess.'

'And I'm sure this new title, Terry's Guide, that was the alternative suggested by Nikki.'

'Who's Nikki?'

'Doesn't matter. Anyway, apart from a few strange spellings, the text of the chapters match the ones I wrote in my unfinished book. I only twigged once I started reading it.'

'Bullshit.'

'It's true, I couldn't have worked it out any sooner.'

'No, I mean bullshit that the text matches,' said Mitch, 'it can't. It's bullshit.'

'It's not bullshit, Mitch, it matches. It's word for word.'

Mitch took a moment. 'All right,' he said, 'let's say it does match. So what? What does this have to do with the Gate?'

'Well that's the exit point,' said Christian, 'it's obvious.'

'Exit point?'

'To leave the dream, to wake up.'

This made no sense. This was just more bullshit.

'Look, it doesn't matter,' said Christian, 'all that matters is I want to go to the Gate and you want to take me there. I mean, that was your whole game all along, wasn't it?'

More muffled ecstasy from upstairs marked out Mitch's thinking time.

'Yeah, okay, you got me,' he said, 'but I was just doing my job, you understand. It was nothing personal.'

'It doesn't matter.'

'I keep out of the politics. I don't pick sides.'

'Mitch, really, forget it.'

'You're not pissed?'

'No. Really. It's my fault for not twigging sooner. Seriously, how stupid am I? The afterlife, animated severed limbs, bodies doing perfectly fine without a head, the whole thing's total nonsense, isn't it?'

'It is?'

'Of course it is.'

'Right ... right,' said Mitch.

'That's why what you did, what you needed to do, doesn't matter. It doesn't matter because none of this' – Christian whirled his arms – 'none of this matters.' He picked up the book. 'This is my book,' he continued, 'proof therefore that this' – he whirled his free arm again – 'is not real. All this, this whole reality, only exists inside my head.' Christian's face fell. 'Oh no, oh I'm so sorry, Mitch.'

'Sorry for what?'

'Well, um, this is a bit awkward, but, oh jeez, how to put this. Mitch, um, I'm afraid you ... don't exist.'

'Is that so?'

'Yes. You're a figment of my imagination, I'm afraid. Um, sorry about that.'

Mitch would have raised his eyebrows if he had any to raise.

'But it's not all bad,' said Christian, 'okay, so you're just a figment of my imagination, but you're a pretty damned central figment. You're not just some nobody I brushed past in the street, no, you're my guide.'

'Okay ...' said Mitch.

'In fact,' said Christian, 'something tells me you're one of those people who uses their middle name instead of their first name, am I right?'

'Maybe,' said Mitch, edging forward a fraction.

'I knew it. And would your real name just happen to be ... Virgil?'

'No. No, it's Dewy.'

'Oh,' said Christian, looking puzzled.

'Why, is that a problem?' said Mitch.

'No, no, just a detail. After all, what's in a name,' said Christian. He looked across at Mitch. 'Dewy. My guide Dewy.'

'*Mitch* works just fine if it's all right with you.'

'Oh, sure. No problem.'

Mitch narrowed the space where his eyes weren't. 'Straight up, you think this is all a dream, and I'm your guide back to reality?'

'I have no doubt.'

'So this is why you're fine about your girl banging the fat dude?'

'Exactly, because he's only banging her in my head.'

'And you believe this all because you think you wrote this book?'

'I don't think I did, I know I did.'

'All right then,' said Mitch, taking the book and opening it up, 'prove it. What's the first word of page ... one hundred and twenty-four?'

'It doesn't work like that.'

'Oh yeah, 'cos that'd be stupid, wouldn't it?' said Mitch. He closed the book and grabbed Christian by the collar.

'Hey, what are you doing?'

'I've had enough of this bullshit,' said Mitch, 'we're going to the Gate, and we're going now.'

'No, not yet. You must let me read the book first, so I can remember.'

'I don't know what your game is, but I'm done, so come on, get moving.' He started marching Christian into the hallway.

'No, Mitch, wait, *wait*.'

Mitch stopped. 'This better be good.'

'Give me one shot and I'll prove it to you. If I fail, I swear I'll go willingly to the Gate, as soon as you like.'

Mitch said nothing.

'Come on, one shot,' said Christian, 'and it'll be a lot easier to get me there if I go willingly.'

'You swear?' said Mitch. 'You swear to come quietly if you fail?'

'I swear.'

'And what if you win?'

'We still go, but you let me read the book before we leave.'

Mitch thought it over. Letting Christian read more of the book would be dangerous, but there was no way Christian could replicate the text – he was just another dead man in denial. There was no way to lose.

'Okay, deal,' said Mitch.

'Okay,' said Christian.

'Right then,' said Mitch, stepping back and opening the book, 'second and final chance, what's the first word at the top of page three hundred and forty-five?'

'Mitch, I told you, it doesn't work like that. I never saw it all finished in my mind. It would only come to me in bits, I'd sit down to write, and when the mood was set, the words would come to me. So that will be the test. You give me a topic, a random section from a random chapter, or you choose one, if you like, and I'll write it, then we see if it matches.'

'Well, sounds okay, I guess,' said Mitch. He went back to the book, and flicked through. 'Let's go for ...'

'Wait,' said Christian.

'What now?'

'First we need to recreate my writing environment.'

Mitch flexed his shoulders. 'Right. Okay, what do we need?'

'Well, we need to get away from the house for a start, it's too quiet.'

'And go where?'

'Somewhere where we can watch a bit of TV.'

'TV?'

'Yes, just a bit. You can't face the blank page from a cold start, might get a brain strain, you've got to warm up to it, we need something to get the juices flowing.'

'Well okay, but don't try anything.'

Mitch and Christian drifted down Vestments, trawling the houses for occupancy and TVs turned on. No one was at home in the first six dwellings, but at number thirty-four they found a house husband masturbating to an old episode of *EastEnders*.

'Here we go,' said Mitch.

'A soap?' said Christian. 'Oh no, come on, I have some standards. Besides, you're not actually suggesting we sit in with this guy, are you? You have seen what he's doing?'

'So what? He's in the privacy of his own home.'

'And so are we.'

'What's the big deal? We all do it. Least we all used to.'

Christian said nothing.

'I kinda like it,' said Mitch, opening a hand towards the straining man, 'don't get me wrong, I'm not light in the loafers, I just miss being able to bash one out. But look, it's like he's having one for the both of us, ay.'

'Well he's welcome to it,' said Christian.

'You know, when I was first dead I got depressed, real depressed. I was sure it couldn't get any worse, especially what with my head not turning up and all. But when I realised I'd never have sex again, not even with myself, Jesus, now that's depressing. Straight up, how fuckin' grim is that?'

The man continued to pound away. He was putting in the effort but seemed disengaged.

'It's so true what they say,' said Mitch, 'you don't know what you've got till it's gone.'

'Profound,' said Christian.

As the scene switched to the Queen Vic pub, the man paused before resuming at an increased stroke rate.

'Pat, Pat, Pat,' he moaned, in low cockney tones.

'Look, I can't take any more of this,' said Christian and made for the exit.

Number thirty-six was empty, as were the next three houses, but at forty-four they found two students watching an old episode of *Monarch of the Glen*.

'This'll do,' said Christian, and they settled in.

And then they watched the news.

And then they watched the students make cups of tea.

And then Mitch assumed they were ready.

And then Christian said, 'Not quite … there's one final step.'

'And that is?' said Mitch.

'*Countdown.*'

'Countdown? Countdown to what?'

Chapter Twenty-Seven

Dexter was making his way through the hastily established complex of boudoirs, massage rooms, dressing rooms, isolation tank rooms, hair and nail salons, saunas, aromatherapy rooms and an entire wing of walk-in wardrobes, on his way to the morning meeting with Gordon. After checking with various assistants, he established that Gordon was in makeup room six, and that was now where the meeting would be held.

Since the return and apparent persistence of his softer disposition, Gordon had not only regained his penchant for silk stockings and panties, but also become increasingly open about himself, or 'the real me' as he was putting it. Now he no longer walked, he *glided*, or so he claimed, stepping out in everything he could get his hands on, from mini-skirts to flowing summer numbers, from cocktail dresses to ball gowns. Though he'd keep things professional for the office, of course, typically going with a blouse, split-hem skirt and heels.

And the flowering was beginning to influence his work style, too. He no longer just told people to do it his way – now he asked for opinions, he consulted, he listened, then told them to do it his way. And there were radical new policies, too: improved leisure facilities for the lower ranks – table tennis *and* draughts – as well as a commitment to slightly higher-quality carpeting in communal areas. Yes, times were changing.

A miasma of perming fluid, scented candles and acetate greeted Dexter well before he opened the door. On entering the room, he found Gordon perched in a swivel chair, papyrus bib around his neck, hair gathered and pinned back.

They exchanged greetings.

'And I believe you know Sarah,' said Gordon, via the mirror, as Dexter took one of the sofa seats.

'I do,' said Dexter, and he exchanged a smile and a nod.

'She's my first, Dex.'

'I'm sorry?'

'First woman in the service, apart from the secretaries of course. Wrote the policy last night. Mortal norms have moved, Dex, we need to move with them, get ourselves acquainted with newfangled thinking, however bizarre ...'

Dexter swapped another glance with Sarah. She eyed the ceiling before carrying on.

'... and Sarah is our first, the first woman in the service, a trailblazer.' Gordon returned to his reflection, but his smile turned to a frown. 'That's too much, woman. I told you, I told you, you overdid the foundation.'

'Well I'm sorry,' said Sarah, 'but they didn't teach us extreme makeup and beauty at Stanford.'

'Well what did they teach?'

'I majored in international relations.'

'Well they need to buck their ideas up. Can't have international relations without makeup. Imagine if Thatcher had met Carter without a bit of lippy. Bang goes Trident, hello World War Three. Mind you, would have been good for our numbers.'

Sarah put the powder brush down. She looked like she was about to reply.

Dexter gave a measured shake of his head.

She shook hers and carried on with the bronzer.

There was a knock at the door. A secretary entered and announced that Cheung and Bhakta were here for the meeting.

'Leave us,' said Gordon, to Sarah.

'But it's not finished,' she said, 'it's ... no, actually, it's fine, just needs a final ...' She took the eyeliner, spun Gordon to face her, and added a swastika to each of Gordon's cheeks. 'There,' she said, and spun him back to the mirror.

'Explain,' said Gordon, sharply.

'Latest thing,' said Sarah, her hands on Gordon's seatback, 'they're all going for this look in Chelsea.'

'But it's–'

'Exactly,' she said, 'it's radical, progressive, and it shows you mean business. No one ever messed with the SS.' She smiled, winked at Dexter and left the room.

'Well, I do mean business,' said Gordon as he showcased each cheek to himself. 'What are you looking at?' he said, catching Dexter's smile.

'Nothing, Gordon, nothing at all.'

Gordon held the stare, before reaching for a Brigitte Bardot blonde bouffant wig. He dipped forward, stretched it onto his scalp, and sat back with a flick of his head. 'Not bad,' he said, teasing out some of the curls, 'not bad at all.' He made a couple more adjustments and then spun round to face the door. 'Come,' he boomed.

Cheung and Bhakta entered.

Dexter's mouth dropped open.

Bhakta was wearing a sunflower and tulip print cotton skirt, heels and a black-and-cream striped blouse. Cheung had somehow got himself into a purple body stocking that looked four sizes too small, but he had at least chosen flats. Both had makeup worse than Gordon's, even after the swastikas.

'Hey good morning, Gordon,' said Cheung.

'I know we're a little early,' said Bhakta, 'but then there's a lot to–'

'What,' bellowed Gordon, 'the blazes is going on?'

'I'm sorry?' said Cheung.

'This is a place of business. Explain your appearance.'

'We thought, um,' said Bhakta.

'We thought it's good now,' said Cheung, 'to go tranny, like you, Gordon.'

'You both look ridiculous,' said Gordon.

They looked at each other.

'You can't put florals next to stripes,' said Gordon, gesticulating at Bhakta, 'and you, Larry, I'd have expected better from you.'

'But, but–'

'Haven't you ever heard of matching for vegetable body shape? A body stocking is good on a string-bean shape, or perhaps a carrot shape. You, Larry, are a potato shape.'

'So, um …'

'So wear something that would suit a potato.'

'But–'

'Get out of my sight.'

'It's just–'

'Out,' shouted Gordon, and he pointed to the door.

Their chins dipped and they left the room.

'Honestly. Did you see that?' he said, to Dexter. 'I tell you I'm surrounded by cretins.'

'Gordon …'

'One can over-purge, I suppose,' said Gordon, swivelling back to face the mirror and make some further adjustments to his curls.

'Gordon … look, are you all right?'

'Of course, why shouldn't I be?'

'Well,' said Dexter, 'you don't think perhaps you've underestimated the impact?'

'Of?'

'Of your son, your other self, his death.'

'It's a tragedy, Dex, no one's denying it, but we have to move on. Yes, his mortal life is over, but look on the bright side, now he's closer to me, I'm closer to me. He'll be right here soon, I'm sure of it.'

'You're not under stress, at all?'

'Not a bit. I'm excited. This is a good thing. Now there'll be two of me to run the place, imagine the productivity. Not to mention all those wasted years to catch up on, I'll finally have some family around here, someone to talk to, someone to be with, someone to take me shopping.'

'Shopping?'

Gordon swivelled back to face Dexter. 'Everyone needs shopping, Dex. Entire economies run on shopping.' He swivelled back to the mirror and picked up a lipstick. 'Besides, look at the big picture. We're nearly there, we've nearly done it. I can feel it in my waters. My boy's going to bring home the bacon. I bet he's pumping the prophet for the master codes as we speak. And once here we'll find a way to get them out there, in the mortal realm, and then the revolution can begin.'

Dexter failed to force a smile.

Gordon put down the lipstick. 'You don't seem thrilled,' he said.

'I'm sorry, Gordon, I am *thrilled*, really.'

'But?'

'Well. I just hope it's all been worth the price.'

'It?'

'It. Your change.'

'I don't follow?'

'Oh come on, the dresses, the makeup, the tights, the lippy. The panties.'

'What's that got to do with my son?'

'The timing. It's too much of a coincidence. This all started what, eleven, twelve, years after the spawning? And now he's dead you're worse than ever.'

'What exactly are you saying?'

'That something went wrong. Creating the boy has caused this, this behaviour.'

'How dare you …'

'Look, Gordon, I hold up my hands. I should have said something years ago–'

'… how dare you try to justify me.'

'*What?*'

Gordon thrust back the chair, stood and turned to Dexter. 'There always has to be a reason, doesn't there, with people like you. Can't be that this is who I am, that this is my true nature.'

'True nature? You were more alpha than Moses for six thousand years, now you're as fruity as a bag of Jaffas, how can this be your true nature?'

'Merely latent.'

'Gordon, these urges are a condition, they are not you.'

'Don't try to tell me how I feel.'

'I'm only being straight with you, Gordon.'

The King of Limbo clopped a few ungainly paces. 'Yes,' he said, tapping his chin.

'Yes what?' said Dexter.

'Yes I see now. That's it, isn't it, being straight with me. So straight you might shatter?'

'What on earth are you talking about?'

'You're jealous.'

'What?'

'Come on, admit it, I've seen the way you look at me.' He turned to linger on his own reflection in the mirror. 'But don't feel bad, I'd be jealous too, if I were you.'

'Gordon, I'm not that way inclined.'

'I don't mean that, man,' said Gordon, snapping back, 'I'm not that way either. I mean you're jealous of my freedom, freedom from outdated dogmas, freedom to do as I please, freedom to–'

'To hold board meetings dressed like Widow Twankey?'

'There's no need to be a naughty boy, Dexter. Now come on, admit it, you'd at least like to try some stockings.'

'Gordon,' said Dexter, holding up his hands, 'I don't have any desire for any of this.'

'Come on, of course you do. I've got some spare ones, you know, over there in my handbag. You could try them now.' Gordon took a step closer. 'Come on, you'll find them most liberating.'

Dexter shuffled back in his seat. 'I can't do this,' he said.

Gordon stepped closer still and held lingering eye contact, before breaking off. 'Suit yourself,' he said, checking his hemline in the mirror, 'I suppose we can't all be divas.'

Chapter Twenty-Eight

Mitch had baulked at the prospect of yet further delay before Christian would be ready to start the test, but his competitive instincts soon had him embroiled in the afternoon TV quiz show that was Channel Four's *Countdown*.

Only when the closing credits rolled did Mitch reflect on the ease with which Christian had manoeuvred him into wasting so much time with this and the other TV offerings. He felt foolish and something close to dirty, though it was tempered with a fair slice of professional admiration. But it didn't matter, because Christian had declared he was ready to begin.

So they returned to 22 Vestments for Christian to sit the most important exam of his existence.

'Got everything you need?' asked Mitch.

'I think so,' said Christian, eyeing his E-grade stationery kit: a wad of crinkled blank sheets – the backs of a handful of Mitch's P16 collection forms – and the crude pencil he'd been given by Hargreaves, in what now seemed like an age ago.

'Right,' said Mitch. He opened the guide and thumbed through the pages of the front section. 'You're gonna write from "Walk the Earth" chapter forty-seven, "Bits of People". Section five, "Behavioural Training".

And your subject is gonna be verses eleven through thirty-two, "Ears, Noses and Testicles".'

'Ears, noses and testicles?'

'That's what I said,' said Mitch, and he closed the book.

Christian picked up the pencil and began.

Mitch retreated to the kitchen to afford Christian a degree of privacy, but kept close, glancing round the door every minute or so. He decided to use the time for contingency planning. Christian could well go back on his word after he failed the test. It would be a long hard slog to the Gate if he had to drag him, but he decided the classic headlock would be best, if he was forced down that path. Sink into the ground to neck level, too. It would be exhausting, but secure, and not too uncomfortable for the man at the front. Still, he'd never attempted it over this kind of distance before.

Mitch was mentally going over the check-in procedures for the fast-track lane at the Gate when his thoughts were interrupted by a shout from the living room.

'Done.'

'What,' said Mitch, drifting through, 'but you've only had, like, fifteen minutes.'

'All I needed,' said Christian.

'Let's see it then,' said Mitch.

Christian got up and handed over the crinkled pages.

Mitch gave them a quick scan. The first five were filled with spidery writing, but he stopped and stared when he got to the last one. 'We didn't say anything about drawings.'

'I felt it needed one,' said Christian.

Mitch sat down in the armchair.

'It's in there, isn't it?' said Christian, beaming. He began to parade around the room.

Mitch opened the guide at the bookmarked test section. He already knew the answer, but had to check because he didn't believe the answer. He flicked on a couple of pages and there it was: a superbly crafted woodcut print of a man looking down his nose at a line-up of testicles and their owners, with pictorial inserts detailing the basic set of 'jump', 'stay' and 'roll' training moves. The illustration was a good deal more elegant than Christian's pencil scrawl, but there was no mistake, they were the same – identical in content, composition and proportion. Mitch receded into the upholstery of the armchair.

But the text, what about the text? He began checking Christian's copy, comparing line by line against the book.

'There's still one thing I don't get,' said Christian, as he looked out onto the garden.

'Oh yeah?' said Mitch, not looking up.

'I reckon I've solved most of the little problems, the little holes in the book world universe, all apart from one ...'

Mitch still didn't look up.

'... a justification for it all being in English.'

'What?' said Mitch.

'The book,' said Christian, turning. 'Obviously I've written it in English, but when I include quotes from Heaven, their songs, their sayings, the titles of their plays, and that, well they're all in English too. Those pages I've just written now, that little side paragraph on the organisations that exist to protect bits of people, what was it, the RSPCBOP, it's an English name. Royal Society for the Prevention of Cruelty to Bits of People. Do you see? Through the whole book I make this unwritten assumption that the language of the afterlife is English.'

Mitch didn't reply but paused in his checking.

'It doesn't stack up, does it?' said Christian. 'God's been around since the beginning, so he'd be speaking some ancient language, and so would the rest of the afterlife, certainly the rest of Heaven.'

'I don't want to think about it,' said Mitch, 'and neither should you.'

'Well, I've tried not to, but it still bugs me.'

'I'm serious, Christian. I don't want you to think about it. Remember the soup? This is the same, this is exactly the same.'

'Okay. Whatever.'

Mitch finished the last page. He cast them to one side. He stood up and gripped his shoulders.

'Well?' said Christian.

'You got it, you got it all,' said Mitch, 'even the fuckin' punctuation.'

'Yes,' said Christian, with a fist pump. He stepped over to Mitch and offered a high five that was not returned.

'So?' said Mitch, eventually.

'So what?'

'So how do you do it?'

'I've told you. It's my book, it's my unconscious.'

'Come on, I didn't die yesterday, what's the trick?'

'No trick.'

'You've memorised it, haven't you?'

'What, the whole book in one day?'

'Well, we only tested you on one section.'

'Which you picked.'

'Maybe you got lucky.'

'Fine, pick another, anything you like.'

No reply from Mitch as Christian began parading about the room. 'And if it was a trick,' said Christian, 'why would I do it? What on earth would I have to gain? I know you want to take me to the Gate, I know you can make me to go whether I like it or not.'

Mitch sat down again.

'You have to accept it, Mitch, this *is* my book, and this, all of this world, is inside my head, every last thing, including you.'

More silence.

Mitch didn't believe for one moment he wasn't real. That was total bullshit. He was street smart, he was sharp; if he wasn't real, he'd have noticed by now – he'd always been really great at stuff like that. But he had to accept that Christian did have detailed knowledge of the book. This was a dangerous development. First, how did this affect the judgement rules? Even if Christian hadn't read or written out the banned section, it seemed a good bet he'd know it, on some level, even if he couldn't access it without the help of a complex daytime-TV ritual. So did that count as banned knowledge? Would it stop him getting in? There was no way of knowing, and there was nothing he could do about it. Second, whatever the fuck was going on, there was a lot Hotswap and the angels hadn't told him. They'd made it seem like a regular pickup, urgent – okay, important – sure, but nothing weird and fucked up like this. Bastards. What the fuck was he now in the middle of? But then, maybe nothing had changed. He was still close, real close to making this delivery. So long as he could get him to the Gate, and so long as his luck held and Christian still qualified for Heaven, he'd still get what he wanted. Okay, so deliver the cargo, take the reward, walk away. That was it. As for the bigger scheme, well, leave that for the angels.

'All right,' said Mitch, 'I guess all that matters is our interests are aligned. So what are we waitin' for? Let's hit the road.'

'Excellent. I'm right with you,' said Christian, 'right after I've read the book.'

'What?'

'That was the deal.'

Mitch clenched his fists. He wanted to pound his forehead but had to make do with his chest. 'All right,' he said, eventually, 'all right.' He picked up the book and handed it over. 'Off you go then. I guess another hour won't hurt.'

'What?'

'What do you mean what?'

'I mean I'm gonna need more time.'

'How much time?'

'Well, I dunno, couple of months maybe?'

'A couple of months?'

'Yes. It's a big book and I'm a slow reader. Besides, I need to make sure I remember everything, every last detail.'

'No way, no fuckin' way,' said Mitch, shaking the space where his head wasn't, 'we're already late, real late, have you any idea how many others will be looking for you? They track people, like I track people. They'll find us and they won't be easy going like me.'

'All right, so let's go somewhere else then, somewhere we won't be found.'

'No.'

'Come on, I know loads of safe places.'

'We're in the Zone, buddy, there are no safe places. There are no walls, just images of walls.'

'Mitch, you said I could read the book before we go, that was the deal.'

'I said you could read some of the book.'

'No, you said I could read the book.'

Mitch gripped his shoulders tight. 'A day. I'll give you a day.'

'Oh come on. Look, how about a month. I can do it in a month, if I really push.'

'Two days, that's it.'

'All right, fourteen.'

'Two.'

'Ten?'

'Two.'

'Seven?'

'Two.'

'Four?'

'Two.'

A long pause.

'All right, okay,' Christian said. He sat down with the book and released the clasp.

'And no looking at the banned section,' said Mitch.

'Hey, no way, I need to see the whole book.'

'How many times? You doofus, it's dangerous, it's pure poison.'

'Oh come on, Mitch.'

'No. Look, whatever is going on here, knowledge is still deadly – especially the back section of that book, maybe. How do you know it's not part of your little mind game. Just as going through the Gate will make you wake up, how do you know reading the banned stuff won't blow your chances and trap you here for good, maybe really kill you?'

'Well, I guess the short answer is I don't know, for sure.'

'Right.'

'But the back section's bound to have some dynamite stuff, isn't it? It's like you said, it must be banned for a reason. It's bound to add some spice, publishers love that, or it could even form an entire second book. They say it's always tough to follow up a first time bestseller, so it could save me a lot of grief next year.'

'I've told you, it's too dangerous. End of story.'

'Look I agree, I agree it's a risk, I hear you. But some risks are worth taking, surely?'

'Not this one.'

Christian folded his arms.

'Look, tell you what,' said Mitch, 'I'll give you an extra day. That's three days, okay. But no looking at the banned section.'

Christian still said nothing.

'Okay?' said Mitch.

'Okay,' muttered Christian, looking away.

'You have to swear, Christian, you swear you will stick to this deal. You get three days, you don't look at the banned section, then you come with me to the Gate. That's it.'

'I said okay.'

'Swear.'

'Okay, jeez, I swear. Okay?'

'Okay.'

Chapter Twenty-Nine

Early the next morning Christian was standing at the top of Vestments trying to keep calm and think clearly. Where to go? Where to be safe? Anywhere in Bracknell would be too dangerous. He needed distance. But he couldn't head out on the motorways or any of the main roads – too predictable. He couldn't go via the town either, for the same reasons. Any route or path he pondered seemed to be one he'd already drifted with Mitch.

Hidden in the rhododendron bushes of number nineteen, two smartly suited men looked on. They looked at each other, and then looked back at Christian. They watched as he put his hand over his eyes, stretched out an arm, and spun round on the spot, completing five hurried revolutions.

The men made a couple of quick notes and then continued to watch as Christian opened his eyes and sprinted off in the direction of his outstretched arm.

A sheet of panic flashed through Mitch when he woke to find himself alone in the living room. He got to his feet and checked the house, sprinting through walls, floors and ceilings, checking every room, then the garden and then the neighbouring houses. Nothing. He rushed back to the house and back into the living room.

What had happened? What the fuck had he missed? Think, think.

He looked around, more carefully this time.

Had he been snatched? Another shepherd? The angels, maybe?

'Fuuuuuuuuck.'

But then he'd heard nothing in the night, not a sound; his knapsack was where he left it, everything seemed to be undisturbed; there were no signs of struggle or sabotage. And then he spotted a note tucked into his knapsack, written on the back of a folded P16.

Sorry. Too good an opportunity to miss. No need to panic, I won't let you down — meet you back at the church in three six months.

Sorry about breaking the deal. I know I swore I wouldn't, but I thought, well, as you're just a figment of my imagination, it's probably fine.

Take it easy,
Christian.

Mitch screwed up the note, threw it into the wall and yelled, 'Little fucker. Fucking fucking fucker.'

Chapter Thirty

Dexter was in his one-to-one with Gordon. It was not being held in the main office, or indeed any office, and it was no longer strictly a one-to-one, either. Like everything else, it was now subordinate to Gordon's increasingly demanding fashion and beauty regime. Today it would be held in parallel with a fitting at the rooms of Gordon's newly commissioned couture dressmaker.

The space smelled like soldering fumes blending with volatile organic compounds, like a kettle catching fire in a carpet shop. It was cramped and chaotic, with every shelf and surface cluttered with textiles, tools, thread, notes and technical documentation. Garments of every description hung from roof rails, making the workbench in the middle of the room a clearing in a cloth forest. At the back, but still dominating the space, was a large, brown-glass-domed beige cupboard that looked like it was made from Bakelite, its sides scratched and scuffed, its doors no longer quite aligned, its control panel matted and worn. Bipton could have easily had it replaced but afterlife tailors, like mortal tailors, trust their old equipment. Not that this provisioner would ever be used on the Lord of Limbo – when that was required, a stooge of matching build would be prodded forward to do his duty. This time the job was beyond Bipton's ability to configure the machine anyway. This job was being done the old old way.

'You know what,' said Gordon, standing proud as Bipton attempted to shoehorn him into the largest little black dress seen in any realm and any time.

Dexter was sitting on a small stool and was keeping his eyes fixed on his notes. 'What?' he said.

'I feel glorious.'

'That's your new buzzword, isn't it,' said Dexter, 'they're all picking up on it, you know. Abdurrahman said he felt glorious yesterday, so did Banberg. Nishimura even said he was slingwhabous.'

'How's that on the hips, sire?' asked Bipton.

'Terrible,' said Gordon, without looking at the tailor, 'make it look tighter, Bippy, but without being tighter.'

Bipton looked worried.

'They're not empty sentiments,' said Gordon, to Dexter, 'I've never felt so alive, and Limbo is feeling it too.'

'Well. Good for you,' said Dexter.

'You're not feeling it?'

'No, no it's not that.'

'So you are feeling it? Finally joining the party, eh? Well better late than never.'

And Dexter did feel it. Troubling though Gordon's unfettered gloriousness was, the longer it stayed, the more convinced Dexter had become that Grímsson and Spitback might actually be right. He sat back from his notes and allowed himself a smile. 'Finally the most populous realm will become the upper realm. As it should be. Blue skies and sunshine, Gordon ... our Promised Land.'

'Exactly,' said Gordon. 'We're on the up, my boy, we're going into fucking orbit. Our plan, our great endeavour, it's finally coming together. And I've been thinking, we should go further.'

'Oh yes?'

'Yes. We should ride the wave of change. For the first time in my life, I'm not just thinking about flogging our galley slaves to do more toiling. Now I'm thinking about where they do their toiling while we flog them. I want change. I want open attitudes to match those open skies. I want a realm where a tax lawyer can strut our corridors dressed as Carmen Miranda, where a facilities manager can chair meetings in leather hot pants, where a local councillor can declare he loves cock and receive nothing worse than a round of applause.'

'There, sire,' said Bipton, creeping back like he was retreating from an unexploded bomb, 'how's that?'

Dexter looked up, but for a moment only. It was a heinous vision, resembling a middle-aged sow at the end of its hen night.

'I like it, Bippy, I like it,' said Gordon.

Bipton bowed.

'Something's not quite right though,' said Gordon, drumming his chest. 'Dex. Get over here.'

'Must I?' said Dexter.

'Yes.'

Dexter put down his notes and got to his feet.

'It doesn't feel right, here at the top,' said Gordon, looking down at the dress and fiddling with it.

Dexter stopped mid-stride.

'I don't bite,' said Gordon, 'now come on, why doesn't it work in the bust?'

Dexter edged closer and reluctantly examined the material.

'Get a proper feel, man.'

'I–'

Gordon gave a tut before grasping Dexter's hand and thrusting it inside the top of the dress. 'Now, be honest, what do you think?'

'I really really don't know what you want me to say, Gordon, but I am quite scared.'

'Just tell me. Do you think these feel like a woman's breasts?'

'No, Gordo. Not in the slightest.'

'Exactly,' said Gordon, 'exactly. It's time I had a boob job.'

'What?' said Dexter, withdrawing his hand. 'Gordo, we don't ... we can't ...'

'Bippy,' said Gordon, fixing the little man with a wide-eyed stare, 'sort it out.'

'Me, sire?' said Bipton, shaking. 'But, but, I'm a tailor, sire.'

'You were a tailor, Bippy, then I made you my couture dressmaker.'

'Yes, sire, thank you, sire.'

'And now I'm making you my plastic surgeon, so get on it.'

The tailor froze. He looked over to Dexter but got nothing more than a shrug.

'Run, Bippy, run,' said Gordon. 'I want to be a double D within the week.'

Bipton scuttled off.

'Gordo, I don't want to rain on your parade, but are you sure about all of this? You don't think you're getting a bit carried away?'

'I've never been so sure of anything,' said Gordon. He stood back to admire the image of loveliness in the mirror. 'Now, tell me everything you know about anal bleaching.'

Chapter Thirty-One

Having traversed housing estates, parks, open fields and woodland, Christian had stumbled upon railway tracks – what he reasoned must be the London to Reading line. He was confident he'd given Mitch the slip, but he needed more distance, he needed to be sure, so he decided to follow the tracks.

Now, in late afternoon, he found himself at Earley station, not far from Reading itself. And this sparked an idea. He knew the nearby university campus – not well, but well enough: several school science trips and a fluffed interview in sixth form. Enough history to know how to find it, but not enough for a third party to put it on their list of Christian's likely hideaways. It would be easy enough to blend in, too; in fact, it would be perfect – he'd be just another student lost in a book.

He left the tracks and skirted his way through the suburban streets and into the Whiteknights Campus.

At first he'd thought the library would be the best bet – a quiet place to read and lights on until late in the evening – but then something caught his eye on the large signposted map of the campus: the university chaplaincy. That had a library too, or at least he seemed to recall mention of it at the presentation before his entrance interview. That was an even better bet. It was a university, a mecca for rational thinking. A theology library would be deserted. And it would be the last place Mitch would think of looking. The eye of the storm, the hideaway within the hideaway.

As he made his way through the campus, his mind's eye pictured a substantial concrete building, smaller than the main library, of course, but still a good size. So when he arrived at a tiny red-brick bungalow, he found himself looking behind it to see where the rest of it was. Perhaps the bungalow was just the entrance? A gateway to a multilevel complex of underground vaults, room after room of dusty religious works and arte-facts? But no. Exploration revealed that inside the bungalow was the inside of a bungalow. Furthermore, the theology library only took up one room of it: three walls of books, table, chairs, whiteboard, globe and guitar – that was it. However, it was still and silent and infused with the soft smell of knowledge (of a sort). It would do fine. And so he settled down to read.

In the main, the quiet atmosphere held up well. Students came and went throughout the day, mostly in ones and twos, and mostly just returning or borrowing books rather than staying to read. And after a few hours, Christian felt certain he was beyond the reach of Mitch. However, what Christian hadn't countered for was the interest of other ghosts. And when it came to early evening, he caught sight of a figure outside the window, a figure with a blue-green glow.

The man, rangy and earnest, was soon standing slightly too close to Christian, introducing himself as Malcolm, and telling Christian how he'd been coming to the library for the past six years in an effort to work out 'what on God's green earth is going on'. It made Christian thankful he'd taken the precaution of pushing his Terry's Guide through the table, moments earlier, but also mad at himself for his lack of discretion with his own blue-green glow, Malcolm having approached as if Christian was wearing a felt-tipped name badge at a gay dating ice-breaker. And it was only now Christian realised that Mitch may not be the only shepherd after him. At least the conversation with Malcolm confirmed he wasn't one of them, or if he was, he wasn't an especially dangerous or cunning one. Even so, Christian resolved to stay in the cone of the ceiling light during darkness and not be tempted to stray to the window again.

. . .

A night and a morning later and Christian was well into the book. He'd planned to read in page order, cover to cover, skipping only what he was sure he'd written out already, but temptation got the better of him and he'd soon found himself dipping in here, there and everywhere. And this, of course, included the forbidden fruit of the banned section. Though after all the hype, it almost completely failed to deliver. Not only well short of revelation, much of it was long-winded and parochial. There were entire chapters devoted to contact with the Almighty and why you shouldn't attempt it, extensive indexed sections detailing skills in constant demand in Heaven and how you should make yourself available to the administration if you have them, and endless customs regulations for those lucky enough to be going on overdimensions business trips and holidays back into the Zone. And the few parts that were interesting were off the other end of the scale, coming across as far-fetched, even for fantasy comic fiction – in particular the chapters attempting to bolster something akin to the traditional six-day creation myth, and the dismissive, brief and bizarre sections on Limbo and Hell. Why had he structured it like this? It made no sense.

But disappointment soon gave way to anxiety. Many of his rules and regulations were unjust and some were out-and-out cruel. It would have been fair enough if they were funny, or made a point while they were doing it, but they weren't and didn't. And it was the same for his 'Perfectly Normal Laws Of Nature' that applied in the Zone, and the consequences for those affected – an eternity stuck in stilettoes; breast implants worn on the outside; disabled dead bonded to wheelchairs they no longer needed. And in all cases, passage through the Gate of Judgement was the only release. None of this was a cause for concern for the residents of the afterlife, to whom the cruelty applied, because of course they didn't exist. The concern was for where they resided, namely inside Christian's head. He was the author, the creator of this world. There was no one else to blame. He tried to tell himself it was black comedy, so black even he couldn't see the jokes, but no matter how he twisted it, he couldn't help but conclude that his subconscious was a far darker, pettier and altogether more slippery place than he'd ever imagined.

In among all the cruelty and arbitrary nastiness, one thing hit him harder than anything else – according to the book, the dead could not contact the living, full stop. It sent him back to his recent pain, all the failed attempts to contact Beatrice, the night he'd spent weeping at her feet while she watched the Eurovision Song Contest. But then thankfully none of that was real, he reminded himself again, before again feeling stupid because his pain hadn't been real either. He'd been taken in by a preposterous account for what he was experiencing, the tallest of tall tales, a fairy story, and what's worse his own fairy story. What a fool.

But it still didn't explain why. Why had he made his universe this way? It was fantasy, he could have set things up however he liked. It would have been nice for Heaven to help out the poor and downtrodden of the mortal realm, with an unseen hand, once in a while, instead of it being prohibited. It would have been nice for the dead to be able to contact the living – comforting for afterlife and mortal characters alike, had he returned to a narrative format, not to mention being a great plot device – but then, he thought, it was, above all else, fiction. He remembered his novel writing advice. No one wants to read about people who get along with one another and have a lovely time quietly achieving their easily achievable goals. Yes, that was it, he'd simply taken that lesson to heart. The cruelty was really a good thing. Yes, a good thing …

Other things just left him scratching his head, though, or rather, the lack of other things, in particular when skimming through the sections detailing the judgement criteria. The ancient no-brainers were still in there: theft, murder, lies – couldn't miss those out – but why hadn't he taken the opportunity to close some of the well-known Abrahamic gaps like rape, paedophilia and slavery; infanticide, torture and genocide? He did smile at his blanket ban on granting estate agents entry to Heaven, though, and even let out a little cheer when digesting the judgement meted out on anyone who had ever joined the clergy, preached a sermon or pressed a certain kind of pamphlet on an unsuspecting householder. But then he thought back to Tony and his quiet life at the vicarage. It wouldn't be funny, let alone fair, for him to end up in Hell. But the text was clear: the sin – spelled 'syn' in the pages – of preaching bought you a one-way ticket downstairs. No exceptions.

But Christian was surprised, tickled and delighted at some of the things he read and saw. In particular the inside jacket cover generated a huge smile, followed by a laugh – a laugh out loud, which was something Christian rarely did when he was on his own. The source of the delight was the author profile, complete with woodcut cheesy portrait. It was Erdygrot. His dream-state friend from childhood, now elevated to Lord of all creation. That wouldn't make publication, of course, it was a private joke with an audience of one, but he gave his subconscious a pat on the back all the same. Because now he thought about it, Erdygrot was a perfect fit for the personification of the deluded, clueless, workshy God he'd envisioned might have found himself somehow inexplicably at the top of the tree.

And so he continued to read and continued to attempt to commit every word to memory. But in the late afternoon, he stopped in shock when he noticed someone out of the corner of his eye, walking up the path to the entrance. It was someone he recognised but didn't immediately accept was actually there, because she was a long way out of context. A long way indeed.

'Long time no see,' said Nikki.

Christian just stared back at her, barely acknowledging the power-trouser makeover. And then he smiled, and then he laughed. The absurdity of it all – Nikki turning up here in his world, for no reason, it was the icing on the evidence-of-dream cake. But just as quickly, he stopped laughing and found his smile slipping back and sticking in his throat.

'Christian,' she said.

There was a problem – a problem with reality. Not real reality, of course, but his dream reality. Now for the first time it struck him how stable it had all been up to this point. Perhaps he hadn't noticed because that's how everyday real reality tends to be, too. Okay, so this dream world was dislocated and confounding, and contained not just the weird but the downright impossible, but until now everything had still had an inner cohesion. Cause and effect had still been in effect. But now Nikki was here, standing right in front of him. An effect with no cause.

'Christian?'

If she could just appear, as if by magic, then so could anything.

Instant vulnerability, a sinking sense of exposure. Perhaps the cocoon of the library, the sanctuary he'd congratulated himself on finding a day earlier, offered no real protection at all, as useful as a greenhouse in a game of hide-and-seek. If Nikki could just appear, perhaps a livid Mitch could too? Perhaps anything could just appear. What was to stop a T-Rex popping into existence in the prayer room, or the hard-wearing carpet beneath him giving way to send him tumbling into a subterranean lava flow?

He got up from the table and moved to the edge of the room. He sat down in the floor and the wall, drew his knees up to his chest and hugged himself.

'Christian, Christian, it's me, it's Nikki.' She bent down and placed a hand on his shoulder. 'Are you okay?'

He looked up into her eyes. *What are you doing here?* he thought, and then repeated the question out loud.

'I came to find you,' she said. 'You were the only person I could think of.'

'There's no reason for you to be here.'

She looked puzzled. 'I just thought we could help each other out. As you can see, I'm dead now too. It's all been such a shock for me, I don't mind saying.'

'No, that's not it at all, is it?' said Christian, shaking his head. 'There is no cause – you're a ghost in the machine.'

'Why are you being like this?' she said. 'I thought you'd understand?' She turned away. 'I'm finding this all so terribly difficult as it is.' She started to whimper.

'Why would I bring you here?' he said, drumming his chin. 'Why here? Why now?' He looked away as he gave it some thought, unmoved by the apparent emotional turmoil his unconscious's version of Nikki was suffering. 'Wait, wait,' he said, 'of course, it's obvious, you're here to manage me again, aren't you?'

'Manage you?' she said, breaking off from her suffering rather quickly.

His concern lifted. There were still cause and effect potholes, great big ones, and he wasn't looking forward to being hassled again, but at least he could now see why, in a roundabout kind of way, his unconscious had introduced Nikki to the proceedings.

'Look, I'm reading it as fast as I can, okay, but it's a big book.'

'What's a big book?'

'Well this of course.' He went to the table and retrieved the book. 'What do you think I've been browsing here? The Bhagavad Gita?'

She froze before losing her balance and falling back onto and into the floor.

'Like learning to walk all over again, isn't it?' said Christian. 'Nice detail though,' he added, giving his unconscious a tip of the hat. He sat down again in the floor at the edge of the room and opened the book.

She pulled herself up, shifted forward onto her knees and crawled towards him, her eyes like CDs. 'But that's the book,' she said.

'Cool, eh?' said Christian, beginning to enjoy himself again.

'May I?' she said.

'Why?'

'Come on, I only want to look.'

'Well. All right. But don't try anything.' He passed it over.

She sat back, folding her legs to the side, and held the book, reverently at first, but her movements soon quickened, her fingers and thumbs jittering as she flipped through the pages. 'What's this?' she said, examining the loose buckle straps.

'It was over the banned section.'

'Banned section?'

'Yes, the whole second half. Judgement, Heaven, Limbo, Hell.'

'This is a full edition?' she said, eyes now locked on the pages.

'Meaning there's a … less than full edition?' said Christian. 'Oh you're not thinking of an abridged one, are you? For the Americans? It's a bit demeaning …'

She flicked to the inside back cover, freezing momentarily at the woodcut portrait of the proud author.

'… hey, it could be a good marketing gimmick for the real book though, actually issuing it with a buckle and strap, you know, along with a warning – *Do not read the second section, open at your own risk*. People love that kind of stuff. Cheesy yet mysterious …'

She was now working back a page at a time.

'… I suppose that'll increase costs though,' said Christian, 'could be tricky fitting one to the paperback version, too …'

He was still failing to acknowledge Nikki's singular focus as she checked through the index, the publication notes, the rather short list of other books by the same author, and then the last page of the last chapter of the last book of the second section.

'… perhaps we could combine it with a cardboard outer case,' he continued, 'oh but then what about the e-book version? We could look at some sort of encryption, I suppose, email in for the password and a cuddly toy … cuddly spleen, maybe? Anyway, that kind of thing.'

He now saw that her hands and the book had dropped to her lap. 'What's up?' he said.

'There's no appendix,' she said, 'nothing after the last chapter.'

'Isn't there?'

'No.'

'Oh.'

'Well, actually there wouldn't be,' she said, 'I suppose, but I thought, perhaps …'

'Oh yes,' said Christian, 'yes, we talked about it, didn't we, and I had a go at it in the end, got all those doodles and the hex. Hey, is it odd it's not here, when the rest of it is?'

She shut the book. 'Christian, did you read much of the back section,' she said, 'the banned bits?'

'Why?'

'Just curious.'

'Well, yes, I've been dipping in here and there.'

'Right, right' – a half smile – 'good, and have you shared this with anyone? Told anyone what you've read?'

'No, but then I only started yesterday.'

'Excellent,' she said, and handed the book back to him. 'And where exactly did you get it?'

'Well, the short version is I stole it from a figment of my imagination.'

'Come again?'

'A figment of my imagination,' said Christian, 'an imaginary shepherd. He's called Mitch Langford. You can't miss him. Well-dressed fellow. Charcoal suit, black polar neck, Canadian accent, no head.'

'You stole it from a headless shepherd who's a figment of your imagination?' She looked around the room. 'Oh wow, holy shit. You don't think any of this is real, do you?'

'Er, no, of course it isn't.'

'Because … you think you're still alive.'

'I don't think so. I know so.'

'Right, right …' she said, seeming distracted, ' … look this imaginary shepherd, who you stole the book from, is he looking for it?'

'I don't know. Probably. He'll be a bit upset, I imagine.'

'Does he know you're here?'

'I don't think so, but then I didn't think you knew I was here. So, I think what probably matters is whether my unconscious can think of a good reason, or even a bad reason, for him to find out.'

'And do you think it can?'

'Well, no, but then there's quite a lot it hasn't been telling me lately.'

'Well, it doesn't matter. He can't touch you, Christian, not now.'

'Really? Why?'

'It doesn't matter,' said Nikki, 'doesn't matter.'

'So anyway,' said Christian, 'I'm, um, sorry to burst your bubble.'

'What bubble?'

'Your reality bubble. You think you're real, I assume, but you're not, you're, well, just another figment of my imagination.'

'Don't worry about it.'

'Really?'

'Really.'

He looked at her properly for the first time since her arrival. She seemed calm; she seemed relaxed. 'Well, I must say you're taking it rather well,' he said, 'though, perhaps it's easier for you.'

'How so?'

'Well, it doesn't mean you don't exist at all, does it? You still exist outside, in real life, it's just the version of you I'm talking to right now doesn't exist. But then, does that make it any easier for you? I mean, when I wake, the you in front of me now will cease to exist, which is still pretty final for you, the *you* you, I mean. Um, sorry about that.'

'As I said, don't worry about it.'

'You're really okay with that?'

'I am.'

He looked her up and down again. 'Ah, I get it,' he said, 'you don't believe me, do you? That's why you're taking it so well.'

Nikki shrugged.

'But then, perhaps you have no choice,' said Christian. 'Perhaps you're hard-wired to believe you're real, believe it with all your heart. I suppose you wouldn't be able to function if you embraced the ugly truth, that you were just a figment of someone's imagination. What would be the point?'

'Point of what?'

'Point of anything.'

'Well yes,' she said, 'exactly. But then surely the same applies to you, Christian, what's your point? Why are you bothering to read the book at all if this is all a dream?'

'To remember, of course.'

'Ah ... yes, so you can write it when you wake up?'

'Bingo.'

'Of course, of course. But what are you going to do about the missing appendix?'

'What about it?'

'Well I think the book really needs it.'

'No,' he said, holding up the book, 'if it needed it, it would be here already.'

'Or,' said Nikki, 'it's so revelatory it's not even been written in your mind yet? Not even your unconscious knows. But now, here you are, inside your unconscious. Think about that for a moment. It's quite an opportunity.'

'Well–'

'Write it from here. Trust me, Christian, this is the difference between a mere bestseller and the most influential book ever written. You must write the appendix, you must write it here and now.'

'See, I said you're here to manage me.'

'Too right, soldier, now let's get you some stationery. As it happens, I've got a surprisingly large amount on hand.'

'No, really, Nik, I'm serious, it doesn't need an appendix. There's so much material already. The first section alone could be split into several paperbacks. And then there's the whole second section–'

'Write it. That's an order. You'll never get another chance to get this close to your unconscious.'

'No, no, look–'

'Christian–'

'No, *look*,' he said, smacking his hand onto the face of the book, 'you're not going to bugger this up for me a second time. I've already got my work cut out trying to remember what's in here as it is. It's not easy, you know, I thought I was doing okay, but I tested myself this morning and the truth is not much has stuck. And even if I can learn it here, I still don't know how much I'll be able to remember when I wake. Will I have total recall for the first thirty seconds, and then just the usual microscope view of random sections? There's no way to know. So I've got to be pragmatic, I've got to be selective. In short, stuff the appendix.'

Silence.

'All right, how about this,' said Nikki, eventually, 'you write the appendix, and I let you feel me up.'

'W-what?'

'You heard. I'm serious.' She sat up on her ballerinas.

He thought about it. He watched her eyes widen, drawing him in. He watched her hand move to her figure-hugging blouse, caressing the ethereal silk.

'Come on,' she said, 'don't tell me you've never thought about it. Write the appendix, and you can do anything you like. Anything.'

'No.'

'Why not? It's just a dream. The real me will never know. It'll be between you and you, your own dirty little secret, so why not have a little fun? Why not have a lot of fun?'

'It's not right.'

'So what, now you're the big moral purist, are you?'

'That's not what I mean. I mean I don't get it. Something doesn't feel right. I don't understand why you're behaving like this.'

'Don't look a gift horse in the mouth, Christian,' she said, arching her back and pushing out her chest.

'No,' said Christian.

She grabbed his hand and drew it to towards her. 'Come on, Christian, darling, you know you–'

'No,' he said, and batted her arm away.

She stood up. She turned and glanced out of the window.

'Listen,' she said, turning back to him and jabbing out a finger, 'you may think you know what's going on here, but you don't. You have no idea what you're mixed up in or what's at stake. I don't *want* to tell you, but if you leave me no choice, I will. Now, please, for your own good, write the appendix.'

'No, Nikki, I won't. And there's nothing you can do to make me.'

He opened the book and started reading where he'd left off.

'Christian.'

He ignored her.

'*Christian.*'

Still nothing.

'All right then,' she said, 'you leave me no choice.'

'Over what?'

'Over telling you the truth.'

'Oh this'll be good,' said Christian, his eyes not lifting from the page.

'The truth is–'

Christian slammed the book shut. 'That I'm not dreaming,' he said, 'that I am dead. Dead as Darwin, Dickens and … King Arthur.'

'Well. Yes.'

'That's exactly what Stuart said, or rather, that's what, you know, dream-Stuart said.'

'You've met Stuart here?'

'I have.'

'But he's right,' she said, 'it's the truth. You are dead.'

'Oh come off it,' said Christian, putting the book to one side, 'if I'm dead, then you're dead.'

'Yes.'

'So Stuart dies, I die and now you die. Bit of a stretch, isn't it?'

'It's true. All of it.'

'Go on then. Indulge me, how did you die? Wait, let me guess, killed by a falling filing cabinet?'

'I threw myself off a roof.'

'Even better,' he said, ignoring the sincerity in her voice, 'because that really fits, doesn't it? You always were a suicide waiting to happen.'

She sat back down opposite him. 'I threw myself off for you, Christian.'

More sincerity. It was unnerving. He'd always found it difficult to feign sincerity and now his unconscious was giving him a masterclass. But, he reminded himself, his unconscious was still all this was.

'All right, I'll ask you another,' he said, 'if I'm dead, and you're dead, how the hell did you find me?'

'I had some help, and I admit, some luck. I wasn't sure you'd still be here, in the Zone.'

Christian said nothing. It seemed she believed what she was saying. Stick to reason, he told himself, sincerity or otherwise; this is merely her personal perception; it counts for nothing, doubly so because it's a figment of your imagination's personal perception.

Nikki smiled.

'What's so funny?' he said.

'You know it's true, don't you?'

'As if.'

'That's what your instincts are telling you.'

'It doesn't matter what my instincts are telling me. My instincts told me England were going to win the World Cup. *Reason* is what matters, and there's no rational explanation for any of this other than a dream. Even if you can explain dying, and finding me, that's just a sideshow, because it still leaves the main event ...' He picked up the book. 'How do you explain this, my finished book, just turning up here in the Zone?'

'But that's just it, the book *is* your explanation.' She took the book from his hands and opened it at the inside back cover. 'You see, I know who this is,' she said, pointing at the woodcut portrait.

'No you don't.'

'No, Christian, *you* don't. You think you do, but you don't.'

'All right then, who do I think it is?'

'You think it's someone from your imagination, from your childhood. The person you always see when you dream.'

'How ... how do you know that?'

'Because–'

'Wait, I'm such an idiot.' He looked her in the eyes. 'You're part of my unconscious,' he said, 'part of me, so you have access to the rest of my unconscious, so of course you'd know about Erdygrot.'

'Erdygrot? That's what you call him?'

'Yes.'

'Nice,' she said, with a smile. 'Anyway,' she continued, 'that's not how I know. I know because you're special, Christian. You dream about him because you're like me. You see, I'm special too.'

'So what, now you're saying you dream about Erdy as well? So one part of my unconscious is dreaming about another part of my unconscious?'

'No, not him. Never him. But I dream about someone else, or rather, for me I am someone else when I dream, sort of. It's hard to explain. It's not quite the same for me, you see. The nature of my connection is even stronger than yours.'

'What are you talking about? *Connection*, what connection?'

'Mine isn't important,' she said, 'but yours, well, that should explain a few things for you.'

'Look, Erdy's just a dream character. I made him up when I was a kid.'

'Did you really make him up? Or was he always there? In your dreams, in your mind, since the beginning.'

'Possibly. I can't remember that far back. But anyway, what does that prove? Nothing.'

'So sure?'

'Yes. Completely.'

'So why isn't he here then?'

'What?'

'Every dream you've ever had,' said Nikki, 'he's been present, hasn't he? I'm guessing sometimes front and centre, but mostly lurking in the background. But he's always there, right?'

'Right ...'

'So where is he now? If this is a dream, where is he, in this world?'

'He, he ... he is here. He is.'

'Where? When?'

'When I, when I ... oh fuck, oh fuck, oh fuck ...'

'When you what?'

He hadn't noticed. How could he not have noticed? 'When I go to sleep,' he said, softly, 'he's there when I go to sleep. He's there when I dream.' Christian drew his hands to his face, pressing his palms to his cheeks like a shooting stick, before pushing them out, hard up to his ears, stretching the skin until his lips smarted.

Dead.

Colton Lazars

DEAD.

His eyes defocused. His head tilted. 'This is real,' he said, 'it's all real. I'm real. Dead real. This is me.' He looked down at his trainers, at his suit, at his AC/DC T-shirt. 'This is really me?'

She nodded.

'But wait, wait a moment,' he said, snapping back to the here and now. 'Christian–'

'Ha,' he whooped, into Nikki's face, 'haaa-aaaaaa, haaaa-aaaaaaaaa-aaaaaa.'

'What?' said Nikki.

'The book,' he said. He held up the tome. 'If I'm dead, how did my book get finished here without me? It's impossible.'

'Oh, Christian, you still don't get it, do you? It's here because it's not your book.'

'Oh come on,' he said, 'of course it's my book.'

'No. It isn't.'

She couldn't be right, it wasn't possible, but once again her sincerity shook him. 'W-well whose is it then?'

She opened the back cover and tapped the woodcut author portrait.

'*Him?*' said Christian. 'That makes no sense at all. He wouldn't have the motivation. I've never so much as seen him tie his shoelaces.'

'Given enough time, even the most unproductive people, *the most unproductive people, Christian,* can accomplish great things.'

'No, no, it's not possible ...'

'I told you, Christian, I told you. You don't know who this is.' She tapped the portrait again.

'Erdy ...' said Christian.

Nikki shook her head. 'That's the name you gave him, but you didn't create him.'

'Yes I did.'

'No. You didn't. You have assumed what men have assumed for millennia, Christian, you have assumed your world is for you, that it revolves around you. Well it doesn't. You're a pawn in a game bigger than you can imagine.'

'So who is he then?'

'Oh come on. You still don't get it?'

Christian said nothing.

'He's been around a long time. A looooong time,' she said, 'a lot longer than you or me. A lot longer than just about anyone, certainly anyone who's ever had anything to do with this world.'

'What, what you're saying he's ...'

'Yes, Christian' – she held up the book and showcased the portrait – 'meet the Lord of all creation, the Almighty, the Numero Uno. Terry to his friends.'

'That's, that's complete bollocks,' spluttered Christian. 'Even if it were true, why would I start writing his book?'

'If you take a moment, you can work it out.'

'Work what out?'

'Think, Christian. The person who wrote this book – why does he appear in your dreams? Why do you have this deep hard-wired connection?'

'Wait ... no way, no freaking way ... you mean ... you actually mean?'

'Yes,' nodded Nikki, solemnly.

'I'm ... I'm Jesus?' Christian screwed up his face.

'No, you cretin,' said Nikki, 'of course you're not fucking Jesus. You're a prophet. A true-blue first-order prophet of Heaven, first in four centuries, first scripture prophet in two millennia. This is why he's in your dreams, this is why his book fills your unconscious, this is why it was your destiny to write it, to share his words.'

'But ...'

'That's why you have an ultra-low soul number.'

'What? But how ... how do you know?'

'Let me guess, something in the seventies or low eighties perhaps?'

'Seventy ... something.'

'Jezebel was number three,' said Nikki. 'Moses was six, Socrates eleven, Galileo sixty-eight, so it's believed, and of course Jesus was thirteen, fourteen, thirty-five, forty-two through forty-six, fifty-five and seventy-three. They're reserved numbers, you see. These days everyone else gets given something in the forty billions, but not the prophets, not the chosen ones.'

'But, but, I am, I was, an atheist. How, how can you have an atheist prophet?'

'Yes, that threw me too, in the beginning. Seems we had some settings wrong, some levers at the wrong polarity, so you were made imperfect.'

'But ...'

'It's the staff, you see. Our people. They're focused, dedicated, devoted, but not that smart, not that great under pressure.'

Christian's neck muscles began to judder.

The happy band of Christian's intellect, pride and incredulity now faced its last stand. Surrounded and confronted by Christian's visceral instinct hordes, now armed to the teeth with the weapon of the enemy – pure cold logic. The few made the only choice available – capitulation and surrender.

'Oh. Right,' he said.

Christian's faculties began to evaporate. He went limp and unplugged himself from reality for a while. It seemed like the sensible thing to do while the firestorm of truth and consequences was razing his particular view of the universe, along with who he thought he was and what he assumed he'd been doing in it.

An hour later Christian was still curled in a ball on the library floor, hugging his whole head and whimpering, as he had been since his world had fallen apart. He couldn't see much point in doing anything else. All meaning and purpose had been wiped. He was a blank hard drive; he had no operating system.

'Look, we don't have time for this,' said Nikki, again, 'you have to snap out of it. You are a rational person, Christian. You must accept the facts and face up to reality. Logic demands it.'

He opened an eye and peered up at her. 'Leave me alone,' he said.

'You see? You see what you've made me reduce you to? I told you, I told you to trust me, Christian. I didn't want to do this, but you left me no choice.'

'Oh yes, because it's all my fault, isn't it.'

'Yes. It is. If you'd just applied yourself and done a few days' work, Heaven would now have much bigger fish to fry and you might still be alive. Even now, here in the Zone, all you had to do was write the appendix, and I'd have happily left you in your little dream delusion, no need to wake up to the ugly truth, no need to grow up. Well, you reap what you sow, *sir*, you reap what you sow.'

'Oh sod off, just sod off and leave me alone.'

'That's not going to happen,' said Nikki, 'you think I've come this far just to walk away? I'm not going anywhere. Now, get a grip.'

'Get a grip?' he said, turning towards her again. 'What on earth to?' He closed his eyes. 'This can't be happening, it can't. It can't. It can't.'

'That's just it, Christian, it's not happening, it's happened. You have to face facts. Look, all right, so you're not who you thought you were, I understand, it's a shock, but have you stopped to think you might be so much more? You still don't understand your role in all this. The truth is you are one of the most important people who ever lived, who ever died.'

'You said I was a pawn.'

'Yes, okay, but a really top pawn. Sometimes the pawn can topple the king.'

'Christian the pawn, Christian the top pawn. Lord of the pawns.' He returned to his ball, curling in tight.

'Focus, Christian. We've come so far, too far to lose it now.'

'There you go again, *lose it now*. There's nothing left for me to lose.'

'Yes there is,' she said, 'of course there is, you just don't know it yet. You've come off the plateau of your old understanding, your old view of the world. Now you're in the trough of despair, but there's a clear path in front of you, a steady climb to a far loftier summit, a high plateau of real understanding of who you are, of how this world works, and the nature of your special role in it, a rarefied purity of existence few can contemplate.'

'I'm not interested. I'm going to stay in my trough, I'm going to live as a pawn.'

'You must trust me, Christian. All will become clear in time, but for now you must do exactly as I say. It is your only chance of salvation.'

'And again. My salvation? There is no me to save. I'm someone else.' He brought his hands up to his mouth and touched his lips. 'I don't know who is speaking, I don't know whose voice this is.' He curled up tighter still and began to cry and mumble, sucking his thumb for the first time in twenty-seven and a half years.

Nikki looked out at the encroaching evening. The library's last earthly occupant had long since left; the lights were off. Only the diffuse distant yellow from the street lamps was holding back the darkness. 'You need time to process things,' she said, 'we'll stay here tonight, Christian, I offer you that as a kindness.'

He said nothing.

'You'll feel better in the morning,' she said.

Chapter Thirty-Two

Christian was woken by the light streaming through the windows. It hadn't had to try too hard. The night had been a week long and what little sleep he had managed had been spent in the company of a gloating smoking Erdygrot, leaning back in his chair with his loafered feet up on the table as Christian was forced to proxy sign the first billion copies of the new third edition of *Terry's Field Guide To the Afterlife*.

Nikki was already awake, sitting cross-legged on the floor, watching him, though he knew she'd been asleep through most of the night. Why hadn't she made more of an effort to guard him – indeed any effort to guard him? Even more, why hadn't he taken advantage to make an easy escape?

'How do you feel?' she asked.

'I don't feel anything.'

'That's perhaps not a bad thing. A new day, a new beginning.'

Christian didn't want a beginning. He wanted an ending. For the second time in his death, all he wanted to do was to stop existing. He pressed his index finger to his chest, to his imaginary oblivion button, he pressed and he held it there.

But much as he craved it, he knew suicide wasn't a solution. For starters, he was already dead, and besides, being dead was the source of all his problems in the first place. There was no way out. Dead was the new alive, and existence, so it seemed, was here to stay. But for how long?

How– He stopped mid-thought, his toes on the edge of the existential cliff, his mind awake to the long drop below. He needed another thought, and quick. Something, anything. He thought about raspberries. Soft, red, seedy fruit. It bought him a few seconds. What next? Quick, quick, quick. Tipp-Ex, pine nuts, Partick Thistle. Next? *Next?* Lone thoughts were no good – he needed a train of them. He needed a proper distraction, a foothold, a waypoint back towards sanity. He thought about the person he used to be – what would that person do? Have the morning off. Useless. Come on, think, think, something practical, something immediate. How about some information? Information about the world. Data; bearings. Yes, that would do as a start. It would distract him, get his feet back on the ground, and it could even be useful. He sat up. 'So the book,' he said, slowly, 'the things it says ... are they true?'

'Possibly. The first section definitely.'

'So I can't contact Bea?'

Nikki didn't answer straight away. 'You need to look forward, now,' she said.

Some train of thought this was. He waited for the latest wave of despair to knock him down and drag him under, but no impact came, or if it did he didn't feel it. 'I don't think I even ... I don't think ... I don't know ... I, I just ...' He managed a small shrug of the shoulders.

'You're doing fine, you're making progress,' said Nikki.

He stared blankly through her. 'So shepherds are real?'

She nodded.

Fucking lying Canadian cocksucker, thought Christian: Mitch really was a headless spectral bounty-hunter who delivered ghosts to the Gate of Judgement and that was what he'd been trying to do all along, even though Christian still didn't know why.

'All those things in the book,' he said, 'those arbitrary judgements, all those rules.'

'All true, possibly.'

'It's a nightmare, a real-life Grimms' fairy tale. Some of the things I remember writing, I wrote as a joke. Magicians being barred from Heaven, and TV magicians going straight to Hell. I'm no fan of TV magicians, but they don't deserve eternal damnation, not all of them anyway. I wish I could go back and change it.'

'But it wasn't your writing,' said Nikki, 'you never had any choice over what you wrote, and even if you did, it wouldn't change how things are here.'

'Oh yes, I forgot. I'm just a pawn.'

'You can be so much more, you really can.' She stood and turned towards the window. 'Look,' she said, pointing to the sunrise outside, 'it's a new day. A clean slate. This is the moment, this is where you start to climb out of the pit.'

'And just when I was beginning to like it.'

She sat down next to him again. 'Everything that's wrong with how things are now, we are trying to change.'

'*We?* I don't even know who *we* is.'

'*We* are the solution. The force that's going to change the face of the afterlife, give ethereals a reason to get up in the morning, create real purpose again.'

Christian said nothing.

'Well doesn't that sound exciting?' she said.

Still nothing.

'Christian, you are a prophet, you have the power to influence billions, you have the power to change the world.'

'But I don't want to be a prophet. The very idea makes me sick. Remember who you're talking to used to be.'

'I can't believe what I'm hearing,' she said. 'You are the envy of everyone who's ever lived. Everyone who's searched in vain for meaning in a meaningless existence. Your life, like mine, has a crystal clear purpose. It's defined by it. Without it you wouldn't even exist. And you choose to turn your back on it? How dare you.'

'I've told you I don't care.'

She stood up and went to the window. 'Well, don't knock what you don't understand,' she said, before turning back to him, 'no bad thing being a prophet, so I've heard. Special afterlife privileges, a seat at the Lord's side ... under normal circumstances. An eternity of basking in the radiance of the creator's no doubt genial company. At least that's what I assume it says in the brochure.'

'Normal circumstances?'

'Well yes, bit different for you. Can't imagine what your fate will be if you end up there.'

'Why?'

'Well,' she said, 'you've leaked a lot of sensitive information, by copying out the book. You've blabber-mouthed the trade secrets. Terry won't be best pleased.'

'I thought he liked his word spread?'

'Oh sure, in the old days, grass-roots stuff with the odd yak herder in the desert, but not these days, not with newspapers, not with the internet, and definitely not these words – these are for afterlife-eyes only, and even then only the residents of Heaven.' She strode to the bookcase and ran her hand through the New Age and Spiritual shelf. 'No, no, he's not gonna be at all happy. You're the trusted aide who went to the papers, the butler who kissed and told.'

'But I didn't know any of this, I didn't know what I was doing.'

'That's not going to wash with him,' said Nikki, shaking her head, 'you think he'll just say, "Well thanks for your honesty, son, don't do it again"? No chance. So you see how lucky you are that I ran into you, before you chose to go to the Gate, or got dragged there?'

'But wait, look I know I'm a … I was a … an atheist, but if Heaven is real, then surely in that of all places there must be some room for forgiveness, for understanding?'

Nikki laughed hard. 'I can't believe you're asking me that. I mean, you have read the book?'

'Oh. Yes. Bugger.'

'But don't despair,' she said, 'you don't have to go to Heaven, you don't have to face that music. Follow me, Christian, complete your destiny, write the appendix and follow me to Limbo.'

'Limbo?'

'Yes.'

'Oh.'

'Once again, you don't seem every enthusiastic.'

'That's because I'm not.'

'What have you got against Limbo?'

'It seemed an oppressive and soulless place, from what I read.'

'No, no, no, it's wonderful. Business, commerce, productivity, these things dominate and permeate all aspects of life.'

'Exactly.'

Nikki frowned. 'But this is where you belong. It's the purpose your empty mortal life never knew.'

'My mortal life was just fine, thank you.'

'You're still not getting it,' she said, shaking her head.

Christian shrugged.

'Oh come on,' she said, 'do I need to spell it out?'

He shrugged again.

'You're a prophet of Heaven, but an agent of Limbo. We made you. Our people went above enemy floors and made you. Christian, you're one of us.'

'What?' he said, gripping his ears before dragging his hands down his cheeks. 'Oh it gets better and better …'

She sat down next to him. 'I know it's not easy,' she said, 'but once you embrace your true self, you will feel better.'

'I didn't ask to be created, I didn't ask for any of this. I'm not interested.'

'Stick with me on this. Look, think back, remember giving literature both barrels? Well write the appendix and you can give God both barrels.'

'I've said I'm not interested.'

'But you're a lifelong atheist. How can you turn down a chance to take down the big guy?'

'Being an atheist isn't about hating God. How can you hate something that doesn't exist?'

'But he does exist. You know that now.'

'Well, yes. I still don't hate him though. I'm … indifferent to him. He's nothing to do with me.'

'Nothing to do with you? He killed you.'

'What?'

'Oh come on, surely you don't think it was an accident?'

'Of course it was an accident, that hearse, the heavy traffic …'

'And Stuart as well?'

'Stuart?'

'The pope's plane just happens to hit my house, right where you'd be sitting if you hadn't skived off sick?'

'Coincidence.'

'Oh come on.'

'Well all right, I suppose it's a possibility.'

'It's more than a possibility, it's a certainty. So do something about it, get yourself some justice.'

'Look, stop,' he said, gripping his ears again, 'just stop, will you.'

'Why?'

'You need to wind back, I don't understand. Why will writing the appendix get me justice? Why's it so important?'

'You're right,' she said, 'you need the background.' She sat back and, piece by piece, spelled it all out. The code sequence that would lead science to evidence of creation, how the world was indeed formed in about a week. How this revelation would turn even the hardest sceptic into a believer overnight – mass conversions, mass repentance, no longer a matter of faith, but a matter of fact. How that would mean no more souls getting into Heaven, and how that would trigger a full reset of the afterlife realms, bringing down the current order.

'It's, it's astonishing,' said Christian, 'and offensive. Offensive to, well, to intelligence.'

'Sometimes the truth hurts,' said Nikki.

'So that's why Heaven tried to kill me.'

'Did kill you, most probably.'

'But hang on, hang on … I only wrote the book because you told me to.'

'What?'

'You made me do it.'

'No–'

'Yes. I'd still have been on my novel if it wasn't for you, might even have finished by now. Heaven would have no interest in me … I'd be alive, I'd be *alive* and still be with Bea.' He clenched his fist and drew his arm back, his elbow high, as he eyeballed Nikki. He held, and held, before thrusting it into the bath foam nothingness of the wall. 'You selfish arrogant bitch. This is my life we're talking about … was my life … my fucking life.'

'Which would never have come into being in the first place without my father,' said Nikki. 'Yes, there was always going to be a risk we'd get discovered, and yes that would endanger your mortal life, but we gave you that life in the first place. You could never have had one without the other.'

'Well I'm definitely not helping you now. You can take a running jump.'

'You must pick a side, Christian. I know you're hurting, but you must see you have no choice but to join us. Unless of course you want to face your fate in Heaven.'

Christian gripped his whole head.

'Come on,' said Nikki, 'do it. Join me and let me help you. We'll help each other.'

'How? How can you possibly help me now?'

'You come with me to Limbo, that's how. Come to Limbo and you'll live out eternity like an executive. And we can go as soon as you've written out the appendix. Come on, I know you can do it. It's what you were made to do.'

'Literally, it would seem.'

'Now you're getting it,' said Nikki. She held the smile, but it soon faded. 'Like it or not, this *is* your destiny.'

'I won't write it and I never will.'

She stood and looked out of the window. 'This is your last chance,' she said. 'We can do it the easy way, or the hard way.'

'Sorry, dear Nikki, it's still a no. Perhaps you should have a bash at it yourself.'

She shook her head. 'You could have had it all, you could have–'

'I'm not listening to any more of this,' he said, and got to his feet. 'I'm done, so good luck with your revolution. I'm off, and if I never see you again, it'll be a lifetime too soon.' He took a step towards the door but she raised a hand to his shoulder.

'I'm sorry, Christian, but you're going to have to come with me.'

'Oh is that right? Gonna make me, are you? You and whose army?'

She smiled, holding eye contact for a moment, before stepping back and raising her palms.

He drifted into the small hallway and out through the door. He stopped mid-stride. The scene outside was somewhat different from when he'd last looked out of the window the previous afternoon. The view of the road and university buildings was now obscured by an immense amphitheatre of suited people, chatting among themselves. At the front, the first two rows sat on swivel business chairs, but all the rows behind stood, apparently in mid-air, in wide curved tiers, right up beyond the tops of the buildings. Christian watched as the thousands of faces turned to look at him, and as they did, they fell silent, as if waiting for the first line of the play.

He stood still, trying to take it in.

Nikki appeared behind Christian and placed an arm around his shoulder.

'This one,' she said.

In the Moon Landing Questions Lounge, God waved Neil back to the lunar module and nodded for Gabriel to sit.

God lifted his visor and sat on the rock opposite. 'And?' he said.

'Update from Candleslack,' said Gabriel, waving a piece of papyrus.

God brought his gloved hands together in a muted clap. 'Found our monkey already has he?'

'Um, no. Still rattling cages, it seems,' said Gabriel. 'Bit of an odd footnote, though. Says his scouts have sighted a ...' he checked the message, *'business column.'*

'Business column?'

'Yes, long train of ethereal office-types marching out of Guildford.'

'What the hell for?'

'We think they're on their way to a conference.'

'They're fuckin' dead, Gabe, why would they go to a conference?'

'Well, why did they go to them when they were alive?'

God screwed up his nose. 'Fair point,' he said.

Once again Christian was being taken on a journey. This time there were no stealth tactics, no trekking through the fields to remain unnoticed, no concerns about a give-away blue-green glow. This time he was being marched at the head of a force that feared no one.

Since Nikki had collected the loyal but small ethereal Manager Garrison from the site of their mass death at iChemiclast Industries, many more administerially inclined lost souls had joined the cause – dead departmental managers, expired chief executives, cut-down-in-their-prime team leaders and office juniors. All were now offered a home. At last an end to their purposeless wanderings. An end to their hunger for org structures to slide into, bureaucracies to bask in, and mission statements to ponder on long weekends. And Nikki's was a broad church. Many of the wider unwashed corporate-lost were also welcomed – accountants, sales and marketing personnel, compliance officers and quality control inspectors; auditors, actuaries, lawyers and solicitors. All the shirt-and-tied tribes were there, all apart from the investment bankers, of course. And the numbers soon told; indeed, Nikki's New Model Manager Army had attracted the white-collar dead faster than an all-expenses fact-finder to Barbados, and the ranks now topped 20,000. And it was an eclectic sight, eclectic for a desk-based force, anyway – sixties grey Glen plaids marched with modern Paul Smiths; high-buttoned tweeds with eighties Armanis; twinsets with trouser suits. A sprinkling of frock coats and zoot-suits enriched the blend further still. All of management death was here. All different. All the same.

They strode on like a giant levitating python, scales of navy blue, black and grey. Two wide ribbons of ghosts, one atop the other, hogging all six lanes of the M4, one hundred and fifty metres above the traffic. The politically savvy movers and shakers – now rebranded brigadiers and generals – marched with Nikki at the head. Behind them came a heavy cordon of elite Corporate Guard HR managers, escorting Christian. Then came the management accountants, actuarial managers and departmental heads, and finally the generic massed ranks of journeyman management in four brigades, all kept in line by alpha male 'middlers' – to a man either over six foot one or under five foot seven – barking out motivational sound bites interspersed with details of the latest revisions to the expense processing procedures.

Christian had been a passenger from the start, deciding he could hardly be expected to expend energy on his own abduction. Not that it made any difference. His escort of HR managers breezed him along by his collar, sleeves and, from the layer below, his trouser legs, like a kite on a stiff breeze.

Moving without his own propulsion was something he'd not experienced since his death. Apart from the continual light tug on his clothing, the ride was smooth, and strangely calming, like a monorail ride cutting above the rush-hour gridlock. And though this army of managers was his apparent enemy, from within it gave an uneasy sense of familiarity and security. There was nothing in the Zone, nothing he'd seen anyway, that could touch this force.

He soon found his mind wandering. Perhaps this was the right approach now? Relax, drift, be carried on the tide. If everything he used to be was a facade, if everything he wanted was beyond reach, then perhaps it was indeed time to let go.

No.

No ... no ... *no.*

He slapped himself, briefly unbalancing the beaky man hanging onto his right sleeve.

'Settle down,' said the man, 'if you struggle, it'll only make things worse.'

Christian slapped himself again, harder this time. 'I'm still me,' he said. 'I get to say who I am.'

'Please yourself,' said the man, 'just say it quietly.'

'Where are we going?' asked Christian.

'You don't need to know. You had your chance.'

'Who says?'

'Nikki Tooting. That's who.'

'I want to speak to her.'

'Well I'm sure she doesn't want to speak to you.'

'Look I have rights, I demand a phone ...'

'There are no–'

'Well, no, obviously, but, well, surely I have the right to ... to pass a note to a stranger?'

'Sorry,' said the man.

Christian gave a thin smile, and then made a point of looking forlorn, before going back to gazing out of the space where the plane window would be, despite the space being occupied by twenty suits. The beaky man eventually relaxed too, his eyes returning to face front.

In an instant Christian brought his hands together as hard as he could, slamming the beaky man into his opposite number. Cries went up.

'All stop, all stop!'

'Stop ahead, stop!'

Christian and his escorts were shoved forward as the ranks behind concertinaed into them, and the ranks behind them in turn blundered in, buckling the column.

Amid a scrum of suits, Christian did his best to seize the moment; his arms were free and in a whirling frenzy he managed to keep them away from the flailing grasps of his captors. But his legs were stuck, not only doggedly still gripped by his trouser escorts, but now trapped in an airborne melee of managers. He struggled and thrashed on, but soon found his arms restrained once again, and with the addition of a few swift slaps to the head, he was persuaded to submit. Order was soon restored, and the army marched on.

Christian's escort party now included two extra guards – facilities managers brought up from the rear, each taking a firm hold of his jacket tails. There would be no further chance of escape. But Christian took heart in his resistance, futile though it had been – a flicker of hope, a realisation his spirits were not quite dead.

The army marched on. Christian did not resist, but began to pay more attention to the ground passing under them. It wasn't easy, but through the fleeting suit-gaps he could make out some details and gain some insights, chief of which was they were using a motorway to navigate, as he had done. And then he saw something that brought back painful memories of his deathday – a great line of people, perhaps seven or eight wide, snaking its way over the landscape.

'What's that?' asked Christian.

'I'm not talking to you,' said the beaky man.

'I only want to know what that is.'

'I'm on performance improvement now.'

'Look I'm sorry about that.'

'Are you?'

'Yes.'

'You don't look sorry.'

'Well, see it from my point of view,' said Christian, 'I have been taken prisoner. Can you blame me?'

'I'm still not talking to you.'

'Come on, I'm not going to try anything again, I promise. It's so dull with nothing to do but listen to those bloody policy and procedure updates.'

'Excuse me but those are vital. Can't lose touch with expense policy, one slip and boom, could be weeks before you get reimbursed.'

'Look, all I want to know is what's ...' He lost his train of thought. 'I'm sorry, expenses? What sort of expenses can you possibly be incurring? You're dead.'

'Lots of things.'

'Name one.'

'Well, I don't know exactly, but you should always be prepared.'

'Really?'

'Yes, I remember there was this training course in Farnborough once, I arrived without a tie, thinking it was business casual, well, turned out–'

'Look, look it doesn't matter,' said Christian, 'forget the expense discussion. Now I promise I won't try to escape, and I promise I'll leave you alone to listen to the updates, if you'll please just tell me what that is down there.'

The man regarded Christian for a long moment, before turning and peering down to his left, stretching to get a clear view. Christian pointed to the endless line of people below.

'Well it's the Queue, of course,' said the man.

'The queue? The queue for what?'

The beaky man paused before answering. 'The queue for the Gate, the Great Queue, what else would it be for?'

Christian got a better view as the managers made a course correction with the motorway – the queue's path seemed erratic, some long straight stretches, while in other places it followed tight curves, sometimes flexing back in on itself, and it stretched out so far that Christian could not see an end or a beginning, or even tell if one section joined another.

'Just how long is this queue?' asked Christian.

'Long,' said the man, 'but that's Heaven for you.'

'I'm sorry?'

'Couldn't organise a meet 'n greet at a hospitality conference.'

'I don't follow.'

'Well it's simple logistics, isn't it?' said the beaky man. 'Industrial revolution, cities, healthcare, population explosion, more people are born, more people die. But do they open up more judgement gates? Fat chance. It's like they think waiting time's only relevant if you're mortal.'

'Well how long is the waiting time?'

'Up above seventy-six last year, so they say.'

'Seventy-six? Seventy-six what? Hours? Surely not days?' Christian tilted his head to get a better look.

'Years,' said the man.

'I'm sorry,' said Christian.

'Years.'

'Seventy-six *years?*'

'Like I say, that's Heaven for you.'

Of course, even in a world full of bizarre sights, the appearance of an airborne column of 20,000 office workers marching in close formation did not go unnoticed. Most ethereal onlookers stood and gawped, some felt the return of an old sense of dread, and a few felt there may be a chance of some much needed action and began following. Not for seventy years had massed ranks of the dead marched low across the skies of Northern Europe, and not for more than two hundred and fifty had they done so over England. However, curious and shocking though it was, it was not greeted with immediate alarm by those who had most to lose – the angels. They'd observed the formation after its emergence from Guildford, tracked it, kept watch from a distance, but the desperate call to action was only sounded when their scouts witnessed the abduction of Christian at

Reading University. It spawned a full-blown crisis. The angels' quarry, held at the head of a mighty army, an army whose purpose, origin and motive they knew not the first thing about, an army they could not hope to challenge in battle, and yet in a few hours they would do just that.

Throughout history, wars of the dead have followed a different pattern to wars of the living. The lethargy of technological progress in all afterlife realms means only primitive weapons are available, and the scarcity of tools and materials in the Zone means even these basic armaments are rare this side of the Gate. But much more significant is the problem of it being almost impossible to injure, let alone kill, someone who is already dead. Weapons can still be used to inflict pain, to intimidate, or to keep an enemy at spear's length, but mostly the few implements carried into an afterlife battle are done so only because, for that particular endeavour, it's reassuring to be holding something long and pointy while you're doing it.

Therefore, afterlife battles tend to take the form of very large-scale wrestling matches. Skill, speed, balance, strength, bravery, tenacity and of course knowledge of actual wrestling all play their part, but even if ropes, chains or handcuffs are available – and in general they are not – once an opponent is defeated, soldiers from the victors' side must be allocated to keep the vanquished subdued. Skimp on this and defeated opponents will just scamper off to rejoin the fight. And therefore in almost every afterlife battle in history, fortune has followed weight of numbers. There is no legend of the 300 in afterlife folklore; there is no Rorke's Drift; there is no Alamo.

In this latest of afterlife battles, supplementary equipment would not feature in the plans of either side, with both forces having been assembled at haste. However, this didn't mean weapons were entirely absent. Within the management ranks, plenty of the newly dead old guard, and long-time dead new recruits, came with biros or fountain pens fused to their hands – a hindrance in civilian afterlife, but now, in battle, they became fearsome close-quarters weapons, with the added bonus that they could not be stripped from them and used by the enemy. More recently deceased management came with keyboards attached to the hands, making for handy mini shields-cum-battering plates. And many of the youngest recent arrivals came with a computer mouse bonded to the palm. For wireless mice, the owner had a readymade small blunt cudgel, but for the lucky few with corded mice, the laptop often found on the other end made for a formidable mace. Envied assets in the New Model Manager Army.

While the angels were empty clawhanded, they did have wrought iron armrods literally up their sleeves. But up their sleeves was where they would have to stay after Candleslack issued a strict decree that everyone had to remain cloaked throughout any engagement. Revealing themselves to the managers, or onlookers for that matter, was not the concern – he'd still rather avoid it, but if need be could live with the fallout; the concern was if the prophet was to see angels. That would be a different matter, that could crystallise as banned knowledge of what lay beyond, or even trigger his conversion, an epiphany of instant faith. Either scenario would prevent his extraction to Heaven.

This was nothing new, of course, they all knew the rules, but even so the decree was met with consternation in the angelic ranks. Not only did fighting undercover in fur coat, smock or gown mean forgoing the armrod weapons benefit, it also meant clipping what was their greatest combat asset – their huge reach.

Tactically, they'd been caught napping. The scouts had got word to Candleslack soon enough, but by the time he and his generals had arrived at the university, the managers were already beginning to disembark. So the angels had little choice but to form up on the move, scrambling to organise themselves into some sort of fighting force while at the same time trailing the managers, keeping in touch while staying out of sight.

And if things weren't bad enough, they had that most foreboding disadvantage of all, the worst disadvantage in any afterlife battle. Angel Field Ops was a small organisation designed for covert influence, reconnaissance and messaging – just a few hundred operatives. Many had answered the emergency muster, but even so, they'd be staring down the barrel of being outnumbered one hundred to one.

The only cause for hope was the element of surprise. They would still get to decide where and when to make their stand.

By midday Candleslack had his theories on where the managers were heading. He hoped he was wrong, but by the middle of the afternoon knew he was not. There wasn't much time. He took the bulk of his force on ahead to take up positions, their much higher top speed allowing them to cut a wide path around and then past the managers, before rejoining the M4 to set up an ambush at Heston Services. There they drifted upwards until they were above the cloud cover. And there they waited.

And as they watched the shadows lengthen, fire sparked in their bellies and grew. Perhaps it was bravado, perhaps it was fatalism, but there was some reason in there too – most of them were hardened campaigners, not soldiers as such, but streetwise in the ways of the Zone, and physically, the mature angels at least were many times stronger than even the toughest former mortal, and these former mortals didn't look like they'd done a real day's work in their lives. If the angels could strike hard, strike fast, and unleash fear and panic in the ranks of the untested double-breasted, it might be enough – get in, get Bootstrap, get out. And if nothing else, the angels had formed an army that, for once, really did have God on its side. Not that this would make the slightest bit of difference.

The management army was sighted just before five. Twenty minutes later it was right under them. They'd hoped for their cloud cover to clear, to have that last final advantage of the sun behind them. But this was England, and so, coming out of heavy grey cumulonimbus, the angels attacked.

Candleslack committed a full third of his force in the first wave, striking at points all along the front half of the manager column, dive-bombing into the ranks at full-sprint-drift, tearing into the suits like cavalry through infantry.

Then the second wave joined the attack, individual angels looking for fresh vulnerabilities in the lines near the head, near their prize, and diving in at them, each time sending a dozen suits tumbling. But though the bites taken were often large, they were fleeting, with reinforcements of blues, blacks and greys quickly stepping in to shore up the position. And the angels' puppeteered wool-stuffed fists, no matter how hard they were thrust, weren't laying anyone out, less still striking terror into the hearts of the enemy. Soon the managers were regrouping. They were growing in confidence, too – now they grabbed out at the attackers, and when a suit managed to hold on, others soon joined, halting and then swamping the angel, clamping the mighty sheathed armwings in full nelsons, with bear hugs, hammerlocks and figure-fours also in evidence, before dragging the victim away into captivity.

After seventeen short minutes, the entire first and second waves – almost two-thirds of the angelic force – had been defeated and captured, and yet the management ranks seemed hardly to have broken formation.

Greater risks would now have to be taken. The order was sounded, and in the clouds above Travelodge Heathrow M4 westbound, the remaining angels removed their robes, fur coats, smocks and gowns. They ripped out their armrods and took them in clenched clawhand. Only Candleslack and his six Housecarls remained cloaked in their navy-blue boiler suits – they alone would wait in the clouds, wait for the chance to make a decisive surgical strike.

And so the final phase began. The third wave dived into battle, sweeping out and down in a wide arc, and then in low behind the managers, cruising up their spine and down into the neck of the column, just back from the bulging head, where they were certain the prophet was being held.

Now the sight of angels in full flow, brilliant-white armwings with spans of six metres, sent real fear through the management ranks – even in the eyes of MBAed executives boasting experience across multiple industry sectors and territories. For the first time, the chain of command broke down. In places, the long twin ribbons came apart, and all down its length the column divided into uncoordinated segments. Now the angels tore into the ranks, bringing armrods down onto the skulls of actuaries, clawhands scratching deep across the backs of city jobbers. Again and again the angels dive-bombed in, each time tearing managers away from the desperate mass at the head, before hurling them down through traffic and under the asphalt of the motorway.

It was working. The managers were being peeled away like the layers of a business-onion, and many of the suits being dispatched were not resurfacing.

But again the suits regrouped. Three of the senior infrastructure manager generals came forward from the middle brigades to command a rearguard action at the head, restocking the massed protection around Christian, ordering more and more managers to clamber in. Soon it was a sprawling ball, surfaced by the soles of a thousand brogues, and getting bigger all the time. And then the free management forces began charging forward from the tail, targeting angels, picking them off one by one. And so the tide turned again, and as it did, it came crashing in faster and faster.

More and more angels were being taken down and manhandled out to the rear. The situation was bleak. Finally Candleslack and his Housecarls went in anyway. A final dive at full pelt, piercing deep into the ball as they attempted to batter their way to Christian. But they too were soon taken.

All was lost.

The managers had taken the best the angels could throw, and in the final analysis had lost little more than a hundred from their general number, and only seventeen from the senior-executive ranks. The angels had fought with gallantry, and yet the white force had been whitewashed.

For the managers, one final obstacle remained. Victory was within reach.

Chapter Thirty-Three

In the purple amethyst mood light of the Blofeld's Lair Lounge, God rolled yet another six and moved his second piece onto the finishing straight. He sat back in his charcoal leather wingback and reached for another cinnamon spam slider, all the while looking across at his weary opponent.

Albert rolled the die. One, again. He popped out his tongue, tugged at his hair and moved his first piece another single space.

As God retook the die in his free hand, the velvet upholstered door was thrust open.

'A knock would be nice, Gabe,' said God, without looking up.

'There's ... there's been a battle in the Zone,' said Gabriel, ruffles rippling through his plumage, 'a full-blown engagement.'

'And?'

'And we were one of the sides ... we were the losing side.'

'We?'

'Candleslack, and, we're not sure, a hundred and sixty, maybe a hundred and seventy angels.'

'Fuck me,' said God.

He pinged the die into the fireplace and turned to his opponent. 'Looks like my victory will have to wait, Al.' He gave a half nod to the open door and Albert took his leave. God stretched before gesturing to the empty seat.

Gabriel sat.

'Tel, we urgently need to–'

'Hold your horses there, Gabe,' said God. He took a bite of his slider before moving Albert's first piece back a few spaces. 'Now, from the top, who were we fighting?'

'That army of managers, Tel, the business column.'

'Over what?' asked God, eyes still on the board.

'They've … they've got the monkey.'

God froze and flicked his eyes to Gabriel's. '*They've* got him?'

'So it seems,' said Gabriel.

'And what, we tried to take him?'

'Yes.'

'And it didn't work?'

'No …'

'And they still have him now?'

Gabriel nodded.

God squeezed down on the buns of his slider, extruding the spam core until it plopped out onto the Ludo board. 'So what the fuck do they want with him?'

'We don't know,' said Gabriel, 'our best theory is they've made him their keynote speaker.'

'What?' God jumped up, catching the edge of the board with his foot, showering Gabriel with Ludo pieces and meat-flavoured matter. 'They know he's a sayer?'

The archangel dipped his armwingtips. 'Now, Tel, just hold on,' he said, 'we have to remember he was an office type in life. That is his true nature. He's one of their own, it's possible they've just … warmed to him.'

'But still, what if he blabs, at the conference? Who knows who'd be listening?'

'Well, indeed. And we think that's why Candleslack made his move. He couldn't take the risk, he had to go for it.'

'You *think* that's why?'

'There's been no official report. All we have is fragmented accounts from the few angels who made it back.'

God's hair and beard sparked and crackled. He walked a few paces, turned, walked a few more, turned again and walked to the mantelpiece. 'And how many went in, did you say?'

'A hundred and sixty, perhaps a hundred and seventy. Everyone who could be mustered.'

'Bloody hell, open war in the Zone, open fuckin' war. This is bad, Gabe.'

Gabriel puffed his cheeks and gave a slow nod. 'So I'm assuming you want to cancel?'

'Cancel what?' asked God.

'The A V gala luncheon. It's tomorrow.'

'Is it?'

'Yes, it is.'

'Really?'

'Yes.'

God ruffled his hair. 'Comes round quick, doesn't it?'

'Yes, Tel, it does,' said Gabriel, 'so do we call it off?'

'No chance.'

'Really? I just thought, under the circumstances, the battle.'

'Gabe. Let me tell you what this is,' said God, 'this is our Brighton Bomb. Did Maggie cancel the Tory conference? Of course she bloody didn't. Six Bloody Marys, darts with Willie Whitelaw, then off to the first session. Business as usual, Gabe, business as fuckin' usual.'

Chapter Thirty-Four

The Manager Army was only an hour from the Gate as night began to fall. Nikki was desperate to push on, but despite her troops' loyalty she did not enjoy absolute power and could not override the decision to camp, the board of director generals insisting that stopping for another reorganisation was necessary, despite already having had five in the previous two days.

And so, as they passed Hammersmith, the column began its steady descent. With a lack of any obvious open ground for a defensive position, the navigation committee issued instructions to commence a landing on the Thames. The long column gradually aligned itself to the curve of the old river as the massed ranks descended lower and lower, before coming to a halt alongside Craven Cottage football ground.

The battalion of management infantry at the rear were ordered outward to form a circular perimeter. Then, all around its circumference, lines of individual managers began shinning up imaginary poles, up and then inward to observation positions, until a network of managers formed a protective dome, towering high above the camp, extending out beyond the London Wetlands, across into Fulham, and as far south as Putney Bridge.

Following the relayed calls of 'Secure', another battalion detached from the rear and split into two dozen platoon work parties. Soon each was heading out into the surrounding suburbs to forage and pillage for papyrus, pencils, paperclips and whatever other useful ethereal bits and bobs they could find – a manager army marches on its stationery.

Though the angel force was spent, hidden beyond the perimeter other interested parties were watching. The shepherds. Many had worked out what was going on well before the angels and had been tracking the manager column from the outset. But they had played no part in the Battle of Heston Services, despite hurried angelic attempts to deputise them with the usual promises and more. The shepherds wanted what was on offer, of course, each pursuing their own particular prize, but not at any price. They would not be part of any grand gesture, any last desperate assault. As ever, their approach would be stealthy, professional, individual, clinical.

'If you'd like to step out, that would be much appreciated,' said Hodge, the compliance officer in charge of stationery foraging party delta-four.

The tree house remained silent.

'We can see your boots,' shouted an accountant from the back.

'Yes, all right, I'll do the talking if you don't mind,' said Hodge.

They watched as the black boots were drawn up into the tree house.

'If you, er, wouldn't mind,' whispered Hodge, gesturing to his troops.

The party moved in and surrounded the target.

'Now come along,' said Hodge, addressing the tree house, 'we don't want to hurt you ... well, I don't want to hurt you, but I promise you, I ... er, we most probably will if you're going to insist on being silly.'

Mitch Langford slowly stepped out and down from his hiding place and gave himself up.

Back inside the perimeter, attention had turned to reports, strategy meetings and the reconvening, dissolving and recombining of scores of think-tanks, focus groups and committees in the never-ending quest for greater efficiency. At the inner circle, the board of director generals had finally accepted the minutes from the previous evening's meeting and had progressed to the main agenda. But Nikki was finding it hard to get moti-vated. Now, so close to the Gate, the absurdity of it all was impossible to ignore. But she didn't whine or protest. She swallowed it all and kept her eyes on the big picture. Yes, it was ludicrous to camp for the night just to find ways to make the final thirty-minute drift optimal; yes, it was frustrating; yes, for once it really was a case of management without common sense; but she reminded herself of the imperious position she was in. If she wouldn't be able to sleep soundly tonight, it wouldn't be through worrying about tomorrow – it would be through a six-year-old's excitement on Christmas Eve. She allowed herself a smile.

Fishguard, Nikki's old General Manager at iChemiclast Industries, now a major – but no better – in the manager ranks, entered the meeting and made his way over.

'The shepherds,' he whispered to Nikki, leaning in, 'I've assembled them for you.'

'Excellent,' said Nikki.

'No hurry,' said Fishguard, as he looked up at the disdain on the faces of the board.

'I'm afraid I have to duck out,' said Nikki, to everyone, 'urgent business. Do carry on.'

They left the meeting and were soon making their way to the southwestern corner of the camp.

'Plenty of goodies in their kit bags,' said Fishguard, 'we're making use of what we can.'

'And the books?' said Nikki.

'Three copies.'

'And no appendices, no notes in the backs?'

Fishguard shook his head. 'Not so much as a scribble, but they were only shepherd editions anyway.'

'And the angels?'

'Not one copy among the lot of them. I imagine they dumped them before the attack.'

They were soon stepping up into the air and approaching a large shoulder-to-shoulder formation of manager guards.

'They're in here,' said Fishguard.

'Wait,' said Nikki, stopping.

Fishguard stopped a stride ahead. 'What's up?'

'I'm forgetting my Sun Tzu.'

'Go on ...'

'Perhaps we don't need to fight tomorrow after all. Bryan, where are we keeping prisoner number one?'

· · ·

Christian was sitting in the corner of the space – his strange levitating cell. No floor and no ceiling, only walls, and even then only ethereal human walls of management guards, most of whom held him permanently in their sights.

He heard voices beyond the enclosure. As faces turned to the far wall, a gap opened up and Nikki walked in. All four walls of managers stiffened up straight. There were a few tentative salutes, with everyone else soon following.

'Relax, everyone,' said Nikki, as she approached the prisoner. 'Hello, Christian.'

He looked down at his trainers.

'Don't I get a hello?' she said.

'I don't want to talk to you.'

'Really? I was told you were demanding just that and nothing else earlier today.'

'I've changed my mind.'

'Well I want to talk to you. I've come to ask you one last time.'

He stood up, went to the other side of the cell and sat down again.

She didn't follow. She remained standing. 'Tomorrow things are going to get, well, nasty,' she said, 'but they don't have to.'

No reply.

'The silent treatment, eh?' she said. 'Last vestige of the defiant prisoner.'

Christian inspected his fingernails.

'Okay, so it seems I have to earn your attention this evening. What to do?' She smiled. 'All right, do you remember your little problem with the language, all those weeks ago?'

'What?' said Christian.

'When you first started the guide, you weren't happy about English being the language of the afterlife?'

'So?'

'So did you ever solve it?'

'I suppose not.'

'Ooh and it's got a lot bigger now, wouldn't you say? Can't sweep it under the carpet so easily now you know it's all real. Now the problem's real too.'

He didn't make eye contact, but gave a couple of slow nods.

She ran her eyes along the faces in the walls of managers and put her fingers in her ears, repeating the gesture until they all did the same. Then she held out a finger and spun it round until they had all turned their backs.

'There, now we can talk properly,' she said. She drifted over and sat down next to him. 'Thought you might have looked it up. I'm pretty sure there'll be a chapter on it.'

'Perhaps. I didn't see one,' he said.

'Well, it doesn't matter, because I'm going to tell you the answer.'

He said nothing, but made momentary eye contact.

'You're curious, aren't you? That rational mind needs to know.'

'Maybe.'

'Right, well, where to start. Okay, do you remember your little spelling mistakes? You'd catch most of them, but some made it into the daily copy.'

'Of course.'

'They weren't ordinary spelling mistakes, were they though? They weren't words you'd ever normally get wrong. That silent extra "i" in "salvation", "English" starting with an "i", that kind of thing.'

'Typos.'

'No, no, you transcribed every word perfectly.'

'So in Heaven they spell "English" with an "i"?'

'They do.'

'Why?'

'No, no,' she said, shaking her head, 'the right question is why, here on Earth, is it spelled with an "e".'

'Because that's the spelling.'

'Yes, but why is that the spelling?'

'It's just how it evolved to be spelled.'

'No. It's because that's as near as they could get it.'

'They? Who do you mean, they?'

'Well who do you think?'

'I think you're talking bollocks.'

'And those strange words,' she said, 'made-up words to your eyes – gainrising for resurrection, welkinfire for meteor.'

'Merely cultural colour.'

'Or perhaps the ones that got away.'

'Meaning?'

'Meaning English, as you know it, is only what it is because of external influence, because of a grand plan.'

'Grand plan? What utter nonsense. English has evolved over millennia, it's well documented. It's not been introduced like VAT or ... aubergines.'

'I'm not disputing that,' said Nikki, sitting up on her ballerinas, 'but its evolution is the result of thousands of years of development and influence.'

'That's exactly my point. Evolution of speech, immigration, ideas ...'

'*Manipulation* of speech, *engineered* immigration, *planted* ideas.'

'What?'

'Centuries of tireless tweaking, adjusting and prodding.'

'What? By who? That doesn't make any–'

'Stage one. Survey the emerged early languages and cultures. Choose your host region – good set of base phonemes, a conquered people open to influence, plus the right geography. Coastlines are good, islands are better. Then there's proximity to potential feeder languages ...'

'This is–'

'Stage two. Manipulation. Mould the language, knead it into shape over the centuries. Bring in the right influences, in the right amounts, in the right order, keep out what you don't need. Start with an influx of Germanic tribes with their ancient base nouns, mix with a dollop of Latin. Add a pinch of Viking to break up the grammar. Turn on the Norman tap for a few hundred years, then turn it off again. Let all that ferment, then send a few rats on a ship to prune back the Latin. Bugger up Henry's latest marriage to hasten the break with Rome, creating a wave of English Bibles to anchor the advantage ...'

'I don't–'

'Stage three. Enrichment. Spice up the brew with idioms, metaphor and parlance, seed great writers with divine inspiration to create the right words, phrasing and usage.'

'Writers? What writers? Name one, name just–'

'Chaucer, Shakespeare, Tyndale, Dickens, Ad–'

'No, no, this is ridiculous ...'

'Stage four. Take it to the world while defending the heartland. Give Britain unrivalled economic and sea power.'

'How? How would you even begin to–'

'The slave trade, the East India Company, the scientific method, the Industrial Revolution, the marine chronometer, the telegraph, steam power and railways. And all the while keep a hand on the scales to save it from invasion for a thousand years.'

'Oh now come on.'

'And in time claim the United States, Australia, the Caribbean, India, the whole British empire.'

'But–'

'Stage five. The final stage. Cement English as the world's language. Hollywood, Elvis Presley, The Beatles. The BBC, computing, the internet. Harry Potter, Stephen Fry and *Top Gear*.'

'Really?'

'We believe so. When you look at the evidence in its entirety, an all-pervasive external influence is the only credible explanation.'

'No, no …'

'Seriously, Christian, you're rational. You're logical. So what's more likely? It was choreographed by an unseen hand, or it really did happen like we're told? That some tiny grey-skied island off the arse end of Europe somehow won the biggest empire in the history of the planet, enslaved and subjugated millions, invented science, industry, popular culture, and gave the world its global language?'

'The triumph of British endeavour,' said Christian. 'Well, apart from the slavery bit. And the subjugation.'

'What about the huge slices of good fortune at every turn? Godwinson just happens to get an arrow in the eye at Hastings, Heminges and Condell just happen to decide it might be nice to preserve the works of Shakespeare, the Pilgrim Fathers only survive because they just happen to bump into the only native in five hundred miles who speaks English.'

'Coincidence.'

She laughed. 'Oh come on, now who's being naive?'

'But the wars, invasions, defence – you can't engineer things like that.'

She laughed again. 'But that's the most direct influence of all. Think about it, calm seas for the Norman Conquest, but not for the Spanish Armada, "God blew and they were scattered." Then there's the soggy ground at Waterloo, the First World War stalemate in the mud, yet in the rematch months of storms and fog magically open up for D-Day. Eisenhower even gave God the credit, for pity's sake.'

'All right, well, what about Britain now? The empire failed, all that's left is an ember, how do you explain that?'

'Because English is now unsurpassable as the world's language.'

'So?'

'So Britain has served its purpose. Don't you see? That's your final piece of evidence.'

Christian's head dropped forward. 'It's, it's beyond words,' he said, 'it's incredible.'

'So now you see the bigger picture, now you see the lies?'

'But why? Why go to all the bother? Surely he's God, surely he's smart enough and omnipotent enough to be fluent in any language, in every language?'

'Oh, Christian, think, will you? Your dream friend, what did you call him, Herdy?'

'Erdy ... grot. Oh. Oh yes.'

'Now you understand?'

Christian looked up and out at the early morning London skyline, above the backs of the heads in the wall of managers, past the roof of Craven Cottage to the blue skies beyond. 'Yes, I think I do,' he said. 'Let other people shoulder the work, get the entire human race to speak your language so you don't have to bother to learn theirs?'

'You got it. So now I hope you can see what we're up against. And this is just one example. The truth is, Heaven can't stop meddling. Oh he says he wants free will, creativity, man to be the master of his destiny. He claims to be all hands off, but what he really wants, what he really does, is to keep humankind in bondage, serving him instead of itself.'

'It's sick, it's suffocating,' said Christian.

'Exactly. So join us. Join us and help change it.'

'But you're no better,' said Christian, 'you want to control just as much as they do.'

'Yes. But to do good, to give the people the structure their meaningless lives need, to guide them to achieve, to grow in an empowerment-rich environment.'

'Why? Why can't you just leave them alone to work things out for themselves?'

'Because we can only build utopia if everyone comes to heel. You start letting one person skive off, sooner or later they're all at it.'

'Utopia?'

'The perfect afterlife society,' said Nikki, 'a new top realm built on unlimited immortal productivity. Work feeding work feeding work feeding work. We can do it, Christian, we really can.'

'You're as mad as they are selfish.'

'You're not listening, you're–'

'Stop, just stop,' he said, 'my mind's made up. I don't want any part of this. Heaven, Limbo, you can keep them both.'

'Well. Maybe you'd be better in the lowest place then?'

'Well maybe. At least they don't seem to be exploiting humanity or trying to turn humanity into a corporation. And they haven't bothered me at all so far. No, I've got no beef with them whatsoever.' He folded his arms.

Nikki stood. 'I've tried to explain the cause, Christian, but if you won't help us for the greater good, you must at least do it for your own preservation. I am your only friend in this world. The shepherd was deceiving you, you know this now, and you know he's still out there. You probably know there's more like him. All of them bent on delivering you to the Gate, to your judgement …'

Christian looked away.

'… and I know you witnessed the attack today. Perhaps you saw the other other-worldly forces that want to capture you? Perhaps you only felt the ripples. Either way, you have no concept of what stalks you, their power, their wrath.'

Still he ignored her.

'Can't you see?' she asked. 'I'm not just your only friend here, I'm your guardian fucking angel. My army is the only thing preventing you being torn apart by the wolves. It's time you realised which side your bread is buttered.'

She turned and drifted to where she'd come in. She clicked her fingers.

The gap opened up again. A manager entered, handed Nikki a box and departed. She took the box over to Christian and sat down. She opened the lid to reveal a healthy ream of blank papyrus pages, an inkwell and a quill.

'Think about what I said. Writing out the appendix is the right thing to do. And even if you can't see that, know that things will soon be a great deal harder for you if these pages are blank come the morning. I have already given you one last chance. You will not get another.' She turned to leave. 'The fate of the world is in your hands, Christian, as is your own.'

Chapter Thirty-Five

The night passed without incident, with not a single skirmish or angelic attempt to infiltrate the dome perimeter.

Nikki had woken at first light, alive on ethereal adrenaline. Knowing it would be futile to try to get back to sleep, she'd instead tried to kill time with the book. It'd felt strange, having it in her hands – the thing she'd spent a lifetime thinking about, and a second lifetime watching Christian tap out at a few sentences a day. This copy, the copy she'd confiscated from Christian, didn't have the prized appendix, of course, but still, here it was, right in her hands. Yet in the sunrise of this great morning, she'd been unable to stomach more than a chapter. It was one thing proof-reading Christian's daily output – then there was justification, then there was detachment – but now, reading as a mere reader, the arrogance, the pomposity, the sheer self-righteousness oozed out of every sentence, at least the ones God had written himself, anyway. Now she'd felt dirty, letting *him* into her head. So after barely half an hour, she'd put the book to one side and set off for a long dawn stroll along the riverbank. And soon the bad taste in her mouth cleared and sweetened again, because the great day was here. One way or another, before the sun would set, Limbo would possess the weapons to change the world for ever.

Along the path she passed through joggers, early-bird commuters – *work hard, commuters, work hard, I'll be seeing you soon* – and a smattering of morning-after-the-night-before shattered revellers. None of them knew how their world would soon change, none of them had an inkling, and she loved it.

When she returned to her command, she gave the order for the army to make ready, which meant they could be on their way inside two hours. It wouldn't take long to pack up, there being almost nothing *to* pack up, but she had to allow time for the orders to filter through the various divisional committees and subcommittees. It mattered not. She would make use of the time, for there was one other item on her agenda.

Now, at eight fifteen, she was sitting at her field command post on the quay, watching the rest of London wake up and the dome dismantle itself, watching as she waited for Fishguard to return from Christian's holding cell.

When he arrived he was carrying pages, but his gait and expression already told the story.

'Nothing?' said Nikki.

'Not quite,' said Fishguard.

'Oh?'

'But nothing useful.'

'Let me see.'

'You're, um, you're not going to like it.'

'Come on, hand them over.'

Fishguard stretched his lips, but obliged.

The top page was blank save for a wide 'm' shape at the bottom edge of the page.

'What's this?' she said.

'I said you're not going to like it.'

She turned the page, to find something similar, only this time drawn slightly higher.

'Here,' said Fishguard, putting his clipboard aside in the air next to him and taking back the pages. 'I'll show you the full effect.'

He took the wad in his left hand and with his right flicked through the pages. The 'm' expanded into a double 'm' as it rose, eventually revealing itself to be a drawing of the back of a fist. It rose steadily through the frame, settling in the centre for a few pages, before the middle finger rose to full extension.

'See?' said Fishguard.

'Cheeky little ...'

'Well executed though, wouldn't you say,' said Fishguard. 'Do you want to see it again? It's better the second time through.'

'No I fucking don't.'

'Well. Anyway, there you go.'

'Stubborn, stupid, arrogant little worm,' said Nikki.

'Merely a delay,' said Fishguard, reclaiming his clipboard, 'besides, I know this will sound like bravado, but I think it's better this way. It means our sacrifice was, well, it wasn't for nothing. Now we can march to glory.'

She was still looking at the pages, but then looked up. 'Yes, yes, you're right, Bryan,' she said, and placed a hand on his shoulder for a moment.

He smiled and gave a nod.

'Now,' she said, 'the shepherds?'

'Ready for inspection,' said Fishguard.

'And prisoner number one?'

'We've got him standing by.'

'Good. Let's get on with it then.'

Mitch, along with eight other shepherds, was being held in an airborne line-up, twenty metres above the Thames and awaiting persons unknown. Like each of his cohorts, he was being firmly held by two burly businessmen clamping his hands behind his back. And around them all stood more suited businessmen, three or four deep, forming a closed cordon about the size of a tennis court. Mitch had noticed the extra personnel stationed at water level, too, as well as the ones overhead. There would be no chance of escape.

The banks of suits parted. A man and a woman entered. Mitch recognised neither, but the woman was senior, that much was clear. She was hot stuff, too.

Mitch watched as the woman ran her eyes along the row of prisoners and took a stroll up the line. He still had no idea who these people were – not just the man and the woman, but any of the suited types who'd captured him. He didn't know what this army was for, or why it was holding Christian, and if his fellow prisoners knew any more, then they certainly weren't letting on. Three of them were known to him: Parphan Chansiri, his right hand and forearm still absent, unknown to all still lying forgotten at the bottom of a chest freezer in the backstreets of Kowloon; Jane Dumbarton, a former landscape gardener who he'd been told was holding out for promised contact with a beloved former client; and Jonny Jones, a chancer happy to stay in angelic bondage merely in exchange for a ready supply of trinkets from Heaven. Comrades in custody, but nevertheless, the competition. A few guarded words and the usual unpleasantries was as far as it went, as far as it ever went.

The others in the line-up he did not know. Local opportunists maybe, though two wore head coverings, suggesting they also had more skin in this game than the rest. One wore what appeared to be a bronze kettle, supported by a wooden collar, and featuring angled mirrors suspended from the handle above the opening. The second wore a helmet made from a barrel or bucket, similar to the one Mitch himself had lost, making him wonder quite how custom his old unit had really been, only this one was red, and carried an inverted label saying 'COD CARAMELS'.

Mitch's own recently scavenged headgear was the least convincing – a coarse sacking bag stretched over a frame of sticks, creating an air of the Elephant Man, all the more disturbing because in several places its surface encroached well into the space an observer might reasonably expect to be occupied by Mitch's head.

'Why you hold me?' said Chansiri, as Nikki walked past, 'I not fuckin' shepherd.'

'Oh, we cramping your style, mate?' said Jonny.

'I've done nothing wrong,' said Jane.

'Please be quiet,' said Nikki, 'all of you.' She strolled down the line. 'Which one of you is Mitch Langford?'

Silence.

'All right,' said Nikki, 'take off the headgear, please.'

Slight shifting of feet.

'Oh come on, gentlemen, there's no need to be shy. We're all friends here.'

She waited.

Mitch, Kettle Man and Cod Caramels began to remove their headgear.

Gasps and cries escaped from the guards. Only the other shepherds and Nikki seemed unsurprised to find nothing but flaps of neck skin on top of each torso.

For Kettle Man, like Mitch, it was all empty space above the collar. But Cod Caramels was unlucky enough to come with lens-corrected blue-frame spectacles, perched in absurd ignorance on the space where his head wasn't.

'Thank you, gentlemen,' said Nikki.

She nodded to Fishguard who made his way over to the managers at the back of the perimeter and passed on an order. A moment later the management waves parted. A tight phalanx of HR guards entered and followed Fishguard back to where Nikki was standing.

Fishguard glanced at Nikki, received a nod, and then signalled to the guards at the front, who then stood aside, to reveal Christian in the centre of the phalanx, being held firm at the arms and shoulders.

Christian clocked Nikki but said nothing.

'Hello, Christian,' she said, before turning back to face the shepherd line-up.

At first Christian seemed confused as he took in the surroundings, the arena of managers, the strange line-up, but then he spotted Mitch.

'Bastard,' shouted Christian, as he tried to lunge forward, testing the hold of his captors.

'Thank you, Christian, thank you so much,' said Nikki.

'Christian,' said Mitch, calling over, 'hey, hey, are you okay, buddy?'

'Buddy? I'm not your buddy, you–'

'It's okay, really,' said Mitch, struggling and failing to free his hands, 'we're cool, I'm not mad at you.'

'You're not mad at *me*?' said Christian.

'Yeah, don't give it another thought. I'm here to help, I er, I know it looks bad but I'll get you out of this, you can count on it.'

Laughter rang out through the ranks.

Fishguard took a step forward and whispered something to Nikki, but she waved him away and continued to watch.

'And why, exactly, would you want to help me out?' asked Christian.

'Because ...' Mitch lowered his voice. 'Because I'm your ...'

'You're my what?'

'You know.'

'No. Tell me.'

Mitch dropped the volume further, but with only the low hum of distant river traffic, and waves on the bank, everyone could still hear just fine. 'I'm your guide, of course.'

Christian laughed, as did some of the other prisoners. 'No you're not,' said Christian, 'I know what you are, what you really are ... *shepherd*.'

Beats of silence, and then Mitch's shoulders slumped, and he seemed to sink two inches nearer the surface of the Thames.

'You've got some nerve,' said Christian. 'My guide. My saviour. Here to help? Here to help yourself more like. You're pond scum, you're worse than, than hedge fund managers ...'

An 'ooh' went up from the managers.

'... how do you live with yourself?'

Everyone turned to Mitch.

'Well done, Christian,' he said, 'well done, you worked it out. Well done ...'

Silence.

'... as for how I live with myself, how do you think I live with myself? I don't have a fuckin' head, buddy. I've done nothing you wouldn't do, if you were in my boots. This is the real world. So grow up and get used to it.'

'Excuse me,' said Nikki, quietly addressing Fishguard's second in command, 'what's your name?'

'Len Benson, miss.'

'Len, these two are staying here with me,' she said, gesturing to Mitch and Christian, 'can you please take these others to Poland.'

'I'm sorry, Poland, ma'am?'

Len looked to Fishguard for support. Fishguard shrugged.

'Yes. Take twenty managers and escort the rest of the prisoners to Poland.'

'Poland ...'

'Yes, or Luxembourg, if you prefer.'

'Luxembourg?'

'Or Portugal for that matter. Anywhere in continental Europe will do. Your choice. I just need them taking far away.'

'Right. And, um, what should we do with them when we get there?'

'Oh, just use your initiative.'

'Right ...'

'Well don't let me stop you, Len.'

And so a bewildered Len Benson waved for Mitch's guards to move him forward, before issuing orders and leading the remaining prisoners away. Christian and Mitch didn't even seem to have noticed as they descended further into their trough of recrimination.

'I've been doing this near twenty years,' said Mitch, his chest now puffed out, 'and I've never met anyone so delusional. You're like a kid.'

'Yeah, well at least I still have my integrity, at least I'm not a mercenary,' said Christian.

'Mercenary?'

'I don't exploit people's hopes and fears, and their futures, just to make my way.'

'You have no idea. You have no idea why I do this. If you did, you'd know you were wrong.'

'Well of course I know why. It's your head, isn't it?'

There was no reply.

'That's what they've promised you? They'll turn off the freezer for you, right?'

'You'd still do the same in my place.'

'No. I would not.'

'Quiet,' said Nikki.

'You would,' said Mitch, still being held, 'you have no idea what it's like. You'd do the same, and more besides, you'd do anything.'

'I said quiet,' said Nikki.

Christian ignored her and began a rambling reply on why he was the best judge of what he would and would not do.

As the argument continued, Nikki turned to the managers holding Christian's shoulders.

'Guards ... I'm sorry, what are your names?' she said.

'Mikhail Leibnitz,' said Mikhail Leibnitz.

'And?'

'Bert,' said Bert.

'Right, Mikhail, Bert, would you please gag the prisoner?'

The guards looked at each other.

'Just use your hands,' she said.

Mikhail put his large hands over Christian's mouth. It didn't really stop Christian from shouting, but it did at least muffle the volume.

'Now then, Mr Langford,' said Nikki, drifting over, 'I have something that belongs to you.'

She clicked her fingers and an aide brought forward the book.

She took it in her hands.

'Full edition, we noted,' said Nikki, holding it up, 'no shepherd version for you?'

'Of course not,' said Mitch, 'shepherd editions ...'

She smiled, released the clasp, and opened up the book somewhere towards the back, the buckle straps flopping free in the process.

'As you'll see,' she said, 'the second section is open, and, I think you'll find, has been well thumbed.'

Mitch said nothing.

'Release him,' said Nikki.

The guards obliged.

She handed him the book.

Mitch took it, glanced down, and looked over to Christian.

'Look, missy, I don't even know who you are,' said Mitch.

'Would you like to know?'

Mitch shifted his weight but said nothing.

'No. I thought not,' she said, with a smile. 'Now, I'm not going to have you sent to Poland. I'm not even going to have you held. I'm going to let you go.'

'Oh is that right?' said Mitch. 'Just like that?'

'Yes, just like that.' She gave Fishguard a nod. 'My guards will escort you to our perimeter. From there you are a free man. Go and tell your shepherd friends, and your employers, their prize has been spoiled. The game is over.'

Mitch stepped over towards Christian.

The guards moved to intercept, but Nikki raised her hand.

'You bozo,' said Mitch, before punching Christian hard in the stomach.

Christian doubled up, only staying on his feet because of the guards holding onto him.

Mitch turned away. His guards returned to his side. Fishguard signalled to those in the arena cordon and a path opened.

'Yeah, well the joke's on you, buddy,' shouted Christian, wheezily, 'the joke's on you, read your book, because the joke's on you.'

Chapter Thirty-Six

With Christian installed in his protective cordon at the head, and the last managers back in their ranks at the rear, the great army was ready for its final journey.

Nikki gave the order and the force moved off, gently ramping up to the new one hundred and forty metre cruising height – as approved by the Altitude Subcommittee of the Navigational Dynamics Department the previous evening. Now they met not even token resistance as they pressed on towards their target, angels nor shepherds standing in their way.

And yet the air was full of anti-climax. Primed for confrontation, most of the managers hadn't had a chance to engage by the time the angels had been defeated, some hadn't even been readied. Their time would come, though, their superiors told them, for one challenge remained.

In no time at all, the army was beginning its descent. Approaching from the west, it passed over Hyde Park, and then, after clipping the roof of Buckingham Palace, executed an eighteen-degree turn to the left and landed on The Mall, taking up most of it. Once down they reorganised into a single wide layer. Senior managers broke off from the front and made their way back down the column, dispatching orders, non-disclosure agreements, and releasing information on the next and final phase of their campaign – The Queue. Most had seen it during their approach, snaking its way through the streets of London. And if they hadn't seen it, they'd certainly heard of it. In recent evenings, tales of its legends and folklore had even been rivalling seminars on the Capability Maturity Model in camp. But few had guessed how it was now unavoidably entwined with their mission.

The size of the army meant it took almost an hour for the briefing to be cascaded to all troops. Nikki was pumped, sparking with nerves of antici-pation, and now, finally, her mighty force of pinstripes, blues and greys was ready to go over the top for the big push.

Troops from the rear were brought forward to form a vanguard, including all the former iChemiclast managers – their final reward, their final honour. And then the column began to move off on the last few yards of its journey. Soon they were turning left at the Duke of York Column, drifting up the steps, dividing like a zip to pass round its base, and then they stopped.

Fifty metres ahead stood the front of the Great Queue, the greatest ever to have formed in all of creation. Twelve bodies wide and densely packed, its tail stretched as far as they could see, trailing up the incline of Regent Street, while its head curved to the army's left, through the small park that was Waterloo Gardens, across Carlton House Terrace and towards one of the grand old whitewashed buildings where it disappeared into a crowd, all cheering at the spectacle of those walking wilfully to their judgement. And in among the onlookers, the ghosts hopeful of limb or organ adoption, a lucky few drifting away with hands and feet in their arms, the distraught appendages still straining back to their soon-to-depart former masters who'd had no choice but to give them up. All must leave this realm whole – no more, no less.

A final and thankfully brief meeting of the inner circle was convened behind the vanguard, and once the final set of minutes was approved, the final tabled agenda item completed, and the final item of any other busi-ness heard, the command was sounded.

The army began to edge forward.

Those in the vanguard could now see that the Battle of Heston Services had been a mere pre-season warm-up. Here, now, was the real deal; this had the potential to get ugly. It had the potential to get ugly because they were about to do something heinous, something universally derided throughout Queue lore. They were about to push in.

By the standards of zonal gatherings, the Manager Army was huge, but even so, it was dwarfed by the staggering abacus-busting numbers in the Queue. No one knew quite how many it held, partly because its number was an ever-shifting total, but mainly because no one ever had the energy or motivation to undertake such a monumental exercise in zonal survey-ing. But even the most conservative estimates put the total at north of two and a half billion.

Therefore, with a force 130,000 times smaller, afterlife military history suggested the managers were foolish to even contemplate an assault on the winding behemoth, and this would indeed be the case, were it not for two things. First, and of greatest significance, the vast majority of the Queue's numbers were well out of deployment range – most were not even within the right time zone, let alone a quick drift of Pall Mall; and second, the managers would not be taking on an army, they would be taking on a queue. The managers were a unified force with common mind and purpose, any one of their number willing to sacrifice themselves for the cause. The queuers were individuals. True, there was a common interest in what lay at the end of the line, and there was a shared sense of natural order and queue etiquette. And in this particular queue there was an unusual degree of organisation and discipline, even extending to an emergent federation of linear democracies, which had formed after the great queue wars of the nineteen seventies. Yet if it came down to it, not one of their number would put themselves out if they felt they might lose their place.

But even so, an all-out attack would not be easy, and its outcome far from certain. A physical engagement would be dangerous, unpredictable. So first, they would try to push in in plain sight, without the Queue realis-ing. In other words, they would try diplomacy.

Fishguard exchanged a few final words with Captain Beresford, now his second in command, then stepped forward alone and approached the Queue. He moved slowly, carefully, making sure he was seen, but avoiding eye contact, and keeping his head bowed, until he was just a few metres from the queuers.

Anyone at the front of a very long queue can get a little agitated, a little paranoid, when approached by a potential pusher. The people Fishguard was now approaching were at the front of a very, very, very, *very* long queue, and their nuclear-grade bubbling disquiet rose with every step he took. Legs twitched, feet tapped and the huge body of ethereal bodies began to sway and pulsate like a cuttlefish saying, 'Keep your fucking distance.' Onlookers in the crowd, near where the Queue disappeared into the whitewashed buildings, began to pick up on the rumblings; some of them began to step back.

'Watch him, watch him,' cried a voice from the Queue.

'He's going to push in, he's going to push in.'

'P-p-p-pusher.'

Fishguard slowly held up his hands and lifted his chin. 'Please, I must have your attention,' he said.

The crowd began to unify. It began to sway, towards and then away from him, lapping to within a few metres of his feet.

'Please, you have nothing to fear,' he said. He stood his ground and waited.

Eventually the shouting and posturing faded. The Queue calmed, but remained on simmer.

Fishguard cleared his throat. 'I represent the deceased incarnation of the Lord of Limbo, the LimboChrist,' he said. 'We require your compliance in an operation of great importance. If you concede to assist, you will experience no material inconvenience, and we will soon be on our way. If you choose to resist, it will come at great personal cost.'

'Speak bloody English,' came a cry from the Queue.

'Shut up, I'm trying to listen,' came another.

'He's trying to push in.'

'P-p-p-pusher.'

All the onlookers were now edging back.

'Please, please,' said Fishguard, lifting his palms but dropping his gaze low, again trying to calm the Queue.

'He's not trying to push in, he's just talking about compliance,' said a voice from the Queue's far side.

'Well what does that mean?' said another.

'I don't know, I'm trying to find out.'

'Sounds like pushing in to me.'

The Queue began to move again, ripples of malcontent running up and down its length as far back as Fishguard could see.

'I can assure you, no one is going to be pushing in,' said Fishguard, 'we just need your help.'

The Queue calmed again.

'All I require is a brief delay in your entry to the Gate.'

'Delay?'

'Half an hour. Forty-five minutes tops.'

'You know how long we've been waiting, guv?'

'Exactly,' said Fishguard, 'so what's another half hour? Relatively speaking, it's the blink of an eye.'

'He's pushing in.'

'P-pusher, p-p-p-pusher.'

'Hang on, hang on,' came a voice from farther back. 'Why do you need us to wait?'

A blanket of quiet fell. All awaited Fishguard's answer.

'I just need to escort some VIPs through,' he said.

'Through? Through where?'

'Through the Gate,' said Fishguard, softly, his head bowed.

Beats of silence.

Fishguard flicked his eyes to those of the queuers.

'He *is* pushing in.'

'P-p-pusher.'

'Get him!'

Fishguard turned to run, but it was too late. Before he could complete his first stride, the Queue had him, ten hands grabbing at his Marks and Spencer epidermis, dragging him in and up, and then, like a reflex swallow, passing him down the length of the Queue, buffeting and rolling him as he went.

One for the back! One for the back!
One for the back! One for the back!

The cry was repeated like an echo, down the Queue's length, alerting the next segment to the arrival of a pusher, on and on, fainter and fainter, as Fishguard was sped off on a luge run down Regent Street and out of sight.

'Forward,' shouted Beresford, with a thrust of his fountain pen.

And so began the Battle of Waterloo Gardens. The vanguard advanced as one, with large numbers from the rear pushing on behind, eager to engage, increasing the density and potency of the attack. Forward they went, battle cries ringing out as they upped the jog into a full drift-sprint.

Moments before impact, they closed ranks to form a packed wedge and drove square-on into the flank of the Queue.

The Queue braced. It had been more than thirty years since they'd seen active service but its members didn't need the command, instinctively linking hands with neighbours, moments before they were steamrollered back through the gardens and into the walls of the buildings. Many hands were forced apart in the impact, but as a whole, the Queue's integrity held, and like an enormous elastic band it stretched, and stretched, soaking up the energy and drawing the managers in. The army's progress slowed to a jog, then a walk, then a crawl, and then it stopped. For a moment there was equilibrium, but then all their efforts came back at them in fast reaction, reversing their advance, crushing the front ranks down under the ground and compressing the rest as the Queue recoiled into them. The shockwave rippled back through the management ranks, flooring the rest of the vanguard and the entire brigade behind it.

Both sides seemed not to know what to do, perhaps from shock, perhaps from realising for the first time what they were caught up in. But the managers were first to regroup. While the Queue was still re-forming, still hastily re-establishing broken neighbourly links, the managers surged forward again, forcing the Queue back farther this time, and this time the managers kept pushing, meeting the growing elastic force of the Queue as it stretched, the tension dragging more and more of the downward segments into the struggle. Three more management battalions joined up from the rear, piling in behind, pushing on like massed number eights, harder and harder, ratcheting up the pressure with every metre. And then, when they could push no further, the cry from behind, 'Brace, brace, brace.'

In an instant, the managers tightened into a rigid column, leaning hard into the Queue, each manager's arms and shoulders to the suit in front, all the way back, holding and pushing, maintaining the position. And then, as before, the Queue's elastic recoil began. But just when they needed to stay flexible, a wave of panic gripped the queuers as one pair of hands after another over-tensed, no one wanting to be the breaking point, no one wanting to lose their place. It was too much. The managers held firm, and the recoiling Queue impaled itself on the business wedge, splitting and tearing clean through. A huge chasm opened as the release of pent-up tension dragged the ragged flailing ends of the head and tail down either side of the column and sent the managers forward. Anguished cries erupted as queuers were separated from those they had walked, stood and waited with for more than half a century. They'd been so near the end, so close to judgement, so close they'd already said their goodbyes, as ready as they'd ever be to again go their separate ways, but not now, not like this.

The army seized its moment, riding the momentum to push farther forward, and to the command of 'right, right, right', turning and surging at the Queue's thrashing tail, scooping it up and ramming it back right through the oblivious mortals perusing their papers in the Reform Club, on and out onto Pall Mall. The managers met little resistance, their advance matching a reflex retreat as queuers again tightened the bonds with their neighbours, protecting what they had.

But shock and fear soon gave way to anger and vengeance. The tail regrouped and lashed forward, swamping the front rows of the manager advance. Bodies smashed into bodies as the two forces began a series of engagements, the writhing severed neck of the Queue flicking back and forth like a cobra, smashing and crushing managers with each swipe; the committed but rigid manager ranks struggled to adapt to the chaotic battle pattern and the traumatic sight of stray managers getting picked off and taken up by the Queue, up and over, and spirited away.

Meanwhile, back on Carlton House Terrace, a raging horde of elite sales executives had been unleashed, sweeping in from the southwestern end, whirling laptop maces above their heads, backed up by the office-chaired account-manager mounted cavalry. They charged at the Queue's ragged decapitated head, screaming aggressive and controversial marketing slogans as they bore down. Some of the queuers panicked, but most stood their ground, still feeling they had a chance, like wildebeest in the herd. Despite everything, they were only metres from the Gate, with just a few tens of people in front – perhaps there was still time. But when half their number were swept up on the first pass, along with several stragglers from the crowd of onlookers, order broke down, the head of the once proud and civil Queue became a chaotic maul, as neighbour fought neighbour, kicking and pushing to get to the Gate. A lucky few managed it, getting into the reception area of number seven, along with a couple of opportunists from the onlookers, before the rest were picked off by the second pass and carried away screaming and thrashing.

. . .

Fifteen minutes later, the Manager Army had achieved its initial objectives – to sever the Queue; to clear the head; to establish a front to keep the tail at bay. All that remained was a short-term hold of the position. But this was already proving to be a major challenge. The erratic behaviour of the Queue's tail had forced the managers into committing to an ever-widening front, now stretching all along Pall Mall, from Commonwealth House to the Serious Fraud Office, with manager forces twenty deep and ten high in places. All four brigades were now in action, but the demands were being cranked up all the time. The frantic and panicking Queue was becoming ever more unpredictable, its wide and now venomous head constantly charging and probing for a way round or through, swallowing dozens of managers with each strike, and its size was continually swelling as news zipped down its length and rear segments pushed forward in response. The managers would not be able to hold out for long.

Behind the front line, the scene was now one of strained order. The board of director generals were still at the controls, for the moment, but many of its members were voicing deep concerns; some were losing their nerve. But not Nikki. She had left them to it and come forward from the command centre on The Mall, up the steps and across into the green calm of Waterloo Gardens.

She turned and took in the spoils – unrestricted access to number seven, Carlton House Terrace.

She stepped upwards into the air to get a better view, up until she stood on a par with the grand pedestalled statues of military men that bordered the gardens, and then those few steps higher – this was hers now, at least for the moment.

She lingered a little before returning to ground level and taking a tour of the gardens, running her fingers through the rose bushes and the trunks of the plane trees, barely able to feel either. Many times she had wanted to come here in her mortal life, but had always denied herself, never knowing if the enemy might be watching. The risk was tiny, of course, but better to take no risk at all.

For everyone else, discovering its secret only in death gave this place no significance. In mortal life, to them, this was just another part of London. In death, the Gate had to be somewhere, so it was no revelation that it should be here. Yes, scientists were sometimes amused, yes, often they were disgusted, but for most people, this piece of land – the street, the building, the garden – was insignificant. Like the Londoner on their way to New York, Heathrow airport is the important thing, not the ground it happens to be built on. But Nikki was different; she had been one of the few who had known in life. She'd drawn such strength from knowing what was here, knowing it with all her heart, despite there being no evidence from her mortal senses, *because* there was no evidence from her mortal senses. And now she was here. Now she'd be able to see what she'd previously only known was hidden inside number seven.

Chapter Thirty-Seven

In the Grand Ballroom of the Caesar's Palace Mega-Lounge of the True Jerusalem Palace complex, the annual Anti-Veneration gala luncheon had been in full swing for several hours. Bow ties were being undone, stilettoes were being discarded, and the Jeragne was really flowing – some people were even drinking it.

Everyone who was anyone was there. The cabinet, the section heads, the upper, middle and lower angelic councils, with all their plus ones, and five times that number drawn from the cream of the Kingdom's celebrities, musicians, philosophers, porn stars, actors and artists.

The pre-lunch programme had followed the familiar traditions, beginning with the parade and novelty hat competition and the songs celebrating God's 1,645 years of uninterrupted suppression of subservience – which everyone had sung with gusto. Then came the speeches and the presentation of the huge piles of gifts for the host – always *gifts*, never *tributes*.

And of course central to the occasion were the near-deadly platefuls of ethereal soft matter, or as Terry called it, 'the grub'. Eighteen of the twenty courses had been served, with most guests discreetly secreting the bulk of it under the tables – the carpet was Paisley for a reason. All that remained were the traditional kipper and marmite crèmes brûlées, and the much more terrifying 'coffee and mints'. Yet no one here was attending under protest. Even under the cloud of recent events, they'd all have happily suffered a third hour of singing, or forced down yet greater culinary crimes, because to attend the Anti-Veneration celebrations meant access to the biggest and cheesiest of big cheeses, and to be seen while getting it. When it came to True Jerusalem society, you were either here or you weren't, and a little thing like a war in the Zone wasn't going to stop anyone. Besides, it gave everyone something to talk about. Everyone.

'Come on, you've been dodgin' this all day,' said God.

'Dodging what?' said Gabriel.

God nodded to the empty chairs on the Angel Field Ops table.

'I don't know what you want me to say, Tel, no change from this morning, no one further's come through.'

God clenched a fist and pressed it into his anchovy vanilla slice, but said nothing.

'Look, I'm sure we'll hear word soon,' said Gabriel. 'Anyway, it's time for the speeches.' He rose to his feet. He took up his spoon and was about to tinkle his glass when the sound of a scuffle outside caused him to pause. The noise grew louder, there were shouts, thumps against the door, a brief pause, and then the doors were flung open.

Everyone turned to see Harold and all twelve apostles march into the centre of the ballroom, stop and stand before God and the top table.

The room fell silent.

Mark and Matthew, at the head of the apostle group, carefully and deliberately scanned left and right, eyeballing many of the guests, before stepping aside to reveal two bald-headed servants facing each other, each wearing nothing but a loin cloth and a leather over-the-shoulder pouch.

The servants took two sidestepped paces out, before reversing to open the space between them.

Gasps and whispers as people realised the man himself was here.

Jesus walked forward, the servants bowing and crabbing ahead of him and scattering rose petals from the leather pouches before each deital footstep.

'All right, son,' said God, leaning back in his chair.

'Father,' said Jesus.

'Right,' said God, 'what's all this then?'

Harold stepped forward. 'This is, this is a citizen's arrest,' he said.

A patter of laughter made its way around the tables, but died when God, Gabriel and the top table failed to join in.

'You sure you know what you're doing, son?' said God.

'I am doing what must be done,' said Harold.

Gabriel stood. 'Remove this man,' he said, calling to the guards now gathering at the back of the room.

'No,' said God, his tone calm and measured.

'No?' said Gabriel.

'No,' said God.

Gabriel sat.

God turned back to Harold. 'The floor's all yours, son,' he said, and made a wide sweeping gesture.

Harold could only look to Matthew and the others.

'Come on then,' said God, 'you've got us all juiced up. Let's hear it.'

Harold opened his mouth.

'Not so easy, is it?' said God 'Not so–'

'Terry, God,' said Harold. He took a step forward. 'You have authorised murder. You have ordered killings, the premeditated execution of a mortal. Other mortals have lost their lives as a consequence.'

Murmurs rippled around the tables.

'Terry, Lord,' said Gabriel, 'we don't have to–'

God raised a finger to Gabriel, but kept his eyes on Harold. 'Is that right, son?' said God. 'Well don't let us stop you mid-flow.'

'I, I have records,' said Harold, 'detailed accounts of events, meetings, dates and times, details of witnesses. Shepherds were dispatched for collections before their targets had died, ladies and gentlemen and angels.'

More murmurs from the crowd.

Now Jesus stepped forward, his flanking petal-scattering servants moving with him.

The room fell silent once more.

'Is this true, Father?' asked Jesus.

God stood. 'Look, boy,' he said, 'don't give me the whole "Father" routine.'

'Is it true?' asked Jesus.

Everyone turned to Terry.

'Oh come on, it's not like you need to ask. You know it's true.'

Stifled gasps around the tables.

Jesus bowed his head. 'I wanted to believe there had been a mistake, Father. I thought, perhaps, you'd just been on the mushroom soup again.'

'Nope,' said God, popping the 'p', 'no such excuse. It's all true, every last bit of it.'

An instant crisp silence. Not a sound, not a whisper.

'What,' said God, hands to his hips as he scanned the dumbstruck faces.

No one moved. No one spoke. Everyone watched and waited.

'What exactly is the big revelation here?' he continued. 'I'm fuckin' God, in case any of you hadn't noticed. Yes I had him killed. And I'd do it again.' He made a fist and extended forefinger and thumb to form a pistol. '*Bang*. Dead. End of story.'

'So you admit it,' said Harold.

'Sure,' said God, and he blew the non-smoke from the muzzle of his hand pistol.

Harold spun round, taking in the room, making as much eye contact as possible, holding out an arm of witness recruitment.

'You all heard him, ladies and gentlemen and angels. A confession. You all heard.'

'Yep,' said God, once more popping the 'p'.

'Oh, Father,' said Jesus, shaking and hanging his head.

More silence. All eyes were now on the son, the saviour.

He lifted his head, his eyes now aflame. 'Father,' said Jesus, 'you leave me but one course of action.' Jesus's eyes widened and his pupils shrank to pinpricks. His beard began to spark.

Everyone either edged forward on their seats or ran for cover.

'I ... I ... I ... I forgive you, Father.'

'Beg pardon?' said Harold.

'He is forgiven,' proclaimed Jesus, taking a turn on the spot.

Cheers rang out. Jesus ran forward, arms open and joy in his eyes. He embraced his father before holding his hand aloft to rapturous applause.

It was a full minute before the room fell silent once again. Now all eyes turned to Harold.

Gabriel puffed out his thin lips before his eyes moved from Harold to the guards at the back. He flicked a gesture with his clawhand.

Two guards stepped forward, bustled past the apostles now remonstrating with Jesus, and took hold of Harold.

Gabriel walked over. The archangel motioned to speak, but in the end just shook his head. 'Take him away,' he muttered.

The guards marched Harold off. Behind him he heard people go back to their conversations and the band start up. In amongst it, he could just make out God talking to Jesus.

'Thanks, son. Look, it's been way too long. We should talk.'

Chapter Thirty-Eight

Though the Queue had been pushed back out onto Pall Mall, Nikki didn't have the street all to herself. Apart from the occasional mortal pedestrian and motor vehicle, several hundred managers were banked up into a bowl, crowding around something just beyond the Turf Club, at the western end of the terrace.

'One hundred,' came a rich loud voice from inside the group, followed by a ripple of applause and a few cheers and jeers.

One of the managers broke off and came over. It was Tom Hanley, formerly a thrusting junior executive in the iChemiclast sales team, and now a Lieutenant Colonel in the Corporate Guard of the Manager Army.

'Ready when you are,' he said.

'Thanks, Tom,' said Nikki, 'let's get started then.'

They began to make their way over towards the bowl of guards, but Nikki stopped and turned when she saw Christian's phalanx of HR managers drifting up the street from the Duke of York Column.

'I'll be right with you,' she said.

'We don't have much time,' said Hanley.

'This won't take long.'

The escort phalanx stopped as Nikki approached.

'Is our guest still safe and sound?' she asked.

'He's doing fine,' said the sergeant, 'message from five company, though. They're getting light on numbers, pretty much everyone's at the front. We, er, don't have a rear perimeter any more.'

'Hello?' said Christian.

'That's fine ... Alan,' said Nikki, reading from the sergeant's ID badge, 'I think we'll be okay.'

'Hello?' said Christian. 'Look, I'm not deaf, you know, I can hear every word.'

Nikki waved her hand and the front rows of guards stood aside. 'What on earth is this?' she said, seeing the sacking over Christian's head, the same sacking that had been part of the improvised headgear confiscated from Mitch the previous evening. 'This is Christian Bootstrap, the great prophet of Limbo, the last sayer of Heaven, have some respect.'

Alan shifted his weight onto his toes. 'We were told to keep him blindfolded for the final approach, ma'am.'

'Okay,' said Nikki, 'fair enough.' She looked over to Hanley, and then back to Alan. 'You've done well,' she said, 'you've all done well.' She scanned the faces, delivering each her infinitely practised, full eye contact encouragement glance, before flicking her hand for the sack to be removed. A guard obliged.

'I demand to know where we are,' said Christian, squinting in the bright sunshine.

'Of course, Christian, of course,' said Nikki, 'well, we're here.'

'And where is here?'

'Just, *here*,' she said. She broke out into a smile.

'Hey, I recognise this place,' he said, looking around and then beyond Nikki, 'I think I came here on a school trip.'

'Wonderful, wonderful, how nice for you. Well, anyway, we'll be going through soon, so have a good last look.'

'Through? Through where?'

'Through the Gate of course. Why else do you think we've come here?'

'The Gate?' said Christian, looking at the leafy street.

'It's in there,' said Nikki, nodding towards the entrance to number seven.

'Hang on, hang on,' said Christian, leaning round for a better look, 'that's the Royal Society.'

'Yes,' said Nikki, matter-of-factly. She turned back to the guards, 'Now–'

'I'm sorry, but the Royal Society?'

'Yes?'

'That's the gateway to the rest of the afterlife?'

'Well the Gate's inside it. In the gents, so I'm told.'

'The gents?' Christian stared at the building in horror.

'Well it had to be somewhere, Christian.'

'But this is the home of science. To put it here, it's, it's an outrage.'

'Back to front as ever, Christian. The Gate's been here for millennia. It predates the Royal Society, it predates the whole street and most of London.'

'Oh. Oh right.'

'So if anything, it's the scientists who are being insensitive.'

Christian tried and failed to find a reply.

'Tragic, isn't it,' said Nikki, turning to give Christian her full attention, 'all the weight of science hasn't provided so much as a scrap of evidence of an afterlife, and all along the gateway to it is sitting right here at science central, right under their noses. Just think, most of them probably walk right through it every day as they head for a cubicle.'

'I suppose so,' said Christian, his voice forlorn.

'Boss,' said Hanley, approaching, 'we need to get started.'

'Okay, Tom,' said Nikki, 'we're nearly done.'

Christian felt the guards take hold of his collar.

'So that's your plan, is it?' said Christian. 'Force me to write the appendix, threaten to push me through if I don't?'

'No,' said Nikki, laughing, 'why, is that what you think? Is that why you think we've come here?'

'Well, yes,' said Christian.

'Oh no, it's much simpler than that. You see, you're about to come through the Gate with me, to Limbo, *then* we'll get you to write the appendix.'

'What? But, why? I don't–'

'We're just being pragmatic, Christian. Strategic thinking, you see. Once you're safely in Limbo, you'll be out of reach of anyone who can help you. Then we will do whatever's required to make you write. And trust me, you'll soon come to heel, you'll be pleading for me to proofread your first draft within hours.'

'But that makes no sense, what use is the information to you over there? Surely you need to release it on Earth, to the living?'

'And we will, Christian, and we will. Heaven isn't the only realm that can spawn prophets, you know.'

'Boss,' said Hanley, 'really, we must–'

'All right,' said Nikki. 'All right.' She turned to leave.

'But how can you even be sure I'll arrive in Limbo?' said Christian. 'That's out of your hands, isn't it? Out of anyone's hands. We all get judged by the same rules.'

'Yes, by and large,' said Nikki.

'And you know I've never been a believer ...'

Nikki stopped, turned and smiled.

'... I've never killed anyone, I've never stolen anything, I'm not Danish ...'

Her smile broadened.

'What's so funny?' he said.

'You really don't know, do you?' said Nikki.

'Know what?'

'Boss, we don't have time for this,' said Hanley.

'I said wait,' said Nikki. 'Christian,' she continued, 'you read the second section.'

'And?'

'Oh come on. I thought you said you'd read the chapters on judgement, the details of the rules?'

'Yes ... well ... I definitely gave them a skim.'

Nikki laughed again. 'Oh, how fitting. Never were too thorough, were you? Dear oh dear, what would poor old Stuart say ... Well now, my dear Christian, in reading the banned section, you now possess prohibited knowledge, the secrets of the lands beyond the Gate, so I'm afraid that's you barred from Heaven, and there's nothing they can do about it, however much they want you.'

'Oh ...' said Christian.

'Like I say, Christian, take a last look.'

Nikki turned to rejoin Hanley and the managers beyond the Turf Club.

'Wait, wait ... hey, *wait*.' As Christian's manager guards closed up around him once again, the last thing he saw was a familiar amphitheatre of suits in the background, but this time with an occasional flash of white from within.

Chapter Thirty-Nine

Dexter was in the gloom of his office, hammering out the details for the third relaxation in the dress code that week, when he heard happy shouts, cheers and a commotion in the corridor. Three seconds later, Gordon, dressed like a tart on the town, bounded in, almost turning a high-heeled ankle, with Cheung, Bhakta and several others piling in after him.

'He's coming, he's on his way,' said Gordon, before rejigging his boob tube.

Dexter stood. 'Who's coming?'

'The boy, of course,' said Gordon.

'It's super great,' said Cheung.

'I think we should declare tomorrow a public double work day, to celebrate,' said Bhakta.

'Hear, hear,' said a voice from the back.

'Let's go triple!' said Cheung.

Cheers of approval and then everyone started talking at once. More people started trying to get into the small office, causing a jam in the doorway.

'Enough,' said Dexter, 'enough.'

He moved out from behind his desk. 'Out, out, the lot of you, I need to talk to Gordon.'

'Yes, but–'

'Out.' He herded them all out, forcing the last few through the door before closing and locking it. 'Now,' he said, turning to Gordon, 'what's this all about?'

'The boy's coming.'

'Calm, please, Gordon, sit down, will you?'

'Can't sit. Too excited. The boy, he's on his way.'

'We've already discussed this, Gordon. Look, I know you think you feel these things, but–'

'No, no, no, I'm not talking about my kundalini, I'm talking something even more convincing.'

'Okay ...'

'The latest arrivals from the Gate. They're all talking about it. A great army, marching under a great leader.'

'What?'

'An army of managers. Administrators, accountants, office professionals. All our creed is there.'

'Well, now, well, that is interesting,' said Dexter. He tapped his teeth with his pencil.

'Interesting?' said Gordon.

'Yes.'

'That's all you have to say?'

'Well it is interesting.'

'It's more than that, it's fucking proof. They must be being led by the boy, who else?'

'I suppose it's possible,' said Dexter.

'Possible?'

'Yes.'

'Well there's even more evidence, actually,' said Gordon.

'Go on.'

'The arrivals at the Gate.'

'And ...'

'They've dried up. Stopped. No one's come through in the last half hour.'

'So ...'

'So it's obvious. The army have blocked off the Queue.'

'I don't follow.'

'So my boy can come through in triumph. Come through with the codes. He's done it, he's only gone and done it, and now he's coming home.'

'Well, yes, I suppose that could be the reason,' said Dexter.

'Oh come on, it must be.'

'Well, I wouldn't say must be. They could be working through a whole load who are all going upstairs, you know, a troop of philosophers or something.'

'For half an hour? No, no, no.'

'Or maybe downstairs? A whole load of Gestapo officers, perhaps – the timing would be about right. Or it could be an enormous darts team?'

'Might stem the flow for a couple of minutes maybe,' said Gordon, 'but not thirty.'

'True,' said Dexter. He sat down in the guest chair. 'Well then, perhaps he really is coming. Gee whiz.' He loosened his tie and undid his top button.

'Pretty amazing, isn't it?' said Gordon. He sat in Dexter's chair, leaned back and put his strappy pink heels up on the desk.

Dexter tried to take it all in, while trying not to take in the vision of Gordon's fishnets. 'You know, I didn't want to acknowledge it, until we were sure,' said Dexter. 'After all this time, I can't believe the plan's finally come together.'

'Well you can believe now. My boy is here, as good as. So there's no time to waste.'

'Exactly,' said Dexter, 'we should get down to Arrivals.' He stood, but Gordon remained seated.

'I'm going there now,' said Gordon, 'but not you, no, you have something more important to do.'

'Oh,' said Dexter, 'what's that then?'

'The celebrations of course. This will be the proudest moment in our cultural history. So you need to get planning, Dex. Now this is my vision – we let him settle in for a bit, readjust and whatnot, then the entire city comes together for a huge festival.'

'But, Gordon, what about the debrief, you know, on the appendix, the codes?'

'Of course, of course, that goes without saying, but the immediate focus needs to be on the celebration.'

'But–'

'That's an order, Dex.'

'Well. Okay then,' said Dexter, and he sat down.

'Now for starters, I want a big gay pride parade,' said Gordon.

'I'm sorry?'

'Actually, not just gay pride. Lesbian pride, and trans ... Which trans am I?'

'Transvestite.'

'Transvestite pride,' said Gordon, 'yes, and the other trans pride. I want everyone, all the oddballs, all the weirdoes, every single one of 'em, in the parade, out and proud.'

'You can't be serious?'

'I am serious. I want poofs on a float. Cowboy hats, arseless chaps, the lot.'

'We don't really have ... Gordon, this is Limbo, remember? You know, blues and greys, steady as she goes. Homosexuals, well, they're more Heaven's thing, aren't they?'

'Balls, man. We have poofs too, you just have to look for them. Find them, Dexter, wheedle them out. Get me a hundred poofs. Get them or you'll be on the float yourself, you and all the section heads.'

Chapter Forty

Nikki and Hanley drifted into the manager amphitheatre to a hushed silence and the sight of an angel, front and centre, being forced to throw something small at a large piece of wood with a spoked wheel drawn on it.

'And that's the second leg,' shouted the logistics manager who was hosting, to rampant cheers.

The guards released their grip and the angel fell to his knees, before being dragged off.

The cheers fell away as stationery wagers were settled, but rose again as the managers spotted Nikki. They all stood, saluted and applauded.

Nikki waved and gave nods of thanks.

But not everyone was cheering. A metre above the ground, over to the left, in neat lines, sat a forced audience of almost 150 angels. Some had their legs and armwings bound – a variety of ropes, chains and manacles in evidence – while others were being held by suits. All were quiet with defeat and, now, the weight of humiliation. Several managers patrolled between the rows, tapping their keyboards to their thighs or twirling their mice as they eyeballed the prisoners.

Behind and around the angelic rows, some 500 managers made up the bowl of the amphitheatre. Most were just enjoying the action, adding spice with some gambling, some were swapping battle stories, others were catching up on their filing.

'All these are all good to go,' said Hanley, pointing to the lines of angels, 'and we're finishing off the last few right now.'

Nikki looked along the lines. She failed to recognise the stout toad-like angel at the far end of the second row, but would do so before the day was out.

'So,' said Hanley, 'shall we get started?'

'Yes,' said Nikki. 'The time has come.'

They turned and headed for the entrance to the Royal Society. She felt an ethereal adrenaline surge. She was about to see the fabled Gate, the mythical portal to the afterlife realms.

They drifted in through the small car park, up five steps and on through into the reception area. A line of manager guards followed, escorting the first batch of angels.

'This way,' said Hanley, as he led them down a flight of stairs, across a hallway and through a door. Inside they found a spacious but unremarkable gents toilet. Unremarkable that is, apart from the addition of an unattended wooden desk, and, next to it, a small turnstile – a single cross of oak-bar spokes mounted in a sandstone cube on top of a sandstone pillar, framed by two smaller pillars.

Nikki looked at Hanley.

Hanley looked at Nikki. 'What?' he said.

'This is it?' she said.

'Well, yes.'

She gave him the exact look she'd given him in life when he'd once commented that 0.1% profit was still better than no profit.

'Look, don't shoot the messenger,' he said, 'I didn't build it.'

'Are we sure this is it?' asked Nikki.

Hanley gestured to a small white lettered sign on top of the wooden desk: 'Gateway to the Afterlife. Queue here. No refunds or returns.'

'Well, all right,' said Nikki. 'I suppose I shouldn't have expected anything better. In fact, this is exactly what I should have expected. Anyway, right, have we tested it yet?'

'We're waiting for the man,' said Hanley, pointing to a handwritten card that read 'Back in five minutes'.

'What on earth?' said Nikki.

'Seems it's locked,' said Hanley. He pushed on the turnstile, jiggling the free play in the mechanism.

'Well where is he?' said Nikki.

Hanley shrugged.

'How about just throwing them over the top?' said Nikki.

'I don't think that'll work,' he said, shaking his head.

'Why?'

'I just get the feeling it won't.'

'Well let's try, shall we?' said Nikki.

She clicked her fingers and gave a nod to the guards. They marched the first angel forward. He was one of the weaker specimens, which is why he'd found himself at the front of the queue.

'Climb over that,' Nikki said to the angel as she pointed to the turnstile.

'Please, please don't make me,' said Tinglewee, backing away, straining at the hold of his guards, 'I won't say anything, I swear I won't. We, we have no choice, you don't know what it's like.'

Shouts from the other angels, demands for strength and courage.

'Why does it always have to be the hard way?' said Nikki. 'Gentlemen, can you please oblige?'

The guards pushed the angel forward.

'No, no,' said Tinglewee, 'please no.'

He struggled and thrashed as he tried to free his armwings, all the while craning his head and looking back in desperation to his comrades, themselves struggling against the heavy restraint of their captors. But there was nothing they could do.

'Move it,' said the first guard, 'no sense in struggling.'

Another guard stepped forward and brought his keyboard down hard across the face of the angel, meeting his cheek with a clickety slap.

Hanley stepped in too, and together they manhandled the angel up onto the turnstile, the prisoner's slippered paddle-shaped feet kicking out, before finding the turnstile bar and bracing against the pressure coming from behind.

'Please,' said the angel, desperation in his voice.

With a heave, the managers lifted the angel, pivoting him up so he stood on the bar, teetering on the brink.

Time slowed as Nikki braced for her first taste of judgement. Some of the managers took a step back, all too aware of the tales – the blinding light, the cries of the damned and the acrid stench of brimstone.

With one final shove they had Tinglewee dispatched, sending him toppling through and landing head first up to his chest in the floor tiles on the other side of the turnstile.

'I don't think it's worked,' said Hanley.

'You don't say,' said Nikki. 'All right, fetch him back.'

While the guards were retrieving the now gibbering Tinglewee, a small man in a matted black uniform and cap, all trimmed and covered in intricate mother-of-pearl button designs, ambled in and made his way round to the back of desk, where he sat down and started fiddling with some papers. He eventually tapped them into alignment and put them to one side. He then opened a drawer, removed some more papers and began to tidy those, seemingly oblivious to the commotion around him.

'What the ...' said Nikki.

'Public sector slackers ...' muttered Hanley.

The man put the second batch of papers on top of the first, adjusted his chair, straightened his tie, attached a clip-on name tag that said 'Peter Seint' and removed the 'Back in five minutes' sign.

'Can I help you, miss?' he said.

'We've been waiting,' said Nikki, 'where've you been?'

'I was on a break.'

'Excuse me, but is this not the sacred Gate of Judgement, The Toran, passage to the three realms of the afterlife?'

'So?'

'So it's not the bloody Post Office.'

'There was no one waiting.'

'What sort of excuse is that?'

'Treacle, it's the first time there's not been a queue since June nineteen fifty-three. So I went out for a gander.'

'Well good for you, hope you enjoyed it, now if you wouldn't mind?'

'Don't seem so different out there, you know, 'part from the cars o'course,' said the attendant, 'I 'eard they were all different these days, though I must say I weren't expectin' 'em to look anyfing like that ... Funny, ain't it, 'ow you build up this picture in yer mind, but only see how wrong it is when you clap yer mincers on the real thing? Course, when I was last out there ...'

Nikki put her hands on her hips and glared at him.

The man stopped and shook his head. 'Ain't even got two seconds for a bit of polite conversation, 'ave you? No, no, I get it, you're in a hurry, you're all in a hurry, no time for a bit of courtesy these days is there, no no.'

'That's right. There isn't,' said Nikki.

'All right,' he said, and gave a low sigh, 'who's first then?'

'He is,' said Hanley, pointing to Tinglewee, now back on their side of the turnstile.

'Right then,' said the man, 'soul card?'

Hanley withdrew a wad of white cards from his inside jacket pocket and handed over the first one.

'This ain't you then?' said the man, looking at the card and then up at Hanley.

'No, it's him,' said Hanley, nodding to Tinglewee.

The attendant turned his head to one side and looked the panic-stricken angel up and down. 'Why's his mouth being held shut?'

'He's got ethereal flu,' said Hanley, 'don't want to spread the germs, do we now?'

'Ethereal flu …' said the man, unmoved.

'Look, you've got his soul card,' said Hanley, stepping closer, 'he's champing at the bit, can't wait to get judged, can you, fella …'

Tinglewee tried to shake his head, but instead found it being enthusiastically nodded for him.

'… now, please, do your job and let him through. Unless you fancy a trip to the other side yourself?'

The attendant puffed out his cheeks, opened a desk drawer, retrieved a token and nudged it across the counter with one finger, before resting his chin on his hand.

Hanley put the token in the slot. The guards shoved the angel up to the turnstile and pushed.

The bars began to rotate with a millstone rumble. Once again, time slowed as Nikki braced for her first taste of ancient justice.

A spark of static. And then Tinglewee disappeared, leaving only a whiff of ozone.

Silence.

The guards let out a few cheers.

'Nice,' said Hanley.

'Is that it?' said Nikki, turning to Hanley.

'Well, yes, I suppose so,' said Hanley.

'Is that it?' said Nikki, turning to the attendant.

He gave a slow nod.

'Right, let's have the next one,' said Hanley, beckoning to the guards.

Nikki watched another nine angels get dispatched to their judgement, taking a morbid curiosity in the range of reactions – more of the panicked pleading and futile struggling, some sheep-like acceptance, but a lot of stoic dignity, too – until she was satisfied everything was running smoothly.

'I'm going to get the main package,' Nikki told Hanley, before turning to head up the stairs. But she stopped mid-stride when she recognised the angel now at the front of the queue. 'Wait, wait a moment,' she said, holding up a hand to the guards. She moved over to the stout toad-like angel now one step from his destiny.

Candleslack looked back at her blankly.

'Well I never,' said Nikki, 'talk about middle-aged spread … and a promotion, I see?' she said, flicking the epaulettes on the angel's tunic.

'Have we met, miss?' said Candleslack.

'In a manner of speaking,' she said. A smug smile flooded her face.

He continued to look blank.

She stepped closer, her slim waist brushing his gut. 'You don't know who I am, do you, *Candleslack*? Even after all this, even now, you still have no idea?'

Candleslack arched his head back a little and furrowed his brow, before bringing his forehead down like a lump hammer on Nikki's nose, sending her rocking on her heels and back over onto the desk, startling the attendant.

Hanley punched Candleslack hard on the top of his head. The guards weighed in, punching and kicking the angel to the floor.

'Are you okay?' asked Hanley, taking Nikki's arm and pulling her to her feet. 'He can't hurt you, you know, not really, not now you're dead.'

'Yes, I fucking know, okay, I'm not fucking stupid.'

'I was just …'

'Put him in,' screeched Nikki, cradling her nose with one hand and pointing to Candleslack with the other.

The guards hauled Candleslack to his feet. Hanley took the token and popped it into the slot.

'Do give my regards to Stan,' shouted Nikki as the turnstile rotated and Candleslack vanished.

Chapter Forty-One

Heaven's light of day was fading, the sun already halfway through its daily retreat, halfway to becoming the manimoon.

Harold was bound tight to a traboogel tray, his smashed wrists clamped behind him, primed in the central launch chute on the dispatch platform at the top of True Jerusalem's thirty-metre-high north perimeter wall. Below him, the near-vertical shallow concave face dropped into the unknown of a long fade to absolute black – the Well of Souls.

Jutting out from the walls and across from the dispatch platform, a raised crescent-shaped observation balcony, supported by two mighty corbelled granite arms, hosted a pop-up bar where God and the who's who of Heaven looked on, leaning on the oak balustrade and making the most of happy hour.

Either side of Harold, but positioned slightly lower, were two other prisoners. Not criminals exactly, or at all, even, from what Harold had overheard. Merely two unfortunates in the wrong place at the wrong time, plucked from the streets of Paradise to provide 'ceremonial balance'.

'The mechanism is primed?' said Gabriel, inspecting the levers and ropes, just back from Harold on the dispatch platform.

'Oiled this morning, sir,' said Catchpole.

'And the track?'

'Greased.'

'And you've tested it?'

'Yup. Two hundredweight of Bratwurst, Guv, shot off clean as a whistle.'

'Good, good.'

Gabriel stepped over to Harold. 'Won't be long now,' said the archangel, softly, 'soon be dusk. Terry is one for tradition.'

'Gabriel, please, there must be–'

'Let's ... let's not, Harold. This is going to be difficult enough as it is.' Gabriel cast his eye over Harold's bindings and the tray release pin.

'I didn't say a word, you know,' said Harold.

'About what?' asked Gabriel.

'About' – he saw that Catchpole was hovering and lowered his voice – 'about not moving the shepherds before the strike, about losing Bootstrap.'

Gabriel put a clawhand on Harold's shoulder. 'Thank you,' he said.

Gabriel turned and climbed back up the short flight of steps to the access gantry, where Matthew and the apostles approached him. After a brief exchange, the archangel waved them through and down to Harold.

'We came to support you, comrade,' said Matthew.

'Where's Jesus?' asked Harold. 'I thought you said he'd be here?'

'He'd love to have been here,' said Mark, his hands clasped in front of him, 'but you know, he's a busy *busy* fellow.'

'Well did he talk to Terry?' asked Harold.

'Quite possibly,' said Mark, with a nod he didn't quite commit to.

'And?'

'Well,' said Matthew, cutting in, 'you're still on the launch chute, so, nuff said?'

'Long way down,' said Luke, with a lift of the eyebrows, as he peered over the edge.

'But–'

'Troof is,' said Matthew, 'Terry's a strong character. No surprise there, he is God! But anyway, once he's made his mind up, well ...'

Mark held up his hands, looked to the sky and chuckled. 'What can you do?'

Harold's chin sank into his chest and he started to tremble.

'But it ain't all bad news, brother,' said Matthew.

'Really?' said Harold.

'Really,' said Matthew. 'You see, we didn't take no for an answer, so we lodged a protest in the regional courts.'

Mark offered a thin smile and raised a limp fist.

'Will that work?' asked Harold. 'Is there time?'

Luke gave an almost gleeful shake of the head.

'No point sugar-coating it,' said Matthew, 'no.'

'But it will make a most piquant statement of principle,' said Mark.

'Principle,' said Matthew, with gusto.

'Prin-cip-el,' said John.

'Principle,' said Luke, over-earnestly, with a rub of his chin and a stifled snigger.

'*Principle?*' said Harold.

'Well, that's what's important, innit?' said Matthew. 'Said so yourself.'

'But, but what about me?'

Mark and Matthew beamed.

'For you, there are no words, Harry,' said Matthew. 'You're the first martyr in centuries and the first ever in Heaven. We'll always drink a toast to you when the nectar's goin' round.'

'Yes, very *very* well done,' said Mark.

'Y-you,' said John, 'you told 'em, Larry.'

'It's *Harry*,' said Mark, glaring at John.

Luke started a slow clap and a chant.

'*Larry, Larry, Larry.*'

A chorus of trumpets opened up above them. The chanting died.

'Good luck, Harry,' said Matthew, 'be nice to think we'll be reunited one day. But, again, I'll spare you that pain – because we won't.' He peered out over the edge of the wall and then looked back to Harold. 'Try to steer with your feet.'

The apostles stepped away, climbed back up the steps and scurried off via the gantry's rear exit when they saw God making his way down from the observation balcony.

God exchanged a word with Gabriel, before the two descended the steps to the dispatch platform and made their way over to Harold.

'Well, you blew it, son,' said God.

The Almighty flicked his cigarette butt over the wall and placed his hand on the release lever.

'Terry,' said Gabriel, leaning into God's ear, 'aren't you going to let Catchpole do that?'

'Never let it be said I don't take responsibility, Gabe,' said God. He turned to Harold. 'Any last words, son?'

Harold seemed surprised, but after a moment gave a slow nod. 'Yes, yes, I do have something to say, if this must be my end.' He cleared his throat and lifted his gaze to the observation deck. 'What I say to you now, I ... I ...' By now, many in the gallery had gone back to their drinks and chit-chat. 'What I, what ...'

Gabriel raised his clawhands to the gallery, armwings stretching wider, and wider, out to full span. He waited.

The chatter and clinking of glasses faded to a background whisper, and then to complete silence. Gabriel held his stance, and held his gaze to the gallery, before retracting his armwings. All eyes were now on Harold.

'What I say to you now ...'

'Speak up, we–'

'What I say to you now,' said Harold, his voice now full and resonant, 'I say for all realms. I say it for the mortal plane, for the Zone, and for the lower places. And I say it most of all for here, for this godforsaken land. And what I say is for all peoples of this world, for angels, for deities, and for all of humankind, but especially for humankind ...'

Silence.

'... what I say to you is–'

God pulled the lever and Harold plummeted.

'Right,' said God, 'who's up for a burger?'

Chapter Forty-Two

Nikki made her way up the stairs, past the angels on judgement row and their guards, through the reception area and back out onto the street. The darts gathering had broken up, all the captured angels having now played. Most of the managers had left, dispatched to shore up the defences at the front, with just a final few remaining while they completed the last exchanges of stationery winnings and said their farewells.

She took a moment to compose herself, before heading back over to Christian's phalanx of guards. And then she saw something she didn't expect. Everyone was still right where she'd left them, only now the guards were all sitting, cross-legged, staring up at Christian.

'And here endeth the lesson,' said Christian.

A small round of applause pattered up from the congregation.

'What's going on?' said Nikki.

'My dear Nikki,' said Christian, 'I'm afraid you've missed the service.'

'The service?'

She noticed Christian had folded his soul card in two and slotted it onto the collar of his black T-shirt.

'If you'd just like to pass that around,' said Christian, handing his sack hat to the first guard, who placed a small packet of staples inside, before passing it to the next guard, who sheepishly began patting his pockets.

'Yes,' said Christian, turning back to Nikki, 'my sermon on the dangers of getting involved in advertising, how it's a sure path to the fires of Hell, which absolutely positively do exist. You see, I did remember some of the things I read.' It was Christian's turn to smile, and he didn't just smile: he shone.

'You delivered a sermon,' said Nikki, 'that's preaching with intent.' She looked down at the guards. 'Why on earth did you listen to him?'

'Well, we were a bit bored, to be honest, boss,' said Alan. 'We didn't let him escape or anything, we've had him in plain sight all the time.'

'You've been taken in, you fools,' said Nikki.

'Oh, I don't know, I thought it was pretty good,' said Alan, 'lots of stuff about advertising creatives going to Hell. I liked that bit. I hate advertising creatives, think they're so clever ...'

'You've never even met one,' said his number two.

'Well that's a measure of just how much I hate them,' said Alan.

'What have you done?' said Nikki, turning to Christian.

'I've taken myself out of the game,' said Christian.

'We're about ready for him,' shouted Hanley, trotting over from number seven, 'what's, er, what's going on?'

Nikki took Christian by his jacket lapels. 'You idiot,' she said, 'you stupid reckless idiot, you've damned yourself to Hell, possibly.'

'Yes, I know. And not possibly, *certainly*. I am now bound to the fires of Hell, and of that you can be sure, my child.' He placed a hand on her forehead. 'Forgive her, Lord, for she know not–'

'But why?' she said, smacking his hand away. 'Why would you do that?'

'To stop you taking me to Limbo, of course.'

'What's he done?' asked Hanley.

'He's preached,' said Nikki.

'Preached?' said Hanley.

'Yep, a sermon ...'

'I even did a collection,' said Christian, gleefully pointing to the now half-full sack making its way around the guards.

'Oh cock,' said Hanley. He stepped back a few paces, sat down in the kerb, and put his hands on the top of his head.

'So, what, you think Hell's a better option, do you?' said Nikki, to Christian.

'Well no, I'm sure it's just as terrible as it's cracked up to be, but so what, it's not like I'm going there.'

'Yes you are, of course you are,' she said, 'Hell is real. Don't you get it? There is no way to undo this.'

'Even better.'

'What?'

'It's you who doesn't get it,' said Christian. 'You see, I'm not going to Hell, ever, because I'm not going through the Gate, ever. I'm not playing this silly game any longer. I'm not going to be judged. I will be my judge.'

'What do you mean you're "not playing"? This is real life, Christian, you can't not play, you don't have a choice.'

'Why don't I have a choice?'

'You just don't. Everybody goes through.'

'Well not me. So there. I'm not playing. You, Limbo and your whole revolution can fuck off. Hell can fuck off. Heaven and God, they can fuck off too.'

Silence.

Some of the guards started to shuffle back.

'You don't want to say that,' said Nikki.

'Say what?' said Christian.

'You can't tell God to ... to fuck off,' whispered Nikki.

'Why not? I meant it. He can fuck off. He can go fuck himself, and being God I imagine he can really do it.'

'Oooh,' said Hanley, with a wince.

All the guards were now back up on their feet and stepping backwards as they gazed worriedly into the sky.

'I'm telling you, you can't say that,' said Nikki.

'No, Nikki,' said Christian, 'this is the guy who according to you tried to kill me, maybe did kill me. And you think I'm worried about offending him? Besides, what's he going to do, kill me again? Condemn me to Hell again? And anyway, what do you care? You're working for the other side, or at least one of the other sides.'

'He is my enemy,' said Nikki, 'but there are still limits, common decency. There are some things we never say.'

'Oh is that right?' said Christian. He leaned back, opened his eyes to the heavens and said, 'God, in case you missed it ... fuck ... off.'

The guards backed off even further, some now glancing behind them, already picking their escape routes.

'Hey, *hey*,' yelled Nikki, sensing the brewing exodus, 'stop that. Stop. Return to your posts.'

'Get back here,' said Hanley, getting to his feet, 'one more step and you're all on a verbal.'

But the guards kept retreating.

'Fair warning,' said Hanley, 'this is fair warning, you'll all be on a verbal.'

A moment later the guards turned and fled.

'Right, right, that's it, verbal warnings for all of you,' shouted Hanley, stretching out an accusing finger, 'it's written warnings next.' But the guards weren't looking back. And then they were gone.

Nikki turned and grabbed Christian by his jacket lapels.

'Hey, get off,' he said.

She tightened and twisted her grip as Christian yelped. For a moment she tightened further still, her eyes widening, her focus seeming to slip from the moment. But then she eased off. 'Look,' she said, releasing him and then placing her hands flat on his lapels, 'look, look, think about it for one moment. You're mad as hell, I'm mad as hell, but in all this, Heaven is the real problem. Too right they killed you, they are your enemy, *he* is your enemy, that's what this is all about. So come on, it's still not too late, write the appendix, write it here and now, complete your work and realise the meaning of your life. It's the only way to defeat him.'

'I've told you a thousand times. I don't care and I'm not doing it.'

'How ... how can you be so selfish? What about me, Christian? If you don't reveal the information, I'll be losing everything I've ever lived for, everything I have died for.'

'Well, excuse me, but that's not my problem, and anyway, in case you hadn't noticed, I've lost a *wee bit* here too. Not only does it appear I was summoned into existence for your stupid cause, but I have died for it, too, so I think I've already given about fifty pounds of flesh. So once again, no, I'm not interested, and in summary I hope you'll understand when I reiterate that you can fuck off too. Fuck off. Fuck off. Fuck. Off.'

She shook her head. 'A fool to the end.'

Her eyes widened. Her hair began to stand on end, pinprick sparks arcing off the tips into the ether.

She launched herself at him, slashing her nails across his face.

Christian cried out in pain.

She closed her fists and landed three heavy punches to his head, punches far harder than anything Hargreaves had thrown.

'Right, let's go,' she said. She took Christian by the collar and began dragging him towards number seven.

'What, what are you doing?' said Christian, dazed.

'You've got an appointment to keep, with Stan.'

'Boss,' said Hanley.

'Don't want to keep him waiting,' said Nikki.

'But you'll send me to Hell, you'll never get the information,' said Christian.

'Shut it,' she screeched and stopped to belt him hard across the face again before striding on, already halfway there.

'Boss ... boss, wait,' said Hanley.

She was almost at the steps leading to the entrance.

'Wait,' said Hanley, grabbing her arm and forcing her to a stop. 'Stockport, we still have Stockport.'

'How do you know about Stockport?' she said.

'Bryan told me. He thought it could still have a part to play. Look, it can work. It really can. What do we have to lose?'

A pause as Nikki looked at Christian and reacquainted herself with the scene around her.

'Yes. Yes you're right,' she said, not taking her eyes off Christian, 'you're right.' She relaxed her stance.

'Stockport?' said Christian.

'You think this is over?' said Nikki. 'This isn't over until I say it's over.' She turned back to Hanley. 'Tom, go to the front, bring back an escort party for us, fifty managers, no less, tell the rest to hold out for another hour then sound the retreat. Stockport is now in effect.'

'Stockport?' said Christian, again.

'You'll be fine on your own with him?' asked Hanley.

'Yes, yes, I'll be fine,' said Nikki, 'now go.'

'Right, right, I'll be as quick as I can.'

As soon as Hanley was out of sight, Christian sprang into action. With all his might, he brought his fist down on Nikki's arms.

She was caught by surprise, but held firm.

He tried again, harder this time, putting everything he had into a hefty blow.

She held firm again, and then started to laugh.

'Go on, try again,' she said.

He tried again.

'Tell you what, I'll just hold you with one arm. Go on, see if you can get away.'

She released one hand.

'I'm not going to give you the satisfaction,' said Christian, before violently struggling again.

It was only now, in this moment, that he finally realised he was dealing with something that was not human. Or at least, this is the explanation he found easiest to accept.

'Stockport?' he said again. 'So what, that's a code word is it?'

'No, it's a town in Greater Manchester.'

'Yes, well yes I know it is. So?'

'So as of now it's our new plan B.'

'Plan B?'

'Christian, we are managers, surely you didn't think we wouldn't have contingency plans?'

'Oh.'

'Yes, Stockport. Home to the largest retail fulfilment centre in Europe. Eight hundred thousand square feet of enclosed grey space, and no reason for anyone ethereal to venture inside, not ghosts, not angels. That is where we will take you, that is where we will hold you, and that is where we will break you. Twenty-four-seven strip-lighting, the ever-present hum of toil, the never-ending stream of stock coming in, orders going out, the cold machinery of business. You may hold out for a while, perhaps a long while, but sooner or later you will feel compelled to write the appendix, because, quite simply, there will be nothing else to do and no way out until you do it.'

'But the angels, I saw them,' said Christian, 'they know about me, don't they? They want me as much as you. You're not going to have it all your own way.'

'I do not fear Heaven,' she said. 'Even if they do track us to Stockport, I will have raised an army ten times the size of this one. You know how many people work for corporations these days? How many become consumed by career, bit by bit, day by day? Slowly seduced, until eventually they accept it, then yearn for it, and in time become defined by it. Inevitable decline and a hollow retirement cements it all in place. By the time they die, they're already dead, and already mine. I have the numbers, and more will join each day. So let Heaven come, let Heaven send every angel, and I will still defeat them. You see, Christian, this will only end when you write the appendix. It is why you exist, and only when you submit to it will you be free. That is why–'

Nikki plunged into the pavement up to her waist, dragging Christian down with her by his lapels.

She screamed and seemed to panic, releasing her grip on him as she swiped around her legs for whatever unseen shark was savaging her. She dropped again, her screams rising, the pavement now at her chest. And then an arm shot up out of the paving slabs, a charcoal-suit-covered arm with a hand that stretched to gag Nikki's mouth. The arm rose higher to reveal a torso, a torso that supported no head.

'Mitch,' said Christian, 'what the–'

'Are you okay?' said Mitch, wrestling to get Nikki gagged and under control.

'I have no answer for that,' said Christian, pulling himself up onto the pavement, 'but what the hell are you doing? Why are you doing this?'

'Sorry, it's–'

Nikki freed an arm but only to elbow Mitch in the space where his nose wasn't.

'Oh ... of course,' said Christian, 'now I get it, you want to take me through the Gate, get your reward. Well, fella, you're too late too, because–'

'I know. I saw everything,' said Mitch, then a grunt as he got a firm hold of Nikki once again, 'I heard your sermon.'

'You know you've lost, then?'

'Yes.'

'So what are you doing here?'

'To fuckin' help, what does it look like?'

'Oh yeah, right, you're here to help. Forgive me if I don't find that convincing, *shepherd.*' Christian turned and started walking towards number seven.

'Well where are you going?' said Mitch, still struggling to hold Nikki.

'Where do you think? I'm never going to be free here, am I? You, her, the angels. So I'll have to take my chances in Hell.'

'Look, hold up, ya big doofus,' said Mitch, 'just stop for a goddamn second.'

Nikki elbowed her hands free and went for Mitch's neck cavity.

'Huuuuoooooow,' cried Mitch, as Nikki jammed her fingers in and tried to wrench it apart. He smashed his fists into her head and then forced his arms under hers to break her hold. 'Please don't do that again, miss,' he wheezed, and spun her round and bent her hands high up her back, in between her shoulder blades.

'Ouuuuuuwwwww,' she yelped, before Mitch gagged her again.

'Buddy, I really am here to help. You gotta trust me.'

'Trust you? Oh sure, of course, why didn't you say so.'

'Look, I'm sorry about trying to deliver you, okay, but they had me over a barrel, I had no choice.'

'Just following orders I suppose?'

'It was always my choice, and I'm not hiding from that, but it's over now, okay?'

'Yes, yes it is.' He turned back towards the building.

'Christian, I read the book, that "Carrots for Donkeys" chapter, in the banned section, I read it.'

Christian stopped.

'I know now,' said Mitch, 'I know it was all bullshit, what they were offering.'

Christian turned. 'So you know they'll never help you? The angels, I mean.'

'Guess I lapped it up the same as the other desperate shmucks.'

'Sorry,' said Christian. He drifted back over to Mitch and Nikki, and sat down.

Mitch now had Nikki under a degree of control, his hand held firm over her mouth, his other pinning her wrists high up her back.

'Oh shit,' said Christian. 'I'm sorry, I didn't think.'

'Didn't think what?'

'Telling you to read that chapter. That's banned knowledge, you won't get into Heaven now either, even if your head does show up.'

'Christian, you didn't tell me anything I didn't already know, not really. Been in this game too long, seen too much. Besides, it's not somewhere I planned on visiting. It was never about that, ay.'

'Yes, yes I understand.'

'I can't believe you told God to fuck off,' said Mitch.

'Oh not you too.'

Mitch laughed, almost losing his grip on Nikki, and then said, 'but you're right. He can fuck off. He should give it serious consideration.'

'Too right.'

'Anyway,' said Mitch, 'we don't have much time.'

'Time for what?'

'Time to get you out of here.'

'What's the point? I'm a wanted man.'

Nikki struggled again, but again Mitch maintained his hold.

'Buddy, you gotta be positive. Look, the heat's already dropped. The shepherds, the angels, they already know you're barred from Heaven, probably, no, definitely. You're already yesterday's news.'

'They still won't forget though, they're not gonna leave me alone.'

'So slip away, become someone else.'

'What, and live on the run?'

'Be easy. You don't stand out like I do, and it's not like there's Interpol here. Give it a few weeks and they won't even remember what you look like.'

'I don't know.'

'I've left you the book, too. It'll help.'

'I don't want to see that book ever again.'

'Don't be a doofus. Take it. It's way more useful than I made out.'

'Well, okay, where is it?'

'Two feet under the doorstep of the rear entrance to Spearmint Rhino, in Bloomsbury, all you gotta do is pick it up.'

'And what about her?' said Christian, pointing to Nikki. 'She'll definitely remember what I look like.'

'Yeah, I know. Which is why I'm dealing with it.'

'How? You can't hold her for ever.'

'I won't have to. Now I've got it under control, so go.'

'What do you mean under control?'

'We're going down,' said Mitch.

'Down? Down where?'

'All the way.'

'What? You mean ...'

'There's no other way, and we're out of time, so good luck, my friend.'

'Wait,' said Christian, 'wait, I want to give her a chance.'

'You want to what? Have you lost your freakin' mind?'

'I'm serious.'

'Buddy, she's bad news. I've got four ex-wives, I know what I'm talkin' about. You know she's behind all this? Behind you being what you are? I got the whole story from the angels, they–'

'She can change, I know she can. She didn't want to be her any more than I wanted to be me.'

'This is a bad idea.'

'Nikki,' said Christian, 'Nik, what I said before, I meant it. If I can throw off my destiny, change my fate, so can you. You didn't choose who you were born to be either. We're the same, you and I. Come on, what do you say?'

She looked up at him, Mitch's hand still clamped over her mouth.

'Let her speak, Mitch.'

'Buddy ...'

'Let her speak.'

Mitch waited, but then removed his hand.

'I ... I don't know what to say,' said Nikki, 'I ... I ...' And then something caught her eye.

They all turned. A parked taxi partly blocked the view, but they could all see a large group of battle-weary managers returning from the front, drifting in through Waterloo Gardens, just a few metres away.

Christian caught Nikki's eye. He shook his head.

'Help, managers, help,' screamed Nikki, 'here, over here.'

'Little tramp,' said the shepherd. He arched his back, pulling Nikki close with a forearm under her throat and then grabbing Christian's right lapel, before dragging them both down with him under the pavement.

Christian flailed his arms, panicking at the sudden pitch-black, super-dense nothingness of road and rock, like being pulled under water without a chance to take a breath, before emerging moments later into a dimly lit basement storeroom full of boxes, books, old scientific apparatus, and a large stack of old board games.

Mitch and Nikki rolled on the floor as the shepherd re-established control, while Christian extracted himself, shaking and dazed, from a Van de Graaff generator.

'You'll be safe here,' said Mitch, sitting up with a once-again restrained Nikki, 'wait till the heat's off, though, yeah?'

Muffled shouts of 'Boss' and 'Nikki' could be heard from the street above.

Nikki tried to reply with muffled yells through Mitch's hand.

'Right, time to end this,' said Mitch. He checked his positioning before arching his back, once again.

'But wait, what about you?' said Christian.

'I'll be fine. You know me. I'll be fine.' He tapped the space where his head wasn't.

'Wait, surely there's another–'

'There isn't.'

'But–'

'There fuckin' isn't, Christian. Now. Don't follow us any lower. It's crust and mantle all the way down.'

Mitch tightened his grip.

'Wait,' shouted Christian.

'What.'

'Mitch, thanks. I mean it. Thanks.'

For a moment Mitch said nothing. A twitch of his neck cavity suggested he was nodding. 'See you round, my friend.'

Mitch thrust backwards, taking Nikki with him. Their feet sprang into the air as their heads disappeared into the floor. Christian watched as Mitch's legs kicked hard, taking them down, Nikki's thrashing in a desperate effort to break free.

Moments later the soles of Mitch's boots disappeared, as did Nikki's ballerinas.

They were gone.

Chapter Forty-Three

Two weeks later, Heaven was still none the wiser as to what had happened. They'd received multiple reports and accounts of the Manager Army's attack on the Queue, they knew the force had dispersed soon after and that the Queue had re-formed, restoring the supply of souls. But that was about it.

Atop twenty-two storeys and under an unbroken azure sky, God dropped the last of his McSlurry burger – haggis bolognaise, processed-pork patty, white bap – on the sky-blue super-lux shag pile and slouched further down the cloud sofa.

'So, Tel, what do you think we should do?' asked Gabriel.

'How long d'you say it's been?' said God.

'A fortnight.'

'And still no sign?'

'Not a dickybird.'

'You know, I can understand the monkey going missing,' said God. 'He's probably realised by now he needs to keep his head down, but what happened to Slacks, what happened to all our boys?'

'I don't get it either,' said Gabriel.

'It's a mystery,' said God.

'So what shall we do about it?'

'Well, let's tell our lads in the field to keep an eye out, yes? For Slacks and Co as well as the monkey.'

'We've already done that, Tel.'

'Right. Good then.'

'So what else?'

'Well, I think that'll do, won't it?' said God.

'Yes, I suppose,' said Gabriel, eventually. 'So how about we get back to sorting out the nerd play then? Walter's finally made those updates.'

'Yeah, that sounds good. But ...'

'But?'

God slipped himself into a full recline, reached into the remains of his burger and withdrew two gherkin slices.

'Let's leave it till next week, eh?' said God, placing a gherkin slice over each eyelid. 'I fancy an early start to the weekend.'

'But it's Tuesday, Tel.'

'Exactly, Gabe. Exactly.'

Gabriel looked like he was about to speak. But instead he just smiled and closed his folder.

Dexter prodded open the door to Gordon's bedroom. The light from the corridor barely lifted the darkness. His boss was lying prostrate on the bed, as he had been these last two weeks, cast down, floored with an all-enveloping lethargy that had Grímsson and the doctors stumped.

'How are you today, Gordo?' said Dexter, in his most positive-without-being-obviously-positive voice.

No reply.

'Thought you may be up for some golf. Just the front nine, clear the cobwebs? They've got those new quartz floodlights fitted. Now you can almost see where you're driving.'

A low grisly groan emanated from the mass on the bed, a mass that Dexter noticed was still wearing – almost wearing – the same silk negligee from earlier in the week.

Dexter walked across the room and turned on the wall-mounted privet.

Wuuumpphh.

'Off,' groaned Gordon, grasping for a pillow and putting it over his head.

Dexter placed his hand on the touchstone. The New York skyline appeared against a crisp blue sky.

'Come on, Gordon, look, Wall Street's just waking up.'

'*Off*,' said Gordon, pulling the pillow tighter and letting out another long moan.

Dexter sighed and powered down the hedge. 'You at least need to come to the parade this afternoon. It's your big day.'

And it was. He'd had to call in all his favours, twist every arm, and use every negotiation trick in his locker, but against the odds, Dexter had done it – Limbo's first ever gay, lesbian, transvestite and transgender pride festival. Limbo, the spiritual heart of conformity, the magnetic north of convention, and yet, because of Dexter's determination, somewhere beyond the low slopes of the north side of the city, 486 middle managers were now removing all their body hair and slipping into little more than a sprinkling of sequins.

Dexter moved closer.

'You need to make the effort. You need to be seen.'

No response.

'It'll give you a boost, too. I can get Manners to wheel you down if you're not up to walking. Then perhaps we could talk about the plan. You remember the plan? The big plan? We need to know what you want us to do, Gordon, what to do next?'

In truth, it was only Dexter who wanted to know what Gordon wanted to do next. The board, Grímsson, Spitback and the section heads had soon grown accustomed to the powers that had inevitably been delegated to them for the duration of Gordon's incapacitation. That his condition lingered suited them just fine.

And it was still unclear what had happened, and where things had gone wrong, despite a stream of news over the last fortnight – scattered accounts from civilian arrivals through the Gate, hardly official, but enough to build up a picture. They'd learned that Gordon's other self, the person they now knew to be Gordon's daughter – Dexter was still waiting for the right moment to break that news – had indeed led an army, resisted an assault by the angels, and mounted her own successful attack on the Queue, but had then gone missing. They didn't know whether she had ever found the prophet, or what had gone wrong.

Finally they had established that the great New Model Manager Army had disbanded. Without leadership, most of their number had drifted back to their old afterlives, or headed off to engage in self-paced individual development programmes.

'We need your instructions, Gordon. You are still the King of Limbo.'

There was more substance to Dexter's tone now, countering the notes of desperation.

'Come,' whispered Gordon, eventually. He was barely audible.

'Come?' said Dexter, moving his ear to Gordon's lips.

'Come ... back ... when ... when I'm feeling better.'

A hooded figure passed through the double doors and entered the foyer of St Benedict's Catholic High School, breezing unnoticed through the tide of pupils heading for the exit.

Last night it had visited 22 Vestments. It had seen a classically proportioned woman, making the most of what she had, curled next to a chubby-cheeked man making the most of what he had.

Today it had visited the churchyard of St Egbert's and its vicarage. Today it had drifted through Caterpillar Park and the grey streets of Bracknell. And now it was here.

Through narrow eyeholes, it picked a course, drifting on through the main hall, stage and backstage, before turning right and down the corridor to the chemistry labs. There, it slowed, before advancing silently into the office of the Head of the Department. The mortal head, lacking the dedication of the man he replaced, had already left for the staffroom, but that did not mean the office was empty.

An earnest-looking man aged about thirty with copper red hair and a strangely styled beard was counselling a sheepish, slightly younger-looking man dressed in a tight-fitting school uniform, the second man's tie askew and shoulders hunched.

'You're smart,' said Hargreaves, to his young charge, 'but you can do so much better.' The pupil lifted his head to speak, but in the end said nothing. 'Smart gets you a foot in the door, but it's useless without hard work. This is the real world of the Spirit Zone, lad, and no one's going to hand you success on a plate.'

'Well. Hello,' said the hooded figure.

Hargreaves stopped and turned his head, and without taking his eyes from the hooded figure, told his pupil they would continue the discussion before class the next day.

He waited until his pupil had gone.

'How many times,' said Hargreaves, breaking eye contact, 'I don't know anything, I haven't seen anything.' He stood. 'Now please leave. This is a school, this is–'

'Calm down, Stuart,' said the hooded figure and he lifted the sack from his head.

'Christian,' said Hargreaves, stepping forward, 'well blow me. Great to see you, lad.'

They exchanged a handshake and then a hearty hug.

'I'm glad you're okay,' said Hargreaves.

'Why wouldn't I be?' asked Christian.

'I heard rumours. I've had visitors.'

'Well, I'm fine, I'm fine. Reports of my death have been … well, they've been spot on, I suppose, but no, I'm fine, I'm fine.'

'I'm glad. Now please, sit,' said Hargreaves, gesturing to the vacant chair.

They each sunk into the nothing of their seats.

'So why the headgear?' asked Hargreaves.

'Thought it sensible not to show my face in public.'

'Well, yes, seems you've become something of a celebrity. Like I say, I've had visitors, asking if I'd seen you.'

'What sort of visitors?'

'They never say. Got the impression they weren't wanting to take you out for a cream tea though.'

'What did you tell them?'

'Nothing. What was there to tell? Didn't frighten me anyway. Told them to sling their hooks.'

'Thanks, Stuart. Really, thanks.'

'So anyway, what can I do for you?'

'I'm glad you asked me that. I'm going away. There are some things I need.'

'Sure. Fire away.'

'Information,' said Christian.

'Go on.'

'I need a list of cryonics facilities in America. Company names, addresses.'

'Cryonics? Freezing people?'

'Yes, or at least bits of people. I thought if you asked around, with your contacts, the professor programme, maybe? There could be someone who may know.'

'Right, right. Well, sure. There's a few people I can ask, I think. Give me a couple of days, okay?'

'Thanks.'

'So you're gonna do a bit of travel, eh?'

'Yes, I am. Better late than never.'

Hargreaves gave a warm nod.

'You know, it used to scare me,' said Christian, 'proper travel, I mean, to be honest. But now I'm excited.'

'The new Christian?' said Hargreaves.

'More like the opposite. I've realised, well, wherever I am, I'm still me. Right?'

'Right,' said Hargreaves, with a nod and a smile. 'And your girl?'

Christian shook his head.

'I'm sorry,' said Hargreaves.

'Don't be. It's for the best. In every way it's for the best, I know that now.'

'And ... Catherine?'

'She's on a different path, you know, literally, I suppose. But that's fine too, it really is.'

'Right,' said Hargreaves, 'I'm glad it's okay. Well, like I say, give me a couple of days, yes? For the information. I'll see what I can uncover.'

'Thanks, I mean it,' said Christian.

They stood.

'Oh yes, there's something else. Where I'm heading, it'll be a long journey and there may be a long wait at the end of it. So I wondered if, maybe ...'

'Wait here,' said Hargreaves, smiling the broadest of smiles, before leaving the room. He returned a few minutes later carrying a wad of poor-quality papyrus, three homemade-looking pencils and a small sharpening knife, and handed them all to Christian.

'Thank you,' said Christian. He put the pencils and the knife into his jacket pocket and tucked the papyrus under his arm.

He shook Hargreaves's hand and turned to leave.

'So are you going to finish your book?' asked Hargreaves.

Christian turned. 'No. No it's time for something new.'

Afterword

It is the east coast of Australia. Southern Queensland. Springtime. A writer is 26,148 words into his first novel. For the last three nights he has not slept well, every night seeing only one thing in his dreams. The image of a stocky, scruffy, beardy man in his fifties, who hangs about, hands in the pockets of his cream corduroy suit, with occasional indifferent glances to his scuffed shoes. At this point the writer decides to make something plain to anyone who will ever read his book. He inserts the following into the copyright page, just in case:

> *Believing that the content of this book may reflect reality can possibly seriously damage your chances of getting into Heaven (which probably does not exist). Furthermore, if you recommend this book to others (this includes favourable reviews on websites and in newspapers), on the basis of it offering possible insights into the true nature of the universe, you can, possibly, seriously increase your chances of spending eternity in Hell (which probably does not exist) for committing the possibly heinous crime of promoting belief in God (who probably does not exist).*

Thank you for reading my book. I must say, it feels rather strange to finally address you after all these pages together. Unless you're one of those people who always reads the last page first and have happened across this? (In which case, I must apologise for the unwarranted familiarity.) Anyway,

I hope you enjoyed it. If you did, would you mind taking a moment to leave a review? I'd be most grateful. If you didn't, then perhaps sleep on it. After all, you can always do it tomorrow …

Colton Lazars

For additional content, thoughts and ideas, visit
www.coltonlazars.com

Acknowledgments

I owe a huge debt of thanks to those who have been kind enough to critique and proofread the book in its various drafts. The feedback was always valuable and insightful and I will be forever grateful. Special thanks go to those who were exposed to the book when it was in embryonic form. To receive chapters out of sequence, over a long period of time, with regular changes of character names, character natures, character existence, plot, scenes and settings will have been discombobulating. Thank you.

Immense thanks to Larry Azmo for the cover design and interior images.

I must also acknowledge the positive and significant influence of several of my school teachers. This book, and indeed my entire perspective on life, would not have been possible without their tireless dedication to bizarreness, incompetence and mild injustice, though it must be said, rarely delivered with malice and usually with good humour. In addition, there is nothing quite like the rarefied theological tedium of a Church of England primary school education for establishing a solid foundation for atheism and critical thinking in adulthood. The small dose that protects against the disease.

Printed in Great Britain
by Amazon

40834779R00463